THE WORLD'S CLASSICS

THE ORDEAL OF RICHARD FEVEREL

GEORGE MEREDITH (1828–1909) was born in Portsmouth, the son of a bankrupt tailor. Educated in Germany and apprenticed to a solicitor, he married the daughter of Thomas Love Peacock in 1849, a union which ended abruptly nine years later when his wife eloped with another man. His second marriage was longer (1864–85) and more successful. Meredith's earliest publication was *Poems* (1851), and he continued through his long career in letters to consider himself a poet first and a novelist second. *Modern Love* (1862) is perhaps his best-known volume of poetry. Between 1856 and his death over fifty years later, he published sixteen full-length novels as well as a great many poems and shorter tales. He achieved fame with *The Ordeal of Richard Feverel* in 1859, but it took another twenty years, until the publication of *The Egoist* (1879), to assure him a pre-eminent place among the English novelists of his time. By the 1880s he had become one of the leading literary men of his day, a position he held until his death. He was awarded the OM in 1905.

JOHN HALPERIN is Centennial Professor of English at Vanderbilt University. His publications include *Trollope and Politics, Gissing: A Life in Books, C. P. Snow: An Oral Biography, The Life of Jane Austen*, and two books on the Victorian novel. He has edited works by Trollope, Meredith, Gissing, and Henry James, and volumes of original essays on Jane Austen, on the theory of the novel, and on Trollope. He was a Guggenheim Fellow in 1978–9.

THE WORLD'S CLASSICS

GEORGE MEREDITH

The Ordeal of Richard Feverel

A History of a Father and Son

Edited with an Introduction by
JOHN HALPERIN

Oxford   New York
OXFORD UNIVERSITY PRESS
1984

Oxford University Press, Walton Street, Oxford OX2 6DP

London New York Toronto
Delhi Bombay Calcutta Madras Karachi
Kuala Lumpur Singapore Hong Kong Tokyo
Nairobi Dar es Salaam Cape Town
Melbourne Auckland
and associated companies in
Beirut Berlin Ibadan Mexico City Nicosia

Oxford is a trade mark of Oxford University Press

Introduction, Select Bibliography, Chronology, and Notes © John Halperin 1984

This edition first published 1984 as a World's Classics paperback

British Library Cataloguing in Publication Data

Meredith, George, 1828–1909
The ordeal of Richard Feverel. —
(The World's classics)
I. Title   II. Halperin, John
823'.8 [F]   PR5006.07
ISBN 0–19–281637–3

Library of Congress Cataloging in Publication Data

Meredith, George, 1828–1909.
The ordeal of Richard Feverel.
(The World's classics)
Bibliography: p.
I. Halperin, John, 1941–   . II.Title.
III. Series.
PR5006.07 1984   823'.8   84–849
ISBN 0–19–281637–3 (pbk.)

Printed in Great Britain by
Hazell Watson & Viney Ltd
Aylesbury, Bucks

CONTENTS

ACKNOWLEDGEMENTS

I should like to thank John Bridges, Franklin Brooks, Donald Greene, James F. Kilroy, Max F. Schulz, Robert Tracy, and H. L. Weatherby, Jr., for invaluable and unstinting help during the preparation of the present volume for publication.

J. H.

INTRODUCTION

> Mamma, whose views on education are remarkably strict, has
> brought me up to be extremely short-sighted; it is part of her
> system.
>
> Gwendolen in *The Importance of Being Earnest*

MEREDITH's masterpiece, *The Ordeal of Richard Feverel*
(1859), has sometimes been criticized for being incon-
sistent. How should one respond to a novel, it has been
asked, which is two-thirds comedy (Chapter XXIX
signals 'The Last Act of a Comedy') and ends with a
series of monumental tragedies?

Well, life too is a mixed genre; and many things which
may seem amusing enough ultimately turn out, as Hardy
says, to be not quite so amusing after all.

A reference to Hardy is not irrelevant here. For in
writing a story which quite deliberately refuses to provide the mid-Victorian reader with the expected happy
ending and a full round of poetic justice, Meredith—
born thirteen years after Trollope, sixteen after Dickens,
seventeen after Thackeray, and eighteen after Mrs
Gaskell—was in fact signalling a new direction for the
novel. He is generally, and rightly, classified with the
'later' Victorian novelists (Hardy, Gissing, Butler,
Moore), who tended to find themselves at odds with
contemporary standards and conventions and whose
novels present us with what Matthew Arnold termed a
'criticism of life' (which Hardy thought of as the function
of art) rather than with various examples of ways of

accommodating ourselves to it. While Dickens, Trollope, and Mrs Gaskell find plenty of things to complain about and to ridicule, in their novels the world is perceived as a place in which, finally, things are made to make sense, poetic justice flourishes, everyone gets his just reward. Do what is right, and you must come through: Thackeray and Wilkie Collins sometimes question this; the others, never. This is by no means the view of the later novelists; in their works we find no such confidence in the organization of the universe. The discoveries of the 'New Sciences' and the difficulty of maintaining religious faith, the failure of economic prosperity (in the 1870s) and the collapse of the One Nation ideal—these, as well as creative sensibilities which, in good 'modern' fashion, had been alienated, prevented the later generation of novelists from seeing their world as a benign place.

A pivotal figure here is George Eliot. The fact that *Adam Bede* appeared in the same year as *The Ordeal of Richard Feverel* has sometimes tempted literary historians to point to 1859 as a watershed moment for the novel. In this same year, doing business as usual, Dickens published *A Tale of Two Cities*, Mrs Gaskell published *Round the Sofa and Other Tales*, Trollope published one of his most mediocre novels, *The Bertrams*, Wilkie Collins's *The Woman in White* was appearing serially, and Thackeray brought out what is arguably the worst book ever produced by a great novelist, *The Virginians*. (*The Origin of Species* also appeared in 1859.) But *Adam Bede* and *The Ordeal of Richard Feverel* pointed in a different direction. These are novels which emphasize psychological development and analysis of character over the demands —or perhaps in place of the demands—of plot, and many of the other conventional requirements of early Victorian story-telling. Perhaps 1859 was indeed the year in which the novel began to change. While such generalizations are both dangerous and often wildly overstated, this one may contain a few seeds of truth.

Like *Adam Bede*, *The Ordeal of Richard Feverel* focuses on the psyches of its characters; and, like *Adam Bede*, it has a highly controversial (for the time) seduction in it. The camera swings away at the crucial moment in both novels, however, in obeisance to contemporary taste; for novelists of this period were dependent for their livelihood on the puritanical requirements of Charles Evans Mudie and his colleagues in the circulating library business. How the libraries reacted quite simply determined sales.

The seduction in *Adam Bede* is that of an inexperienced girl by a rich man—the standard type—and Arthur Donnithorne is given plenty of time to repent of his action before the novel comes to an end. And while Hetty's baby is not allowed to live, she—unlike Tess, later—does survive, though in vastly changed circumstances. Dinah and Adam come together at the end, and the novel closes on a happy note. Born nine years before Meredith, George Eliot, though a transitional figure, is temperamentally closer to the early Victorian novelists than to her successors in the field. Her faith in the goodness of people, her 'religion of humanity', allowed her to let her foolish people commit their folly early in the story, repent at their leisure, and survive. The idea that she is a tragic novelist surely invites re-examination.

In *The Ordeal of Richard Feverel*, the seduction is that of a virtuous boy by a woman of the world, and occurs near the end of the novel—different premises indeed. There is no happy ending. For these reasons—and for its irreverence—Meredith's novel got itself into serious trouble with the circulating libraries. While *Adam Bede*, doctrinally clean, was an immediate best-seller, *The Ordeal of Richard Feverel* initially became little more than a *succès de scandale*, not at all the same thing, and by no means as gratifying to an impecunious author as a healthy sale. But Meredith did not see life as a Dickens novel. For him acts had consequences, and the consequences of rash and foolish conduct were not easily sidestepped or atoned for.

It may be argued, then, that the appearance of *The Ordeal of Richard Feverel*, even more emphatically than that of *Adam Bede*, marks the beginning of the end of the 'old' Victorian novel and the advent of something new. It was Meredith, not George Eliot, whom Gissing worshipped (*Feverel* was his favourite novel); nor was Gissing the only late Victorian novelist to lionize Meredith. It is difficult to appreciate now how towering a figure Meredith was for the novelists of the 1890s. Trollope was in eclipse, Dickens thought fit only for children. Though Henry James read George Eliot and Gissing read Charlotte Brontë, Meredith and Hardy were the contemporary heroes, and the old-fashioned novel with a happy ending was an object of mirth. Writers simply didn't perceive their world that way any more. Meredith, who was born in 1828, had been seeing the universe as an ominous place, and writing about it that way, for a long time by the 1890s. He was a giant to the younger men in his trade, who noticed no similarity between the world they lived in and that depicted by George Eliot or Trollope or Dickens.

The setting of Meredith's great novel is shadowy, the chronology obscure. Still, one can place its action, roughly, from the late 1820s to the mid-1830s (like almost all Victorian novels, this one is set in the recent past). These dates are suggested by the fact that Austin Wentworth, after four years abroad, is greeted upon his return (XLI) by Adrian with news of the Reform Bill (1832) and its consequences; by the dependence of most of the characters on carriages and horses for long trips, and trains only infrequently—in the 1840s they would have been jumping on one train after another (like Dickens in many of his novels, Meredith wants the atmosphere of an earlier time; horses instead of trains brought with them the ambience of the late Regency and George IV); by the description of Blaize as a 'free-trade farmer', a characterization that would have been relevant in the Twenties and Thirties but not in the Fifties, after the Corn Laws had been repealed; by the brief debate in the novel over the comparative merits of Byron and Wordsworth, which would not have been possible later (in the 1840s, say), when Wordsworth was a revered figure and Byron a bad joke; by the mere presence in the story of a duel, something in which no mid-Victorian gentleman, no matter how highly strung, would have become involved, for Prince Albert had made duelling not only illegal but, more importantly, both immoral and unfashionable (the duel in which Trollope's Phineas Finn gets himself embroiled is highly anomalous); and by the libidinous evening party at Richmond, replete with unbuttoned ladies and lascivious lords—again, a scene simply impossible to imagine a few years after Victoria ascended the throne, in 1837 (the Twenties and Thirties were the last decades, until the Seventies and Eighties, when such things could be written about: the Nancy of *Oliver Twist*, published 1837–9, could not, and indeed was not, repeated in any form in Dickens's later novels). For such amorous adventures as Richard's, Meredith needed an earlier time, when a hero with romantic illusions could jump on a horse.

But the debates over science that were taking place in the middle of the nineteenth century are very much present in the novel's main target, the spurious 'scientific' System by which Sir Austin Feverel brings up his son.

Meredith believed in evolution—the view of character development in his novels is patently evolutionary—and his protagonists are often changed by a kind of organic growth. Undoubtedly he welcomed *The Origin of Species* and the publications by Lyell and Darwin and others which had preceded it. But one can believe in evolution and at the same time abhor the application of scientific principles to human conduct, and there can be no doubt that this is what Meredith is doing in *The Ordeal of Richard Feverel*—whose villain is neither Lord Mountfalcon nor Lady Mountfalcon nor anyone other than Sir Austin Feverel himself.

Only by involving himself with other people in society can a person learn what he is: it is this (very sound) principle which Sir Austin violently opposes. Now one of Meredith's most constant themes is what he calls the 'comedy of egoism', which arises, he believes, out of man's failure to perceive his rightful place in the human hierarchy and his vision of himself as being at the centre of the world. Meredith's important *Essay on Comedy and the Uses of the Comic Spirit* (1877), as well as the famous Prelude to his only other great novel, *The Egoist* (1879), make clear his commitment to the idea that the egoist must be ridiculed, not tolerated—and certainly not taken seriously or at his own valuation of himself. Meredith speaks of the virtues, indeed the necessity, of laughter, and of the need to recognize folly, advocating 'Olympian' mockery rather than sympathy for the egoist. What Meredith calls the 'Comic Spirit' provides moral progress by deflating egoism and establishing in its place a sense of proportion. It is the perspective of this 'Comic Spirit' from which the story is told, and which we encounter in the narrative voice, from first to last, in *The Ordeal of Richard Feverel*; the result of this is an ironic, sometimes jeering tone which makes the novel complex, and perhaps hard going for the reader unused to Meredithian mockery.

One form egoism frequently takes in Meredith's novels is the unreasonable desire of some to possess others entirely. Among the amazing gallery of egoists, hedonists, and solipsists in *The Ordeal of Richard Feverel*—extensively revised by Meredith in 1878 (see Note on the Text); that is, during the same period in which he wrote the *Essay on Comedy* and *The Egoist*—Sir Austin (like Dickens's Dombey) is prominent for his desire to possess completely the heart and soul of his son. 'I require not only that my son should obey; I would have him guiltless of the impulse to gainsay my wishes,' declares the baronet (XVI). The boy must not only be obedient; he must be innocent of Thoughtcrime. Indeed, there is something Orwellian about Sir Austin; he is the Victorians' most spectacular anticipation of Big Brother. In his wish 'to be Providence to his son' (IV), he destroys him. Richard's 'ordeal' is his moral education, which is the edifice of his father and which, due to his father's System, suffers fatal delays in construction. 'His son's ordeal was to be his own,' Meredith remarks of the baronet (XXVIII). Acts have consequences. What we do, how we act, inevitably affects others besides ourselves: it is one of Meredith's most deeply felt precepts. Unfortunately for the hapless Richard, all of Sir Austin's diseased chickens come home to roost in the breast of his romantic, idealistic, and tragically inexperienced son.

It is clearly wrong to have a 'system' of any kind in dealing with others, especially those who are close to us. Meredith believed that the novel must affirm human freedom in the face of scientific determinism. Sir Austin places his faith in the scientific control of human nature; but human nature cannot be 'controlled'—either scientifically or in any other way. Instinct, which finally 'beats'

the System, is alien to it, as is humour. It is indicative
that the baronet has no sense of humour: 'the faculty of
laughter . . . was denied him'(XXII). 'Honest passion',
the novel reminds us, 'has an instinct that can be safer
than conscious wisdom' (XXIX). But it is instinct that
Sir Austin fears above all—and rightly so. The System
works, more or less, so long as Richard is young and
malleable, without instincts of his own. Eventually he
begins to think for himself. The combination of heroic
idealism and personal naivety prove to be catastrophic.

Love—and what can be more instinctive than that?—
marks the end of the System (the chapter titled 'The Last
Act of a Comedy' is that in which Richard is married);
for science, as we have seen, takes no cognizance of
instinct. The breach between Richard and his father
begins when the boy is commanded to burn his poetry.
Art, of course, is always anathema to tyrants, who fear
what they cannot control; love, we remember, is the
great enemy of the Party in *Nineteen Eighty-Four*. The gulf
between Sir Austin and his son becomes impassable
when Lucy enters the picture and Richard falls in love
with her. The baronet refuses to accept her because she is
not his own choice. There is an obvious irony here. The
System has worked so far in that it has rendered Richard
capable of choosing for his wife the one woman in the
world with whom he has a chance of happiness. Indeed,
when Richard meets and loves Lucy, 'Then truly the
System triumphed' (XV), as Meredith observes. But the
System, being a system, does not 'know its rightful hour
of exaltation' (XIX). A bad scientist as well as a bad
father, Sir Austin cannot refrain from tinkering with a
process which has, after all, turned out an admirable
adolescent. In the paroxysm of jealousy and anger which
overtakes him, the baronet never gives the marriage a
chance to work; he has been baulked in his chosen role as

his son's one God. Nothing the boy does without his consent and encouragement can be acceptable. 'It was the first of the angels who made the road to hell' (XXI), he remarks; but he seems to have forgotten that the original sin was Pride. That Sir Austin takes the Devil's side is clear enough. After Richard's marriage, in his determination to close his heart and mind against his son, the baronet 'did not battle with the tempter. He took him into his bosom at once, as if he had been ripe for him, and received his suggestions, and bowed to his dictates' (XXXIII).

'Love of any human object is the soul's ordeal,' Sir Austin observes (XXI); Meredith obviously agrees with him. But *how* we love is important. Sir Austin, and ultimately Richard too, can be seen as people who love the wrong way. To love possessively—so jealously as to turn vindictive and unreasonable—is the wrong way. But to love too selflessly, without any ego, is also dangerous, for it leaves us with no defences, vulnerable to the smallest pinprick. Richard's blind romantic love, while morally preferable to his father's more selfish brand, is dangerous too. It is indicative that he is described as 'an engine . . . at high pressure' (XXIX); as having 'the character of a bullet with a treble charge of powder behind it' (XLI); and, in an image which recurs, as 'strung like an arrow drawn to the head' (e.g., XV). Those who recommend to his father what Lord Heddon calls 'a little racketing' (XVIII) for Richard are undoubtedly right. Had the boy been allowed some experience of the world before meeting the Mountfalcons and their set—had he, in short, stopped living in a dream of knight-errantry—the final tragedies might have been avoided. But Richard, until the end, exists in a world of his own, as his father does—different worlds, to be sure, but equally divorced from reality. One cannot make a career out of 'saving' women any more than one can bring up a child scientifically. The old family doctor who declares that Richard 'ought to see the world, and know what he is made of' (XXIII) is ignored. So is Lord Heddon's prophetic warning: 'Early excesses the frame will recover from; late ones break the constitution' (XVIII). Even Mrs. Doria sees that Richard's 'education acts like a disease on him. He cannot regard anything sensibly. He is for ever in some mad excess of his fancy, and what he will come to at last heaven only knows!' (XXXV). The problem, of course, is the father. He understands as little of the world as his son; the egoist perceives nothing, being blinded by self-regard. Indeed, we are told that 'Sir Austin . . . knew less of his son than the servant of his household' (XII). When the baronet advises Mr. Thompson (XVII) to let Ripton see the vices of London in order to take away their mystery and allure, we know that he won't allow Richard the same freedom. Feverels, of course, are not Thompsons. It is all pride, Satanic pride.

Richard should have been sent to school, like Ralph Morton, where he would have learned a few things worth knowing. 'Mystery is the great danger to youth' (XXV), as Adrian rightly declares. But the father cannot let the son out of his sight; is it to be expected that God should send his only son to Eton? The father knows nothing; the son is brought up to know nothing. 'The danger of a little knowledge of things is disputable,' the novel reminds us (XXX), *'but beware the little knowledge of one's self!'* (the italics are Meredith's). Sir Austin never has any self-knowledge—not even, as Lady Blandish makes clear, at the end, when he fails to see that he is responsible for all that has happened. 'As he wished the world to see him, he believed himself' (XL); yes, *believed himself*. It is here that the baronet's egoism is thrown into greatest relief, in his putting himself and his own wishes before the welfare of the son he claims to love. 'He lost the tenderness he should have had for his experiment—the living, burning youth at his elbow' (XXII). For this, he cannot be forgiven. Even when vaguely cognizant of some possible guilt, Sir Austin manages to turn his conduct to his own advantage: 'His was an order of mind that would accept the most burdensome charges and by some species of moral usury make a profit out of them' (XL).

What ultimately renders the novel so moving and so indelible is the attractiveness of Richard Feverel himself, a character we so readily and enthusiastically admire and commune with until, in the final third of the novel, the results of his pernicious 'education' catch up with him and he behaves like an imbecile. The tale is brilliantly and beautifully written from first to last, however, and even in the final section Meredith is able to preserve our feeling for Richard—most notably in the much-praised chapter called 'Nature Speaks' (XLIII), in which, alone in the German forest, Richard achieves some insight into himself and into the meaning of his past actions. But it is the trimming of the bright flame— the fact that 'Richard will never be what he promised' (XLVI)—that we must come to terms with at the end. By then it is too late; Richard is a failure. Meredith wishes us to see that acts *do* have consequences, that how we treat others *is* important, and that human interaction, since the ultimate results of it cannot be fully known or understood at the time, is a fragile thing, more deserving of our consideration than what we may conceive our own momentary needs and desires to be. And so there is no happy ending.

In the book's final chapters, though Sir Austin has met Lucy and realized that only through 'blind fortuity' could Richard have found such a perfect mate and that 'instinct' has indeed 'beaten science' (XLIII), he has still understood little more than that, as he says, 'it is useless to base any system on a human being'. Meredith comments on Sir Austin's error: 'If, instead of saying, Base no system on a human being, he had said, Never experimentalize with one, he would have been nearer the truth' (XXX). Humans can be nurtured by love, but not by science. It is this lesson that Richard learns in the German forest—the value of unselfish love of another. But too much has happened that cannot be undone; Richard cannot escape fully the mad fancies and illusions fostered in him by his pernicious upbringing. Egoism and sentimentality, taken in large doses, are capable of turning comedy into tragedy after all. 'The Fates must indeed be hard, the Ordeal severe, the Destiny dark, that could destroy so bright a Spring!' (XII). Indeed they are. And so it is that in our last view of Richard Feverel we see the defeated hero lying silently in his bed, striving to imprint the image of his dead wife upon his mind.

JOHN HALPERIN

NOTE ON THE TEXT

The Ordeal of Richard Feverel was published by Chapman and
Hall in three volumes on 20 June 1859; the original price in
boards was 31*s*. 6*d*. The novel appeared in two volumes in the
Tauchnitz series. A revised edition in one volume was brought
out in 1878 by Kegan Paul & Co. A sixpenny edition was
published by Newnes in 1899, and another in 1900 by
Constable. The revised (1878) version of the novel appeared as
part of the De Luxe Edition of Meredith's works, 39 vols.
(1898–1912). The 1878 version was also reprinted in what has
become the standard edition of the works: the Memorial
Edition, 29 vols. (1909–12). *The Ordeal of Richard Feverel* was
published in the Everyman Library series in 1935; since then
there have been several paperback versions, none of which was
in print in 1983.

The present edition is a reproduction of Volume II of the
Memorial Edition and follows the 1878 revised version of the
novel rather than the 1859 original. Meredith preferred the
later to the original version, needless to say—and with good
reason. In the revised edition, the opening (and rambling) four
chapters of the first edition were conflated into one. The
sections thus excised depict, satirically, troops of ladies pursuing Sir Austin Feverel; the ladies are irrelevant to what
follows in the novel, and painlessly dispensed with. The first
edition also contains a chapter in which a Mrs Grandison, the
mother of a daughter who might be a candidate to marry
Richard, figures; like the ladies in the original opening
chapters, the Grandisons have no real connection with the
main action of the story and thus are not missed in the revised
edition.

The 1878 edition rather than that of 1859 must be the preferred one, and that is what is reproduced here. Meredith revised *The Ordeal of Richard Feverel* when he was an experienced author at the height of his powers; his changes are an improvement on the original, erasing as they do some extraneous material and focusing our attention more narrowly on what is important; the novelist, in 1878, neither removed nor added anything which marks the book as a product of 1859; and in any case the author himself usually deserves the last word on the question of which version of his work goes down to posterity.

SELECT BIBLIOGRAPHY

There is no definitive bibliography of Meredith's works; the best of the bibliographies is Michael Collie, *George Meredith: A Bibliography* (1974). The only bibliography of criticism available is *George Meredith: An Annotated Bibliography 1925–1975*, ed. John Charles Olmsted (1978). *The Letters of George Meredith*, 3 vols., ed. C. L. Cline (1970), is the standard edition. There is no satisfactory life; the best of the biographies remains Lionel Stevenson, *The Ordeal of George Meredith* (1953).

A selection of contemporary criticism is given in *Meredith: The Critical Heritage*, ed. Ioan Williams (1971). Useful essays on Meredith in more general works may be found in John Halperin, *Egoism and Self-Discovery in the Victorian Novel* (1974) and Robert M. Polhemus, *Comic Faith: The Great Tradition from Austen to Joyce* (1980).

Recommended critical studies: Gillian Beer, *Meredith: A Change of Masks* (1970); Norman Kelvin, *A Troubled Eden: Nature and Society in the Works of George Meredith* (1961); Joseph Moses, *The Novelist as Comedian: George Meredith and the Ironic Sensibility* (1983); V S. Pritchett, *George Meredith and English Comedy* (1969); Judith Wilt, *The Readable People of George Meredith* (1975); and Walter F. Wright, *Art and Substance in George Meredith* (1953).

A CHRONOLOGY OF
GEORGE MEREDITH

1828   Born in Portsmouth on 12 February.

1842–4   Schooling at the Moravian School at Neuwied, on the Rhine.

1845   Apprenticeship to Richard S. Charnock, a solicitor.

1849   Publication of 'Chilianwallah', his first printed poem (July).

        Marriage to Mary Ellen Peacock Nicolls (August).

1851   *Poems* (1 vol., J. W. Parker).

1853   Birth of son, Arthur Gryffydh (June).

1856   First novel, *The Shaving of Shagpat: An Arabian Entertainment* (1 vol., Chapman & Hall).

1857   *Farina: A Legend of Cologne* (1 vol., Smith, Elder).

1858   Elopement of Mary Ellen Meredith with Henry Wallis.

1859   *The Ordeal of Richard Feverel* (3 vols., Chapman & Hall).

1860–8   Writing for *The Ipswich Journal*.

1860–95   Reading for Chapman & Hall.

1860   *Evan Harrington; or, He would be a Gentleman*, serialized in *Once a Week*, February–October; published in America by Harper, 1 vol.

1861   *Evan Harrington* (3 vols., Bradbury & Evans).

        Death of Mary Ellen Meredith (October).

1862   *Modern Love and Poems of the English Roadside, with Poems and Ballads* (1 vol., Chapman & Hall).

1864   Marriage to Marie Vulliamy (September).

        Emilia in England, serialized in *Revue des deux Mondes*, November–December; published by Chapman & Hall, 3 vols.; later renamed *Sandra Belloni* and published in 1 vol., 1886.

1865   Birth of son, William Maxse (July).

        Rhoda Fleming, A Story (3 vols., Tinsley).

1866   Correspondent for the Italian war, for the *Morning Post* (summer).

        Vittoria, serialized in the *Fortnightly Review*, January–December.

1867   *Vittoria* (3 vols., Chapman & Hall).

1870–1   *The Adventures of Harry Richmond*, serialized in the *Cornhill Magazine*, September 1870–November 1871.

1871   Birth of daughter, Marie Eveleen (June).

        The Adventures of Harry Richmond (3 vols., Smith, Elder).

1874–5   *Beauchamp's Career*, serialized in the *Fortnightly Review*, August 1874–December 1875.

1876   *Beauchamp's Career* (3 vols., Chapman & Hall).

1877   *The House on the Beach* in the *New Quarterly Magazine*, January.

        Lecture on 'Comedy and the Uses of the Comic Spirit' (February).

        Essay on Comedy in the *New Quarterly Magazine*, April; published in 1 vol. by Constable in England and Charles Scribner's Sons in America, 1897.

        The House on the Beach: A Realistic Tale (1 vol., Harper).

        The Case of General Ople and Lady Camper in the *New Quarterly Magazine*, July; published in 1 vol. by John W. Lovell in America and George Munro in Britain in 1890.

1879   *The Egoist: A Comedy in Narrative* (3 vols., Kegan Paul).

1879–80   *The Egoist*, serialized under the title 'Sir Willoughby Patterne the Egoist', in the *Glasgow Weekly Herald*, June 1879–January 1880.

1880   *The Tragic Comedians: A Study in a well-known Story* (2 vols., Chapman & Hall).

1880–1   *The Tragic Comedians*, serialized in the *Fortnightly Review*, October 1880–February 1881.

1883   *Poems and Lyrics of the Joy of the Earth* (1 vol., Macmillan).

1884   *Diana of the Crossways: A Novel*, serialized in the *Fortnightly Review*, June–December.

1885   *Diana of the Crossways* (3 vols., Chapman & Hall).

        Death of Marie Vulliamy Meredith (September).

1887   *Ballads and Poems of Tragic Life* (1 vol., Macmillan, and Roberts in America).

1888   *The Pilgrim's Scrip* (1 vol., Roberts).

        A Reading of Earth (1 vol., Macmillan and Roberts).

1889   *Jump-to-Glory Jane: A Poem, Universal Review*, October.

        Jump-to-Glory Jane (1 vol., Swan, Sonnenschein; privately printed).

1890   *The Tale of Chloe: An Episode in the History of Beau Beamish* (1 vol., John W. Lovell, America; published by Constable in 1900).

1890–1 *One of Our Conquerors*, serialized October 1890–May 1891 simultaneously in the *Fortnightly Review*, *The Sun* (New York), and *The Australasian*.

1891   *One of Our Conquerors* (3 vols., Chapman & Hall).

1892   *Poems: The Empty Purse with Odes to the Comic Spirit: To Youth in Memory and Verses* (1 vol., Macmillan and Roberts).

1893–4 *Lord Ormont and His Aminta*, serialized in the *Pall Mall Magazine*, December 1893–August 1894.

1894   *Lord Ormont and His Aminta* (3 vols., Chapman & Hall).

1895   *The Amazing Marriage*, serialized in *Scribner's Magazine*, January–December; published by Constable and Charles Scribner's Sons, 2 vols.

1897   *Selected Poems* (1 vol., Constable and Charles Scribner's Sons).

1898   *Odes in Contribution to the Song of French History*, in *Cosmopolis*, March–May; published in 1 vol. by Constable and Charles Scribner's Sons.

        Essays, Vol. XXXII of the De Luxe Edition (see Select Bibliography; Constable).

        Poems, Vol. XXXI of the De Luxe Edition (contains some new poems; those in Vols. XXIX–XXX are reprints; Constable).

        Nature Poems (1 vol., Constable).

1900   *The Story of Bhanavar the Beautiful* (1 vol., Constable).

1901   *A Reading of Life, with Other Poems* (1 vol., Constable and Charles Scribner's Sons).

1902   *Short Stories*, Pocket Edition (1 vol., Constable and Charles Scribner's Sons).

1905   Order of Merit conferred.

1908   *Tercentenary of Milton's Birth* (1 vol., Oxford University Press; privately printed).

1909   *Twenty Poems* (1 vol.; privately printed; contributions to *Household Words*).

       Last Poems (1 vol., Constable and Charles Scribner's Sons).

       Poems Written in Early Youth (mostly from the 1851 and 1862 volumes.; 1 vol., Constable and Charles Scribner's Sons).

       Love in a Valley (1 vol., R. Fletcher Seymour, America).

       Death on 18 May.

1910   *Celt and Saxon* (unfinished novel), serialized in the *Fortnightly Review*, January–August, and in *The Forum* (New York), January–June.

       Celt and Saxon (1 vol., Constable).

       Miscellaneous Prose, Vol. XXXIV of the De Luxe Edition (Constable).

CONTENTS

CONTENTS

THE ORDEAL OF RICHARD FEVEREL

THE

ORDEAL OF RICHARD FEVEREL

CHAPTER I

THE INMATES OF RAYNHAM ABBEY

SOME years ago a book was published under the title
of 'The Pilgrim's Scrip.'* It consisted of a selection of
original aphorisms by an anonymous gentleman, who in
this bashful manner gave a bruised heart to the world.

He made no pretension to novelty. 'Our new thoughts
have thrilled dead bosoms,' he wrote; by which avowal it
may be seen that youth had manifestly gone from him,
since he had ceased to be jealous of the ancients. There
was a half-sigh floating through his pages for those days
of intellectual coxcombry, when ideas come to us affecting
the embraces of virgins, and swear to us they are ours
alone, and no one else have they ever visited: and we
believe them.

For an example of his ideas of the sex he said:

'I expect that Woman will be the last thing civilized
by Man.'

Some excitement was produced in the bosoms of ladies
by so monstrous a scorn of them.

One adventurous person betook herself to the Heralds'
College, and there ascertained that a Griffin between two
Wheatsheaves, which stood on the title-page of the book,

3

formed the crest of Sir Austin Absworthy Bearne Feverel,
Baronet, of Raynham Abbey, in a certain Western county
folding Thames: a man of wealth and honour, and a somewhat lamentable history.

The outline of the baronet's story was by no means new.
He had a wife, and he had a friend.* His marriage was for
love; his wife was a beauty; his friend was a sort of poet.
His wife had his whole heart, and his friend all his confidence. When he selected Denzil Somers from among his
college chums, it was not on account of any similarity of
disposition between them, but from his intense worship of
genius, which made him overlook the absence of principle
in his associate for the sake of such brilliant promise.
Denzil had a small patrimony to lead off with, and that
he dissipated before he left college; thenceforth he was
dependent upon his admirer, with whom he lived, filling
a nominal post of bailiff to the estates, and launching forth
verse of some satiric and sentimental quality; for being
inclined to vice, and occasionally, and in a quiet way,
practising it, he was of course a sentimentalist and a sa-
tirist, entitled to lash the Age and complain of human
nature. His earlier poems, published under the pseudo-
nym of Diaper Sandoe, were so pure and bloodless in their
love passages, and at the same time so biting in their
moral tone, that his reputation was great among the virtuous, who form the larger portion of the English book-
buying public. Election-seasons called him to ballad-
poetry on behalf of the Tory party. Diaper possessed
undoubted fluency, but did little, though Sir Austin was
ever expecting much of him.

A languishing, inexperienced woman, whose husband
in mental and in moral stature is more than the ordinary
height above her, and who, now that her first romantic
admiration of his lofty bearing has worn off, and her fretful little refinements of taste and sentiment are not in-

stinctively responded to, is thrown into no wholesome household collision with a fluent man, fluent in prose and rhyme. Lady Feverel, when she first entered on her duties at Raynham, was jealous of her husband's friend. By degrees she tolerated him. In time he touched his guitar in her chamber, and they played Rizzio and Mary together.*

> 'For I am not the first who found
> The name of Mary fatal!'

says a subsequent sentimental alliterative love-poem of Diaper's.*

Such was the outline of the story. But the baronet could fill it up. He had opened his soul to these two. He had been noble Love to the one, and to the other perfect Friendship. He had bid them be brother and sister whom he loved, and live a Golden Age with him at Raynham. In fact, he had been prodigal of the excellences of his nature, which it is not good to be, and, like Timon,* he became bankrupt, and fell upon bitterness.

The faithless lady was of no particular family; an orphan daughter of an admiral who educated her on his half-pay, and her conduct struck but at the man whose name she bore.

After five years of marriage, and twelve of friendship, Sir Austin was left to his loneliness with nothing to ease his heart of love upon save a little baby boy in a cradle. He forgave the man: he put him aside as poor for his wrath. The woman he could not forgive; she had sinned every way. Simple ingratitude to a benefactor was a pardonable transgression, for he was not one to recount and crush the culprit under the heap of his good deeds. But her he had raised to be his equal, and he judged her as his equal. She had blackened the world's fair aspect for him.

In the presence of that world, so different to him now, he preserved his wonted demeanour, and made his features

a flexible mask. Mrs. Doria Forey, his widowed sister,
said that Austin might have retired from his Parliamentary
career for a time, and given up gaieties and that kind of
thing; her opinion, founded on observation of him in
public and private, was, that the light thing who had
taken flight was but a feather on her brother's Feverel-
heart, and his ordinary course of life would be resumed.
There are times when common men cannot bear the weight
of just so much. Hippias Feverel, one of his brothers,
thought him immensely improved by his misfortune, if
the loss of such a person could be so designated; and seeing that Hippias received in consequence free quarters at
Raynham, and possession of the wing of the Abbey she
had inhabited, it is profitable to know his thoughts. If
the baronet had given two or three blazing dinners in the
great hall he would have deceived people generally, as he
did his relatives and intimates. He was too sick for that:
fit only for passive acting.

The nursemaid waking in the night beheld a solitary
figure darkening a lamp above her little sleeping charge,
and became so used to the sight as never to wake with a
start. One night she was strangely aroused by a sound of
sobbing. The baronet stood beside the cot in his long
black cloak and travelling cap. His fingers shaded a
lamp, and reddened against the fitful darkness that ever
and anon went leaping up the wall. She could hardly
believe her senses to see the austere gentleman, dead
silent, dropping tear upon tear before her eyes. She lay
stone-still in a trance of terror and mournfulness, mechanically counting the tears as they fell, one by one. The
hidden face, the fall and flash of those heavy drops in the
light of the lamp he held, the upright, awful figure, agitated at regular intervals like a piece of clockwork by the
low murderous catch of his breath: it was so piteous to
her poor human nature that her heart began wildly pal-

pitating. Involuntarily the poor girl cried out to him, 'Oh, sir!' and fell a-weeping. Sir Austin turned the lamp on her pillow, and harshly bade her go to sleep, striding from the room forthwith. He dismissed her with a purse the next day.

Once, when he was seven years old, the little fellow woke up at night to see a lady bending over him. He talked of this the next day, but it was treated as a dream; until in the course of the day his uncle Algernon was driven home from Lobourne cricket-ground with a broken leg. Then it was recollected that there was a family ghost; and, though no member of the family believed in the ghost, none would have given up a circumstance that testified to its existence; for to possess a ghost is a distinction above titles.

Algernon Feverel lost his leg, and ceased to be a gentleman in the Guards. Of the other uncles of young Richard, Cuthbert, the sailor, perished in a spirited boat expedition against a slaving negro chief up the Niger. Some of the gallant lieutenant's trophies of war decorated the little boy's play-shed at Raynham, and he bequeathed his sword to Richard, whose hero he was. The diplomatist and beau, Vivian, ended his flutterings from flower to flower by making an improper marriage, as is the fate of many a beau, and was struck out of the list of visitors. Algernon generally occupied the baronet's disused town-house, a wretched being, dividing his time between horse and card exercise: possessed, it was said, of the absurd notion that a man who has lost his balance by losing his leg may regain it by sticking to the bottle. At least, whenever he and his brother Hippias got together, they never failed to try whether one leg, or two, stood the bottle best. Much of a puritan as Sir Austin was in his habits, he was too good a host, and too thorough a gentleman, to impose them upon his guests. The brothers, and other relatives, might do as they would while they did not disgrace the name, and then it was final: they must depart to behold his countenance no more.

Algernon Feverel was a simple man, who felt, subsequent to his misfortune, as he had perhaps dimly fancied it before, that his career lay in his legs, and was now irrevocably cut short. He taught the boy boxing, and shooting, and the arts of fence, and superintended the direction of his animal vigour with a melancholy vivacity. The remaining energies of Algernon's mind were devoted to animadversions on swift bowling. He preached it over the county, struggling through laborious literary compositions, addressed to sporting newspapers, on the Decline of Cricket. It was Algernon who witnessed and chronicled young Richard's first fight, which was with young Tom Blaize of Belthorpe Farm, three years the boy's senior.

Hippias Feverel was once thought to be the genius of the family. It was his ill luck to have strong appetites and a weak stomach; and, as one is not altogether fit for the battle of life who is engaged in a perpetual contention with his dinner, Hippias forsook his prospects at the Bar, and, in the embraces of dyspepsia, compiled his ponderous work on the Fairy Mythology of Europe. He had little to do with the Hope of Raynham beyond what he endured from his juvenile tricks.

A venerable lady, known as Great Aunt Grantley, who had money to bequeath to the heir, occupied with Hippias the background of the house and shared her caudles*with him. These two were seldom seen till the dinner-hour, for which they were all day preparing, and probably all night remembering, for the Eighteenth Century was an admirable trencherman, and cast age aside while there was a dish on the table.

Mrs. Doria Forey was the eldest of the three sisters of the baronet, a florid affable woman, with fine teeth, exceedingly fine light wavy hair, a Norman nose, and a reputation for understanding men; and that, with these practical creatures, always means the art of managing them. She had married an expectant younger son of a good family, who deceased before the fulfilment of his prospects; and, casting about in her mind the future chances of her little daughter and sole child, Clare, she marked down a probability. The far sight, the deep determination, the resolute perseverance of her sex, where a daughter is to be provided for and a man to be overthrown, instigated her to invite herself to Raynham, where, with that daughter, she fixed herself.

The other two Feverel ladies were the wife of Colonel Wentworth and the widow of Mr. Justice Harley: and the only thing remarkable about them was that they were mothers of sons of some distinction.

Austin Wentworth's story was of that wretched character which to be comprehended, that justice should be dealt him, must be told out and openly; which no one dares now do.

For a fault in early youth, redeemed by him nobly, according to his light, he was condemned to undergo the world's harsh judgement: not for the fault—for its atonement.

'—Married his mother's housemaid,' whispered Mrs. Doria, with a ghastly look, and a shudder at young men of republican sentiments, which he was reputed to entertain.

'The compensation for Injustice,' says the 'Pilgrim's Scrip,' 'is, that in that dark Ordeal we gather the worthiest around us.'

And the baronet's fair friend, Lady Blandish, and some few true men and women, held Austin Wentworth high.

He did not live with his wife; and Sir Austin, whose mind was bent on the future of our species, reproached him with being barren to posterity, while knaves were propagating.

The principal characteristic of the second nephew, Adrian Harley, was his sagacity. He was essentially the wise youth, both in counsel and in action.

'In action,' the 'Pilgrim's Scrip' observes, 'Wisdom goes by majorities.'

Adrian had an instinct for the majority, and, as the world invariably found him enlisted in its ranks, his apellation of wise youth was acquiesced in without irony.

The wise youth, then, had the world with him, but no friends. Nor did he wish for those troublesome appendages of success. He caused himself to be required by people who could serve him; feared by such as could injure. Not that he went out of the way to secure his end, or risked the expense of a plot. He did the work as easily as he ate his daily bread. Adrian was an epicurean;* one whom Epicurus would have scourged out of his garden, certainly: an epicurean of our modern notions. To satisfy his appetites without rashly staking his character was the wise youth's problem for life. He had no intimates except Gibbon and Horace,* and the society of these fine aristocrats of literature helped him to accept humanity as it had been, and was; a supreme ironic procession, with laughter of Gods in the background. Why not laughter of mortals also? Adrian had his laugh in his comfortable corner. He possessed peculiar attributes of a heathen God. He was a disposer of men: he was polished, luxurious, and happy —at their cost. He lived in eminent self-content, as one lying on soft cloud, lapped in sunshine. Nor Jove, nor Apollo, cast eye upon the maids of earth with cooler fire of selection, or pursued them in the covert with more sacred impunity. And he enjoyed his reputation for virtue as something additional. Stolen fruits are said to be sweet; undeserved rewards are exquisite.

The best of it was, that Adrian made no pretences. He did not solicit the favourable judgement of the world. Nature and he attempted no other concealment than the ordinary mask men wear. And yet the world would proclaim him moral, as well as wise, and the pleasing converse every way of his disgraced cousin Austin.

In a word, Adrian Harley had mastered his philosophy at the early age of one-and-twenty. Many would be glad to say the same at that age twice-told: they carry in their breasts a burden with which Adrian's was not loaded. Mrs. Doria was nearly right about his heart. A singular mishap (at his birth, possibly, or before it) had unseated that organ, and shaken it down to his stomach, where it was a much lighter, nay, an inspiring weight, and encouraged him merrily onward. Throned there it looked on little that did not arrive to gratify it. Already that region was a trifle prominent in the person of the wise youth, and carried, as it were, the flag of his philosophical tenets in front of him. He was charming after dinner, with men or with women: delightfully sarcastic: perhaps a little too unscrupulous in his moral tone, but that his moral reputation belied him, and it must be set down to generosity of disposition.

Such was Adrian Harley, another of Sir Austin's intellectual favourites, chosen from mankind to superintend the education of his son at Raynham. Adrian had been destined for the Church. He did not enter into Orders. He and the baronet had a conference together one day, and from that time Adrian became a fixture in the Abbey. His father died in his promising son's college term, bequeathing him nothing but his legal complexion, and Adrian became stipendiary officer in his uncle's household.

A playfellow of Richard's occasionally, and the only comrade of his age that he ever saw, was Master Ripton Thompson, the son of Sir Austin's solicitor, a boy without a character.

A comrade of some description was necessary, for Richard was neither to go to school nor to college. Sir Austin considered that the schools were corrupt, and maintained that young lads might by parental vigilance be kept pretty secure from the Serpent until Eve sided with him: a period that might be deferred, he said. He had a system of education for his son. How it worked we shall see.

CHAPTER II

SHOWING HOW THE FATES SELECTED THE FOURTEENTH BIRTHDAY TO TRY THE STRENGTH OF THE SYSTEM

OCTOBER shone royally on Richard's fourteenth birthday. The brown beechwoods and golden birches glowed to a brilliant sun. Banks of moveless cloud hung about the horizon, mounded to the west, where slept the wind. Promise of a great day for Raynham, as it proved to be, though not in the manner marked out.

Already archery-booths and cricketing-tents were rising on the lower grounds towards the river, whither the lads of Bursley and Lobourne, in boats and in carts, shouting for a day of ale and honour, jogged merrily to match themselves anew, and pluck at the living laurel from each other's brows, like manly Britons. The whole park was beginning to be astir and resound with holiday cries. Sir Austin Feverel, a thorough good Tory, was no game-preserver, and could be popular whenever he chose, which Sir Miles Papworth, on the other side of the river, a fast-handed Whig and terror to poachers, never could be. Half the village of Lobourne was seen trooping through the avenues of the park. Fiddlers and gipsies clamoured at the gates for admission: white smocks, and slate, surmounted by hats of serious brim, and now and then a scarlet cloak, smacking of the old country, dotted the grassy sweeps to the levels.

And all the time the star of these festivities was receding further and further, and eclipsing himself with his reluctant serf Ripton, who kept asking what they were to do and where they were going, and how late it was in the day, and suggesting that the lads of Lobourne would be calling out for them, and Sir Austin requiring their presence, without getting any attention paid to his misery or remonstrances. For Richard had been requested by his father to submit to medical examination like a boor enlisting for a soldier, and he was in great wrath.

He was flying as though he would have flown from the shameful thought of what had been asked of him. By and by he communicated his sentiments to Ripton, who said they were those of a girl: an offensive remark, remembering which, Richard, after they had borrowed a couple of guns at the bailiff's farm, and Ripton had fired badly, called his friend a fool.

Feeling that circumstances were making him look wonderfully like one, Ripton lifted his head and retorted defiantly, 'I 'm not!'

This angry contradiction, so very uncalled for, annoyed Richard, who was still smarting at the loss of the birds, owing to Ripton's bad shot, and was really the injured party. He therefore bestowed the abusive epithet on Ripton anew, and with increase of emphasis.

'You shan't call me so, then, whether I am or not,' says Ripton, and sucks his lips.

This was becoming personal. Richard sent up his brows, and stared at his defier an instant. He then informed him that he certainly should call him so, and would not object to call him so twenty times.

'Do it, and see!' returns Ripton, rocking on his feet, and breathing quick.

With a gravity of which only boys and other barbarians are capable, Richard went through the entire number, stressing the epithet to increase the defiance and avoid monotony, as he progressed, while Ripton bobbed his head every time in assent, as it were, to his comrade's accuracy, and as a record for his profound humiliation. The dog they had with them gazed at the extraordinary performance with interrogating wags of the tail.

Twenty times, duly and deliberately, Richard repeated the obnoxious word.

At the twentieth solemn iteration of Ripton's capital shortcoming, Ripton delivered a smart back-hander on Richard's mouth, and squared precipitately; perhaps sorry when the deed was done, for he was a kind-hearted lad, and as Richard simply bowed in acknowledgment of the blow he thought he had gone too far. He did not know the young gentleman he was dealing with. Richard was extremely cool.

'Shall we fight here?' he said.

'Anywhere you like,' replied Ripton.

'A little more into the wood, I think. We may be interrupted.' And Richard led the way with a courteous reserve that somewhat chilled Ripton's ardour for the contest. On the skirts of the wood, Richard threw off his jacket and waistcoat, and, quite collected, waited for Ripton to do the same. The latter boy was flushed and restless; older and broader, but not so tight-limbed and well-set. The Gods, sole witnesses of their battle, betted dead against him. Richard had mounted the white cockade of the Feverels, and there was a look in him that asked for tough work to extinguish. His brows, slightly lined upward at the temples, converging to a knot about the well-set straight nose; his full grey eyes, open nostrils, and planted feet, and a gentlemanly air of calm and alertness, formed a spirited picture of a young combatant. As for Ripton, he was all abroad, and fought in school-boy style—that is, he rushed at the foe head foremost, and struck like a windmill. He was a lumpy boy. When he did hit, he made himself felt; but he was at the mercy of science. To see him come dashing in, blinking and puffing and whirling his arms abroad while the felling blow went straight between them, you perceived that he was fighting a fight of desperation, and knew it. For the dreaded alternative glared him in the face that, if he yielded, he must look like what he had been twenty times calumniously called; and he would die rather than yield, and swing his windmill till he dropped. Poor boy! he dropped frequently. The gallant fellow fought for appearances, and down he went. The Gods favour one of two parties. Prince Turnus*was a noble youth; but he had not Pallas*at his elbow. Ripton was a capital boy; he had no science. He could not prove he was not a fool! When one comes to think of it, Ripton did choose the only possible way, and we should all of us have considerable difficulty in proving the negative by any other. Ripton came on the unerring fist again and again; and if it was true, as he said in short colloquial gasps, that he required as much beating as an egg to be beaten thoroughly, a fortunate interruption alone saved our friend from resembling that substance. The boys heard summoning voices, and beheld Mr. Morton of Poer Hall and Austin Wentworth stepping towards them.

A truce was sounded, jackets were caught up, guns shouldered, and off they trotted in concert through the depths of the wood, not stopping till that and half-a-dozen fields and a larch plantation were well behind them.

When they halted to•take breath, there was a mutual study of faces. Ripton's was much discoloured, and looked fiercer with its natural war-paint than the boy felt. Nevertheless, he squared up dauntlessly on the new ground, and

Richard, whose wrath was appeased, could not refrain from asking him whether he had not really had enough.

'Never!' shouts the noble enemy.

'Well, look here,' said Richard, appealing to common sense, 'I'm tired of knocking you down. I'll say you're not a fool, if you'll give me your hand.'

Ripton demurred an instant to consult with honour, who bade him catch at his chance.

He held out his hand. 'There!' and the boys grasped hands and were fast friends. Ripton had gained his point, and Richard decidedly had the best of it. So they were on equal ground. Both could claim a victory, which was all the better for their friendship.

Ripton washed his face and comforted his nose at a brook, and was now ready to follow his friend wherever he chose to lead. They continued to beat about for birds. The birds on the Raynham estates were found singularly cunning, and repeatedly eluded the aim of these prime shots, so they pushed their expedition into the lands of their neighbours, in search of a stupider race, happily oblivious of the laws and conditions of trespass; unconscious, too, that they were poaching on the demesne of the notorious Farmer Blaize, the free-trade farmer*under the shield of the Papworths, no worshipper of the Griffin between two Wheatsheaves; destined to be much allied with Richard's fortunes from beginning to end. Farmer Blaize hated poachers, and especially young chaps poaching, who did it mostly from impudence. He heard the audacious shots popping right and left, and going forth to have a glimpse at the intruders, and observing their size, swore he would teach my gentlemen a thing, lords or no lords.

Richard had brought down a beautiful cock-pheasant, and was exulting over it, when the farmer's portentous figure burst upon them, cracking an avenging horsewhip. His salute was ironical.

'Havin' good sport, gentlemen, are ye?'

'Just bagged a splendid bird!' radiant Richard informed him.

'Oh!' Farmer Blaize gave an admonitory flick of the whip.

'Just let me clap eye on 't, then.'

'Say, please,' interposed Ripton, who was not blind to doubtful aspects.

Farmer Blaize threw up his chin, and grinned grimly.

'Please to you, sir? Why, my chap, you looks as if ye didn't much mind what come t' yer nose, I reckon. You looks an old poacher, you do. Tall ye what 'tis!' He changed his banter to business, 'That bird 's mine! Now you jest hand him over, and sheer off, you dam young scoundrels! I know ye!' And he became exceedingly opprobrious, and uttered contempt of the name of Feverel.

Richard opened his eyes.

'If you wants to be horsewhipped, you 'll stay where y' are!' continued the farmer. 'Giles Blaize never stands nonsense!'

'Then we 'll stay,' quoth Richard.

'Good! so be 't! If you will have 't, have 't, my men!'

As a preparatory measure, Farmer Blaize seized a wing of the bird, on which both boys flung themselves desperately, and secured it minus the pinion.

'That 's your game,' cried the farmer. 'Here 's a taste of horsewhip for ye. I never stands nonsense!' and sweetch went the mighty whip, well swayed. The boys tried to close with him. He kept his distance and lashed without mercy. Black blood was made by Farmer Blaize that day! The boys wriggled, in spite of themselves. It was like a relentless serpent coiling, and biting, and stinging their young veins to madness. Probably they felt the disgrace of the contortions they were made to go through more than the pain, but the pain was fierce, for the farmer

laid about from a practised arm, and did not consider that
he had done enough till he was well breathed and his ruddy
jowl inflamed. He paused, to receive the remainder of
the cock-pheasant in his face.

'Take your beastly bird,' cried Richard.

'Money, my lads, and interest,' roared the farmer,
lashing out again.

Shameful as it was to retreat, there was but that course
open to them.   They decided to surrender the field.

'Look! you big brute,' Richard shook his gun, hoarse
with passion, 'I'd have shot you, if I'd been loaded.
Mind! if I come across you when I'm loaded, you coward,
I'll fire!'

The un-English nature of this threat exasperated Farmer
Blaize, and he pressed the pursuit in time to bestow a few
farewell stripes as they were escaping tight-breeched into
neutral territory. At the hedge they parleyed a minute,
the farmer to inquire if they had had a mortal good tan-
ning and were satisfied, for when they wanted a further
instalment of the same they were to come for it to Belthorpe Farm, and there it was in pickle: the boys meantime exploding in menaces and threats of vengeance, on
which the farmer contemptuously turned his back.   Ripton had already stocked an armful of flints for the enjoyment of a little skirmishing.   Richard, however, knocked
them all out, saying, 'No! Gentlemen don't fling stones;
leave that to the blackguards.'

'Just one shy at him!' pleaded Ripton, with his eye on
Farmer Blaize's broad mark, and his whole mind drunken
with a sudden revelation of the advantages of light troops
in opposition to heavies.

'No,' said Richard, imperatively, 'no stones,' and
marched briskly away. Ripton followed with a sigh.
His leader's magnanimity was wholly beyond him. A
good spanking mark at the farmer would have relieved

Master Ripton; it would have done nothing to console Richard Feverel for the ignominy he had been compelled to submit to. Ripton was familiar with the rod, a monster much despoiled of his terrors by intimacy. Birch-fever was past with this boy. The horrible sense of shame, self-loathing, universal hatred, impotent vengeance, as if the spirit were steeped in abysmal blackness, which comes upon a courageous and sensitive youth condemned for the first time to taste this piece of fleshly bitterness, and suffer what he feels is a defilement, Ripton had weathered and forgotten. He was seasoned wood, and took the world pretty wisely; not reckless of castigation, as some boys become, nor over-sensitive as to dishonour, as his friend and comrade beside him was.

Richard's blood was poisoned. He had the fever on him severely. He would not allow stone-flinging, because it was a habit of his to discountenance it. Mere gentlemanly considerations had scarce shielded Farmer Blaize, and certain very ungentlemanly schemes were coming to ghastly heads in the tumult of his brain; rejected solely from their glaring impracticability even to his young intelligence. A sweeping and consummate vengeance for the indignity alone should satisfy him. Something tremendous must be done, and done without delay. At one moment he thought of killing all the farmer's cattle; next of killing him; challenging him to single combat with the arms, and according to the fashion of gentlemen. But the farmer was a coward; he would refuse. Then he, Richard Feverel, would stand by the farmer's bedside, and rouse him; rouse him to fight with powder and ball in his own chamber, in the cowardly midnight, where he might tremble, but dare not refuse.

'Lord!' cried simple Ripton, while these hopeful plots were raging in his comrade's brain, now sparkling for immediate execution, and anon lapsing disdainfully dark in their chances of fulfilment, 'how I wish you'd have let me notch him, Ricky! I'm a safe shot. I never miss. I should feel quite jolly if I'd spanked him once. We should have had the best of him at that game. I say!' and a sharp thought drew Ripton's ideas nearer home, 'I wonder whether my nose is as bad as he says! Where can I see myself?'

To these exclamations Richard was deaf, and he trudged steadily forward, facing but one object.

After tearing through innumerable hedges, leaping fences, jumping dykes, penetrating brambly copses, and getting dirty, ragged, and tired, Ripton awoke from his dream of Farmer Blaize and a blue nose to the vivid consciousness of hunger; and this grew with the rapidity of light upon him, till in the course of another minute he was enduring the extremes of famine, and ventured to question his leader whither he was being conducted. Raynham was out of sight. They were a long way down the valley, miles from Lobourne, in a country of sour pools, yellow brooks, rank pasturage, desolate heath. Solitary cows were seen; the smoke of a mud cottage; a cart piled with peat; a donkey grazing at leisure, oblivious of an unkind world; geese by a horse-pond, gabbling as in the first loneliness of creation; uncooked things that a famishing boy cannot possibly care for, and must despise. Ripton was in despair.

'Where *are* you going to?' he inquired with a voice of the last time of asking, and halted resolutely.

Richard now broke his silence to reply, 'Anywhere.'

'Anywhere!' Ripton took up the moody word. 'But ain't you awfully hungry?' he gasped vehemently, in a way that showed the total emptiness of his stomach.

'No,' was Richard's brief response.

'Not hungry!' Ripton's amazement lent him increased vehemence. 'Why, you haven't had anything to eat since breakfast! Not hungry? I declare I'm starving. I feel such a gnawing I could eat dry bread and cheese!'

Richard sneered: not for reasons that would have actuated a similar demonstration of the philosopher.

'Come,' cried Ripton, 'at all events, tell us where you're going to stop.'

Richard faced about to make a querulous retort. The injured and hapless visage that met his eye disarmed him. The lad's nose, though not exactly of the dreaded hue, was really becoming discoloured. To upbraid him would be cruel. Richard lifted his head, surveyed the position, and exclaiming 'Here!' dropped down on a withered bank, leaving Ripton to contemplate him as a puzzle whose every new move was a worse perplexity.

CHAPTER III

THE MAGIAN CONFLICT

AMONG boys there are laws of honour and chivalrous codes, not written or formally taught, but intuitively understood by all, and invariably acted upon by the loyal and the true. The race is not nearly civilized, we must remember. Thus, not to follow your leader whithersoever he may think proper to lead; to back out of an expedition because the end of it frowns dubious, and the present fruit of it is discomfort; to quit a comrade on the road, and return home without him: these are tricks which no boy of spirit would be guilty of, let him come to any description of mortal grief in consequence. Better so than have his own conscience denouncing him sneak. Some boys who behave boldly enough are not troubled by this conscience, and the eyes and the lips of their fellows have to supply the deficiency. They do it with just as haunting, and even more horrible pertinacity, than the inner voice, and the result, if the probation be not very severe and searching, is the same. The leader can rely on the faithfulness of his host: the comrade is sworn to serve. Master Ripton Thompson was naturally loyal. The idea of turning off and forsaking his friend never once crossed his mind, though his condition was desperate, and his friend's behaviour that of a Bedlamite.* He announced several times impatiently that they would be too late for dinner. His friend did not budge. Dinner seemed nothing to him. There he lay plucking grass, and patting the old dog's nose, as if incapable of conceiving what a thing hunger was. Ripton took half-a-dozen turns up and down, and at last flung himself down beside the taciturn boy, accepting his fate.

Now, the chance that works for certain purposes sent a smart shower from the sinking sun, and the wet sent two strangers for shelter in the lane behind the hedge where the boys reclined. One was a travelling tinker,* who lit a pipe and spread a tawny umbrella. The other was a burly young countryman, pipeless and tentless. They saluted with a nod, and began recounting for each other's benefit the day-long doings of the weather, as it had affected their individual experience and followed their prophecies. Both had anticipated and foretold a bit of rain before night, and therefore both welcomed the wet with satisfaction. A monotonous betweenwhiles kind of talk they kept droning, in harmony with the still hum of the air. From the weather theme they fell upon the blessings of tobacco; how it was the poor man's friend, his company, his consolation, his comfort, his refuge at night, his first thought in the morning.

'Better than a wife!' chuckled the tinker. 'No curtain-lecturin' with a pipe. Your pipe an't a shrew.'

'That be it!' the other chimed in. 'Your pipe doan't mak' ye out wi' all the cash Saturday evenin'.'

'Take one,' said the tinker, in the enthusiasm of the moment, handing a grimy short clay. Speed-the-Plough filled from the tinker's pouch, and continued his praises.

'Penny a day, and there y' are, primed! Better than a wife? Ha, ha!'

'And you can get rid of it, if ye wants for to, and when ye wants,' added tinker.

'So ye can!' Speed-the-Plough took him up. 'And ye doan't want for to. Leastways, t' other case. I means pipe.'

'And,' continued tinker, comprehending him perfectly, 'it don't bring repentance after it.'

'Not nohow, master, it doan't! And'—Speed-the-Plough cocked his eye—'it doan't eat up half the victuals, your pipe doan't.'

Here the honest yeoman gesticulated his keen sense of a clincher, which the tinker acknowledged; and having, so to speak, sealed up the subject by saying the best thing that could be said, the two smoked for some time in silence to the drip and patter of the shower.

Ripton solaced his wretchedness by watching them through the briar hedge. He saw the tinker stroking a white cat, and appealing to her, every now and then, as his missus, for an opinion or a confirmation; and he thought that a curious sight. Speed-the-Plough was stretched at full length, with his boots in the rain, and his head amidst the tinker's pots, smoking, profoundly contemplative. The minutes seemed to be taken up alternately by the grey puffs from their mouths.

It was the tinker who renewed the colloquy. Said he, 'Times is bad!'

His companion assented, 'Sure-ly!'

'But it somehow comes round right,' resumed the

tinker. 'Why, look here. Where's the good o' moping?
I sees it all come round right and tight. Now I travels
about. I 've got my beat. 'Casion calls me t 'other day to
Newcastle!—Eh?'

'Coals!' ejaculated Speed-the-Plough sonorously.

'Coals!' echoed the tinker. 'You ask what I goes
there for, mayhap? Never you mind. One sees a mort*
o' life in my trade. Not for coals it isn't. And I don't
carry 'em there, neither. Anyhow, I comes back. London's my mark. Says I, I 'll see a bit o' the sea, and steps
aboard a collier.* We were as nigh wrecked as the prophet
Paul.'*

'A—who's him?' the other wished to know.

'Read your Bible,' said the tinker. 'We pitched and
tossed—'tain't that game at sea 'tis on land, I can tell ye!
I thinks, down we 're agoing—say your prayers, Bob
Tiles! That was a night, to be sure! But God's above
the devil, and here I am, ye see.'

Speed-the-Plough lurched round on his elbow and regarded him indifferently. 'D 'ye call that doctrin'? He
bean 't al 'ays, or I shoo'n't be scrapin' my heels wi' nothin'
to do, and, what's warse, nothin' to eat. Why, look heer.
Luck's luck, and bad luck's the con-trary. Varmer
Bollop, t 'other day, has's rick burnt down. Next night
his gran'ry's burnt. What do he tak' and go and do? He
takes and goes and hangs unsel', and turns us out of his
employ. God warn't above the devil then, I thinks, or I
can't make out the reckonin'."

The tinker cleared his throat, and said it was a bad
case.

'And a darn'd bad case. I 'll tak' my oath on 't!' cried
Speed-the-Plough. 'Well, look heer! Heer's another
darn'd bad case. I threshed for Varmer Blaize—Blaize
o' Beltharpe—afore I goes to Varmer Bollop. Varmer
Blaize misses pilkins.* He swears our chaps steals pilkins.

'Twarn't me steals 'em. What do *he* tak' and go and do?
He takes and tarns us off, me and another, neck and crop,
to scuffle about and starve, for all *he* keers. God warn't
above the devil then, I thinks. Not nohow, as I can see!'

The tinker shook his head, and said that was a bad case
also.

'And you can't mend it,' added Speed-the-Plough.
'It's bad, and there it be. But I'll tell ye what, master.
Bad wants payin' for.' He nodded and winked mysteriously. 'Bad has its wages as well's honest work, I'm
thinkin'. Varmer Bollop I don't owe no grudge to: Varmer Blaize I do. And I shud like to stick a Lucifer in
his rick some dry windy night.' Speed-the-Plough
screwed up an eye villainously. 'He wants hittin' in the
wind,—jest where the pocket is, master, do Varmer Blaize,
and he'll cry out "O Lor'!" Varmer Blaize will. You
won't get the better o' Varmer Blaize by no means, as I
makes out, if ye doan't hit into him jest there.'

The tinker sent a rapid succession of white clouds from
his mouth, and said that would be taking the devil's side
of a bad case. Speed-the-Plough observed energetically
that, if Farmer Blaize was on the other, he should be on
that side.

There was a young gentleman close by, who thought
with him. The hope of Raynham had lent a careless half-
compelled attention to the foregoing dialogue, wherein a
common labourer and a travelling tinker had propounded
and discussed one of the most ancient theories of trans-
mundane dominion and influence on mundane affairs. He
now started to his feet, and came tearing through the briar
hedge, calling out for one of them to direct them the nearest
road to Bursley. The tinker was kindling preparations
for his tea, under the tawny umbrella. A loaf was set forth,
on which Ripton's eyes, stuck in the edge, fastened rav-
enously. Speed-the-Plough volunteered information that

Bursley was a good three mile from where they stood, and a good eight mile from Lobourne.

'I 'll give you half-a-crown for that loaf, my good fellow,' said Richard to the tinker.

'It 's a bargain,' quoth the tinker, 'eh, missus?'

His cat replied by humping her back at the dog.

The half-crown was tossed down, and Ripton, who had just succeeded in freeing his limbs from the briar, prickly as a hedgehog, collared the loaf.

'Those young squires be sharp-set, and no mistake,' said the tinker to his companion. 'Come! we 'll to Bursley after 'em, and talk it out over a pot o' beer.' Speed-the-Plough was nothing loth, and in a short time they were following the two lads on the road to Bursley, while a horizontal blaze shot across the autumn land from the Western edge of the rain-cloud.

CHAPTER IV

ARSON

SEARCH for the missing boys had been made everywhere over Raynham, and Sir Austin was in grievous discontent. None had seen them save Austin Wentworth and Mr. Morton. The baronet sat construing their account of the flight of the lads when they were hailed, and resolved it into an act of rebellion on the part of his son. At dinner he drank the young heir's health in ominous silence. Adrian Harley stood up in his place to propose the health. His speech was a fine piece of rhetoric. He warmed in it till, after the Ciceronic model, inanimate objects were personified, and Richard's table-napkin and vacant chair were invoked to follow the steps of a peerless father, and

uphold with his dignity the honour of the Feverels. Austin
Wentworth, whom a soldier's death compelled to take his
father's place in support of the toast, was tame after such
magniloquence. But the reply, the thanks which young
Richard should have delivered in person were not forthcoming. Adrian's oratory had given but a momentary
life to napkin and chair. The company of honoured friends,
and aunts, and uncles, and remotest cousins, were glad to
disperse and seek amusement in music and tea. Sir Austin
did his utmost to be hospitably cheerful, and requested
them to dance. If he had desired them to laugh he would
have been obeyed, and in as hearty a manner.

'How triste!' said Mrs. Doria Forey to Lobourne's
curate, as that most enamoured automaton went through
his paces beside her with professional stiffness.

'One who does not suffer can hardly assent,' the curate
answered, basking in her beams.

'Ah, you are good!' exclaimed the lady. 'Look at my
Clare. She will not dance on her cousin's birthday with
any one but him. What are we to do to enliven these
people?'

'Alas, madam! you cannot do for all what you do for
one,' the curate sighed, and wherever she wandered in
discourse, drew her back with silken strings to gaze on his
enamoured soul.

He was the only gratified stranger present. The others
had designs on the young heir. Lady Attenbury of Long-
ford House had brought her highly-polished specimen of
marketware, the Lady Juliana Jaye, for a first introduction to him, thinking he had arrived at an age to estimate
and pine for her black eyes and pretty pert mouth. The
Lady Juliana had to pair off with a dapper Papworth, and
her mama was subjected to the gallantries of Sir Miles,
who talked land and steam-engines to her till she was sick,
and had to be impertinent in self-defence. Lady Blandish,

the delightful widow, sat apart with Adrian, and enjoyed his sarcasms on the company. By ten at night the poor show ended, and the rooms were dark, dark as the prognostics multitudinously hinted by the disappointed and chilled guests concerning the probable future of the hope of Raynham. Little Clare kissed her mama, curtsied to the lingering curate, and went to bed like a very good girl. Immediately the maid had departed, little Clare deliberately exchanged night attire for that of day. She was noted as an obedient child. Her light was always allowed to burn in her room for half-an-hour, to counteract her fears of the dark. She took the light, and stole on tiptoe to Richard's room. No Richard was there. She peeped in further and further. A trifling agitation of the curtains shot her back through the door and along the passage to her own bedchamber with extreme expedition. She was not much alarmed, but feeling guilty she was on her guard. In a short time she was prowling about the passages again. Richard had slighted and offended the little lady, and was to be asked whether he did not repent such conduct toward his cousin; not to be asked whether he had forgotten to receive his birthday kiss from her; for, if he did not choose to remember that, Miss Clare would never remind him of it, and to-night should be his last chance of a reconciliation. Thus she meditated, sitting on a stair, and presently heard Richard's voice below in the hall, shouting for supper.

'Master Richard has returned,' old Benson the butler tolled out intelligence to Sir Austin.

'Well?' said the baronet.

'He complains of being hungry,' the butler hesitated, with a look of solemn disgust.

'Let him eat.'

Heavy Benson hesitated still more as he announced that the boy had called for wine. It was an unprecedented thing. Sir Austin's brows were portending an arch, but

Adrian suggested that he wanted possibly to drink his birthday, and claret was conceded.

The boys were in the vortex of a partridge-pie when Adrian strolled in to them. They had now changed characters. Richard was uproarious. He drank a health with every glass; his cheeks were flushed and his eyes brilliant. Ripton looked very much like a rogue on the tremble of detection, but his honest hunger and the partridge-pie shielded him awhile from Adrian's scrutinizing glance. Adrian saw there was matter for study, if it were only on Master Ripton's betraying nose, and sat down to hear and mark.

'Good sport, gentlemen, I trust to hear?' he began his quiet banter, and provoked a loud peal of laughter from Richard.

'Ha, ha! I say, Rip: "Havin' good sport, gentlemen, are ye?" You remember the farmer! Your health, parson! We haven't had our sport yet. We're going to have some first-rate sport. Oh, well! we haven't much show of birds. We shot for pleasure, and returned them to the proprietors. You're fond of game, parson! Ripton is a dead shot in what Cousin Austin calls the Kingdom of "would-have-done" and "might-have-been." Up went the birds, and cries Rip, "I've forgotten to load!" Oh, ho!—Rip! some more claret. —Do just leave that nose of yours alone.—Your health, Ripton Thompson! The birds hadn't the decency to wait for him, and so, parson, it's their fault, and not Rip's, you haven't a dozen brace at your feet. What have you been doing at home, Cousin Rady?'

'Playing Hamlet, in the absence of the Prince of Denmark. The day without you, my dear boy, must be dull, you know.'

'"He speaks: can I trust what he says is sincere?
There's an edge to his smile that cuts much like a sneer."

Sandoe's poems! You know the couplet, Mr. Rady. Why
shouldn't I quote Sandoe? You know you like him, Rady.
But, if you 've missed me, I 'm sorry. Rip and I have had
a beautiful day. We 've made new acquaintances. We 've
seen the world. I 'm the monkey that has seen the world,
and I 'm going to tell you all about it. First, there 's a
gentleman who takes a rifle for a fowling-piece. Next,
there 's a farmer who warns everybody, gentleman and
beggar, off his premises. Next, there 's a tinker and a
ploughman, who think that God is always fighting with
the devil which shall command the kingdoms of the earth.
The tinker 's for God, and the ploughman——'

'I 'll drink your health, Ricky,' said Adrian, interrupting.

'Oh, I forgot, parson;—I mean no harm, Adrian. I 'm
only telling what I 've heard.'

'No harm, my dear boy,' returned Adrian. 'I 'm perfectly aware that Zoroaster*is not dead. You have been
listening to a common creed. Drink the Fire-worshippers,*
if you will.'

'Here's to Zoroaster, then!' cried Richard. 'I say,
Rippy! we 'll drink the Fire-worshippers to-night, won't
we?'

A fearful conspiratorial frown, that would not have disgraced Guido Fawkes,* was darted back from the plastic
features of Master Ripton.

Richard gave his lungs loud play.

'Why, what did you say about Blaizes, Rippy? Didn't
you say it was fun?'

Another hideous and silencing frown was Ripton's
answer. Adrian watched the innocent youths, and knew
that there was talking under the table. 'See,' thought
he, 'this boy has tasted his first scraggy morsel of life to-
day, and already he talks like an old stager, and has, if I
mistake not, been acting too. My respected chief,' he
apostrophized Sir Austin, 'combustibles are only the more

dangerous for compression. This boy will be ravenous
for Earth when he is let loose, and very soon make his
share of it look as foolish as yonder game-pie!'—a prophecy Adrian kept to himself.

Uncle Algernon shambled in to see his nephew before the
supper was finished, and his more genial presence brought
out a little of the plot.

'Look here, uncle!' said Richard. 'Would you let a
churlish old brute of a farmer strike you without making
him suffer for it?'

'I fancy I should return the compliment, my lad,'
replied his uncle.

'Of course you would! So would I. And he shall suffer
for it.' The boy looked savage, and his uncle patted him
down.

'I've boxed his son; I'll box him,' said Richard, shouting for more wine.

'What, boy! Is it old Blaize has been putting you up?'

'Never mind, uncle!' The boy nodded mysteriously.

Look there! Adrian read on Ripton's face, he says
'never mind,' and lets it out!

'Did we beat to-day, uncle?'

'Yes, boy; and we'd beat them any day they bowl
fair. I'd beat them on one leg. There's only Natkins
and Featherdene among them worth a farthing.'

'We beat!' cries Richard. 'Then we'll have some
more wine, and drink their healths.'

The bell was rung; wine ordered. Presently comes in
heavy Benson, to say supplies are cut off. One bottle,
and no more. The Captain whistled: Adrian shrugged.

The bottle, however, was procured by Adrian subsequently. He liked studying intoxicated urchins.

One subject was at Richard's heart, about which he was
reserved in the midst of his riot. Too proud to inquire
how his father had taken his absence, he burned to hear

whether he was in disgrace. He led to it repeatedly, and it was constantly evaded by Algernon and Adrian. At last, when the boy declared a desire to wish his father good-night, Adrian had to tell him that he was to go straight to bed from the supper-table. Young Richard's face fell at that, and his gaiety forsook him. He marched to his room without another word.

Adrian gave Sir Austin an able version of his son's behaviour and adventures; dwelling upon this sudden taciturnity when he heard of his father's resolution not to see him. The wise youth saw that his chief was mollified behind his moveless mask, and went to bed, and Horace, leaving Sir Austin in his study. Long hours the baronet sat alone. The house had not its usual influx of Feverels that day. Austin Wentworth was staying at Poer Hall, and had only come over for an hour. At midnight the house breathed sleep. Sir Austin put on his cloak and cap, and took the lamp to make his rounds. He apprehended nothing special, but with a mind never at rest he constituted himself the sentinel of Raynham. He passed the chamber where the Great-Aunt Grantley lay, who was to swell Richard's fortune, and so perform her chief business on earth. By her door he murmured, 'Good creature! you sleep with a sense of duty done,' and paced on, reflecting, 'She has not made money a demon of discord,' and blessed her. He had his thoughts at Hippias's somnolent door, and to them the world might have subscribed.

A monomaniac at large, watching over sane people in slumber! thinks Adrian Harley, as he hears Sir Austin's footfall, and truly that was a strange object to see.—Where is the fortress that has not one weak gate? where the man who is sound at each particular angle? Ay, meditates the recumbent cynic, more or less mad is not every mother's son? Favourable circumstances—good air, good company, two or three good rules rigidly adhered to—keep the world out of Bedlam. But, let the world fly into a passion, and is not Bedlam the safest abode for it?

Sir Austin ascended the stairs, and bent his steps leisurely toward the chamber where his son was lying in the left wing of the Abbey. At the end of the gallery which led to it he discovered a dim light. Doubting it an illusion, Sir Austin accelerated his pace. This wing had aforetime a bad character. Notwithstanding what years had done to polish it into fair repute, the Raynham kitchen stuck to tradition, and preserved certain stories of ghosts seen there, that effectually blackened it in the susceptible minds of new housemaids and under-cooks, whose fears would not allow the sinner to wash his sins. Sir Austin had heard of the tales circulated by his domestics underground. He cherished his own belief, but discouraged theirs, and it was treason at Raynham to be caught traducing the left wing. As the baronet advanced, the fact of a light burning was clear to him. A slight descent brought him into the passage, and he beheld a poor human candle standing outside his son's chamber. At the same moment the door closed hastily. He entered Richard's room. The boy was absent. The bed was unpressed: no clothes about: nothing to show that he had been there that night. Sir Austin felt vaguely apprehensive. Has he gone to my room to await me? thought the father's heart. Something like a tear quivered in his arid eyes as he meditated and hoped this might be so. His own sleeping-room faced that of his son. He strode to it with a quick heart. It was empty. Alarm dislodged anger from his jealous heart, and dread of evil put a thousand questions to him that were answered in air. After pacing up and down his room he determined to go and ask the boy Thompson, as he called Ripton, what was known to him.

The chamber assigned to Master Ripton Thompson was at the northern extremity of the passage, and overlooked

Lobourne and the valley to the West. The bed stood
between the window and the door. Sir Austin found the
door ajar, and the interior dark. To his surprise, the boy
Thompson's couch, as revealed by the rays of his lamp,
was likewise vacant. He was turning back when he fancied he heard the sibilation of a whispering in the room.
Sir Austin cloaked the lamp and trod silently toward the
window. The heads of his son Richard and the boy
Thompson were seen crouched against the glass, holding
excited converse together. Sir Austin listened, but he
listened to a language of which he possessed not the key.
Their talk was of fire, and of delay: of expected agrarian
astonishment: of a farmer's huge wrath: of violence exercised upon gentlemen, and of vengeance: talk that the boys
jerked out by fits, and that came as broken links of a chain
impossible to connect. But they awoke curiosity. The
baronet condescended to play the spy upon his son.

Over Lobourne and the valley lay black night and innumerable stars.

'How jolly I feel!' exclaimed Ripton, inspired by
claret; and then, after a luxurious pause—'I think that
fellow has pocketed his guinea, and cut his lucky.'*

Richard allowed a long minute to pass, during which
the baronet waited anxiously for his voice, hardly recognizing it when he heard its altered tones.

'If he has, I'll go; and I'll do it myself.'

'You would?' returned Master Ripton. 'Well, I'm
hanged!—I say, if you went to school, wouldn't you get
into rows! Perhaps he hasn't found the place where the
box was stuck in. I think he funks it. I almost wish you
hadn't done it, upon my honour—eh? Look there! what
was that? That looked like something.—I say! do you
think we shall ever be found out?'

Master Ripton intoned this abrupt interrogation very
seriously.

'I don't think about it,' said Richard, all his faculties bent on signs from Lobourne.

'Well, but,' Ripton persisted, 'suppose we are found out?'

'If we are, I must pay for it.'

Sir Austin breathed the better for this reply. He was beginning to gather a clue to the dialogue. His son was engaged in a plot, and was, moreover, the leader of the plot. He listened for further enlightenment.

'What was the fellow's name?' inquired Ripton.

His companion answered, 'Tom Bakewell.'

'I'll tell you what,' continued Ripton. 'You let it all clean out to your cousin and uncle at supper.—How capital claret is with partridge-pie! What a lot I ate!—Didn't you see me frown?'

The young sensualist was in an ecstasy of gratitude to his late refection, and the slightest word recalled him to it. Richard answered him—

'Yes; and felt your kick. It doesn't matter. Rady's safe, and uncle never blabs.'

'Well, my plan is to keep it close. You 're never safe if you don't.—I never drank much claret before,' Ripton was off again. 'Won't I now, though! claret 's my wine. You know, it may come out any day, and then we 're done for,' he rather incongruously appended.

Richard only took up the business-thread of his friend's rambling chatter, and answered—

'You 've got nothing to do with it, if we are.'

'Haven't I, though! I didn't stick-in the box but I 'm an accomplice, that 's clear. Besides,' added Ripton, 'do you think I should leave you to bear it all on your shoulders? I ain't that sort of chap, Ricky, I can tell you.'

Sir Austin thought more highly of the boy Thompson. Still it looked a detestable conspiracy, and the altered manner of his son impressed him strangely. He was not the boy of yesterday. To Sir Austin it seemed as if a gulf had suddenly opened between them. The boy had embarked, and was on the waters of life in his own vessel. It was as vain to call him back as to attempt to erase what Time has written with the Judgment Blood! This child, for whom he had prayed nightly in such a fervour and humbleness to God, the dangers were about him, the temptations thick on him, and the devil on board piloting. If a day had done so much, what would years do? Were prayers and all the watchfulness he had expended of no avail?

A sensation of infinite melancholy overcame the poor gentleman—a thought that he was fighting with a fate in this beloved boy.

He was half disposed to arrest the two conspirators on the spot, and make them confess, and absolve themselves; but it seemed to him better to keep an unseen eye over his son: Sir Austin's old system prevailed.

Adrian characterized this system well, in saying that Sir Austin wished to be Providence to his son.

If immeasurable love were perfect wisdom, one human being might almost impersonate Providence to another. Alas! love, divine as it is, can do no more than lighten the house it inhabits—must take its shape, sometimes intensify its narrowness—can spiritualize, but not expel, the old lifelong lodgers above-stairs and below.

Sir Austin decided to continue quiescent.

The valley still lay black beneath the large autumnal stars, and the exclamations of the boys were becoming fevered and impatient. By-and-by one insisted that he had seen a twinkle. The direction he gave was out of their anticipations. Again the twinkle was announced. Both boys started to their feet. It was a twinkle in the right direction now.

"He's done it!' cried Richard, in great heat. 'Now

you may say old Blaize 'll soon be old Blazes, Rip. I hope he's asleep.'

'I'm sure he's snoring!—Look there! He's alight fast enough. He's dry. He'll burn.—I say,' Ripton reassumed the serious intonation, 'do you think they'll ever suspect us?'

'What if they do? We must brunt it.'

'Of course we will. But, I say! I wish you hadn't given them the scent, though. I like to look innocent. I can't when I know people suspect me. Lord! look there! Isn't it just beginning to flare up!'

The farmer's grounds were indeed gradually standing out in sombre shadows.

'I'll fetch my telescope,' said Richard. Ripton, somehow not liking to be left alone, caught hold of him.

'No; don't go and lose the best of it. Here, I'll throw open the window, and we can see.'

The window was flung open, and the boys instantly stretched half their bodies out of it; Ripton appearing to devour the rising flames with his mouth: Richard with his eyes.

Opaque and statuesque stood the figure of the baronet behind them. The wind was low. Dense masses of smoke hung amid the darting snakes of fire, and a red malign light was on the neighbouring leafage. No figures could be seen. Apparently the flames had nothing to contend against, for they were making terrible strides into the darkness.

'Oh!' shouted Richard, overcome by excitement, 'if I had my telescope! We must have it! Let me go and fetch it! I will!'

The boys struggled together, and Sir Austin stepped back. As he did so, a cry was heard in the passage. He hurried out, closed the chamber, and came upon little Clare lying senseless along the floor.

CHAPTER V

ADRIAN PLIES HIS HOOK

In the morning that followed this night, great gossip was interchanged between Raynham and Lobourne. The village told how Farmer Blaize, of Belthorpe Farm, had his rick feloniously set fire to; his stables had caught fire, himself had been all but roasted alive in the attempt to rescue his cattle, of which numbers had perished in the flames. Raynham counterbalanced arson with an authentic ghost seen by Miss Clare in the left wing of the Abbey—the ghost of a lady, dressed in deep mourning, a scar on her forehead, and a bloody handkerchief at her breast, frightful to behold! and no wonder the child was frightened out of her wits, and lay in a desperate state awaiting the arrival of the London doctors. It was added that the servants had all threatened to leave in a body, and that Sir Austin to appease them had promised to pull down the entire left wing, like a gentleman; for no decent creature, said Lobourne, could consent to live in a haunted house.

Rumour for the nonce had a stronger spice of truth than usual. Poor little Clare lay ill, and the calamity that had befallen Farmer Blaize, as regards his rick, was not much exaggerated. Sir Austin caused an account of it to be given him at breakfast, and appeared so scrupulously anxious to hear the exact extent of injury sustained by the farmer that heavy Benson went down to inspect the scene. Mr. Benson returned, and, acting under Adrian's malicious advice, framed a formal report of the catastrophe, in which the farmer's breeches figured, and certain cooling applications to a part of the farmer's person. Sir

Austin perused it without a smile. He took occasion to have it read out before the two boys, who listened very demurely, as to an ordinary newspaper incident; only when the report particularized the garments damaged, and the unwonted distressing position Farmer Blaize was reduced to in his bed, an indecorous fit of sneezing laid hold of Master Ripton Thompson, and Richard bit his lip and burst into loud laughter, Ripton joining him, lost to consequences.

'I trust you feel for this poor man,' said Sir Austin to his son, somewhat sternly. He saw no sign of feeling.

It was a difficult task for Sir Austin to keep his old countenance toward the hope of Raynham, knowing him the accomplice-incendiary, and believing the deed to have been unprovoked and wanton. But he must do so, he knew, to let the boy have a fair trial against himself. Be it said, moreover, that the baronet's possession of his son's secret flattered him. It allowed him to act, and in a measure to feel, like Providence; enabled him to observe and provide for the movements of creatures in the dark. He therefore treated the boy as he commonly did, and Richard saw no change in his father to make him think he was suspected.

The youngster's game was not so easy against Adrian. Adrian did not shoot or fish. Voluntarily he did nothing to work off the destructive nervous fluid, or whatever it may be, which is in man's nature; so that two culprit boys once in his power were not likely to taste the gentle hand of mercy, and Richard and Ripton paid for many a trout and partridge spared. At every minute of the day Ripton was thrown into sweats of suspicion that discovery was imminent, by some stray remark or message from Adrian. He was as a fish with the hook in his gills, mysteriously caught without having nibbled; and dive into what depths he would he was sensible of a summoning force that compelled him perpetually toward the gasping surface, which he seemed inevitably approaching when the dinner-bell sounded. There the talk was all of Farmer Blaize. If it dropped, Adrian revived it, and his caressing way with Ripton was just such as a keen sportsman feels toward the creature that has owned his skill, and is making its appearance for the world to acknowledge the same. Sir Austin saw the manœuvres, and admired Adrian's shrewdness. But he had to check the young natural lawyer, for the effect of so much masked examination upon Richard was growing baneful. This fish also felt the hook in his gills, but this fish was more of a pike, and lay in different waters, where there were old stumps and black roots to wind about, and defy alike strong pulling and delicate handling. In other words, Richard showed symptoms of a disposition to take refuge in lies.

'You know the grounds, my dear boy,' Adrian observed to him. 'Tell me; do you think it easy to get to the rick unperceived? I hear they suspect one of the farmer's turned-off hands.'

'I tell you I don't know the grounds,' Richard sullenly replied.

'Not?' Adrian counterfeited courteous astonishment. 'I thought Mr. Thompson said you were over there yesterday?'

Ripton, glad to speak a truth, hurriedly assured Adrian that it was not he had said so.

'Not? You had good sport, gentlemen, hadn't you?'

'Oh, yes!' mumbled the wretched victims, reddening as they remembered, in Adrian's slightly drawled rusticity of tone, Farmer Blaize's first address to them.

'I suppose you were among the Fire-worshippers last night, too?' persisted Adrian. 'In some countries, I hear, they manage their best sport at night-time, and beat up for game with torches. It must be a fine sight. After all, the country would be dull if we hadn't a rip here and there to treat us to a little conflagration.'

'A rip!' laughed Richard, to his friend's disgust and alarm at his daring. 'You don't mean this Rip, do you?'

'Mr. Thompson fire a rick? I should as soon suspect you, my dear boy.—You are aware, young gentlemen, that it is rather a serious thing—Eh? In this country, you know, the landlord has always been the pet of the Laws. By the way,' Adrian continued, as if diverging to another topic, 'you met two gentlemen of the road in your explorations yesterday, Magians.* Now, if I were a magistrate of the county, like Sir Miles Papworth, my suspicions would light upon those gentlemen. A tinker and a ploughman, I think you said, Mr. Thompson. Not? Well, say two ploughmen.'

'More likely two tinkers,' said Richard.

'Oh! if you wish to exclude the ploughman—was he out of employ?'

Ripton, with Adrian's eyes inveterately fixed on him, stammered an affirmative.

'The tinker, or the ploughman?'

'The ploughm—' Ingenuous Ripton looking about, as if to aid himself whenever he was able to speak the truth, beheld Richard's face blackening at him, and swallowed back half the word.

'The ploughman!' Adrian took him up cheerily. 'Then we have here a ploughman out of employ. Given a plough-man out of employ and a rick burnt. The burning of a rick is an act of vengeance, and a ploughman out of employ is a vengeful animal. The rick and the ploughman are advancing to a juxtaposition. Motive being established, we have only to prove their proximity at a certain hour, and our ploughman voyages beyond seas.'

'Is it transportation for rick-burning?' inquired Ripton aghast.

Adrian spoke solemnly: 'They shave your head. You are manacled. Your diet is sour bread and cheese-parings. You work in strings of twenties and thirties. ARSON is branded on your backs in an enormous A. Theological works are the sole literary recreation of the well-conducted and deserving. Consider the fate of this poor fellow, and what an act of vengeance brings him to! Do you know his name?'

'How should I know his name?' said Richard, with an assumption of innocence painful to see.

Sir Austin remarked that no doubt it would soon be known, and Adrian perceived that he was to quiet his line, marvelling a little at the baronet's blindness to what was so clear. He would not tell, for that would ruin his future influence with Richard; still he wanted some present credit for his discernment and devotion. The boys got away from dinner, and, after deep consultation, agreed upon a course of conduct, which was to commiserate Farmer Blaize loudly, and make themselves look as much like the public as it was possible for two young malefactors to look, one of whom already felt Adrian's enormous A devouring his back with the fierceness of the Promethean eagle,* and isolating him for ever from mankind. Adrian relished their novel tactics sharply, and led them to lengths of lamentation for Farmer Blaize. Do what they might, the hook was in their gills. The farmer's whip had reduced them to bodily contortions: these were decorous compared with the spiritual writhings they had to perform under Adrian's manipulation. Ripton was fast becoming a coward, and Richard a liar, when next morning Austin Wentworth came over from Poer Hall bringing news that one Mr. Thomas Bakewell, yeoman, had been arrested on suspicion of the crime of Arson and lodged in jail, awaiting the magisterial pleasure of Sir Miles Papworth. Austin's eye rested on Richard as he spoke these terrible tidings.

The hope of Raynham returned his look, perfectly calm, and had, moreover, the presence of mind not to look at Ripton.

CHAPTER VI

JUVENILE STRATAGEMS

As soon as they could escape, the boys got away together into an obscure corner of the park, and there took counsel of their extremity.

'Whatever shall we do now?' asked Ripton of his leader.

Scorpion girt with fire was never in a more terrible prison-house than poor Ripton, around whom the rageing element he had assisted to create seemed to be drawing momently narrower circles.

'There's only one chance,' said Richard, coming to a dead halt, and folding his arms resolutely.

His comrade inquired with the utmost eagerness what that chance might be?

Richard fixed his eyes on a flint, and replied: 'We must rescue that fellow from jail.'

Ripton gazed at his leader, and fell back with astonishment. 'My dear Ricky! but how are we to do it?'

Richard, still perusing his flint, replied: 'We must manage to get a file in to him and a rope. It can be done, I tell you. I don't care what I pay. I don't care what I do. He must be got out.'

'Bother that old Blaize!' exclaimed Ripton, taking off his cap to wipe his frenzied forehead, and brought down his friend's reproof.

'Never mind old Blaize now. Talk about letting it out! Look at you. I'm ashamed of you. You talk about Robin Hood and King Richard!* Why, you haven't an atom of courage. Why, you let it out every second of the day. Whenever Rady begins speaking you start; I can see the perspiration rolling down you. Are you afraid?——And then you contradict yourself. You never keep to one story. Now, follow me. We must risk everything to get him out. Mind that! And keep out of Adrian's way as much as you can. And keep to one story.'

With these sage directions the young leader marched his companion-culprit down to inspect the jail where Tom Bakewell lay groaning over the results of the super-mundane conflict, and the victim of it that he was.

In Lobourne Austin Wentworth had the reputation of the poor man's friend; a title he earned more largely ere he went to the reward God alone can give to that supreme virtue. Dame Bakewell, the mother of Tom, on hearing of her son's arrest, had run to comfort him and render him what help she could; but this was only sighs and tears, and, oh deary me! which only perplexed poor Tom, who bade her leave an unlucky chap to his fate, and not make himself a thundering villain. Whereat the dame begged him to take heart, and he should have a true comforter. 'And though it's a gentleman that's coming to you, Tom —for he never refuses a poor body,' said Mrs. Bakewell, 'it's a true Christian, Tom! and the Lord knows if the sight of him mayn't be the saving of you, for he's light to look on, and a sermon to listen to, he is!'

Tom was not prepossessed by the prospect of a sermon, and looked a sullen dog enough when Austin entered his cell. He was surprised at the end of half an hour to find himself engaged in man-to-man conversation with a gentleman and a Christian. When Austin rose to go, Tom begged permission to shake his hand.

'Take and tell young master up at the Abbey that I an't the chap to peach. He'll know. He's a young gentleman as 'll make any man do as he wants 'em! He's a mortal wild young gentleman! And I 'm a Ass! That 's where 'tis. But I an't a blackguard. Tell him that, sir!'

This was how it came that Austin eyed young Richard seriously while he told the news at Raynham. The boy was shy of Austin more than of Adrian. Why, he did not know; but he made it a hard task for Austin to catch him alone, and turned sulky that instant. Austin was not clever like Adrian: he seldom divined other people's ideas, and always went the direct road to his object; so instead of beating about and setting the boy on the alert at all points, crammed to the muzzle with lies, he just said, 'Tom Bakewell told me to let you know he does not intend to peach on you,' and left him.

Richard repeated the intelligence to Ripton, who cried aloud that Tom was a brick.

'He shan't suffer for it,' said Richard, and pondered on a thicker rope and sharper file.

'But will your cousin tell?' was Ripton's reflection.

'He!' Richard's lip expressed contempt. 'A ploughman refuses to peach, and you ask if one of our family will?'

Ripton stood for the twentieth time reproved on this point.

The boys had examined the outer walls of the jail, and arrived at the conclusion that Tom's escape might be managed if Tom had spirit, and the rope and file could be anyway reached to him. But to do this, somebody must gain admittance to his cell, and who was to be taken into their confidence?

'Try your cousin,' Ripton suggested, after much debate. Richard, smiling, wished to know if he meant Adrian.

'No, no!' Ripton hurriedly reassured him. 'Austin.'

The same idea was knocking at Richard's head.

'Let's get the rope and file first,' said he, and to Bursley they went for those implements to defeat the law, Ripton procuring the file at one shop and Richard the rope at

another, with such masterly cunning did they lay their
measures for the avoidance of every possible chance of detection. And better to assure this, in a wood outside
Bursley Richard stripped to his shirt and wound the rope
round his body, tasting the tortures of anchorites*and penitential friars, that nothing should be risked to make Tom's
escape a certainty. Sir Austin saw the marks at night, as
his son lay asleep, through the half-opened folds of his
bed-gown.

It was a severe stroke when, after all their stratagems
and trouble, Austin Wentworth refused the office the boys
had zealously designed for him. Time pressed. In a few
days poor Tom would have to face the redoubtable Sir
Miles, and get committed, for rumours of overwhelming
evidence to convict him were rife about Lobourne, and
Farmer Blaize's wrath was unappeasable. Again and again
young Richard begged his cousin not to see him disgraced,
and to help him in this extremity. Austin smiled on him.

'My dear Ricky,' said he, 'there are two ways of getting out of a scrape: a long way and a short way. When
you 've tried the roundabout method, and failed, come to
me, and I 'll show you the straight route.'

Richard was too entirely bent upon the roundabout
method to consider this advice more than empty words,
and only ground his teeth at Austin's unkind refusal.

He imparted to Ripton, at the eleventh hour, that they
must do it themselves, to which Ripton heavily assented.

On the day preceding poor Tom's doomed appearance
before the magistrate, Dame Bakewell had an interview
with Austin, who went to Raynham immediately, and
sought Adrian's counsel upon what was to be done. Homeric
laughter and nothing else could be got out of Adrian when
he heard of the doings of these desperate boys: how they
had entered Dame Bakewell's smallest of retail shops, and
purchased tea, sugar, candles, and comfits of every descrip-

tion, till the shop was clear of customers: how they had then hurried her into her little back-parlour, where Richard had torn open his shirt and revealed the coils of rope, and Ripton displayed the point of a file from a serpentine recess in his jacket: how they had then told the astonished woman that the rope she saw and the file she saw were instruments for the liberation of her son; that there existed no other means on earth to save him, they, the boys, having unsuccessfully attempted all: how upon that Richard had tried with the utmost earnestness to persuade her to disrobe and wind the rope round her own person: and Ripton had aired his eloquence to induce her to secrete the file: how, when she resolutely objected to the rope, both boys began backing the file, and in an evil hour, she feared, said Dame Bakewell, she had rewarded the gracious permission given her by Sir Miles Papworth to visit her son, by tempting Tom to file the Law. Though, thanks be to the Lord! Dame Bakewell added, Tom had turned up his nose at the file, and so she had told young Master Richard, who swore very bad for a young gentleman.

'Boys are like monkeys,' remarked Adrian, at the close of his explosions, 'the gravest actors of farcical nonsense that the world possesses. May I never be where there are no boys! A couple of boys left to themselves will furnish richer fun than any troop of trained comedians. No: no Art arrives at the artlessness of nature in matters of comedy. You can't simulate the ape. Your antics are dull. They haven't the charming inconsequence of the natural animal. Look at these two! Think of the shifts they are put to all day long! They know I know all about it, and yet their serenity of innocence is all but unruffled in my presence. You're sorry to think about the end of the business, Austin? So am I! I dread the idea of the curtain going down. Besides, it will do Ricky a world of good. A practical lesson is the best lesson.'

'Sinks deepest,' said Austin, 'but whether he learns good or evil from it is the question at stake.'

Adrian stretched his length at ease.

'This will be his first nibble at experience, old Time's fruit, hateful to the palate of youth! for which season only hath it any nourishment! Experience! You know Coleridge's capital simile?*—Mournful you call it? Well! all wisdom is mournful. 'Tis therefore, coz, that the wise do love the Comic Muse. Their own high food would kill them. You shall find great poets, rare philosophers, night after night on the broad grin before a row of yellow lights and mouthing masks. Why? Because all's dark at home. The stage is the pastime of great minds. That's how it comes that the stage is now down. An age of rampant little minds, my dear Austin! How I hate that cant of yours about an Age of Work—you, and your Mortons, and your parsons Brawnley, rank radicals all of you, base materialists! What does Diaper Sandoe sing of your Age of Work? Listen!

> "An Age of petty tit for tat,
>   An Age of busy gabble:
> An Age that's like a brewer's vat,
>   Fermenting for the rabble!
>
> An Age that's chaste in Love, but lax
>   To virtuous abuses:
> Whose gentlemen and ladies wax
>   Too dainty for their uses.
>
> An Age that drives an Iron Horse,
>   Of Time and Space defiant;
> Exulting in a Giant's Force,
>   And trembling at the Giant.
>
> An Age of Quaker hue and cut,
>   By Mammon misbegotten;
> See the mad Hamlet mouth and strut!
>   And mark the Kings of Cotton!

From this unrest, lo, early wreck'd,
 A Future staggers crazy,
Ophelia of the Ages, deck'd
 With woeful weed and daisy!"'

Murmuring, 'Get your parson Brawnley to answer that!'
Adrian changed the resting-place of a leg, and smiled.
The AGE was an old battle-field between him and Austin.

'My parson Brawnley, as you call him, has answered it,'
said Austin, 'not by hoping his best, which would probably leave the Age to go mad to your satisfaction, but by
doing it. And he has and will answer your Diaper Sandoe
in better verse, as he confutes him in a better life.'

'You don't see Sandoe's depth,' Adrian replied. 'Consider that phrase, "Ophelia of the Ages"! Is not Brawnley,
like a dozen other leading spirits—I think that's your term
—just the metaphysical Hamlet to drive her mad? She,
poor maid! asks for marriage and smiling babes, while my
lord lover stands questioning the Infinite, and rants to the
Impalpable.'

Austin laughed. 'Marriage and smiling babes she would
have in abundance, if Brawnley legislated. Wait till you
know him. He will be over at Poer Hall shortly, and you
will see what a Man of the Age means. But now, pray,
consult with me about these boys.'

'Oh, those boys!' Adrian tossed a hand. 'Are there
boys of the Age as well as men? Not? Then boys are
better than men: boys are for all Ages. What do you
think, Austin? They've been studying Latude's Escape.*
I found the book open in Ricky's room, on the top of Jonathan Wild.* Jonathan preserved the secrets of his profession, and taught them nothing. So they're going to make
a Latude of Mr. Tom Bakewell. He's to be Bastille Bakewell, whether he will or no. Let them. Let the wild colt
run free! We can't help them. We can only look on. We
should spoil the play.'

Adrian always made a point of feeding the fretful beast Impatience with pleasantries—a not congenial diet; and Austin, the most patient of human beings, began to lose his self-control.

'You talk as if Time belonged to you, Adrian. We have but a few hours left us. Work first, and joke afterwards. The boy's fate is being decided now.'

'So is everybody's, my dear Austin!' yawned the epicurean.

'Yes, but this boy is at present under our guardianship —under yours especially.'

'Not yet! not yet!' Adrian interjected languidly. 'No getting into scrapes when I have him. The leash, young hound! the collar, young colt! I'm perfectly irresponsible at present.'

'You may have something different to deal with when you are responsible, if you think that.'

'I take my young prince as I find him, coz: a Julian, or a Caracalla: a Constantine, or a Nero.* Then, if he will play the fiddle to a conflagration, he shall play it well: if he must be a disputatious apostate, at any rate he shall understand logic and men, and have the habit of saying his prayers.'

'Then you leave me to act alone?' said Austin, rising.

'Without a single curb!' Adrian gesticulated an acquiesced withdrawal. 'I'm sure you would not, still more certain you cannot, do harm. And be mindful of my prophetic words: Whatever's done, old Blaize will have to be bought off. There's the affair settled at once. I suppose I must go to the chief to-night and settle it myself. We can't see this poor devil condemned, though it's nonsense to talk of a boy being the prime instigator.'

Austin cast an eye at the complacent languor of the wise youth, his cousin, and the little that he knew of his fellows told him he might talk for ever here, and not be

comprehended. The wise youth's two ears were stuffed
with his own wisdom. One evil only Adrian dreaded, it
was clear—the action of the law.

As he was moving away, Adrian called out to him, 'Stop,
Austin! There! don't be anxious! You invariably take
the glum side. I 've done something. Never mind what.
If you go down to Belthorpe, be civil, but not obsequious.
You remember the tactics of Scipio Africanus against the
Punic elephants?* Well, don't say a word—in thine ear,
coz: I 've turned Master Blaize's elephants. If they
charge, 'twill be a feint, and back to the destruction of his
serried ranks! You understand. Not? Well, 'tis as well.
Only let none say that I sleep. If I must see him to-night,
I go down knowing he has not got us in his power.' The
wise youth yawned, and stretched out a hand for any book
that might be within his reach. Austin left him to look
about the grounds for Richard.

CHAPTER VII

DAPHNE'S BOWER

A LITTLE laurel-shaded temple of white marble looked
out on the river from a knoll bordering the Raynham
beechwoods, and was dubbed by Adrian Daphne's Bower.
To this spot Richard had retired, and there Austin found
him with his head buried in his hands, a picture of desperation, whose last shift has been defeated. He allowed
Austin to greet him and sit by him without lifting his
head. Perhaps his eyes were not presentable.

'Where 's your friend?' Austin began.

'Gone!' was the answer, sounding cavernous from
behind hair and fingers. An explanation presently fol-

lowed, that a summons had come for him in the morning from Mr. Thompson; and that Mr. Ripton had departed against his will.

In fact, Ripton had protested that he would defy his parent and remain by his friend in the hour of adversity and at the post of danger. Sir Austin signified his opinion that a boy should obey his parent, by giving orders to Benson for Ripton's box to be packed and ready before noon; and Ripton's alacrity in taking the baronet's view of filial duty was as little feigned as his offer to Richard to throw filial duty to the winds. He rejoiced that the Fates had agreed to remove him from the very hot neighbour-hood of Lobourne, while he grieved, like an honest lad, to see his comrade left to face calamity alone. The boys parted amicably, as they could hardly fail to do, when Ripton had sworn fealty to the Feverels with a warmth that made him declare himself bond, and due to appear at any stated hour and at any stated place to fight all the farmers in England, on a mandate from the heir of the house.

'So you 're left alone,' said Austin, contemplating the boy's shapely head. 'I 'm glad of it. We never know what 's in us till we stand by ourselves.'

There appeared to be no answer forthcoming. Vanity, however, replied at last, 'He wasn't much support.'

'Remember his good points now he 's gone, Ricky.'

'Oh! he was staunch,' the boy grumbled.

'And a staunch friend is not always to be found. Now, have you tried your own way of rectifying this business, Ricky?'

'I have done everything.'

'And failed!'

There was a pause, and then the deep-toned evasion—'Tom Bakewell 's a coward!'

'I suppose, poor fellow,' said Austin, in his kind way,

'he doesn't want to get into a deeper mess. I don't think he's a coward.'

'He is a coward,' cried Richard. 'Do you think if I had a file I would stay in prison? I'd be out the first night! And he might have had the rope, too—a rope thick enough for a couple of men his size and weight. Ripton and I and Ned Markham swung on it for an hour, and it didn't give way. He's a coward, and deserves his fate. I've no compassion for a coward.'

'Nor I much,' said Austin.

Richard had raised his head in the heat of his denunciation of poor Tom. He would have hidden it had he known the thought in Austin's clear eyes while he faced them.

'I never met a coward myself,' Austin continued. 'I have heard of one or two. One let an innocent man die for him.'

'How base!' exclaimed the boy.

'Yes, it was bad,' Austin acquiesced.

'Bad!' Richard scorned the poor contempt. 'How I would have spurned him! He was a coward!'

'I believe he pleaded the feelings of his family in his excuse, and tried every means to get the man off. I have read also in the confessions of a celebrated philosopher,* that in his youth he committed some act of pilfering, and accused a young servant-girl of his own theft, who was condemned and dismissed for it, pardoning her guilty accuser.'

'What a coward!' shouted Richard. 'And he confessed it publicly?'

'You may read it yourself.'

'He actually wrote it down, and printed it?'

'You have the book in your father's library. Would you have done so much?'

Richard faltered. No! he admitted that he never could have told people.

'Then who is to call that man a coward?' said Austin.
'He expiated his cowardice as all who give way in moments
of weakness, and are not cowards, must do.   The coward
chooses to think "God does not see. I shall escape." He
who is not a coward, and has succumbed, knows that God
has seen all, and it is not so hard a task for him to make
his heart bare to the world. Worse, I should fancy it, to
know myself an impostor when men praised me.'

Young Richard's eyes were wandering on Austin's
gravely cheerful face. A keen intentness suddenly fixed
them, and he dropped his head.

'So I think you 're wrong, Ricky, in calling this poor
Tom a coward because he refuses to try your means of
escape,' Austin resumed. 'A coward hardly objects to
drag in his accomplice. And, where the person involved
belongs to a great family, it seems to me that for a poor
plough-lad to volunteer not to do so speaks him anything
but a coward.'

Richard was dumb. Altogether to surrender his rope
and file was a fearful sacrifice, after all the time, trepidation, and study he had spent on those two saving instruments. If he avowed Tom's manly behaviour, Richard
Feverel was in a totally new position. Whereas, by keeping Tom a coward, Richard Feverel was the injured one,
and to seem injured is always a luxury; sometimes a necessity, whether among boys or men.

In Austin the Magian conflict would not have lasted
long. He had but a blind notion of the fierceness with
which it raged in young Richard. Happily for the boy,
Austin was not a preacher. A single insistance, a cant
phrase, a fatherly manner, might have wrecked him, by
arousing ancient or latent opposition. The born preacher
we feel instinctively to be our foe. He may do some good
to the wretches that have been struck down and lie gasping
on the battlefield: he rouses antagonism in the strong.

Richard's nature, left to itself, wanted little more than an indication of the proper track, and when he said, 'Tell me what I can do, Austin?' he had fought the best half of the battle. His voice was subdued. Austin put his hand on the boy's shoulder.

'You must go down to Farmer Blaize.'

'Well!' said Richard, sullenly divining the deed of penance.

'You'll know what to say to him when you're there.'

The boy bit his lip and frowned. 'Ask a favour of that big brute, Austin? I can't!'

'Just tell him the whole case, and that you don't intend to stand by and let the poor fellow suffer without a friend to help him out of his scrape.'

'But, Austin,' the boy pleaded, 'I shall have to ask him to help off Tom Bakewell! How can I ask him, when I hate him?'

Austin bade him go, and think nothing of the consequences till he got there.

Richard groaned in soul.

'You've no pride, Austin.'

'Perhaps not.'

'You don't know what it is to ask a favour of a brute you hate.'

Richard stuck to that view of the case, and stuck to it the faster the more imperatively the urgency of a movement dawned upon him.

'Why,' continued the boy, 'I shall hardly be able to keep my fists off him!'

'Surely you've punished him enough, boy?' said Austin.

'He struck me!' Richard's lip quivered. 'He dared not come at me with his hands. He struck me with a whip. He'll be telling everybody that he horsewhipped me, and that I went down and begged his pardon. Begged his pardon! A Feverel beg his pardon! Oh, if I had my will!'

'The man earns his bread, Ricky. You poached on his grounds. He turned you off, and you fired his rick.'

'And I'll pay him for his loss. And I won't do any more.'

'Because you won't ask a favour of him?'

'No! I will not ask a favour of him.'

Austin looked at the boy steadily. 'You prefer to receive a favour from poor Tom Bakewell?'

At Austin's enunciation of this obverse view of the matter Richard raised his brow. Dimly a new light broke in upon him. 'Favour from Tom Bakewell, the ploughman? How do you mean, Austin?'

'To save yourself an unpleasantness you permit a country lad to sacrifice himself for you? I confess I should not have so much pride.'

'Pride!' shouted Richard, stung by the taunt, and set his sight hard at the blue ridges of the hills.

Not knowing for the moment what else to do, Austin drew a picture of Tom in prison, and repeated Tom's volunteer statement. The picture, though his intentions were far from designing it so, had to Richard, whose perception of humour was infinitely keener, a horrible chaw-bacon smack about it. Visions of a grinning lout, open from ear to ear, unkempt, coarse, splay-footed, rose before him and afflicted him with the strangest sensations of disgust and comicality, mixed up with pity and remorse—a sort of twisted pathos. There lay Tom; hobnail Tom! a bacon-munching, reckless, beer-swilling animal! and yet a man; a dear brave human heart notwithstanding; capable of devotion and unselfishness. The boy's better spirit was touched, and it kindled his imagination to realise the abject figure of poor clodpole Tom, and surround it with a halo of mournful light. His soul was alive. Feelings

he had never known streamed in upon him as from an
ethereal casement, an unwonted tenderness, an embracing
humour, a consciousness of some ineffable glory, an irra-
diation of the features of humanity. All this was in the
bosom of the boy, and through it all the vision of an actual
hobnail Tom, coarse, unkempt, open from ear to ear;
whose presence was a finger of shame to him and an op-
pression of clodpole; yet toward whom he felt just then a
loving-kindness beyond what he felt for any living creature.
He laughed at him, and wept over him. He prized him,
while he shrank from him. It was a genial strife of the
angel in him with constituents less divine; but the angel
was uppermost and led the van—extinguished loathing,
humanized laughter, transfigured pride—pride that would
persistently contemplate the corduroys of gaping Tom,
and cry to Richard, in the very tone of Adrian's ironic
voice, 'Behold your benefactor!'

Austin sat by the boy, unaware of the sublimer tumult
he had stirred. Little of it was perceptible in Richard's
countenance. The lines of his mouth were slightly drawn;
his eyes hard set into the distance. He remained thus
many minutes. Finally he jumped to his legs, saying,
'I'll go at once to old Blaize and tell him.'

Austin grasped his hand, and together they issued out
of Daphne's Bower, in the direction of Lobourne.

CHAPTER VIII

THE BITTER CUP

FARMER BLAIZE was not so astonished at the visit of
Richard Feverel as that young gentleman expected him
to be. The farmer, seated in his easy-chair in the little
low-roofed parlour of an old-fashioned farm-house, with

a long clay pipe on the table at his elbow, and a veteran
pointer at his feet, had already given audience to three
distinguished members of the Feverel blood, who had come
separately, according to their accustomed secretiveness,
and with one object. In the morning it was Sir Austin
himself. Shortly after his departure, arrived Austin
Wentworth; close on his heels, Algernon, known about
Lobourne as the Captain, popular wherever he was known.
Farmer Blaize reclined in considerable elation. He had
brought these great people to a pretty low pitch. He had
welcomed them hospitably, as a British yeoman should;
but not budged a foot in his demands: not to the baronet:
not to the Captain: not to good young Mr. Wentworth.
For Farmer Blaize was a solid Englishman; and, on hearing from the baronet a frank confession of the hold he had
on the family, he determined to tighten his hold, and only
relax it in exchange 'for tangible advantages—compensation to his pocket, his wounded person, and his still more
wounded sentiments: the total indemnity being, in round
figures, three hundred pounds, and a spoken apology from
the prime offender, young Mister Richard. Even then
there was a reservation. Provided, the farmer said, nobody had been tampering with any of his witnesses. In
that case Farmer Blaize declared the money might go,
and he would transport Tom Bakewell, as he had sworn
he would. And it goes hard, too, with an accomplice, by
law, added the farmer, knocking the ashes leisurely out of
his pipe. He had no wish to bring any disgrace anywhere;
he respected the inmates of Raynham Abbey, as in duty
bound; he should be sorry to see them in trouble. Only
no tampering with his witnesses. He was a man for Law.
Rank was much: money was much: but Law was more.
In this country Law was above the sovereign. To tamper
with the Law was treason to the realm.

'I come to you direct,' the baronet explained. 'I

tell you candidly in what way I discovered my son to be mixed up in this miserable affair. I promise you indemnity for your loss, and an apology that shall, I trust, satisfy your feelings, assuring you that to tamper with witnesses is not the province of a Feverel. All I ask of you in return is, not to press the prosecution. At present it rests with you. I am bound to do all that lies in my power for this imprisoned man. How and wherefore my son was prompted to suggest, or assist in, such an act, I cannot explain, for I do not know.'

'Hum!' said the farmer. 'I think I do.'

'You know the cause?' Sir Austin stared. 'I beg you to confide it to me.'

''Least I can pretty nigh neighbour it with a guess,' said the farmer. 'We an't good friends, Sir Austin, me and your son, just now—not to say cordial. I, ye see, Sir Austin, I'm a man as don't like young gentlemen a-poachin' on his grounds without his permission,—in special when birds is plentiful on their own. It appear he do like it. Consequently I has to flick this whip—as them fellers at the races: All in this 'ere Ring 's mine! as much as to say; and who's been hit, he's had fair warnin'. I'm sorry for 't, but that 's just the case.'

Sir Austin retired to communicate with his son, when he should find him.

Algernon's interview passed off in ale and promises. He also assured Farmer Blaize that no Feverel could be affected by his proviso.

No less did Austin Wentworth. The farmer was satisfied.

'Money 's safe, I know,' said he; 'now for the 'pology!' and Farmer Blaize thrust his legs further out, and his head further back.

The farmer naturally reflected that the three separate visits had been conspired together. Still the baronet's frankness, and the baronet's not having reserved himself for the third and final charge, puzzled him. He was considering whether they were a deep, or a shallow lot, when young Richard was announced.

A pretty little girl with the roses of thirteen springs in her cheeks, and abundant beautiful bright tresses, tripped before the boy, and loitered shyly by the farmer's armchair to steal a look at the handsome new-comer. She was introduced to Richard as the farmer's niece, Lucy Desborough, the daughter of a lieutenant in the Royal Navy, and, what was better, though the farmer did not pronounce it so loudly, a real good girl.

Neither the excellence of her character, nor her rank in life, tempted Richard to inspect the little lady. He made an awkward bow, and sat down.

The farmer's eyes twinkled. 'Her father,' he continued, 'fought and fell for his coontry. A man as fights for 's coontry 's a right to hould up his head—ay! with any in the land. Desb'roughs o' Dorset! d 'ye know that family, Master Feverel?'

Richard did not know them, and, by his air, did not desire to become acquainted with any offshoot of that family.

'She can make puddens and pies,' the farmer went on, regardless of his auditor's gloom. 'She 's a lady, as good as the best of 'em. I don't care about their being Catholics —the Desb'roughs o' Dorset are gentlemen. And she 's good for the pianer, too! She strums to me of evenin's. I 'm for the old tunes: she 's for the new. Gal-like! While she 's with me she shall be taught things use'l. She can parley-voo a good 'un and foot it, as it goes; been in France a couple of year. I prefer the singin' of 't to the talking of 't. Come, Luce! toon up—eh?—Ye wun't? That song about the Viffendeer—a female'—Farmer Blaize volunteered the translation of the title—'who wears the—you guess what! and marches along with the French sojers: a pretty brazen bit o' goods, I sh'd fancy.'*

THE BITTER CUP 61

Mademoiselle Lucy corrected her uncle's French, but objected to do more. The handsome cross boy had almost taken away her voice for speech, as it was, and sing in his company she could not; so she stood, a hand on her uncle's chair to stay herself from falling, while she wriggled a dozen various shapes of refusal, and shook her head at the farmer with fixed eyes.

'Aha!' laughed the farmer, dismissing her, 'they soon learn the difference 'twixt the young 'un and the old 'un. Go along, Luce! and learn yer lessons for to-morrow.'

Reluctantly the daughter of the Royal Navy glided away. Her uncle's head followed her to the door, where she dallied to catch a last impression of the young stranger's lowering face, and darted through.

Farmer Blaize laughed and chuckled. 'She an't so fond of her uncle as that, every day! Not that she an't a good nurse—the kindest little soul you'd meet of a winter's walk! She'll read t' ye, and make drinks, and sing, too, if ye likes it, and she won't be tired. A obstinate good 'un, she be! Bless her!'

The farmer may have designed, by these eulogies of his niece, to give his visitor time to recover his composure, and establish a common topic. His diversion only irritated and confused our shame-eaten youth. Richard's intention had been to come to the farmer's threshold: to summon the farmer thither, and in a loud and haughty tone then and there to take upon himself the whole burden of the charge against Tom Bakewell. He had strayed, during his passage to Belthorpe, somewhat back to his old nature; and his being compelled to enter the house of his enemy, sit in his chair, and endure an introduction to his family, was more than he bargained for. He commenced blinking hard in preparation for the horrible dose to which delay and the farmer's cordiality added inconceivable bitters. Farmer Blaize was quite at his ease; nowise in a hurry. He spoke of the weather and the harvest: of recent doings up at the Abbey: glanced over that year's cricketing; hoped that no future Feverel would lose a leg to the game. Richard saw and heard Arson in it all. He blinked harder as he neared the cup. In a moment of silence, he seized it with a gasp.

'Mr. Blaize! I have come to tell you that I am the person who set fire to your rick the other night.'

An odd contraction formed about the farmer's mouth. He changed his posture, and said, 'Ay? that's what ye 're come to tell me, sir?'

'Yes!' said Richard firmly.

'And that be all?'

'Yes!' Richard reiterated.

The farmer again changed his posture. 'Then, my lad, ye 've come to tell me a lie!'

Farmer Blaize looked straight at the boy, undismayed by the dark flush of ire he had kindled.

'You dare to call me a liar!' cried Richard, starting up.

'I say,' the farmer renewed his first emphasis, and smacked his thigh thereto, 'that's a lie!'

Richard held out his clenched fist. 'You have twice insulted me. You have struck me: you have dared to call me a liar. I would have apologized—I would have asked your pardon, to have got off that fellow in prison. Yes! I would have degraded myself that another man should not suffer for my deed——'

'Quite proper!' interposed the farmer.

'And you take this opportunity of insulting me afresh. You're a coward, sir! nobody but a coward would have insulted me in his own house.'

'Sit ye down, sit ye down, young master,' said the farmer, indicating the chair and cooling the outburst with his hand. 'Sit ye down. Don't ye be hasty. If ye hadn't been hasty t' other day, we sh'd a been friends yet.

Sit ye down, sir. I sh'd be sorry to reckon you out a liar, Mr. Feverel, or anybody o' your name. I respects yer father, though we 're opp'site politics. I 'm willin' to think well o' you. What I say is, that as you say an't the trewth. Mind! I don't like you none the worse for 't. But it an't what is. That 's all! You knows it as well 's I!'

Richard, disdaining to show signs of being pacified, angrily reseated himself. The farmer spoke sense, and the boy, after his late interview with Austin, had become capable of perceiving vaguely that a towering passion is hardly the justification for a wrong course of conduct.

'Come,' continued the farmer, not unkindly, 'what else have you to say?'

Here was the same bitter cup he had already once drained brimming at Richard's lips again! Alas, poor human nature! that empties to the dregs a dozen of these evil drinks, to evade the single one which Destiny, less cruel, had insisted upon.

The boy blinked and tossed it off.

'I came to say that I regretted the revenge I had taken on you for your striking me.'

Farmer Blaize nodded.

'And now ye 've done, young gentleman?'

Still another cupful!

'I should be very much obliged,' Richard formally began, but his stomach was turned; he could but sip and sip, and gather a distaste which threatened to make the penitential act impossible. 'Very much obliged,' he repeated: 'much obliged, if you would be so kind,' and it struck him that had he spoken this at first he would have given it a wording more persuasive with the farmer and more worthy of his own pride: more honest, in fact: for a sense of the dishonesty of what he was saying caused him to cringe and simulate humility to deceive the farmer, and the more he said the less he felt his words, and, feeling them less, he inflated them more. 'So kind,' he stammered, 'so kind' (fancy a Feverel asking this big brute to be so kind!) 'as to do me the favour' (*me* the favour!) 'to exert yourself' (it's all to please Austin) 'to endeavour to—hem! to' (there's no saying it!)——

The cup was full as ever. Richard dashed at it again.

'What I came to ask is, whether you would have the kindness to try what you could do' (what an infamous shame to have to beg like this!) 'do to save—do to ensure —whether you would have the kindness—' It seemed out of all human power to gulp it down. The draught grew more and more abhorrent. To proclaim one's iniquity, to apologize for one's wrongdoing; thus much could be done; but to beg a favour of the offended party—that was beyond the self-abasement any Feverel could consent to. Pride, however, whose inevitable battle is against itself, drew aside the curtains of poor Tom's prison, crying a second time, 'Behold your Benefactor!' and, with the words burning in his ears, Richard swallowed the dose:

'Well, then, I want you, Mr. Blaize,—if you don't mind —will you help me to get this man Bakewell off his punishment?'

To do Farmer Blaize justice, he waited very patiently for the boy, though he could not quite see why he did not take the gate at the first offer.

'Oh!' said he, when he heard and had pondered on the request. 'Hum! ha! we'll see about it t'morrow. But if he's innocent, you know, we shan't mak'n guilty.'

'It was I did it!' Richard declared.

The farmer's half-amused expression sharpened a bit.

'So, young gentleman! and you're sorry for the night's work?'

'I shall see that you are paid the full extent of your losses.'

'Thank 'ee,' said the farmer drily.

'And, if this poor man is released to-morrow, I don't care what the amount is.'

Farmer Blaize deflected his head twice in silence. 'Bribery,' one motion expressed: 'Corruption,' the other.

'Now,' said he, leaning forward, and fixing his elbows on his knees, while he counted the case at his finger's ends, 'excuse the liberty, but wishin' to know where this 'ere money 's to come from, I sh'd like jest t 'ask if so be Sir Austin know o' this?'

'My father knows nothing of it,' replied Richard.

The farmer flung back in his chair. 'Lie number Two,' said his shoulders, soured by the British aversion to being plotted at, and not dealt with openly.

'And ye 've the money ready, young gentleman?'

'I shall ask my father for it.'

'And he 'll hand 't out?'

'Certainly he will!'

Richard had not the slightest intention of ever letting his father into his counsels.

'A good three hundred pounds, ye know?' the farmer suggested.

No consideration of the extent of damages, and the size of the sum, affected young Richard, who said boldly, 'He will not object when I tell him I want that sum.'

It was natural Farmer Blaize should be a trifle suspicious that a youth's guarantee would hardly be given for his father's readiness to disburse such a thumping bill, unless he had previously received his father's sanction and authority.

'Hum!' said he, 'why not 'a told him before?'

The farmer threw an objectionable shrewdness into his query, that caused Richard to compress his mouth and glance high.

Farmer Blaize was positive 'twas a lie.

'Hum! Ye still hold to 't you fired the rick?' he asked.

'The blame is mine!' quoth Richard, with the loftiness of a patriot of old Rome.

'Na, na!' the straightforward Briton put him aside. 'Ye did 't, or ye didn't do 't.   Did ye do 't, or no ?'

Thrust in a corner, Richard said, 'I did it.'

Farmer Blaize reached his hand to the bell.   It was answered in an instant by little Lucy, who received orders to fetch in a dependent at Belthorpe going by the name of the Bantam, and made her exit as she had entered, with her eyes on the young stranger.

'Now,' said the farmer, 'these be my principles.   I 'm a plain man, Mr. Feverel.   Above board with me, and you 'll find me handsome.   Try to circumvent me, and I 'm a ugly customer.   I 'll show you I 've no animosity. Your father pays—you apologize.   That 's enough for me! Let Tom Bakewell fight 't out with the Law, and I 'll look on.   The Law wasn't on the spot, I suppose? so the Law ain't much witness.   But I am.   Leastwise the Bantam is.   I tell you, young gentleman, the Bantam saw 't!   It 's no mortal use whatever your denyin' that ev'dence.   And where 's the good, sir, I ask?   What comes of 't?   Whether it be you, or whether it be Tom Bakewell—ain't all one? If I holds back, ain't it sim'lar?   It 's the trewth I want! And here 't comes,' added the farmer, as Miss Lucy ushered in the Bantam, who presented a curious figure for that rare divinity to enliven.

CHAPTER IX

A FINE DISTINCTION

In build of body, gait and stature, Giles Jinkson, the Bantam, was a tolerably fair representative of the Punic elephant, whose part, with diverse anticipations, the generals of the Blaize and Feverel forces, from opposing ranks, expected him to play. Giles, surnamed the Bantam, on account of some forgotten sally of his youth or infancy, moved and looked elephantine. It sufficed that Giles was well fed to assure that Giles was faithful—if uncorrupted. The farm which supplied to him ungrudging provender had all his vast capacity for work in willing exercise: the farmer who held the farm his instinct reverenced as the fountain-source of beef and bacon, to say nothing of beer, which was plentiful at Belthorpe, and good. This Farmer Blaize well knew, and he reckoned consequently that here was an animal always to be relied on—a sort of human composition out of dog, horse, and bull, a cut above each of these quadrupeds in usefulness, and costing proportionately more, but on the whole worth the money, and therefore invaluable, as everything worth its money must be to a wise man. When the stealing of grain had been made known at Belthorpe, the Bantam, a fellow-thresher with Tom Bakewell, had shared with him the shadow of the guilt. Farmer Blaize, if he hesitated which to suspect, did not debate a second as to which he would discard; and when the Bantam said he had seen Tom secreting pilkins in a sack, Farmer Blaize chose to believe him, and off went poor Tom, told to rejoice in the clemency that spared his appearance at Sessions.

The Bantam's small sleepy orbits saw many things, and just at the right moment, it seemed. He was certainly the first to give the clue at Belthorpe on the night of the conflagration, and he may, therefore, have seen poor Tom retreating stealthily from the scene, as he averred he did. Lobourne had its say on the subject. Rustic Lobourne hinted broadly at a young woman in the case, and, moreover, told a tale of how these fellow-threshers had, in noble rivalry, one day turned upon each other to see which of the two threshed the best; whereof the Bantam still bore marks, and malice, it was said. However, there he stood, and tugged his forelocks to the company, and if Truth really had concealed herself in him she must have been hard set to find her unlikeliest hiding-place.

'Now,' said the farmer, marshalling forth his elephant with the confidence of one who delivers his ace of trumps, 'tell this young gentleman what ye saw on the night of the fire, Bantam!'

The Bantam jerked a bit of a bow to his patron, and then swung round, fully obscuring him from Richard.

Richard fixed his eyes on the floor, while the Bantam in rudest Doric*commenced his narrative. Knowing what was to come, and thoroughly nerved to confute the main incident, Richard barely listened to his barbarous locution: but when the recital arrived at the point where the Bantam affirmed he had seen 'T'm Baak'll wi's owen hoies,'*Richard faced him, and was amazed to find himself being mutely addressed by a series of intensely significant grimaces, signs, and winks.

'What do you mean? Why are you making those faces at me?' cried the boy indignantly.

Farmer Blaize leaned round the Bantam to have a look at him, and beheld the stolidest mask ever given to man.

'Bain't makin' no faces at nobody,' growled the sulky elephant.

The farmer commanded him to face about and finish.

'A see T'm Baak'll,' the Bantam recommenced, and again the contortions of a horrible wink were directed at Richard. The boy might well believe this churl was lying, and he did, and was emboldened to exclaim:

'You never saw Tom Bakewell set fire to that rick!'

The Bantam swore to it, grimacing an accompaniment.

'I tell you,' said Richard, 'I put the lucifers* there myself!"

The suborned elephant was staggered. He meant to telegraph to the young gentleman that he was loyal and true to certain gold pieces that had been given him, and that in the right place and at the right time he should prove so. Why was he thus suspected? Why was he not understood?

'A thowt I see 'un, then,' muttered the Bantam, trying a middle course.

This brought down on him the farmer, who roared, 'Thought! Ye thought! What d' ye mean? Speak out, and don't be thinkin'. Thought? What the devil's that?'

'How could he see who it was on a pitch-dark night?' Richard put in.

'Thought!' the farmer bellowed louder. 'Thought— Devil take ye, when ye took yer oath on 't. Hulloa! What are ye screwin' yer eye at Mr. Feverel for?—I say, young gentleman, have you spoke to this chap before now?'

'I?' replied Richard. 'I have not seen him before.'

Farmer Blaize grasped the two arms of the chair he sat on, and glared his doubts.

'Come,' said he to the Bantam, 'speak out, and ha' done wi 't. Say what ye saw, and none o' yer thoughts. Damn yer thoughts! Ye saw Tom Bakewell fire that there rick!' The farmer pointed at some musk-pots in the window. 'What business ha' you to be a-thinkin'? You 're a witness? Thinkin' an't ev'dence. What 'll ye say to-morrow before magistrate! Mind! what you says to-day, you 'll stick by to-morrow.'

Thus adjured, the Bantam hitched his breech. What on earth the young gentleman meant he was at a loss to speculate. He could not believe that the young gentleman wanted to be transported, but if he had been paid to help that, why, he would. And considering that this day's evidence rather bound him down to the morrow's, he determined, after much ploughing and harrowing through obstinate shocks of hair, to be not altogether positive as to the person. It is possible that he became thereby more a mansion of truth than he previously had been; for the night, as he said, was so dark that you could not see your hand before your face; and though, as he expressed it, you might be mortal sure of a man, you could not identify him upon oath, and the party he had taken for Tom Bakewell, and could have sworn to, might have been the young gentleman present, especially as he was ready to swear it upon oath.

So ended the Bantam.

No sooner had he ceased, than Farmer Blaize jumped up from his chair, and made a fine effort to lift him out of the room from the point of his toe. He failed, and sank back groaning with the pain of the exertion and disappointment.

'They 're liars, every one!' he cried. 'Liars, perj'rers, bribers, and c'rrupters!—Stop!' to the Bantam, who was slinking away. 'You 've done for yerself already! You swore to it!'

'A din't!' said the Bantam doggedly.

'You swore to 't!' the farmer vociferated afresh.

The Bantam played a tune upon the handle of the door, and still affirmed that he did not; a double contradiction at which the farmer absolutely raged in his chair, and was hoarse, as he called out a third time that the Bantam had sworn to it.

'Noa!' said the Bantam, ducking his poll. 'Noa!' he repeated in a lower note; and then, while a sombre grin betokening idiotic enjoyment of his profound casuistical quibble worked at his jaw:—

'Not up'n o-ath!' he added, with a twitch of the shoulder and an angular jerk of the elbow.

Farmer Blaize looked vacantly at Richard, as if to ask him what he thought of England's peasantry after the sample they had there. Richard would have preferred not to laugh, but his dignity gave way to his sense of the

ludicrous, and he let fly a shout. The farmer was in no
laughing mood. He turned a wide eye back to the door,
'Lucky for 'm,' he exclaimed, seeing the Bantam had
vanished, for his fingers itched to break that stubborn head.
He grew very puffy, and addressed Richard solemnly:

'Now, look ye here, Mr. Feverel! You 've been a-tamper-
ing with my witness. It 's no use denyin'! I say y' 'ave,
sir! You, or some of ye. I don't care about no Feverel!
My witness there has been bribed. The Bantam 's been
bribed,' and he shivered his pipe with an energetic thump
on the table—'bribed! I knows it! I could swear to 't——!'

'Upon oath?' Richard inquired, with a grave face.

'Ay, upon oath!' said the farmer, not observing the
impertinence.

'I 'd take my Bible oath on 't! He 's been corrupted, my
principal witness! Oh! it 's damn cunnin', but it won't do
the trick. I 'll transpoort Tom Bakewell, sure as a gun.
He shall travel, that man shall. Sorry for you, Mr. Feverel
—sorry you haven't seen how to treat me proper—you, or
yours. Money won't do everything—no! it won't. It 'll
c'rrupt a witness, but it won't clear a felon. I 'd ha'
'scused you, sir! You 're a boy and 'll learn better. I
asked no more than payment and a 'pology; and that I 'd
ha' taken content—always provided my witnesses weren't
tampered with. Now you must stand yer luck, all o'
ye.'

Richard stood up and replied, 'Very well, Mr. Blaize.'

'And if,' continued the farmer, 'Tom Bakewell don't
drag you into 't after 'm, why, you 're safe, as I hope ye 'll
be, sincere!'

'It was not in consideration of my own safety that I
sought this interview with you,' said Richard, head erect.

'Grant ye that,' the farmer responded. 'Grant ye that!
Yer bold enough, young gentleman—comes of the blood
that should be! If y' had only ha' spoke trewth!—I believe

yer father—believe every word he said. I do wish I could
ha' said as much for Sir Austin's son and heir.'

'What!' cried Richard, with an astonishment hardly to
be feigned, 'you have seen my father?'

But Farmer Blaize had now such a scent for lies that he
could detect them where they did not exist, and mumbled
gruffly,

'Ay, we knows all about that!'

The boy's perplexity saved him from being irritated.
Who could have told his father? An old fear of his
father came upon him, and a touch of an old inclination
to revolt.

'My father knows of this?' said he, very loudly, and
staring, as he spoke, right through the farmer. 'Who
has played me false? Who would betray me to him? It
was Austin! No one knew it but Austin. Yes, and it was
Austin who persuaded me to come here and submit to
these indignities. Why couldn't he be open with me? I
shall never trust him again——!'

'And why not you with me, young gentleman?' said
the farmer. 'I sh'd trust you if ye had.'

Richard did not see the analogy. He bowed stiffly and
bade him good afternoon.

Farmer Blaize pulled the bell. ''Company the young
gentleman out, Lucy,' he waved to the little damsel in
the doorway. 'Do the honours. And, Mr. Richard, ye
might ha' made a friend o' me, sir, and it 's not too late so
to do. I 'm not cruel, but I hate lies. I whipped my boy
Tom, bigger than you, for not bein' above board, only
yesterday—ay! made 'un stand within swing o' this chair,
and take 's measure. Now, if ye 'll come down to me, and
speak trewth before the trial—if it 's only five minutes
before 't; or if Sir Austin, who 's a gentleman, 'll say there 's
been no tamperin' with any o' my witnesses, his word for 't
—well and good! I 'll do my best to help off Tom Bakewell.

And I 'm glad, young gentleman, you 've got a conscience about a poor man, though he 's a villain. Good afternoon, sir.'

Richard marched hastily out of the room, and through the garden, never so much as deigning a glance at his wistful little guide, who hung at the garden gate to watch him up the lane, wondering a world of fancies about the handsome proud boy.

CHAPTER X

RICHARD PASSES THROUGH HIS PRELIMINARY ORDEAL, AND IS THE OCCASION OF AN APHORISM

To have determined upon an act something akin to heroism in its way, and to have fulfilled it by lying heartily, and so subverting the whole structure built by good resolution, seems a sad downfall if we forget what human nature, in its green weedy spring, is composed of. Young Richard had quitted his cousin Austin fully resolved to do his penance and drink the bitter cup; and he had drunk it; drained many cups to the dregs; and it was to no purpose. Still they floated before him, brimmed, trebly bitter. Away from Austin's influence, he was almost the same boy who had slipped the guinea into Tom Bakewell's hand, and the lucifers into Farmer Blaize's rick. For good seed is long ripening; a good boy is not made in a minute. Enough that the seed was in him. He chafed on his road to Raynham at the scene he had just endured, and the figure of Belthorpe's fat tenant burnt like hot copper on the tablet of his brain, insufferably condescending, and, what was worse, in the right. Richard, obscured as his mind's eye was by wounded pride, saw that clearly, and hated his enemy for it the more.

Heavy Benson's tongue was knelling dinner as Richard arrived at the Abbey. He hurried up to his room to dress. Accident, or design, had laid the book of Sir Austin's aphorisms open on the dressing-table. Hastily combing his hair, Richard glanced down and read—

'The Dog returneth to his vomit: the Liar must eat his Lie.'

Underneath was interjected in pencil: 'The Devil's mouthful!'

Young Richard ran downstairs feeling that his father had struck him in the face.

Sir Austin marked the scarlet stain on his son's cheek-bones. He sought the youth's eye, but Richard would not look, and sat conning his plate, an abject copy of Adrian's succulent air at that employment. How could he pretend to the relish of an epicure when he was pain-fully endeavouring to masticate The Devil's mouthful?

Heavy Benson sat upon the wretched dinner. Hippias, usually the silent member, as if awakened by the unnatu-ral stillness, became sprightly, like the goatsucker owl*at night, and spoke much of his book, his digestion, and his dreams, and was spared both by Algernon and Adrian. One inconsequent dream he related, about fancying him-self quite young and rich, and finding himself suddenly in a field cropping razors around him, when, just as he had, by steps dainty as those of a French dancing-master, reached the middle, he to his dismay beheld a path clear of the bloodthirsty steel-crop, which he might have taken at first had he looked narrowly; and there he was.

Hippias's brethren regarded him with eyes that plainly said they wished he had remained there. Sir Austin, however, drew forth his note-book, and jotted down a re-flection. A composer of aphorisms can pluck blossoms even from a razor-crop. Was not Hippias's dream the very counterpart of Richard's position? He, had he looked narrowly, might have taken the clear path: he, too, had been making dainty steps till he was surrounded by the grinning blades. And from that text Sir Austin preached to his son when they were alone. Little Clare was still too unwell to be permitted to attend the dessert, and father and son were soon closeted together.

It was a strange meeting. They seemed to have been separated so long. The father took his son's hand; they sat without a word passing between them. Silence said most. The boy did not understand his father: his father frequently thwarted him: at times he thought his father foolish: but that paternal pressure of his hand was eloquent to him of how warmly he was beloved. He tried once or twice to steal his hand away, conscious it was melting him. The spirit of his pride, and old rebellion, whispered him to be hard, unbending, resolute. Hard he had entered his father's study: hard he had met his father's eyes. He could not meet them now. His father sat beside him gently; with a manner that was almost meekness, so he loved this boy. The poor gentleman's lips moved. He was praying internally to God for him.

By degrees an emotion awoke in the boy's bosom. Love is that blessed wand which wins the waters from the hardness of the heart. Richard fought against it, for the dignity of old rebellion. The tears would come; hot and struggling over the dams of pride. Shamefully fast they began to fall. He could no longer conceal them, or check the sobs. Sir Austin drew him nearer and nearer, till the beloved head was on his breast.

An hour afterwards, Adrian Harley, Austin Wentworth, and Algernon Feverel were summoned to the baronet's study.

Adrian came last. There was a style of affable omnipotence about the wise youth as he slung himself into a chair, and made an arch of the points of his fingers, through

which to gaze on his blundering kinsmen. Careless as one
may be whose sagacity has foreseen, and whose benevolent efforts have forestalled, the point of danger at the
threshold, Adrian crossed his legs, and only intruded on
their introductory remarks so far as to hum half audibly
at intervals—

'Ripton and Richard were two pretty men,'

in parody of the old ballad.* Young Richard's red eyes,
and the baronet's ruffled demeanour, told him that an
explanation had taken place, and a reconciliation. That
was well. The baronet would now pay cheerfully. Adrian
summed and considered these matters, and barely listened
when the baronet called attention to what he had to say:
which was elaborately to inform all present, what all present very well knew, that a rick had been fired, that his son
was implicated as an accessory to the fact, that the perpe-
trator was now imprisoned, and that Richard's family were,
as it seemed to him, bound in honour to do their utmost
to effect the man's release.

Then the baronet stated that he had himself been down
to Belthorpe, his son likewise: and that he had found every
disposition in Blaize to meet his wishes.

The lamp which ultimately was sure to be lifted up to
illumine the acts of this secretive race began slowly to
dispread its rays; and, as statement followed statement,
they saw that all had known of the business: that all had
been down to Belthorpe: all save the wise youth Adrian,
who, with due deference and a sarcastic shrug, objected
to the proceeding, as putting them in the hands of the
man Blaize. His wisdom shone forth in an oration so persuasive and aphoristic that had it not been based on a plea
against honour, it would have made Sir Austin waver.
But its basis was expediency, and the baronet had a better
aphorism of his own to confute him with.

'Expediency is man's wisdom, Adrian Harley. Doing right is God's.'

Adrian curbed his desire to ask Sir Austin whether an attempt to counteract the just working of the law was doing right. The direct application of an aphorism was unpopular at Raynham.

'I am to understand then,' said he, 'that Blaize consents not to press the prosecution.'

'Of course he won't,' Algernon remarked. 'Confound him! he'll have his money, and what does he want besides?'

'These agricultural gentlemen are delicate customers to deal with. However, if he really consents——'

'I have his promise,' said the baronet, fondling his son.

Young Richard looked up to his father, as if he wished to speak. He said nothing, and Sir Austin took it as a mute reply to his caresses, and caressed him the more. Adrian perceived a reserve in the boy's manner, and as he was not quite satisfied that his chief should suppose him to have been the only idle, and not the most acute and vigilant member of the family, he commenced a cross-examination of him by asking who had last spoken with the tenant of Belthorpe?

'I think I saw him last,' murmured Richard, and relinquished his father's hand.

Adrian fastened on his prey. 'And left him with a distinct and satisfactory assurance of his amicable intentions?'

'No,' said Richard.

'Not?' the Feverels joined in astounded chorus.

Richard sidled away from his father, and repeated a shamefaced 'No.'

'Was he hostile?' inquired Adrian, smoothing his palms, and smiling.

'Yes,' the boy confessed.

Here was quite another view of their position. Adrian,

generally patient of results, triumphed strongly at having evoked it, and turned upon Austin Wentworth, reproving him for inducing the boy to go down to Belthorpe. Austin looked grieved. He feared that Richard had failed in his good resolve.

'I thought it his duty to go,' he observed.

'It was!' said the baronet emphatically.

'And you see what comes of it, sir,' Adrian struck in. 'These agricultural gentlemen, I repeat, are delicate customers to deal with. For my part I would prefer being in the hands of a policeman. We are decidedly collared by Blaize. What were his words, Ricky? Give it in his own Doric.'

'He said he would transport Tom Bakewell.'

Adrian smoothed his palms, and smiled again. Then they could afford to defy Mr. Blaize, he informed them significantly, and made once more a mysterious allusion to the Punic elephant, bidding his relatives be at peace. They were attaching, in his opinion, too much importance to Richard's complicity. The man was a fool, and a very extraordinary arsonite, to have an accomplice at all. It was a thing unknown in the annals of rick-burning. But one would be severer than law itself to say that a boy of fourteen had instigated to crime a full-grown man. At that rate the boy was "father of the man" with a vengeance, and one might hear next that "the baby was father of the boy." They would find common sense a more benevolent ruler than poetical metaphysics.

When he had done, Austin, with his customary directness, asked him what he meant.

'I confess, Adrian,' said the baronet, hearing him expostulate with Austin's stupidity, 'I for one am at a loss. I have heard that this man, Bakewell, chooses voluntarily not to inculpate my son. Seldom have I heard anything that so gratified me. It is a view of innate noble-

ness in the rustic's character which many gentlemen
might take example from. We are bound to do our utmost for the man.' And, saying that he should pay a
second visit to Belthorpe, to inquire into the reasons for
the farmer's sudden exposition of vindictiveness, Sir Austin
rose.

Before he left the room Algernon asked Richard if the
farmer had vouchsafed any reasons, and the boy then
spoke of the tampering with the witnesses, and the Bantam's 'Not upon oath!' which caused Adrian to choke
with laughter. Even the baronet smiled at so cunning a
distinction as that involved in swearing a thing, and not
swearing it upon oath.

'How little,' he exclaimed, 'does one yeoman know
another! To elevate a distinction into a difference is the
natural action of their minds. I will point that out to
Blaize. He shall see that the idea is native born.'

Richard saw his father go forth. Adrian, too, was ill
at ease.

'This trotting down to Belthorpe spoils all,' said he.
'The affair would pass over to-morrow—Blaize has no
witnesses. The old rascal is only standing out for more
money.'

'No, he isn't,' Richard corrected him. 'It's not that.
I'm sure he believes his witnesses have been tampered
with, as he calls it.'

'What if they have, boy?' Adrian put it boldly. 'The
ground is cut from under his feet.'

'Blaize told me that if my father would give his word
there had been nothing of the sort, he would take it. My
father will give his word.'

'Then,' said Adrian, 'you had better stop him from
going down.'

Austin looked at Adrian keenly, and questioned him
whether he thought the farmer was justified in his sus-

picions. The wise youth was not to be entrapped. He had only been given to understand that the witnesses were tolerably unstable, and, like the Bantam, ready to swear lustily, but not upon the Book. How given to understand, he chose not to explain, but he reiterated that the chief should not be allowed to go down to Belthorpe.

Sir Austin was in the lane leading to the farm when he heard steps of some one running behind him. It was dark, and he shook off the hand that laid hold of his cloak, roughly, not recognizing his son.

'It's I, sir,' said Richard panting. 'Pardon me. You mustn't go in there.'

'Why not?' said the baronet, putting his arm about him.

'Not now,' continued the boy. 'I will tell you all to-night. I must see the farmer myself. It was my fault, sir. I—I lied to him—the Liar must eat his Lie. Oh, forgive me for disgracing you, sir. I did it—I hope I did it to save Tom Bakewell. Let me go in alone, and speak the truth.'

'Go, and I will wait for you here,' said his father.

The wind that bowed the old elms, and shivered the dead leaves in the air, had a voice and a meaning for the baronet during that half-hour's lonely pacing up and down under the darkness, awaiting his boy's return. The solemn gladness of his heart gave nature a tongue. Through the desolation flying overhead—the wailing of the Mother of Plenty across the bare-swept land—he caught intelligible signs of the beneficent order of the universe, from a heart newly confirmed in its grasp of the principle of human goodness, as manifested in the dear child who had just left him; confirmed in its belief in the ultimate victory of good within us, without which nature has neither music nor meaning, and is rock, stone, tree, and nothing more.

In the dark, the dead leaves beating on his face, he had
a word for his note-book: 'There is for the mind but one
grasp of happiness: from that uppermost pinnacle of wisdom, whence we see that this world is well designed.'

CHAPTER XI

IN WHICH THE LAST ACT OF THE BAKEWELL COMEDY IS CLOSED IN A LETTER

OF all the chief actors in the Bakewell Comedy, Master
Ripton Thompson awaited the fearful morning which was
to decide Tom's fate, in dolefullest mood, and suffered the
gravest mental terrors. Adrian, on parting with him, had
taken casual occasion to speak of the position of the criminal in modern Europe, assuring him that International
Treaty now did what Universal Empire had aforetime
done, and that among Atlantic barbarians now, as among
the Scythians*of old, an offender would find precarious
refuge and an emissary haunting him.

In the paternal home, under the roofs of Law, and removed from the influence of his conscienceless young chief,
the staggering nature of the act he had put his hand to,
its awful felonious aspect, overwhelmed Ripton. He saw
it now for the first time. 'Why, it 's next to murder!' he
cried out to his amazed soul, and wandered about the house
with a prickly skin. Thoughts of America, and commencing life afresh as an innocent gentleman, had crossed his
disordered brain. He wrote to his friend Richard, pro-
posing to collect disposable funds, and embark, in case
of Tom's breaking his word, or of accidental discovery.
He dared not confide the secret to his family, as his leader
had sternly enjoined him to avoid any weakness of that

kind; and, being by nature honest and communicative, the restriction was painful, and melancholy fell upon the boy. Mama Thompson attributed it to love. The daughters of parchment rallied him concerning Miss Clare Forey. His hourly letters to Raynham, and silence as to everything and everybody there, his nervousness, and unwonted propensity to sudden inflammation of the cheeks, were set down for sure signs of the passion. Miss Letitia Thompson, the pretty and least parchmentary one, destined by her Papa for the heir of Raynham, and perfectly aware of her brilliant future, up to which she had, since Ripton's departure, dressed and grimaced, and studied cadences (the latter with such success, though not yet fifteen, that she languished to her maid, and melted the small factotum footman)—Miss Letty, whose insatiable thirst for intimations about the young heir Ripton could not satisfy, tormented him daily in revenge, and once, quite unconsciously, gave the lad a fearful turn; for after dinner, when Mr. Thompson read the paper by the fire, preparatory to sleeping at his accustomed post, and Mama Thompson and her submissive female brood sat tasking the swift intricacies of the needle, and emulating them with the tongue, Miss Letty stole behind Ripton's chair, and introduced between him and his book the Latin initial letter, large and illuminated, of the theme she supposed to be absorbing him, as it did herself. The unexpected vision of this accusing Captain of the Alphabet, this resplendent and haunting A, fronting him bodily, threw Ripton straight back in his chair, while Guilt, with her ancient indecision what colours to assume on detection, flew from red to white, from white to red, across his fallen chaps. Letty laughed triumphantly. Amor,* the word she had in mind, certainly has a connection with Arson.

But the delivery of a letter into Master Ripton's hands furnished her with other and likelier appearances to study.

For scarce had Ripton plunged his head into the missive
than he gave way to violent transports, such as the healthy-
minded little damsel, for all her languishing cadences,
deemed she really could express were a downright declaration to be made to her. The boy did not stop at table.
Quickly recollecting the presence of his family, he rushed
to his own room. And now the girl's ingenuity was taxed
to gain possession of that letter. She succeeded, of course,
she being a huntress with few scruples and the game un-
guarded. With the eyes of amazement she read this
foreign matter:

'Dear Ripton,—If Tom had been committed I would
have shot old Blaize. Do you know my father was behind
us that night when Clare saw the ghost and heard all we
said before the fire burst out. It is no use trying to conceal anything from him. Well as you are in an awful state
I will tell you all about it. After you left Ripton I had a
conversation with Austin and he persuaded me to go down
to old Blaize and ask him to help off Tom. I went for I
would have done anything for Tom after what he said to
Austin and I defied the old churl to do his worst. Then
he said if my father paid the money and nobody had tampered with his witnesses he would not mind if Tom did get
off and he had his chief witness in called the Bantam very
like his master I think and the Bantam began winking at
me tremendjously as you say, and said he had sworn he
saw Tom Bakewell but not upon oath. He meant not on
the Bible. He could swear to it but not on the Bible. I
burst out laughing and you should have seen the rage old
Blaize was in. It was splendid fun. Then we had a consultation at home Austin Rady my father Uncle Algernon
who has come down to us again and your friend in prosperity and adversity R. D. F. My father said he would go
down to old Blaize and give him the word of a gentleman

we had not tampered with his witnesses and when he was gone we were all talking and Rady says he must not see the farmer. I am as certain as I live that it was Rady bribed the Bantam. Well I ran and caught up my father and told him not to go in to old Blaize but I would and eat my words and tell him the truth. He waited for me in the lane. Never mind what passed between me and old Blaize. He made me beg and pray of him not to press it against Tom and then to complete it he brought in a little girl a niece of his and says to me she 's your best friend after all and told me to thank her. A little girl twelve years of age. What business had she to mix herself up in my matters. Depend upon it Ripton wherever there is mischief there are girls I think. She had the insolence to notice my face, and ask me not to be unhappy. I was polite of course but I would not look at her. Well the morning came and Tom was had up before Sir Miles Papworth. It was Sir Miles gout gave us the time or Tom would have been had up before we could do anything. Adrian did not want me to go but my father said I should accompany him and held my hand all the time. I shall be careful about getting into these scrapes again. When you have done anything honourable you do not mind but getting among policemen and magistrates makes you ashamed of yourself. Sir Miles was very attentive to my father and me and dead against Tom. We sat beside him and Tom was brought in Sir Miles told my father that if there was one thing that showed a low villain it was rick-burning. What do you think of that. I looked him straight in the face and he said to me he was doing me a service in getting Tom committed and clearing the country of such fellows and Rady began laughing. I hate Rady. My father said his son was not in haste to inherit and have estates of his own to watch and Sir Miles laughed too. I thought we were discovered at first. Then they began the exam-

ination of Tom. The Tinker was the first witness and
he proved that Tom had spoken against old Blaize and
said something about burning his rick. I wished I had
stood in the lane to Bursley with him alone. Our country lawyer we engaged for Tom cross-questioned him and
then he said he was not ready to swear to the exact words
that had passed between him and Tom. I should think
not. Then came another who swore he had seen Tom
lurking about the farmer's grounds that night. Then
came the Bantam and I saw him look at Rady. I was
tremendjously excited and my father kept pressing my
hand. Just fancy my being brought to feel that a word
from that fellow would make me miserable for life and he
must perjure himself to help me. That comes of giving
way to passion. My father says when we do that we are
calling in the devil as doctor. Well the Bantam was told
to state what he had seen and the moment he began Rady
who was close by me began to shake and he was laughing
I knew though his face was as grave as Sir Miles. You
never heard such a rigmarole but I could not laugh. He
said he thought he was certain he had seen somebody by
the rick and it was Tom Bakewell who was the only man
he knew who had a grudge against Farmer Blaize and if
the object had been a little bigger he would not mind
swearing to Tom and would swear to him for he was dead
certain it was Tom only what he saw looked smaller and
it was pitch-dark at the time. He was asked what time
it was he saw the person steal away from the rick and
then he began to scratch his head and said supper-time.
Then they asked what time he had supper and he said
nine o'clock by the clock and we proved that at nine
o'clock Tom was drinking in the ale-house with the Tinker
at Bursley and Sir Miles swore and said he was afraid he
could not commit Tom and when he heard that Tom looked
up at me and I say he is a noble fellow and no one shall

sneer at Tom while I live. Mind that. Well Sir Miles
asked us to dine with him and Tom was safe and I am to
have him and educate him if I like for my servant and I
will. And I will give money to his mother and make her
rich and he shall never repent he knew me. I say Rip.
The Bantam must have seen *me*. It was when I went to
stick in the lucifers. As we were all going home from
Sir Miles's at night he has lots of red-faced daughters but
I did not dance with them though they had music and
were full of fun and I did not care to I was so delighted
and almost let it out. When we left and rode home Rady
said to my father the Bantam was not such a fool as he
was thought and my father said one must be in a state
of great personal exaltation to apply that epithet to any
man and Rady shut his mouth and I gave my pony a clap
of the heel for joy. I think my father suspects what Rady
did and does not approve of it. And he need not have
done it after all and might have spoilt it. I have been
obliged to order him not to call me Ricky for he stops
short at Rick so that everybody knows what he means.
My dear Austin is going to South America. My pony is
in capital condition. My father is the cleverest and best
man in the world. Clare is a little better. I am quite
happy. I hope we shall meet soon my dear Old Rip and
we will not get into any more tremendjous scrapes will we.
—I remain, your sworn friend,

'RICHARD DORIA FEVEREL.'

'*P.S.* I am to have a nice River Yacht. Good-bye,
Rip. Mind you learn to box. Mind you are not to show
this to any of your friends on pain of my displeasure.

'N.B. Lady B. was so angry when I told her that I
had not come to her before. She would do anything in
the world for me. I like her next best to my father and
Austin. Good-bye old Rip.'

Poor little Letitia, after three perusals of this ingenuous epistle, where the laws of punctuation were so disregarded, resigned it to one of the pockets of her brother Ripton's best jacket, deeply smitten with the careless composer. And so ended the last act of the Bakewell Comedy, on which the curtain closes with Sir Austin's pointing out to his friends the beneficial action of the System in it from beginning to end.

CHAPTER XII

THE BLOSSOMING SEASON

LAYING of ghosts is a public duty, and as the mystery of the apparition that had frightened little Clare was never solved on the stage of events at Raynham, where dread walked the Abbey, let us go behind the scenes a moment. Morally superstitious as the baronet was, the character of his mind was opposed to anything like spiritual agency in the affairs of men, and, when the matter was made clear to him, it shook off a weight of weakness and restored his mental balance; so that from this time he went about more like the man he had once been, grasping more thoroughly the great truth, that This World is well designed. Nay, he could laugh on hearing Adrian, in reminiscence of the ill luck of one of the family members at its first manifestation, call the uneasy spirit, Algernon's Leg.

Mrs. Doria was outraged. She maintained that her child had seen——. Not to believe in it was almost to rob her of her personal property. After satisfactorily studying his old state of mind in her, Sir Austin, moved by pity, took her aside one day and showed her that her Ghost could write words in the flesh. It was a letter from the unhappy lady who had given Richard birth,—brief cold lines, simply telling him his house would be disturbed by her no more. Cold lines, but penned by what heart-broken abnegation, and underlying them what anguish of soul! Like most who dealt with him, Lady Feverel thought her husband a man fatally stern and implacable, and she acted as silly creatures will act when they fancy they see a fate against them: she neither petitioned for her right nor claimed it: she tried to ease her heart's yearning by stealth, and now she renounced all. Mrs. Doria, not wanting in the family tenderness and softness, shuddered at him for accepting the sacrifice so composedly: but he bade her to think how distracting to this boy would be the sight of such relations between mother and father. A few years, and as man he should know, and judge, and love her. 'Let this be her penance, not inflicted by me!' Mrs. Doria bowed to the System for another, not opining when it would be her turn to bow for herself.

Further behind the scenes we observe Rizzio and Mary grown older, much disenchanted: she discrowned, dishevelled,—he with gouty fingers on a greasy guitar. The Diaper Sandoe of promise lends his pen for small hires. His fame has sunk; his bodily girth has sensibly increased. What he can do, and will do, is still his theme; meantime the juice of the juniper*is in requisition, and it seems that those small hires cannot be performed without it. Returning from her wretched journey to her wretcheder home, the lady had to listen to a mild reproof from easy-going Diaper,—a reproof so mild that he couched it in blank verse: for, seldom writing metrically now, he took to talking it. With a fluent sympathetic tear, he explained to her that she was damaging her interests by these proceedings; nor did he shrink from undertaking to elucidate

wherefore. Pluming a smile upon his succulent mouth,
he told her that the poverty she lived in was utterly un-
befitting her gentle nurture, and that he had reason to
believe—could assure her—that an annuity was on the
point of being granted her by her husband. And Diaper
broke his bud of a smile into full flower as he delivered
this information. She learnt that he had applied to her
husband for money. It is hard to have one's last prop of
self-respect cut away just when we are suffering a martyr's
agony at the stake. There was a five minutes' tragic colloquy in the recesses behind the scenes,—totally tragic to
Diaper, who had fondly hoped to bask in the warm sun
of that annuity, and re-emerge from his state of grub.
The lady then wrote the letter Sir Austin held open to
his sister. The atmosphere behind the scenes is not
wholesome, so, having laid the Ghost, we will return and
face the curtain.

That infinitesimal dose of THE WORLD which Master
Ripton Thompson had furnished to the System with such
instantaneous and surprising effect was considered by Sir
Austin to have worked well, and to be for the time quite
sufficient, so that Ripton did not receive a second invitation to Raynham, and Richard had no special intimate
of his own age to rub his excessive vitality against, and
wanted none. His hands were full enough with Tom
Bakewell. Moreover, his father and he were heart in
heart. The boy's mind was opening, and turned to his
father affectionately reverent. At this period, when the
young savage grows into higher influences, the faculty
of worship is foremost in him. At this period Jesuits will
stamp the future of their chargeling flocks; and all who
bring up youth by a System, and watch it, know that it
is the malleable moment. Boys possessing any mental
or moral force to give them a tendency, then predestinate
their careers; or, if under supervision, take the impress

that is given them: not often to cast it off, and seldom
to cast it off altogether.

In Sir Austin's Note-book was written: 'Between
Simple Boyhood and Adolescence—The Blossoming Sea-
son—on the threshold of Puberty, there is one Unselfish
Hour—say, Spiritual Seed-time.'

He took care that good seed should be planted in Richard,
and that the most fruitful seed for a youth, namely, Example, should be of a kind to germinate in him the love of
every form of nobleness.

'I am only striving to make my son a Christian,' he
said, answering them who persisted in expostulating with
the System. And to these instructions he gave an aim:
'First be virtuous,' he told his son, 'and then serve your
country with heart and soul.' The youth was instructed
to cherish an ambition for statesmanship, and he and his
father read history and the speeches of British orators to
some purpose; for one day Sir Austin found him leaning cross-legged, and with his hand to his chin, against
a pedestal supporting the bust of Chatham,* contemplating the hero of our Parliament, his eyes streaming with
tears.

People said the baronet carried the principle of Example so far that he only retained his boozing dyspeptic
brother Hippias at Raynham in order to exhibit to his
son the woeful retribution nature wreaked upon a life of
indulgence; poor Hippias having now become a walking
complaint. This was unjust, but there is no doubt he
made use of every illustration to disgust or encourage his
son that his neighbourhood afforded him, and did not
spare his brother, for whom Richard entertained a contempt in proportion to his admiration of his father, and
was for flying into penitential extremes which Sir Austin
had to soften.

The boy prayed with his father morning and night.

'How is it, sir,' he said one night, 'I can't get Tom Bakewell to pray?'

'Does he refuse?' Sir Austin asked.

'He seems to be ashamed to,' Richard replied. 'He wants to know what is the good? and I don't know what to tell him.'

'I 'm afraid it has gone too far with him,' said Sir Austin, 'and until he has had some deep sorrows he will not find the divine want of Prayer. Strive, my son, when you represent the people, to provide for their education. He feels everything now through a dull impenetrable rind. Culture is half-way to Heaven. Tell him, my son, should he ever be brought to ask how he may know the efficacy of Prayer, and that his prayer will be answered, tell him (he quoted THE PILGRIM'S SCRIP):

'"Who rises from Prayer a better man, his prayer is answered."'

'I will, sir,' said Richard, and went to sleep happy.

Happy in his father and in himself, the youth now lived. Conscience was beginning to inhabit him, and he carried some of the freightage known to men; though in so crude a form that it overweighed him, now on this side, now on that.

The wise youth Adrian observed these further progressionary developments in his pupil, soberly cynical. He was under Sir Austin's interdict not to banter him, and eased his acrid humours inspired by the sight of a felonious young rick-burner turning saint, by grave affectations of sympathy and extreme accuracy in marking the not widely-distant dates of his various changes. The Bread-and-water phase lasted a fortnight: the Vegetarian (an imitation of his cousin Austin), little better than a month: the religious, somewhat longer: the religious-propagandist (when he was for converting the heathen of Lobourne and Bursley, and the domestics of the Abbey, including

Tom Bakewell), longer still, and hard to bear;—he tried
to convert Adrian! All the while Tom was being exercised like a raw recruit. Richard had a drill-sergeant
from the nearest barracks down for him, to give him a
proper pride in himself, and marched him to and fro with
immense satisfaction, and nearly broke his heart trying
to get the round-shouldered rustic to take in the rudi-
ments of letters: for the boy had unbounded hopes for
Tom, as a hero in grain.

Richard's pride also was cast aside. He affected to be,
and really thought he was, humble. Whereupon Adrian,
as by accident, imparted to him the fact that men were
animals, and he an animal with the rest of them.

'*I* an animal!' cries Richard in scorn, and for weeks he
was as troubled by this rudiment of self-knowledge as Tom
by his letters. Sir Austin had him instructed in the wonders of anatomy, to restore his self-respect.

SEED-TIME passed thus smoothly, and adolescence came
on, and his cousin Clare felt what it was to be of an opposite sex to him. She too was growing, but nobody cared
how she grew. Outwardly even her mother seemed absorbed in the sprouting of the green off-shoot of the Feverel tree, and Clare was his handmaiden, little marked by
him.

Lady Blandish honestly loved the boy. She would tell
him: 'If I had been a girl, I would have had you for my
husband.' And he with the frankness of his years would
reply: 'And how do you know I would have had you?'
causing her to laugh and call him a silly boy, for had
he not heard her say she would have had him? Terrible
words, he knew not then the meaning of!

'You don't read your father's Book,' she said. Her
own copy was bound in purple velvet, gilt-edged, as deco-
rative ladies like to have holier books, and she carried it
about with her, and quoted it, and (Adrian remarked to

Mrs. Doria) hunted a noble quarry, and deliberately aimed at him therewith, which Mrs. Doria chose to believe, and regretted her brother would not be on his guard.

'See here,' said Lady Blandish, pressing an almondy finger-nail to one of the Aphorisms, which instanced how age and adversity must clay-enclose us ere we can effectually resist the magnetism of any human creature in our path. 'Can you understand it, child?'

Richard informed her that when she read he could.

'Well, then, my squire,' she touched his cheek and ran her fingers through his hair, 'learn as quick as you can not to be all hither and yon with a hundred different attractions, as I was before I met a wise man to guide me.'

'Is my father very wise?' Richard asked.

'I think so,' the lady emphasized her individual judgement.

'Do you——' Richard broke forth, and was stopped by a beating of his heart.

'Do I—what?' she calmly queried.

'I was going to say, do you—I mean, I love him so much.'

Lady Blandish smiled and slightly coloured.

They frequently approached this theme, and always retreated from it; always with the same beating of heart to Richard, accompanied by the sense of a growing mystery, which, however, did not as yet generally disturb him.

Life was made very pleasant to him at Raynham, as it was part of Sir Austin's principle of education that his boy should be thoroughly joyous and happy; and whenever Adrian sent in a satisfactory report of his pupil's advancement, which he did pretty liberally, diversions were planned, just as prizes are given to diligent school-boys, and Richard was supposed to have all his desires gratified while he attended to his studies. The System flourished. Tall, strong, bloomingly healthy, he took the lead of his

companions on land and water, and had more than one
bondsman in his service besides Ripton Thompson—the
boy without a Destiny! Perhaps the boy with a Destiny
was growing up a trifle too conscious of it. His generosity to his occasional companions was princely, but was
exercised something too much in the manner of a prince;
and, notwithstanding his contempt for baseness, he would
overlook that more easily than an offence to his pride,
which demanded an utter servility when it had once been
rendered susceptible. If Richard had his followers he
had also his feuds. The Papworths were as subservient
as Ripton, but young Ralph Morton, the nephew of Mr.
Morton, and a match for Richard in numerous promising
qualities, comprising the noble science of fisticuffs, this
youth spoke his mind too openly, and moreover would not
be snubbed. There was no middle course for Richard's
comrades between high friendship or absolute slavery.
He was deficient in those cosmopolite habits and feelings
which enable boys and men to hold together without caring much for each other; and, like every insulated mortal,
he attributed the deficiency, of which he was quite aware,
to the fact of his possessing a superior nature. Young
Ralph was a lively talker: therefore, argued Richard's
vanity, he had no intellect. He was affable: therefore
he was frivolous. The women liked him: therefore he
was a butterfly. In fine, young Ralph was popular, and
our superb prince, denied the privilege of despising, ended
by detesting him.

Early in the days for their contention for leadership,
Richard saw the absurdity of affecting to scorn his rival.
Ralph was an Eton boy, and hence, being robust, a swimmer and a cricketer. A swimmer and a cricketer is nowhere to be scorned in youth's republic. Finding that
manœuvre would not do, Richard was prompted once or
twice to entrench himself behind his greater wealth and

his position; but he soon abandoned that also, partly because his chilliness to ridicule told him he was exposing himself, and chiefly that his heart was too chivalrous. And so he was dragged into the lists by Ralph, and experienced the luck of champions. For cricket, and for diving, Ralph bore away the belt: Richard's middle-stump tottered before his ball, and he could seldom pick up more than three eggs underwater to Ralph's half-dozen. He was beaten, too, in jumping and running. Why will silly mortals strive to the painful pinnacles of championship? Or why, once having reached them, not have the magnanimity and circumspection to retire into private life immediately? Stung by his defeats, Richard sent one of his dependent Papworths to Poer Hall, with a challenge to Ralph Barthrop Morton; matching himself to swim across the Thames and back, once, twice, or thrice, within a less time than he, Ralph Barthrop Morton, would require for the undertaking. It was accepted, and a reply returned, equally formal in the trumpeting of Christian names, wherein Ralph Barthrop Morton acknowledged the challenge of Richard Doria Feverel, and was his man. The match came off on a midsummer morning, under the direction of Captain Algernon. Sir Austin was a spectator from the cover of a plantation by the riverside, unknown to his son, and, to the scandal of her sex, Lady Blandish accompanied the baronet. He had invited her attendance, and she, obeying her frank nature, and knowing what THE PILGRIM'S SCRIP said about prudes, at once agreed to view the match, pleasing him mightily. For was not here a woman worthy of the Golden Ages of the world? one who could look upon man as a creature divinely made, and look with a mind neither tempted, nor taunted, by the Serpent! Such a woman was rare. Sir Austin did not discompose her by uttering his praises. She was conscious of his approval only in an increased gentleness of manner, and something in his voice and communications, as if he were speaking to a familiar, a very high compliment from him. While the lads were standing ready for the signal to plunge from the steep decline of greensward into the shining waters, Sir Austin called upon her to admire their beauty, and she did, and even advanced her head above his shoulder delicately. In so doing, and just as the start was given, a bonnet became visible to Richard. Young Ralph was heels in air before he moved, and then he dropped like lead. He was beaten by several lengths.

The result of the match was unaccountable to all present, and Richard's friends unanimously pressed him to plead a false start. But though the youth, with full confidence in his better style and equal strength, had backed himself heavily against his rival, and had lost his little river-yacht to Ralph, he would do nothing of the sort. It was the Bonnet had beaten him, not Ralph. The Bonnet, typical of the mystery that caused his heart those violent palpitations, was his dear, detestable enemy.

And now, as he progressed from mood to mood, his ambition turned toward a field where Ralph could not rival him, and where the Bonnet was etherealized, and reigned glorious mistress. A check to the pride of a boy will frequently divert him to the path where lie his subtlest powers. Richard gave up his companions, servile or antagonistic: he relinquished the material world to young Ralph, and retired into himself, where he was growing to be lord of kingdoms: where Beauty was his handmaid, and History his minister, and Time his ancient harper, and sweet Romance his bride; where he walked in a realm vaster and more gorgeous than the great Orient, peopled with the heroes that have been. For there is no princely wealth, and no loftiest heritage, to equal this early one that is made bountifully common to so many, when the ripening blood has put a spark to the imagination, and the earth is seen through rosy mists of a thousand fresh-awakened nameless and aimless desires; panting for bliss and taking it as it comes; making of any sight or sound, perforce of the enchantment they carry with them, a key to infinite, because innocent, pleasure. The passions then are gambolling cubs; not the ravaging gluttons they grow to. They have their teeth and their talons, but they neither tear nor bite. They are in counsel and fellowship with the quickened heart and brain. The whole sweet system moves to music.

Something akin to the indications of a change in the spirit of his son, which were now seen, Sir Austin had marked down to be expected, as due to his plan. The blushes of the youth, his long vigils, his clinging to solitude, his abstraction, and downcast but not melancholy air, were matters for rejoicing to the prescient gentleman. 'For it comes,' said he to Dr. Clifford of Lobourne, after consulting him medically on the youth's behalf and being assured of his soundness, 'it comes of a thoroughly sane condition. The blood is healthy, the mind virtuous: neither instigates the other to evil, and both are perfecting toward the flower of manhood. If he reach that pure —in the untainted fulness and perfection of his natural powers—I am indeed a happy father! But one thing he will owe to me: that at one period of his life he knew paradise, and could read God's handwriting on the earth! Now those abominations whom you call precocious boys—your little pet monsters, doctor!—and who can wonder that the world is what it is? when it is full of them—as they will have no divine time to look back upon in their own lives, how can they believe in innocence and goodness, or be other than sons of selfishness and the Devil? But my boy,' and the baronet dropped his voice to a key that was touching to hear, 'my boy, if he fall, will fall

from an actual region of purity. He dare not be a sceptic
as to that. Whatever his darkness, he will have the guid-
ing light of a memory behind him. So much is secure.'

To talk nonsense, or poetry, or the dash between the
two, in a tone of profound sincerity, and to enunciate
solemn discordances with received opinion so seriously as
to convey the impression of a spiritual insight, is the
peculiar gift by which monomaniacs, having first persuaded
themselves, contrive to influence their neighbours, and
through them to make conquest of a good half of the
world, for good or for ill. Sir Austin had this gift. He
spoke as if he saw the truth, and, persisting in it so long,
he was accredited by those who did not understand him,
and silenced them that did.

'We shall see,' was all the argument left to Dr. Clifford, and other unbelievers.

So far certainly the experiment had succeeded. A
comelier, braver, better boy was nowhere to be met. His
promise was undeniable. The vessel, too, though it lay
now in harbour and had not yet been proved by the buffets
of the elements on the great ocean, had made a good trial
trip, and got well through stormy weather, as the records
of the Bakewell Comedy witnessed to at Raynham. No
augury could be hopefuller. The Fates must indeed be
hard, the Ordeal severe, the Destiny dark, that could destroy so bright a Spring! But, bright as it was, the baronet
relaxed nothing of his vigilant supervision. He said to
his intimates: 'Every act, every fostered inclination, almost
every thought, in this Blossoming Season, bears its seed
for the Future. The living Tree now requires incessant
watchfulness.' And, acting up to his light, Sir Austin
did watch. The youth submitted to an examination
every night before he sought his bed; professedly to give
an account of his studies, but really to recapitulate his
moral experiences of the day. He could do so, for he was

pure. Any wildness in him that his father noted, any remoteness or richness of fancy in his expressions, was set down as incidental to the Blossoming Season. There is nothing like a theory for binding the wise. Sir Austin, despite his rigid watch and ward, knew less of his son than the servant of his household. And he was deaf, as well as blind. Adrian thought it his duty to tell him that the youth was consuming paper. Lady Blandish likewise hinted at his mooning propensities. Sir Austin from his lofty watch-tower of the System had foreseen it, he said. But when he came to hear that the youth was writing poetry, his wounded heart had its reasons for being much disturbed.

'Surely,' said Lady Blandish, 'you knew he scribbled?'

'A very different thing from writing poetry,' said the baronet. 'No Feverel has ever written poetry.'

'I don't think it 's a sign of degeneracy,' the lady remarked. 'He rhymes very prettily to me.'

A London phrenologist, and a friendly Oxford Professor of poetry, quieted Sir Austin's fears.

The phrenologist said he was totally deficient in the imitative faculty; and the Professor, that he was equally so in the rhythmic, and instanced several consoling false quantities in the few effusions submitted to him. Added to this, Sir Austin told Lady Blandish that Richard had, at his best, done what no poet had ever been known to be capable of doing: he had, with his own hands, and in cold blood, committed his virgin manuscript to the flames: which made Lady Blandish sigh forth, 'Poor boy!'

Killing one's darling child is a painful imposition. For a youth in his Blossoming Season, who fancies himself a poet, to be requested to destroy his first-born, without a reason (though to pretend a reason cogent enough to justify the request were a mockery), is a piece of abhorrent despotism, and Richard's blossoms withered under it. A strange man had been introduced to him, who traversed and bisected his skull with sagacious stiff fingers, and crushed his soul while, in an infallible voice, declaring him the animal he was: making him feel such an animal! Not only his blossoms withered, his being seemed to draw in its shoots and twigs. And when, coupled thereunto (the strange man having departed, his work done), his father, in his tenderest manner, stated that it would give him pleasure to see those same precocious, utterly valueless, scribblings among the cinders, the last remaining mental blossoms spontaneously fell away. Richard's spirit stood bare. He protested not. Enough that it could be wished! He would not delay a minute in doing it. Desiring his father to follow him, he went to a drawer in his room, and from a clean-linen recess, never suspected by Sir Austin, the secretive youth drew out bundle after bundle: each neatly tied, named, and numbered: and pitched them into flames. And so Farewell my young Ambition! and with it farewell all true confidence between Father and Son.

CHAPTER XIII

THE MAGNETIC AGE

It was now, as Sir Austin had written it down, The Magnetic Age: the Age of violent attractions, when to hear mention of love is dangerous, and to see it, a communication of the disease. People at Raynham were put on their guard by the baronet, and his reputation for wisdom was severely criticized in consequence of the injunctions he thought fit to issue through butler and housekeeper down to the lower household, for the preservation of his son from any visible symptom of the passion. A footman and two housemaids are believed to have been dismissed on the report of heavy Benson that they were in or inclining to the state; upon which an under-cook and a dairymaid voluntarily threw up their places, averring that 'they did not want no young men, but to have their sex spied after by an old wretch like that,' indicating the ponderous butler, 'was a little too much for a Christian woman,' and then they were ungenerous enough to glance at Benson's well-known marital calamity, hinting that some men met their deserts. So intolerable did heavy Benson's espionage become, that Raynham would have grown depopulated of its womankind had not Adrian interfered, who pointed out to the baronet what a fearful arm his butler was wielding. Sir Austin acknowledged it despondently. 'It only shows,' said he, with a fine spirit of justice, 'how all but impossible it is to legislate where there are women!'

'I do not object,' he added; 'I hope I am too just to object to the exercise of their natural inclinations. All I ask from them is discreetness.'

'Ay,' said Adrian, whose discreetness was a marvel.

'No gadding about in couples,' continued the baronet, 'no kissing in public. Such occurrences no boy should witness. Whenever people of both sexes are thrown together, they will be silly; and where they are high-fed, uneducated, and barely occupied, it must be looked for as a matter of course. Let it be known that I only require discreetness.'

Discreetness, therefore, was instructed to reign at the Abbey. Under Adrian's able tuition the fairest of its domestics acquired that virtue.

Discreetness, too, was enjoined to the upper household. Sir Austin, who had not previously appeared to notice the case of Lobourne's hopeless curate, now desired Mrs. Doria to interdict, or at least discourage, his visits, for the appearance of the man was that of an embodied sigh and groan.

'Really, Austin!' said Mrs. Doria, astonished to find her brother more awake than she had supposed, 'I have never allowed him to hope.'

'Let him see it, then,' replied the baronet; 'let him see it.'

'The man amuses me,' said Mrs. Doria. 'You know, we have few amusements here, we inferior creatures. I confess I should like a barrel-organ better; that reminds one of town and the opera; and besides, it plays more than one tune. However, since you think my society bad for him, let him stop away.'

With the self-devotion of a woman she grew patient and sweet the moment her daughter Clare was spoken of, and the business of her life in view. Mrs. Doria's maternal heart had betrothed the two cousins, Richard and Clare; had already beheld them espoused and fruitful. For this she yielded the pleasures of town; for this she immured herself at Raynham; for this she bore with a thousand follies, exactions, inconveniences, things abhorrent to her, and heaven knows what forms of torture and self-denial, which are smilingly endured by that greatest of voluntary martyrs—a mother with a daughter to marry. Mrs. Doria, an amiable widow, had surely married but for her daughter Clare. The lady's hair no woman could possess without feeling it her pride. It was the daily theme of her lady's-maid,—a natural aureole to her head. She was gay, witty, still physically youthful enough to claim a destiny; and she sacrificed it to accomplish her daughter's! sacrificed, as with heroic scissors, hair, wit, gaiety—let us not attempt to enumerate how much! more than may be said. And she was only one of thousands; thousands who have no portion of the hero's reward; for he may reckon on applause, and condolence, and sympathy, and honour; they, poor slaves! must look for nothing but the opposition of their own sex and the sneers of ours. Oh, Sir Austin! had you not been so blinded, what an Aphorism might have sprung from this point of observation! Mrs. Doria was coolly told, between sister and brother, that during the Magnetic Age her daughter's presence at Raynham was undesirable. Instead of nursing offence, her sole thought was the mountain of prejudice she had to contend against. She bowed, and said, Clare wanted sea-air—she had never quite recovered the shock of that dreadful night. How long, Mrs. Doria wished to know, might the Peculiar Period be expected to last?

'That,' said Sir Austin, 'depends. A year, perhaps. He is entering on it. I shall be most grieved to lose you, Helen. Clare is now—how old?'

'Seventeen.'

'She is marriageable.'

'Marriageable, Austin! at seventeen! don't name such a thing. My child shall not be robbed of her youth.'

'Our women marry early, Helen.'

'My child shall not!'

The baronet reflected a moment. He did not wish to lose his sister.

'As you are of that opinion, Helen,' said he, 'perhaps we may still make arrangements to retain you with us. Would you think it advisable to send Clare—she should know discipline—to some establishment for a few months?' . . .

'To an asylum, Austin?' cried Mrs. Doria, controlling her indignation as well as she could.

'To some select superior seminary, Helen. There are such to be found.'

'Austin!' Mrs. Doria exclaimed, and had to fight with a moisture in her eyes. 'Unjust! absurd!' she mur-

mured. The baronet thought it a natural proposition
that Clare should be a bride or a schoolgirl.

'I cannot leave my child,' Mrs. Doria trembled. 'Where
she goes, I go. I am aware that she is only one of our
sex, and therefore of no value to the world, but she is my
child. I will see, poor dear, that you have no cause to
complain of her.'

'I thought,' Sir Austin remarked, 'that you acquiesced
in my views with regard to my son.'

'Yes—generally,' said Mrs. Doria, and felt culpable that
she had not before, and could not then, tell her brother
that he had set up an Idol in his house—an Idol of flesh!
more retributive and abominable than wood or brass or
gold. But she had bowed to the Idol too long—she had
too entirely bound herself to gain her project by subserv-
iency. She had, and she dimly perceived it, committed
a greater fault in tactics, in teaching her daughter to bow
to the Idol also. Love of that kind Richard took for tribute. He was indifferent to Clare's soft eyes. The parting kiss he gave her was ready and cold as his father could
desire. Sir Austin now grew eloquent to him in laudation
of manly pursuits: but Richard thought his eloquence
barren, his attempts at companionship awkward, and all
manly pursuits and aims, life itself, vain and worthless.
To what end? sighed the blossomless youth, and cried
aloud, as soon as he was relieved of his father's society,
what was the good of anything? Whatever he did—which-
ever path he selected, led back to Raynham. And whatever he did, however wretched and wayward he showed
himself, only confirmed Sir Austin more and more in the
truth of his previsions. Tom Bakewell, now the youth's
groom, had to give the baronet a report of his young master's proceedings, in common with Adrian, and while there
was no harm to tell Tom spoke out. 'He do ride like
fire every day to Pig's Snout,' naming the highest hill

in the neighbourhood, 'and stand there and stare, never movin', like a mad 'un. And then hoam agin all slack as if he 'd been beaten in a race by somebody.'

'There is no woman in that!' mused the baronet. 'He would have ridden back as hard as he went,' reflected this profound scientific humanist, 'had there been a woman in it. He would shun vast expanses, and seek shade, concealment, solitude. The desire for distances betokens emptiness and undirected hunger: when the heart is possessed by an image we fly to wood and forest, like the guilty.'

Adrian's report accused his pupil of an extraordinary access of cynicism.

'Exactly,' said the baronet. 'As I foresaw. At this period an insatiate appetite is accompanied by a fastidious palate. Nothing but the quintessences of existence, and those in exhaustless supplies, will satisfy this craving, which is not to be satisfied! Hence his bitterness. Life can furnish no food fitting for him. The strength and purity of his energies have reached to an almost divine height, and roam through the Inane. Poetry, love, and such-like, are the drugs earth has to offer to high natures, as she offers to low ones debauchery. 'Tis a sign, this sourness, that he is subject to none of the empiricisms that are afloat. Now to keep him clear of them!'

The Titans had an easier task in storming Olympus.* As yet, however, it could not be said that Sir Austin's System had failed. On the contrary, it had reared a youth, handsome, intelligent, well-bred, and, observed the ladies, with acute emphasis, innocent. Where, they asked, was such another young man to be found?

'Oh!' said Lady Blandish to Sir Austin, 'if men could give their hands to women unsoiled—how different would many a marriage be! She will be a happy girl who calls Richard husband.'

'Happy, indeed!' was the baronet's caustic ejaculation. 'But where shall I meet one equal to him, and his match?'

'I was innocent when I was a girl,' said the lady.

Sir Austin bowed a reserved opinion.

'Do you think no girls innocent?'

Sir Austin gallantly thought them all so.

'No, that you know they are not,' said the lady, stamping. 'But they are more innocent than boys, I am sure.'

'Because of their education, madam. You see now what a youth can be. Perhaps, when my System is published, or rather—to speak more humbly—when it is practised, the balance may be restored, and we shall have virtuous young men.'

'It 's too late for poor me to hope for a husband from one of them,' said the lady, pouting and laughing.

'It is never too late for beauty to waken love,' returned the baronet, and they trifled a little. They were approaching Daphne's Bower, which they entered, and sat there to taste the coolness of a descending midsummer day.

The baronet seemed in a humour for dignified fooling; the lady for serious converse.

'I shall believe again in Arthur's knights,' she said. 'When I was a girl I dreamed of one.'

'And he was in quest of the San Greal?'

'If you like.'

'And showed his good taste by turning aside for the more tangible San Blandish?'

'Of course you consider it would have been so,' sighed the lady, ruffling.

'I can only judge by our generation,' said Sir Austin, with a bend of homage.

The lady gathered her mouth. 'Either we are very mighty or you are very weak.'

'Both, madam.'

'But whatever we are, and if we are bad, bad! we love virtue, and truth, and lofty souls, in men: and, when we meet those qualities in them, we are constant, and would die for them—die for them. Ah! you know men but not women.'

'The knights possessing such distinctions must be young, I presume?' said Sir Austin.

'Old, or young!'

'But if old, they are scarce capable of enterprise?'

'They are loved for themselves, not for their deeds.'

'Ah!'

'Yes—ah!' said the lady. 'Intellect may subdue women—make slaves of them; and they worship beauty perhaps as much as you do. But they only love for ever and are mated when they meet a noble nature.'

Sir Austin looked at her wistfully.

'And did you encounter the knight of your dream?'

'Not then.' She lowered her eyelids. It was prettily done.

'And how did you bear the disappointment?'

'My dream was in the nursery. The day my frock was lengthened to a gown I stood at the altar. I am not the only girl that has been made a woman in a day, and given to an ogre instead of a true knight.'

'Good God!' exclaimed Sir Austin, 'women have much to bear.'

Here the couple changed characters. The lady became gay as the baronet grew earnest.

'You know it is our lot,' she said. 'And we are allowed many amusements. If we fulfil our duty in producing children, that, like our virtue, is its own reward. Then, as a widow, I have wonderful privileges.'

'To preserve which, you remain a widow?'

'Certainly,' she responded. 'I have no trouble now in patching and piecing that rag the world calls—a char-

acter. I can sit at your feet every day unquestioned.
To be sure, others do the same, but they are female
eccentrics, and have cast off the rag altogether.'

Sir Austin drew nearer to her. 'You would have made
an admirable mother, madam.'

This from Sir Austin was very like positive wooing.

'It is,' he continued, 'ten thousand pities that you
are not one.'

'Do you think so?' She spoke with humility.

'I would,' he went on, 'that heaven had given you a
daughter.'

'Would you have thought her worthy of Richard?'

'Our blood, madam, should have been one!'

The lady tapped her toe with her parasol. 'But I am
a mother,' she said. 'Richard is my son. Yes! Richard
is my boy,' she reiterated.

Sir Austin most graciously appended, 'Call him ours,
madam,' and held his head as if to catch the word from
her lips, which, however, she chose to refuse, or defer.
They made the coloured West a common point for their
eyes, and then Sir Austin said:

'As you will not say "ours," let me. And, as you have
therefore an equal claim on the boy, I will confide to you
a project I have lately conceived.'

The announcement of a project hardly savoured of a
coming proposal, but for Sir Austin to confide one to a
woman was almost tantamount to a declaration. So
Lady Blandish thought, and so said her soft, deep-eyed
smile, as she perused the ground while listening to the
project. It concerned Richard's nuptials. He was now
nearly eighteen. He was to marry when he was five and
twenty. Meantime a young lady, some years his junior,
was to be sought for in the homes of England, who would
be every way fitted by education, instincts, and blood—
on each of which qualifications Sir Austin unreservedly

enlarged—to espouse so perfect a youth and accept the honourable duty of assisting in the perpetuation of the Feverels. The baronet went on to say that he proposed to set forth immediately, and devote a couple of months, to the first essay in his Cœlebite search.*

'I fear,' said Lady Blandish, when the project had been fully unfolded, 'you have laid down for yourself a difficult task. You must not be too exacting.'

'I know it.' The baronet's shake of the head was piteous.

'Even in England she will be rare. But I confine myself to no class. If I ask for blood it is for untainted, not what you call high blood. I believe many of the middle classes are frequently more careful—more pure-blooded —than our aristocracy. Show me among them a God-fearing family who educate their children—I should prefer a girl without brothers and sisters—as a Christian damsel should be educated—say, on the model of my son, and she may be penniless, I will pledge her to Richard Feverel.'

Lady Blandish bit her lip. 'And what do you do with Richard while you are absent on this expedition?'

'Oh!' said the baronet, 'he accompanies his father.'

'Then give it up. His future bride is now pinafored and bread-and-buttery. She romps, she cries, she dreams of play and pudding. How can he care for her? He thinks more at his age of old women like me. He will be certain to kick against her, and destroy your plan, believe me, Sir Austin.'

'Ay? ay? do you think that?' said the baronet.

Lady Blandish gave him a multitude of reasons.

'Ay! true,' he muttered. 'Adrian said the same. He must not see her. How could I think of it! The child is naked woman. He would despise her. Naturally!'

'Naturally!' echoed the lady.

'Then, madam,' and the baronet rose, 'there is one thing for me to determine upon. I must, for the first time in his life, leave him.'

'Will you, indeed?' said the lady.

'It is my duty, having thus brought him up, to see that he is properly mated,—not wrecked upon the quicksands of marriage, as a youth so delicately trained might be; more easily than another! Betrothed, he will be safe from a thousand snares. I may, I think, leave him for a term. My precautions have saved him from the temptations of his season.'

'And under whose charge will you leave him?' Lady Blandish inquired.

She had emerged from the temple and stood beside Sir Austin on the upper steps under a clear summer twilight.

'Madam!' he took her hand, and his voice was gallant and tender, 'under whose but yours?'

As the baronet said this, he bent above her hand, and raised it to his lips.

Lady Blandish felt that she had been wooed and asked in wedlock. She did not withdraw her hand. The baronet's salute was flatteringly reverent. He deliberated over it, as one going through a grave ceremony. And he, the scorner of women, had chosen her for his homage! Lady Blandish forgot that she had taken some trouble to arrive at it. She received the exquisite compliment in all its unique honey sweet: for in love we must deserve nothing or the fine bloom of fruition is gone.

The lady's hand was still in durance, and the baronet had not recovered from his profound inclination, when a noise from the neighbouring beechwood startled the two actors in this courtly pantomime. They turned their heads, and beheld the hope of Raynham on horseback surveying the scene. The next moment he had galloped away.

CHAPTER XIV

AN ATTRACTION

ALL night Richard tossed on his bed with his heart in a rapid canter, and his brain bestriding it, traversing the rich untasted world, and the great Realm of Mystery, from which he was now restrained no longer. Months he had wandered about the gates of the Bonnet, wondering, sighing, knocking at them, and getting neither admittance nor answer. He had the key now. His own father had given it to him. His heart was a lightning steed, and bore him on and on over limitless regions bathed in superhuman beauty and strangeness, where cavaliers and ladies leaned whispering upon close greenswards, and knights and ladies cast a splendour upon savage forests, and tilts and tourneys were held in golden courts lit to a glorious day by ladies' eyes, one pair of which, dimly visioned, constantly distinguishable, followed him through the boskage and dwelt upon him in the press, beaming while he bent above a hand glittering white and fragrant as the frosted blossom of a May night.

Awhile the heart would pause and flutter to a shock: he was in the act of consummating all earthly bliss by pressing his lips to the small white hand. Only to do that, and die! cried the Magnetic Youth: to fling the Jewel of Life into that one cup and drink it off! He was intoxicated by anticipation. For that he was born. There was, then, some end in existence, something to live for! to kiss a woman's hand, and die! He would leap from the couch, and rush to pen and paper to relieve his swarming sensations. Scarce was he seated when the pen was dashed aside, the paper sent flying with the exclamation,

'Have I not sworn I would never write again?' Sir Austin had shut that safety-valve. The nonsense that was in the youth might have poured harmlessly out, and its urgency for ebullition was so great that he was repeatedly oblivious of his oath, and found himself seated under the lamp in the act of composition before pride could speak a word. Possibly the pride even of Richard Feverel had been swamped if the act of composition were easy at such a time, and a single idea could stand clearly foremost; but myriads were demanding the first place; chaotic hosts, like ranks of stormy billows, pressed impetuously for expression, and despair of reducing them to form, quite as much as pride, to which it pleased him to refer his incapacity, threw down the powerless pen, and sent him panting to his outstretched length and another head-long career through the rosy-girdled land.

Toward morning the madness of the fever abated some-what, and he went forth into the air. A lamp was still burning in his father's room, and Richard thought, as he looked up, that he saw the ever-vigilant head on the watch. Instantly the lamp was extinguished, the win-dow stood cold against the hues of dawn.

Strong pulling is an excellent medical remedy for cer-tain classes of fever. Richard took to it instinctively. The clear fresh water, burnished with sunrise, sparkled against his arrowy prow; the soft deep shadows curled smiling away from his gliding keel. Overhead solitary morning unfolded itself, from blossom to bud, from bud to flower; still, delicious changes of light and colour, to whose influences he was heedless as he shot under wil-lows and aspens, and across sheets of river-reaches, pure mirrors to the upper glory, himself the sole tenant of the stream. Somewhere at the founts of the world lay the land he was rowing toward; something of its shad-owed lights might be discerned here and there. It was not a dream, now he knew. There was a secret abroad. The woods were full of it; the waters rolled with it, and the winds. Oh, why could not one in these days do some high knightly deed which should draw down ladies' eyes from their heaven, as in the days of Arthur! To such a meaning breathed the unconscious sighs of the youth, when he had pulled through his first feverish energy.

He was off Bursley, and had lapsed a little into that musing quietude which follows strenuous exercise, when he heard a hail and his own name called. It was no lady, no fairy, but young Ralph Morton, an irruption of miserable masculine prose. Heartily wishing him abed with the rest of mankind, Richard rowed in and jumped ashore. Ralph immediately seized his arm, saying that he desired earnestly to have a talk with him, and dragged the Magnetic Youth from his water-dreams, up and down the wet mown grass. That he had to say seemed to be difficult of utterance, and Richard, though he barely listened, soon had enough of his old rival's gladness at seeing him, and exhibited signs of impatience; whereat Ralph, as one who branches into matter somewhat foreign to his mind, but of great human interest and importance, put the question to him:

'I say, what woman's name do you like best?'

'I don't know any,' quoth Richard indifferently. 'Why are you out so early?'

In answer to this, Ralph suggested that the name of Mary might be considered a pretty name.

Richard agreed that it might be; the housekeeper at Raynham, half the women cooks, and all the housemaids, enjoyed that name; the name of Mary was equivalent for women at home.

'Yes, I know,' said Ralph. "We have lots of Marys. It's so common. Oh! I don't like Mary best. What do you think of Lucy?'

Richard thought it just like another.

'Do you know,' Ralph continued, throwing off the mask and plunging into the subject, "I'd do anything on earth for some names—one or two. It's not Mary, nor Lucy. Clarinda's pretty, but it's like a novel. Claribel, I like. Names beginning with "Cl" I prefer. The "Cl's" are always gentle and lovely girls you would die for! Don't you think so?'

Richard had never been acquainted with any of them to inspire that emotion. Indeed these urgent appeals to his fancy in feminine names at five o'clock in the morning slightly surprised him, though he was but half awake to the outer world. By degrees he perceived that Ralph was changed. Instead of the lusty boisterous boy, his rival in manly sciences, who spoke straightforwardly and acted up to his speech, here was an abashed and blush-persecuted youth, who sued piteously for a friendly ear wherein to pour the one idea possessing him. Gradually, too, Richard apprehended that Ralph likewise was on the frontiers of the Realm of Mystery, perhaps further toward it than he himself was; and then, as by a sympathetic stroke, was revealed to him the wonderful beauty and depth of meaning in feminine names. The theme appeared novel and delicious, fitted to the season and the hour. But the hardship was, that Richard could choose none from the number; all were the same to him; he loved them all.

'Don't you really prefer the "Cl's"?' said Ralph persuasively.

'Not better than the names ending in "a" and "y,"' Richard replied, wishing he could, for Ralph was evidently ahead of him.

'Come under these trees,' said Ralph. And under the trees Ralph unbosomed. His name was down for the army: Eton was quitted for ever. In a few months he would have to join his regiment, and before he left he must say good-bye to his friends. . . . Would Richard tell him Mrs. Forey's address? he had heard she was somewhere by the sea. Richard did not remember the address, but said he would willingly take charge of any letter and forward it.

Ralph dived his hand into his pocket. 'Here it is. But don't let anybody see it.'

'My aunt's name is not Clare,' said Richard, perusing what was composed of the exterior formula. 'You've addressed it to Clare herself."

That was plain to see.

'Emmeline Clementina Matilda Laura, Countess Blandish,' Richard continued in a low tone, transferring the names, and playing on the musical strings they were to him. Then he said, 'Names of ladies! How they sweeten their names!'

He fixed his eyes on Ralph. If he discovered anything further he said nothing, but bade the good fellow good-bye, jumped into his boat, and pulled down the tide. The moment Ralph was hidden by an abutment of the banks, Richard reperused the address. For the first time it struck him that his cousin Clare was a very charming creature: he remembered the look of her eyes, and especially the last reproachful glance she gave him at parting. What business had Ralph to write to her? Did she not belong to Richard Feverel? He read the words again and again: Clare Doria Forey. Why, Clare was the name he liked best—nay, he loved it. Doria, too— she shared his own name with him. Away went his heart, not at a canter now, at a gallop, as one who sights the quarry. He felt too weak to pull. Clare Doria Forey —oh, perfect melody! Sliding with the tide, he heard it fluting in the bosom of the hills.

When nature has made us ripe for love, it seldom occurs

that the Fates are behindhand in furnishing a temple for the flame.

Above green-flashing plunges of a weir, and shaken by the thunder below, lilies, golden and white, were swaying at anchor among the reeds. Meadow-sweet hung from the banks thick with weed and trailing bramble, and there also hung a daughter of earth. Her face was shaded by a broad straw hat with a flexible brim that left her lips and chin in the sun, and, sometimes nodding, sent forth a light of promising eyes. Across her shoulders, and behind, flowed large loose curls, brown in shadow, almost golden where the ray touched them. She was simply dressed, befitting decency and the season. On a closer inspection you might see that her lips were stained. This blooming young person was regaling on dewberries. They grew between the bank and the water. Apparently she found the fruit abundant, for her hand was making pretty progress to her mouth. Fastidious youth, which revolts at woman plumping her exquisite proportions on bread-and-butter, and would (we must suppose) joyfully have her scraggy to have her poetical, can hardly object to dewberries. Indeed the act of eating them is dainty and induces musing. The dewberry is a sister to the lotus, and an innocent sister. You eat: mouth, eye, and hand are occupied, and the undrugged mind free to roam. And so it was with the damsel who knelt there. The little skylark went up above her, all song, to the smooth southern cloud lying along the blue: from a dewy copse dark over her nodding hat the blackbird fluted, calling to her with thrice mellow note: the kingfisher flashed emerald out of green osiers:* a bow-winged heron travelled aloft, seeking solitude: a boat slipped toward her, containing a dreamy youth; and still she plucked the fruit, and ate, and mused, as if no fairy prince were invading her territories, and as if she wished not for one, or knew not her wishes. Surrounded by the green shaven meadows, the pastoral summer buzz, the weir-fall's thundering white, amid the breath and beauty of wild flowers, she was a bit of lovely human life in a fair setting; a terrible attraction. The Magnetic Youth leaned round to note his proximity to the weir-piles, and beheld the sweet vision. Stiller and stiller grew nature, as at the meeting of two electric clouds. Her posture was so graceful, that though he was making straight for the weir, he dared not dip a scull. Just then one enticing dewberry caught her eyes. He was floating by unheeded, and saw that her hand stretched low, and could not gather what it sought. A stroke from his right brought him beside her. The damsel glanced up dismayed, and her whole shape trembled over the brink. Richard sprang from his boat into the water. Pressing a hand beneath her foot, which she had thrust against the crumbling wet sides of the bank to save herself, he enabled her to recover her balance, and gain safe earth, whither he followed her.

CHAPTER XV

FERDINAND AND MIRANDA*

He had landed on an island of the still-vexed Bermoothes.* The world lay wrecked behind him: Raynham hung in mists, remote, a phantom to the vivid reality of this white hand which had drawn him thither away thousands of leagues in an eye-twinkle. Hark, how Ariel*sang overhead! What splendour in the heavens! What marvels of beauty about his enchanted brows! And, O you wonder! Fair Flame! by whose light the glories of being are now first seen. . . . Radiant Miranda! Prince Ferdinand is at your feet.

Or is it Adam, his rib*taken from his side in sleep, and thus transformed, to make him behold his Paradise, and lose it? . . .

The youth looked on her with as glowing an eye. It was the First Woman to him.

And she—mankind was all Caliban*to her, saving this one princely youth.

So to each other said their changeing eyes in the moment they stood together; he pale, and she blushing.

She was indeed sweetly fair, and would have been held fair among rival damsels. On a magic shore, and to a youth educated by a System, strung like an arrow drawn to the head, he, it might be guessed, could fly fast and far with her. The soft rose in her cheeks, the clearness of her eyes, bore witness to the body's virtue; and health and happy blood were in her bearing. Had she stood before Sir Austin among rival damsels, that Scientific Humanist, for the consummation of his System, would have thrown her the handkerchief for his son. The wide summer-hat, nodding over her forehead to her brows, seemed to flow with the flowing heavy curls, and those fire-threaded mellow curls, only half-curls, waves of hair call them, rippling at the ends, went like a sunny red-veined torrent down her back almost to her waist: a glorious vision to the youth, who embraced it as a flower of beauty, and read not a feature. There were curious features of colour in her face for him to have read. Her brows, thick and brownish against a soft skin showing the action of the blood, met in the bend of a bow, extending to the temples long and level: you saw that she was fashioned to peruse the sights of earth, and by the pliability of her brows that the wonderful creature used her faculty, and was not going to be a statue to the gazer. Under the dark thick brows an arch of lashes shot out, giving a wealth of darkness to the full frank blue eyes, a mystery of meaning—more than brain was ever meant to fathom: richer, henceforth, than all mortal wisdom to Prince Ferdinand. For when nature turns artist, and produces contrasts of colour on a fair face, where is the Sage, or what the Oracle, shall match the depth of its lightest look?

Prince Ferdinand was also fair. In his slim boating-attire his figure looked heroic. His hair, rising from the parting to the right of his forehead, in what his admiring Lady Blandish called his plume, fell away slanting silkily to the temples across the nearly imperceptible upward curve of his brows there—felt more than seen, so slight it was—and gave to his profile a bold beauty, to which his bashful, breathless air was a flattering charm. An arrow drawn to the head, capable of flying fast and far with her! He leaned a little forward, drinking her in with all his eyes, and young Love has a thousand. Then truly the System triumphed, just ere it was to fall; and could Sir Austin have been content to draw the arrow to the head, and let it fly, when it would fly, he might have pointed to his son again, and said to the world, 'Match him!' Such keen bliss as the youth had in the sight of her, an innocent youth alone has powers of soul in him to experience.

'O Women!' says THE PILGRIM's SCRIP, in one of its solitary outbursts, 'Women, who like, and will have for hero, a rake! how soon are you not to learn that you have taken bankrupts to your bosoms, and that the putrescent gold that attracted you is the slime of the Lake of Sin!'

If these two were Ferdinand and Miranda, Sir Austin was not Prospero,* and was not present, or their fates might have been different.

So they stood a moment, changing eyes, and then Miranda spoke, and they came down to earth, feeling no less in heaven.

She spoke to thank him for his aid. She used quite common simple words; and used them, no doubt, to express a common simple meaning: but to him she was uttering magic, casting spells, and the effect they had on him was manifested in the incoherence of his replies, which were too foolish to be chronicled.

The couple were again mute. Suddenly Miranda, with an exclamation of anguish, and innumerable lights and shadows playing over her lovely face, clapped her hands, crying aloud, 'My book! my book!' and ran to the bank.

Prince Ferdinand was at her side. 'What have you lost?' he said.

'My book!' she answered, her delicious curls swinging across her shoulders to the stream. Then turning to him, 'Oh, no, no! let me entreat you not to,' she said; 'I do not so very much mind losing it.' And in her eagerness to restrain him she unconsciously laid her gentle hand upon his arm, and took the force of motion out of him.

'Indeed, I do not really care for the silly book,' she continued, withdrawing her hand quickly, and reddening. 'Pray, do not!'

The young gentleman had kicked off his shoes. No sooner was the spell of contact broken than he jumped in. The water was still troubled and discoloured by his introductory adventure, and, though he ducked his head with the spirit of a dabchick, the book was missing. A scrap of paper floating from the bramble just above the water, and looking as if fire had caught its edges and it had flown from one adverse element to the other, was all he could lay hold of; and he returned to land disconsolately, to hear Miranda's murmured mixing of thanks and pretty expostulations.

'Let me try again,' he said.

'No, indeed!' she replied, and used the awful threat: 'I will run away if you do,' which effectually restrained him.

Her eye fell on the fire-stained scrap of paper, and brightened, as she cried, 'There, there! you have what I want. It is that. I do not care for the book. No, please! You are not to look at it. Give it me.'

Before her playfully imperative injunction was fairly spoken, Richard had glanced at the document and discovered a Griffin between two Wheatsheaves: his crest in silver: and below—O wonderment immense! his own handwriting!

He handed it to her. She took it, and put it in her bosom.

Who would have thought, that, where all else perished, Odes, Idyls, Lines, Stanzas, this one Sonnet to the stars should be miraculously reserved for such a starry fate—passing beatitude!

As they walked silently across the meadow, Richard strove to remember the hour and the mood of mind in which he had composed the notable production. The stars were invoked, as seeing and foreseeing all, to tell him where then his love reclined, and so forth; Hesper* was complacent enough to do so, and described her in a couplet—

'Through sunset's amber see me shining fair,
    As her blue eyes shine through her golden hair.'

And surely no words could be more prophetic. Here were two blue eyes and golden hair; and by some strange chance, that appeared like the working of a divine finger, she had become the possessor of the prophecy, she that was to fulfil it! The youth was too charged with emotion to speak. Doubtless the damsel had less to think of, or had some trifling burden on her conscience, for she seemed to grow embarrassed. At last she drew up her chin to look at her companion under the nodding brim of her hat (and the action gave her a charmingly freakish air), crying, 'But where are you going to? You are wet through. Let me thank you again; and, pray, leave me, and go home and change instantly.'

'Wet?' replied the magnetic muser, with a voice of tender interest; 'not more than one foot, I hope. I will leave you while you dry your stockings in the sun.'

At this she could not withhold a shy laugh.

'Not I, but you. You would try to get that silly book for me, and you are dripping wet. Are you not very uncomfortable?'

In all sincerity he assured her that he was not.

'And you really do not feel that you are wet?'

He really did not: and it was a fact that he spoke truth.

She pursed her dewberry mouth in the most comical way, and her blue eyes lightened laughter out of the half-closed lids.

'I cannot help it,' she said, her mouth opening, and sounding harmonious bells of laughter in his ears. 'Pardon me, won't you?'

His face took the same soft smiling curves in admiration of her.

'Not to feel that you have been in the water, the very moment after!' she musically interjected, seeing she was excused.

'It's true,' he said; and his own gravity then touched him to join a duet with her, which made them no longer feel strangers, and did the work of a month of intimacy. Better than sentiment, laughter opens the breast to love; opens the whole breast to his full quiver, instead of a corner here and there for a solitary arrow. Hail the occasion propitious, O British young! and laugh and treat love as an honest God, and dabble not with the senti-

mental rouge. These two laughed, and the souls of each
cried out to other, 'It is I, it is I.'

They laughed and forgot the cause of their laughter,
and the sun dried his light river clothing, and they strolled
toward the blackbird's copse, and stood near a stile in
sight of the foam of the weir and the many-coloured rings
of eddies streaming forth from it.

Richard's boat, meanwhile, had contrived to shoot the
weir, and was swinging, bottom upward, broadside with
the current down the rapid backwater.

'Will you let it go?' said the damsel, eyeing it curiously.

'It can't be stopped,' he replied, and could have added:
'What do I care for it now!'

His old life was whirled away with it, dead, drowned.
His new life was with her, alive, divine.

She flapped low the brim of her hat. 'You must really
not come any farther,' she softly said.

'And will you go, and not tell me who you are?' he
asked, growing bolder as the fears of losing her came across
him. 'And will you not tell me before you go'—his face
burned—'how you came by that—that paper?'

She chose to select the easier question for answer: 'You
ought to know me; we have been introduced.' Sweet was
her winning off-hand affability.

'Then who, in heaven's name, are you? Tell me! I
never could have forgotten you.'

'You have, I think,' she said.

'Impossible that we could ever have met, and I forget you!'
She looked up to him.

'Do you remember Belthorpe?'

'Belthorpe! Belthorpe!' quoth Richard, as if he had
to touch his brain to recollect there was such a place.
'Do you mean old Blaize's farm?'

'Then I am old Blaize's niece.' She tripped him a
soft curtsey.

The magnetized youth gazed at her. By what magic was it that this divine sweet creature could be allied with that old churl!

'Then what—what is your name?' said his mouth, while his eyes added, 'O wonderful creature! How came you to enrich the earth?'

'Have you forgot the Desboroughs of Dorset, too?' she peered at him from a side-bend of the flapping brim.

'The Desboroughs of Dorset?' A light broke in on him. 'And have you grown to this? That little girl I saw there!'

He drew close to her to read the nearest features of the vision. She could no more laugh off the piercing fervour of his eyes. Her volubility fluttered under his deeply wistful look, and now neither voice was high, and they were mutually constrained.

'You see,' she murmured, 'we are old acquaintances.'

Richard, with his eyes still intently fixed on her, returned, 'You are very beautiful!'

The words slipped out. Perfect simplicity is unconsciously audacious. Her overpowering beauty struck his heart, and, like an instrument that is touched and answers to the touch, he spoke.

Miss Desborough made an effort to trifle with this terrible directness; but his eyes would not be gainsaid, and checked her lips. She turned away from them, her bosom a little rebellious. Praise so passionately spoken, and by one who has been a damsel's first dream, dreamed of nightly many long nights, and clothed in the virgin silver of her thoughts in bud, praise from him is coin the heart cannot reject, if it would. She quickened her steps.

'I have offended you!' said a mortally wounded voice across her shoulder.

That he should think so were too dreadful.

'Oh, no, no! you would never offend me.' She gave him her whole sweet face.

'Then why—why do you leave me?'

'Because,' she hesitated, 'I must go.'

'No. You must not go. Why must you go? Do not go.'

'Indeed I must,' she said, pulling at the obnoxious broad brim of her hat; and, interpreting a pause he made for his assent to her rational resolve, shyly looking at him, she held her hand out, and said, 'Good-bye,' as if it were a natural thing to say.

The hand was pure white—white and fragrant as the frosted blossom of a Maynight. It was the hand whose shadow, cast before, he had last night bent his head reverentially above, and kissed—resigning himself thereupon over to execution for payment of the penalty of such daring—by such bliss well rewarded.

He took the hand, and held it, gazing between her eyes.

'Good-bye,' she said again, as frankly as she could, and at the same time slightly compressing her fingers on his in token of adieu. It was a signal for his to close firmly upon hers.

'You will not go?'

'Pray, let me,' she pleaded, her sweet brows suing in wrinkles.

'You will not go?' Mechanically he drew the white hand nearer his thumping heart.

'I must,' she faltered piteously.

'You will not go?'

'Oh, yes! yes!'

'Tell me. Do you wish to go?'

The question was a subtle one. A moment or two she did not answer, and then forswore herself, and said, Yes.

'Do you—you wish to go?' He looked with quivering eyelids under hers.

A fainter Yes responded.

'You wish—wish to leave me?' His breath went with the words.

'Indeed I must.'

Her hand became a closer prisoner.

All at once an alarming delicious shudder went through her frame. From him to her it coursed, and back from her to him. Forward and back love's electric messenger rushed from heart to heart, knocking at each, till it surged tumultuously against the bars of its prison, crying out for its mate. They stood trembling in unison, a lovely couple under these fair heavens of the morning.

When he could get his voice it said, 'Will you go?'

But she had none to reply with, and could only mutely bend upward her gentle wrist.

'Then, farewell!' he said, and, dropping his lips to the soft fair hand, kissed it, and hung his head, swinging away from her, ready for death.

Strange, that now she was released she should linger by him. Strange, that his audacity, instead of the executioner, brought blushes and timid tenderness to his side, and the sweet words, 'You are not angry with me?'

'With you, O Beloved!' cried his soul. 'And you forgive me, fair charity!'

'I think it was rude of me to go without thanking you again,' she said, and again proffered her hand.

The sweet heaven-bird shivered out his song above him. The gracious glory of heaven fell upon his soul. He touched her hand, not moving his eyes from her, nor speaking, and she, with a soft word of farewell, passed across the stile, and up the pathway through the dewy shades of the copse, and out of the arch of the light, away from his eyes.

And away with her went the wild enchantment. He looked on barren air. But it was no more the world of yesterday. The marvellous splendours had sown seeds in him, ready to spring up and bloom at her gaze; and in his bosom now vivid conjuration of her tones, her face, her shape, makes them leap and illumine him like fitful summer lightnings—ghosts of the vanished sun.

There was nothing to tell him that he had been making love and declaring it with extraordinary rapidity; nor did he know it. Soft flushed cheeks! sweet mouth! strange sweet brows! eyes of softest fire! how could his ripe eyes behold you, and not plead to keep you? Nay, how could he let you go? And he seriously asked himself that question.

To-morrow this place will have a memory—the river and the meadow, and the white falling weir: his heart will build a temple here; and the skylark will be its high-priest, and the old blackbird its glossy-gowned chorister, and there will be a sacred repast of dewberries. To-day the grass is grass: his heart is chased by phantoms and finds rest nowhere. Only when the most tender freshness of his flower comes across him does he taste a moment's calm; and no sooner does it come than it gives place to keen pangs of fear that she may not be his for ever.

Ere long he learns that her name is Lucy. Ere long he meets Ralph, and discovers that in a day he has distanced him by a sphere. He and Ralph and the curate of Lobourne join in their walks, and raise classical discussions on ladies' hair, fingering a thousand delicious locks, from those of Cleopatra to the Borgia's.* 'Fair! fair! all of them fair!' sighs the melancholy curate, 'as are those women formed for our perdition! I think we have in this country what will match the Italian or the Greek.' His mind flutters to Mrs. Doria, Richard blushes before the vision of Lucy, and Ralph, whose heroine's hair is a dark luxuriance, dissents, and claims a noble share in the slaughter of men for dark-haired Wonders. They have no mutual confidences, but they are singularly kind to each other, these three children of instinct.

CHAPTER XVI

UNMASKING OF MASTER RIPTON THOMPSON

LADY BLANDISH, and others who professed an interest in the fortunes and future of the systematized youth, had occasionally mentioned names of families whose alliance according to apparent calculations, would not degrade his blood: and over these names, secretly preserved on an open leaf of the note-book, Sir Austin, as he neared the metropolis, distantly dropped his eye. There were names historic and names mushroomic; names that the Conqueror*might have called in his muster-roll; names that had been, clearly, tossed into the upper stratum of civilized life by a mill-wheel or a merchant-stool. Against them the baronet had written M. or Po. or Pr.—signifying, Money, Position, Principles, favouring the latter with special brackets. The wisdom of a worldly man, which he could now and then adopt, determined him, before he commenced his round of visits, to consult and sound his solicitor and his physician thereanent;* lawyers and doc-tors being the rats who know best the merits of a house, and on what sort of foundation it may be standing.

Sir Austin entered the great city with a sad mind. The memory of his misfortune came upon him vividly, as if no years had intervened, and it were but yesterday that he found the letter telling him that he had no wife and his son no mother. He wandered on foot through the streets the first night of his arrival, looking strangely at the shops and shows and bustle of the world from which he had divorced himself; feeling as destitute as the poorest vagrant. He had almost forgotten how to find his way about, and came across his old mansion in his efforts to

regain his hotel. The windows were alight—signs of
merry life within. He stared at it from the shadow of
the opposite side. It seemed to him he was a ghost
gazing upon his living past. And then the phantom
which had stood there mocking while he felt as other men
—the phantom, now flesh and blood reality, seized and
convulsed his heart, and filled its unforgiving crevices
with bitter ironic venom. He remembered by the time
reflection returned to him that it was Algernon, who had
the house at his disposal, probably giving a card-party,
or something of the sort. In the morning, too, he remembered that he had divorced the world to wed a System,
and must be faithful to that exacting Spouse, who, now
alone of things on earth, could fortify and recompense
him.

Mr. Thompson received his client with the dignity and
emotion due to such a rent-roll and the unexpectedness
of the honour. He was a thin stately man of law, garbed
as one who gave audience to acred bishops, and carrying
on his countenance the stamp of paternity to the parch-
ment-skins, and of a virtuous attachment to Port wine
sufficient to increase his respectability in the eyes of moral
Britain. After congratulating Sir Austin on the fortunate issue of two or three suits, and being assured that
the baronet's business in town had no concern therewith,
Mr. Thompson ventured to hope that the young heir was
all his father could desire him to be, and heard with satisfaction that he was a pattern to the youth of the Age.

'A difficult time of life, Sir Austin!' said the old lawyer,
shaking his head. 'We must keep our eyes on them—
keep awake! The mischief is done in a minute.'

'We must take care to have seen where we planted,
and that the root was sound, or the mischief will do itself
in spite of, or under the very spectacles of, supervision,'
said the baronet.

His legal adviser murmured 'Exactly,' as if that were
his own idea, adding, 'It is my plan with Ripton, who
has had the honour of an introduction to you, and a very
pleasant time he spent with my young friend, whom he
does not forget. Ripton follows the Law. He is articled
to me, and will, I trust, succeed me worthily in your confidence. I bring him into town in the morning; I take
him back at night. I think I may say that I am quite
content with him.'

'Do you think,' said Sir Austin, fixing his brows, 'that
you can trace every act of his to its motive?'

The old lawyer bent forward and humbly requested that
this might be repeated.

'Do you'—Sir Austin held the same searching expression—'do you establish yourself in a radiating centre of
intuition: do you base your watchfulness on so thorough
an acquaintance with his character, so perfect a knowledge of the instrument, that all its movements—even the
eccentric ones—are anticipated by you, and provided for?'

The explanation was a little too long for the old lawyer
to entreat another repetition. Winking with the painful
deprecation of a deaf man, Mr. Thompson smiled urbanely,
coughed conciliatingly, and said he was afraid he could
not affirm that much, though he was happily enabled to
say that Ripton had borne an extremely good character
at school.

'I find,' Sir Austin remarked, as sardonically he relaxed
his inspecting pose and mien, 'there are fathers who are
content to be simply obeyed. Now I require not only
that my son should obey; I would have him guiltless of
the impulse to gainsay my wishes—feeling me in him
stronger than his undeveloped nature, up to a certain
period, where my responsibility ends and his commences.
Man is a self-acting machine. He cannot cease to be a
machine; but, though self-acting, he may lose the powers

of self-guidance, and in a wrong course his very vitalities
hurry him to perdition.   Young, he is an organism ripening
to the set mechanic diurnal round, and while so he needs
all the angels to hold watch over him that he grow straight
and healthy, and fit for what machinal duties he may have
to perform' . . .

Mr. Thompson agitated his eyebrows dreadfully.   He
was utterly lost.   He respected Sir Austin's estates too
much to believe for a moment he was listening to downright folly.   Yet how otherwise explain the fact of his
excellent client being incomprehensible to him?   For a
middle-aged gentleman, and one who has been in the
habit of advising and managing, will rarely have a notion
of accusing his understanding; and Mr. Thompson had
not the slightest notion of accusing his.   But the baronet's
condescension in coming thus to him, and speaking on
the subject nearest his heart, might well affect him, and
he quickly settled the case in favour of both parties, pro-
nouncing mentally that his honoured client had a meaning, and so deep it was, so subtle, that no wonder he experienced difficulty in giving it fitly significant words.

Sir Austin elaborated his theory of the Organism and
the Mechanism, for his lawyer's edification.   At a recurrence of the word 'healthy' Mr. Thompson caught him
up—

'I apprehended you!   Oh, I agree with you, Sir Austin!
entirely!   Allow me to ring for my son Ripton.   I think,
if you condescend to examine him, you will say that
regular habits, and a diet of nothing but law-reading—
for other forms of literature I strictly interdict—have
made him all that you instance.'

Mr. Thompson's hand was on the bell.   Sir Austin
arrested him.

'Permit me to see the lad at his occupation,' said he.

Our old friend Ripton sat in a room apart with the

confidential clerk, Mr. Beazley, a veteran of law, now little better than a document, looking already signed and sealed, and shortly to be delivered, who enjoined nothing from his pupil and companion save absolute silence, and sounded his praises to his father at the close of days when it had been rigidly observed—not caring, or considering, the finished dry old document that he was, under what kind of spell a turbulent commonplace youth could be charmed into stillness for six hours of the day. Ripton was supposed to be devoted to the study of Blackstone.* A tome of the classic legal commentator lay extended outside his desk, under the partially lifted lid of which nestled the assiduous student's head—law being thus brought into direct contact with his brain-pan. The office-door opened, and he heard not; his name was called, and he remained equally moveless. His method of taking in Blackstone seemed absorbing as it was novel.

'Comparing notes, I daresay,' whispered Mr. Thompson to Sir Austin. 'I call that study!'

The confidential clerk rose, and bowed obsequious senility.

'Is it like this every day, Beazley?' Mr. Thompson asked with parental pride.

'Ahem!' the old clerk replied, 'he is like this every day, sir. I could not ask more of a mouse.'

Sir Austin stepped forward to the desk. His proximity roused one of Ripton's senses, which blew a call to the others. Down went the lid of the desk. Dismay, and the ardours of study, flashed together in Ripton's face. He slouched from his perch with the air of one who means rather to defend his position than welcome a superior, the right hand in his waistcoat pocket fumbling a key, the left catching at his vacant stool.

Sir Austin put two fingers on the youth's shoulder, and said, leaning his head a little on one side, in a way habitual to him, 'I am glad to find my son's old comrade thus profitably occupied. I know what study is myself. But beware of prosecuting it too excitedly! Come! you must not be offended at our interruption; you will soon take up the thread again. Besides, you know, you must get accustomed to the visits of your client.'

So condescending and kindly did this speech sound to Mr. Thompson, that, seeing Ripton still preserve his appearance of disorder and sneaking defiance, he thought fit to nod and frown at the youth, and desired him to inform the baronet what particular part of Blackstone he was absorbed in mastering at that moment.

Ripton hesitated an instant, and blundered out, with dubious articulation, 'The Law of Gravelkind.'

'What Law?' said Sir Austin, perplexed.

'Gravelkind,' again rumbled Ripton's voice.

Sir Austin turned to Mr. Thompson for an explanation. The old lawyer was shaking his law-box.

'Singular!' he exclaimed. 'He will make that mistake! What law, sir?'

Ripton read his error in the sternly painful expression of his father's face, and corrected himself. 'Gavelkind, sir.'

'Ah!' said Mr. Thompson, with a sigh of relief. 'Gavelkind, indeed! Gavelkind! An old Kentish——' He was going to expound, but Sir Austin assured him he knew it, and a very absurd law it was, adding, 'I should like to look at your son's notes, or remarks on the judiciousness of that family arrangement, if he has any.'

'You were making notes, or referring to them, as we entered,' said Mr. Thompson to the sucking lawyer; 'a very good plan, which I have always enjoined on you. Were you not?'

Ripton stammered that he was afraid he had not any notes to show, worth seeing.

'What were you doing then, sir?'

'Making notes,' muttered Ripton, looking incarnate subterfuge.

'Exhibit!'

Ripton glanced at his desk and then at his father; at Sir Austin, and at the confidential clerk. He took out his key. It would not fit the hole.

'Exhibit!' was peremptorily called again.

In his praiseworthy efforts to accommodate the key-hole, Ripton discovered that the desk was already unlocked. Mr. Thompson marched to it, and held the lid aloft. A book was lying open within, which Ripton immediately hustled among a mass of papers and tossed into a dark corner, not before the glimpse of a coloured frontispiece was caught by Sir Austin's eye.

The baronet smiled, and said, 'You study Heraldry, too? Are you fond of the science?'

Ripton replied that he was very fond of it—extremely attached, and threw a further pile of papers into the dark corner.

The notes had been less conspicuously placed, and the search for them was tedious and vain. Papers, not legal, or the fruits of study, were found, that made Mr. Thompson more intimate with the condition of his son's exchequer; nothing in the shape of a remark on the Law of Gavelkind.

Mr. Thompson suggested to his son that they might be among those scraps he had thrown carelessly into the dark corner. Ripton, though he consented to inspect them, was positive they were not there.

'What have we here?' said Mr. Thompson, seizing a neatly folded paper addressed to the Editor of a law publication, as Ripton brought them forth, one by one. Forthwith Mr. Thompson fixed his spectacles and read aloud:

'*To the Editor of the* Jurist.

'Sir,—In your recent observations on the great case of Crim——'

Mr. Thompson hem'd! and stopped short, like a man who comes unexpectedly upon a snake in his path.   Mr. Beazley's feet shuffled.   Sir Austin changed the position of an arm.

'It 's on the other side, I think,' gasped Ripton.

Mr. Thompson confidently turned over, and intoned with emphasis.

'To Absalom, the son of David, the little Jew usurer of Bond Court, Whitecross Gutters, for his introduction to Venus, I O U Five pounds, when I can pay.

'Signed: RIPTON THOMPSON.'

Underneath this fictitious legal instrument was discreetly appended:

'(Mem.   Document not binding.)'

There was a pause: an awful under-breath of sanctified wonderment and reproach passed round the office.   Sir Austin assumed an attitude.   Mr. Thompson shed a glance of severity on his confidential clerk, who parried by throwing up his hands.

Ripton, now fairly bewildered, stuffed another paper under his father's nose, hoping the outside perhaps would satisfy him: it was marked 'Legal Considerations.'   Mr. Thompson had no idea of sparing or shielding his son.   In fact, like many men whose self-love is wounded by their offspring, he felt vindictive, and was ready to sacrifice him up to a certain point, for the good of both.   He therefore opened the paper, expecting something worse than what he had hitherto seen, despite its formal heading, and he was not disappointed.

The 'Legal Considerations' related to the Case regarding which Ripton had conceived it imperative upon him to address a letter to the Editor of the *Jurist*, and was

indeed a great case, and an ancient; revived apparently
for the special purpose of displaying the forensic abilities
of the Junior Counsel for the Plaintiff, Mr. Ripton Thompson, whose assistance the Attorney-General, in his opening
statement, congratulated himself on securing; a rather
unusual thing, due probably to the eminence and renown
of that youthful gentleman at the Bar of his country. So
much was seen from the copy of a report purporting to be
extracted from a newspaper, and prefixed to the Junior
Counsel's remarks, or Legal Considerations, on the conduct of the Case, the admissibility and non-admissibility
of certain evidence, and the ultimate decision of the
judges.

Mr. Thompson, senior, lifted the paper high, with the
spirit of one prepared to do execution on the criminal, and
in the voice of a town-crier, varied by a bitter accentua-
tion and satiric sing-song tone, deliberately read:

'VULCAN *v.* MARS.*

'The Attorney-General, assisted by Mr. Ripton Thompson, appeared on behalf of the Plaintiff. Mr. Serjeant
Cupid, Q.C., and Mr. Capital Opportunity, for the De-
fendant.'

'Oh!' snapped Mr. Thompson, senior, peering venom at
the unfortunate Ripton over his spectacles, ' your notes are
on that issue, sir! Thus you employ your time, sir!'

With another side-shot at the confidential clerk, who
retired immediately behind a strong entrenchment of
shrugs, Mr. Thompson was pushed by the devil of his
rancour to continue reading:

"This Case is too well known to require more than a
partial summary of particulars. . . .'

'Ahem! we will skip the particulars, however partial,' said Mr. Thompson. 'Ah!—what do you mean here, sir, —but enough! I think we may be excused your Legal Considerations on such a Case. This is how you employ your law-studies, sir! You put them to this purpose? Mr. Beazley! you will henceforward sit alone. I must have this young man under my own eye. Sir Austin! permit me to apologize to you for subjecting you to a scene so disagreeable. It was a father's duty not to spare him.'

Mr. Thompson wiped his forehead, as Brutus*might have done after passing judgement on the scion of his house.

'These papers,' he went on, fluttering Ripton's precious lucubrations in a waving judicial hand, 'I shall retain. The day will come when he will regard them with shame. And it shall be his penance, his punishment, to do so! Stop!' he cried, as Ripton was noiselessly shutting his desk, 'have you more of them, sir; of a similar description? Rout them out! Let us know you at your worst. What have you there—in that corner?'

Ripton was understood to say he devoted that corner to old briefs on important cases.

Mr. Thompson thrust his trembling fingers among the old briefs, and turned over the volume Sir Austin had observed, but without much remarking it, for his suspicions had not risen to print.

'A Manual of Heraldry?' the baronet politely, and it may be ironically, inquired, before it could well escape.

'I like it very much,' said Ripton, clutching the book in dreadful torment.

'Allow me to see that you have our arms and crest correct.' The baronet proffered a hand for the book.

'A Griffin between two Wheatsheaves,' cried Ripton, still clutching it nervously.

Mr. Thompson, without any notion of what he was doing, drew the book from Ripton's hold; whereupon the two seniors laid their grey heads together over the title-page. It set forth in attractive characters beside a col-oured frontispiece, which embodied the promise displayed there, the entrancing adventures of Miss Random, a strange young lady.

Had there been a Black Hole within the area of those law regions to consign Ripton to there and then, or an Iron Rod handy to mortify his sinful flesh, Mr. Thompson would have used them. As it was, he contented himself by looking Black Holes and Iron Rods at the detected youth, who sat on his perch insensible to what might hap-pen next, collapsed.

Mr. Thompson cast the wicked creature down with a 'Pah!' He, however, took her up again, and strode away with her. Sir Austin gave Ripton a forefinger, and kindly touched his head, saying, 'Good-bye, boy! At some future date Richard will be happy to see you at Raynham.'

Undoubtedly this was a great triumph to the System!

CHAPTER XVII

GOOD WINE AND GOOD BLOOD

THE conversation between solicitor and client was re-sumed.

'Is it possible,' quoth Mr. Thompson, the moment he had ushered his client into his private room, 'that you will consent, Sir Austin, to see him and receive him again?'

'Certainly,' the baronet replied. 'Why not? This by no means astonishes me. When there is no longer danger to my son he will be welcome as he was before. He is a schoolboy. I knew it. I expected it. The results of your principle, Thompson!'

'One of the very worst books of that abominable class!'
exclaimed the old lawyer, opening at the coloured frontispiece, from which brazen Miss Random smiled bewitchingly out, as if she had no doubt of captivating Time and
all his veterans on a fair field. 'Pah!' he shut her to
with the energy he would have given to the office of publicly slapping her face; 'from this day I diet him on bread
and water—rescind his pocket-money!—How he could
have got hold of such a book! How he—! And what ideas!
Concealing them from me as he has done so cunningly!
He trifles with vice! His mind is in a putrid state! I might
have believed—I did believe—I might have gone on believing—my son Ripton to be a moral young man!' The
old lawyer interjected on the delusion of fathers, and sat
down in a lamentable abstraction.

'The lad has come out!' said Sir Austin. 'His adop-
tion of the legal form is amusing. He trifles with vice,
true: people newly initiated are as hardy as its intimates,
and a young sinner's amusements will resemble those of
a confirmed debauchee. The satiated, and the insatiate, appetite alike appeal to extremes. You are astonished at this revelation of your son's condition. I expected it; though assuredly, believe me, not this sudden
and indisputable proof of it. But I knew that the seed
was in him, and therefore I have not latterly invited him
to Raynham. School, and the corruption there, will bear
its fruits sooner or later. I could advise you, Thompson,
what to do with him: it would be my plan.'

Mr. Thompson murmured, like a true courtier, that he
should esteem it an honour to be favoured with Sir Austin
Feverel's advice: secretly resolute, like a true Briton,
to follow his own.

'Let him, then,' continued the baronet, 'see vice in
its nakedness. While he has yet some innocence, nau-
seate him! Vice, taken little by little, usurps gradually

the whole creature. My counsel to you, Thompson, would be, to drag him through the·sinks of town.'

Mr. Thompson began to blink again.

'Oh, I shall punish him, Sir Austin! Do not fear me, sir. I have no tenderness for vice.'

'That is not what is wanted, Thompson. You mistake me. He should be dealt with gently. Heavens! do you hope to make him hate vice by making him a martyr for its sake? You must descend from the pedestal of age to become its Mentor: cause him to see how certainly and pitilessly vice itself punishes: accompany him into its haunts——'

'Over town?' broke forth Mr. Thompson.

'Over town,' said the baronet.

'And depend upon it,' he added, 'that, until fathers act thoroughly up to their duty, we shall see the sights we see in great cities, and hear the tales we hear in little villages, with death and calamity in our homes, and a legacy of sorrow and shame to the generations to come. I do aver,' he exclaimed, becoming excited, 'that, if it were not for the duty to my son, and the hope I cherish in him, I, seeing the accumulation of misery we are handing down to an innocent posterity—to whom, through our sin, the fresh breath of life will be foul—I—yes! I would hide my name! For whither are we tending? What home is pure absolutely? What cannot our doctors and lawyers tell us?"

Mr. Thompson acquiesced significantly.

'And what is to come of this?' Sir Austin continued. 'When the sins of the fathers are multiplied by the sons, is not perdition the final sum of things? And is not life, the boon of heaven, growing to be the devil's game utterly? But for my son, I would hide my name. I would not bequeath it to be cursed by them that walk above my grave!'

This was indeed a terrible view of existence. Mr. Thompson felt uneasy. There was a dignity in his client, an impressiveness in his speech, that silenced remonstrating reason and the cry of long years of comfortable respectability. Mr. Thompson went to church regularly; paid his rates and dues without overmuch, or at least more than common, grumbling. On the surface he was a good citizen, fond of his children, faithful to his wife, devoutly marching to a fair seat in heaven on a path paved by something better than a thousand a year. But here was a man sighting him from below the surface, and though it was an unfair, únaccustomed, not to say un-English, method of regarding one's fellow-man, Mr. Thompson was troubled by it. What though his client exaggerated? Facts were at the bottom of what he said. And he was acute—he had unmasked Ripton! Since Ripton's exposure he winced at a personal application in the text his client preached from. Possibly this was the secret source of part of his anger against that peccant youth.

Mr. Thompson shook his head, and, with dolefully puckered visage and a pitiable contraction of his shoulders, rose slowly up from his chair. Apparently he was about to speak, but he straightway turned and went meditatively to a side-recess in the room, whereof he opened a door, drew forth a tray and a decanter labelled PORT, filled a glass for his client, deferentially invited him to partake of it; filled another glass for himself, and drank.

That was his reply.

Sir Austin never took wine before dinner. Thompson had looked as if he meant to speak: he waited for Thompson's words.

Mr. Thompson saw that, as his client did not join him in his glass, the eloquence of that Porty reply was lost on his client.

Having slowly ingurgitated and meditated upon this

precious draught, and turned its flavour over and over
with an aspect of potent Judicial wisdom (one might have
thought that he was weighing mankind in the balance),
the old lawyer heaved, and said, sharpening his lips over
the admirable vintage, 'The world is in a very sad state,
I fear, Sir Austin!'

His client gazed at him queerly.

'But that,' Mr. Thompson added immediately, ill-
concealing by his gaze the glowing intestinal congratulations going on within him, 'that is, I think you would say,
Sir Austin—if I could but prevail upon you—a tolerably
good character wine!'

'There's virtue somewhere, I see, Thompson!' Sir
Austin murmured, without disturbing his legal adviser's
dimples.

The old lawyer sat down to finish his glass, saying, that
such a wine was not to be had everywhere.

They were then outwardly silent for a space. Inwardly
one of them was full of riot and jubilant uproar: as if the
solemn fields of law were suddenly to be invaded and possessed by troops of Bacchanals:* and to preserve a decently
wretched physiognomy over it, and keep on terms with
his companion, he had to grimace like a melancholy clown
in a pantomime.

Mr. Thompson brushed back his hair. The baronet
was still expectant. Mr. Thompson sighed deeply, and
emptied his glass. He combated the change that had
come over him. He tried not to see Ruby. He tried to
feel miserable, and it was not in him. He spoke, drawing
what appropriate inspirations he could from his client's
countenance, to show that they had views in common:
'Degenerating sadly, I fear!'

The baronet nodded.

'According to what my wine-merchants say,' continued Mr. Thompson, 'there can be no doubt about it.'

Sir Austin stared.

'It's the grape, or the ground, or something,' Mr. Thompson went on. 'All I can say is, our youngsters will have a bad look-out! In my opinion Government should be compelled to send out a Commission to inquire into the cause. To Englishmen it would be a public calamity. It surprises me—I hear men sit and talk despondently of this extraordinary disease of the vine, and not one of them seems to think it incumbent on him to act, and do his best to stop it.' He fronted his client like a man who accuses an enormous public delinquency. 'Nobody makes a stir! The apathy of Englishmen will become proverbial. Pray, try it, Sir Austin! Pray, allow me. Such a wine cannot disagree at any hour. Do! I am allowanced two glasses three hours before dinner. Stomachic. I find it agree with me surprisingly: quite a new man. I suppose it will last our time. It must! What should we do? There's no Law possible without it. Not a lawyer of us could live. Ours is an occupation which dries the blood.'

The scene with Ripton had unnerved him, the wine had renovated, and gratitude to the wine inspired his tongue. He thought that his respected client, of the whimsical mind, though undoubtedly correct moral views, had need of a glass.

'Now that very wine—Sir Austin—I think I do not err in saying, that very wine your respected father, Sir Pylcher Feverel, used to taste whenever he came to consult my father, when I was a boy. And I remember one day being called in, and Sir Pylcher himself poured me out a glass. I wish I could call in Ripton now, and do the same. No! Leniency in such a case as that!—The wine would not hurt him—I doubt if there be much left for him to welcome his guests with. Ha! ha! Now if I could persuade you, Sir Austin, as you do not take wine before dinner, some day to favour me with your company at my little country cottage—I have a wine there—the fellow to that—I think you would, I do think you would—' Mr. Thompson meant to say, he thought his client would arrive at something of a similar jocund contemplation of his fellows in their degeneracy that inspirited lawyers after potation, but condensed the sensual promise into 'highly approve.'

Sir Austin speculated on his legal adviser with a sour mouth comically compressed.

It stood clear to him that Thompson before his Port, and Thompson after, were two different men. To indoctrinate him now was too late: it was perhaps the time to make the positive use of him he wanted.

He pencilled on a handy slip of paper: 'Two prongs of a fork; the World stuck between them—Port and the Palate: 'Tis one which fails first—Down goes World'; and again the hieroglyph—'Port-spectacles.' He said, 'I shall gladly accompany you this evening, Thompson,' words that transfigured the delighted lawyer, and consigned the skeleton of a great Aphorism to his pocket, there to gather flesh and form, with numberless others in a like condition.

'I came to visit my lawyer,' he said to himself. 'I think I have been dealing with The World in epitome!'

CHAPTER XVIII

THE SYSTEM ENCOUNTERS THE WILD OATS SPECIAL PLEA

THE rumour circulated that Sir Austin Feverel, the recluse of Raynham, the rank misogynist, the rich baronet, was in town, looking out a bride for his only son and uncorrupted heir. Doctor Benjamin Bairam was the excellent authority. Doctor Bairam had safely delivered Mrs. Deborah Gossip of this interesting bantling,* which was forthwith dandled in dozens of feminine laps. Doctor Bairam could boast the first interview with the famous recluse. He had it from his own lips that the object of the baronet was to look out a bride for his only son and uncorrupted heir; 'and,' added the doctor, 'she'll be lucky who gets him.' Which was interpreted to mean, that he would be a catch; the doctor probably intending to allude to certain extraordinary difficulties in the way of a choice.

A demand was made on the publisher of THE PILGRIM'S SCRIP for all his outstanding copies. Conventionalities were defied. A summer-shower of cards fell on the baronet's table.

He had few male friends. He shunned the Clubs as nests of scandal. The cards he contemplated were mostly those of the sex, with the husband, if there was a husband, evidently dragged in for propriety's sake. He perused the cards and smiled. He knew their purpose. What terrible light Thompson and Bairam had thrown on some of them! Heavens! in what a state was the blood of this Empire.

Before commencing his campaign he called on two ancient intimates, Lord Heddon, and his distant cousin Darley Absworthy, both Members of Parliament, useful men, though gouty, who had sown in their time a fine crop of wild oats, and advocated the advantage of doing so, seeing that they did not fancy themselves the worse for it. He found one with an imbecile son and the other with consumptive daughters. 'So much,' he wrote in the Note-book, 'for the Wild Oats theory!'

Darley was proud of his daughters' white and pink skins. 'Beautiful complexions,' he called them. The eldest was in the market, immensely admired. Sir Austin was introduced to her. She talked fluently and sweetly. A youth not on his guard, a simple school-boy youth, or even a man, might have fallen in love with her, she was so affable and fair. There was something poetic about her. And she was quite well, she said, the baronet frequently questioning her on that point. She intimated that she was robust; but towards the close of their conversation her hand would now and then travel to her side, and she breathed painfully an instant, saying, 'Isn't it odd? Dora, Adela, and myself, we all feel the same queer sensation—about the heart, I think it is—after talking much.'

Sir Austin nodded and blinked sadly, exclaiming to his soul, 'Wild oats! wild oats!'

He did not ask permission to see Dora and Adela.

Lord Heddon vehemently preached wild oats.

'It 's all nonsense, Feverel,' he said, 'about bringing up a lad out of the common way. He 's all the better for a little racketing when he 's green—feels his bone and muscle—learns to know the world. He 'll never be a man if he hasn't played at the old game one time in his life, and the earlier the better. I 've always found the best fellows were wildish once. I don't care what he does when he 's a green-horn; besides, he 's got an excuse for it then. You can't expect to have a man, if he doesn't take a man's food. You 'll have a milksop. And, depend upon it, when he does break out he 'll go to the devil, and nobody pities him. Look what those fellows, the grocers, do when they get hold of a young—what d' ye call 'em?— apprentice. They know the scoundrel was born with a sweet tooth. Well! they give him the run of the shop, and in a very short time he soberly deals out the goods, a devilish deal too wise to abstract a morsel even for the pleasure of stealing. I know you have contrary theories. You hold that the young grocer should have a soul above sugar. It won't do! Take my word for it, Feverel, it's a dangerous experiment, that of bringing up flesh and blood in harness. No colt will bear it, or he's a tame beast. And look you: take it on medical grounds. Early excesses the frame will recover from: late ones break the constitution. There's the case in a nutshell. How's your son?'

'Sound and well!' replied Sir Austin. 'And yours?'

'Oh, Lipscombe's always the same!' Lord Heddon sighed peevishly. 'He's quiet—that's one good thing; but there's no getting the country to take him, so I must give up hopes of that.'

Lord Lipscombe entering the room just then, Sir Austin surveyed him, and was not astonished at the refusal of the country to take him.

'Wild oats!' he thought, as he contemplated the headless, degenerate, weedy issue and result.

Both Darley Absworthy and Lord Heddon spoke of the marriage of their offspring as a matter of course. 'And if I were not a coward,' Sir Austin confessed to himself, 'I should stand forth and forbid the banns! This universal ignorance of the inevitable consequence of sin is frightful! The wild oats plea is a torpedo that seems to have struck the world, and rendered it morally insensible.' However, they silenced him. He was obliged to spare their feelings on a subject to him so deeply sacred. The healthful image of his noble boy rose before him, a triumphant living rejoinder to any hostile argument.

He was content to remark to his doctor, that he thought the third generation of wild oats would be a pretty thin crop!

Families against whom neither Thompson lawyer nor Bairam physician could recollect a progenitorial blot, either on the male or female side, were not numerous. 'Only,' said the doctor, 'you really must not be too exacting in these days, my dear Sir Austin. It is impossible to contest your principle, and you are doing mankind incalculable service in calling its attention to this the gravest of its duties: but as the stream of civilization progresses we must be a little taken in the lump, as it were. The world is, I can assure you—and I do not look only above the surface, you can believe—the world is awakening to the vital importance of the question.'

'Doctor,' replied Sir Austin, 'if you had a pure-blood Arab barb*would you cross him with a screw?'*

'Decidedly not,' said the doctor.

'Then permit me to say, I shall employ every care to match my son according to his merits,' Sir Austin returned. 'I trust the world is awakening, as you observe. I have been to my publisher, since my arrival in town, with a manuscript "Proposal for a New System of Education of our British Youth," which may come in opportunely. I think I am entitled to speak on that subject.'

'Certainly,' said the doctor. 'You will admit, Sir Austin, that, compared with continental nations—our neighbours, for instance—we shine to advantage, in morals, as in everything else. I hope you admit that?'

'I find no consolation in shining by comparison with a lower standard,' said the baronet. 'If I compare the enlightenment of your views—for you admit my principle— with the obstinate incredulity of a country doctor's, who sees nothing of the world, you are hardly flattered, I presume?'

Doctor Bairam would hardly be flattered at such a comparison, assuredly, he interjected.

'Besides,' added the baronet, 'the French make no pretences, and thereby escape one of the main penalties of hypocrisy. Whereas we!—but I am not their advocate, credit me. It is better, perhaps, to pay our homage to virtue. At least it delays the spread of entire corruptness.'

Doctor Bairam wished the baronet success, and diligently endeavoured to assist his search for a mate worthy of the pure-blood barb, by putting several mamas, whom he visited, on the alert.

CHAPTER XIX

A DIVERSION PLAYED ON A PENNY-WHISTLE

AWAY with Systems! Away with a corrupt World! Let us breathe the air of the Enchanted Island.

Golden lie the meadows: golden run the streams; red gold is on the pine-stems. The sun is coming down to earth, and walks the fields and the waters.

The sun is coming down to earth, and the fields and the waters shout to him golden shouts. He comes, and his heralds run before him, and touch the leaves of oaks and planes and beeches lucid green, and the pine-stems redder gold; leaving brightest footprints upon thickly-weeded banks, where the foxglove's last upper-bells incline, and bramble-shoots wander amid moist rich herbage. The plumes of the woodland are alight; and beyond them, over the open, 'tis a race with the long-thrown shadows; a race across the heaths and up the hills, till, at the farthest bourne of mounted eastern cloud, the heralds of the sun lay rosy fingers and rest.

Sweet are the shy recesses of the woodland. The ray treads softly there. A film athwart the pathway quivers many-hued against purple shade fragrant with warm pines, deep moss-beds, feathery ferns. The little brown squirrel drops tail and leaps; the inmost bird is startled to a chance tuneless note. From silence into silence things move.

Peeps of the revelling splendour above and around enliven the conscious full heart within. The flaming West, the crimson heights, shower their glories through voluminous leafage. But these are bowers where deep bliss dwells, imperial joy, that owes no fealty to yonder glories, in which the young lamb gambols and the spirits of men are glad. Descend, great Radiance! embrace creation with beneficent fire, and pass from us! You and the vice-regal light that succeeds to you, and all heavenly pageants, are the ministers and the slaves of the throbbing content within.

For this is the home of the enchantment. Here, secluded from vexed shores, the prince and princess of the island meet: here like darkling nightingales they sit, and into eyes and ears and hands pour endless ever-fresh treasures of their souls.

Roll on, grinding wheels of the world: cries of ships going down in a calm, groans of a System which will not know its rightful hour of exultation, complain to the universe. You are not heard here.

He calls her by her name, Lucy: and she, blushing at her great boldness, has called him by his, Richard. Those two names are the key-notes of the wonderful harmonies the angels sing aloft.

'Lucy! my beloved!'

'O Richard!'

Out in the world there, on the skirts of the woodland, a sheep-boy pipes to meditative eve on a penny-whistle.

Love's musical instrument is as old, and as poor: it has but two stops; and yet, you see, the cunning musician does thus much with it!

Other speech they have little; light foam playing upon waves of feeling, and of feeling compact, that bursts only when the sweeping volume is too wild, and is no more than their sigh of tenderness spoken.

Perhaps love played his tune so well because their natures had unblunted edges, and were keen for bliss, confiding in it as natural food. To gentlemen and ladies he fine-draws upon the viol, ravishingly; or blows into the mellow bassoon; or rouses the heroic ardours of the trumpet; or, it may be, commands the whole Orchestra for them. And they are pleased. He is still the cunning musician. They languish, and taste ecstasy: but it is, however sonorous, an earthly concert. For them the spheres move not to two notes. They have lost, or forfeited and never known, the first supersensual spring of the ripe senses into passion; when they carry the soul with them, and have the privileges of spirits to walk disembodied, boundlessly to feel. Or one has it, and the other is a dead body. Ambrosia*let them eat, and drink the nectar: here sit a couple to whom Love's simple bread and water is a finer feast.

Pipe, happy sheep-boy, Love! Irradiated angels, unfold your wings and lift your voices!

They have outflown philosophy. Their instinct has shot beyond the ken of science. They were made for their Eden.

'And this divine gift was in store for me!'

So runs the internal outcry of each, clasping each: it is their recurring refrain to the harmonies. How it illumined the years gone by and suffused the living Future!

'You for me: I for you!'

'We are born for each other!'

They believe that the angels have been busy about them from their cradles. The celestial hosts have worthily striven to bring them together. And, O victory! O wonder! after toil and pain, and difficulties exceeding, the celestial hosts have succeeded!

'Here we two sit who are written above as one!'

Pipe, happy Love! pipe on to these dear innocents!

The tide of colour has ebbed from the upper sky. In the West the sea of sunken fire draws back; and the stars leap forth, and tremble, and retire before the advancing moon, who slips the silver train of cloud from her shoulders, and, with her foot upon the pine-tops, surveys heaven.

'Lucy, did you never dream of meeting me?'

'O Richard! yes; for I remembered you.'

'Lucy! and did you pray that we might meet?'

'I did!'

Young as when she looked upon the lovers in Paradise, the fair Immortal journeys onward. Fronting her, it is not night but veiled day. Full half the sky is flushed. Not darkness, not day, but the nuptials of the two.

'My own! my own forever! You are pledged to me? Whisper!"

He hears the delicious music.

'And you are mine?'

A soft beam travels to the fern-covert under the pine-wood where they sit, and for answer he has her eyes: turned to him an instant, timidly fluttering over the depths of his, and then downcast; for through her eyes her soul is naked to him.

'Lucy! my bride! my life!'

The night-jar spins his dark monotony on the branch of the pine. The soft beam travels round them, and listens to their hearts. Their lips are locked.

Pipe no more, Love, for a time! Pipe as you will you cannot express their first kiss; nothing of its sweetness, and of the sacredness of it nothing. St. Cecilia* up aloft, before the silver organ-pipes of Paradise, pressing fingers upon all the notes of which Love is but one, from her you may hear it.

So Love is silent. Out in the world there, on the skirts of the woodland, the self-satisfied sheep-boy delivers a last complacent squint down the length of his penny-whistle, and, with a flourish correspondingly awry, he also marches into silence, hailed by supper. The woods are still. There is heard but the night-jar spinning on the pine-branch, circled by moonlight.

CHAPTER XX

CELEBRATES THE TIME-HONOURED TREATMENT OF A DRAGON
BY THE HERO

ENCHANTED Islands have not yet rooted out their old brood of dragons. Wherever there is romance, these monsters come by inimical attraction. Because the heavens are certainly propitious to true lovers, the beasts of the abysses are banded to destroy them, stimulated by innumerable sad victories; and every love-tale is an Epic War of the upper and lower powers. I wish good fairies were a little more active. They seem to be cajoled into security by the happiness of their favourites; whereas the wicked are always alert and circumspect. They let the little ones shut their eyes to fancy they are not seen, and then commence.

These appointments and meetings, involving a start from the dinner-table at the hour of contemplative digestion and prime claret; the hour when the wise youth Adrian delighted to talk at his ease—to recline in dreamy consciousness that a work of good was going on inside him; these abstractions from his studies, excesses of gaiety, and glumness, heavings of the chest, and other odd signs, but mainly the disgusting behaviour of his pupil at the dinner-table, taught Adrian to understand, though the young gentleman was clever in excuses, that he had somehow learnt there was another half to the divided Apple of Creation, and had embarked upon the great voyage of discovery of the difference between the two halves. With his usual coolness Adrian debated whether he might be in the observatory or the practical stage of the voyage. For himself, as a man and a philosopher, Adrian had no objection to its being either; and he had only to consider which was temporarily

most threatening to the ridiculous System he had to support. Richard's absence annoyed him. The youth was
vivacious, and his enthusiasm good fun; and besides, when
he left table, Adrian had to sit alone with Hippias and the
Eighteenth Century, from both of whom he had extracted
all the amusement that could be got, and he saw his digestion menaced by the society of two ruined stomachs,
who bored him just when he loved himself most. Poor
Hippias was now so reduced that he had profoundly to
calculate whether a particular dish, or an extra glass of
wine, would have a bitter effect on him and be felt through
the remainder of his years. He was in the habit of uttering
his calculations half aloud, wherein the prophetic doubts
of experience, and the succulent insinuations of appetite,
contended hotly. It was horrible to hear him, so let us
pardon Adrian for tempting him to a decision in favour of
the moment.

'Happy to take wine with you,' Adrian would say, and
Hippias would regard the decanter with a pained forehead,
and put up the doctor.

'Drink, nephew Hippy, and think of the doctor to-
morrow!' the Eighteenth Century cheerily ruffles her cap
at him, and recommends her own practice.

'It's this literary work!' interjects Hippias, handling his
glass of remorse. 'I don't know what else it can be. You
have no idea how anxious I feel. I have frightful dreams.
I'm perpetually anxious.'

'No wonder,' says Adrian, who enjoys the childish simplicity to which an absorbed study of his sensational existence has brought poor Hippias. 'No wonder. Ten years
Fairy Mythology! Could any one hope to sleep in peace
after that? As to your digestion, no one has a digestion
who is in the doctor's hands. They prescribe from dogmas,
and don't count on the system. They have cut you down
from two bottles to two glasses. It's absurd. You can't

sleep, because your system is crying out for what it's accustomed to.'

Hippias sips his Madeira with a niggardly confidence, but assures Adrian that he really should not like to venture on a bottle now: it would be rank madness to venture on a bottle now, he thinks. Last night only, after partaking, under protest, of that rich French dish, or was it the duck? —Adrian advised him to throw the blame on that vulgar bird.—Say the duck, then. Last night, he was no sooner stretched in bed, than he seemed to be of an enormous size: all his limbs—his nose, his mouth, his toes—were elephantine! An elephant was a pigmy to him. And his hugeousness seemed to increase the instant he shut his eyes. He turned on this side; he turned on that. He lay on his back; he tried putting his face to the pillow; and he continued to swell. He wondered the room could hold him—he thought he must burst it—and absolutely lit a candle, and went to the looking-glass to see whether he was bearable.

By this time Adrian and Richard were laughing uncontrollably. He had, however, a genial auditor in the Eighteenth Century, who declared it to be a new disease, not known in her day, and deserving investigation. She was happy to compare sensations with him, but hers were not of the complex order, and a potion soon righted her. In fact, her system appeared to be a debatable ground for aliment and medicine, on which the battle was fought, and, when over, she was none the worse, as she joyfully told Hippias. Never looked ploughman on prince, or village belle on Court Beauty, with half the envy poor nineteenth-century Hippias expended in his gaze on the Eighteenth. He was too serious to note much the laughter of the young men.

This 'Tragedy of a Cooking-Apparatus,' as Adrian designated the malady of Hippias, was repeated regularly every evening. It was natural for any youth to escape as quick as he could from such a table of stomachs.

Adrian bore with his conduct considerately, until a letter from the baronet, describing the house and maternal System of a Mrs. Caroline Grandison, and the rough grain of hopefulness in her youngest daughter, spurred him to think of his duties, and see what was going on. He gave Richard half-an-hour's start, and then put on his hat to follow his own keen scent, leaving Hippias and the Eighteenth Century to piquet.*

In the lane near Belthorpe he met a maid of the farm not unknown to him, one Molly Davenport by name, a buxom lass, who, on seeing him, invoked her Good Gracious, the generic maid's familiar, and was instructed by reminiscences vivid, if ancient, to giggle.

'Are you looking for your young gentleman?' Molly presently asked.

Adrian glanced about the lane like a cool brigand, to see if the coast was clear, and replied to her, 'I am, miss. I want you to tell me about him.'

'Dear!' said the buxom lass, 'was you coming for me to-night to know?'

Adrian rebuked her: for her bad grammar, apparently. ''Cause I can't stop out long to-night,' Molly explained, taking the rebuke to refer altogether to her bad grammar.

'You may go in when you please, miss. Is that any one coming? Come here in the shade.'

'Now, get along!' said Miss Molly.

Adrian spoke with resolution. 'Listen to me, Molly Davenport!' He put a coin in her hand, which had a medical effect in calming her to attention. 'I want to know whether you have seen him at all?'

'Who? Your young gentleman? I sh'd think I did. I seen him to-night only. Ain't he growed handsome? He's al'ays about Beltharp now. It ain't to fire no more ricks. He's afire 'unself. Ain't you seen 'em together? He's after the missis——"

Adrian requested Miss Davenport to be respectful, and confine herself to particulars. This buxom lass then told him that her young missis and Adrian's young gentleman were a pretty couple, and met one another every night. The girl swore for their innocence.

'As for Miss Lucy, she haven't a bit of art in her, nor have he.'

'They're all nature, I suppose,' said Adrian. 'How is it I don't see her at church?'

'She's Catholic, or somethink,' said Molly. 'Her fey-ther was, and a leftenant. She've a Cross in her bedroom. She don't go to church. I see you there last Sunday a-lookin' so solemn,' and Molly stroked her hand down her chin to give it length.

Adrian insisted on her keeping to facts. It was dark, and in the dark he was indifferent to the striking contrasts suggested by the lass, but he wanted to hear facts, and he again bribed her to impart nothing but facts. Upon which she told him further, that her young lady was an innocent artless creature who had been to school upwards of three years with the nuns, and had a little money of her own, and was beautiful enough to be a lord's lady, and had been in love with Master Richard ever since she was a little girl. Molly had got from a friend of hers up at the Abbey, Mary Garner, the housemaid who cleaned Master Richard's room, a bit of paper once with the young gentleman's handwriting, and had given it to her Miss Lucy, and Miss Lucy had given her a gold sovereign for it—just for his handwriting! Miss Lucy did not seem happy at the farm, because of that young Tom, who was always leering at her, and to be sure she was quite a lady, and could play, and sing, and dress with the best.

'She looks like angels in her nightgown!' Molly wound up.

The next moment she ran up close, and speaking for the first time as if there were a distinction of position between them, petitioned: 'Mr. Harley! you won't go for doin' any harm to 'em 'cause of what I said, will you now? Do say you won't now, Mr. Harley! She is good, though she's a Catholic. She was kind to me when I was ill, and I wouldn't have her crossed—I'd rather be showed up myself, I would!'

The wise youth gave no positive promise to Molly, and she had to read his consent in a relaxation of his austerity. The noise of a lumbering foot plodding down the lane caused her to be abruptly dismissed. Molly took to flight, the lumbering foot accelerated its pace, and the pastoral appeal to her flying skirts was heard—'Moll! yau theyre! It be I—Bantam!' But the sprightly Silvia* would not stop to his wooing, and Adrian turned away laughing at these Arcadians.*

Adrian was a lazy dragon. All he did for the present was to hint and tease. 'It's the Inevitable!' he said, and asked himself why he should seek to arrest it. He had no faith in the System. Heavy Benson had. Benson of the slow thick-lidded antediluvian eye and loose-crumpled skin; Benson, the Saurian,* the woman-hater; Benson was wide awake. A sort of rivalry existed between the wise youth and Heavy Benson. The fidelity of the latter dependant had moved the baronet to commit to him a portion of the management of the Raynham estate, and this Adrian did not like. No one who aspires to the honourable office of leading another by the nose can tolerate a party in his ambition. Benson's surly instinct told him he was in the wise youth's way, and he resolved to give his master a striking proof of his superior faithfulness. For some weeks the Saurian eye had been on the two secret creatures. Heavy Benson saw letters come and go in the day, and now the young gentleman was off and out every night, and seemed to be on wings. Benson knew whither he went, and the object he went for. It was a woman—that was enough. The Saurian eye had actually seen the sinful thing lure the hope of Raynham into the shades. He composed several epistles of warning to the baronet of the work that was going on; but before sending one he wished to record a little of their guilty conversation; and for this purpose the faithful fellow trotted over the dews to eavesdrop, and thereby aroused the good fairy, in the person of Tom Bakewell, the sole confidant of Richard's state.

Tom said to his young master, 'Do you know what, sir? You be watched!'

Richard, in a fury, bade him name the wretch, and Tom hung his arms, and aped the respectable protrusion of the butler's head.

'It 's he, is it?' cried Richard. 'He shall rue it, Tom. If I find him near me when we 're together he shall never forget it.'

'Don't hit too hard, sir,' Tom suggested. 'You hit mortal hard when you 're in earnest, you know.'

Richard averred he would forgive anything but that, and told Tom to be within hail to-morrow night—he knew where. By the hour of the appointment it was out of the lover's mind.

Lady Blandish dined that evening at Raynham, by Adrian's pointed invitation. According to custom, Richard started up and off, with few excuses. The lady exhibited no surprise. She and Adrian likewise strolled forth to enjoy the air of the Summer night. They had no intention of spying. Still they may have thought, by meeting Richard and his innamorata, there was a chance of laying a foundation of ridicule to sap the passion. They may have thought so—they were on no spoken understanding.

'I have seen the little girl,' said Lady Blandish. 'She is pretty—she would be telling if she were well set up. She speaks well. How absurd it is of that class to educate their women above their station! The child is really too good for a farmer. I noticed her before I knew of this; she

has enviable hair. I suppose she doesn't paint her eyelids.
Just the sort of person to take a young man. I thought
there was something wrong. I received, the day before
yesterday, an impassioned poem evidently not intended for
me. My hair was gold. My meeting him was foretold.
My eyes were homes of light fringed with night. I sent it
back, correcting the colours.'

'Which was death to the rhymes,' said Adrian. 'I saw
her this morning. The boy hasn't bad taste. As you say,
she is too good for a farmer. Such a spark would explode
any System. She slightly affected mine. The Huron* is
stark mad about her.'

'But we must positively write and tell his father,' said
Lady Blandish.

The wise youth did not see why they should exaggerate
a trifle. The lady said she would have an interview with
Richard, and then write, as it was her duty to do. Adrian
shrugged, and was for going into the scientific explanation of
Richard's conduct, in which the lady had to discourage him.

'Poor boy!" she sighed. 'I am really sorry for him. I
hope he will not feel it too strongly. They feel strongly,
father and son.'

'And select wisely,' Adrian added.

'That's another thing,' said Lady Blandish.

Their talk was then of the dulness of neighbouring county
people, about whom, it seemed, there was little or no scandal afloat: of the lady's loss of the season in town, which
she professed not to regret, though she complained of her
general weariness: of whether Mr. Morton of Poer Hall would
propose to Mrs. Doria, and of the probable despair of the
hapless curate of Lobourne; and other gossip, partly in
French.

They rounded the lake, and got upon the road through
the park to Lobourne. The moon had risen. The atmosphere was warm and pleasant.

'Quite a lover's night,' said Lady Blandish.

'And I, who have none to love—pity me!' The wise youth attempted a sigh.

'And never will have,' said Lady Blandish, curtly. 'You *buy* your loves.'

Adrian protested. However, he did not plead verbally against the impeachment, though the lady's decisive insight astonished him. He began to respect her, relishing her exquisite contempt, and he reflected that widows could be terrible creatures.

He had hoped to be a little sentimental with Lady Blandish, knowing her romantic. This mixture of the harshest common sense and an air of '*I* know you men,' with romance and refined temperament, subdued the wise youth more than a positive accusation supported by witnesses would have done. He looked at the lady. Her face was raised to the moon. She knew nothing—she had simply spoken from the fulness of her human knowledge, and had forgotten her words. Perhaps, after all, her admiration, or whatever feeling it was, for the baronet, was sincere, and really the longing for a virtuous man. Perhaps she had tried the opposite set pretty much. Adrian shrugged. Whenever the wise youth encountered a mental difficulty he instinctively lifted his shoulders to equal altitudes, to show that he had no doubt there was a balance in the case—plenty to be said on both sides, which was the same to him as a definite solution.

At their tryst in the wood, abutting on Raynham Park, wrapped in themselves, piped to by tireless Love, Richard and Lucy sat, toying with eternal moments. How they seem as if they would never end! What mere sparks they are when they have died out! And how in the distance of time they revive, and extend, and glow, and make us think them full the half, and the best of the fire, of our lives!

With the onward flow of intimacy, the two happy lovers

ceased to be so shy of common themes, and their speech did
not reject all as dross that was not pure gold of emotion.

Lucy was very inquisitive about everything and everybody at Raynham. Whoever had been about Richard
since his birth, she must know the history of, and he for a
kiss will do her bidding.

Thus goes the tender duet:

'You should know my cousin Austin, Lucy.—Darling!
Beloved!'

'My own! Richard!'

'You should know my cousin Austin. You shall know
him. He would take to you best of them all, and you to
him. He is in the tropics now, looking out a place—it's a
secret—for poor English working-men to emigrate to and
found a colony in that part of the world:—my white angel!'

'Dear love!'

'He is such a noble fellow! Nobody here understands
him but me. Isn't it strange? Since I met you I love him
better! That's because I love all that's good and noble
better now—Beautiful! I love—I love you!'

'My Richard!'

'What do you think I've determined, Lucy? If my
father——but no! my father does love me.—No! he will
not; and we will be happy together here. And I will win
my way with you. And whatever I win will be yours; for
it will be owing to you. I feel as if I had no strength but
yours—none! and you make me—O Lucy!'

His voice ebbs. Presently Lucy murmurs—

'Your father, Richard.'

'Yes, my father?'

'Dearest Richard! I feel so afraid of him.'

'He loves me, and will love you, Lucy.'

'But I am so poor and humble, Richard.'

'No one I have ever seen is like you, Lucy.'

'You think so, because you——'

'What?'

'Love me,' comes the blushing whisper, and the duet gives place to dumb variations, performed equally in concert.

It is resumed.

'You are fond of the knights, Lucy. Austin is as brave as any of them.—My own bride! Oh, how I adore you! When you are gone, I could fall upon the grass you tread upon, and kiss it. My breast feels empty of my heart— Lucy! if we lived in those days, I should have been a knight, and have won honour and glory for you. Oh! one can do nothing now. My lady-love! My lady-love!—A tear?— Lucy?'

'Dearest! Ah, Richard! I am not a lady.'

'Who dares say that? Not a lady—the angel I love!'

'Think, Richard, who I am.'

'My beautiful! I think that God made you, and has given you to me.'

Her eyes fill with tears, and, as she lifts them heavenward to thank her God, the light of heaven strikes on them, and she is so radiant in her pure beauty that the limbs of the young man tremble.

'Lucy! O heavenly spirit! Lucy!'

Tenderly her lips part—'I do not weep for sorrow.'

The big bright drops lighten, and roll down, imaged in his soul.

They lean together—shadows of ineffable tenderness playing on their thrilled cheeks and brows.

He lifts her hand, and presses his mouth to it. She has seen little of mankind, but her soul tells her this one is different from others, and at the thought, in her great joy, tears must come fast, or her heart will break—tears of boundless thanksgiving. And he, gazing on those soft, ray-illumined, dark-edged eyes, and the grace of her loose falling tresses, feels a scarce-sufferable holy fire streaming through his members.

It is long ere they speak in open tones.

'O happy day when we met!'

What says the voice of one, the soul of the other echoes.

'O glorious heaven looking down on us!'

Their souls are joined, are made one for evermore beneath that bending benediction.

'O eternity of bliss!'

Then the diviner mood passes, and they drop to earth.

'Lucy! come with me to-night, and look at the place where you are some day to live. Come, and I will row you on the lake. You remember what you said in your letter that you dreamt?—that we were floating over the shadow of the Abbey to the nuns at work by torchlight felling the cypress, and they handed us each a sprig. Why, darling, it was the best omen in the world, their felling the old trees. And you write such lovely letters. So pure and sweet they are. I love the nuns for having taught you.'

'Ah, Richard! See! we forget! Ah!' she lifts up her face pleadingly, as to plead against herself, 'even if your father forgives my birth, he will not my religion. And, dearest, though I would die for you I cannot change it. It would seem that I was denying God; and—oh! it would make me ashamed of my love.'

'Fear nothing!' He winds her about with his arm. 'Come! He will love us both, and love you the more for being faithful to your father's creed. You don't know him, Lucy. He seems harsh and stern—he is full of kindness and love. He isn't at all a bigot. And besides, when he hears what the nuns have done for you, won't he thank them, as I do? And—oh! I must speak to him soon, and you must be prepared to see him soon, for I cannot bear your remaining at Belthorpe, like a jewel in a sty. Mind! I'm not saying a word against your uncle. I declare I love everybody and everything that sees you and touches you. Stay! it *is* a wonder how you could have grown there. But you were not born there, and your father had good blood. Desborough!—there was a Colonel Desborough—never mind! Come!'

She dreads to. She begs not to. She is drawn away.

The woods are silent, and then—

'What think you of that for a pretty pastoral?' says a very different voice.

Adrian reclined against a pine overlooking the fern-covert. Lady Blandish was recumbent upon the brown pine-droppings, gazing through a vista of the lower greenwood which opened out upon the moon-lighted valley, her hands clasped round one knee, her features almost stern in their set hard expression.

They had heard, by involuntarily overhearing about as much as may be heard in such positions, a luminous word or two.

The lady did not answer. A movement among the ferns attracted Adrian, and he stepped down the decline across the pine-roots to behold heavy Benson below, shaking fernseed and spidery substances off his crumpled skin.

'Is that you, Mr. Hadrian?' called Benson, starting, as he puffed, and exercised his handkerchief.

'Is it *you*, Benson, who have had the audacity to spy upon these Mysteries?' Adrian called back, and coming close to him, added, 'You look as if you had just been well thrashed.'

'Isn't it dreadful, sir?' snuffled Benson. 'And his father in ignorance, Mr. Hadrian!'

'He shall know, Benson! He shall know how you have endangered your valuable skin in his service. If Mr. Richard had found you there just now I wouldn't answer for the consequences.'

'Ha!' Benson spitefully retorted. 'This won't go on, Mr. Hadrian. It shan't, sir. It will be put a stop to tomorrow, sir. I call it corruption of a young gentleman like

him, and harlotry, sir, I call it.   I'd have every jade flogged
that made a young innocent gentleman go on like that, sir.'

'Then why didn't you stop it yourself, Benson?   Ah, I
see! you waited—what?   This is not the first time you
have been attendant on Mr. Apollo* and Miss Dryope?*
You have written to headquarters?'

'I did my duty, Mr. Hadrian.'

The wise youth returned to Lady Blandish, and informed
her of Benson's zeal.   The lady's eyes flashed.   'I hope
Richard will treat him as he deserves,' she said.

'Shall we home?' Adrian inquired.

'Do me a favour,' the lady replied.   'Get my carriage
sent round to meet me at the park-gates.'

'Won't you——?'

'I want to be left alone.'

Adrian bowed and left her.   She was still sitting with
her hands clasped round one knee, gazing towards the dim
ray-strewn valley.

'An odd creature!' muttered the wise youth.   'She's as
odd as any of them.   She ought to be a Feverel.   I suppose
she's graduating for it.   Hang that confounded old ass of
a Benson!   He has had the impudence to steal a march
on me!'

The shadow of the cypress was lessening on the lake.   The
moon was climbing high.   As Richard rowed the boat, Lucy
sang to him softly.   She sang first a fresh little French
song, reminding him of a day when she had been asked to
sing to him before, and he did not care to hear.   'Did I
live?' he thinks.   Then she sang to him a bit of one of
those majestic old Gregorian chants,* that, wherever you
may hear them, seem to build up cathedral walls about
you.   The young man dropped the sculls.   The strange
solemn notes gave a religious tone to his love, and wafted
him into the knightly ages and the reverential heart of
chivalry.

Hanging between two heavens on the lake: floating to her voice: the moon stepping over and through white shoals of soft high clouds above and below: floating to her voice—no other breath abroad! His soul went out of his body as he listened.

They must part. He rows her gently shoreward.

'I never was so happy as to-night,' she murmurs.

'Look, my Lucy. The lights of the old place are on the lake. Look where you are to live.'

'Which is your room, Richard?'

He points it out to her.

'O Richard! that I were one of the women who wait on you! I should ask nothing more. How happy she must be!'

'My darling angel-love. You shall be happy; but all shall wait on you, and I foremost, Lucy.'

'Dearest! may I hope for a letter?'

'By eleven to-morrow. And I?'

'Oh! you will have mine, Richard.'

'Tom shall wait for it. A long one, mind! Did you like my last song?'

She puts her hand quietly against her bosom, and he knows where it rests. O love! O heaven!

They are aroused by the harsh grating of the bow of the boat against the shingle. He jumps out, and lifts her ashore.

'See!' she says, as the blush of his embrace subsides—'See!' and prettily she mimics awe and feels it a little, 'the cypress does point towards us. O Richard! it does!'

And he, looking at her rather than at the cypress, delighting in her arch grave ways—

'Why, there's hardly any shadow at all, Lucy. She mustn't dream, my darling! or dream only of me.'

'Dearest! but I do.'

'To-morrow, Lucy! The letter in the morning, and you at night. O happy to-morrow!'

'You will be sure to be there, Richard?'

'If I am not dead, Lucy.'

'O Richard! pray, pray do not speak of that. I shall not survive you.'

'Let us pray, Lucy, to die together, when we are to die. Death or life with you! Who is it yonder? I see some one—is it Tom? It's Adrian!'

'Is it Mr. Harley?' The fair girl shivered.

'How dares he come here!' cried Richard.

The figure of Adrian, instead of advancing, discreetly circled the lake. They were stealing away when he called. His call was repeated. Lucy entreated Richard to go to him; but the young man preferred to summon his attendant, Tom, from within hail, and send him to know what was wanted.

'Will he have seen me? Will he have known me?' whispered Lucy tremulously.

'And if he does, love?' said Richard.

'Oh! if he does, dearest—I don't know, but I feel such a presentiment. You have not spoken of him to-night, Richard. Is he good?'

'Good?' Richard clutched her hand for the innocent maiden phrase. 'He's very fond of eating; that's all I know of Adrian.'

Her hand was at his lips when Tom returned.

'Well, Tom.'

'Mr. Adrian wishes particular to speak to you,' sir, said Tom.

'Do go to him, dearest! Do go!' Lucy begs him.

'Oh, how I hate Adrian!' The young man grinds his teeth.

'Do go!' Lucy urges him. 'Tom—good Tom—will see me home. To-morrow, dear love! To-morrow!'

'You wish to part from me?'

'Oh, unkind! but you must not come with me now. It may be news of importance, dearest. Think, Richard!'

'Tom! go back!'

At the imperious command the well-drilled Tom strides off a dozen paces, and sees nothing. Then the precious charge is confided to him. A heart is cut in twain.

Richard made his way to Adrian. 'What is it you want with me, Adrian?'

'Are we seconds, or principals, O fiery one?' was Adrian's answer. 'I want nothing with you, except to know whether you have seen Benson.'

'Where should I see Benson? What do I know of Benson's doings?'

'Of course not—such a secret old fist as he is! I want some one to tell him to order Lady Blandish's carriage to be sent round to the park-gates. I thought he might be round your way over there—I came upon him accidentally just now in Abbey-wood. What's the matter, boy?'

'You saw him *there*?'

'Hunting Diana, I suppose. He thinks she's not so chaste as they say,' continued Adrian. 'Are you going to knock down that tree?'

Richard had turned to the cypress, and was tugging at the tough wood. He left it and went to an ash.

'You'll spoil that weeper,' Adrian cried. 'Down she comes! But good-night, Ricky. If you see Benson, mind you tell him.'

Doomed Benson following his burly shadow hove in sight on the white road while Adrian spoke. The wise youth chuckled and strolled round the lake, glancing over his shoulder every now and then.

It was not long before he heard a bellow for help—the roar of a dragon in his throes. Adrian placidly sat down on the grass, and fixed his eyes on the water. There, as the roar was being repeated amid horrid resounding echoes, the wise youth mused in this wise—

'"The Fates are Jews with us when they delay a punishment," says THE PILGRIM'S SCRIP, or words to that effect. The heavens evidently love Benson, seeing that he gets his punishment on the spot. Master Ricky is a peppery young man. He gets it from the ap Gruffudh.* I rather believe in race. What a noise that old ruffian makes! He'll require poulticing with THE PILGRIM'S SCRIP. We shall have a message to-morrow, and a hubbub, and perhaps all go to town, which won't be bad for one who's been a prey to all the desires born of dulness. Benson howls: there's life in the old dog yet! He bays the moon. Look at her. She doesn't care. It's the same to her whether we coo like turtle-doves or roar like twenty lions. How complacent she looks! And yet she has just as much sympathy for Benson as for Cupid. She would smile on if both were being birched. Was that a raven or Benson? He howls no more. It sounds guttural: frog-like—something between the brek-kek-kek and the hoarse raven's croak. The fellow'll be killing him. It's time to go to the rescue. A deliverer gets more honour by coming in at the last gasp than if he forestalled catastrophe.—Ho, there, what's the matter?'

So saying, the wise youth rose, and leisurely trotted to the scene of battle, where stood St. George puffing over the prostrate Dragon.

'Holloa, Ricky! is it you?' said Adrian. 'What's this? Whom have we here?—Benson, as I live!'

'Make this beast get up,' Richard returned, breathing hard, and shaking his great ash-branch.

'He seems incapable, my dear boy. What have you been up to?—Benson! Benson!—I say, Ricky, this looks bad.'

'He's shamming!' Richard clamoured like a savage. 'Spy upon me, will he? I tell you, he's shamming. He

hasn't had half enough. Nothing's too bad for a spy.
Let him get up!'

'Insatiate youth! do throw away that enormous weapon.'

'He has written to my father,' Richard shouted. 'The
miserable spy! Let him get up!'

'Ooogh! I won't!' huskily groaned Benson. 'Mr.
Hadrian, you're a witness he's—my back—!' Cavernous
noises took up the tale of his maltreatment.

'I daresay you love your back better than any part of
your body now,' Adrian muttered. 'Come, Benson! be a
man. Mr. Richard has thrown away the stick. Come, and
get off home, and let's see the extent of the damage.'

'Ooogh! he's a devil! Mr. Hadrian, sir, he's a devil!'
groaned Benson, turning half over in the road to ease his
aches.

Adrian caught hold of Benson's collar and lifted him to
a sitting posture. He then had a glimpse of what his hopeful pupil's hand could do in wrath. The wretched butler's
coat was slit and welted; his hat knocked in; his flabby
spirit so broken that he started and trembled if his pitiless
executioner stirred a foot. Richard stood over him, grasping his great stick; no dawn of mercy for Benson in any
corner of his features.

Benson screwed his neck round to look up at him, and
immediately gasped, 'I won't get up! I won't! He's
ready to murder me again!—Mr. Hadrian! if you stand by
and see it, you're liable to the law, sir—I won't get up
while he's near.' No persuasion could induce Benson to
try his legs while his executioner stood by.

Adrian took Richard aside: 'You've almost killed the
poor devil, Ricky. You must be satisfied with that. Look
at his face.'

'The coward bobbed while I struck,' said Richard. 'I
marked his back. He ducked. I told him he was getting
it worse.'

At so civilized a piece of savagery, Adrian opened his mouth wide.

'Did you really? I admire that. You told him he was getting it worse.''

Adrian opened his mouth again to shake another roll of laughter out.

'Come,' he said, 'Excalibur* has done his work. Pitch him into the lake. And see—here comes the Blandish. You can't be at it again before a woman. Go and meet her, and tell her the noise was an ox being slaughtered. Or say Argus.'*

With a whirr that made all Benson's bruises moan and quiver, the great ash-branch shot aloft, and Richard swung off to intercept Lady Blandish.

Adrian got Benson on his feet. The heavy butler was disposed to summon all the commiseration he could feel for his bruised flesh. Every half-step he attempted was like a dislocation. His groans and grunts were frightful.

'How much did that hat cost, Benson?' said Adrian, as he put it on his head.

'A five-and-twenty shilling beaver, Mr. Hadrian!' Benson caressed its injuries.

'The cheapest policy of insurance I remember to have heard of!' said Adrian.

Benson staggered, moaning at intervals to his cruel comforter—

'He's a devil, Mr. Hadrian! He's a devil, sir, I do believe, sir. Ooogh! he's a devil!—I can't move, Mr. Hadrian. I must be fetched. And Dr. Clifford must be sent for, sir. I shall never be fit for work again. I haven't a sound bone in my body, Mr. Hadrian.'

'You see, Benson, this comes of your declaring war upon Venus.* I hope the maids will nurse you properly. Let me see: you are friends with the housekeeper, aren't you? All depends upon that.'

'I'm only a faithful servant, Mr. Hadrian,' the miserable butler snarled.

'Then you've got no friend but your bed. Get to it as quick as possible, Benson."

'I can't move.' Benson made a resolute halt. 'I must be fetched,' he whinnied. 'It's a shame to ask me to move, Mr. Hadrian.'

'You will admit that you are heavy, Benson,' said Adrian, 'so I can't carry you. However, I see Mr. Richard is very kindly returning to help me.'

At these words heavy Benson instantly found his legs, and shambled on.

Lady Blandish met Richard in dismay.

'I have been horribly frightened,' she said. 'Tell me, what was the meaning of those cries I heard?'

'Only some one doing justice on a spy,' said Richard, and the lady smiled, and looked on him fondly, and put her hand through his hair.

'Was that all? I should have done it myself if I had been a man. Kiss me.'

CHAPTER XXI

RICHARD IS SUMMONED TO TOWN TO HEAR A SERMON

By twelve o'clock at noon next day the inhabitants of Raynham Abbey knew that Berry, the baronet's man, had arrived post-haste from town, with orders to conduct Mr. Richard thither, and that Mr. Richard had refused to go, had sworn he would not, defied his father, and despatched Berry to the Shades. Berry was all that Benson was not. Whereas Benson hated woman, Berry admired her warmly. Second to his own stately person, woman occupied his reflections, and commanded his homage. Berry was of majestic port, and used dictionary words. Among the maids of Raynham his conscious calves produced all the discord and the frenzy those adornments seem destined to create in tender bosoms. He had, moreover, the reputation of having suffered for the sex; which assisted his object in inducing the sex to suffer for him. What with his calves, and his dictionary words, and the attractive halo of the mysterious vindictiveness of Venus surrounding him, this Adonis*of the lower household was a mighty man below, and he moved as one.

On hearing the tumult that followed Berry's arrival, Adrian sent for him, and was informed of the nature of his mission, and its results.

'You should come to me first,' said Adrian. 'I should have imagined you were shrewd enough for that, Berry?'

'Pardon me, Mr. Adrian,' Berry doubled his elbow to explain. 'Pardon me, sir. Acting recipient of special injunctions, I was not a free agent.'

'Go to Mr. Richard again, Berry. There will be a little confusion if he holds back. Perhaps you had better throw out a hint or so of apoplexy. A slight hint will do. And here—Berry! when you return to town, you had better not mention anything—to quote Johnson—of Benson's spiflication.'

'Certainly not, sir.'

The wise youth's hint had the desired effect on Richard.

He dashed off a hasty letter by Tom to Belthorpe, and, mounting his horse, galloped to the Bellingham station.

Sir Austin was sitting down to a quiet early dinner at his hotel, when the Hope of Raynham burst into his room.

The baronet was not angry with his son. On the contrary, for he was singularly just and self-accusing while pride was not up in arms, he had been thinking all day after the receipt of Benson's letter that he was deficient in cordiality, and did not, by reason of his excessive anxiety, make himself sufficiently his son's companion: was not enough, as he strove to be, mother and father to him; preceptor and friend; previsor and associate. He had not to ask his conscience where he had lately been to blame towards the System. He had slunk away from Raynham in the very crisis of the Magnetic Age, and this young woman of the parish (as Benson had termed sweet Lucy in his letter) was the consequence.

Yes! pride and sensitiveness were his chief foes, and he would trample on them. To begin, he embraced his son: hard upon an Englishman at any time—doubly so to one so shamefaced at emotion in cool blood, as it were. It gave him a strange pleasure, nevertheless. And the youth seemed to answer to it; he was excited. Was his love, then, beginning to correspond with his father's as in those intimate days before the Blossoming Season?

But when Richard, inarticulate at first in his haste, cried out, 'My dear, dear father! You are safe! I feared— You are better, sir? Thank God!' Sir Austin stood away from him.

'Safe?' he said. 'What has alarmed you?'

Instead of replying, Richard dropped into a chair, and seized his hand and kissed it.

Sir Austin took a seat, and waited for his son to explain.

'Those doctors are such fools!' Richard broke out. 'I was sure they were wrong. They don't know headache from apoplexy. It's worth the ride, sir, to see you. You left Raynham so suddenly—But you are well! It was not an attack of real apoplexy?'

His father's brows contorted, and he said, No, it was not. Richard pursued:

'If you were ill, I couldn't come too soon, though, if coroner's inquests sat on horses, those doctors would be found guilty of mare-slaughter. Cassandra 'll be knocked up. I was too early for the train at Bellingham, and I wouldn't wait. She did the distance in four hours and three-quarters. Pretty good, sir, wasn't it?'

'It has given you appetite for dinner, I hope,' said the baronet, not so well pleased to find that it was not simple obedience that had brought the youth to him in such haste.

'I'm ready,' replied Richard. 'I shall be in time to return by the last train to-night. I will leave Cassandra in your charge for a rest.'

His father quietly helped him to soup, which he commenced gobbling with an eagerness that might pass for appetite.

'All well at Raynham?' said the baronet.

'Quite, sir.'

'Nothing new?'

'Nothing, sir.'

'The same as when I left?'

'No change whatever!'

'I shall be glad to get back to the old place,' said the baronet. 'My stay in town has certainly been profitable. I have made some pleasant acquaintances who may probably favour us with a visit there in the late autumn—people you may be pleased to know. They are very anxious to see Raynham.'

'I love the old place,' cried Richard. 'I never wish to leave it.'

'Why, boy, before I left you were constantly begging to see town.'

'Was I, sir? How odd! Well! I don't want to remain here. I've seen enough of it.'

'How did you find your way to me?'

Richard laughed, and related his bewilderment at the miles of brick, and the noise, and the troops of people, concluding, 'There's no place like home!'

The baronet watched his symptomatic brilliant eyes, and favoured him with a double-dealing sentence—

'To anchor the heart by any object ere we have half traversed the world, is youth's foolishness, my son. Reverence time! A better maxim that than your Horatian.'*

'He knows all!' thought Richard, and instantly drew away leagues from his father, and threw up fortifications round his love and himself.

Dinner over, Richard looked hurriedly at his watch, and said, with much briskness, 'I shall just be in time, sir, if we walk. Will you come with me to the station?'

The baronet did not answer.

Richard was going to repeat the question, but found his father's eyes fixed on him so meaningly that he wavered, and played with his empty glass.

'I think we will have a little more claret,' said the baronet.

Claret was brought, and they were left alone.

The baronet then drew within arm's-reach of his son, and began:

'I am not aware what you may have thought of me, Richard, during the years we have lived together; and indeed I have never been in a hurry to be known to you; and, if I had died before my work was done, I should not have complained at losing half my reward, in hearing you thank me. Perhaps, as it is, I never may. Everything, save selfishness, has its recompense. I shall be content if you prosper.'

He fetched a breath and continued: 'You had in your infancy a great loss.' Father and son coloured simultaneously. 'To make that good to you I chose to isolate myself from the world, and devote myself entirely to your welfare; and I think it is not vanity that tells me now that the son I have reared is one of the most hopeful of God's creatures. But for that very reason you are open to be tempted the most, and to sink the deepest. It was the first of the angels who made the road to hell.'

He paused again. Richard fingered at his watch.

'In our House, my son, there is peculiar blood. We go to wreck very easily. It sounds like superstition; I cannot but think we are tried as most men are not. I see it in us all. And you, my son, are compounded of two races. Your passions are violent. You have had a taste of revenge. You have seen, in a small way, that the pound of flesh draws rivers of blood. But there is now in you another power. You are mounting to the table-land of life, where mimic battles are changed to real ones. And you come upon it laden equally with force to create and to destroy.' He deliberated to announce the intelligence, with deep meaning: 'There are women in the world, my son!'

The young man's heart galloped back to Raynham.

'It is when you encounter them that you are thoroughly on trial. It is when you know them that life is either a mockery to you, or, as some find it, a gift of blessedness. They are our ordeal. Love of any human object is the soul's ordeal; and they are ours, loving them, or not.'

The young man heard the whistle of the train. He saw the moon-lighted wood, and the vision of his beloved. He could barely hold himself down and listen.

'I believe,' the baronet spoke with little of the cheerfulness of belief, 'good women exist.'

Oh, if he knew Lucy!

'But,' and he gazed on Richard intently, 'it is given to very few to meet them on the threshold—I may say, to none. We find them after hard buffeting, and usually, when we find the one fitted for us, our madness has misshaped our destiny, our lot is cast. For women are not the end, but the means, of life. In youth we think them the former, and thousands, who have not even the excuse of youth, select a mate—or worse—with that sole view. I believe women punish us for so perverting their uses. They punish Society.'

The baronet put his hand to his brow as his mind travelled into consequences.

'Our most diligent pupil learns not so much as an earnest teacher,' says THE PILGRIM'S SCRIP; and Sir Austin, in schooling himself to speak with moderation of women, was beginning to get a glimpse of their side of the case.

Cold Blood now touched on love to Hot Blood.

Cold Blood said, 'It is a passion coming in the order of nature, the ripe fruit of our animal being.'

Hot Blood felt: 'It is a divinity! All that is worth living for in the world.'

Cold Blood said: 'It is a fever which tests our strength, and too often leads to perdition.'

Hot Blood felt: 'Lead whither it will, I follow it.'

Cold Blood said: 'It is a name men and women are much in the habit of employing to sanctify their appetites.'

Hot Blood felt: 'It is worship; religion; life!'

And so the two parallel lines ran on.

The baronet became more personal:

'You know my love for you, my son. The extent of it you cannot know; but you must know that it is something very deep, and—I do not wish to speak of it—but a father must sometimes petition for gratitude, since the only true expression of it is his son's moral good. If you care for my love, or love me in return, aid me with all your energies to keep you what I have made you, and guard you from the snares besetting you. It was in my hands once. It is ceasing to be so. Remember, my son, what my love is. It is different, I fear, with most fathers: but I am bound up in your welfare: what you do affects me vitally. You will take no step that is not intimate with my happiness, or my misery. And I have had great disappointments, my son.'

So far it was well. Richard loved his father, and even in his frenzied state he could not without emotion hear him thus speak.

Unhappily, the baronet, who by some fatality never could see when he was winning the battle, thought proper in his wisdom to water the dryness of his sermon with a little jocoseness, on the subject of young men fancying themselves in love, and, when they were raw and green, absolutely wanting to be—that most awful thing, which the wisest and strongest of men undertake in hesitation and after self-mortification and penance—married! He sketched the Foolish Young Fellow—the object of general ridicule and covert contempt. He sketched the Woman—the strange thing made in our image, and with all our faculties —passing to the rule of one who in taking her proved that he could not rule himself, and had no knowledge of her save as a choice morsel which he would burn the whole world, and himself in the bargain, to possess. He harped upon the Foolish Young Fellow, till the foolish young fellow felt his skin tingle and was half suffocated with shame and rage.

After this, the baronet might be as wise as he pleased: he had quite undone his work. He might analyze Love and anatomize Woman. He might accord to her her due position, and paint her fair: he might be shrewd, jocose, gentle, pathetic, wonderfully wise: he spoke to deaf ears.

Closing his sermon with the question, softly uttered: 'Have you anything to tell me, Richard?' and hoping for a confession, and a thorough re-establishment of confidence, the callous answer struck him cold: 'I have not.'

The baronet relapsed in his chair, and made diagrams of his fingers.

Richard turned his back on further dialogue by going to the window. In the section of sky over the street twinkled two or three stars; shining faintly, feeling the moon. The moon was rising: the woods were lifting up to her: his star

of the woods would be there. A bed of moss set about
flowers in a basket under him breathed to his nostril of the
woodland keenly, and filled him with delirious longing.

A succession of hard sighs brought his father's hand on
his shoulder.

'You have nothing you could say to me, my son? Tell
me, Richard! Remember, there is no home for the soul
where dwells a shadow of untruth!'

'Nothing at all, sir,' the young man replied, meeting him
with the full orbs of his eyes.

The baronet withdrew his hand, and paced the room.

At last it grew impossible for Richard to control his impatience, and he said: 'Do you intend me to stay here, sir?
Am I not to return to Raynham at all to-night?'

His father was again falsely jocular:

'What? and catch the train after giving it ten minutes'
start?'

'Cassandra will take me,' said the young man earnestly.
'I needn't ride her hard, sir. Or perhaps you would lend
me your Winkelried? I should be down with him in little
better than three hours.'

'Even then, you know, the park-gates would be locked.'

'Well, I could stable him in the village. Dowling knows
the horse, and would treat him properly. May I have him,
sir?'

The cloud cleared off Richard's face as he asked. At
least, if he missed his love that night he would be near her,
breathing the same air, marking what star was above her
bed-chamber, hearing the hushed night-talk of the trees
about her dwelling: looking on the distances that were like
hope half fulfilled and a bodily presence bright as Hesper,
since he knew her. There were two swallows under the
eaves shadowing Lucy's chamber-windows: two swallows,
mates in one nest, blissful birds, who twittered and cheep-
cheeped to the sole-lying beauty in her bed. Around these

birds the lover's heart revolved, he knew not why. He associated them with all his close-veiled dreams of happiness. Seldom a morning passed when he did not watch them leave the nest on their breakfast-flight, busy in the happy stillness of dawn. It seemed to him now that if he could be at Raynham to see them in to-morrow's dawn he would be compensated for his incalculable loss of to-night: he would forgive and love his father, London, the life, the world. Just to see those purple backs and white breasts flash out into the quiet morning air! He wanted no more.

The baronet's trifling had placed this enormous boon within the young man's visionary grasp.

He still went on trying the boy's temper.

'You know there would be nobody ready for you at Raynham. It is unfair to disturb the maids.'

Richard overrode every objection.

'Well, then, my son,' said the baronet, preserving his half-jocular air, 'I must tell you that it is my wish to have you in town.'

'Then you have not been ill at all, sir!' cried Richard, as in his despair he seized the whole plot.

'I have been as well as you could have desired me to be,' said his father.

'Why did they lie to me?' the young man wrathfully exclaimed.

'I think, Richard, you can best answer that,' rejoined Sir Austin, kindly severe.

Dread of being signalized as the Foolish Young Fellow prevented Richard from expostulating further. Sir Austin saw him grinding his passion into powder for future explosion, and thought it best to leave him for awhile.

CHAPTER XXII

INDICATES THE APPROACHES OF FEVER

For three weeks Richard had to remain in town and
endure the teachings of the System in a new atmosphere.
He had to sit and listen to men of science who came to
renew their intimacy with his father, and whom of all men
his father wished him to respect and study; practically scientific men being, in the baronet's estimation, the only
minds thoroughly mated and enviable. He had to endure
an introduction to the Grandisons, and meet the eyes of
his kind, haunted as he was by the Foolish Young Fellow.
The idea that he might by any chance be identified with
him held the poor youth in silent subjection. And it was
horrible. For it was a continued outrage on the fair image
he had in his heart. The notion of the world laughing at
him because he loved sweet Lucy stung him to momentary frenzies, and developed premature misanthropy in
his spirit. Also the System desired to show him whither
young women of the parish lead us, and he was dragged
about at night-time to see the sons and daughters of darkness, after the fashion prescribed to Mr. Thompson; how
they danced and ogled down the high road to perdition.
But from this sight possibly the teacher learnt more than
his pupil, since we find him seriously asking his meditative
hours, in the Note-book: 'Wherefore Wild Oats are only
of one gender?' a question certainly not suggested to him
at Raynham; and again— 'Whether men might not be
attaching too rigid an importance? . . .' to a subject
with a dotted tail apparently, for he gives it no other in
the Note-book. But, as I apprehend, he had come to plead
in behalf of women here, and had deduced something from

positive observation. To Richard the scenes he witnessed were strange wild pictures, likely if anything to have increased his misanthropy, but for his love.

Certain sweet little notes from Lucy sustained the lover during the first two weeks of exile. They ceased; and now Richard fell into such despondency that his father in alarm had to take measures to hasten their return to Raynham. At the close of the third week Berry laid a pair of letters, bearing the Raynham post-mark, on the breakfast-table, and, after reading one attentively, the baronet asked his son if he was inclined to quit the metropolis.

'For Raynham, sir?' cried Richard, and relapsed, saying, 'As you will!' aware that he had given a glimpse of the Foolish Young Fellow.

Berry accordingly received orders to make arrangements for their instant return to Raynham.

The letter Sir Austin lifted his head from to bespeak his son's wishes was a composition of the wise youth Adrian's, and ran thus:

'Benson is doggedly recovering. He requires great indemnities. Happy when a faithful fool is the main sufferer in a household! I quite agree with you that our faithful fool is the best servant of great schemes. Benson is now a piece of history. I tell him that this is indemnity enough, and that the sweet Muse usually insists upon gentlemen being half-flayed before she will condescend to notice them; but Benson, I regret to say, rejects the comfort so fine a reflection should offer, and had rather keep his skin and live opaque. Heroism seems partly a matter of training. Faithful folly is Benson's nature: the rest has been thrust upon him.

'The young person has resigned the neighbourhood. I had an interview with the fair Papist myself, and also with the man Blaize. They were both sensible, though one swore

and the other sighed. She is pretty. I hope she does not
paint. I can affirm that her legs are strong, for she walks
to Bellingham twice a week to take her Scarlet bath, when,
having confessed and been made clean by the Romish unction, she walks back the brisker, of which my Protestant
muscular system is yet aware. It was on the road to Bellingham I engaged her. She is well in the matter of hair.
Madam Godiva* might challenge her, it would be a fair
match. Has it never struck you that Woman is nearer the
vegetable than Man?—Mr. Blaize intends her for his son—
a junction that every lover of fairy mythology must desire
to see consummated. Young Tom is heir to all the *agré-
mens* of the Beast. The maids of Lobourne say (I hear)
that he is a very Proculus*among them. Possibly the en-
vious men say it for the maids. Beauty does not speak bad
grammar—and altogether she is better out of the way.'

The other letter was from Lady Blandish, a lady's letter,
and said:

'I have fulfilled your commission to the best of my
ability, and heartily sad it has made me. She is indeed
very much above her station—pity that it is so! She is
almost beautiful—*quite* beautiful at times, and not in *any
way* what you have been led to fancy. The poor child had
no story to tell. I have again seen her, and talked with her
for an hour as kindly as I could. I could gather nothing
more than we know. It is just a woman's history as it invariably commences. Richard is the god of her idolatry.
She will renounce him, and sacrifice herself for his sake.
Are we so bad? She asked me what she was to do. She
would do whatever was imposed upon her—all but pretend
to love another, and that she never would, and, I believe,
never will. You know I am sentimental, and I confess we
dropped a *few tears* together. Her uncle has sent her for the

Winter to the institution where it appears she was educated, and where they are very fond of her and want to
keep her, which it would be a good thing if they were to
do. The man is a good sort of man. She was entrusted to
him by her father, and he never interferes with her religion, and is very scrupulous about all that pertains to it,
though, as he says, he is a Christian himself. In the Spring
(but the poor child does not know this) she is to come back,
and be married to his lout of a son. I am *determined* to
prevent that. May I not reckon on your promise to aid me?
When you see her, I am sure you will. It would be sacri-
lege to look on and permit such a thing. You know, they
are *cousins*. She asked me, where in the world was there
one like Richard? What could I answer? They were your
own words, and spoken with a depth of conviction! I hope
he is really calm. I shudder to think of him when he comes,
and discovers what I have been doing. I hope I have been
really doing right! A good deed, you say, never dies; but
we cannot always know—I must rely on you. Yes, it is,
I should think, easy to suffer martyrdom when one is sure
of one's cause! but then one *must* be sure of it. I have
done nothing lately but to repeat to myself that saying of
yours, No. 54, C. 7, P.S.; and it has consoled me, I cannot
say why, except that all wisdom consoles, whether it applies
directly or not:

'"*For this reason so many fall from God, who have attained
to Him; that they cling to Him with their Weakness, not with
their Strength.*"

'I like to know of what you were thinking when you composed this or that saying—what *suggested* it. May not one
be admitted to inspect the machinery of wisdom? I feel
curious to know how thoughts—*real* thoughts—are born.
Not that I hope to win the secret. Here is the beginning

of one (but we poor women can never put together even two of the three ideas which you say go to form a thought): "When a wise man makes a false step, will he not go farther than a fool?" It has just flitted through me.

'I cannot get on with Gibbon, so wait your return to recommence the readings. I dislike the *sneering essence* of his writings. I keep referring to his face, until the dislike seems to become personal. How different is it with Wordsworth! And yet I cannot escape from the thought that he is always solemnly thinking of himself (but I *do* reverence him). But this is curious; Byron was a greater egoist, and yet I do not feel the same with him. He reminds me of a beast of the desert, savage and beautiful; and the former is what one would imagine a superior donkey reclaimed from the heathen to be—a *very* superior donkey, I mean, with great power of speech and great natural complacency, and whose stubbornness you must admire as part of his mission. The worst is that no one will imagine anything sublime in a superior donkey, so my simile is unfair and false. Is it not strange? I love Wordsworth best, and yet Byron has the greater power over me. How is that?'

('Because,' Sir Austin wrote beside the query in pencil, 'women are cowards, and succumb to Irony and Passion, rather than yield their hearts to Excellence and Nature's Inspiration.')

The letter pursued:

'I have finished Boiardo and have taken up Berni.* The latter offends me. I suppose we women do not really care for humour. You are right in saying we have none ourselves, and "cackle" instead of laugh. It is true (of me, at least) that "Falstaff is only to us an incorrigible fat man." I want to know what he *illustrates*. And Don

Quixote—what end can be served in making a noble mind
ridiculous?—I hear you say—practical! So it is. We
are very narrow, I know. But we like wit—practical
again! Or in your words (when I really *think* they generally come to my aid—perhaps it is that it is often all *your*
thought); we "prefer the rapier thrust, to the broad embrace of Intelligence."'

He trifled with the letter for some time, re-reading chosen
passages as he walked about the room, and considering he
scarce knew what. There are ideas language is too gross
for, and shape too arbitrary, which come to us and have
a definite influence upon us, and yet we cannot fasten on
the filmy things and make them visible and distinct to ourselves, much less to others. Why did he twice throw a
look into the glass in the act of passing it? He stood for
a moment with erect head facing it. His eyes for the
nonce seemed little to peruse his outer features; the grey-
gathered brows, and the wrinkles much action of them had
traced over the circles half up his high straight forehead;
the iron-grey hair that rose over his forehead and fell away
in the fashion of Richard's plume. His general appearance showed the tints of years; but none of their weight,
and nothing of the dignity of his youth, was gone. It was
so far satisfactory, but his eyes were wide, as one who
looks at his essential self through the mask we wear.
Perhaps he was speculating as he looked on the sort of
aspect he presented to the lady's discriminative regard.
Of her feelings he had not a suspicion. But he knew with
what extraordinary lucidity women can, when it pleases
them, and when their feelings are not quite boiling under
the noonday sun, seize all the sides of a character, and
put their fingers on its weak point. He was cognizant of
the total absence of the humorous in himself (the want that
must shut him out from his fellows), and perhaps the clear-

thoughted, intensely self-examining gentleman filmily conceived, Me also, in common with the poet, she gazes on as one of the superior—grey beasts!

He may have so conceived the case; he was capable of that great-mindedness, and could snatch at times very luminous glances at the broad reflector which the world of fact lying outside our narrow compass holds up for us to see ourselves in when we will. Unhappily, the faculty of laughter, which is due to this gift, was denied him; and having seen, he, like the companion of friend Balaam,* could go no farther. For a good wind of laughter had relieved him of much of the blight of self-deception, and oddness, and extravagance; had given a healthier view of our atmosphere of life; but he had it not.

Journeying back to Bellingham in the train, with the heated brain and brilliant eye of his son beside him, Sir Austin tried hard to feel infallible, as a man with a System should feel; and because he could not do so, after much mental conflict, he descended to entertain a personal antagonism to the young woman who had stepped in between his experiment and success. He did not think kindly of her. Lady Blandish's encomiums of her behaviour and her beauty annoyed him. Forgetful that he had in a measure forfeited his rights to it, he took the common ground of fathers, and demanded, 'Why he was not justified in doing all that lay in his power to prevent his son from casting himself away upon the first creature with a pretty face he encountered?' Deliberating thus, he lost the tenderness he should have had for his experiment—the living, burning youth at his elbow, and his excessive love for him took a rigorous tone. It appeared to him politic, reasonable, and just, that the uncle of this young woman, who had so long nursed the prudent scheme of marrying her to his son, should not only not be thwarted in his object but encouraged and even assisted. At least, not thwarted. Sir Austin had no glass before him while these ideas hardened in his mind, and he had rather forgotten the letter of Lady Blandish.

Father and son were alone in the railway carriage. Both were too preoccupied to speak. As they neared Bellingham, the dark was filling the hollows of the country. Over the pine-hills beyond the station a last rosy streak lingered across a green sky. Richard eyed it while they flew along. It caught him forward: it seemed full of the spirit of his love, and brought tears of mournful longing to his eyelids. The sad beauty of that one spot in the heavens seemed to call out to his soul to swear to his Lucy's truth to him: was like the sorrowful visage of his fleur-de-luce,* as he called her, appealing to him for faith. That tremulous tender way she had of half-closing and catching light on the nether-lids, when sometimes she looked up in her lover's face—a look so mystic-sweet that it had grown to be the fountain of his dreams: he saw it yonder, and his blood thrilled.

Know you those wand-like touches of I know not what, before which our grosser being melts, and we, much as we hope to be in the Awaking, stand etherealized, trembling with new joy? They come but rarely; rarely even in love, when we fondly think them revelations. Mere sensations they are, doubtless: and we rank for them no higher in the spiritual scale than so many translucent glorious *polypi* that quiver on the shores, the hues of heaven running through them. Yet in the harvest of our days it is something for the animal to have had such mere fleshly polypian experiences to look back upon, and they give him an horizon—pale seas of luring splendour. One who has had them (when they do not bound him) may find the Isles of Bliss sooner than another. Sensual faith in the upper glories is something. 'Let us remember,' says THE PILGRIM'S SCRIP, 'that Nature, though heathenish, reaches at her best to the footstool of the Highest. She is not all dust, but a living portion of the spheres. In aspiration it is our error to despise

her, forgetting that through Nature only can we *ascend*.
Cherished, trained, and purified, she is then partly worthy
the divine mate who is to make her wholly so. St. Simeon*
saw the Hog in Nature, and took Nature for the Hog.'

It was one of these strange bodily exaltations which
thrilled the young man, he knew not how it was, for sadness and his forebodings vanished. The soft wand touched
him. At that moment, had Sir Austin spoken openly,
Richard might have fallen upon his heart. He could not.
He chose to feel injured on the common ground of fathers,
and to pursue his System by plotting. Lady Blandish had
revived his jealousy of the creature who menaced it, and
jealousy of a System is unreflecting and vindictive as jealousy of woman.

Heath-roots and pines breathed sharp in the cool autumn
evening about the Bellingham station. Richard stood a
moment as he stepped from the train, and drew the country
air into his lungs with large heaves of the chest. Leaving
his father to the felicitations of the station-master, he went
into the Lobourne road to look for his faithful Tom, who
had received private orders through Berry to be in attendance with his young master's mare, Cassandra, and was
lurking in a plantation of firs unenclosed on the borders
of the road, where Richard, knowing his retainer's zest for
conspiracy too well to seek him anywhere but in the part
most favoured with shelter and concealment, found him
furtively whiffing tobacco.

'What news, Tom? Is there an illness?'

Tom sent his undress cap on one side to scratch at
dilemma, an old agricultural habit to which he was still
a slave in moments of abstract thought or sudden difficulty.

'No, I don't want the rake, Mr. Richard,' he whinnied
with a false grin, as he beheld his master's eye vacantly
following the action.

'Speak out!" he was commended. 'I haven't had a letter for a week!'

Richard learnt the news. He took it with surprising outward calm, only getting a little closer to Cassandra's neck, and looking very hard at Tom without seeing a speck of him, which had the effect on Tom of making him sincerely wish his master would punch his head at once rather than fix him in that owl-like way.

'Go on!' said Richard huskily. 'Yes? She 's gone! Well?'

Tom was brought to understand he must make the most of trifles, and recited how he had heard from a female domestic at Belthorpe of the name of Davenport, formerly known to him, that the young lady never slept a wink from the hour she knew she was going, but sat up in her bed till morning crying most pitifully, though she never complained. Hereat the tears unconsciously streamed down Richard's cheeks. Tom said he had tried to see her, but Mr. Adrian kept him at work, ciphering at a terrible sum—that and nothing else all day! saying, it was to please his young master on his return. 'Likewise something in Lat'n,' added Tom. 'Nom'tive Mouser! 'nough to make ye mad, sir!' he exclaimed with pathos. The wretch had been put to acquire a Latin declension.

Tom saw her on the morning she went away, he said: she was very sorrowful-looking, and nodded kindly to him as she passed in the fly along with young Tom Blaize. 'She have got uncommon kind eyes, sir,' said Tom, 'and cryin' don't spoil them.' For which his hand was wrenched.

Tom had no more to tell, save that, in rounding the road, the young lady had hung out her hand, and seemed to move it forward and back, as much as to say, Good-bye, Tom! 'And though she couldn't see me,' said Tom, 'I took off my hat. I did take it so kind of her to think of a chap like me.' He was at high-pressure sentiment—what with his education for a hero and his master's love-stricken state.

'You saw no more of her, Tom?'

'No, sir. That was the last!'

'That was the last you saw of her, Tom?'

'Well, sir, I saw nothin' more.'

'And so she went out of sight!'

'Clean gone, that she were, sir.'

'Why did they take her away? what have they done with her? where have they taken her to?'

These red-hot questionings were addressed to the universal heaven rather than to Tom.

'Why didn't she write?' they were resumed. 'Why did she leave? She's mine. She belongs to me! Who dared take her away? Why did she leave without writing?—— Tom!'

'Yes, sir,' said the well-drilled recruit, dressing himself up to the word of command. He expected a variation of the theme from the change of tone with which his name had been pronounced, but it was again, 'Where have they taken her to?' and this was even more perplexing to Tom than his hard sum in arithmetic had been. He could only draw down the corners of his mouth hard, and glance up queerly.

'She *had* been crying—you saw that, Tom?'

'No mistake about that, Mr. Richard. Cryin' all night and all day, I sh'd say.'

'And she was crying when you saw her?'

'She look'd as if she'd just done for a moment, sir.'

'But her face was white?'

'White as a sheet.'

Richard paused to discover whether his instinct had caught a new view from these facts. He was in a cage, always knocking against the same bars, fly as he might. Her tears were the stars in his black night. He clung to them as golden orbs. Inexplicable as they were, they were at least pledges of love.

The hues of sunset had left the West. No light was there but the stedfast pale eye of twilight. Thither he was drawn. He mounted Cassandra, saying: 'Tell them something, Tom. I shan't be home to dinner,' and rode off toward the forsaken home of light over Belthorpe, wherein he saw the wan hand of his Lucy, waving farewell, receding as he advanced. His jewel was stolen,—he must gaze upon the empty box.

CHAPTER XXIII

CRISIS IN THE APPLE-DISEASE

NIGHT had come on as Richard entered the old elm-shaded, grass-bordered lane leading down from Raynham to Belthorpe. The pale eye of twilight was shut. The wind had tossed up the bank of Western cloud, which was now flying broad and unlighted across the sky, broad and balmy—the charioted South-west at full charge behind his panting coursers. As he neared the farm his heart fluttered and leapt up. He was sure she must be there. She must have returned. Why should she have left for good without writing? He caught suspicion by the throat, making it voiceless, if it lived: he silenced reason. Her not writing was now a proof that she had returned. He listened to nothing but his imperious passion, and murmured sweet words for her, as if she were by: tender cherishing epithets of love in the nest. She was there—she moved somewhere about like a silver flame in the dear old house, doing her sweet household duties. His blood began to sing: O happy those within, to see her, and be about her! By some extraordinary process he contrived to cast a sort of glory round the burly person of Farmer Blaize himself. And oh! to have companionship with a seraph one must know a seraph's bliss, and was not young Tom to be envied? The smell of late clematis brought on the wind enwrapped him, and went to his brain, and threw a light over the old red-brick house, for he remembered where it grew, and the winter rose-tree, and the jessamine, and the passion-flower: the garden in front with the standard roses tended by her hands; the long wall to the left striped by the branches of the cherry, the peep of a further garden through the wall, and then the orchard, and the fields beyond—the happy circle of her dwelling! it flashed before his eyes while he looked on the darkness. And yet it was the reverse of hope which kindled this light and inspired the momentary calm he experienced: it was despair exaggerating delusion, wilfully building up on a groundless basis. 'For the tenacity of true passion is terrible,' says THE PILGRIM'S SCRIP: 'it will stand against the hosts of heaven, God's great array of Facts, rather than surrender its aim, and must be crushed before it will succumb—sent to the lowest pit!' He knew she was not there; she was gone. But the power of a will strained to madness fought at it, kept it down, conjured forth her ghost, and would have it as he dictated. Poor youth! the great array of facts was in due order of march.

He had breathed her name many times, and once overloud; almost a cry for her escaped him. He had not noticed the opening of a door and the noise of a foot along the gravel walk. He was leaning over Cassandra's uneasy neck watching the one window intently, when a voice addressed him out of the darkness.

'Be that you, young gentleman?—Mr. Fev'rel?'

Richard's trance was broken. 'Mr. Blaize!' he said, recognizing the farmer's voice.

'Good even'n t' you, sir,' returned the farmer. 'I knew the mare though I didn't know you. Rather bluff to-night it be. Will ye step in, Mr. Fev'rel? it 's beginnin' to spit— going to be a wildish night, I reckon.'

Richard dismounted. The farmer called one of his men to hold the mare, and ushered the young man in. Once there, Richard's conjurations ceased. There was a deadness about the rooms and passages that told of her absence. The walls he touched—these were the vacant shell of her. He had never been in the house since he knew her, and now what strange sweetness, and what pangs!

Young Tom Blaize was in the parlour, squared over the table in open-mouthed examination of an ancient book of the fashions for a summer month which had elapsed during his mother's minority. Young Tom was respectfully studying the aspects of the radiant beauties of the polite work. He also was a thrall of woman, newly enrolled, and full of wonder.

'What, Tom!' the farmer sang out as soon as he had opened the door; 'there ye be! at yer Folly agin, are ye? What good 'll them fashens do to you, I 'd like t' know? Come, shut up, and go and see to Mr. Fev'rel's mare. He 's al'ays at that ther' Folly now. I say there never were a better name for a book than that ther' Folly! Talk about attitudes!'

The farmer laughed his fat sides into a chair, and motioned his visitor to do likewise.

'It 's a comfort they 're most on 'em females,' he pursued, sounding a thwack on his knee as he settled himself agreeably in his seat. 'It don't matter much what they does, except pinchin' in—waspin' it—at the waist. Give me nature, I say—woman as she 's made! eh, young gentleman?'

'You seem very lonely here,' said Richard, glancing round, and at the ceiling.

'Lonely?' quoth the farmer. 'Well, for the matter o' that, we be!—jest now, so 't happens; I 've got my pipe, and Tom 've got his Folly. He 's on one side the table, and I 'm on t'other. He gaapes, and I gazes. We are a bit lonesome. But there—it 's *for* the best!'

Richard resumed, 'I hardly expected to see you to-night, Mr. Blaize.'

'Y' acted like a man in coming, young gentleman, and I does ye honour for it!' said Farmer Blaize, with sudden energy and directness.

The thing implied by the farmer's words caused Richard to take a quick breath. They looked at each other, and looked away, the farmer thrumming on the arm of his chair.

Above the mantel-piece, surrounded by tarnished indifferent miniatures of high-collared, well-to-do yeomen of the anterior generation, trying their best not to grin, and high-waisted old ladies smiling an encouraging smile through plentiful cap-puckers, there hung a passably executed half-figure of a naval officer in uniform, grasping a telescope under his left arm, who stood forth clearly as not of their kith and kin. His eyes were blue, his hair light, his bearing that of a man who knows how to carry his head and shoulders. The artist, while giving him an epaulette to indicate his rank, had also recorded the juvenility which a lieutenant in the naval service can retain after arriving at that position, by painting him with smooth cheeks and fresh ruddy lips. To this portrait Richard's eyes were directed. Farmer Blaize observed it, and said—

'Her father, sir!'

Richard moderated his voice to praise the likeness.

'Yes,' said the farmer, 'pretty well. Next best to havin' *her*, though it's a long way off that!'

'An old family, Mr. Blaize—is it not?' Richard asked, in as careless a tone as he could assume.

'Gentlefolks—what's left of 'em,' replied the farmer with an equally affected indifference.

'And that's her father?' said Richard, growing bolder to speak of her.

'That's her father, young gentleman!'

'Mr. Blaize,' Richard turned to face him, and burst out, 'where is she?'

'Gone, sir! packed off!—Can't have her here now.' The farmer thrummed a step brisker, and eyed the young man's wild face resolutely.

'Mr. Blaize,' Richard leaned forward to get closer to him. He was stunned, and hardly aware of what he was saying or doing: 'Where has she gone? Why did she leave?'

'You needn't to ask, sir—ye know,' said the farmer, with a side shot of his head.

'But *she* did not—it was not her wish to go?'

'No! I think she likes the place. Mayhap she likes 't too well!'

'Why did you send her away to make her unhappy, Mr. Blaize?'

The farmer bluntly denied it was he was the party who made her unhappy. 'Nobody can't accuse *me*. Tell ye what, sir. I wunt have the busybodies set to work about her, and there 's all the matter. So let you and I come to an understandin'.'

A blind inclination to take offence made Richard sit upright. He forgot it the next minute, and said humbly: 'Am I the cause of her going?'

'Well!' returned the farmer, 'to speak straight—ye be!'

'What can I do, Mr. Blaize, that she may come back again?' the young hypocrite asked.

'Now,' said the farmer, 'you 're coming to business. Glad to hear ye talk in that sensible way, Mr. Fev'rel. You may guess I wants her bad enough. The house ain't itself now she 's away, and I ain't myself. Well, sir! This ye can do. If you gives me your promise not to meddle with her at all—I can't mak' out how you come to be acquainted; not to try to get her to be meetin' you—and if you 'd 'a seen her when she left, you would—when did ye meet?— last grass, wasn't it?—your word as a gentleman not to be writing letters, and spyin' after her—I 'll have her back at once. Back she shall come!'

'Give her up!' cried Richard.

'Ay, that 's it!' said the farmer. 'Give her up.'

The young man checked the annihilation of time that was on his mouth.

'You sent her away to protect her from me, then?' he said savagely.

'That 's not quite it, but that 'll do,' rejoined the farmer.

'Do you think I shall harm her, sir?'

'People seem to think she 'll harm you, young gentleman,' the farmer said with some irony.

'Harm *me*—she? What people?'

'People pretty intimate with you, sir.'

'What people? Who spoke of us?' Richard began to scent a plot, and would not be baulked.

'Well, sir, look here,' said the farmer. 'It ain't no secret, and if it be, I don't see why I 'm to keep it. It appears your education 's peculiar!' The farmer drawled out the word as if he were describing the figure of a snake. 'You ain't to be as other young gentlemen. All the better! You 're a fine bold young gentleman, and your father 's a right to be proud of ye. Well, sir—I'm sure I thank him for 't—he comes to hear of you and Luce, and of course he don't want nothin' o' that—more do I. I meets him there! What 's more I won't have nothin' of it. She be my gal. She were left to my protection. And she 's a lady, sir. Let me tell ye, ye won't find many on 'em so well looked to as she be—my Luce! Well, Mr. Fev'rel, it 's you, or it 's her—one of ye must be out o' the way. So we 're told. And Luce—I do believe she 's just as anxious about yer education as yer father—she says she 'll go, and wouldn't write, and 'd break it off for the sake o' your education. And she 've kep' her word, haven't she?— She 's a true 'n. What she says she 'll do!—True blue she be, my Luce! So now, sir, you do the same, and I 'll thank ye.'

Any one who has tossed a sheet of paper into the fire, and seen it gradually brown with heat, and strike to flame, may conceive the mind of the lover as he listened to this speech.

His anger did not evaporate in words, but condensed and sank deep. 'Mr. Blaize,' he said, 'this is very kind of the people you allude to, but I am of an age now to think and act for myself—I love her, sir!' His whole countenance changed, and the muscles of his face quivered.

'Well!' said the farmer, appeasingly, 'we all do at your age—somebody or other. It 's natural!'

'I love her!' the young man thundered afresh, too much possessed by his passion to have a sense of shame in the confession. 'Farmer!' his voice fell to supplication, 'will you bring her back?'

Farmer Blaize made a queer face. He asked—what for? and where was the promise required?—But was not the lover's argument conclusive? He said he loved her! and he could not see why her uncle should not in consequence immediately send for her, that they might be together. All very well, quoth the farmer, but what 's to come of it?— What was to come of it? Why, love, and more love! And a bit too much! the farmer added grimly.

'Then you refuse me, farmer,' said Richard. 'I must look to you for keeping her away from me, not to—to— these people. You will not have her back, though I tell you I love her better than my life?'

Farmer Blaize now had to answer him plainly, he had a reason and an objection of his own. And it was, that her character was at stake, and God knew whether she herself might not be in danger. He spoke with a kindly candour, not without dignity. He complimented Richard personally, but young people were young people; baronets' sons were not in the habit of marrying farmers' nieces.

At first the son of a System did not comprehend him. When he did, he said: 'Farmer! if I give you my word of honour, as I hope for heaven, to marry her when I am of age, will you have her back?'

He was so fervid that, to quiet him, the farmer only shook his head doubtfully at the bars of the grate, and let his chest fall slowly. Richard caught what seemed to him a glimpse of encouragement in these signs, and observed: 'It's not because you object to me, Mr. Blaize?'

The farmer signified it was not that.

'It's because my father is against me,' Richard went on, and undertook to show that love was so sacred a matter that no father could entirely and for ever resist his son's inclinations. Argument being a cool field where the farmer could meet and match him, the young man got on the tramroad of his passion, and went ahead. He drew pictures of Lucy, of her truth, and his own. He took leaps from life to death, from death to life, mixing imprecations and prayers in a torrent. Perhaps he did move the stolid old Englishman a little, he was so vehement, and made so visible a sacrifice of his pride.

Farmer Blaize tried to pacify him, but it was useless. His jewel he must have.

The farmer stretched out his hand for the pipe that allayeth botheration. 'May smoke heer now,' he said. 'Not when—somebody's present. Smoke in the kitchen then. Don't mind smell?'

Richard nodded, and watched the operations while the farmer filled, and lighted and began to puff, as if his fate hung on them.

'Who'd a' thought, when you sat over there once, of its comin' to this?' ejaculated the farmer, drawing ease and reflection from tobacco. 'You didn't think much of her that day, young gentleman! I introduced ye. Well! things comes about. Can't you wait till she returns in due course, now?'

This suggestion, the work of the pipe, did but bring on him another torrent.

'It's queer,' said the farmer, putting the mouth of the pipe to his wrinkled-up temples.

Richard waited for him, and then he laid down the pipe altogether, as no aid in perplexity, and said, after leaning his arm on the table and staring at Richard an instant:

'Look, young gentleman! My word's gone. I've spoke it. I've given 'em the 'surance she shan't be back till the Spring, and then I'll have her, and then—well! I do hope, for more reasons than one, ye'll both be wiser—I've got my own notions about her. But I an't the man to force a gal to marry 'gainst her inclines. Depend upon it I'm not your enemy, Mr. Fev'rel. You're jest the one to mak' a young gal proud. So wait,—and see. That's my 'dvice. Jest tak' and wait. I've no more to say.'

Richard's impetuosity had made him really afraid of speaking his notions concerning the projected felicity of young Tom, if indeed they were serious.

The farmer repeated that he had no more to say; and Richard, with 'Wait till the Spring! Wait till the Spring!' dinning despair in his ears, stood up to depart. Farmer Blaize shook his slack hand in a friendly way, and called out at the door for young Tom, who, dreading allusions to his Folly, did not appear. A maid rushed by Richard in the passage, and slipped something into his grasp, which fixed on it without further consciousness than that of touch. The mare was led forth by the Bantam. A light rain was falling down strong warm gusts, and the trees were noisy in the night. Farmer Blaize requested Richard at the gate to give him his hand, and say all was well. He liked the young man for his earnestness and honest outspeaking. Richard could not say all was well, but he gave his hand, and knitted it to the farmer's in a sharp squeeze, when he got upon Cassandra, and rode into the tumult.

A calm, clear dawn succeeded the roaring West, and threw its glowing grey image on the waters of the Abbey-lake. Before sunrise Tom Bakewell was abroad, and met the missing youth, his master, jogging Cassandra leisurely along the Lobourne park-road, a sorry couple to look at. Cassandra's flanks were caked with mud, her head drooped: all that was in her had been taken out by that wild night. On what heaths and heavy fallows had she not spent her noble strength, recklessly fretting through the darkness!

'Take the mare,' said Richard, dismounting and patting her between the eyes. 'She's done up, poor old gal! Look to her, Tom, and then come to me in my room.'

Tom asked no questions.

Three days would bring the anniversary of Richard's birth, and though Tom was close, the condition of the mare, and the young gentleman's strange freak in riding her out all night becoming known, prepared everybody at Raynham for the usual bad-luck birthday, the prophets of which were full of sad gratification. Sir Austin had an unpleasant office to require of his son; no other than that of humbly begging Benson's pardon, and washing out the undue blood he had spilt in taking his Pound of Flesh. Heavy Benson was told to anticipate the demand for pardon, and practised in his mind the most melancholy Christian deportment he could assume on the occasion. But while his son was in this state, Sir Austin considered that he would hardly be brought to see the virtues of the act, and did not make the requisition of him, and heavy Benson remained drawn up solemnly expectant at doorways, and at the foot of the staircase, a Saurian Caryatid, wherever he could get a step in advance of the young man, while Richard heedlessly passed him, as he passed everybody else, his head bent to the ground, and his legs bearing him like random instruments of whose service he was unconscious. It was a shock to Benson's implicit belief in his patron; and he was not consoled by the philosophic explanation, 'That Good in a strong many-compounded nature is of slower growth than any other mortal thing, and must not be forced.' Damnatory doctrines best pleased Benson. He was ready to pardon, as a Christian should, but he did want his enemy before him on his knees. And now, though the Saurian Eye saw more than all the other eyes in the house, and saw that there was matter in hand between Tom and his master to breed exceeding discomposure to the System, Benson, as he had not received his indemnity, and did not wish to encounter fresh perils for nothing, held his peace.

Sir Austin partly divined what was going on in the breast of his son, without conceiving the depths of distrust his son cherished or quite measuring the intensity of the passion that consumed him. He was very kind and tender with him. Like a cunning physician who has, nevertheless, overlooked the change in the disease superinduced by one false dose, he meditated his prescriptions carefully and confidently, sure that he knew the case, and was a match for it. He decreed that Richard's erratic behaviour should pass unnoticed. Two days before the birthday, he asked him whether he would object to having company? To which Richard said: 'Have whom you will, sir.' The preparation for festivity commenced accordingly.

On the birthday eve he dined with the rest. Lady Blandish was there, and sat penitently at his right. Hippias prognosticated certain indigestion for himself on the morrow. The Eighteenth Century wondered whether she should live to see another birthday. Adrian drank the two-years' distant term of his tutorship, and Algernon went over the list of the Lobourne men who would cope with Bursley on the morrow. Sir Austin gave ear and a word to all, keeping his mental eye for his son. To please Lady Blandish also, Adrian ventured to make trifling jokes about London's

Mrs. Grandison; jokes delicately not decent, but so delicately so, that it was not decent to perceive it.

After dinner Richard left them. Nothing more than commonly peculiar was observed about him, beyond the excessive glitter of his eyes, but the baronet said, 'Yes, yes! that will pass.' He and Adrian, and Lady Blandish, took tea in the library, and sat till a late hour discussing casuistries relating mostly to the Apple-disease. Converse very amusing to the wise youth, who could suggest to the two chaste minds situations of the shadiest character, with the air of a seeker after truth, and lead them, unsuspecting, where they dared not look about them. The Aphorist had elated the heart of his constant fair worshipper with a newly rounded, if not newly-conceived sentence, when they became aware that they were four. Heavy Benson stood among them. He said he had knocked, but received no answer. There was, however, a vestige of surprise and dissatisfaction on his face beholding Adrian of the company, which had not quite worn away, and gave place, when it did vanish, to an aspect of flabby severity.

'Well, Benson? well?' said the baronet.

The unmoving man replied: 'If you please, Sir Austin— Mr. Richard!'

'Well!'

'He's out!'

'Well?'

'With Bakewell!'

'Well?'

'And a carpet-bag!'

The carpet-bag might be supposed to contain that funny thing called a young hero's romance in the making.

Out Richard was, and with a carpet-bag, which Tom Bakewell carried. He was on the road to Bellingham, under heavy rain, hasting like an escaped captive, wild with joy, while Tom shook his skin, and grunted at his discomforts. The mail train was to be caught at Bellingham. He knew where to find her now, through the intervention of Miss Davenport, and thither he was flying, an arrow loosed from the bow: thither, in spite of fathers and friends and plotters, to claim her, and take her, and stand with her against the world.

They were both thoroughly wet when they entered Bellingham, and Tom's visions were of hot drinks. He hinted the necessity for inward consolation to his master, who could answer nothing but 'Tom! Tom! I shall see her tomorrow!' It was bad—travelling in the wet, Tom hinted again, to provoke the same insane outcry, and have his arm seized and furiously shaken into the bargain. Passing the principal inn of the place, Tom spoke plainly for brandy.

'No!' cried Richard, 'there's not a moment to be lost!' and as he said it, he reeled, and fell against Tom, muttering indistinctly of faintness, and that there was no time to lose. Tom lifted him in his arms, and got admission to the inn. Brandy, the country's specific, was advised by host and hostess, and forced into his mouth, reviving him sufficiently to cry out, 'Tom! the bell's ringing: we shall be late,' after which he fell back insensible on the sofa where they had stretched him. Excitement of blood and brain had done its work upon him. The youth suffered them to undress him and put him to bed, and there he lay, forgetful even of love; a drowned weed borne onward by the tide of the hours. There his father found him.

Was the Scientific Humanist remorseful? He had looked forward to such a crisis as that point in the disease his son was the victim of, when the body would fail and give the spirit calm to conquer the malady, knowing very well that the seeds of the evil were not of the spirit. Moreover, to see him and have him was a repose after the alarm Benson had sounded. 'Mark!' he said to Lady Blandish, 'when he recovers he will not care for her.'

The lady had accompanied him to the Bellingham inn on first hearing of Richard's seizure.

'What an iron man you can be,' she exclaimed, smothering her intuitions. She was for giving the boy his bauble; promising it him, at least, if he would only get well and be the bright flower of promise he once was.

'Can you look on him,' she pleaded, 'can you look on him and persevere?'

It was a hard sight for this man who loved his son so deeply. The youth lay in his strange bed, straight and motionless, with fever on his cheeks and altered eyes.

Old Dr. Clifford of Lobourne was the medical attendant, who, with head-shaking, and gathering of lips, and reminiscences of ancient arguments, guaranteed to do all that leech could do in the matter. The old doctor did admit that Richard's constitution was admirable, and answered to his prescriptions like a piano to the musician. 'But,' he said at a family consultation, for Sir Austin had told him how it stood with the young man, 'drugs are not much in cases of this sort. Change! That's what's wanted, and as soon as may be. Distraction! He ought to see the world, and know what he is made of. It's no use my talking, I know,' added the doctor.

'On the contrary,' said Sir Austin, 'I am quite of your persuasion. And the world he shall see—now.'

'We have dipped him in Styx, you know, doctor,' Adrian remarked.

'But, doctor,' said Lady Blandish, 'have you known a case of this sort before?'

'Never, my lady,' said the doctor, 'they're not common in these parts. Country people are tolerably healthy-minded.'

'But people—and country people—have died for love, doctor?'

The doctor had not met any of them.

'Men or women?' inquired the baronet.

Lady Blandish believed mostly women.

'Ask the doctor whether they were healthy-minded women,' said the baronet. 'No! you are both looking at the wrong end. Between a highly-cultured being, and an emotionless animal, there is all the difference in the world. But of the two, the doctor is nearer the truth. The healthy nature is pretty safe. If he allowed for organization he would be right altogether. To feel, but not to feel to excess, that is the problem.'

> 'If I can't have the one I chose,
> To some fresh maid I will propose,'

Adrian hummed a country ballad.

CHAPTER XXIV

OF THE SPRING PRIMROSE AND THE AUTUMNAL

WHEN the young Experiment again knew the hours that rolled him onward, he was in his own room at Raynham. Nothing had changed: only a strong fist had knocked him down and stunned him, and he opened his eyes to a grey world: he had forgotten what he lived for. He was weak and thin, and with a pale memory of things. His functions were the same, everything surrounding him was the same: he looked upon the old blue hills, the far-lying fallows, the river, and the woods: he knew them, they seemed to have lost recollection of him. Nor could he find in familiar human faces the secret of intimacy of heretofore. They were the same faces: they nodded and smiled to him. What was lost he could not tell. Something had been knocked out of him! He was sensible of his father's sweetness of manner, and he was grieved that he could not reply to it, for every sense of shame and reproach had strangely gone. He felt very useless. In place of the fiery love for one, he now bore about a cold charity to all.

Thus in the heart of the young man died the Spring Primrose, and while it died another heart was pushing forth the Primrose of Autumn.

The wonderful change in Richard, and the wisdom of her admirer, now positively proved, were exciting matters to Lady Blandish. She was rebuked for certain little rebellious fancies concerning him that had come across her enslaved mind from time to time. For was he not almost a prophet? It distressed the sentimental lady that a love like Richard's could pass off in mere smoke, and words such as she had heard him speak in Abbey-wood resolve to emptiness. Nay, it humiliated her personally, and the baronet's shrewd prognostication humiliated her. For how should he know, and dare to say, that love was a thing of the dust that could be trodden out under the heel of science? But he had said so, and he had proved himself right. She heard with wonderment that Richard of his own accord had spoken to his father of the folly he had been guilty of, and had begged his pardon. The baronet told her this, adding that the youth had done it in a cold unwavering way, without a movement of his features: had evidently done it to throw off the burden of the duty he had conceived. He had thought himself bound to acknowledge that he had been the Foolish Young Fellow, wishing, possibly, to abjure the fact by an act of penance. He had also given satisfaction to Benson, and was become a renovated peaceful spirit, whose main object appeared to be to get up his physical strength by exercise and no expenditure of speech.

In her company he was composed and courteous; even when they were alone together he did not exhibit a trace

of melancholy. Sober he seemed, as one who has recovered
from a drunkenness and has determined to drink no more.
The idea struck her that he might be playing a part, but
Tom Bakewell, in a private conversation they had, informed her that he had received an order from his young
master, one day while boxing with him, not to mention the
young lady's name to him as long as he lived; and Tom
could only suppose that she had offended him. Theoreti-
cally wise Lady Blandish had always thought the baronet;
she was unprepared to find him thus practically sagacious.
She fell many degrees; she wanted something to cling to;
so she clung to the man who struck her low. Love, then,
was earthly; its depths could be probed by science! A
man lived who could measure it from end to end; foretell
its term; handle the young cherub as were he a shot owl!
We who have flown into cousinship with the empyrean,
and disported among immortal hosts, our base birth as a
child of Time is made bare to us!—our wings are cut! Oh,
then, if science is this victorious enemy of love, let us love
science! was the logic of the lady's heart; and secretly
cherishing the assurance that she should confute him yet,
and prove him utterly wrong, she gave him the fruits of
present success, as it is a habit of women to do; involuntarily partly. The fires took hold of her. She felt soft
emotions such as a girl feels, and they flattered her. It
was like youth coming back. Pure women have a second
youth. The Autumn primrose flourished.

We are advised by THE PILGRIM'S SCRIP that—
'The ways of women, which are Involution, and their
practices, which are Opposition, are generally best hit upon
by guesswork, and a bold word';—it being impossible to
track them and hunt them down in the ordinary style.

So that we may not ourselves become involved and opposed, let us each of us venture a guess and say a bold word
as to how it came that the lady, who trusted love to be

eternal, grovelled to him that shattered her tender faith, and loved him.

Hitherto it had been simply a sentimental dalliance, and gossips had maligned the lady. Just when the gossips grew tired of their slander, and inclined to look upon her charitably, she set about to deserve every word they had said of her; which may instruct us, if you please, that gossips have only to persist in lying to be crowned with verity, or that one has only to endure evil mouths for a period to gain impunity. She was always at the Abbey now. She was much closeted with the baronet. It seemed to be understood that she had taken Mrs. Doria's place. Benson in his misogynic soul perceived that she was taking Lady Feverel's: but any report circulated by Benson was sure to meet discredit, and drew the gossips upon himself; which made his meditations tragic. No sooner was one woman defeated than another took the field! The object of the System was no sooner safe than its great author was in danger!

'I can't think what has come to Benson,' he said to Adrian.

'He seems to have received a fresh legacy of several pounds of lead,' returned the wise youth, and imitating Dr. Clifford's manner. 'Change is what he wants! distraction! send him to Wales for a month, sir, and let Richard go with him. The two victims of woman may do each other good.'

'Unfortunately I can't do without him,' said the baronet.

'Then we must continue to have him on our shoulders all day, and on our chests all night!' Adrian ejaculated.

'I think while he preserves this aspect we won't have him at the dinner-table,' said the baronet.

Adrian thought that would be a relief to their digestions; and added: 'You know, sir, what he says?'

Receiving a negative, Adrian delicately explained to him

that Benson's excessive ponderosity of demeanour was
caused by anxiety for the safety of his master.

'You must pardon a faithful fool, sir,' he continued, for
the baronet became red, and exclaimed:

'His stupidity is past belief! I have absolutely to bolt
my study-door against him.'

Adrian at once beheld a charming scene in the interior
of the study, not unlike one that Benson had visually witnessed. For, like a wary prophet, Benson, that he might
have warrant for what he foretold of the future, had a care
to spy upon the present: warned haply by THE PILGRIM'S
SCRIP, of which he was a diligent reader, and which says,
rather emphatically: 'Could we see Time's full face, we
were wise of him.' Now to see Time's full face, it is sometimes necessary to look through keyholes, the veteran having a trick of smiling peace to you on one cheek and grimacing confusion on the other behind the curtain. Decency
and a sense of honour restrain most of us from being thus
wise and miserable for ever. Benson's excuse was that he
believed in his master, who was menaced. And moreover,
notwithstanding his previous tribulation, to spy upon
Cupid was sweet to him. So he peeped, and he saw a sight.
He saw Time's full face; or, in other words, he saw the wiles
of woman and the weakness of man: which is our history, as
Benson would have written it, and a great many poets and
philosophers have written it.

Yet it was but the plucking of the Autumn primrose that
Benson had seen: a somewhat different operation from the
plucking of the Spring one: very innocent! Our staid
elderly sister has paler blood, and has, or thinks she has,
a reason or two about the roots. She is not all instinct.
'For this high cause, and for that I know men, and know
him to be the flower of men, I give myself to him!' She
makes that lofty inward exclamation while the hand is
detaching her from the roots. Even so strong a self-justi-

fication she requires. She has not that blind glory in excess which her younger sister can gild the longest leap with. And if, moth-like, she desires the star, she is nervously cautious of candles. Hence her circles about the dangerous human flame are wide and shy. She must be drawn nearer and nearer by a fresh *reason*. She loves to sentimentalize. Lady Blandish had been sentimentalizing for ten years. She would have preferred to pursue the game. The dark-eyed dame was pleased with her smooth life and the soft excitement that did not ruffle it. Not willingly did she let herself be won.

'Sentimentalists,' says THE PILGRIM'S SCRIP, 'are they who seek to enjoy without incurring the Immense Debtorship for a thing done.'

'It is,' the writer says of Sentimentalism elsewhere, 'a happy pastime and an important science to the timid, the idle, and the heartless; but a damning one to them who have anything to forfeit.'

However, one who could set down the dying for love, as a sentimentalism, can hardly be accepted as a clear authority. Assuredly he was not one to avoid the incurring of the immense debtorship in any way: but he was a bondman still to the woman who had forsaken him, and a spoken word would have made it seem his duty to face that public scandal which was the last evil to him. What had so horrified the virtuous Benson, Richard had already beheld in Daphne's Bower; a simple kissing of the fair white hand! Doubtless the keyhole somehow added to Benson's horror. The two similar performances, so very innocent, had wondrous opposite consequences. The first kindled Richard to adore Woman; the second destroyed Benson's faith in Man. But Lady Blandish knew the difference between the two. She understood why the baronet did not speak; excused, and respected him for it. She was content, since she must love, to love humbly, and she had, besides, her pity for his

sorrows to comfort her. A hundred fresh reasons for loving
him arose and multiplied every day. He read to her the
secret book in his own handwriting, composed for Richard's
Marriage Guide: containing Advice and Directions to a
Young Husband, full of the most tender wisdom and delicacy; so she thought; nay, not wanting in poetry, though
neither rhymed nor measured. He expounded to her the
distinctive character of the divers ages of love, giving the
palm to the flower she put forth, over that of Spring, or
the Summer rose. And while they sat and talked, 'My
wound has healed,' he said. 'How?' she asked. 'At the
fountain of your eyes,' he replied, and drew the joy of new
life from her blushes, without incurring further debtorship
for a thing done.

CHAPTER XXV

IN WHICH THE HERO TAKES A STEP

LET it be some apology for the damage caused by the
careering hero, and a consolation to the quiet wretches,
dragged along with him at his chariot-wheels, that he is
generally the last to know when he has made an actual
start; such a mere creature is he, like the rest of us, albeit
the head of our fates. By this you perceive the true hero,
whether he be a prince or a pot-boy, that he does not plot;
Fortune does all for him. He may be compared to one to
whom, in an electric circle, it is given to carry the *battery*.
We caper and grimace at his will; yet not his the will, not
his the power. 'Tis all Fortune's, whose puppet he is. She
deals her dispensations through him. Yea, though our
capers be never so comical, he laughs not. Intent upon his
own business, the true hero asks little services of us here

and there; thinks it quite natural that they should be acceded to, and sees nothing ridiculous in the lamentable contortions we must go through to fulfil them. Probably he is the elect of Fortune, because of that notable faculty of being intent upon his own business: 'Which is,' says THE PILGRIM'S SCRIP, 'with men to be valued equal to that force which in water *makes a stream.*' This prelude was necessary to the present chapter of Richard's history.

It happened that in the turn of the year, and while old earth was busy with her flowers, the fresh wind blew, the little bird sang, and Hippias Feverel, the Dyspepsy, amazed, felt the Spring move within him. He communicated his delightful new sensations to the baronet, his brother, whose constant exclamation with regard to him, was: 'Poor Hippias! All his machinery is bare!' and had no hope that he would ever be in a condition to defend it from view. Nevertheless Hippias had that hope, and so he told his brother, making great exposure of his machinery to effect the explanation. He spoke of all his physical experiences exultingly, and with wonder. The achievement of common efforts, not usually blazoned, he celebrated as triumphs, and, of course, had Adrian on his back very quickly. But he could bear him, or anything, now. It was such ineffable relief to find himself looking out upon the world of mortals instead of into the black phantasmal abysses of his own complicated frightful structure. 'My mind doesn't so much seem to haunt itself, now,' said Hippias, nodding shortly and peering out of intense puckers to convey a glimpse of what hellish sufferings his had been: 'I feel as if I had come aboveground.'

A poor Dyspepsy may talk as he will, but he is the one who never gets sympathy, or experiences compassion: and it is he whose groaning petitions for charity do at last rout that Christian virtue. Lady Blandish, a charitable soul, could not listen to Hippias, though she had a heart for little mice and flies, and Sir Austin had also small patience with his brother's gleam of health, which was just enough to make his disease visible. He remembered his early follies and excesses, and bent his ear to him as one man does to another who complains of having to pay a debt legally incurred.

'I think,' said Adrian, seeing how the communications of Hippias were received, 'that when our Nemesis takes lodgings in the stomach, it 's best to act the Spartan, smile hard, and be silent.'

Richard alone was decently kind to Hippias; whether from opposition, or real affection, could not be said, as the young man was mysterious. He advised his uncle to take exercise, walked with him, cultivated cheerful impressions in him, and pointed out innocent pursuits. He made Hippias visit with him some of the poor old folk of the village, who bewailed the loss of his cousin Austin Wentworth, and did his best to waken him up, and give the outer world a stronger hold on him. He succeeded in nothing but in winning his uncle's gratitude. The season bloomed scarce longer than a week for Hippias, and then began to languish. The poor Dyspepsy's eager grasp at beatification relaxed: he went underground again. He announced that he felt 'spongy things'—one of the more constant throes of his malady. His bitter face recurred: he chewed the cud of horrid hallucinations. He told Richard he must give up going about with him: people telling of their ailments made him so uncomfortable—the birds were so noisy, pairing— the rude bare soil sickened him.

Richard treated him with a gravity equal to his father's. He asked what the doctors said.

'Oh! the doctors!' cried Hippias with vehement scepticism. 'No man of sense believes in medicine for chronic disorder. Do you happen to have heard of any new remedy

then, Richard? No? They advertize a great many cures
for indigestion, I assure you, my dear boy. I wonder
whether one can rely upon the authenticity of those signatures? I see no reason why there should be *no* cure for
such a disease?—Eh? And it's just one of the things a
quack, as they call them, would hit upon sooner than one
who is in the beaten track. Do you know, Richard, my
dear boy, I've often thought that if we could by any means
appropriate to our use some of the extraordinary digestive
power that a boa constrictor has in his gastric juices, there is
really no manner of reason why we should not comfortably
dispose of as much of an ox as our stomachs will hold, and
one might eat French dishes without the wretchedness of
thinking what's to follow. And this makes me think that
those fellows *may*, after all, have got some truth in them:
some secret that, of course, they require to be paid for. We
distrust each other in this world too much, Richard. I've
felt inclined once or twice—but it's absurd!—If it only
alleviated a few of my sufferings *I* should be satisfied. I've
no hesitation in saying that I should be quite satisfied if it
only did away with one or two, and left me free to eat and
drink as other people do. Not that I mean to try them.
It's only a fancy—Eh? What a thing health is, my dear
boy! Ah! if I were like you! I was in love once!'

'Were you!' said Richard, coolly regarding him.

'I've forgotten what I felt!' Hippias sighed. 'You've
very much improved, my dear boy.'

'So people say,' quoth Richard.

Hippias looked at him anxiously: 'If I go to town and
get the doctor's opinion about trying a new course—Eh,
Richard? will you come with me? I should like your company. We could see London together, you know. Enjoy
ourselves,' and Hippias rubbed his hands.

Richard smiled at the feeble glimmer of enjoyment promised by his uncle's eyes, and said he thought it better they

should stay where they were—an answer that might mean anything. Hippias immediately became possessed by the beguiling project. He went to the baronet, and put the matter before him, instancing doctors as the object of his journey, not quacks, of course; and requesting leave to take Richard. Sir Austin was getting uneasy about his son's manner. It was not natural. His heart seemed to be frozen: he had no confidences: he appeared to have no ambition—to have lost the virtues of youth with the poison that had passed out of him. He was disposed to try what effect a little travelling might have on him, and had himself once or twice hinted to Richard that it would be good for him to move about, the young man quietly replying that he did not wish to quit Raynham at all, which was too strict a fulfilment of his father's original views in educating him there entirely. On the day that Hippias made his proposal, Adrian, seconded by Lady Blandish, also made one. The sweet Spring season stirred in Adrian as well as in others: not to pastoral measures: to the joys of the operatic world and bravura glories. He also suggested that it would be advisable to carry Richard to town for a term, and let him know his position, and some freedom. Sir Austin weighed the two proposals. He was pretty certain that Richard's passion was consumed, and that the youth was now only under the burden of its ashes. He had found against his heart, at the Bellingham inn: a great lock of golden hair. He had taken it, and the lover, after feeling about for it with faint hands, never asked for it. This precious lock (Miss Davenport had thrust it into his hand at Belthorpe as Lucy's last gift), what sighs and tears it had weathered! The baronet laid it in Richard's sight one day, and beheld him take it up, turn it over, and drop it down again calmly, as if he were handling any common curiosity. It pacified him on that score. The young man's love was dead. Dr. Clifford said rightly: he wanted dis-

tractions. The baronet determined that Richard should go.
Hippias and Adrian then pressed their several suits as to
which should have him. Hippias, when he could forget
himself, did not lack sense. He observed that Adrian was
not at present a proper companion for Richard, and would
teach him to look on life from the false point.

'You don't understand a young philosopher,' said the
baronet.

'A young philosopher 's an old fool!' returned Hippias,
not thinking that his growl had begotten a phrase.

His brother smiled with gratification, and applauded him
loudly: 'Excellent! worthy of your best days! You 're
wrong, though, in applying it to Adrian. He has never
been precocious. All he has done has been to bring sound
common sense to bear upon what he hears and sees. I think,
however,' the baronet added, 'he may want faith in the
better qualities of men.' And this reflection inclined him
not to let his son be alone with Adrian. He gave Richard
his choice, who saw which way his father's wishes tended,
and decided so to please him. Naturally it annoyed Adrian
extremely. He said to his chief:

'I suppose you know what you are doing, sir. I don't
see that we derive any advantage from the family name
being made notorious for twenty years of obscene suffering,
and becoming a byword for our constitutional tendency
to stomachic distension before we fortunately encountered
Quackem's Pill. My uncle's tortures have been huge, but
I would rather society were not intimate with them under
their several headings.' Adrian enumerated some of the
most abhorrent. 'You know him, sir. If he conceives a
duty, he will do it in the face of every decency—all the
more obstinate because the conception is rare. If he feels a
little brisk the morning after the pill, he sends the letter
that makes us famous! We go down to posterity with
heightened characteristics, to say nothing of a contem-

porary celebrity nothing less than our being turned inside-out to the rabble. I confess I don't desire to have my machinery made bare to them.'

Sir Austin assured the wise youth that Hippias had arranged to go to Dr. Bairam. He softened Adrian's chagrin by telling him that in about two weeks they would follow to London: hinting also at a prospective Summer campaign. The day was fixed for Richard to depart, and the day came. Madame the Eighteenth Century called him to her chamber and put into his hand a fifty-pound note, as her contribution toward his pocket-expenses. He did not want it, he said, but she told him he was a young man, and would soon make that fly when he stood on his own feet. The old lady did not at all approve of the System in her heart, and she gave her grand-nephew to understand that, should he require more, he knew where to apply, and secrets would be kept. His father presented him with a hundred pounds—which also Richard said he did not want—he did not care for money. 'Spend it or not,' said the baronet, perfectly secure in him.

Hippias had few injunctions to observe. They were to take up quarters at the hotel, Algernon's general run of company at the house not being altogether wholesome. The baronet particularly forewarned Hippias of the imprudence of attempting to restrict the young man's movements, and letting him imagine he was under surveillance. Richard having been, as it were, pollarded by despotism, was now to grow up straight, and bloom again, in complete independence, as far as he could feel. So did the sage decree; and we may pause a moment to reflect how wise were his previsions, and how successful they must have been, had not Fortune, the great foe to human cleverness, turned against him, or he against himself.

The departure took place on a fine March morning. The bird of Winter sang from the budding tree; in the blue sky

sang the bird of Summer. Adrian rode between Richard and
Hippias to the Bellingham station, and vented his disgust
on them after his own humorous fashion, because it did not
rain and damp their ardour. In the rear came Lady Blandish and the baronet, conversing on the calm summit of
success.

'You have shaped him exactly to resemble yourself,' she
said, pointing with her riding-whip to the grave stately
figure of the young man.

'Outwardly, perhaps,' he answered, and led to a discussion on Purity and Strength, the lady saying that she
preferred Purity.

'But you do not,' said the baronet. 'And there I admire the always true instinct of women, that they *all* worship Strength in whatever form, and seem to know it to be
the child of heaven; whereas Purity is but a characteristic,
a garment, and can be spotted—how soon! For there are
questions in this life with which we must grapple or be
lost, and when, hunted by that cold eye of intense inner-
consciousness, the clearest soul becomes a cunning fox, if it
have not courage to stand and do battle. Strength indicates
a boundless nature—like the Maker. Strength is a God to
you—Purity a toy. A pretty one, and you seem to be fond
of playing with it,' he added, with unaccustomed slyness.

The lady listened, pleased at the sportive malice which
showed that the constraint on his mind had left him. It
was for women to fight their fight now; she only took part
in it for amusement. This is how the ranks of our enemies
are thinned; no sooner do poor women put up a champion
in their midst than she betrays them.

'I see,' she said archly, 'we are the lovelier vessels;
you claim the more direct descent. Men are seedlings:
Women—slips! Nay, you have said so,' she cried out at
his gestured protestation, laughing.

'But I never printed it.'

'Oh! what you speak answers for print with me.'

Exquisite Blandish! He could not choose but love her.

'Tell me what are your plans?' she asked. 'May a woman know?'

He replied, 'I have none or you would share them. I shall study him in the world. This indifference must wear off. I shall mark his inclinations now, and he shall be what he inclines to. Occupation will be his prime safety. His cousin Austin's plan of life appears most to his taste, and he can serve the people that way as well as in Parliament, should he have no stronger ambition. The clear duty of a man of any wealth is to serve the people as he best can. He shall go among Austin's set, if he wishes it, though personally I find no pleasure in rash imaginations, and undigested schemes built upon the mere instinct of principles.'

'Look at him now,' said the lady. 'He seems to care for nothing; not even for the beauty of the day.'

'Or Adrian's jokes,' added the baronet.

Adrian could be seen to be trying zealously to torment a laugh, or a confession of irritation, out of his hearers, stretching out his chin to one, and to the other, with audible asides. Richard he treated as a new instrument of destruction about to be let loose on the slumbering metropolis; Hippias as one in an interesting condition; and he got so much fun out of the notion of these two journeying together, and the mishaps that might occur to them, that he esteemed it almost a personal insult for his hearers not to laugh. The wise youth's dull life at Raynham had afflicted him with many peculiarities of the professional joker.

'Oh! the Spring! the Spring!' he cried, as in scorn of his sallies they exchanged their unmeaning remarks on the sweet weather across him. 'You seem both to be uncommonly excited by the operations of turtles, rooks, and daws. Why can't you let them alone?

> "Wind bloweth,
> Cock croweth,
> Doodle-doo;
> Hippy verteth,
> Ricky sterteth,
> Sing Cuckoo!"

There's an old native pastoral!—Why don't you write a Spring sonnet, Ricky? The asparagus-beds are full of promise, I hear, and eke the strawberry. Berries I fancy your Pegasus*has a taste for. What kind of berry was that I saw some verses of yours about once?—amatory verses to some kind of berry—yewberry, blueberry, glueberry! Pretty verses, decidedly warm. Lips, eyes, bosom, legs— legs? I don't think you gave her any legs. No legs and no nose. That appears to be the poetic taste of the day. It shall be admitted that you create the very beauties for a chaste people.

> "O might I lie where leans her lute!"

and offend no moral community. That's not a bad image of yours, my dear boy:

> "Her shape is like an antelope
> Upon the Eastern hills."

But as a candid critic, I would ask you if the likeness can be considered correct when you give her no legs? You will see at the ballet that you are in error about women at present, Richard. That admirable institution which our venerable elders have imported from Gallia*for the instruction of our gaping youth, will edify and astonish you. I assure you I used, from reading THE PILGRIM'S SCRIP, to imagine all sorts of things about them, till I was taken there, and learnt that they are very like us after all, and then they ceased to trouble me. Mystery is the great danger to youth, my son! Mystery is woman's redoubtable weapon, O

Richard of the Ordeal! I'm aware that you've had your lessons in anatomy, but nothing will persuade you that an anatomical figure means flesh and blood. You can't realize the fact. Do you intend to publish when you're in town? It'll be better not to put your name. Having one's name to a volume of poems is as bad as to an advertizing pill.'

'I will send you an early copy, Adrian, when I publish,' quoth Richard. 'Hark at that old blackbird, uncle.'

'Yes!' Hippias quavered, looking up from the usual subject of his contemplation, and trying to take an interest in him, 'fine old fellow!'

'What a chuckle he gives out before he flies! Not unlike July nightingales. You know that bird I told you of—the blackbird that had its mate shot, and used to come to sing to old Dame Bakewell's bird from the tree opposite. A rascal knocked it over the day before yesterday, and the dame says her bird hasn't sung a note since.'

'Extraordinary!' Hippias muttered abstractedly. 'I remember the verses.'

'But where's your moral?' interposed the wrathful Adrian. 'Where's constancy rewarded?

"The ouzel-cock so black of hue,
    With orange-tawny bill;
The rascal with his aim so true;
    The Poet's little quill!"

Where's the moral of that? except that all's game to the poet! Certainly we have a noble example of the devotedness of the female, who for three entire days refuses to make herself heard, on account of a defunct male. I suppose that's what Ricky dwells on.'

'As you please, my dear Adrian,' says Richard, and points out larch-buds to his uncle, as they ride by the young green wood.

The wise youth was driven to extremity. Such a lapse from his pupil's heroics to this last verge of Arcadian coolness, Adrian could not believe in. 'Hark at this old blackbird!' he cried, in his turn, and pretending to interpret his fits of song:

'Oh, what a pretty comedy!—Don't we wear the mask well, my Fiesco?*—Genoa will be our own to-morrow!—Only wait until the train has started—jolly! jolly! jolly! We'll be winners yet!

'Not a bad verse—eh, Ricky? my Lucius Junius!'*

'You do the blackbird well,' said Richard, and looked at him in a manner mildly affable.

Adrian shrugged. 'You're a young man of wonderful powers,' he emphatically observed; meaning to say that Richard quite beat him; for which opinion Richard gravely thanked him, and with this they rode into Bellingham.

There was young Tom Blaize at the station, in his Sunday beaver and gala waistcoat and neckcloth, coming the lord over Tom Bakewell, who had preceded his master in charge of the baggage. He likewise was bound for London. Richard, as he was dismounting, heard Adrian say to the baronet: 'The Beast, sir, appears to be going to fetch Beauty'; but he paid no heed to the words. Whether young Tom heard them or not, Adrian's look took the lord out of him, and he shrunk away into obscurity, where the nearest approach to the fashions which the tailors of Bellingham could supply to him, sat upon him more easily, and he was not stiffened by the eyes of the superiors whom he sought to rival. The baronet, Lady Blandish, and Adrian remained on horseback, and received Richard's adieux across the palings. He shook hands with each of them in the same kindly cold way, eliciting from Adrian a marked encomium on his style of doing it. The train came up, and Richard stepped after his uncle into one of the carriages.

Now surely there will come an age when the presentation of science at war with Fortune and the Fates, will be deemed the true epic of modern life; and the aspect of a scientific humanist who, by dint of incessant watchfulness, has maintained a System against those active forces, cannot be reckoned less than sublime, even though at the moment he but sit upon his horse, on a fine March morning such as this, and smile wistfully to behold the son of his heart, his System incarnate, wave a serene adieu to tutelage, neither too eager nor morbidly unwilling to try his luck alone for a term of two weeks. At present, I am aware, an audience impatient for blood and glory scorns the stress I am putting on incidents so minute, a picture so little imposing. An audience will come to whom it will be given to see the elementary machinery at work: who, as it were, from some slight hint of the straws, will feel the winds of March when they do not blow. To them will nothing be trivial, seeing that they will have in their eyes the invisible conflict going on around us, whose features a nod, a smile, a laugh of ours perpetually changes. And they will perceive, moreover, that in real life all hangs together: the train is laid in the lifting of an eyebrow, that bursts upon the field of thousands. They will see the links of things as they pass, and wonder not, as foolish people now do, that this great matter came out of that small one.

Such an audience, then, will participate in the baronet's gratification at his son's demeanour, wherein he noted the calm bearing of experience not gained in the usual wanton way: and will not be without some excited apprehension at his twinge of astonishment, when, just as the train went sliding into swiftness, he beheld the grave, cold, self-possessed young man throw himself back in the carriage violently laughing. Science was at a loss to account for that. Sir Austin checked his mind from inquiring, that he might keep suspicion at a distance, but he thought it odd, and the jarring sensation that ran along his nerves at the sight, remained with him as he rode home.

Lady Blandish's tender womanly intuition bade her say: 'You see it was the very thing he wanted. He has got his natural spirits already.'

'It was,' Adrian put in his word, 'the exact thing he wanted. His spirits have returned miraculously.'

'Something amused him,' said the baronet, with an eye on the puffing train.

'Probably something his uncle said or did,' Lady Blandish suggested, and led off at a gallop.

Her conjecture chanced to be quite correct. The cause for Richard's laughter was simple enough. Hippias, on finding the carriage-door closed on him, became all at once aware of the bright-haired hope which dwells in Change, for one who does not woo her too frequently; and to express his sudden relief from mental despondency at the amorous prospect, the Dyspepsy bent and gave his hands a sharp rub between his legs: which unlucky action brought Adrian's pastoral,

> 'Hippy verteth,
> Sing cuckoo!'

in such comic colours before Richard, that a demon of laughter seized him.

> 'Hippy verteth!'

Every time he glanced at his uncle the song sprang up, and he laughed so immoderately that it looked like madness come upon him.

'Why, why, why, what are you laughing at, my dear boy?' said Hippias, and was provoked by the contagious exercise to a modest 'ha! ha!'

'Why, what are you laughing at, uncle?' cried Richard.

'I really don't know,' Hippias chuckled.

'Nor I, uncle! Sing, cuckoo!'

They laughed themselves into the pleasantest mood imaginable. Hippias not only came aboveground, he flew about in the very skies, *verting* like any blithe creature of the season. He remembered old legal jokes, and anecdotes of Circuit; and Richard laughed at them all, but more at him—he was so genial, and childishly fresh, and innocently joyful at his own transformation, while a lurking doubt in the bottom of his eyes, now and then, that it might not last, and that he must go underground again, lent him a look of pathos and humour which tickled his youthful companion irresistibly, and made his heart warm to him.

'I tell you what, uncle,' said Richard, 'I think travelling 's a capital thing.'

'The best thing in the world, my dear boy,' Hippias returned. 'It makes me wish I had given up that Work of mine, and tried it before, instead of chaining myself to a task. We 're quite different beings in a minute. I am. Hem! what shall we have for dinner?'

'Leave that to me, uncle. I shall order for you. You know, I intend to make you well. How gloriously we go along! I should like to ride on a railway every day.'

Hippias remarked: 'They say it rather injures the digestion.'

'Nonsense! see how you 'll digest to-night and to-morrow.'

'Perhaps I shall do something yet,' sighed Hippias, alluding to the vast literary fame he had aforetime dreamed of. 'I hope I shall have a good night to-night.'

'Of course you will! What! after laughing like that?'

'Ugh!' Hippias grunted, 'I dare say, Richard, you sleep the moment you get into bed!'

'The instant my head 's on my pillow, and up the moment I wake. Health 's everything!'

'Health's everything!' echoed Hippias, from his immense distance.

'And if you 'll put yourself in my hands,' Richard continued, 'you shall do just as I do. You shall be well and strong, and sing "Jolly!" like Adrian's blackbird. You shall, upon my honour, uncle!'

He specified the hours of devotion to his uncle's recovery —no less than twelve a day—that he intended to expend, and his cheery robustness almost won his uncle to leap up recklessly and clutch health as his own.

'Mind,' quoth Hippias, with a half-seduced smile, 'mind your dishes are not too savoury!'

'Light food and claret! Regular meals and amusement! Lend your heart to all, but give it to none!' exclaims young Wisdom, and Hippias mutters, 'Yes! yes!' and intimates that the origin of his malady lay in his not following that maxim earlier.

'Love ruins us, my dear boy,' he said, thinking to preach Richard a lesson, and Richard boisterously broke out—

> 'The love of Monsieur Francatelli,
> It was the ruin of—*et cœtera*.'

Hippias blinked, exclaiming, 'Really, my dear boy! I never saw you so excited.'

'It 's the railway! It 's the fun, uncle!'

'Ah!' Hippias wagged a melancholy head, 'you 've got the Golden Bride! Keep her if you can. That 's a pretty fable of your father's. I gave him the idea, though. Austin filches a great many of my ideas!'

'Here 's the idea in verse, uncle—

> "O sunless walkers by the tide!
> O have you seen the Golden Bride!
> They say that she is fair beyond
> All women; faithful, and more fond!"

You know, the young inquirer comes to a group of penitent
sinners by the brink of a stream. They howl, and answer:

> "Faithful she is, but she forsakes:
>   And fond, yet endless woe she makes:
>   And fair! but with this curse she 's cross'd;
>   To know her not till she is lost!"

Then the doleful party march off in single file solemnly, and
the fabulist pursues—

> "She hath a palace in the West:
>   Bright Hesper lights her to her rest:
>   And him the Morning Star awakes
>   Whom to her charmed arms she takes.
>
> So lives he till he sees, alas!
>   The maids of baser metal pass."

And prodigal of the happiness she lends him, he asks to
share it with one of them. There is the Silver Maid, and
the Copper, and the Brassy Maid, and others of them. First,
you know, he tries Argentine, and finds her only twenty to
the pound, and has a worse experience with Copperina, till
he descends to the scullery; and the lower he goes, the less
obscure become the features of his Bride of Gold, and all
her radiance shines forth, my uncle!'

'Verse rather blunts the point. Well, keep to her, now
you 've got her,' says Hippias.

'We will, uncle! Look how the farms fly past! Look
at the cattle in the fields! And how the lines duck, and
swim up!

> "She claims the whole and not the part—
>   The coin of an unused heart!
>   To gain his Golden Bride again,
>   He hunts with melancholy men,"

—and is waked no longer by the Morning Star!'*

'Not if he doesn't sleep till an hour before it rises!'
Hippias interjected. 'You don't rhyme badly. But stick
to prose. Poetry's a Base-metal maid. I'm not sure that
any writing's good for the digestion. I'm afraid it has
spoilt mine.'

'Fear nothing, uncle!' laughed Richard. 'You shall
ride in the park with me every day to get an appetite. You
and I and the Golden Bride. You know that little poem of
Sandoe's?

> "She rides in the park on a prancing bay,
>   She and her squires together;
> Her dark locks gleam from a bonnet of gray,
>   And toss with the tossing feather.
>
> Too calmly proud for a glance of pride
>   Is the beautiful face as it passes;
> The cockneys nod to each other aside,
>   The coxcombs lift their glasses.
>
> And throng to her, sigh to her, you that can breach
>   The ice-wall that guards her securely;
> You have not such bliss, though she smile on you each,
>   As the heart that can image her purely."

Wasn't Sandoe once a friend of my father's? I suppose
they quarrelled. He understands the heart. What does
he make his "Humble Lover" say?

> "True, Madam, you may think to part
>   Conditions by a glacier-ridge,
> But Beauty's for the largest heart,
>   And all abysses Love can bridge!'"

Hippias now laughed; grimly, as men laugh at the emptiness of words.

'Largest heart!' he sneered. 'What's a "glacier-ridge"?
I've never seen one. I can't deny it rhymes with "bridge."
But don't go parading your admiration of that person,

Richard. Your father will speak to you on the subject when he thinks fit.'

'I thought they had quarrelled,' said Richard. 'What a pity!' and he murmured to a pleased ear:

'Beauty 's for the largest heart!'

The flow of their conversation was interrupted by the entrance of passengers at a station. Richard examined their faces with pleasure. All faces pleased him. Human nature sat tributary at the feet of him and his Golden Bride. As he could not well talk his thoughts before them, he looked out at the windows, and enjoyed the changeing landscape, projecting all sorts of delights for his old friend Ripton, and musing hazily on the wondrous things he was to do in the world; of the great service he was to be to his fellow-creatures. In the midst of his reveries he was landed in London. Tom Bakewell stood at the carriage-door. A glance told Richard that his squire had something curious on his mind, and he gave Tom the word to speak out. Tom edged his master out of hearing, and began sputtering a laugh.

'Dash'd if I can help it, sir!' he said. 'That young Tom! He 've come to town dressed that spicy! and he don't know his way about no more than a stag. He 's come to fetch somebody from another rail, and he don't know how to get there, and he ain't sure about which rail 'tis. Look at him, Mr. Richard! There he goes.'

Young Tom appeared to have the weight of all London on his beaver.

'Who has he come for?' Richard asked.

'Don't you know, sir? You don't like me to mention the name,' mumbled Tom, bursting to be perfectly intelligible.

'Is it for her, Tom?'

'Miss Lucy, sir.'

Richard turned away, and was seized by Hippias, who begged him to get out of the noise and pother, and caught hold of his slack arm to bear him into a conveyance; but Richard, by wheeling half to the right, or left, always got his face round to the point where young Tom was manœuvring to appear at his ease. Even when they were seated in the conveyance, Hippias could not persuade him to drive off. He made the excuse that he did not wish to start till there was a clear road. At last young Tom cast anchor by a policeman, and, doubtless at the official's suggestion, bashfully took seat in a cab, and was shot into the whirlpool of London. Richard then angrily asked his driver what he was waiting for.

'Are you ill, my boy?' said Hippias. 'Where's your colour?'

He laughed oddly, and made a random answer that he hoped the fellow would drive fast.

'I hate slow motion after being in the railway,' he said.

Hippias assured him there was something the matter with him.

'Nothing, uncle! nothing!' said Richard, looking fiercely candid.

They say, that when the skill and care of men rescue a drowned wretch from extinction, and warm the flickering spirit into steady flame, such pain it is, the blood forcing its way along the dry channels, and the heavily-ticking nerves, and the sullen heart—the struggle of life and death in him—grim death relaxing his gripe; such pain it is, he cries out no thanks to them that pull him by inches from the depths of the dead river. And he who has thought a love extinct, and is surprised by the old fires, and the old tyranny, he rebels, and strives to fight clear of the cloud of forgotten sensations that settle on him; such pain it is, the old sweet music reviving through his frame, and the charm of his passion fixing him afresh. Still was fair Lucy the one woman to Richard. He had forbidden her name but from an instinct of self-defence. Must the maids of

baser metal dominate him anew, it is in Lucy's shape.
Thinking of her now so near him—his darling! all her
graces, her sweetness, her truth; for, despite his bitter
blame of her, he knew her true—swam in a thousand visions
before his eyes; visions pathetic, and full of glory, that
now wrung his heart, and now elated it. As well might a
ship attempt to calm the sea, as this young man the violent
emotion that began to rage in his breast. 'I shall not see
her!' he said to himself exultingly, and at the same instant
thought, how black was every corner of the earth but that
one spot where Lucy stood! how utterly cheerless the place
he was going to! Then he determined to bear it: to live in
darkness; there was a refuge in the idea of a voluntary
martyrdom. 'For if I chose I could see her—this day
within an hour!—I could see her, and touch her hand, and,
oh, heaven!—But I do not choose.' And a great wave
swelled through him, and was crushed down only to swell
again more stormily.

Then Tom Bakewell's words recurred to him that young
Tom Blaize was uncertain where to go for her, and that she
might be thrown on this Babylon alone. And flying from
point to point, it struck him that they had known at
Raynham of her return, and had sent him to town to be
out of the way—they had been miserably plotting against
him once more. 'They shall see what right they have to
fear me. I 'll shame them!' was the first turn taken by
his wrathful feelings, as he resolved to go, and see her safe,
and calmly return to his uncle, whom he sincerely believed
not to be one of the conspirators. Nevertheless, after forming that resolve, he sat still, as if there were something fatal
in the wheels that bore him away from it—perhaps because
he knew, as some do when passion is lord, that his intelligence juggled with him; though none the less keenly
did he feel his wrongs and suspicions. His Golden Bride
was waning fast. But when Hippias ejaculated to cheer

him: 'We shall soon be there!' the spell broke. Richard
stopped the cab, saying he wanted to speak to Tom, and
would ride with him the rest of the journey. He knew well
enough which line of railway his Lucy must come by. He
had studied every town and station on the line. Before his
uncle could express more than a mute remonstrance, he
jumped out and hailed Tom Bakewell, who came behind
with the boxes and baggage in a companion cab, his head a
yard beyond the window to make sure of his ark of safety,
the vehicle preceding.

'What an extraordinary, impetuous boy it is,' said Hippias. 'We're in the very street!'

Within a minute the stalwart Berry, despatched by the
baronet to arrange everything for their comfort, had opened
the door, and made his bow.

'Mr. Richard, sir?—evaporated?' was Berry's modulated
inquiry.

'Behind—among the boxes, fool!' Hippias growled, as
he received Berry's muscular assistance to alight. 'Lunch
ready—eh!'

'Luncheon was ordered precise at two o'clock, sir—been
in attendance one quarter of an hour. Heah!' Berry sang
out to the second cab, which, with its pyramid of luggage,
remained stationary some thirty paces distant. At his
voice the majestic pile deliberately turned its back on them,
and went off in a contrary direction.

CHAPTER XXVI

RECORDS THE RAPID DEVELOPMENT OF THE HERO

ON the stroke of the hour when Ripton Thompson was
accustomed to consult his gold watch for practical purposes,
and sniff freedom and the forthcoming dinner, a burglarious

foot entered the clerk's office where he sat, and a man of a scowling countenance, who looked a villain, and whom he was afraid he knew, slid a letter into his hands, nodding that it would be prudent for him to read, and be silent. Ripton obeyed in alarm. Apparently the contents of the letter relieved his conscience; for he reached down his hat, and told Mr. Beazley to inform his father that he had business of pressing importance in the West, and should meet him at the station. Mr. Beazley zealously waited upon the paternal Thompson without delay, and together making their observations from the window, they beheld a cab of many boxes, into which Ripton darted and was followed by one in groom's dress. It was Saturday, the day when Ripton gave up his law-readings, magnanimously to bestow himself upon his family, and Mr. Thompson liked to have his son's arm as he walked down to the station; but that third glass of Port which always stood for his second, and the groom's suggestion of aristocratic acquaintances, prevented Mr. Thompson from interfering; so Ripton was permitted to depart.

In the cab Ripton made a study of the letter he held. It had the preciseness of an imperial mandate.

'DEAR RIPTON,—You are to get lodgings for a lady immediately. Not a word to a soul. Then come along with Tom.   R. D. F.'

'Lodgings for a lady!' Ripton meditated aloud: 'What sort of lodgings? Where am I to get lodgings? Who's the lady?—I say!' he addressed the mysterious messenger. 'So you're Tom Bakewell, are you, Tom?'

Tom grinned his identity.

'Do you remember the rick, Tom? Ha! ha! We got out of that neatly. We might all have been transported, though. I could have convicted you, Tom, safe! It's no use coming across a practised lawyer. Now tell me.' Ripton having flourished his powers, commenced his examination: 'Who 's this lady?'

'Better wait till you see Mr. Richard, sir,' Tom resumed his scowl to reply.

'Ah!" Ripton acquiesced. 'Is she young, Tom?'

Tom said she was not old.

'Handsome, Tom?'

'Some might think one thing, some another,' Tom said.

'And where does she come from now?' asked Ripton, with the friendly cheerfulness of a baffled counsellor.

'Comes from the country, sir.'

'A friend of the family, I suppose? a relation?'

Ripton left this insinuating query to be answered by a look. Tom's face was a dead blank.

'Ah!' Ripton took a breath, and eyed the mask opposite him. 'Why, you 're quite a scholar, Tom! Mr. Richard is well? All right at home?'

'Come to town this mornin' with his uncle,' said Tom. 'All well, thank ye, sir.'

'Ha!' cried Ripton, more than ever puzzled, 'now I see. You all came to town to-day, and these are your boxes outside. So, so! But Mr. Richard writes for me to get lodgings for a lady. There must be some mistake—he wrote in a hurry. He wants lodgings for you all—eh?'

' 'M sure *I* d'n know what he wants,' said Tom. 'You 'd better go by the letter, sir.'

Ripton reconsulted that document. '"Lodgings for a lady, and then come along with Tom. Not a word to a soul." I say! that looks like—but he never cared for *them*. You don't mean to say, Tom, he 's been running away with anybody?'

Tom fell back upon his first reply: 'Better wait till ye see Mr. Richard, sir,' and Ripton exclaimed: 'Hanged if you ain't the tightest witness I ever saw! I shouldn't like to have you in a box. Some of you country fellows beat any number of cockneys. You do!'

Tom received the compliment stubbornly on his guard, and Ripton, as nothing was to be got out of him, set about considering how to perform his friend's injunctions; deciding firstly, that a lady fresh from the country ought to lodge near the parks, in which direction he told the cabman to drive. Thus, unaware of his high destiny, Ripton joined the hero, and accepted his character in the New Comedy.

It is, nevertheless, true that certain favoured people do have beneficent omens to prepare them for their parts when the hero is in full career, so that they really may be nerved to meet him; ay, and to check him in his course, had they that signal courage. For instance, Mrs. Elizabeth Berry, a ripe and wholesome landlady of advertized lodgings, on the borders of Kensington, noted, as she sat rocking her contemplative person before the parlour fire this very March afternoon, a supernatural tendency in that fire to burn *all on one side:* which signifies that a wedding approaches the house. Why—who shall say? Omens are as impassable as heroes. It may be because in these affairs the fire is thought to be all on one side. Enough that the omen exists, and spoke its solemn warning to the devout woman. Mrs. Berry, in her circle, was known as a certificated lecturer against the snares of matrimony. Still that was no reason why she should not like a wedding. Expectant, therefore, she watched the one glowing cheek of Hymen,* and with pleasing tremours beheld a cab of many boxes draw up by her bit of garden, and a gentleman emerge from it in the act of consulting an advertizement paper. The gentleman required lodgings for a lady. Lodgings for a lady Mrs. Berry could produce, and a very roseate smile for a gentleman; so much so that Ripton forgot to ask about the terms, which made the landlady in Mrs. Berry leap up to embrace him as the happy man. But her experienced woman's eye

checked her enthusiasm. He had not the air of a bridegroom: he did not seem to have a weight on his chest, or
an itch to twiddle everything with his fingers. At any rate,
he was not the bridegroom for whom omens fly abroad.
Promising to have all ready for the lady within an hour,
Mrs. Berry fortified him with her card, curtsied him back
to his cab, and floated him off on her smiles.

The remarkable vehicle which had woven this thread of
intrigue through London streets, now proceeded sedately
to finish its operations. Ripton was landed at a hotel in
Westminster. Ere he was halfway up the stairs, a door
opened, and his old comrade in adventure rushed down.
Richard allowed no time for salutations. 'Have you done
it?' was all he asked. For answer Ripton handed him
Mrs. Berry's card. Richard took it, and left him standing
there. Five minutes elapsed, and then Ripton heard the
gracious rustle of feminine garments above. Richard came
a little in advance, leading and half-supporting a figure in
a black silk mantle and small black straw bonnet; young
—that was certain, though she held her veil so close he
could hardly catch the outlines of her face; girlishly slender,
and sweet and simple in appearance. The hush that came
with her, and her soft manner of moving, stirred the silly
youth to some of those ardours that awaken the Knight
of Dames in our bosoms. He felt that he would have given
considerable sums for her to lift her veil. He could see
that she was trembling—perhaps weeping. It was the
master of her fate she clung to. They passed him without
speaking. As she went by, her head passively bent, Ripton had a glimpse of noble tresses and a lovely neck; great
golden curls hung loosely behind, pouring from under her
bonnet. She looked a captive borne to the sacrifice. What
Ripton, after a sight of those curls, would have given for
her just to lift her veil an instant and strike him blind with
beauty, was, fortunately for his exchequer, never de-

manded of him. And he had absolutely been composing
speeches as he came along in the cab! gallant speeches
for the lady, and sly congratulatory ones for his friend, to
be delivered as occasion should serve, that both might
know him a man of the world, and be at their ease. He
forgot the smirking immoralities he had revelled in. This
was clearly serious. Ripton did not require to be told that
his friend was in love, and meant that life and death business called marriage, parents and guardians consenting or
not.

Presently Richard returned to him, and said hurriedly,
'I want you now to go to my uncle at our hotel. Keep
him quiet till I come. Say I had to see you—say anything. I shall be there by the dinner hour. Rip! I must
talk to you alone after dinner.'

Ripton feebly attempted to reply that he was due at
home. He was very curious to hear the plot of the New
Comedy; and besides, there was Richard's face questioning
him sternly and confidently for signs of unhesitating obedience. He finished his grimaces by asking the name and
direction of the hotel. Richard pressed his hand. It is
much to obtain even that recognition of our devotion from
the hero.

Tom Bakewell also received his priming, and, to judge
by his chuckles and grins, rather appeared to enjoy the
work cut out for him. In a few minutes they had driven
to their separate destinations; Ripton was left to the unusual exercise of his fancy. Such is the nature of youth
and its thirst for romance, that only to act as a subordinate
is pleasant. When one unfurls the standard of defiance to
parents and guardians, he may be sure of raising a lawless
troop of adolescent ruffians, born rebels, to any amount.
The beardless crew know that they have not a chance of
pay; but what of that when the rosy prospect of thwarting
their elders is in view? Though it is to see another eat the

Forbidden Fruit, they will run all his risks with him. Gaily Ripton took rank as lieutenant in the enterprise, and the moment his heart had sworn the oaths, he was rewarded by an exquisite sense of the charms of existence. London streets wore a sly laugh to him. He walked with a dandi-fied heel. The generous youth ogled aristocratic carriages, and glanced intimately at the ladies, overflowingly happy. The crossing-sweepers blessed him. He hummed lively tunes, he turned over old jokes in his mouth unctuously, he hugged himself, he had a mind to dance down Piccadilly, and all because a friend of his was running away with a pretty girl, and he was in the secret.

It was only when he stood on the doorstep of Richard's hotel, that his jocund mood was a little dashed by remem-bering that he had then to commence the duties of his office, and must fabricate a plausible story to account for what he knew nothing about—a part that the greatest of sages would find it difficult to perform. The young, how-ever, whom sages well may envy, seldom fail in lifting their inventive faculties to the level of their spirits, and two minutes of Hippias's angry complaints against the friend he serenely inquired for, gave Ripton his cue.

'We're in the very street—within a stone's throw of the house, and he jumps like a harlequin out of my cab into another; he must be mad—that boy's got madness in him! —and carries off all the boxes—my dinner-pills, too! and keeps away the whole of the day, though he promised to go to the doctor, and had a dozen engagements with me,' said Hippias, venting an enraged snarl to sum up his grievances.

Ripton at once told him that the doctor was not at home.

'Why, you don't mean to say he's been to the doctor?' Hippias cried out.

'He has called on him twice, sir,' said Ripton, expres-sively. 'On leaving me he was going a third time. I shouldn't wonder that 's what detains him—he 's so determined.'

By fine degrees Ripton ventured to grow circumstantial, saying that Richard's case was urgent and required immediate medical advice; and that both he and his father were of opinion Richard should not lose an hour in obtaining it.

'He 's alarmed about himself,' said Ripton, and tapped his chest.

Hippias protested he had never heard a word from his nephew of any physical affliction.

'He was afraid of making you anxious, I think, sir.'

Algernon Feverel and Richard came in while he was hammering at the alphabet to recollect the first letter of the doctor's name. They had met in the hall below, and were laughing heartily as they entered the room. Ripton jumped up to get the initiative.

'Have you seen the doctor?' he asked, significantly plucking at Richard's fingers.

Richard was all abroad at the question.

Algernon clapped him on the back. 'What the deuce do you want with doctor, boy?'

The solid thump awakened him to see matters as they were. 'Oh, ay! the doctor!' he said, smiling frankly at his lieutenant. 'Why, he tells me he 'd back me to do Milo's trick*in a week from the present day.—Uncle,' he came forward to Hippias, 'I hope you 'll excuse me for running off as I did. I was in a hurry. I left something at the railway. This stupid Rip thinks I went to the doctor about myself. The fact was, I wanted to fetch the doctor to see you here—so that you might have no trouble, you know. You can't bear the sight of his instruments and skeletons—I 've heard you say so. You said it set all your marrow in revolt—"fried your marrow," I think were the words, and made you see twenty thousand different ways of sliding down to the chambers of the Grim King. Don't you remember?'

Hippias emphatically did not remember, and he did not believe the story. Irritation at the mad ravishment of his pill-box rendered him incredulous. As he had no means of confuting his nephew, all he could do safely to express his disbelief in him, was to utter petulant remarks on his powerlessness to appear at the dinner-table that day: upon which—Berry just then trumpeting dinner—Algernon seized one arm of the Dyspepsy, and Richard another, and the laughing couple bore him into the room where dinner was laid, Ripton sniggering in the rear, the really happy man of the party.

They had fun at the dinner-table. Richard would have it; and his gaiety, his by-play, his princely superiority to truth and heroic promise of overriding all our laws, his handsome face, the lord and possessor of beauty that he looked, as it were a star shining on his forehead, gained the old complete mastery over Ripton, who had been, mentally at least, half patronizing him till then, because he knew more of London and life, and was aware that his friend now depended upon him almost entirely.

After a second circle of the claret, the hero caught his lieutenant's eye across the table, and said:

'We must go out and talk over that law-business, Rip, before you go. Do you think the old lady has any chance?'

'Not a bit!' said Ripton authoritatively.

'But it's worth fighting—eh, Rip?'

'Oh, certainly!' was Ripton's mature opinion.

Richard observed that Ripton's father seemed doubtful. Ripton cited his father's habitual caution. Richard made a playful remark on the necessity of sometimes acting in opposition to fathers. Ripton agreed to it—in certain cases.

'Yes, yes! in certain cases,' said Richard.

'Pretty legal morality, gentlemen!' Algernon interjected;
Hippias adding: 'And lay, too!'

The pair of uncles listened further to the fictitious dialogue, well kept up on both sides, and in the end desired a
statement of the old lady's garrulous case; Hippias offering
to decide what her chances were in law, and Algernon to
give a common-sense judgement.

'Rip will tell you,' said Richard, deferentially signalling
the lawyer. 'I'm a bad hand at these matters. Tell them
how it stands, Rip.'

Ripton disguised his excessive uneasiness under endeavours to right his position on his chair, and, inwardly praying
speed to the claret jug to come and strengthen his wits,
began with a careless aspect: 'Oh, nothing! She—very
curious old character! She—a—wears a wig. She—a
—very curious old character indeed! She—a—quite the
old style. There's no doing anything with her!' and Ripton took a long breath to relieve himself after his elaborate
fiction.

'So it appears,' Hippias commented, and Algernon
asked: 'Well? and about her wig? Somebody stole it?'
while Richard, whose features were grim with suppressed
laughter, bade the narrator continue.

Ripton lunged for the claret jug. He had got an old
lady like an oppressive bundle on his brain, and he was as
helpless as she was. In the pangs of ineffectual authorship
his ideas shot at her wig, and then at her one characteristic
of extreme obstinacy, and tore back again at her wig, but
she would not be animated. The obstinate old thing would
remain a bundle. Law studies seemed light in comparison
with this tremendous task of changeing an old lady from a
doll to a human creature. He flung off some claret, perspired freely, and, with a mental tribute to the cleverness
of those author fellows, recommenced: 'Oh, nothing! She
—Richard knows her better than I do—an old lady—

somewhere down in Suffolk. I think we had better advise
her not to proceed. The expenses of litigation are enormous! She—I think we had better advise her to stop
short, and not make any scandal.'

'And not make any scandal!' Algernon took him up.
'Come, come! there's something more than a wig, then?''

Ripton was commanded to proceed, whether she did or
no. The luckless fictionist looked straight at his pitiless leader, and blurted out dubiously, 'She—there's a
daughter.'

'Born with effort!' ejaculated Hippias. 'Must give
her pause after that! and I'll take the opportunity to
stretch my length on the sofa. Heigho! that's true what
Austin says: "The general prayer should be for a full
stomach, and the individual for one that works well; for
on that basis only are we a match for temporal matters,
and able to contemplate eternal." Sententious, but true.
I gave him the idea, though! Take care of your stomachs,
boys! and if ever you hear of a monument proposed to a
scientific cook or gastronomic doctor, send in your sub-
scriptions. Or say to him while he lives, Go forth, and be
a Knight! Ha! They have a good cook at this house.
He suits me better than ours at Raynham. I almost wish I
had brought my manuscript to town, I feel so much better.
Aha! I didn't expect to digest at all without my regular
incentive. I think I shall give it up.—What do you say
to the theatre to-night, boys!'

Richard shouted, 'Bravo, uncle!'

'Let Mr. Thompson finish first,' said Algernon. 'I want
to hear the conclusion of the story. The old girl has a wig
and a daughter. I'll swear somebody runs away with one
of the two! Fill your glass, Mr. Thompson, and forward!'

'So somebody does,' Ripton received his impetus. 'And
they're found in town together,' he made a fresh jerk.
'She—a—that is, the old lady—found them in company.'

'She finds him with her wig on in company!' said Algernon. 'Capital! Here's matter for the lawyers!'

'And you advise her not to proceed, under such circumstances of aggravation?' Hippias observed, humorously twinkling with his stomachic contentment.

'It's the daughter,' Ripton sighed, and surrendering to pressure, hurried on recklessly, 'A runaway match—beautiful girl!—the only son of a baronet—married by special licence. A—the point is,' he now brightened and spoke from his own element, 'the point is whether the marriage can be annulled, as she's of the Catholic persuasion and he's a Protestant, and they're both married under age. That's the point.'

Having come to the point he breathed extreme relief, and saw things more distinctly; not a little amazed at his leader's horrified face.

The two elders were making various absurd inquiries, when Richard sent his chair to the floor, crying, 'What a muddle you're in, Rip! You're mixing half-a-dozen stories together. The old lady I told you about was old Dame Bakewell, and the dispute was concerning a neighbour of hers who encroached on her garden, and I said I'd pay the money to see her righted!'

'Ah,' said Ripton, humbly, 'I was thinking of the other. Her garden! Cabbages don't interest me——'

'Here, come along,' Richard beckoned to him savagely. 'I'll be back in five minutes, uncle,' he nodded coolly to either.

The young men left the room. In the hall-passage they met Berry, dressed to return to Raynham. Richard dropped a helper to the intelligence into his hand, and warned him not to gossip much of London. Berry bowed perfect discreetness.

'What on earth induced you to talk about Protestants and Catholics marrying, Rip?' said Richard, as soon as they were in the street.

'Why,' Ripton answered, 'I was so hard pushed for it, 'pon my honour, I didn't know what to say. I ain't an author, you know; I can't make a story. I was trying to invent a point, and I couldn't think of any other, and I thought that was just the point likely to make a jolly good dispute. Capital dinners they give at those crack hotels. Why did you throw it all upon me? I didn't begin on the old lady.'

The hero mused. 'It's odd! It's impossible you could have known! I'll tell you why, Rip! I wanted to try you. You fib well at long range, but you don't do at close quarters and single combat. You're good behind walls, but not worth a shot in the open. I just see what you're fit for. You're staunch—that I am certain of. You always were. Lead the way to one of the parks—down in that direction. You know?—where she is!'

Ripton led the way. His dinner had prepared this young Englishman to defy the whole artillery of established morals. With the muffled roar of London around them, alone in a dark slope of green, the hero, leaning on his henchman, and speaking in a harsh clear undertone, delivered his explanations. Doubtless the true heroic insignia and point of view will be discerned, albeit in common private's uniform.

'They've been plotting against me for a year, Rip! When you see her, you'll know what it was to have such a creature taken away from you. It nearly killed me. Never mind what she is. She's the most perfect and noble creature God ever made! It's not only her beauty—I don't care so much about that!—but when you've once seen her, she seems to draw music from all the nerves of your body; but she's such an angel. I worship her. And her mind's like her face. She's pure gold. There, you'll see her to-night.

'Well,' he pursued, after inflating Ripton with this rap-

turous prospect, 'they got her away, and I recovered. It
was Mister Adrian's work. What 's my father's objection to
her? Because of her birth? She 's educated; her manners
are beautiful—full of refinement—quick and soft! Can
they show me one of their ladies like her?—she 's the
daughter of a naval lieutenant! Because she 's a Catholic?
What has religion to do with'—he pronounced 'Love!' a
little modestly—as it were a blush in his voice.

'Well, when I recovered I thought I did not care for her.
It shows how we know ourselves! And I cared for nothing.
I felt as if I had no blood. I tried to imitate my dear Austin. I wish to God he were here. I love Austin. He
would understand her. He 's coming back this year, and
then—but it 'll be too late then.—Well, my father 's always
scheming to make me perfect—he has never spoken to me
a word about her, but I can see her in his eyes—he wanted
to give me a change, he said, and asked me to come to town
with my uncle Hippy, and I consented. It was another
plot to get me out of the way! As I live, I had no more idea
of meeting her than of flying to heaven!'

He lifted his face. 'Look at those old elm branches!
How they seem to mix among the stars!—glittering fruits
of Winter!'

Ripton tipped his comical nose upward and was in duty
bound to say, Yes! though he observed no connection
between them and the narrative.

'Well,' the hero went on, 'I came to town. There I
heard she was coming, too—coming home. It must have
been fate, Ripton! Heaven forgive me! I was angry with
her, and I thought I should like to see her once—only once
—and reproach her for being false—for she never wrote to
me. And, oh, the dear angel! what she must have suffered!
—I gave my uncle the slip, and got to the railway she was
coming by. There was a fellow going to meet her—a farmer's son—and, good God! they were going to try and

make her marry him! I remembered it all then. A servant of the farm had told me. That fellow went to the wrong station, I suppose, for we saw nothing of him. There she was—not changed a bit!—looking lovelier than ever! And when she saw me, I knew in a minute that she must love me till death!—You don't know what it is yet, Rip!—Will you believe it?—Though I was as sure she loved me and had been true as steel, as that I shall see her to-night, I spoke bitterly to her. And she bore it meekly—she looked like a saint. I told her there was but one hope of life for me—she must prove she was true, and as I give up all, so must she. I don't know what I said. The thought of losing her made me mad. She tried to plead with me to wait—it was for my sake, I know. I pretended, like a miserable hypocrite, that she did not love me at all. I think I said shameful things. Oh what noble creatures women are! She hardly had strength to move. I took her to that place where you found us.—Rip! she went down on her knees to me. I never dreamed of anything in life so lovely as she looked then. Her eyes were thrown up, bright with a crowd of tears—her dark brows bent together, like Pain and Beauty meeting in one; and her glorious golden hair swept off her shoulders as she hung forward to my hands.—Could I lose such a prize?—If anything could have persuaded me, would not that?—I thought of Dante's Madonna—Guido's Magdalen.*—Is there sin in it? I see none! And if there is, it's all mine! I swear she's spotless of a thought of sin. I see her very soul! Cease to love her? Who dares ask me? Cease to love her? Why, I live on her!—To see her little chin straining up from her throat, as she knelt to me!—there was one curl that fell across her throat . . .'

Ripton listened for more. Richard had gone off in a muse at the picture.

'Well?' said Ripton, 'and how about that young farmer fellow?'

The hero's head was again contemplating the starry branches. His lieutenant's question came to him after an interval.

'Young Tom? Why, it's young Tom Blaize—son of our old enemy, Rip! I like the old man now. Oh! I saw nothing of the fellow.'

'Lord!' cried Ripton, 'are we going to get into a mess with Blaizes again? I don't like that!'

His commander quietly passed his likes or dislikes.

'But when he goes to the train, and finds she's not there?' Ripton suggested.

'I've provided for that. The fool went to the South-east instead of the South-west. All warmth, all sweetness, comes with the South-west!—I've provided for that, friend Rip. My trusty Tom awaits him there, as if by accident. He tells him he has not seen her, and advises him to remain in town, and go for her there to-morrow, and the day following. Tom has money for the work. Young Tom ought to see London, you know, Rip!—like you. We shall gain some good clear days. And when old Blaize hears of it— what then? I have her! she's mine!—Besides, he won't hear for a week. This Tom beats that Tom in cunning, I'll wager. Ha! ha!' the hero burst out at a recollection. 'What do you think, Rip? My father has some sort of System with me, it appears, and when I came to town the time before, he took me to some people—the Grandisons—and what do you think? one of the daughters is a little girl—a nice little thing enough—very funny—and he wants me to wait for her! He hasn't said so, but I know it. I know what he means. Nobody understands him but me. I know he loves me, and is one of the best of men—but just consider! —a *little girl* who just comes up to my elbow. Isn't it ridiculous? Did you ever hear such nonsense?'

Ripton emphasised his opinion that it certainly was foolish.

'No, no! The die's cast!' said Richard. 'They've been plotting for a year up to this day, and this is what comes of it! If my father loves me, he will love her. And if he loves me, he'll forgive my acting against his wishes, and see it was the only thing to be done. Come! step out! what a time we've been!' and away he went, compelling Ripton to the sort of strides a drummer-boy has to take beside a column of grenadiers.

Ripton began to wish himself in love, seeing that it endowed a man with wind so that he could breathe great sighs, while going at a tremendous pace, and experience no sensation of fatigue. The hero was communing with the elements, his familiars, and allowed him to pant as he pleased. Some keen-eyed Kensington urchins, noticing the discrepancy between the pedestrian powers of the two, aimed their wit at Mr. Thompson junior's expense. The pace, and nothing but the pace, induced Ripton to proclaim that they had gone too far, when they discovered that they had overshot the mark by half a mile. In the street over which stood love's star, the hero thundered his presence at a door, and evoked a flying housemaid, who knew not Mrs. Berry. The hero attached significance to the fact that his instincts should have betrayed him, for he could have sworn to that house. The door being shut he stood in dead silence.

'Haven't you got her card?' Ripton inquired, and heard that it was in the custody of the cabman. Neither of them could positively bring to mind the number of the house.

'You ought to have chalked it, like that fellow in the Forty Thieves,' Ripton hazarded a pleasantry which met with no response.

Betrayed by his instincts, the magic slaves of Love! The hero heavily descended the steps.

Ripton murmured that they were done for. His commander turned on him, and said: 'Take all the houses on the opposite side, one after another. I'll take these.' With a wry face Ripton crossed the road, altogether subdued by Richard's native superiority to adverse circumstances.

Then were families aroused. Then did mortals dimly guess that something portentous was abroad. Then were labourers all day in the vineyard, harshly wakened from their evening's nap. Hope and Fear stalked the street, as again and again the loud companion summonses resounded. Finally Ripton sang out cheerfully. He had Mrs. Berry before him, profuse of mellow courtesies.

Richard ran to her and caught her hands: 'She's well?—upstairs?'

'Oh, quite well! only a trifle tired with her journey, and fluttering-like,' Mrs. Berry replied to Ripton alone. The lover had flown aloft.

The wise woman sagely ushered Ripton into her own private parlour, there to wait till he was wanted.

CHAPTER XXVII

CONTAINS AN INTERCESSION FOR THE HEROINE

'In all cases where two have joined to commit an offence, punish one of the two lightly,' is the dictum of THE PILGRIM'S SCRIP.

It is possible for young heads to conceive proper plans of action, and occasionally, by sheer force of will, to check the wild horses that are ever fretting to gallop off with them. But when they have given the reins and the whip to another, what are they to do? They may go down on their knees, and beg and pray the furious charioteer to stop, or moderate his pace. Alas! each fresh thing they do redoubles his ardour. There is a power in their troubled beauty women learn the use of, and what wonder? They have seen it kindle Ilium*to flames so often! But ere they grow matronly in the house of Menelaus,* they weep, and implore, and do not, in truth, know how terribly two-edged is their gift of loveliness. They resign themselves to an incomprehensible frenzy; pleasant to them, because they attribute it to excessive love. And so the very sensible things which they can and do say, are vain.

I reckon it absurd to ask them to be quite in earnest. Are not those their own horses in yonder team? Certainly, if they were quite in earnest, they might soon have my gentleman as sober as a carter. A hundred different ways of disenchanting him exist, and Adrian will point you out one or two that shall be instantly efficacious. For Love, the charioteer, is easily tripped, while honest jog-trot Love keeps his legs to the end. Granted dear women are not quite in earnest, still the mere words they utter should be put to their good account. They do mean them, though their hearts are set the wrong way. 'Tis a despairing, pathetic homage to the judgement of the majority, in whose faces they are flying. Punish Helen,* very young, lightly. After a certain age you may select her for special chastisement. An innocent with Theseus,* with Paris*she is an advanced incendiary.

The fair young girl was sitting as her lover had left her; trying to recall her stunned senses. Her bonnet was unremoved, her hands clasped on her knees; dry tears in her eyes. Like a dutiful slave, she rose to him. And first he claimed her mouth. There was a speech, made up of all the pretty wisdom her wild situation and true love could gather, awaiting him there; but his kiss scattered it to fragments. She dropped to her seat weeping, and hiding her shamed cheeks.

By his silence she divined his thoughts, and took his hand and drew it to her lips.

He bent beside her, bidding her look at him.

'Keep your eyes so.'

She could not.

'Do you fear me, Lucy?'

A throbbing pressure answered him.

'Do you love me, darling?'

She trembled from head to foot.

'Then why do you turn from me?'

She wept: 'O Richard, take me home! take me home!'

'Look at me, Lucy!'

Her head shrank timidly round.

'Keep your eyes on me, darling! Now speak!'

But she could not look and speak too. The lover knew his mastery when he had her eyes.

'You wish me to take you home?'

She faltered: 'O Richard? it is not too late.'

'You regret what you have done for me?'

'Dearest! it is ruin.'

'You weep because you have consented to be mine?'

'Not for me! O Richard!'

'For me you weep? Look at me! For me?'

'How will it end! O Richard!'

'You weep for me?'

'Dearest! I would die for you!'

'Would you see me indifferent to everything in the world? Would you have me lost? Do you think I will live another day in England without you? I have staked all I have on you, Lucy. You have nearly killed me once. A second time, and the earth will not be troubled by me. You ask me to wait, when they are plotting against us on all sides? Darling Lucy! look on me. Fix your fond eyes on me. You ask me to wait when here you are given to me— when you have proved my faith—when we know we love as none have loved. Give me your eyes! Let them tell me I have your heart!'

Where was her wise little speech? How could she match such mighty eloquence? She sought to collect a few more of the scattered fragments.

'Dearest! your father may be brought to consent by and by, and then—Oh! if you take me home now——'

The lover stood up. 'He who has been arranging that fine scheme to disgrace and martyrize you? True, as I live! that's the reason of their having you back. Your old servant heard him and your uncle discussing it. He!—Lucy! he's a good man, but he must not step in between you and me. I say God has given you to me.'

He was down by her side again, his arms enfolding her.

She had hoped to fight a better battle than in the morning, and she was weaker and softer.

Ah! why should she doubt that his great love was the first law to her? Why should she not believe that she would wreck him by resisting? And if she suffered, oh sweet to think it was for his sake! Sweet to shut out wisdom; accept total blindness, and be led by him!

The hag Wisdom annoyed them little further. She rustled her garments ominously, and vanished.

'Oh, my own Richard!' the fair girl just breathed.

He whispered, 'Call me that name.'

She blushed deeply.

'Call me that name,' he repeated. 'You said it once to-day.'

'Dearest!'

'Not that.'

'O darling!'

'Not that.'

'Husband!'

She was won. The rosy gate from which the word had issued was closed with a seal.

Ripton did not enjoy his introduction to the caged bird of beauty that night. He received a lesson in the art of

pumping from the worthy landlady below, up to an hour
when she yawned, and he blinked, and their common candle
wore with dignity the brigand's hat of midnight, and cocked
a drunken eye at them from under it.

CHAPTER XXVIII

RELATES HOW PREPARATIONS FOR ACTION WERE CONDUCTED UNDER THE APRIL OF LOVERS

BEAUTY, of course, is for the hero. Nevertheless, it is
not always he on whom beauty works its most conquering
influence. It is the dull commonplace man into whose slow
brain she drops like a celestial light, and burns lastingly.
The poet, for instance, is a connoisseur of beauty: to the
artist she is a model. These gentlemen by much contemplation of her charms wax critical. The days when they
had hearts being gone, they are haply divided between the
blonde and the brunette; the aquiline nose and the Proserpine;* this shaped eye and that. But go about among simple unprofessional fellows, boors, dunderheads, and here
and there you shall find some barbarous intelligence which
has had just strength enough to conceive, and has taken
Beauty as its Goddess, and knows but one form to worship,
in its poor stupid fashion, and would perish for her. Nay,
more: the man would devote all his days to her, though
he is dumb as a dog. And, indeed, he is Beauty's Dog.
Almost every Beauty has her Dog. The hero possesses
her; the poet proclaims her; the painter puts her upon can-
vas; and the faithful old Dog follows her: and the end of
it all is that the faithful old Dog is her single attendant.
Sir Hero is revelling in the wars, or in Armida's bowers;*
Mr. Poet has spied a wrinkle; the brush is for the rose in

its season. She turns to her old Dog then. She hugs him; and he, who has subsisted on a bone and a pat till there he squats decrepit, he turns his grateful old eyes up to her, and has not a notion that she is hugging sad memories in him: Hero, Poet, Painter, in one scrubby one! Then is she buried, and the village hears languid howls, and there is a paragraph in the newspapers concerning the extraordinary fidelity of an Old Dog.

Excited by suggestive recollections of Nooredeen and the Fair Persian,* and the change in the obscure monotony of his life by his having quarters in a crack hotel, and living familiarly with West-End people—living on the fat of the land (which forms a stout portion of an honest youth's romance), Ripton Thompson breakfasted next morning with his chief at half-past eight. The meal had been fixed overnight for seven, but Ripton slept a great deal more than the nightingale, and (to chronicle his exact state) even half-past eight rather afflicted his new aristocratic senses and reminded him too keenly of law and bondage. He had preferred to breakfast at Algernon's hour, who had left word for eleven. Him, however, it was Richard's object to avoid, so they fell to, and Ripton no longer envied Hippias in bed. Breakfast done, they bequeathed the consoling information for Algernon that they were off to hear a popular preacher, and departed.

'How happy everybody looks!' said Richard, in the quiet Sunday streets.

'Yes—jolly!' said Ripton.

'When I 'm—when this is over, I 'll see that they are, too—as many as I can make happy,' said the hero: adding softly: 'Her blind was down at a quarter to six. I think she slept well!'

'You 've been there this morning?' Ripton exclaimed; and an idea of what love was dawned upon his dull brain.

'Will she see me, Ricky?'

'Yes. She 'll see you to-day. She was tired last night.'
'Positively?'

Richard assured him that the privilege would be his.

'Here,' he said, coming under some trees in the park,
'here 's where I talked to you last night. What a time it
seems! How I hate the night!'

On the way, that Richard might have an exalted opinion
of him, Ripton hinted decorously at a somewhat intimate
and mysterious acquaintance with the sex. Headings of
certain random adventures he gave.

'Well!' said his chief, 'why not marry her?'

Then was Ripton shocked, and cried, 'Oh!' and had a
taste of the feeling of superiority, destined that day to be
crushed utterly.

He was again deposited in Mrs. Berry's charge for a term
that caused him dismal fears that the Fair Persian still refused to show her face, but Richard called out to him, and
up Ripton went, unaware of the transformation he was to
undergo. Hero and Beauty stood together to receive him.
From the bottom of the stairs he had his vivaciously agreeable smile ready for them, and by the time he entered the
room his cheeks were painfully stiff, and his eyes had
strained beyond their exact meaning. Lucy, with one
hand anchored to her lover, welcomed him kindly. He relieved her shyness by looking so extremely silly. They sat
down, and tried to commence a conversation, but Ripton
was as little master of his tongue as he was of his eyes. After
an interval, the Fair Persian having done duty by showing
herself, was glad to quit the room. Her lord and possessor
then turned inquiringly to Ripton.

'You don't wonder now, Rip?' he said.

'No, Richard!' Ripton waited to reply with sufficient
solemnity, 'indeed I don't!'

He spoke differently; he looked differently. He had the
Old Dog's eyes in his head. They watched the door she

had passed through; they listened for her, as dogs' eyes do. When she came in, bonneted for a walk, his agitation was dog-like. When she hung on her lover timidly, and went forth, he followed without an idea of envy, or anything save the secret raptures the sight of her gave him, which are the Old Dog's own. For beneficent Nature requites him. His sensations cannot be heroic, but they have a fulness and a wagging delight as good in their way. And this capacity for humble unaspiring worship has its peculiar guerdon. When Ripton comes to think of Miss Random now, what will he think of himself? Let no one despise the Old Dog. Through him doth Beauty vindicate her sex.

It did not please Ripton that others should have the bliss of beholding her, and as, to his perceptions, everybody did, and observed her offensively, and stared, and turned their heads back, and interchanged comments on her, and became in a minute madly in love with her, he had to smother low growls. They strolled about the pleasant gardens of Kensington all the morning, under the young chestnut buds, and round the windless waters, talking, and soothing the wild excitement of their hearts. If Lucy spoke, Ripton pricked up his ears. She, too, made the remark that everybody seemed to look happy, and he heard it with thrills of joy. 'So everybody is, where you are!' he would have wished to say, if he dared, but was restrained by fears that his burning eloquence would commit him. Ripton knew the people he met twice. It would have been difficult to persuade him they were the creatures of accident.

From the Gardens, in contempt of Ripton's frowned protest, Richard boldly struck into the Park, where solitary carriages were beginning to perform the circuit. Here Ripton had some justification for his jealous pangs. The young girl's golden locks of hair; her sweet, now dreamily sad, face; her gentle graceful figure in the black straight

dress she wore; a sort of half-conventual air she had—a
mark of something not of class, that was partly beauty's,
partly maiden innocence growing conscious, partly remorse
at her weakness and dim fear of the future it was sowing
—did attract the eye-glasses. Ripton had to learn that
eyes are bearable, but eye-glasses an abomination. They
fixed a spell upon his courage; for somehow the youth had
always ranked them as emblems of our nobility, and hearing two exquisite eye-glasses, who had been to front and
rear several times, drawl in gibberish generally imputed to
lords, that his heroine was a charming little creature, just
the size, but had no style,—he was abashed; he did not fly
at them and tear them. He became dejected. Beauty's
dog is affected by the eye-glass in a manner not unlike the
common animal's terror of the human eye.

Richard appeared to hear nothing, or it was homage that
he heard. He repeated to Lucy Diaper Sandoe's verses—

'The cockneys nod to each other aside,
        The coxcombs lift their glasses,'

and projected hiring a horse for her to ride every day in
the park, and shine among the highest.

They had turned to the West, against the sky glittering
through the bare trees across the water, and the bright-
edged rack. The lover, his imagination just then occupied
in clothing earthly glories in celestial, felt where his senses
were sharpest the hand of his darling falter, and instinctively looked ahead. His uncle Algernon was leisurely jolt-
ing towards them on his one sound leg. The dismembered
Guardsman talked to a friend whose arm supported him,
and speculated from time to time on the fair ladies driving
by. The two white faces passed him unobserved. Unfortunately Ripton, coming behind, went plump upon the Captain's live toe—or so he pretended—crying, 'Confound
it, Mr. Thompson! you might have chosen the other.'

The horrible apparition did confound Ripton, who stammered that it was extraordinary.

'Not at all,' said Algernon. 'Everybody makes up to that fellow. Instinct, I suppose!'

He had not to ask for his nephew. Richard turned to face the matter.

'Sorry I couldn't wait for you this morning, uncle,' he said, with the coolness of relationship. 'I thought you never walked so far.'

His voice was in perfect tone—the heroic mask admirable.

Algernon examined the downcast visage at his side, and contrived to allude to the popular preacher. He was instantly introduced to Ripton's sister, Miss Thompson.

The Captain bowed, smiling melancholy approval of his nephew's choice of a minister. After a few stray remarks, and an affable salute to Miss Thompson, he hobbled away, and then the three sealed volcanoes breathed, and Lucy's arm ceased to be squeezed quite so much up to the heroic pitch.

This incident quickened their steps homeward to the sheltering wings of Mrs. Berry. All that passed between them on the subject comprised a stammered excuse from Ripton for his conduct, and a good-humoured rejoinder from Richard, that he had gained a sister by it: at which Ripton ventured to wish aloud Miss Desborough would only think so, and a faint smile twitched poor Lucy's lips to please him. She hardly had strength to reach her cage. She had none to eat of Mrs. Berry's nice little dinner. To be alone, that she might cry and ease her heart of its accusing weight of tears, was all she prayed for. Kind Mrs. Berry, slipping into her bedroom to take off her things, found the fair body in a fevered shudder, and finished by undressing her completely and putting her to bed.

'Just an hour's sleep, or so,' the mellifluous woman

explained the case to the two anxious gentlemen. 'A quiet sleep and a cup of warm tea goes for more than twenty doctors, it do—when there's the flutters,' she pursued. "I know it by myself. And a good cry beforehand's better than the best of medicine."

She nursed them into a make-believe of eating, and retired to her softer charge and sweeter babe, reflecting, 'Lord! Lord! the three of 'em don't make fifty! I'm as old as two and a half of 'em, to say the least.' Mrs. Berry used her apron, and by virtue of their tender years took them all three into her heart.

Left alone, neither of the young men could swallow a morsel.

'Did you see the change come over her?' Richard whispered.

Ripton fiercely accused his prodigious stupidity.

The lover flung down his knife and fork: 'What could I do? If I had said nothing, we should have been suspected. I was obliged to speak. And she hates a lie! See! it has struck her down. God forgive me!'

Ripton affected a serene mind: 'It was a fright, Richard,' he said. 'That's what Mrs. Berry means by flutters. Those old women talk in that way. You heard what she said. And these old women know. I'll tell you what it is. It's this, Richard!—it's because you've got a fool for your friend!'

'She regrets it,' muttered the lover. 'Good God! I think she fears me.' He dropped his face in his hands.

Ripton went to the window, repeating energetically for his comfort: 'It's because you've got a fool for your friend!'

Sombre grew the street they had last night aroused. The sun was buried alive in cloud. Ripton saw himself no more in the opposite window. He watched the deplorable objects passing on the pavement. His aristocratic visions had gone like his breakfast. Beauty had been struck down by his egregious folly, and there he stood—a wretch!

Richard came to him: 'Don't mumble on like that, Rip!' he said. 'Nobody blames you.'

'Ah! you're very kind, Richard,' interposed the wretch, moved at the face of misery he beheld.

'Listen to me, Rip! I shall take her home to-night. Yes! If she's happier away from me!—do you think me a brute, Ripton? Rather than have her shed a tear, I'd ——! I'll take her home to-night!'

Ripton suggested that it was sudden; adding from his larger experience, people perhaps might talk.

The lover could not understand what they should talk about, but he said: 'If I give him who came for her yesterday the clue? If no one sees or hears of me, what can they say? O Rip! I'll give her up. I'm wrecked for ever! What of that? Yes—let them take her! The world in arms should never have torn her from me, but when she cries—Yes! all's over. I'll find him at once.'

He searched in out-of-the-way corners for the hat of resolve. Ripton looked on, wretcheder than ever.

The idea struck him:—'Suppose, Richard, she doesn't want to go?'

It was a moment when, perhaps, one who sided with parents and guardians and the old wise world, might have inclined them to pursue their righteous wretched course, and have given small Cupid a smack and sent him home to his naughty Mother. Alas! (it is THE PILGRIM'S SCRIP interjecting) women are the born accomplices of mischief! In bustles Mrs. Berry to clear away the reflection, and finds the two knights helmed, and sees, though 'tis dusk, that they wear doubtful brows, and guesses bad things for her dear God Hymen in a twinkling.

'Dear! dear!' she exclaimed, 'and neither of you eaten a scrap! And there's my dear young lady off into the prettiest sleep you ever see!'

'Ha?' cried the lover, illuminated.

'Soft as a baby!' Mrs. Berry averred. 'I went to look at her this very moment, and there's not a bit of trouble in her breath. It come and it go like the sweetest regular instrument ever made. The Black Ox haven't trod on *her* foot yet! Most like it was the air of London. But only fancy, if you had called in a doctor! Why, I shouldn't have let her take any of his quackery. Now, there!'

Ripton attentively observed his chief, and saw him doff his hat with a curious caution, and peer into its recess, from which, during Mrs. Berry's speech, he drew forth a little glove—dropped there by some freak of chance.

'Keep me, keep me, now you have me!' sang the little glove, and amused the lover with a thousand conceits.

'When will she wake, do you think, Mrs. Berry?' he asked.

'Oh! we mustn't go for disturbing her,' said the guileful good creature. 'Bless ye! let her sleep it out. And if you young gentlemen was to take my advice, and go and take a walk for to get a appetite—everybody should eat! it's their sacred duty, no matter what their feelings be! and I say it who'm no chicken!—I'll frickashee this—which is a chicken—against your return. I'm a cook, I can assure ye!'

The lover seized her two hands. 'You're the best old soul in the world!' he cried. Mrs. Berry appeared willing to kiss him. 'We won't disturb her. Let her sleep. Keep her in bed, Mrs. Berry. Will you? And we'll call to inquire after her this evening, and come and see her to-morrow. I'm sure you'll be kind to her. There! there!' Mrs. Berry was preparing to whimper. 'I trust her to you, you see. Good-bye, you dear old soul.'

He smuggled a handful of gold into her keeping, and went to dine with his uncles, happy and hungry.

Before they reached the hotel, they had agreed to draw Mrs. Berry into their confidence, telling her (with embellishments) all save their names, so that they might enjoy the counsel and assistance of that trump of a woman, and yet have nothing to fear from her. Lucy was to receive the name of Letitia, Ripton's youngest and best-looking sister. The heartless fellow proposed it in cruel mockery of an old weakness of hers.

'Letitia!' mused Richard. 'I like the name. Both begin with L. There's something soft—womanlike—in the L's.'

Material Ripton remarked that they looked like pounds on paper. The lover roamed through his golden groves. 'Lucy Feverel! that sounds better! I wonder where Ralph is. I should like to help him. He's in love with my cousin Clare. He'll never do anything till he marries. No man can. I'm going to do a hundred things when it's over. We shall travel first. I want to see the Alps. One doesn't know what the earth is till one has seen the Alps. What a delight it will be to her! I fancy I see her eyes gazing up at them.

> "And oh, your dear blue eyes, that heavenward glance
>   With kindred beauty, banished humbleness,
>   Past weeping for mortality's distress—
> Yet from your soul a tear hangs there in trance.
>   And fills, but does not fall;
>   Softly I hear it call
> At heaven's gate, till Sister Seraphs press
> To look on you their old love from the skies:
> Those are the eyes of Seraphs bright on your blue eyes!"

Beautiful! These lines, Rip, were written by a man who was once a friend of my father's. I intend to find him and make them friends again. You don't care for poetry. It's no use your trying to swallow it, Rip!'

'It sounds very nice,' said Ripton, modestly shutting his mouth.

'The Alps! Italy! Rome! and then I shall go to the

East,' the hero continued. 'She's ready to go anywhere with me, the dear brave heart! Oh, the glorious golden East! I dream of the desert. I dream I'm chief of an Arab tribe, and we fly all white in the moonlight on our mares, and hurry to the rescue of my darling! And we push the spears, and we scatter them, and I come to the tent where she crouches, and catch her to my saddle, and away!—Rip! what a life!'

Ripton strove to imagine he could enjoy it.

'And then we shall come home, and I shall lead Austin's life, with her to help me. First be virtuous, Rip! and then serve your country heart and soul. A wise man told me that. I think I shall do something.'

Sunshine and cloud, cloud and sunshine, passed over the lover. Now life was a narrow ring; now the distances extended, were winged, flew illimitably. An hour ago and food was hateful. Now he manfully refreshed his nature, and joined in Algernon's encomiums on Miss Letitia Thompson.

Meantime Beauty slept, watched by the veteran volunteer of the hero's band. Lucy awoke from dreams which seemed reality, to the reality which was a dream. She awoke calling for some friend, 'Margaret!' and heard one say, 'My name is Bessy Berry, my love! not Margaret.' Then she asked piteously where she was, and where was Margaret, her dear friend, and Mrs. Berry whispered, 'Sure you've got a dearer!'

'Ah!' sighed Lucy, sinking on her pillow, overwhelmed by the strangeness of her state.

Mrs. Berry closed the frill of her nightgown and adjusted the bedclothes quietly.

Her name was breathed.

'Yes, my love?' she said.

'Is he here?'

'He's gone, my dear.'

'Gone?—Oh, where?' The young girl started up in disorder.

'Gone, to be back, my love! Ah! that young gentleman!' Mrs. Berry chanted: 'Not a morsel have he eat; not a drop have he drunk!'

'O Mrs. Berry! why did you not make him?' Lucy wept for the famine-struck hero, who was just then feeding mightily.

Mrs. Berry explained that to make one eat who thought the darling of his heart like to die, was a sheer impossibility for the cleverest of women; and on this deep truth Lucy reflected, with her eyes wide at the candle. She wanted one to pour her feelings out to. She slid her hand from under the bedclothes, and took Mrs. Berry's, and kissed it. The good creature required no further avowal of her secret, but forthwith leaned her consummate bosom to the pillow, and petitioned Heaven to bless them both!—Then the little bride was alarmed, and wondered how Mrs. Berry could have guessed it.

'Why,' said Mrs. Berry, 'your love is out of your eyes, and out of everything ye do.' And the little bride wondered more. She thought she had been so very cautious not to betray it. The common woman in them made cheer together after their own April fashion. Following which Mrs. Berry probed for the sweet particulars of this beautiful love-match; but the little bride's lips were locked. She only said her lover was above her in station.

'And you're a Catholic, my dear!'

'Yes, Mrs. Berry!'

'And him a Protestant.'

'Yes, Mrs. Berry!'

'Dear, dear!—And why shouldn't ye be?' she ejaculated, seeing sadness return to the bridal babe. 'So as you was born, so shall ye be! But you'll have to make your arrangements about the children. The girls to worship with you, the boys with him. It's the same God, my dear! You mustn't blush at it, though you do look so pretty. If my young gentleman could see you now!'

'Please, Mrs. Berry!' Lucy murmured.

'Why, he will, you know, my dear!'

'Oh, please, Mrs. Berry!'

'And you that can't bear the thoughts of it! Well, I do wish there was fathers and mothers on both sides and dockments signed, and bridesmaids, and a breakfast! but love is love, and ever will be, in spite of them.'

She made other and deeper dives into the little heart, but though she drew up pearls, they were not of the kind she searched for. The one fact that hung as a fruit upon her tree of Love, Lucy had given her; she would not, in fealty to her lover, reveal its growth and history, however sadly she yearned to pour out all to this dear old Mother Confessor.

Her conduct drove Mrs. Berry from the rosy to the autumnal view of matrimony, generally heralded by the announcement that it is a lottery.

'And when you see your ticket,' said Mrs. Berry, 'you shan't know whether it's a prize or a blank. And, Lord knows! some go on thinking it's a prize when it turns on 'em and tears 'em. I'm one of the blanks, my dear! I drew a blank in Berry. He was a black Berry to me, my dear! Smile away! he truly was, and I a-prizin' him as proud as you can conceive! My dear!' Mrs. Berry pressed her hands flat on her apron. 'We hadn't been a three months man and wife, when that man—it wasn't the honeymoon, which some can't say—that man—Yes! he kicked me. His wedded wife he kicked! Ah!' she sighed to Lucy's large eyes, 'I could have borne that. A blow don't touch the heart,' the poor creature tapped her sensitive side. 'I went on loving of him, for I'm a soft one. Tall as a Grenadier he is, and when out of service grows his moustache.

I used to call him my body-guardsman—like a Queen! I flattered him like the fools we women are. For, take my word for it, my dear, there's nothing here below so vain as a man! That I know. But I didn't deserve it. . . . I'm a superior cook. . . . I did not deserve that noways.' Mrs Berry thumped her knee, and accentuated up her climax: 'I mended his linen. I saw to his adornments—he called his clothes, the bad man! I was a servant to him, my dear! and there—it was nine months—nine months from the day he swear to protect and cherish and that—nine calendar months, and my gentleman is off with another woman! Bone of his bone!—pish!' exclaimed Mrs. Berry, reckoning her wrongs over vividly. ' Here's my ring. A pretty ornament! What do it mean? I'm for tearin' it off my finger a dozen times in the day. It's a symbol? I call it a tomfoolery for the dead-alive to wear it, that's a widow and not a widow, and haven't got a name for what she is in any Dixonary. I've looked, my dear, and'—she spread out her arms—'Johnson*haven't got a name for me!'

At this impressive woe Mrs. Berry's voice quavered into sobs. Lucy spoke gentle words to the poor outcast from Johnson. The sorrows of Autumn have no warning for April. The little bride, for all her tender pity, felt happier when she had heard her landlady's moving tale of the wickedness of man, which cast in bright relief the glory of that one hero who was hers. Then from a short flight of inconceivable bliss, she fell, shot by one of her hundred Argus-eyed fears.

'O Mrs. Berry! I'm so young! Think of me—only just seventeen!'

Mrs. Berry immediately dried her eyes to radiance. 'Young, my dear! Nonsense! There's no so much harm in being young, here and there. I knew an Irish lady was married at fourteen. Her daughter married close over fourteen. She was a grandmother by thirty! When any strange man began, she used to ask him what pattern caps grandmothers wore. They'd stare! Bless you! the grandmother could have married over and over again. It was her daughter's fault, not hers, you know.'

'She was three years younger,' mused Lucy.

'She married beneath her, my dear. Ran off with her father's bailiff's son. "Ah, Berry!" she'd say, "if I hadn't been foolish, I should be my lady now—not Granny!" Her father never forgave her—left all his estates out of the family.'

'Did her husband always love her?' Lucy preferred to know.

'In his way, my dear, he did,' said Mrs. Berry, coming upon her matrimonial wisdom. 'He couldn't help himself. If he left off, he began again. She was so clever, and did make him so comfortable. Cook! there wasn't such another cook out of a Alderman's kitchen; no, indeed! And she a born lady! That tells ye it's the duty of all women! She had her saying—"When the parlour fire gets low, put coals on the ketchen fire!" and a good saying it is to treasure. Such is man! no use in havin' their hearts if ye don't have their stomachs.'

Perceiving that she grew abstruse, Mrs. Berry added briskly: 'You know nothing about that yet, my dear. Only mind me and mark me: don't neglect your cookery. Kissing don't last: cookery do!'

Here, with an aphorism worthy a place in THE PILGRIM'S SCRIP, she broke off to go posseting*for her dear invalid. Lucy was quite well; very eager to be allowed to rise and be ready when the knock should come. Mrs. Berry, in her loving considerateness for the little bride, positively commanded her to lie down, and be quiet, and submit to be nursed and cherished. For Mrs. Berry well knew that ten minutes alone with the hero could only be had while the little bride was in that unattainable position.

Thanks to her strategy, as she thought, her object was gained. The night did not pass before she learnt, from the hero's own mouth, that Mr. Richards, the father of the hero, and a stern lawyer, was adverse to his union with this young lady he loved, because of a ward of his, heiress to an immense property, whom he desired his son to espouse; and because his darling Letitia was a Catholic— Letitia, the sole daughter of a brave naval officer deceased, and in the hands of a savage uncle, who wanted to sacrifice this beauty to a brute of a son. Mrs. Berry listened credulously to the emphatic narrative, and spoke to the effect that the wickedness of old people formed the excuse for the wildness of young ones. The ceremonious administration of oaths of secresy and devotion over, she was enrolled in the hero's band, which now numbered three, and entered upon the duties with feminine energy, for there are no conspirators like women. Ripton's lieutenancy became a sinecure, his rank merely titular. He had never been married—he knew nothing about licences, except that they must be obtained, and were not difficult—he had not an idea that so many days' warning must be given to the clergyman of the parish where one of the parties was resident. How should he? All his forethought was comprised in the ring, and whenever the discussion of arrangements for the great event grew particularly hot and important, he would say, with a shrewd nod: 'We mustn't forget the ring, you know, Mrs. Berry!' and the new member was only prevented by natural commonplace from shouting: 'Oh, drat ye! and your ring too.' Mrs. Berry had acted conspicuously in fifteen marriages, by banns, and by licence, and to have such an obvious requisite dinned in her ears was exasperating. They could not have contracted alliance with an auxiliary more invaluable, an authority so profound; and they acknowledged it to themselves. The hero marched like an automaton at her bidding; Lieutenant

Thompson was rejoiced to perform services as errand-boy in the enterprise.

'It's in hopes you'll be happier than me, I do it,' said the devout and charitable Berry. 'Marriages is made in heaven, they say; and if that's the case, I say they don't take much account of us below!'

Her own woful experiences had been given to the hero in exchange for his story of cruel parents.

Richard vowed to her that he would henceforth hold it a duty to hunt out the wanderer from wedded bonds, and bring him back bound and suppliant.

'Oh, he'll come!' said Mrs. Berry, pursing prophetic wrinkles: 'he'll come of his own accord. Never anywheres will he meet such a cook as Bessy Berry! And he know her value in his heart of hearts. And I do believe, when he do come, I shall be opening these arms to him again, and not slapping his impidence in the face—I'm that soft! I always was—in matrimony, Mr. Richards!'

As when nations are secretly preparing for war, the docks and arsenals hammer night and day, and busy contractors measure time by inches, and the air hums around for leagues as it were myriads of bees, so the house and neighbourhood of the matrimonial soft one resounded in the heroic style, and knew little of the changes of light decreed by Creation. Mrs. Berry was the general of the hour. Down to Doctors' Commons she expedited the hero, instructing him how boldly to face the Law, and fib: for that the Law never could resist a fib and a bold face. Down the hero went, and proclaimed his presence. And lo! the Law danced to him its sedatest lovely bear's-dance. Think ye the Law less susceptible to him than flesh and blood? With a beautiful confidence it put the few familiar questions to him, and nodded to his replies: then stamped the bond, and took the fee. It must be an old vagabond at heart that can permit the irrevocable to go so cheap, even to a hero. For only mark him when he is petitioned by heroes and heroines to undo what he does so easily! That small archway of Doctors' Commons seems the eye of a needle, through which the lean purse has a way, somehow, of slipping more readily than the portly; but once through, all are camels alike, the lean purse an especially big camel.* Dispensing tremendous marriage as it does, the Law can have no conscience.

'I hadn't the slightest difficulty,' said the exulting hero. 'Of course not!' returns Mrs. Berry. 'It's as easy, if ye're in earnest, as buying a plum bun.'

Likewise the ambassador of the hero went to claim the promise of the Church to be in attendance on a certain spot, on a certain day, and there hear oath of eternal fealty, and gird him about with all its forces: which the Church, receiving a wink from the Law, obsequiously engaged to do, for less than the price of a plum-cake.

Meantime, while craftsmen and skilled women, directed by Mrs. Berry, were toiling to deck the day at hand, Raynham and Belthorpe slept,—the former soundly; and one day was as another to them. Regularly every morning a letter arrived from Richard to his father, containing observations on the phenomena of London; remarks (mainly cynical) on the speeches and acts of Parliament; and reasons for not having yet been able to call on the Grandisons. They were certainly rather monotonous and spiritless. The baronet did not complain. That cold dutiful tone assured him there was no internal trouble or distraction. 'The letters of a healthful physique!' he said to Lady Blandish, with sure insight. Complacently he sat and smiled, little witting that his son's ordeal was imminent, and that his son's ordeal was to be his own. Hippias wrote that his nephew was killing him by making appointments which he never kept, and altogether neglecting him in the most shameless way, so that his ganglionic centre was in a ten times worse state than when he left Raynham. He wrote very bitterly, but it was hard to feel compassion for his offended stomach.

On the other hand, young Tom Blaize was not forthcoming, and had despatched no tidings whatever. Farmer Blaize smoked his pipe evening after evening, vastly disturbed. London was a large place—young Tom might be lost in it, he thought; and young Tom had his weaknesses. A wolf at Belthorpe, he was likely to be a sheep in London, as yokels have proved. But what had become of Lucy? This consideration almost sent Farmer Blaize off to London direct, and he would have gone had not his pipe enlightened him. A young fellow might play truant and get into a scrape, but a young man and a young woman were sure to be heard of, *unless* they were acting in complicity. Why, of course, young Tom had behaved like a man, the rascal! and married her outright there, while he had the chance. It was a long guess. Still it was the only reasonable way of accounting for his extraordinary silence, and therefore the farmer held to it that he had done the deed. He argued as modern men do who think the hero, the upsetter of ordinary calculations, is gone from us. So, after despatching a letter to a friend in town to be on the lookout for son Tom, he continued awhile to smoke his pipe, rather elated than not, and mused on the shrewd manner he should adopt when Master Honeymoon did appear.

Toward the middle of the second week of Richard's absence, Tom Bakewell came to Raynham for Cassandra, and privately handed a letter to the Eighteenth Century, containing a request for money, and a round sum. The Eighteenth Century was as good as her word, and gave Tom a letter in return, enclosing a cheque on her bankers, amply providing to keep the heroic engine in motion at a moderate pace. Tom went back, and Raynham and Lobourne slept and dreamed not of the morrow. The System, wedded to

Time, slept, and knew not how he had been outraged—anticipated by seven pregnant seasons. For Time had heard the hero swear to that legalizing instrument, and had also registered an oath. Ah me! venerable Hebrew Time! he is unforgiving. Half the confusion and fever of the world comes of this vendetta he declares against the hapless innocents who have once done him a wrong. They cannot escape him. They will never outlive it. The father of jokes, he is himself no joke; which it seems the business of men to discover.

The days roll round. He is their servant now. Mrs. Berry has a new satin gown, a beautiful bonnet, a gold brooch, and sweet gloves, presented to her by the hero, wherein to stand by his bride at the altar to-morrow; and, instead of being an old wary hen, she is as much a chicken as any of the party, such has been the magic of these articles. Fathers she sees accepting the facts produced for them by their children; a world content to be carved out as it pleases the hero.

At last Time brings the bridal eve, and is blest as a benefactor. The final arrangements are made; the bridegroom does depart; and Mrs. Berry lights the little bride to her bed. Lucy stops on the landing where there is an old clock eccentrically correct that night. 'Tis the palpitating pause before the gates of her transfiguration. Mrs. Berry sees her put her rosy finger on the ONE about to strike, and touch all the hours successively till she comes to the TWELVE that shall sound 'Wife' in her ears on the morrow, moving her lips the while, and looking round archly solemn when she has done; and that sight so catches at Mrs. Berry's heart that, not guessing Time to be the poor child's enemy, she endangers her candle by folding Lucy warmly in her arms, whimpering, 'Bless you for a darling! you innocent lamb! You shall be happy! You shall!'

Old Time gazes grimly ahead.

CHAPTER XXIX

IN WHICH THE LAST ACT OF A COMEDY TAKES THE PLACE OF THE FIRST

ALTHOUGH it blew hard when Cæsar crossed the Rubicon,* the passage of that river is commonly calm; calm as Acheron.* So long as he gets his fare, the ferryman*does not need to be told whom he carries: he pulls with a will, and heroes may be over in half an hour. Only when they stand on the opposite bank, do they see what a leap they have taken. The shores they have relinquished shrink to an infinite remoteness. There they have dreamed: here they must act. There lie youth and irresolution: here manhood and purpose. They are veritably in another land: a moral Acheron divides their life. Their memories scarce seem their own! The PHILOSOPHICAL GEOGRAPHY (about to be published) observed that each man has, one time or other, a little Rubicon—a clear or a foul water to cross. It is asked him: 'Wilt thou wed this Fate, and give up all behind thee?' And 'I will,' firmly pronounced, speeds him over. The above-named manuscript authority informs us, that by far the greater number of carcases rolled by this heroic flood to its sister stream below, are those of fellows who have repented their pledge, and have tried to swim back to the bank they have blotted out. For though every man of us may be a hero for one fatal minute, very few remain so after a day's march even: and who wonders that Madam Fate is indignant, and wears the features of the terrible Universal Fate to him? Fail before her, either in heart or in act, and lo, how the alluring loves in her visage wither and sicken to what it is modelled on! Be your Rubicon big or small, clear or foul, it is the same: you shall not return. On—

or to Acheron!—I subscribe to that saying of THE PIL-
GRIM'S SCRIP:

'The danger of a little knowledge of things is disputable:
but beware the little knowledge of one's self!'

Richard Feverel was now crossing the River of his Ordeal.
Already the mists were stealing over the land he had left:
his life was cut in two, and he breathed but the air that met
his nostrils. His father, his father's love, his boyhood and
ambition, were shadowy. His poetic dreams had taken a
living attainable shape. He had a distincter impression of
the Autumnal Berry and her household than of anything at
Raynham. And yet the young man loved his father, loved
his home: and I dare say Cæsar loved Rome: but whether
he did or no, Cæsar when he killed the Republic was quite
bald, and the hero we are dealing with is scarce beginning
to feel his despotic moustache. Did he know what he was
made of? Doubtless, nothing at all. But honest passion
has an instinct that can be safer than conscious wisdom.
He was an arrow drawn to the head, flying from the bow.
His audacious mendacities and subterfuges did not strike
him as in any way criminal; for he was perfectly sure that
the winning and securing of Lucy would in the end be boisterously approved of, and in that case, were not the means
justified? Not that he took trouble to argue thus, as older
heroes and self-convicting villains are in the habit of doing,
to deduce a clear conscience. Conscience and Lucy went
together.

It was a soft fair day. The Rubicon sparkled in the
morning sun. One of those days when London embraces
the prospect of summer, and troops forth all its babies. The
pavement, the squares, the parks, were early alive with the
cries of young Britain. Violet and primrose girls, and organ
boys with military monkeys, and systematic bands very determined in tone if not in tune, filled the atmosphere, and
crowned the blazing procession of omnibuses, freighted

with business men, Cityward, where a column of reddish brown smoke,—blown aloft by the South-west, marked the scene of conflict to which these persistent warriors repaired. Richard had seen much of early London that morning. His plans were laid. He had taken care to ensure his personal liberty against accidents, by leaving his hotel and his injured uncle Hippias at sunrise. To-day or to-morrow his father was to arrive. Farmer Blaize, Tom Bakewell reported to him, was rageing in town. Another day and she might be torn from him; but to-day this miracle of creation would be his, and then from those glittering banks yonder, let them summon him to surrender her who dared! The position of things looked so propitious that he naturally thought the powers waiting on love conspired in his behalf. And she, too—since she must cross this river, she had sworn to him to be brave, and do him honour, and wear the true gladness of her heart in her face. Without a suspicion of folly in his acts, or fear of results, Richard strolled into Kensington Gardens, breakfasting on the foreshadow of his great joy, now with a vision of his bride, now of the new life opening to him. Mountain masses of clouds, rounded in sunlight, swung up the blue. The flowering chestnut pavilions overhead rustled and hummed. A sound in his ears as of a banner unfolding in the joyful distance lulled him.

He was to meet his bride at the church at a quarter past eleven. His watch said a quarter to ten. He strolled on beneath the long-stemmed trees toward the well dedicated to a saint obscure. Some people were drinking at the well. A florid lady stood by a younger one, who had a little silver mug half-way to her mouth, and evinced undisguised dislike to the liquor of the salutary saint.

'Drink, child!' said the maturer lady. 'That is only your second mug. I insist upon your drinking three full ones every morning we 're in town. Your constitution positively requires iron!'

'But, mama,' the other expostulated, 'it's so nasty. I shall be sick.'

'Drink!' was the harsh injunction. 'Nothing to the German waters, my dear. Here, let me taste.' She took the mug and gave it a flying kiss. 'I declare I think it almost nice—not at all objectionable. Pray, taste it,' she said to a gentleman standing below them to act as cup-bearer.

An unmistakable cis-Rubicon*voice replied: 'Certainly, if it's good fellowship; though I confess I don't think mutual sickness a very engaging ceremony.'

Can one never escape from one's relatives? Richard ejaculated inwardly.

Without a doubt those people were Mrs. Doria, Clare, and Adrian. He had them under his eyes.

Clare, peeping up from her constitutional dose to make sure no man was near to see the possible consequence of it, was the first to perceive him. Her hand dropped.

'Now, pray, drink, and do not fuss!' said Mrs. Doria.

'Mama!' Clare gasped.

Richard came forward and capitulated honourably, since retreat was out of the question. Mrs. Doria swam to meet him: 'My own boy! My dear Richard!' profuse of exclamations. Clare shyly greeted him. Adrian kept in the background.

'Why, we were coming for you to-day, Richard,' said Mrs. Doria, smiling effusion; and rattled on, 'We want another cavalier. This is delightful! My dear nephew! You have grown from a boy to a man. And there's down on his lip! And what brings you here at such an hour in the morning? Poetry, I suppose! Here, take my arm, child.—Clare! finish that mug and thank your cousin for sparing you the third. I always bring her, when we are by a chalybeate,*to take the waters before breakfast. We have to get up at unearthly hours. Think, my dear boy! Mothers

are sacrifices! And so you 've been alone a fortnight with
your agreeable uncle! A charming time of it you must
have had! Poor Hippias! what may be his last nos-
trum?'

'Nephew!' Adrian stretched his head round to the
couple. 'Doses of nephew taken morning and night fourteen days! And he guarantees that it shall destroy an iron
constitution in a month.'

Richard mechanically shook Adrian's hand as he spoke.
'Quite well, Ricky?'

'Yes: well enough,' Richard answered.

'Well?' resumed his vigorous aunt, walking on with
him, while Clare and Adrian followed. 'I really never
saw you looking so handsome. There's something about
your face—look at me—you needn't blush. You 've grown
to an Apollo. That blue buttoned-up frock coat becomes
you admirably—and those gloves, and that easy neck-tie.
Your style is irreproachable, quite a style of your own!
And nothing eccentric. You have the instinct of dress.
Dress shows blood, my dear boy, as much as anything else.
Boy!—you see, I can't forget old habits. You were a boy
when I left, and now!—Do you see any change in him,
Clare?' she turned half round to her daughter.

'Richard is looking very well, mama,' said Clare, glancing
at him under her eyelids.

'I wish I could say the same of you, my dear.—Take
my arm, Richard. Are you afraid of your aunt? I want
to get used to you. Won't it be pleasant, our being all in
town together in the season? How fresh the Opera will be
to you! Austin, I hear, takes stalls. You can come to the
Foreys' box when you like. We are staying with the Foreys
close by here. I think it 's a little too far out, you know;
but they like the neighbourhood. This is what I have
always said: Give him more liberty! Austin has seen it
at last. How do you think Clare looking?'

The question had to be repeated. Richard surveyed his cousin hastily, and praised her looks.

'Pale!' Mrs. Doria sighed.

'Rather pale, aunt.'

'Grown very much—don't you think, Richard?'

'Very tall girl indeed, aunt.'

'If she had but a little more colour, my dear Richard! I 'm sure I give her all the iron she can swallow, but that pallor still continues. I think she does not prosper away from her old companion. She was accustomed to look up to you, Richard——'

'Did you get Ralph's letter, aunt?' Richard interrupted her.

'Absurd!' Mrs. Doria pressed his arm. 'The nonsense of a boy! Why did you undertake to forward such stuff?'

'I 'm certain he loves her,' said Richard, in a serious way.

The maternal eyes narrowed on him. 'Life, my dear Richard, is a game of cross-purposes,' she observed, dropping her fluency, and was rather angered to hear him laugh. He excused himself by saying that she spoke so like his father.

'You breakfast with us,' she freshened off again. 'The Foreys wish to see you; the girls are dying to know you. Do you know, you have a reputation on account of that' —she crushed an intruding adjective—'System you were brought up on. You mustn't mind it. For my part, I think you look a credit to it. Don't be bashful with young women, mind! As much as you please with the old ones. You know how to behave among men. There you have your Drawing-room Guide! I 'm sure I shall be proud of you. Am I not?'

Mrs. Doria addressed his eyes coaxingly.

A benevolent idea struck Richard, that he might employ the minutes to spare, in pleading the case of poor Ralph; and, as he was drawn along, he pulled out his watch to note the precise number of minutes he could dedicate to this charitable office.

'Pardon me,' said Mrs. Doria. 'You want manners, my dear boy. I think it never happened to me before that a man consulted his watch in my presence.'

Richard mildly replied that he had an engagement at a particular hour, up to which he was her servant.

'Fiddlededee!' the vivacious lady sang. 'Now I 've got you, I mean to keep you. Oh! I 've heard all about you. This ridiculous indifference that your father makes so much of! Why, of course, you wanted to see the world! A strong healthy young man shut up all his life in a lonely house—no friends, no society, no amusements but those of rustics! Of course you were indifferent! Your intelligence and superior mind alone saved you from becoming a dissipated country boor.—Where are the others?'

Clare and Adrian came up at a quick pace.

'My damozel dropped something,' Adrian explained.

Her mother asked what it was.

'Nothing, mama,' said Clare, demurely, and they proceeded as before.

Overborne by his aunt's fluency of tongue, and occupied in acute calculation of the flying minutes, Richard let many pass before he edged in a word for Ralph. When he did, Mrs. Doria stopped him immediately.

'I must tell you, child, that I refuse to listen to such rank idiotcy.'

'It 's nothing of the kind, aunt.'

'The fancy of a boy.'

'He 's not a boy. He 's half a year older than I am!'

'You silly child! The moment you fall in love, you all think yourselves men.'

'On my honour, aunt! I believe he loves her thoroughly.'

'Did he tell you so, child?'

'Men don't speak openly of those things,' said Richard.

'Boys do,' said Mrs. Doria.

'But listen to me in earnest, aunt. I want you to be kind to Ralph. Don't drive him to—You may be sorry for it. Let him—do let him write to her, and see her. I believe women are as cruel as men in these things.'

'I never encourage absurdity, Richard.'

'What objection have you to Ralph, aunt?'

'Oh, they 're both good families. It 's not that absurdity, Richard. It will be to his credit to remember that his first fancy wasn't a dairymaid.' Mrs. Doria pitched her accent tellingly. It did not touch her nephew.

'Don't you want Clare ever to marry?' He put the last point of reason to her.

Mrs. Doria laughed. 'I hope so, child. We must find some comfortable old gentleman for her.'

'What infamy!' mutters Richard.

'And I engage Ralph shall be ready to dance at her wedding, or eat a hearty breakfast—We don't dance at weddings now, and very properly. It 's a horrid sad business, not to be treated with levity.—Is that his regiment?' she said, as they passed out of the hussar-sentinelled gardens. 'Tush, tush, child! Master Ralph will recover, as—hem! others have done. A little headache—you call it heartache —and up you rise again, looking better than ever. No doubt, to have a grain of sense forced into your brains, you poor dear children! must be painful. Girls suffer as much as boys, I assure you. More, for their heads are weaker, and their appetites less constant. Do I talk like your father now? Whatever makes the boy fidget at his watch so?'

Richard stopped short. Time spoke urgently.

'I must go,' he said.

His face did not seem good for trifling. Mrs. Doria would trifle in spite.

'Listen, Clare! Richard is going. He says he has an engagement. What possible engagement can a young man have at eleven o'clock in the morning?—unless it's to be married!' Mrs. Doria laughed at the ingenuity of her suggestion.

'Is the church handy, Ricky?' said Adrian. 'You can still give us half an hour if it is. The celibate hours strike at Twelve.' And he also laughed in his fashion.

'Won't you stay with us, Richard?' Clare asked. She blushed timidly, and her voice shook.

Something indefinite—a sharp-edged thrill in the tones made the burning bridegroom speak gently to her.

'Indeed, I would, Clare; I should like to please you, but I have a most imperative appointment—that is, I promised —I must go. I shall see you again——'

Mrs. Doria took forcible possession of him. 'Now, do come, and don't waste words. I insist upon your having some breakfast first, and then, if you really must go, you shall. Look! there's the house. At least you will accompany your aunt to the door.'

Richard conceded this. She little imagined what she required of him. Two of his golden minutes melted into nothingness. They were growing to be jewels of price, one by one more and more precious as they ran, and now so costly-rare—rich as his blood! not to kindest relations, dearest friends, could he give another. The die is cast! Ferryman! push off.

'Good-bye!' he cried, nodding bluffly at the three as one, and fled.

They watched his abrupt muscular stride through the grounds of the house. He looked like resolution on the march. Mrs. Doria, as usual with her out of her brother's hearing, began rating the System.

'See what becomes of that nonsensical education! The boy really does not know how to behave like a common mortal. He has some paltry appointment, or is mad after some ridiculous idea of his own, and everything must be sacrificed to it! That's what Austin calls concentration of the faculties. I think it's more likely to lead to downright insanity than to greatness of any kind. And so I shall tell Austin. It's time he should be spoken to seriously about him.'

'He's an engine, my dear aunt,' said Adrian. 'He isn't a boy, or a man, but an engine. And he appears to have been at high pressure since he came to town—out all day and half the night.'

'He's mad!' Mrs. Doria interjected.

'Not at all. Extremely shrewd is Master Ricky, and carries as open an eye ahead of him as the ships before Troy. He's more than a match for any of us. He is for me, I confess.'

'Then,' said Mrs. Doria, 'he does astonish me!'

Adrian begged her to retain her astonishment till the right season, which would not be long arriving.

Their common wisdom counselled them not to tell the Foreys of their hopeful relative's ungracious behaviour. Clare had left them. When Mrs. Doria went to her room her daughter was there, gazing down at something in her hand, which she guiltily closed.

In answer to an inquiry why she had not gone to take off her things, Clare said she was not hungry. Mrs. Doria lamented the obstinacy of a constitution that no quantity of iron could affect, and eclipsed the looking-glass, saying: 'Take them off here, child, and learn to assist yourself.'

She disentangled her bonnet from the array of her spreading hair, talking of Richard, and his handsome appearance, and extraordinary conduct. Clare kept opening and shutting her hand, in an attitude half-pensive, half-listless. She did not stir to undress. A joyless dimple hung in one pale cheek, and she drew long even breaths.

Mrs. Doria, assured by the glass that she was ready to show, came to her daughter.

'Now, really,' she said, 'you are too helpless, my dear. You cannot do a thing without a dozen women at your elbow. What will become of you? You will have to marry a millionaire.—What 's the matter with you, child?'

Clare undid her tight-shut fingers, as if to some attraction of her eyes, and displayed a small gold hoop on the palm of a green glove.

'A wedding-ring!' exclaimed Mrs. Doria, inspecting the curiosity most daintily.

There on Clare's pale green glove lay a wedding-ring!

Rapid questions as to where, when, how, it was found, beset Clare, who replied: In the Gardens, mama. This morning. When I was walking behind Richard.'

'Are you sure he did not give it you, Clare?'

'Oh no, mama! he did not give it me.'

'Of course not! only he does such absurd things! I thought, perhaps—these boys are so exceedingly ridiculous!' Mrs. Doria had an idea that it might have been concerted between the two young gentlemen, Richard and Ralph, that the former should present this token of hymenæal devotion from the latter to the young lady of his love; but a moment's reflection exonerated boys even from such preposterous behaviour.

'Now, I wonder,' she speculated on Clare's cold face, 'I do wonder whether it 's lucky to find a wedding-ring? What very quick eyes you have, my darling!' Mrs. Doria kissed her. She thought it must be lucky, and the circumstance made her feel tender to her child. Her child did not move to the kiss.

'Let 's see whether it fits,' said Mrs. Doria, almost infantine with surprise and pleasure.

Clare suffered her glove to be drawn off. The ring slid down her long thin finger, and settled comfortably.

'It does!' Mrs. Doria whispered. To find a wedding-ring is open to any woman; but to find a wedding-ring that fits may well cause a superstitious emotion. Moreover, that it should be found while walking in the neighbourhood of the identical youth whom a mother has destined for her daughter, gives significance to the gentle perturbation of ideas consequent on such a hint from Fortune.

'It really fits!' she pursued. 'Now I never pay any attention to the nonsense of omens and that kind of thing' (had the ring been a horseshoe Mrs. Doria would have picked it up and dragged it obediently home), 'but this, I must say, is odd—to find a ring that fits!—singular! It never happened to me. Sixpence is the most I ever discovered, and I have it now. Mind you keep it, Clare—this ring. And,' she laughed, 'offer it to Richard when he comes; say you think he must have dropped it.'

The dimple in Clare's cheek quivered.

Mother and daughter had never spoken explicitly of Richard. Mrs. Doria, by exquisite management, had contrived to be sure that on one side there would be no obstacle to her project of general happiness, without, as she thought, compromising her daughter's feelings unnecessarily. It could do no harm to an obedient young girl to hear that there was no youth in the world like a certain youth. He the prince of his generation, she might softly consent, when requested, to be his princess; and if never requested (for Mrs. Doria envisaged failure), she might easily transfer her softness to squires of lower degree. Clare had always been blindly obedient to her mother (Adrian called them Mrs. Doria Battledoria and the fair Shuttlecockiana),* and her mother accepted in this blind obedience the text of her entire character. It is difficult for those who think very earnestly for their children to know when their children are thinking on their own account. The exercise of their volition we construe as revolt. Our love does not like to be invalided and deposed from its command, and here I think yonder old thrush on the lawn who has just kicked the

last of her lank offspring out of the nest to go shift for itself, much the kinder of the two, though sentimental people
do shrug their shoulders at these unsentimental acts of the
creatures who never wander from nature. Now, excess of
obedience is, to one who manages most exquisitely, as bad
as insurrection. Happily Mrs. Doria saw nothing in her
daughter's manner save a want of iron. Her pallor, her
lassitude, the tremulous nerves in her face, exhibited an
imperious requirement of the mineral.

'The reason why men and women are mysterious to us,
and prove disappointing,' we learn from THE PILGRIM'S
SCRIP, 'is, that we will read them from our own book; just
as we are perplexed by reading ourselves from theirs.'

Mrs. Doria read her daughter from her own book, and she
was gay; she laughed with Adrian at the breakfast-table,
and mock-seriously joined in his jocose assertion that Clare
was positively and by all hymenæal auspices betrothed to
the owner of that ring, be he who he may, and must, whenever he should choose to come and claim her, give her hand
to him (for everybody agreed the owner must be masculine,
as no *woman* would drop a wedding-ring), and follow him
whither he listed all the world over. Amiable giggling
Forey girls called Clare, The Betrothed. Dark man, or
fair ? was mooted. Adrian threw off the first strophe of
Clare's fortune in burlesque rhymes, with an insinuating
gypsy twang. Her aunt Forey warned her to have her
dresses in readiness. Her grandpapa Forey pretended to
grumble at bridal presents being expected from grandpapas.
This one smelt orange-flower, another spoke solemnly of an
old shoe. The finding of a wedding-ring was celebrated
through all the palpitating accessories and rosy ceremonies
involved by that famous instrument. In the midst of the
general hilarity, Clare showed her deplorable want of iron
by bursting into tears.

Did the poor mocked-at heart divine what might be then

enacting? Perhaps, dimly, as we say: that is, without
eyes.

At an altar stand two fair young creatures, ready with
their oaths. They are asked to fix all time to the moment,
and they do so. If there is hesitation at the immense undertaking, it is but maidenly. She conceives as little mental
doubt of the sanity of the act as he. Over them hangs a
cool young curate in his raiment of office. Behind are two
apparently lucid people, distinguished from each other by
sex and age: the former a bunch of simmering black
satin; under her shadow a cock-robin in the dress of a gentleman, big joy swelling out his chest, and pert satisfaction
cocking his head. These be they who stand here in place
of parents to the young couple. All is well. The service
proceeds.

Firmly the bridegroom tells forth his words. This hour
of the complacent giant at least is his, and that he
means to hold him bound through the eternities, men may
hear. Clearly, and with brave modesty, speaks she: no
less firmly, though her body trembles: her voice just vi-
brating while the tone travels on, like a smitten vase.

Time hears sentence pronounced on him: the frail hands
bind his huge limbs and lock the chains. He is used to it:
he lets them do as they will.

Then comes that period when they are to give their troth
to each other. The Man with his right hand takes the
Woman by her right hand: the Woman with her right hand
takes the Man by his right hand.—Devils dare not laugh at
whom Angels crowd to contemplate.

Their hands are joined: their blood flows as one stream.
Adam and fair Eve front the generations. Are they not
lovely? Purer fountains of life were never in two bosoms.

And then they loose their hands, and the cool curate doth
bid the Man to put a ring on the Woman's fourth finger,
counting thumb. And the Man thrusts his hand into one

pocket, and into another, forward and back many times:
into all his pockets. He remembers that he felt for it, and
felt it in his waistcoat pocket, when in the Gardens. And
his hand comes forth empty. And the Man is ghastly to
look at!

Yet, though Angels smile, shall not Devils laugh! The
curate deliberates. The black satin bunch ceases to simmer.
He in her shadow changes from a beaming cock-robin to an
inquisitive sparrow. Eyes multiply questions: lips have no
reply. Time ominously shakes his chain, and in the pause
a sound of mockery stings their ears.

Think ye a hero is one to be defeated in his first battle?
Look at the clock! there are but seven minutes to the stroke
of the celibate hours: the veteran is surely lifting his two
hands to deliver fire, and his shot will sunder them in twain
so nearly united. All the jewellers of London speeding down
with sacks full of the nuptial circlet cannot save them!

The battle must be won on the field, and what does the
hero now? It is an inspiration! For who else would
dream of such a reserve in the rear? None see what he
does; only that the black-satin bunch is remonstratingly
agitated, stormily shaken, and subdued: and as though the
menacing cloud had opened, and dropped the dear token
from the skies at his demand, he produces the symbol of
their consent, and the service proceeds: 'With this ring I
thee wed.'

They are prayed over and blest. For good, or for ill, this
deed is done. The names are registered; fees fly right and
left: they thank, and salute, the curate, whose official coolness melts into a smile of monastic gallantry: the beadle
on the steps waves off a gaping world as they issue forth:
bridegroom and bridesman recklessly scatter gold on him:
carriage doors are banged to: the coachmen drive off, and
the scene closes, everybody happy.

CHAPTER XXX

CELEBRATES THE BREAKFAST

AND the next moment the bride is weeping as if she would dissolve to one of Dian's*Virgin Fountains from the clasp of the Sun-God.* She has nobly preserved the mask imposed by comedies, till the curtain has fallen, and now she weeps, streams with tears. Have patience, O impetuous young man! It is your profession to be a hero. This poor heart is new to it, and her duties involve such wild acts, such brigandage, such terrors and tasks, she is quite unnerved. She did you honour till now. Bear with her now. She does not cry the cry of ordinary maidens in like cases. While the struggle went on her tender face was brave; but, alas! Omens are against her: she holds an ever-present dreadful one on that fatal fourth finger of hers, which has coiled itself round her dream of delight, and takes her in its clutch like a horrid serpent. And yet she must love it. She dares not part from it. She must love and hug it, and feed on its strange honey, and all the bliss it gives her casts all the deeper shadow on what is to come.

Say: Is it not enough to cause feminine apprehension, for a woman to be married in another woman's ring?

You are amazons,* ladies, at Saragossa,* and a thousand citadels—wherever there is strife, and Time is to be taken by the throat. Then shall few men match your sublime fury. But what if you see a vulture, visible only to yourselves, hovering over the house you are gaily led by the torch to inhabit? Will you not crouch and be cowards?

As for the hero, in the hour of victory he pays no heed to omens. He does his best to win his darling to confidence by caresses. Is she not his? Is he not hers? And why,

when the battle is won, does she weep? Does she regret
what she has done?

Oh, never! never! her soft blue eyes assure him, stedfast
love seen swimming on clear depths of faith in them,
through the shower.

He is silenced by her exceeding beauty, and sits perplexed
waiting for the shower to pass.

Alone with Mrs. Berry, in her bedroom, Lucy gave tongue
to her distress, and a second character in the comedy
changed her face.

'O Mrs. Berry! Mrs Berry! what has happened! what
has happened!'

'My darlin' child!' The bridal Berry gazed at the finger of doleful joy. 'I'd forgot all about it! And that's
what've made me feel so queer ever since, then! I've been
seemin' as if I wasn't myself somehow, without my ring.
Dear! dear! what a wilful young gentleman! We ain't a
match for men in that state—Lord help us!'

Mrs. Berry sat on the edge of a chair: Lucy on the edge
of the bed.

'What do you think of it, Mrs. Berry? Is it not terrible?'

'I can't say I should 'a liked it myself, my dear,' Mrs.
Berry candidly responded.

'Oh! why, why, why did it happen!' the young bride
bent to a flood of fresh tears, murmuring that she felt
already old—forsaken.

'Haven't you got a comfort in your religion for all accidents?' Mrs. Berry inquired.

'None for this. I know it's wrong to cry when I am so
happy. I hope he will forgive me.'

Mrs. Berry vowed her bride was the sweetest, softest,
beautifulest thing in life.

'I'll cry no more,' said Lucy. 'Leave me, Mrs. Berry,
and come back when I ring.'

She drew forth a little silver cross, and fell upon her knees to the bed. Mrs. Berry left the room tiptoe.

When she was called to return, Lucy was calm and tearless, and smiled kindly to her.

'It's over now,' she said.

Mrs. Berry sedately looked for her ring to follow.

'He does not wish me to go in to the breakfast you have prepared, Mrs. Berry. I begged to be excused. I cannot eat.'

Mrs. Berry very much deplored it, as she had laid out a superior nuptial breakfast, but with her mind on her ring she nodded assentingly.

'We shall not have much packing to do, Mrs. Berry.'

'No, my dear. It's pretty well all done.'

'We are going to the Isle of Wight, Mrs. Berry.'

'And a very suitable spot ye've chose, my dear!'

'He loves the sea. He wishes to be near it.'

'Don't ye cross to-night, if it's anyways rough, my dear. It isn't adviseable.' Mrs. Berry sank her voice to say, 'Don't ye be soft and give way to him there, or you'll both be repenting it.'

Lucy had only been staving off the unpleasantness she had to speak. She saw Mrs. Berry's eyes pursuing her ring, and screwed up her courage at last.

'Mrs. Berry.'

'Yes, my dear.'

'Mrs. Berry, you shall have another ring.'

'Another, my dear?' Berry did not comprehend. 'One's quite enough for the objeck,' she remarked.

'I mean,' Lucy touched her fourth finger, 'I cannot part with this.' She looked straight at Mrs. Berry.

That bewildered creature gazed at her, and at the ring, till she had thoroughly exhausted the meaning of the words, and then exclaimed, horror-struck: 'Deary me, now! you don't say that? You're to be married again in your own religion.'

The young wife repeated: 'I can never part with it.'

'But, my dear!' the wretched Berry wrung her hands, divided between compassion and a sense of injury. 'My dear!' she kept expostulating like a mute.

'I know all that you would say, Mrs. Berry. I am very grieved to pain you. It is mine now, and must be mine. I cannot give it back.'

There she sat, suddenly developed to the most inflexible little heroine in the three Kingdoms.

From her first perception of the meaning of the young bride's words, Mrs. Berry, a shrewd physiognomist, knew that her case was hopeless, unless she treated her as she herself had been treated, and seized the ring by force of arms; and that she had not heart for.

'What!' she gasped faintly, 'one's own lawful wedding-ring you wouldn't give back to a body?'

'Because it is mine, Mrs. Berry. It was yours, but it is mine now. You shall have whatever you ask for but that. Pray, forgive me! It must be so.'

Mrs. Berry rocked on her chair, and sounded her hands together. It amazed her that this soft little creature could be thus firm. She tried argument.

'Don't ye know, my dear, it's the fatalest thing you're inflictin' upon me, reelly! Don't ye know that bein' bereft of one's own lawful wedding-ring's the fatalest thing in life, and there's no prosperity after it!' For what stands in place o' that, when that's gone, my dear? And what *could* ye give me to compensate a body for the loss o' that? Don't ye know—Oh, deary me!' The little bride's face was so set that poor Berry wailed off in despair.

'I know it,' said Lucy. 'I know it all. I know what I do to you. Dear, dear Mrs. Berry! forgive me! If I parted with my ring I know it would be fatal.'

So this fair young freebooter took possession of her argument as well as her ring.

Berry racked her distracted wits for a further appeal.

'But, my child,' she counterargued, 'you don't understand. It ain't as you think. It ain't a hurt to you now. Not a bit, it ain't. It makes no difference now! Any ring does while the wearer 's a maid. And your Mr. Richard 'll find the very ring he intended for ye. And, of course, that 's the one you 'll wear as his wife. It 's all the same now, my dear. It 's no shame to a maid. Now do—now do—there 's a darlin' !'

Wheedling availed as little as argument.

'Mrs. Berry,' said Lucy, 'you know what my—he spoke: "With this ring I thee wed." It was with *this* ring. Then how could it be with another?'

Berry was constrained despondently to acknowledge that was logic.

She hit upon an artful conjecture:

'Won't it be unlucky your wearin' of the ring which served me so? Think o' that!'

'It may! it may! it may!' cried Lucy.

'And arn't you rushin' into it, my dear?'

'Mrs. Berry,' Lucy said again, 'it was this ring. It cannot—it never can be another. It was this. What it brings me I must bear. I shall wear it till I die!'

'Then what am *I* to do?' the ill-used woman groaned. 'What shall I tell my husband when he come back to me, and see I 've got a new ring waitin' for him? Won't that be a welcome?'

Quoth Lucy: 'How can he know it is not the same, in a plain gold ring?'

'You never see so keen a eyed man in joolry as my Berry!' returned his solitary spouse. 'Not know, my dear? Why, any one would know that 've got eyes in his head. There 's as much difference in wedding-rings as there 's in wedding people! Now, do pray be reasonable, my own sweet!'

'Pray, do not ask me,' pleads Lucy.

'Pray, do think better of it,' urges Berry.

'Pray, pray, Mrs. Berry!' pleads Lucy.

'—And not leave your old Berry all forlorn just when you 're so happy!'

'Indeed I would not, you dear, kind old creature!' Lucy faltered.

Mrs. Berry thought she had her.

'Just when you 're going to be the happiest wife on earth —all you want yours!' she pursued the tender strain. 'A handsome young gentleman! Love and Fortune smilin' on ye——!'

Lucy rose up.

'Mrs. Berry,' she said, 'I think we must not lose time in getting ready, or he will be impatient.'

Poor Berry surveyed her in abject wonder from the edge of her chair. Dignity and resolve were in the ductile form she had hitherto folded under her wing. In an hour the heroine had risen to the measure of the hero. Without being exactly aware what creature she was dealing with, Berry acknowledged to herself it was not one of the common run, and sighed, and submitted.

'It 's like a divorce, that it is!' she sobbed.

After putting the corners of her apron to her eyes, Berry bustled humbly about the packing. Then Lucy, whose heart was full to her, came and kissed her, and Berry bumped down and regularly cried. This over, she had recourse to fatalism.

'I suppose it was to be, my dear! It 's my punishment for meddlin' wi' such matters. No, I 'm not sorry. Bless ye both. Who 'd 'a thought you was so wilful?—you that any one might have taken for one of the silly-softs! You 're a pair, my dear! indeed you are! You was made to meet! But we mustn't show him we 've been crying.—Men don't like it when they 're happy. Let 's wash our faces and try to bear our lot.'

So saying the black-satin bunch careened to a renewed deluge. She deserved some sympathy, for if it is sad to be married in another person's ring, how much sadder to have one's own old accustomed lawful ring violently torn off one's finger and eternally severed from one! But where you have heroes and heroines, these terrible complications ensue.

They had now both fought their battle of the ring, and with equal honour and success.

In the chamber of banquet Richard was giving Ripton his last directions. Though it was a private wedding, Mrs. Berry had prepared a sumptuous breakfast. Chickens offered their breasts: pies hinted savoury secrets: things mystic, in a mash, with Gallic appellatives, jellies, creams, fruits, strewed the table: as a tower in the midst, the cake colossal: the priestly vesture of its nuptial white relieved by hymenæal splendours.

Many hours, much labour and anxiety of mind, Mrs. Berry had expended upon this breakfast, and why? There is one who comes to all feasts that have their basis in Folly, whom criminals of trained instinct are careful to provide against: who will speak, and whose hateful voice must somehow be silenced while the feast is going on. This personage is THE PHILOSOPHER. Mrs. Berry knew him. She knew that he would come. She provided against him in the manner she thought most efficacious: that is, by cheating her eyes and intoxicating her conscience with the due and proper glories incident to weddings where fathers dilate, mothers collapse, and marriage settlements are flourished on high by the family lawyer: and had there been no show of the kind to greet her on her return from the church, she would, and she foresaw she would, have stared at squalor and emptiness, and repented her work. The Philosopher would have laid hold of her by the ear, and called her bad names. Entrenched behind a breakfast-table so legitimately adorned, Mrs. Berry defied him. In the presence of that cake he dared not speak above a whisper. And there were wines to drown him in, should he still think of protesting; fiery wines, and cool: claret sent purposely by the bridegroom for the delectation of his friend.

For one good hour, therefore, the labour of many hours kept him dumb. Ripton was fortifying himself so as to forget him altogether, and the world as well, till the next morning. Ripton was excited, overdone with delight. He had already finished one bottle, and listened, pleasantly flushed, to his emphatic and more abstemious chief. He had nothing to do but to listen, and to drink. The hero would not allow him to shout Victory! or hear a word of toasts; and as, from the quantity of oil poured on it, his eloquence was becoming a natural force in his bosom, the poor fellow was afflicted with a sort of elephantiasis of suppressed emotion. At times he half rose from his chair, and fell vacuously into it again; or he chuckled in the face of weighty, severely-worded instructions; tapped his chest, stretched his arms, yawned, and in short behaved so singularly that Richard observed it, and said: 'On my soul, I don't think you know a word I 'm saying.'

'Every word, Ricky!' Ripton spirted through the opening. 'I 'm going down to your governor, and tell him: Sir Austin! Here 's your only chance of being a happy father— no, no!—Oh! don't you fear me, Ricky! I shall talk the old gentleman over.'

His chief said:

'Look here. You had better not go down to-night. Go down the first thing to-morrow, by the six o'clock train. Give him my letter. Listen to me—give him my letter, and don't speak a word till he speaks. His eyebrows will go up and down, he won't say much. I know him. If he asks you about her, don't be a fool, but say what you think of her sensibly——'

No cork could hold in Ripton when she was alluded to. He shouted: 'She 's an angel!'

Richard checked him: 'Speak sensibly, I say—quietly.
You can say how gentle and good she is—my fleur-de-luce!
And say, this was not her doing. If any one's to blame,
it's I. I made her marry me. Then go to Lady Blandish,
if you don't find her at the house. You may say whatever
you please to her. Give her my letter, and tell her I want
to hear from her immediately. She has seen Lucy, and I
know what she thinks of her. You will then go to Farmer
Blaize. I told you Lucy happens to be his niece—she has
not lived long there. She lived with her aunt Desborough
in France while she was a child, and can hardly be called
a relative to the farmer—there's not a point of likeness
between them. Poor darling! she never knew her mother.
Go to Mr. Blaize, and tell him. You will treat him just as
you would treat any other gentleman. If you are civil, he
is sure to be. And if he abuses me, for my sake and hers
you will still treat him with respect. You hear? And then
write me a full account of all that has been said and done.
You will have my address the day after to-morrow. By the
way, Tom will be here this afternoon. Write out for him
where to call on you the day after to-morrow, in case you
have heard anything in the morning you think I ought to
know at once, as Tom will join me that night. Don't mention to anybody about my losing the ring, Ripton. I
wouldn't have Adrian get hold of that for a thousand
pounds. How on earth I came to lose it! How well she
bore it, Rip! How beautifully she behaved!'

Ripton again shouted: 'An angel!' Throwing up the
heels of his second bottle, he said:

'You may trust your friend, Richard. Aha! when you
pulled at old Mrs. Berry I didn't know what was up. I do
wish you'd let me drink her health?'

'Here's to Penelope!'*said Richard, just wetting his
mouth. The carriage was at the door: a couple of dire
organs, each grinding the same tune, and a vulture-scented

itinerant band (from which not the secretest veiled wedding
can escape) worked harmoniously without in the production
of discord, and the noise acting on his nervous state made
him begin to fume and send in messages for his bride by
the maid.

By and by the lovely young bride presented herself
dressed for the journey, and smiling from stained eyes.

Mrs. Berry was requested to drink some wine, which
Ripton poured out for her, enabling Mrs. Berry thereby to
measure his condition.

The bride now kissed Mrs. Berry, and Mrs. Berry kissed
the bridegroom, on the plea of her softness. Lucy gave
Ripton her hand, with a musical 'Good-bye, Mr. Thompson,'
and her extreme graciousness made him just sensible enough
to sit down before he murmured his fervent hopes for her
happiness.

'I shall take good care of him,' said Mrs. Berry, focus-
sing her eyes to the comprehension of the company.

'Farewell, Penelope!' cried Richard. 'I shall tell the
police everywhere to look out for your lord.'

'Oh my dears! good-bye, and Heaven bless ye both!'

Berry quavered, touched with compunction at the
thoughts of approaching loneliness. Ripton, his mouth
drawn like a bow to his ears, brought up the rear to the
carriage, receiving a fair slap on the cheek from an old
shoe precipitated by Mrs. Berry's enthusiastic female domestic.

White handkerchiefs were waved, the adieux had fallen to
signs: they were off. Then did a thought of such urgency
illumine Mrs. Berry, that she telegraphed, hand in air,
awakening Ripton's lungs, for the coachman to stop, and
ran back to the house. Richard chafed to be gone, but at
his bride's intercession he consented to wait. Presently
they beheld the old black-satin bunch stream through the
street-door, down the bit of garden, and up the astonished

street, halting, panting, capless at the carriage door, a book
in her hand,—a much-used, dog-leaved, steamy, greasy
book, which, at the same time calling out in breathless
jerks, 'There! never ye mind looks! I ain't got a new one.
Read it, and don't ye forget it!' she discharged into Lucy's
lap, and retreated to the railings, a signal for the coachman
to drive away for good.

How Richard laughed at the Berry's bridal gift! Lucy,
too, lost the omen at her heart as she glanced at the title of
the volume. It was Dr. Kitchener on Domestic Cookery!

CHAPTER XXXI

THE PHILOSOPHER APPEARS IN PERSON

GENERAL withdrawing of heads from street-windows,
emigration of organs and bands, and a relaxed atmosphere
in the circle of Mrs. Berry's abode, proved that Dan Cupid
had veritably flown to suck the life of fresh regions. With
a pensive mind she grasped Ripton's arm to regulate his
steps, and returned to the room where her creditor awaited
her. In the interval he had stormed her undefended fortress,
the cake, from which altitude he shook a dolorous head at
the guilty woman. She smoothed her excited apron, sighing. Let no one imagine that she regretted her complicity.
She was ready to cry torrents, but there must be absolute
castigation before this criminal shall conceive the sense of
regret; and probably then she will cling to her wickedness
the more—such is the born Pagan's tenacity! Mrs. Berry
sighed, and gave him back his shake of the head. O you
wanton, improvident creature! said he. O you very wise
old gentleman! said she. He asked her the thing she had
been doing. She enlightened him with the fatalist's reply.

He sounded a bogey's alarm of contingent grave results. She retreated to the entrenched camp of the fact she had helped to make.

'It's done!' she exclaimed. How could she regret what she felt comfort to know was done? Convinced that events alone could stamp a mark on such stubborn flesh, he determined to wait for them, and crouched silent on the cake, with one finger downwards at Ripton's incision there, showing a crumbling chasm and gloomy rich recess.

The eloquent indication was understood. 'Dear! dear!' cried Mrs. Berry, 'what a heap o' cake, and no one to send it to!'

Ripton had resumed his seat by the table and his embrace of the claret. Clear ideas of satisfaction had left him and resolved to a boiling geysir of indistinguishable transports. He bubbled, and waggled, and nodded amicably to nothing, and successfully, though not without effort, preserved his uppermost member from the seductions of the nymph Gravitation, who was on the look-out for his whole length shortly.

'Ha! ha!' he shouted, about a minute after Mrs. Berry had spoken, and almost abandoned himself to the nymph on the spot. Mrs. Berry's words had just reached his wits.

'Why do you laugh, young man?' she inquired, familiar and motherly on account of his condition.

Ripton laughed louder, and caught his chest on the edge of the table and his nose on a chicken. 'That's goo'!' he said, recovering, and rocking under Mrs. Berry's eyes. 'No friend!'

'I did not say, no friend,' she remarked. 'I said, no one; meanin', I know not where for to send it to.'

Ripton's response to this was: You put a Griffin on that cake. Wheatsheaves each side.'

'His crest?' Mrs. Berry said sweetly.

'Oldest baronetcy 'n England!' waved Ripton.

'Yes?' Mrs. Berry encouraged him on.

'You think he's Richards. We're oblige' be very close. And she's the most lovely!—If I hear man say thing 'gainst her. . . . If I hear man say thing 'gainst her! . . .'

'You needn't for to cry over her, young man,' said Mrs. Berry. 'I wanted for to drink their right healths by their right names, and then go about my day's work, and I do hope you won't keep me.'

Ripton stood bolt upright at her words.

'You do?' he said, and filling a bumper he with cheerfully vinous articulation and glibness of tongue proposed the health of Richard and Lucy Feverel, of Raynham Abbey! and that mankind should not require an expeditious example of the way to accept the inspiring toast, he drained his bumper at a gulp. It finished him. The farthing rushlight of his reason leapt and expired. He tumbled to the sofa and there stretched.

Some minutes subsequent to Ripton's signalization of his devotion to the bridal pair, Mrs. Berry's maid entered the room to say that a gentleman was inquiring below after the young gentleman who had departed, and found her mistress with a tottering wineglass in her hand, exhibiting every symptom of unconsoled hysterics. Her mouth gaped, as if the fell creditor had her by the swallow. She ejaculated with horrible exultation that she had been and done it, as her disastrous aspect seemed to testify, and her evident, but inexplicable, access of misery induced the sympathetic maid to tender those caressing words that were all Mrs. Berry wanted to go off into the self-caressing fit without delay; and she had already given the preluding demoniac ironic outburst, when the maid called heaven to witness that the gentleman would hear her; upon which Mrs. Berry violently controlled her bosom, and ordered that he should be shown upstairs instantly to see her the wretch she was. She repeated the injunction.

The maid did as she was told, and Mrs. Berry, wishing first to see herself as she was, mutely accosted the looking-glass, and tried to look a very little better. She dropped a shawl on Ripton and was settled, smoothing her agitation when her visitor was announced.

The gentleman was Adrian Harley. An interview with Tom Bakewell had put him on the track, and now a momentary survey of the table, and its white-vestured cake, made him whistle.

Mrs. Berry plaintively begged him to do her the favour to be seated.

'A fine morning, ma'am,' said Adrian.

'It have been!' Mrs. Berry answered, glancing over her shoulder at the window, and gulping as if to get her heart down from her mouth.

'A very fine Spring,' pursued Adrian, calmly anatomizing her countenance.

Mrs. Berry smothered an adjective to 'weather' on a deep sigh. Her wretchedness was palpable. In proportion to it, Adrian waxed cheerful and brisk. He divined enough of the business to see that there was some strange intelligence to be fished out of the culprit who sat compressing hysterics before him; and as he was never more in his element than when he had a sinner, and a repentant prostrate abject sinner, in hand, his affable countenance might well deceive poor Berry.

'I presume these are Mr. Thompson's lodgings?' he remarked, with a look at the table.

Mrs. Berry's head and the whites of her eyes informed him that they were not Mr. Thompson's lodgings.

'No?' said Adrian, and threw a carelessly inquisitive eye about him. 'Mr. Feverel is out, I suppose?'

A convulsive start at the name, and two corroborating hands dropped on her knees, formed Mrs. Berry's reply.

'Mr. Feverel's man,' continued Adrian, 'told me I

should be certain to find him here. I thought he would be with his friend, Mr. Thompson. I 'm too late, I perceive. Their entertainment is over. I fancy you have been having a party of them here, ma'am?—a bachelors' breakfast!'

In the presence of that cake this observation seemed to mask an irony so shrewd that Mrs. Berry could barely contain herself. She felt she must speak. Making her face as deplorably propitiating as she could, she began:

'Sir, may I beg for to know your name?'

Mr. Harley accorded her request.

Groaning in the clutch of a pitiless truth, she continued: 'And you are Mr. Harley, that was—oh! and you 've come for Mr.——?'

Mr. Richard Feverel was the gentleman Mr. Harley had come for.

'Oh! and it 's no mistake, and he 's of Raynham Abbey?' Mrs. Berry inquired.

Adrian, very much amused, assured her that he was born and bred there.

'His father 's Sir Austin?' wailed the black-satin bunch from behind her handkerchief.

Adrian verified Richard's descent.

'Oh, then, what have I been and done!' she cried, and stared blankly at her visitor. 'I been and married my baby! I been and married the bread out of my own mouth. O Mr. Harley! Mr. Harley! I knew you when you was a boy that big, and wore jackets; and all of you. And it 's my softness that 's my ruin, for I never can resist a man's asking. Look at that cake, Mr. Harley!'

Adrian followed her directions quite coolly. 'Wedding-cake, ma'am!' he said.

'Bride-cake it is, Mr. Harley!'

'Did you make it yourself, ma'am?'

The quiet ease of the question overwhelmed Mrs. Berry and upset that train of symbolic representations by which she was seeking to make him guess the catastrophe and spare her the furnace of confession.

'I did not make it myself, Mr. Harley,' she replied. 'It's a bought cake, and I'm a lost woman. Little I dreamed when I had him in my arms a baby that I should some day be marrying him out of my own house! I little dreamed that! Oh, why did he come to me! Don't you remember his old nurse, when he was a baby in arms, that went away so sudden, and no fault of hers, Mr. Harley! The very mornin' after the night you got into Mr. Benson's cellar, and got so tipsy on his Madeary—I remember it as clear as yesterday!—and Mr. Benson was that angry he threated to use the whip to you, and I helped put you to bed. I'm that very woman.'

Adrian smiled placidly at these reminiscences of his guileless youthful life.

'Well, ma'am! well?' he said. He would bring her to the furnace.

'Won't you see it all, kind sir?' Mrs. Berry appealed to him in pathetic dumb show.

Doubtless by this time Adrian did see it all, and was mentally cursing at Folly, and reckoning the immediate consequences, but he looked uninstructed, his peculiar dimple-smile was undisturbed, his comfortable full-bodied posture was the same. 'Well, ma'am?' he spurred her on.

Mrs. Berry burst forth: 'It were done this mornin', Mr. Harley, in the church, at half-past eleven of the clock, or twenty to, by licence.'

Adrian was now obliged to comprehend a case of matrimony. 'Oh,' he said, like one who is as hard as facts, and as little to be moved: 'Somebody was married this morning; was it Mr. Thompson, or Mr. Feverel?'

Mrs. Berry shuffled up to Ripton, and removed the shawl from him, saying: 'Do he look like a new married bridegroom, Mr. Harley?'

Adrian inspected the oblivious Ripton with philosophic gravity.

'This young gentleman was at church this morning?' he asked.

'Oh! quite reasonable and proper then,' Mrs. Berry begged him to understand.

'Of course, ma'am.' Adrian lifted and let fall the stupid inanimate limbs of the gone wretch, puckering his mouth queerly. 'You were all reasonable and proper, ma'am. The principal male performer, then, is my cousin, Mr. Feverel? He was married by you, this morning, by licence at your parish church, and came here, and ate a hearty breakfast, and left intoxicated.'

Mrs. Berry flew out. 'He never drink a drop, sir. A more moderate young gentleman you never see. Oh! don't ye think that now, Mr. Harley. He was as upright and master of his mind as you be.'

'Ay!' the wise youth nodded thanks to her for the comparison, 'I mean the other form of intoxication.'

Mrs. Berry sighed. She could say nothing on that score.

Adrian desired her to sit down, and compose herself, and tell him circumstantially what had been done.

She obeyed, in utter perplexity at his perfectly composed demeanour.

Mrs. Berry, as her recital declared, was no other than that identical woman who once in old days had dared to behold the baronet behind his mask, and had ever since lived in exile from the Raynham world on a little pension regularly paid to her as an indemnity. She was that woman, and the thought of it made her almost accuse Providence for the betraying excess of softness it had endowed her with. How was she to recognize her baby grown a man? He came in a feigned name; not a word of the family was mentioned. He came like an ordinary mortal, though she felt something more than ordinary to him—she knew she did. He came bringing a beautiful young lady, and on what grounds could she turn her back on them? Why, seeing that all was chaste and legal, why *should* she interfere to make them unhappy—so few the chances of happiness in this world! Mrs. Berry related the seizure of her ring.

'One wrench,' said the sobbing culprit, 'one, and my ring was off!'

She had no suspicions, and the task of writing her name in the vestry-book had been too exacting for a thought upon the other signatures.

'I dare say you were exceedingly sorry for what you had done,' said Adrian.

'Indeed, sir,' moaned Berry, 'I were, and am.'

'And would do your best to rectify the mischief—eh, ma'am?'

'Indeed, and indeed, sir, I would,' she protested solemnly.

'—As, of course, you should—knowing the family. Where may these lunatics have gone to spend the Moon?'

Mrs. Berry swimmingly replied: 'To the Isle——. I don't quite know, sir!' she snapped the indication short, and jumped out of the pit she had fallen into. Repentant as she might be, those dears should not be pursued and cruelly balked of their young bliss! 'To-morrow, if you please, Mr. Harley: not to-day!'

'A pleasant spot,' Adrian observed, smiling at his easy prey

By a measurement of dates he discovered that the bridegroom had brought his bride to the house on the day he had quitted Raynham, and this was enough to satisfy Adrian's mind that there had been concoction and chicanery. Chance, probably, had brought him to the old woman: chance certainly had not brought him to the young one.

'Very well, ma'am,' he said, in answer to her petitions for his favourable offices with Sir Austin in behalf of her little pension and the bridal pair, 'I will tell him you were only a blind agent in the affair, being naturally soft, and that you trust he will bless the consummation. He will be in town to-morrow morning; but one of you two must see him to-night. An emetic kindly administered will set our friend here on his legs. A bath and a clean shirt, and he might go. I don't see why your name should appear at all. Brush him up, and send him to Bellingham by the seven o'clock train. He will find his way to Raynham; he knows the neighbourhood best in the dark. Let him go and state the case. Remember, one of you must go.'

With this fair prospect of leaving a choice of a perdition between the couple of unfortunates, for them to fight and lose all their virtues over, Adrian said, 'Good morning.'

Mrs. Berry touchingly arrested him. 'You won't refuse a piece of his cake, Mr. Harley?'

'Oh, dear, no, ma'am,' Adrian turned to the cake with alacrity. 'I shall claim a very large piece. Richard has a great many friends who will rejoice to eat his wedding-cake. Cut me a fair quarter, Mrs. Berry. Put it in paper, if you please. I shall be delighted to carry it to them, and apportion it equitably according to their several degrees of relationship.'

Mrs. Berry cut the cake. Somehow, as she sliced through it, the sweetness and hapless innocence of the bride was presented to her, and she launched into eulogies of Lucy, and clearly showed how little she regretted her conduct. She vowed that they seemed made for each other; that both were beautiful; both had spirit; both were innocent, and to part them, or make them unhappy, would be, Mrs. Berry wrought herself to cry aloud, oh, such a pity!

Adrian listened to it as the expression of a matter-of-fact opinion. He took the huge quarter of cake, nodded mul-titudinous promises, and left Mrs. Berry to bless his good heart.

'So dies the System!' was Adrian's comment in the street. 'And now let prophets roar! He dies respectably in a marriage-bed, which is more than I should have foretold of the monster. Meantime,' he gave the cake a dramatic tap, 'I'll go sow nightmares.'

CHAPTER XXXII

PROCESSION OF THE CAKE

ADRIAN really bore the news he had heard with creditable disinterestedness, and admirable repression of anything beneath the dignity of a philosopher. When one has attained that felicitous point of wisdom from which one sees all mankind to be fools, the diminutive objects may make what new moves they please, one does not marvel at them: their sedateness is as comical as their frolic, and their frenzies more comical still. On this intellectual eminence the wise youth had built his castle, and he had lived in it from an early period. Astonishment never shook the foundations, nor did envy of greater heights tempt him to relinquish the security of his stronghold, for he saw none. Jugglers he saw running up ladders that overtopped him, and air-balloons scaling the empyrean; but the former came precipitately down again, and the latter were at the mercy of the winds; while he remained tranquil on his solid unambitious ground, fitting his morality to the laws, his conscience to his morality, his comfort to his conscience. Not that voluntarily he cut himself off from his fellows: on the contrary, his sole amusement was their society. Alone he was rather dull, as a man who beholds but one thing must naturally be. Study of the animated varieties of that one thing excited him sufficiently to think life a pleasant play; and the

faculties he had forfeited to hold his elevated position he
could serenely enjoy by contemplation of them in others.
Thus:—wonder at Master Richard's madness: though he
himself did not experience it, he was eager to mark the
effect on his beloved relatives. As he carried along his
vindictive hunch of cake, he shaped out their different attitudes of amaze, bewilderment, horror; passing by some
personal chagrin in the prospect. For his patron had projected a journey, commencing with Paris, culminating on
the Alps, and lapsing in Rome: a delightful journey to
show Richard the highways of History and tear him from
the risk of further ignoble fascinations, that his spirit
might be altogether bathed in freshness and revived. This
had been planned during Richard's absence to surprise him.

Now the dream of travel was to Adrian what the love of
woman is to the race of young men. It supplanted that
foolishness. It was his Romance, as we say; that buoyant
anticipation on which in youth we ride the airs, and which,
as we wax older and too heavy for our atmosphere, hardens
to the Hobby, which, if an obstinate animal, is a safer horse,
and conducts man at a slower pace to the sexton. Adrian
had never travelled. He was aware that his romance was
earthly and had discomforts only to be evaded by the one
potent talisman possessed by his patron. His Alp would
hardly be grand to him without an obsequious landlord in
the foreground: he must recline on Mammon's* imperial
cushions in order to moralize becomingly on the ancient
world. The search for pleasure at the expense of discomfort, as frantic lovers woo their mistresses to partake the
shelter of a hut and batten on a crust, Adrian deemed the
bitterness of beggarliness. Let his sweet mistress be given
him in the pomp and splendour due to his superior emotions,
or not at all. Consequently the wise youth had long nursed
an ineffectual passion, and it argued a great nature in him,
that at the moment when his wishes were to be crowned, he

should look with such slight touches of spleen at the gorgeous composite fabric of Parisian cookery and Roman antiquities crumbling into unsubstantial mockery. Assuredly very few even of the philosophers would have turned away uncomplainingly to meaner delights the moment after.

Hippias received the first portion of the cake.

He was sitting by the window in his hotel, reading. He had fought down his breakfast with more than usual success,' and was looking forward to his dinner at the Foreys with less than usual timidity.

'Ah! glad you 've come, Adrian,' he said, and expanded his chest. 'I was afraid I should have to ride down. This is kind of you. We 'll walk down together through the park. It 's absolutely dangerous to walk alone in these streets. My opinion is, that orange-peel lasts all through the year now, and will till legislation puts a stop to it. I give you my word I slipped on a piece of orange-peel yesterday afternoon in Piccadilly, and I thought I was down! I saved myself by a miracle.'

'You have an appetite, I hope?' Adrian asked.

'I think I shall get one, after a bit of a walk,' chirped Hippias. 'Yes. I think I feel hungry now.'

'Charmed to hear it,' said Adrian, and began unpinning his parcel on his knees. 'How should you define Folly?' he checked the process to inquire.

'Hm!' Hippias meditated; he prided himself on being oracular when such questions were addressed to him. 'I think I should define it to be a slide.'

'Very good definition. In other words, a piece of orange-peel; once on it, your life and limbs are in danger, and you are saved by a miracle. You must present that to the PILGRIM. And the monument of folly, what would that be?'

Hippias meditated anew. 'All the human race on one another's shoulders.' He chuckled at the sweeping sourness of the instance.

'Very good,' Adrian applauded, 'or in default of that, some symbol of the thing, say; such as this of which I have here brought you a chip.'

Adrian displayed the quarter of the cake.

'This is the monument made portable—eh?'

'Cake!' cried Hippias, retreating his chair to dramatize his intense disgust. 'You're right of them that eat it. If I—if I don't mistake,' he peered at it, 'the noxious composition bedizened in that way is what they call wedding-cake. It's arrant poison! Who is it you want to kill? What are you carrying such stuff about for?'

Adrian rang the bell for a knife. 'To present you with your due and proper portion. You will have friends and relatives, and can't be saved from them, not even by miracle. It is a habit which exhibits, perhaps, the unconscious inherent cynicism of the human mind, for people who consider that they have reached the acme of mundane felicity, to distribute this token of esteem to their friends, with the object probably' (he took the knife from a waiter and went to the table to slice the cake) 'of enabling those friends (these edifices require very delicate incision—each particular currant and subtle condiment hangs to its neighbour—a wedding-cake is evidently the most highly civilized of cakes, and partakes of the evils as well as the advantages of civilization!)—I was saying, they send us these love-tokens, no doubt (we shall have to weigh out the crumbs, if each is to have his fair share) that we may the better estimate their state of bliss by passing some hours in purgatory. This, as far as I can apportion it without weights and scales, is your share, my uncle!'

He pushed the corner of the table bearing the cake towards Hippias.

'Get away!' Hippias vehemently motioned, and started from his chair. 'I'll have none of it, I tell you! It's death! It's fifty times worse than that beastly compound Christmas pudding! What fool has been doing this, then? Who dares send me cake? Me! It's an insult.'

'You are not compelled to eat any before dinner,' said Adrian, pointing the corner of the table after him, 'but your share you must take, and appear to consume. One who has done so much to bring about the marriage cannot in conscience refuse his allotment of the fruits. Maidens, I hear, first cook it under their pillows, and extract nuptial dreams therefrom—said to be of a lighter class, taken that way. It's a capital cake, and, upon my honour, you have helped to make it—you have indeed! So here it is.'

The table again went at Hippias. He ran nimbly round it, and flung himself on a sofa exhausted, crying: 'There! . . . My appetite's gone for to-day!'

'Then shall I tell Richard that you won't touch a morsel of his cake?' said Adrian, leaning on his two hands over the table and looking at his uncle.

'Richard?'

'Yes, your nephew: my cousin: Richard! Your companion since you've been in town. He's married, you know. Married this morning at Kensington parish church, by licence, at half-past eleven of the clock, or twenty to. Married, and gone to spend his honeymoon in the Isle of Wight: a very delectable place for a month's residence. I have to announce to you that, thanks to your assistance, the experiment is launched, sir!——'

'Richard married!'

There was something to think and to say in objection to it, but the wits of poor Hippias were softened by the shock. His hand travelled half-way to his forehead, spread out to smooth the surface of that seat of reason, and then fell.

'Surely you knew all about it? you were so anxious to have him in town under your charge. . . .'

'Married?' Hippias jumped up—he had it. 'Why, he's under age! he's an infant.'

'So he is. But the infant is not the less married. Fib like a man and pay your fee—what does it matter? Any one who is breeched can obtain a licence in our noble country. And the interests of morality demand that it should not be difficult. Is it true—can you persuade anybody that you have known nothing about it?'

'Ha! infamous joke! I wish, sir, you would play your pranks on somebody else,' said Hippias, sternly, as he sank back on the sofa. 'You've done me up for the day, I can assure you.'

Adrian sat down to instil belief by gentle degrees, and put an artistic finish to the work. He had the gratification of passing his uncle through varied contortions, and at last Hippias perspired in conviction, and exclaimed, 'This accounts for his conduct to me. That boy must have a cunning nothing short of infernal! I feel . . . I feel it just here,' he drew a hand along his midriff.

'I'm not equal to this world of fools,' he added faintly, and shut his eyes. 'No, I can't dine. Eat? ha! . . . no. Go without me!'

Shortly after, Hippias went to bed, saying to himself, as he undressed, 'See what comes of our fine schemes! Poor Austin!' and as the pillow swelled over his ears, 'I'm not sure that a day's fast won't do me good.' The Dyspepsy had bought his philosophy at a heavy price; he had a right to use it.

Adrian resumed the procession of the cake.

He sighted his melancholy uncle Algernon hunting an appetite in the Row, and looking as if the hope ahead of him were also one-legged. The Captain did not pass without querying the ungainly parcel.

'I hope I carry it ostentatiously enough?' said Adrian. 'Enclosed is wherewithal to quiet the alarm of the land.

Now may the maids and wives of Merry England sleep secure. I had half a mind to fix it on a pole, and engage a band to parade it. This is our dear Richard's wedding-cake. Married at half-past eleven this morning, by licence, at the Kensington parish church; his own ring being lost he employed the ring of his beautiful bride's lachrymose land-lady, she standing adjacent by the altar. His farewell to you as a bachelor, and hers as a maid, you can claim on the spot, if you think proper, and digest according to your powers.'

Algernon let off steam in a whistle. 'Thompson, the solicitor's daughter!' he said. 'I met them the other day, somewhere about here. He introduced me to her. A pretty little baggage.'

'No.' Adrian set him right. ''Tis a Miss Desborough, a Roman Catholic dairymaid. Reminds one of pastoral England in the time of the Plantagenets! He's quite equal to introducing her as Thompson's daughter, and himself as Beelzebub's* son. However, the wild animal is in Hymen's chains, and the cake is cut. Will you have your morsel?'

'Oh, by all means!—not now.' Algernon had an un-wonted air of reflection.—'Father know it?'

'Not yet. He will to-night by nine o'clock.'

'Then I must see him by seven. Don't say you met me.' He nodded, and pricked his horse.

'Wants money!' said Adrian, putting the combustible he carried once more in motion.

The women were the crowning joy of his contempla-tive mind. He had reserved them for his final discharge. Dear demonstrative creatures! Dyspepsia would not weaken their poignant outcries, or self-interest check their fainting fits. On the generic woman one could calcu-late. Well might THE PILGRIM'S SCRIP say of her that, 'She is always at Nature's breast'; not intending it as a compliment. Each woman is Eve throughout the ages; whereas the PILGRIM would have us believe that the Adam in men has become warier, if no wiser; and weak as he is, has learnt a lesson from time. Probably the Pilgrim's meaning may be taken to be, that Man grows, and Woman does not.

At any rate, Adrian hoped for such natural choruses as you hear in the nursery when a bauble is lost. He was awake to Mrs. Doria's maternal predestinations, and guessed that Clare stood ready with the best form of filial obedience. They were only a poor couple to gratify his Mephistophelian humour,* to be sure, but Mrs. Doria was equal to twenty, and they would proclaim the diverse ways with which maidenhood and womanhood took disappointment, while the surrounding Forey girls and other females of the family assembly were expected to develop the finer shades and tapering edges of an agitation to which no woman could be cold.

All went well. He managed cleverly to leave the cake unchallenged in a conspicuous part of the drawing-room, and stepped gaily down to dinner. Much of the conversation adverted to Richard. Mrs. Doria asked him if he had seen the youth, or heard of him.

'Seen him? no! Heard of him? yes!' said Adrian. 'I have heard of him. I heard that he was sublimely happy, and had eaten such a breakfast that dinner was impossible; claret and cold chicken, cake and'——

'Cake at breakfast!' they all interjected.

'That seems to be his fancy just now.'

'What an extraordinary taste!'

'You know, he is educated on a System.'

One fast young male Forey allied the System and the cake in a miserable pun. Adrian, a hater of puns, looked at him, and held the table silent, as if he were going to speak; but he said nothing, and the young gentleman vanished from the conversation in a blush, extinguished by his own spark.

Mrs. Doria peevishly exclaimed, 'Oh! fish-cake, I suppose! I wish he understood a little better the obligations of relationship.'

'Whether he understands them, I can't say,' observed Adrian, 'but I assure you he is very energetic in extending them.'

The wise youth talked innuendoes whenever he had an opportunity, that his dear relative might be rendered sufficiently inflammable by and by at the aspect of the cake; but he was not thought more than commonly mysterious and deep.

'Was his appointment at the house of those Grandison people?' Mrs. Doria asked, with a hostile upper-lip.

Adrian warmed the blindfolded parties by replying, 'Do they keep a beadle at the door?'

Mrs. Doria's animosity to Mrs. Grandison made her treat this as a piece of satirical ingenuousness. 'I dare say they do,' she said.

'And a curate on hand?'

'Oh, I should think a dozen!'

Old Mr. Forey advised his punning grandson Clarence to give that house a wide berth, where he might be disposed of and dished-up at a moment's notice, and the scent ran off at a jest.

The Foreys gave good dinners, and with the old gentleman the excellent old fashion remained in permanence of trooping off the ladies as soon as they had taken their sustenance and just exchanged a smile with the flowers and the dessert, when they rose to fade with a beautiful accord, and the gallant males breathed under easier waistcoats, and settled to the business of the table, sure that an hour for unbosoming and imbibing was their own. Adrian took a chair by Brandon Forey, a barrister of standing.

'I want to ask you,' he said, 'whether an infant in law can legally bind himself.'

'If he's old enough to affix his signature to an instrument, I suppose he can,' yawned Brandon.

'Is he responsible for his acts?'

'I've no doubt we could hang him.'

'Then what he could do for himself, you could do for him?'

'Not quite so much; pretty near.'

'For instance, he can marry?'

'That's not a criminal case, you know.'

'And the marriage is valid?'

'You can dispute it.'

'Yes, and the Greeks and the Trojans can fight. It holds then?'

'Both water and fire!'

The patriarch of the table sang out to Adrian that he stopped the vigorous circulation of the claret.

'Dear me, sir!' said Adrian, 'I beg pardon. The circumstances must excuse me. The fact is, my cousin Richard got married to a dairymaid this morning, and I wanted to know whether it held in law.'

It was amusing to watch the manly coolness with which the announcement was taken. Nothing was heard more energetic than, 'Deuce he has!' and, 'A dairymaid!'

'I thought it better to let the ladies dine in peace,' Adrian continued. 'I wanted to be able to console my aunt——'

'Well, but—well, but,' the old gentleman, much the most excited, puffed—'eh, Brandon? He's a boy, this young ass! Do you mean to tell me a boy can go and marry when he pleases, and any trull he pleases, and the marriage is good? If I thought that I'd turn every woman off my premises. I would! from the housekeeper to the scullery-maid. I'd have no woman near him till—till——'

'Till the young greenhorn was grey, sir?' suggested Brandon.

'Till he knew what women are made of, sir!' the old gentleman finished his sentence vehemently. 'What, d 'ye think, will Feverel say to it, Mr. Adrian?'

'He has been trying the very System you have proposed, sir—one that does not reckon on the powerful action of curiosity on the juvenile intelligence. I 'm afraid it 's the very worst way of solving the problem.'

'Of course it is,' said Clarence. 'None but a fool!——'

'At your age,' Adrian relieved his embarrassment, 'it is natural, my dear Clarence, that you should consider the idea of an isolated or imprisoned manhood something monstrous, and we do not expect you to see what amount of wisdom it contains. You follow one extreme, and we the other. I don't say that a middle course exists. The history of mankind shows our painful efforts to find one, but they have invariably resolved themselves into asceticism, or laxity, acting and reacting. The moral question is, if a naughty little man, by reason of his naughtiness, releases himself from foolishness, does a foolish little man, by reason of his foolishness, save himself from naughtiness?'

A discussion, peculiar to men of the world, succeeded the laugh at Mr. Clarence. Then coffee was handed round and the footman informed Adrian, in a low voice, that Mrs. Doria Forey particularly wished to speak with him. Adrian preferred not to go in alone. 'Very well,' he said, and sipped his coffee. They talked on, sounding the depths of law in Brandon Forey, and receiving nought but hollow echoes from that profound cavity. He would not affirm that the marriage was invalid: he would not affirm that it could not be annulled. He thought not: still he thought it would be worth trying. A consummated and a non-consummated union were two different things. . . .

'Dear me!' said Adrian, 'does the Law recognize that? Why, that's almost human!'

Another message was brought to Adrian that Mrs. Doria Forey *very* particularly wished to speak with him.

'What can be the matter?' he exclaimed, pleased to have his faith in woman strengthened. The cake had exploded, no doubt.

So it proved, when the gentlemen joined the fair society. All the younger ladies stood about the table, whereon the cake stood displayed, gaps being left for those sitting to feast their vision, and intrude the comments and speculations continually arising from fresh shocks of wonder at the unaccountable apparition. Entering with the half-guilty air of men who know they have come from a grosser atmosphere, the gallant males also ranged themselves round the common object of curiosity.

'Here! Adrian!' Mrs. Doria cried. 'Where is Adrian? Pray, come here. Tell me! Where did this cake come from? Whose is it? What does it do here? You know all about it, for you brought it. Clare saw you bring it into the room. What does it mean? I insist upon a direct answer. Now do not make me impatient, Adrian.'

Certainly Mrs. Doria was equal to twenty. By her concentrated rapidity and volcanic complexion it was evident that suspicion had kindled.

'I was really bound to bring it,' Adrian protested.

'Answer me!'

The wise youth bowed: 'Categorically. This cake came from the house of a person, a female, of the name of Berry. It belongs to you partly, partly to me, partly to Clare, and to the rest of our family, on the principle of equal division: for which purpose it is present. . . .'

'Yes! Speak!'

'It means, my dear aunt, what that kind of cake usually does mean.'

'This, then, is the Breakfast! And the ring! Adrian! where is Richard?'

Mrs. Doria still clung to unbelief in the monstrous horror.

But when Adrian told her that Richard had left town, her struggling hope sank. 'The wretched boy has ruined himself!' she said, and sat down trembling.

Oh! that System! The delicate vituperations gentle ladies use instead of oaths, Mrs. Doria showered on that System. She hesitated not to say that her brother had got what he deserved. Opinionated, morbid, weak, justice had overtaken him. Now he would see! but at what a price! at what a sacrifice!

Mrs. Doria commanded Adrian to confirm her fears.

Sadly the wise youth recapitulated Berry's words. 'He was married this morning at half-past eleven of the clock, or twenty to twelve, by licence, at the Kensington parish church.'

'Then that was his appointment!' Mrs. Doria murmured.

'That was the cake for breakfast!' breathed a second of her sex.

'And it was his ring!' exclaimed a third.

The men were silent, and made long faces.

Clare stood cold and sedate. She and her mother avoided each other's eyes.

'Is it that abominable country person, Adrian?'

'The happy damsel is, I regret to say, the Papist dairy-maid,' said Adrian, in sorrowful but deliberate accents.

Then arose a feminine hum, in the midst of which Mrs. Doria cried, 'Brandon!' She was a woman of energy. Her thoughts resolved to action spontaneously.

'Brandon,' she drew the barrister a little aside, 'can they not be followed, and separated? I want your advice. Cannot we separate them? A boy! it is really shameful if he should be allowed to fall into the toils of a designing creature to ruin himself irrevocably. Can we not, Brandon?'

The worthy barrister felt inclined to laugh, but he answered her entreaties: 'From what I hear of the young groom I should imagine the office perilous.'

'I'm speaking of law, Brandon. Can we not obtain an order from one of your Courts to pursue them and separate them instantly?'

'This evening?'

'Yes!'

Brandon was sorry to say she decidedly could not.

'You might call on one of your Judges, Brandon.'

Brandon assured her that the Judges were a hard-worked race, and to a man slept heavily after dinner.

'Will you do so to-morrow, the first thing in the morning? Will you promise me to do so, Brandon?—Or a magistrate! A magistrate would send a policeman after them. My dear Brandon! I beg—I beg you to assist us in this dreadful extremity. It will be the death of my poor brother. I believe he would forgive anything but this. You have no idea what his notions are of blood.'

Brandon tipped Adrian a significant nod to step in and aid.

'What is it, aunt?' asked the wise youth. 'You want them followed and torn asunder by wild policemen?'

'To-morrow!' Brandon queerly interposed.

'Won't that be—just too late?' Adrian suggested.

Mrs. Doria sighed out her last spark of hope.

'You see,' said Adrian. . . .

'Yes! yes!' Mrs. Doria did not require any of his elucidations. 'Pray be quiet, Adrian, and let me speak. Brandon! it cannot be! it's quite impossible! Can you stand there and tell me that boy is legally married? I never will believe it! The law cannot be so shamefully bad as to permit a boy—a mere child—to do such absurd things. Grandpapa!' she beckoned to the old gentleman. 'Grandpapa! pray do make Brandon speak. These lawyers never will. He might stop it, if he would. If I were a man, do you think I would stand here?'

'Well, my dear,' the old gentleman toddled to compose her, 'I'm quite of your opinion. I believe he knows no more than you or I. My belief is they none of them know anything till they join issue and go into Court. I want to see a few female lawyers.'

'To encourage the bankrupt perruquier,* sir?' said Adrian. 'They would have to keep a large supply of wigs on hand.'

'And you can jest, Adrian!' his aunt reproached him. 'But I will not be beaten. I know—I am firmly convinced that no law would ever allow a boy to disgrace his family and ruin himself like that, and nothing shall persuade me that it is so. Now, tell me, Brandon, and pray do speak in answer to my questions, and please to forget you are dealing with a woman. *Can* my nephew be rescued from the consequences of his folly? *Is* what he has done legitimate? *Is* he bound for life by what he has done while a boy?'

'Well—a,' Brandon breathed through his teeth. 'A —hm! the matter's so very delicate, you see, Helen.'

'You're to forget that,' Adrian remarked.

'A—hm! well!' pursued Brandon. 'Perhaps if you could arrest and divide them before nightfall, and make affidavit of certain facts . . .'

'Yes?' the eager woman hastened his lagging mouth.

'Well . . . hm! a . . . in that case . . . a . . . Or if a lunatic, you could prove him to have been of unsound mind. . . .'

'Oh! there's no doubt of his madness on *my* mind, Brandon.'

'Yes! well! in that case . . . Or if of different religious persuasions . . .'

'She *is* a Catholic!' Mrs. Doria joyfully interjected.

'Yes! well! in that case . . . objections might be taken to the form of the marriage . . . Might be proved fictitious . . . Or if he's under, say, eighteen years . . .'

'He *can't* be much more,' cried Mrs. Doria. 'I think,' she appeared to reflect, and then faltered imploringly to Adrian, 'What is Richard's age?'

The kind wise youth could not find it in his heart to strike away the phantom straw she caught at.

'Oh! about that, I should fancy,' he muttered, and found it necessary at the same time to duck and turn his head for concealment. Mrs. Doria surpassed his expectations.

'Yes! well, then . . .' Brandon was resuming with a shrug, which was meant to say he still pledged himself to nothing, when Clare's voice was heard from out the buzzing circle of her cousins: 'Richard is nineteen years and six months old to-day, mama.'

'Nonsense, child.'

'He is, mama.' Clare's voice was very stedfast.

'Non*sense*, I tell you. How *can* you know?'

'Richard is one year and nine months older than me, mama.'

Mrs. Doria fought the fact by years and finally by months. Clare was too strong for her.

'Singular child!' she mentally apostrophized the girl who scornfully rejected straws while drowning.

'But there's the religion still!' she comforted herself, and sat down to cogitate.

The men smiled and looked vacuous.

Music was proposed. There are times when soft music hath not charms; when it is put to as base uses as Imperial Cæsar's dust and is taken to fill horrid pauses. Angelica Forey thumped the piano, and sang: '*I'm a laughing*

Gitana,* *ha—ha! ha—ha!*' Matilda Forey and her cousin
Mary Branksburne wedded their voices, and songfully incited all young people to *Haste to the bower that love has
built,* and defy the wise ones of the world; but the wise
ones of the world were in a majority there, and very few
places of assembly will be found where they are not; so
the glowing appeal of the British ballad-monger passed
into the bosom of the emptiness he addressed. Clare was
asked to entertain the company. The singular child calmly
marched to the instrument, and turned over the appropriate illustrations to the ballad-monger's repertory.

Clare sang a little Irish air. Her duty done, she marched
from the piano. Mothers are rarely deceived by their
daughters in these matters; but Clare deceived her mother;
and Mrs. Doria only persisted in feeling an agony of pity
for her child, that she might the more warrantably pity
herself—a not uncommon form of the emotion, for there
is no juggler like that heart the ballad-monger puts into
our mouths so boldly. Remember that she saw years of
self-denial, years of a ripening scheme, rendered fruitless in
a minute, and by the System which had almost reduced her
to the condition of constitutional hypocrite. She had enough
of bitterness to brood over, and some excuse for self-pity.

Still, even when she was cooler, Mrs. Doria's energetic
nature prevented her from giving up. Straws were straws,
and the frailer they were the harder she clutched them.

She rose from her chair, and left the room, calling to
Adrian to follow her.

'Adrian,' she said, turning upon him in the passage,
'you mentioned a house where this horrible cake . . .
where he was this morning. I desire you to take me to
that woman immediately.'

The wise youth had not bargained for personal servitude.
He had hoped he should be in time for the last act of the
opera that night, after enjoying the comedy of real life.

'My dear aunt . . .' he was beginning to insinuate.

'Order a cab to be sent for, and get your hat,' said Mrs. Doria.

There was nothing for it but to obey. He stamped his assent to the PILGRIM'S dictum, that Women are practical creatures, and now reflected on his own account, that relationship to a young fool may be a vexation and a nuisance. However, Mrs. Doria compensated him.

What Mrs. Doria intended to do, the practical creature did not plainly know; but her energy positively demanded to be used in some way or other, and her instinct directed her to the offender on whom she could use it in wrath. She wanted somebody to be angry with, somebody to abuse. She dared not abuse her brother to his face: him she would have to console. Adrian was a fellow-hypocrite to the System, and would, she was aware, bring her into painfully delicate, albeit highly philosophic, ground by a discussion of the case. So she drove to Bessy Berry simply to inquire whither her nephew had flown.

When a soft woman, and that soft woman a sinner, is matched with a woman of energy, she does not show much fight, and she meets no mercy. Bessy Berry's creditor came to her in female form that night. She then beheld it in all its terrors. Hitherto it had appeared to her as a male, a disembodied spirit of her imagination possessing male attributes, and the peculiar male characteristic of being moved, and ultimately silenced, by tears. As female, her creditor was terrible indeed. Still, had it not been a late hour, Bessy Berry would have died rather than speak openly that her babes had sped to make their nest in the Isle of Wight. They had a long start, they were out of the reach of pursuers, they were safe, and she told what she had to tell. She told more than was wise of her to tell. She made mention of her early service in the family, and of her little pension. Alas! her little pension! Her creditor had come expecting no payment—come, as creditors are wont in such moods, just to take it out of her—to employ the familiar term. At once Mrs. Doria pounced upon the pension.

'That, of course, you know is at an end,' she said in the calmest manner, and Berry did not plead for the little bit of bread to her. She only asked a little consideration for her feelings.

True admirers of women had better stand aside from the scene. Undoubtedly it was very sad for Adrian to be compelled to witness it. Mrs. Doria was not generous. The PILGRIM may be wrong about the sex not growing; but its fashion of conducting warfare we must allow to be barbarous, and according to what is deemed the pristine, or wild cat, method. Ruin, nothing short of it, accompanied poor Berry to her bed that night, and her character bled till morning on the pillow.

The scene over, Adrian reconducted Mrs. Doria to her home. Mice had been at the cake during her absence, apparently. The ladies and gentlemen present put it on the greedy mice, who were accused of having gorged and gone to bed.

'I 'm sure they 're quite welcome,' said Mrs. Doria. 'It 's a farce, this marriage, and Adrian has quite come to my way of thinking. I would not touch an atom of it. Why, they were married in a married woman's ring! Can *that* be legal, as you call it? Oh, I 'm convinced! Don't tell me. Austin will be in town to-morrow, and if he is true to his principles, he will instantly adopt measures to rescue his son from infamy. I want no legal advice. I go upon common sense, common decency. This marriage is false.'

Mrs. Doria's fine scheme had become so much a part of her life, that she could not give it up. She took Clare to her bed, and caressed and wept over her, as she would not have done had she known the singular child, saying,

'Poor Richard! my dear poor boy! we must save him,
Clare! we must save him!' Of the two the mother showed
the greater want of iron on this occasion. Clare lay in her
arms rigid and emotionless, with one of her hands tight-
locked. All she said was: 'I knew it in the morning,
mama.' She slept clasping Richard's nuptial ring.

By this time all specially concerned in the System knew
it. The honeymoon was shining placidly above them.
Is not happiness like another circulating medium? When
we have a very great deal of it, some poor hearts are ach-
ing for what is taken away from them. When we have
gone out and seized it on the highways, certain inscrutable
laws are sure to be at work to bring us to the criminal
bar, sooner or later. Who knows the honeymoon that did
not steal somebody's sweetness? Richard Turpin* went
forth, singing: 'Money or life' to the world: Richard
Feverel has done the same, substituting 'Happiness' for
'Money,' frequently synonyms. The coin he wanted he
would have, and was just as much a highway robber as
his fellow Dick, so that those who have failed to recognize
him as a hero before, may now regard him in that light.
Meanwhile the world he had squeezed looks exceedingly
patient and beautiful. His coin chinks delicious music
to him. Nature and the order of things on earth have no
warmer admirer than a jolly brigand or a young man
made happy by the Jews.

CHAPTER XXXIII

NURSING THE DEVIL

AND now the author of the System was on trial under the
eyes of the lady who loved him. What so kind as they?
Yet are they very rigorous, those soft watchful woman's
eyes. If you are below the measure they have made of

you, you will feel it in the fulness of time. She cannot
but show you that she took you for a giant, and has had
to come down a bit. You feel yourself strangely diminish-
ing in those sweet mirrors, till at last they drop on you
complacently level. But, oh beware, vain man, of ever
waxing enamoured of that wonderful elongation of a male
creature you saw reflected in her adoring upcast orbs!
Beware of assisting to delude her! A woman who is not
quite a fool will forgive your being but a man, if you are
surely that: she will haply learn to acknowledge that
no mortal tailor could have fitted that figure she made
of you respectably, and that practically (though she sighs
to think it) her ideal of you was on the pattern of an overgrown charity-boy in the regulation jacket and breech.
For this she first scorns the narrow capacities of the tailor,
and then smiles at herself. But shouldst thou, when the
hour says plainly, Be thyself, and the woman is willing
to take thee as thou art, shouldst thou still aspire to be
that thing of shanks and wrists, wilt thou not seem contemptible as well as ridiculous? And when the fall comes,
will it not be flat on thy face, instead of to the common
height of men? You may fall miles below her measure of
you, and be safe: nothing is damaged save an overgrown
charity-boy; but if you fall below the common height of
men, you must make up your mind to see her rustle her
gown, spy at the looking-glass, and transfer her allegiance.
The moral of which is, that if we pretend to be what we
are not, women, for whose amusement the farce is performed, will find us out and punish us for it. And it is
usually the end of a sentimental dalliance.

Had Sir Austin given vent to the pain and wrath it was
natural he should feel, he might have gone to unphilo-
sophic excesses, and, however much he lowered his reputation as a sage, Lady Blandish would have excused him:
she would not have loved him less for seeing him closer.

But the poor gentleman tasked his soul and stretched his muscles to act up to her conception of him. He, a man of science in life, who was bound to be surprised by nothing in nature, it was not for him to do more than lift his eyebrows and draw in his lips at the news delivered by Ripton Thompson, that ill bird at Raynham.

All he said, after Ripton had handed the letters and carried his penitential headache to bed, was: 'You see, Emmeline, it is useless to base any system on a human being.'

A very philosophical remark for one who has been busily at work building for nearly twenty years. Too philosophical to seem genuine. It revealed where the blow struck sharpest. Richard was no longer the Richard of his creation—his pride and his joy—but simply a human being with the rest. The bright star had sunk among the mass.

And yet, what had the young man done? And in what had the System failed?

The lady could not but ask herself this, while she condoled with the offended father.

'My friend,' she said, tenderly taking his hand before she retired, 'I know how deeply you must be grieved. I know what your disappointment must be. I do not beg of you to forgive him now. You cannot doubt his love for this young person, and according to his light, has he not behaved honourably, and as you would have wished, rather than bring her to shame? You will think of that. It has been an accident—a misfortune—a terrible misfortune . . .'

'The God of this world is in the machine—not out of it,' Sir Austin interrupted her, and pressed her hand to get the good-night over.

At any other time her mind would have been arrested to admire the phrase; now it seemed perverse, vain, false, and she was tempted to turn the meaning that was in it against himself, much as she pitied him.

'You know, Emmeline,' he added, 'I believe very little in the fortune, or misfortune, to which men attribute their successes and reverses. They are useful impersonations to novelists; but my opinion is sufficiently high of flesh and blood to believe that we make our own history without intervention. Accidents?—Terrible misfortunes? —What are they?—Good-night.'

'Good-night,' she said, looking sad and troubled. 'When I said, "misfortune," I meant, of course, that he is to blame, but—shall I leave you his letter to me?'

'I think I have enough to meditate upon,' he replied, coldly bowing.

'God bless you,' she whispered. 'And—may I say it? do not shut your heart.'

He assured her that he hoped not to do so, and the moment she was gone he set about shutting it as tight as he could.

If, instead of saying, Base no system on a human being, he had said, Never experimentalize with one, he would have been nearer the truth of his own case. He had experimented on humanity in the person of the son he loved as his life, and at once, when the experiment appeared to have failed, all humanity's failings fell on the shoulders of his son. Richard's parting laugh in the train—it was explicable now: it sounded in his ears like the mockery of this base nature of ours at every endeavour to exalt and chasten it. The young man had plotted this. From step to step Sir Austin traced the plot. The curious mask he had worn since his illness; the selection of his incapable uncle Hippias for a companion in preference to Adrian; it was an evident, well-perfected plot. That hideous laugh would not be silenced. Base, like the rest, treacherous, a creature of passions using his abilities solely to gratify them—never surely had humanity such chances as in him! A Manichæan tendency, from which the sententious eulogist of nature had been struggling for years (and which was partly at the bottom of the System), now began to cloud and usurp dominion of his mind. As he sat alone in the forlorn dead-hush of his library, he saw the devil.

How are we to know when we are at the head and fountain of the fates of them we love?

There by the springs of Richard's future, his father sat: and the devil said to him: 'Only be quiet: do nothing: resolutely do nothing: your object now is to keep a brave face to the world, so that all may know you superior to this human nature that has deceived you. For it is the shameless deception, not the marriage, that has wounded you.'

'Ay!' answered the baronet, 'the shameless deception, not the marriage! wicked and ruinous as it must be; a destroyer of my tenderest hopes! my dearest schemes! Not the marriage—the shameless deception!' and he crumpled up his son's letter to him, and tossed it into the fire.

How are we to distinguish the dark chief of the Manichæans when he talks our own thoughts to us?

Further he whispered, 'And your System:—if you would be brave to the world, have courage to cast the dream of it out of you: relinquish an impossible project; see it as it is—dead: too good for men!'

'Ay!' muttered the baronet: 'all who would save them perish on the Cross!'

And so he sat nursing the devil.

By and by he took his lamp, and put on the old cloak and cap, and went to gaze at Ripton. That exhausted debauchee and youth without a destiny slept a dead sleep. A handkerchief was bound about his forehead, and his helpless sunken chin and snoring nose projected up the pillow, made him look absurdly piteous. The baronet remembered how often he had compared his boy with this one: his own bright boy! And where was the difference between them?

'Mere outward gilding!' said his familiar.

'Yes,' he responded, 'I dare say this one never positively plotted to deceive his father: he followed his appetites unchecked, and is internally the sounder of the two.'

Ripton, with his sunken chin and snoring nose under the light of the lamp, stood for human nature, honest, however abject.

'Miss Random, I fear very much, is a necessary establishment!' whispered the monitor.

'Does the evil in us demand its natural food, or it corrupts the whole?' ejaculated Sir Austin. 'And is no angel of avail till that is drawn off? And is that our conflict—to see whether we can escape the contagion of its embrace, and come uncorrupted out of that?'

'The world is wise in its way,' said the voice.

'Though it look on itself through Port wine?' he suggested, remembering his lawyer Thompson.

'Wise in not seeking to be too wise,' said the voice.

'And getting intoxicated on its drug of comfort!'

'Human nature is weak.'

'And Miss Random is an establishment, and Wild Oats an institution!'

'It always has been so.'

'And always will be?'

'So I fear! in spite of your very noble efforts.'

'And leads—whither? And ends—where?'

Richard's laugh, taken up by horrid reverberations, as it were through the lengths of the Lower Halls, replied.

This colloquy of two voices in a brain was concluded by Sir Austin asking again if there were no actual difference between the flower of his hopes and yonder drunken weed,

and receiving for answer that there was a decided dissimi
larity in the smell of the couple; becoming cognizant of
which he retreated.

Sir Austin did not battle with the tempter. He took
him into his bosom at once, as if he had been ripe for him,
and received his suggestions, and bowed to his dictates.
Because he suffered, and decreed that he would suffer
silently, and be the only sufferer, it seemed to him that
he was great-minded in his calamity. He had stood against
the world. The world had beaten him. What then?
He must shut his heart and mask his face; that was all.
To be far in advance of the mass, is as fruitless to mankind, he reflected, as straggling in the rear. For how do we
know that they move behind us at all, or move in our
track? What we win for them is lost; and where we are
overthrown we lie!

It was thus that a fine mind and a fine heart at the
bounds of a nature not great, chose to colour his retro-
gression and countenance his shortcoming; and it was
thus that he set about ruining the work he had done. He
might well say, as he once did, that there are hours when
the clearest soul becomes a cunning fox. For a grief that
was private and peculiar, he unhesitatingly cast the blame
upon humanity; just as he had accused it in the period
of what he termed his own ordeal. How had he borne
that? By masking his face. And he prepared the ordeal
for his son by doing the same. This was by no means
his idea of a man's duty in tribulation, about which he
could be strenuously eloquent. But it was his instinct so
to act, and in times of trial great natures alone are not
at the mercy of their instincts. Moreover it would cost
him pain to mask his face; pain worse than that he endured when there still remained an object for him to open
his heart to in proportion; and he always reposed upon
the Spartan comfort of.bearing pain and being passive.

'Do nothing,' said the devil he nursed; which meant in his case, 'Take me into you and don't cast me out.' Excellent and sane is the outburst of wrath to men, when it stops short of slaughter. For who that locks it up to eat in solitary, can say that it is consumed? Sir Austin had as weak a digestion for wrath, as poor Hippias for a green duckling. Instead of eating it, it ate him. The wild beast in him was not the less deadly because it did not roar, and the devil in him not the less active because he resolved to do nothing.

He sat at the springs of Richard's future, in the forlorn dead-hush of his library there, hearing the cinders click in the extinguished fire, and that humming stillness in which one may fancy one hears the midnight Fates busily stirring their embryos. The lamp glowed mildly on the bust of Chatham.

Toward morning a gentle knock fell at his door. Lady Blandish glided in. With hasty step she came straight to him, and took both his hands.

'My friend,' she said, speaking tearfully, and trembling, 'I feared I should find you here. I could not sleep. How is it with you?'

'Well! Emmeline, well!' he replied, torturing his brows to fix the mask.

He wished it had been Adrian who had come to him. He had an extraordinary longing for Adrian's society. He knew that the wise youth would divine how to treat him, and he mentally confessed to just enough weakness to demand a certain kind of management. Besides Adrian, he had not a doubt, would accept him entirely as he seemed, and not pester him in any way by trying to unlock his heart; whereas, a woman, he feared, would be waxing too womanly, and swelling from tears and supplications to a scene, of all things abhorred by him the most. So he rapped the floor with his foot, and gave the lady no very welcome face when he said it was well with him.

She sat down by his side, still holding one hand firmly, and softly detaining the other.

'Oh, my friend! may I believe you? May I speak to you?' She leaned close to him. 'You know my heart. I have no better ambition than to be your friend. Surely I divide your grief, and may I not claim your confidence? Who has wept more over your great and dreadful sorrows? I would not have come to you, but I do believe that sorrow shared relieves the burden, and it is now that you may feel a woman's aid, and something of what a woman could be to you. . . .'

'Be assured,' he gravely said, 'I thank you, Emmeline, for your intentions.'

'No, no! not for my intentions! And do not thank me. Think of him . . . think of your dear boy . . . Our Richard, as we have called him.—Oh! do not think it a foolish superstition of mine, but I have had a thought this night that has kept me in torment till I rose to speak to you. . . . Tell me first you have forgiven him.'

'A father bears no malice to his son, Emmeline.'

'Your heart has forgiven him?'

'My heart has taken what he gave.'

'And quite forgiven him?'

'You will hear no complaints of mine.'

The lady paused despondingly, and looked at him in a wistful manner, saying with a sigh, 'Yes! I know how noble you are, and different from others!'

He drew one of his hands from her relaxed hold.

'You ought to be in bed, Emmeline.'

'I cannot sleep.'

'Go, and talk to me another time.'

'No, it must be now. You have helped me when I struggled to rise into a clearer world, and I think, humble as I am, I can help you now. I have had a thought this night that if you do not pray for him and bless him . . . it will end miserably. My friend, have you done so?'

He was stung and offended, and could hardly help showing it in spite of his mask.

'Have you done so, Austin?'

'This is assuredly a new way of committing fathers to the follies of their sons, Emmeline!'

'No, not that. But will you pray for your boy, and bless him, before the day comes?'

He restrained himself to pronounce his words calmly:—
'And I must do this, or it will end in misery? How else can it end? Can I save him from the seed he has sown? Consider, Emmeline, what you say. He has repeated his cousin's sin. You see the end of that. . . .'

'Oh, so different! This young person is *not*, is *not* of the class poor Austin Wentworth allied himself to. Indeed it is different. And he—be just and admit his nobleness. I fancied you did. This young person has great beauty, she has the elements of good breeding, she—indeed I think, had she been in another position, you would not have looked upon her unfavourably.'

'She may be too good for my son!' The baronet spoke with sublime bitterness.

'No woman is too good for Richard, and you know it.'

'Pass her.'

'Yes, I will speak only of him. He met her by a fatal accident. We thought his love dead, and so did he till he saw her again. He met her, he thought we were plotting against him, he thought he should lose her for ever, and in the madness of an hour he did this. . . .'

'My Emmeline pleads bravely for clandestine matches.'

'Ah! do not trifle, my friend. Say! would you have had him act as young men in his position generally do to young women beneath them?'

Sir Austin did not like the question. It probed him very severely.

'You mean,' he said, 'that fathers must fold their arms, and either submit to infamous marriages, or have these creatures ruined.'

'I do *not* mean that,' exclaimed the lady, striving for what she did mean, and how to express it. 'I mean that . . . he loved her. Is it not a madness at his age? But what I chiefly mean is—save him from the consequences. No, you shall not withdraw your hand. Think of his pride, his sensitiveness, his great wild nature—wild when he is set wrong: think, how intense it is, set upon love; think, my friend, do not forget his love for you.'

Sir Austin smiled an admirable smile of pity.

'That I should save him, or any one, from consequences, is asking more than the order of things will allow to you, Emmeline, and is not in the disposition of this world. I cannot. Consequences are the natural offspring of acts.* My child, you are talking sentiment, which is the distraction of our modern age in everything—a phantasmal vapour distorting the image of the life we live. You ask me to give him a golden age in spite of himself. All that could be done, by keeping him in the paths of virtue and truth, I did. He is become a man, and as a man he must reap his own sowing.'

The baffled lady sighed. He sat so rigid: he spoke so securely, as if wisdom were to him more than the love of his son. And yet he did love his son. Feeling sure that he loved his son while he spoke so loftily, she reverenced him still, baffled as she was, and sensible that she had been quibbled with.

'All I ask of you is to open your heart to him,' she said. He kept silent.

'Call him a man,—he is, and must ever be the child of your education, my friend.'

'You would console me, Emmeline, with the prospect that, if he ruins himself, he spares the world of young women. Yes, that is something!'

Closely she scanned the mask. It was impenetrable. He could meet her eyes, and respond to the pressure of her hand, and smile, and not show what he felt. Nor did he deem it hypocritical to seek to maintain his elevation in her soft soul, by simulating supreme philosophy over offended love. Nor did he know that he had an angel with him then: a blind angel, and a weak one, but one who struck upon his chance.

'Am I pardoned for coming to you?' she said, after a pause.

'Surely I can read my Emmeline's intentions,' he gently replied.

'Very poor ones. I feel my weakness. I cannot utter half I have been thinking. Oh, if I could!'

'You speak very well, Emmeline.'

'At least, I am pardoned!'

'Surely so.'

'And before I leave you, dear friend, shall I be forgiven? —may I beg it?—will you bless him?'

He was again silent.

'Pray for him, Austin! pray for him ere the night is over.'

As she spoke she slid down to his feet and pressed his hand to her bosom.

The baronet was startled. In very dread of the soft fit that wooed him, he pushed back his chair, and rose, and went to the window.

'It's day already!' he said with assumed vivacity, throwing open the shutters, and displaying the young light on the lawn.

Lady Blandish dried her tears as she knelt, and then joined him, and glanced up silently at Richard's moon

standing in wane toward the West. She hoped it was because of her having been premature in pleading so earnestly, that she had failed to move him, and she accused
herself more than the baronet. But in acting as she had
done, she had treated him as no common man, and she
was compelled to perceive that his heart was at present
hardly superior to the hearts of ordinary men, however
composed his face might be, and apparently serene his
wisdom. From that moment she grew critical of him,
and began to study her idol—a process dangerous to idols.
He, now that she seemed to have relinquished the painful subject, drew to her, and as one who wished to smooth
a foregone roughness, murmured: 'God's rarest blessing
is, after all, a good woman! My Emmeline bears her
sleepless night well. She does not shame the day.' He
gazed down on her with a fondling tenderness.

'I could bear many, many!' she replied, meeting his
eyes, 'and you would see me look better and better, if . . .
if only . . .' but she had no encouragement to end
the sentence.

Perhaps he wanted some mute form of consolation;
perhaps the handsome placid features of the dark-eyed
dame touched him: at any rate their Platonism was advanced by his putting an arm about her. She felt the arm
and talked of the morning.

Thus proximate, they by and by both heard something
very like a groan behind them, and looking round, beheld
the Saurian eye. Lady Blandish smiled, but the baronet's
discomposure was not to be concealed. By a strange fatality every stage of their innocent loves was certain to
have a human beholder.

'Oh, I 'm sure I beg pardon,' Benson mumbled, arresting
his head in a melancholy pendulosity. He was ordered
out of the room.

'And I think I shall follow him, and try to get forty

winks,' said Lady Blandish. They parted with a quiet squeeze of hands.

The baronet then called in Benson.

'Get me my breakfast as soon as you can,' he said, regardless of the aspect of injured conscience Benson sombrely presented to him. 'I am going to town early. And, Benson,' he added, 'you will also go to town this afternoon, or to-morrow, if it suits you, and take your book with you to Mr. Thompson. You will not return here. A provision will be made for you. You can go.'

The heavy butler essayed to speak, but the tremendous blow and the baronet's gesture choked him. At the door he made another effort which shook the rolls of his loose skin pitiably. An impatient signal sent him out dumb, —and Raynham was quit of the one believer in the Great Shaddock*dogma.

CHAPTER XXXIV

CONQUEST OF AN EPICURE

It was the month of July. The Solent*ran up green waves before a full-blowing South-wester. Gay little yachts bounded out like foam, and flashed their sails, light as sea-nymphs. A crown of deep Summer blue topped the flying mountains of cloud.

By an open window that looked on the brine through nodding roses, our young bridal pair were at breakfast, regaling worthily, both of them. Had the Scientific Humanist observed them, he could not have contested the fact, that as a couple who had set up to be father and mother of Britons, they were doing their duty. Files of egg-cups with disintegrated shells, bore witness to it, and they were still at work, hardly talking from rapidity of exercise. Both were dressed for an expedition. She had her bonnet on, and he his yachting-hat. His sleeves were turned over at the wrists, and her gown showed its lining on her lap. At times a chance word might spring a laugh, but eating was the business of the hour, as I would have you to know it always will be where Cupid is in earnest. Tribute flowed in to them from the subject land. Neglected lies Love's penny-whistle on which they played so prettily, and charmed the spheres to hear them. What do they care for the spheres, who have one another? Come, eggs! come, bread and butter! come, tea with sugar in it and milk! and welcome, the jolly hours. That is a fair interpretation of the music in them just now. Yonder instrument was good only for the overture. After all, what finer aspiration can lovers have, than to be free man and woman in the heart of plenty? And is it not a glorious level to have attained? Ah, wretched Scientific Humanist! not to be by any mark the admirable sight of these young creatures feeding. It would have been a spell to exorcise the Manichee,* methinks.

The mighty performance came to an end, and then, with a flourish of his table-napkin, husband stood over wife, who met him on the confident budding of her mouth. The poetry of mortals is their daily prose. Is it not a glorious level to have attained? A short, quick-blooded kiss, radiant, fresh, and honest as Aurora,* and then Richard says without lack of cheer, 'No letter to-day, my Lucy!' whereat her sweet eyes dwell on him a little seriously, but he cries, 'Never mind! he'll be coming down himself some morning. He has only to know her, and all's well! eh?' and so saying he puts a hand beneath her chin, and seems to frame her fair face in fancy, she smiling up to be looked at.

'But one thing I do want to ask my darling,' says Lucy, and dropped into his bosom with hands of petition. 'Take me on board his yacht with him to-day—not leave me with those people! Will he? I'm a good sailor, he knows!'

'The best afloat!' laughs Richard, hugging her, 'but, you know, you darling bit of a sailor, they don't allow more than a certain number on board for the race, and if they hear you've been with me, there'll be cries of foul play! Besides, there's Lady Judith to talk to you about Austin, and Lord Mountfalcon's compliments for you to listen to, and Mr. Morton to take care of you.'

Lucy's eyes fixed sideways an instant.

'I hope I don't frown and blush as I did?' she said, screwing her pliable brows up to him winningly, and he bent his cheek against hers, and murmured something delicious.

'And we shall be separated for—how many hours? one, two, three hours!' she pouted to his flatteries.

'And then I shall come on board to receive my bride's congratulations.'

'And then my husband will talk all the time to Lady Judith.'

'And then I shall see my wife frowning and blushing at Lord Mountfalcon.'

'Am I so foolish, Richard?' she forgot her trifling to ask in an earnest way, and had another Aurorean kiss, just brushing the dew on her lips, for answer.

After hiding a month in shyest shade, the pair of happy sinners had wandered forth one day to look on men and marvel at them, and had chanced to meet Mr. Morton of Poer Hall, Austin Wentworth's friend, and Ralph's uncle. Mr. Morton had once been intimate with the baronet, but had given him up for many years as impracticable and hopeless, for which reason he was the more inclined to regard Richard's misdemeanour charitably, and to lay the faults of the son on the father; and thinking society to be the one thing requisite to the young man, he had introduced him to the people he knew in the island; among others to the Lady Judith Felle, a fair young dame, who introduced him to Lord Mountfalcon, a puissant nobleman; who introduced him to the yachtsmen beginning to congregate; so that in a few weeks he found himself in the centre of a brilliant company, and for the first time in his life tasted what it was to have free intercourse with his fellow-creatures of both sexes. The son of a System was, therefore, launched; not only through the surf, but in deep waters.

Now the baronet had so far compromised between the recurrence of his softer feelings and the suggestions of his new familiar, that he had determined to act toward Richard with justness. The world called it magnanimity, and even Lady Blandish had some thoughts of the same kind when she heard that he had decreed to Richard a handsome allowance, and had scouted Mrs. Doria's proposal for him to contest the legality of the marriage; but Sir Austin knew well he was simply just in not withholding money from a youth so situated. And here again the world deceived him by embellishing his conduct. For what is it to be just to whom we love! He knew it was not magnanimous, but the cry of the world somehow fortified him in the conceit that in dealing perfect justice to his son he was doing all that was possible, because so much more than common fathers would have done. He had shut his heart.

Consequently Richard did not want money. What he wanted more, and did not get, was a word from his father, and though he said nothing to sadden his young bride, she felt how much it preyed upon him to be at variance with the man whom, now that he had offended him and gone against him, he would have fallen on his knees to; the man who was as no other man to him. She heard him of nights when she lay by his side, and the darkness, and

the broken mutterings, of those nights clothed the figure
of the strange stern man in her mind. Not that it affected
the appetites of the pretty pair. We must not expect
that of Cupid enthroned and in condition; under the
influence of sea-air, too. The files of egg-cups laugh at
such an idea. Still the worm did gnaw them. Judge,
then, of their delight when, on this pleasant morning, as
they were issuing from the garden of their cottage to go
down to the sea, they caught sight of Tom Bakewell rushing up the road with a portmanteau on his shoulders, and,
some distance behind him, discerned Adrian.

'It 's all right!' shouted Richard, and ran off to meet
him, and never left his hand till he had hauled him
up, firing questions at him all the way, to where Lucy
stood.

'Lucy! this is Adrian, my cousin.'——'Isn't he an angel?' his eyes seemed to add; while Lucy's clearly answered, 'That he is!'

The full-bodied angel ceremoniously bowed to her, and
acted with reserved unction the benefactor he saw in
their greetings. 'I think we are not strangers,' he was
good enough to remark, and very quickly let them know
he had not breakfasted; on hearing which they hurried
him into the house, and Lucy put herself in motion to
have him served.

'Dear old Rady,' said Richard, tugging at his hand
again, 'how glad I am you 've come! I don't mind telling
you we 've been horridly wretched.'

'Six, seven, eight, nine eggs,' was Adrian's comment on
a survey of the breakfast-table.

'Why wouldn't he write? Why didn't he answer one of
my letters? But here you are, so I don't mind now. He
wants to see us, does he? We 'll go up to-night. I 've
a match on at eleven; my little yacht—I 've called her
the *Blandish*—against Fred Currie's *Begum*. I shall beat,

but whether I do or not, we 'll go up to-night. What 's
the news? What are they all doing?'

'My dear boy!' Adrian returned, sitting comfortably
down, 'let me put myself a little more on an equal footing with you before I undertake to reply. Half that number of eggs will be sufficient for an unmarried man, and
then we 'll talk. They 're all very well, as well as I can
recollect after the shaking my total vacuity has had this
morning. I came over by the first boat, and the sea, the
sea has made me love mother earth, and desire of her
fruits.'

Richard fretted restlessly opposite his cool relative.

'Adrian! what did he say when he heard of it? I want
to know exactly what words he said.'

'Well says the sage, my son! "Speech is the small
change of Silence." He said less than I do.'

'That 's how he took it!' cried Richard, and plunged
in meditation.

Soon the table was cleared, and laid out afresh, and
Lucy preceded the maid bearing eggs on the tray, and
sat down unbonneted, and like a thorough-bred housewife,
to pour out the tea for him.

'Now we 'll commence,' said Adrian, tapping his egg
with meditative cheerfulness; but his expression soon
changed to one of pain, all the more alarming for his
benevolent efforts to conceal it. Could it be possible the
egg was bad? oh, horror! Lucy watched him, and waited
in trepidation.

'This egg has boiled three minutes and three-quarters,'
he observed, ceasing to contemplate it.

'Dear, dear!' said Lucy, 'I boiled them myself exactly
that time. Richard likes them so. And you like them
hard, Mr. Harley?'

'On the contrary, I like them soft. Two minutes and a
half, or three-quarters at the outside. An egg should never

rashly verge upon hardness—never. Three minutes is the excess of temerity.'

'If Richard had told me! If I had only known!' the lovely little hostess interjected ruefully, biting her lip.

'We mustn't expect him to pay attention to such matters,' said Adrian, trying to smile.

'Hang it! there are more eggs in the house,' cried Richard, and pulled savagely at the bell.

Lucy jumped up, saying, 'Oh, yes! I will go and boil some exactly the time you like. Pray let me go, Mr. Harley.'

Adrian restrained her departure with a motion of his hand. 'No,' he said, 'I will be ruled by Richard's tastes, and Heaven grant me his digestion!'

Lucy threw a sad look at Richard, who stretched on a sofa, and left the burden of the entertainment entirely to her. The eggs were a melancholy beginning, but her ardour to please Adrian would not be damped, and she deeply admired his resignation. If she failed in pleasing this glorious herald of peace, no matter by what small misadventure, she apprehended calamity; so there sat this fair dove with brows at work above her serious smiling blue eyes, covertly studying every aspect of the plump-faced epicure, that she might learn to propitiate him. 'He shall not think me timid and stupid,' thought this brave girl, and indeed Adrian was astonished to find that she could both chat and be useful, as well as look ornamental. When he had finished one egg, behold, two fresh ones came in, boiled according to his prescription. She had quietly given her orders to the maid, and he had them without fuss. Possibly his look of dismay at the offending eggs had not been altogether involuntary, and her woman's instinct, inexperienced as she was, may have told her that he had come prepared to be not very well satisfied with anything in Love's cottage. There was mental faculty in those pliable brows to see through, and combat, an unwitting wise youth.

How much she had achieved already she partly divined when Adrian said: 'I think now I'm in case to answer your questions, my dear boy—thanks to Mrs. Richard,' and he bowed to her his first direct acknowledgment of her position. Lucy thrilled with pleasure.

'Ah!' cried Richard, and settled easily on his back.

'To begin, the Pilgrim has lost his Note-book, and has been persuaded to offer a reward which shall maintain the happy finder thereof in an asylum for life. Benson—superlative Benson—has turned his shoulders upon Raynham. None know whither he has departed. It is believed that the sole surviving member of the sect of the Shaddock-Dogmatists is under a total eclipse of Woman.'

'Benson gone?' Richard exclaimed. 'What a tremendous time it seems since I left Raynham!'

'So it is, my dear boy. The honeymoon is Mahomet's minute; or say, the Persian King's water-pail that you read of in the story: You dip your head in it, and when you draw it out, you discover that you have lived a life. To resume: your uncle Algernon still roams in pursuit of the lost one—I should say, hops. Your uncle Hippias has a new and most perplexing symptom; a determination of bride-cake to the nose. Ever since your generous present to him, though he declares he never consumed a morsel of it, he has been under the distressing illusion that his nose is enormous, and I assure you he exhibits quite a maidenly timidity in following it—through a doorway, for instance. He complains of its terrible weight. I have conceived that Benson invisible might be sitting on it. His hand, and the doctor's, are in hourly consultation with it, but I fear it will not grow smaller. The Pilgrim has begotten upon it a new Aphorism: that Size is a matter of opinion.

'Poor uncle Hippy!' said Richard, 'I wonder he doesn't believe in magic. There's nothing supernatural to rival the wonderful sensations he does believe in. Good God! fancy coming to that!'

'I'm sure I'm very sorry,' Lucy protested, 'but I can't help laughing.'

Charming to the wise youth her pretty laughter sounded.

'The Pilgrim has your notion, Richard. Whom does he not forestall? "Confirmed dyspepsia is the apparatus of illusions," and he accuses the Ages that put faith in sorcery, of universal indigestion, which may have been the case, owing to their infamous cookery. He says again, if you remember, that our own Age is travelling back to darkness and ignorance through dyspepsia. He lays the seat of wisdom in the centre of our system, Mrs. Richard: for which reason you will understand how sensible I am of the vast obligation I am under to you at the present moment, for your especial care of mine.'

Richard looked on at Lucy's little triumph, attributing Adrian's subjugation to her beauty and sweetness. She had latterly received a great many compliments on that score, which she did not care to hear, and Adrian's homage to a practical quality was far pleasanter to the young wife, who shrewdly guessed that her beauty would not help her much in the struggle she had now to maintain. Adrian continuing to lecture on the excelling virtues of wise cookery, a thought struck her: Where, where had she tossed Mrs. Berry's book?

'So that's all about the home-people?' said Richard.

'All!' replied Adrian. 'Or stay: you know Clare's going to be married? Not? Your Aunt Helen——'

'Oh, bother my Aunt Helen! What do you think she had the impertinence to write—but never mind! Is it to Ralph?'

'Your Aunt Helen, I was going to say, my dear boy,

is an extraordinary woman. It was from her originally that the Pilgrim first learnt to call the female the practical animal. He studies us all, you know. THE PILGRIM'S SCRIP is the abstract portraiture of his surrounding relatives. Well, your Aunt Helen——'

'Mrs. Doria Battledoria!' laughed Richard.

'——being foiled in a little pet scheme of her own—call it a System if you like—of some ten or fifteen years' standing, with regard to Miss Clare——'

'The fair Shuttlecockiana!'

'——instead of fretting like a man, and questioning Providence, and turning herself and everybody else inside out, and seeing the world upside down, what does the practical animal do? She wanted to marry her to somebody she couldn't marry her to, so she resolved instantly to marry her to somebody she could marry her to: and as old gentlemen enter into these transactions with the practical animal the most readily, she fixed upon an old gentleman; an unmarried old gentleman, a rich old gentleman, and now a captive old gentleman. The ceremony takes place in about a week from the present time. No doubt you will receive your invitation in a day or two.'

'And that cold, icy, wretched Clare has consented to marry an old man!' groaned Richard. 'I'll put a stop to that when I go to town.'

Richard got up and strode about the room. Then he bethought him it was time to go on board and make preparations.

'I'm off,' he said. 'Adrian, you'll take her. She goes in the *Empress*, Mountfalcon's vessel. He starts us. A little schooner-yacht—such a beauty! I'll have one like her some day. Good-bye, darling!' he whispered to Lucy, and his hand and eyes lingered on her, and hers on him, seeking to make up for the priceless kiss they were debarred from. But she quickly looked away from him as he held her:—Adrian stood silent: his brows were up, and his mouth dubiously contracted. He spoke at last.

'Go on the water?'

'Yes. It's only to St. Helen's. Short and sharp.'

'Do you grudge me the nourishment my poor system has just received, my son?'

'Oh, bother your system! Put on your hat, and come along. I'll put you on board in my boat.'

'Richard! I have already paid the penalty of them who are condemned to come to an island. I will go with you to the edge of the sea, and I will meet you there when you return, and take up the Tale of the Tritons:* but, though I forfeit the pleasure of Mrs. Richard's company, I refuse to quit the land.'

'Yes, oh, Mr. Harley!' Lucy broke from her husband, 'and I will stay with you, if you please. I don't want to go among those people, and we can see it all from the shore. Dearest! I don't want to go. You don't mind? Of course, I will go if you wish, but I would so much rather stay'; and she lengthened her plea in her attitude and look to melt the discontent she saw gathering.

Adrian protested that she had much better go; that he could amuse himself very well till their return, and so forth; but she had schemes in her pretty head, and held to it to be allowed to stay in spite of Lord Mountfalcon's disappointment, cited by Richard, and at the great risk of vexing her darling, as she saw. Richard pished, and glanced contemptuously at Adrian. He gave way ungraciously.

'There, do as you like. Get your things ready to leave this evening. No, I'm not angry.'—Who could be? he seemed as he looked up from her modest fondling to ask Adrian, and seized the indemnity of a kiss on her forehead, which, however, did not immediately disperse the shade of annoyance he felt.

'Good heavens!' he exclaimed. 'Such a day as this, and a fellow refuses to come on the water! Well, come along to the edge of the sea.' Adrian's angelic quality had quite worn off to him. He never thought of devoting himself to make the most of the material there was: but somebody else did, and that fair somebody succeeded wonderfully in a few short hours. She induced Adrian to reflect that the baronet had only to see her, and the family muddle would be smoothed at once. He came to it by degrees; still the gradations were rapid. Her manner he liked; she was certainly a nice picture: best of all, she was sensible. He forgot the farmer's niece in her, she was so very sensible. She appeared really to understand that it was a woman's duty to know how to cook.

But the difficulty was, by what means the baronet could be brought to consent to see her. He had not yet consented to see his son, and Adrian, spurred by Lady Blandish, had ventured something in coming down. He was not inclined to venture more. The small debate in his mind ended by his throwing the burden on time. Time would bring the matter about. Christians as well as Pagans are in the habit of phrasing this excuse for folding their arms; 'forgetful,' says THE PILGRIM'S SCRIP, 'that the devil's imps enter into no such armistice.'

As she loitered along the shore with her amusing companion, Lucy had many things to think of. There was her darling's match. The yachts were started by pistol-shot by Lord Mountfalcon on board the *Empress*, and her little heart beat after Richard's straining sails. Then there was the strangeness of walking with a relative of Richard's, one who had lived by his side so long. And the thought that perhaps this night she would have to appear before the dreaded father of her husband.

'O Mr. Harley!' she said, 'is it true—are we to go to-night? And me,' she faltered, 'will he see me?'

'Ah! that is what I wanted to talk to you about,' said
Adrian. 'I made some reply to our dear boy which he
has slightly misinterpreted. Our second person plural is
liable to misconstruction by an ardent mind. I said
"see you," and he supposed—now, Mrs. Richard, I am
sure you will understand me. Just at present perhaps it
would be advisable—when the father and son have settled
their accounts, the daughter-in-law can't be a debtor. . . .'

Lucy threw up her blue eyes. A half-cowardly delight
at the chance of a respite from the awful interview made
her quickly apprehensive.

'O Mr. Harley! you think he should go alone first?'

'Well, that is my notion. But the fact is, he is such an
excellent husband that I fancy it will require more than a
man's power of persuasion to get him to go.'

'But I will persuade him, Mr. Harley.'

'Perhaps, if you would . . .'

'There is nothing I would not do for his happiness,'
murmured Lucy.

The wise youth pressed her hand with lymphatic approbation. They walked on till the yachts had rounded the
point.

'Is it to-night, Mr. Harley?' she asked with some
trouble in her voice now that her darling was out of sight.

'I don't imagine your eloquence even will get him to
leave you to-night,' Adrian replied gallantly. 'Besides,
I must speak for myself. To achieve the passage to an
island is enough for one day. No necessity exists for any
hurry, except in the brain of that impetuous boy. You
must correct it, Mrs. Richard. Men are made to be
managed, and women are born managers. Now, if you
were to let him know that you don't want to go to-night,
and let him guess, after a day or two, that you would
very much rather . . . you might affect a peculiar repug-
nance. By taking it on yourself, you see, this wild young

man will not require such frightful efforts of persuasion. Both his father and he are exceedingly delicate subjects, and his father unfortunately is not in a position to be managed directly. It's a strange office to propose to you, but it appears to devolve upon you to manage the father through the son. Prodigal having made his peace, you, who have done all the work from a distance, naturally come into the circle of the paternal smile, knowing it due to you. I see no other way. If Richard suspects that his father objects for the present to welcome his daughter-in-law, hostilities will be continued, the breach will be widened, bad will grow to worse, and I see no end to it.'

Adrian looked in her face, as much as to say: Now are you capable of this piece of heroism? And it did seem hard to her that she should have to tell Richard she shrank from any trial. But the proposition chimed in with her fears and her wishes: she thought the wise youth very wise: the poor child was not insensible to his flattery, and the subtler flattery of making herself in some measure a sacrifice to the home she had disturbed. She agreed to simulate as Adrian had suggested.

Victory is the commonest heritage of the hero, and when Richard came on shore proclaiming that the *Blandish* had beaten the *Begum* by seven minutes and three-quarters, he was hastily kissed and congratulated by his bride with her fingers among the leaves of Dr. Kitchener, and anxiously questioned about wine.

'Dearest! Mr. Harley wants to stay with us a little, and he thinks we ought not to go immediately—that is, before he has had some letters, and I feel . . . I would so much rather . . .'.

'Ah! that's it, you coward!' said Richard. 'Well, then, to-morrow. We had a splendid race. Did you see us?'

'Oh, yes! I saw you and was sure my darling would win.' And again she threw on him the cold water of that solicitude about wine. 'Mr. Harley must have the best, you know, and we never drink it, and I 'm so silly, I don't know good wine, and if you would send Tom where he can get *good* wine. I have seen to the dinner.'

'So that 's why you didn't come to meet me?'

'Pardon me, darling.'

'Well, I do, but Mountfalcon doesn't, and Lady Judith thinks you ought to have been there.'

'Ah, but my heart was with you!'

Richard put his hand to feel for the little heart: her eyelids softened, and she ran away.

It is to say much of the dinner that Adrian found no fault with it, and was in perfect goodhumour at the conclusion of the service. He did not abuse the wine they were able to procure for him, which was also much. The coffee, too, had the honour of passing without comment. These were sound first steps toward the conquest of an epicure, and as yet Cupid did not grumble.

After coffee they strolled out to see the sun set from Lady Judith's grounds. The wind had dropped. The clouds had rolled from the zenith, and ranged in amphitheatre with distant flushed bodies over sea and land: Titanic crimson head and chest rising from the wave faced Hyperion*falling. There hung Briareus*with deep-indented trunk and ravined brows, stretching all his hands up to unattainable blue summits. North-west the range had a rich white glow, as if shining to the moon, and westward, streams of amber, melting into upper rose, shot out from the dipping disk.

'What Sandoe calls the passion-flower of heaven,' said Richard under his breath to Adrian, who was serenely chanting Greek hexameters, and answered, in the swing of the cæsura,*'He might as well have said cauliflower.'

Lady Judith, with a black lace veil tied over her head, met them in the walk. She was tall and dark; dark-haired, dark-eyed, sweet and persuasive in her accent and manner. 'A second edition of the Blandish,' thinks Adrian. She welcomed him as one who had claims on her affability. She kissed Lucy protectingly, and remarking on the wonders of the evening, appropriated her husband. Adrian and Lucy found themselves walking behind them.

The sun was under. All the spaces of the sky were alight, and Richard's fancy flamed.

'So you're not intoxicated with your immense triumph this morning?' said Lady Judith.

'Don't laugh at me. When it's over I feel ashamed of the trouble I've taken. Look at that glory!—I'm sure you despise me for it.'

'Was I not there to applaud you? I only think such energies should be turned into some definitely useful channel. But you must not go into the Army.'

'What else can I do?'

'You are fit for so much that is better.'

'I never can be anything like Austin.'

'But I think you can do more.'

'Well, I thank you for thinking it, Lady Judith. Something I will do. A man must deserve to live, as you say.'

'Sauces,' Adrian was heard to articulate distinctly in the rear, 'Sauces are the top tree of this science. A woman who has mastered sauces sits on the apex of civilization.'

Briareus reddened duskily seaward. The West was all a burning rose.

'How can men see such sights as those, and live idle?' Richard resumed. 'I feel ashamed of asking my men to work for me.—Or I feel so now.'

'Not when you're racing the *Begum*, I think. There's no necessity for you to turn democrat like Austin. Do you write now?'

'No. What is writing like mine? It doesn't deceive me. I know it's only the excuse I'm making to myself for remaining idle. I haven't written a line since—lately.'

'Because you are so happy.'

'No, not because of that. Of course I'm very happy...' He did not finish.

Vague, shapeless ambition had replaced love in yonder skies. No Scientific Humanist was by to study the natural development, and guide him. This lady would hardly be deemed a very proper guide to the undirected energies of the youth, yet they had established relations of that nature. She was five years older than he, and a woman, which may explain her serene presumption.

The cloud-giants had broken up: a brawny shoulder smouldered over the sea.

'We'll work together in town, at all events,' said Richard. 'Why can't we go about together at night and find out people who want help?'

Lady Judith smiled, and only corrected his nonsense by saying, 'I think we mustn't be too romantic. You will become a knight-errant, I suppose. You have the characteristics of one.'

'Especially at breakfast,' Adrian's unnecessarily emphatic gastronomical lessons to the young wife here came in.

'You must be our champion,' continued Lady Judith: 'the rescuer and succourer of distressed dames and damsels. We want one badly.'

'You do,' said Richard, earnestly: 'from what I hear: from what I know!' His thoughts flew off with him as knight-errant hailed shrilly at exceeding critical moments by distressed dames and damsels. Images of airy towers hung around. His fancy performed miraculous feats. The towers crumbled. The stars grew larger, seemed to throb with lustre. His fancy crumbled with the towers of the air, his heart gave a leap, he turned to Lucy.

'My darling! what have you been doing?' And as if to compensate her for his little knight-errant infidelity, he pressed very tenderly to her.

'We have been engaged in a charming conversation on domestic cookery,' interposed Adrian.

'Cookery! such an evening as this?' His face was a handsome likeness of Hippias at the presentation of bride-cake.

'Dearest! you know it's very useful,' Lucy mirthfully pleaded.

'Indeed I quite agree with you, child,' said Lady Judith, 'and I think you have the laugh of us. I certainly will learn to cook some day.'

'Woman's mission, in so many words,' ejaculated Adrian.

'And pray, what is man's?'

'To taste thereof, and pronounce thereupon.'

'Let us give it up to them,' said Lady Judith to Richard. 'You and I never will make so delightful and beautifully balanced a world of it.'

Richard appeared to have grown perfectly willing to give everything up to the fair face, his bridal Hesper.

Next day Lucy had to act the coward anew, and as she did so, her heart sank to see how painfully it affected him that she should hesitate to go with him to his father. He was patient, gentle; he sat down by her side to appeal to her reason, and used all the arguments he could think of to persuade her.

'If we go together and make him see us both: if he sees he has nothing to be ashamed of in you—rather everything to be proud of; if you are only near him, you will not have to speak a word, and I'm certain—as certain as that I live—that in a week we shall be settled happily at Raynham. I know my father so well, Lucy. Nobody knows him but I.'

Lucy asked whether Mr. Harley did not.

'Adrian? Not a bit. Adrian only knows a part of people, Lucy; and not the best part.'

Lucy was disposed to think more highly of the object of her conquest.

'Is it he that has been frightening you, Lucy?'

'No, no, Richard; oh, dear no!' she cried, and looked at him more tenderly because she was not quite truthful.

'He doesn't know my father at all,' said Richard. But Lucy had another opinion of the wise youth, and secretly maintained it. She could not be won to imagine the baronet a man of human mould, generous, forgiving, full of passionate love at heart, as Richard tried to picture him, and thought him, now that he beheld him again through Adrian's embassy. To her he was that awful figure, shrouded by the midnight. 'Why are you so harsh?' she had heard Richard cry more than once. She was sure that Adrian must be right.

'Well, I tell you I won't go without you,' said Richard, and Lucy begged for a little more time.

Cupid now began to grumble, and with cause. Adrian positively refused to go on the water unless that element were smooth as a plate. The South-west still joked boisterously at any comparison of the sort; the days were magnificent; Richard had yachting engagements; and Lucy always petitioned to stay to keep Adrian company, conceiving it her duty as hostess. Arguing with Adrian was an absurd idea. If Richard hinted at his retaining Lucy, the wise youth would remark: 'It's a wholesome interlude to your extremely Cupidinous behaviour, my dear boy.'

Richard asked his wife what they could possibly find to talk about.

'All manner of things,' said Lucy; 'not only cookery. He is so amusing, though he does make fun of THE PIL-

GRIM'S SCRIP, and I think he ought not. And then, do you know, darling—you won't think me vain?—I think he is beginning to like me a little.'

Richard laughed at the humble mind of his Beauty.

'Doesn't everybody like you, admire you? Doesn't Lord Mountfalcon, and Mr. Morton, and Lady Judith?'

'But he is one of your family, Richard.'

'And they all will, if she isn't a coward.'

'Ah, no!' she sighs, and is chidden.

The conquest of an epicure, or any young wife's conquest beyond her husband, however loyally devised for their mutual happiness, may be costly to her. Richard in his hours of excitement was thrown very much with Lady Judith. He consulted her regarding what he termed Lucy's cowardice. Lady Judith said: 'I think she's wrong, but you must learn to humour little women.'

'Then would you advise me to go up alone?' he asked, with a cloudy forehead.

'What else can you do? Be reconciled yourself as quickly as you can. You can't drag her like a captive, you know?'

It is not pleasant for a young husband, fancying his bride the peerless flower of Creation, to learn that he must humour a little woman in her. It was revolting to Richard.

'What I fear,' he said, 'is, that my father will make it smooth with me, and not acknowledge her: so that whenever I go to him, I shall have to leave her, and tit for tat—an abominable existence, like a ball on a billiard-table. I won't bear that ignominy. And this I know, I know! she might prevent it at once, if she would only be brave, and face it. You, you, Lady Judith, you wouldn't be a coward?'

'Where my old lord tells me to go, I go,' the lady coldly replied. 'There's not much merit in that. Pray, don't cite me. Women are born cowards, you know.'

'But I love the women who are not cowards.'

'The little thing—your wife has not refused to go?'

'No—but tears! Who can stand tears?'

Lucy had come to drop them. Unaccustomed to have his will thwarted, and urgent where he saw the thing to do so clearly, the young husband had spoken strong words: and she, who knew that she would have given her life by inches for him: who knew that she was playing a part for his happiness, and hiding for his sake the nature that was worthy his esteem; the poor little martyr had been weak a moment.

She had Adrian's support. The wise youth was very comfortable. He liked the air of the Island, and he liked being petted. 'A nice little woman! a very nice little woman!' Tom Bakewell heard him murmur to himself according to a habit he had; and his air of rather succulent patronage as he walked or sat beside the innocent Beauty, with his head thrown back and a smile that seemed always to be in secret communion with his marked abdominal prominence, showed that she was gaining part of what she played for. Wise youths who buy their loves, are not unwilling, when opportunity offers, to try and obtain the commodity for nothing. Examinations of her hand, as for some occult purpose, and unctuous pattings of the same, were not infrequent. Adrian waxed now and then Anacreontic*in his compliments. Lucy would say: 'That's worse than Lord Mountfalcon.'

'Better English than the noble lord deigns to employ—allow that?' quoth Adrian.

'He is very kind,' said Lucy.

'To all, save to our noble vernacular,' added Adrian. 'He seems to scent a rival to his dignity there.'

It may be that Adrian scented a rival to his lymphatic emotions.

'We are at our ease here in excellent society,' he wrote

to Lady Blandish. 'I am bound to confess that the Huron has a happy fortune, or a superlative instinct. Blindfold he has seized upon a suitable mate. She can look at a lord, and cook for an epicure. Besides Dr. Kitchener, she reads and comments on THE PILGRIM'S SCRIP. The "Love" chapter, of course, takes her fancy. That picture of Woman, "*Drawn by Reverence and coloured by Love,*" she thinks beautiful, and repeats it, tossing up pretty eyes. Also the lover's petition: "*Give me purity to be worthy the good in her, and grant her patience to reach the good in me.*" 'Tis quite taking to hear her lisp it. Be sure that I am repeating the petition! I make her read me her choice passages. She has not a bad voice.

'The Lady Judith I spoke of is Austin's Miss Menteith, married to the incapable old Lord Felle, or Fellow, as the wits here call him. Lord Mountfalcon is his cousin, and her—what? She has been trying to find out, but they have both got over their perplexity, and act respectively the bad man reproved and the chaste counsellor; a position in which our young couple found them, and haply diverted its perils. They have quite taken them in hand. Lady Judith undertakes to cure the fair Papist of a pretty, modest trick of frowning and blushing when addressed, and his lordship directs the exuberant energies of the original man. 'Tis thus we fulfil our destinies, and are content. Sometimes they change pupils; my lord educates the little dame, and my lady the hope of Raynham. Joy and blessings unto all! as the German poet sings. Lady Judith accepted the hand of her decrepit lord that she might be of potent service to her fellow-creatures. Austin, you know, had great hopes of her.

'I have for the first time in my career a field of lords to study. I think it is not without meaning that I am introduced to it by a yeoman's niece. The language of the two social extremes is similar. I find it to consist in an instinctively lavish use of vowels and adjectives. My lord and Farmer Blaize speak the same tongue, only my lord's has lost its backbone, and is limp, though fluent. Their pursuits are identical; but that one has money, or, as the Pilgrim terms it, *vantage*, and the other has not. Their ideas seem to have a special relationship in the peculiarity of stopping where they have begun. Young Tom Blaize with *vantage* would be Lord Mountfalcon. Even in the character of their parasites I see a resemblance, though I am bound to confess that the Hon. Peter Brayder, who is my lord's parasite, is by no means noxious.

'This sounds dreadfully democrat. Pray, don't be alarmed. The discovery of the affinity between the two extremes of the Royal British Oak has made me thrice conservative. I see now that the national love of a lord is less subservience than a form of self-love; putting a goldlace hat on one's image, as it were, to bow to it. I see, too, the admirable wisdom of our system:—could there be a finer balance of power than in a community where men intellectually nil, have lawful vantage and a goldlace hat on? How soothing it is to intellect—that noble rebel, as the Pilgrim has it—to stand, and bow, and know itself superior! This exquisite compensation maintains the balance: whereas that period anticipated by the Pilgrim, when science shall have produced an *intellectual aristocracy*, is indeed horrible to contemplate. For what despotism is so black as one the mind cannot challenge? 'Twill be an iron Age. Wherefore, madam, I cry, and shall continue to cry, "*Vive* Lord Mountfalcon! long may he sip his Burgundy! long may the bacon-fed carry him on their shoulders!"

'Mr. Morton (who does me the honour to call me Young Mephisto, and Socrates missed) leaves to-morrow to get Master Ralph out of a scrape. Our Richard has just been elected member of a Club for the promotion of nausea.

Is he happy? you ask. As much so as one who has had the misfortune to obtain what he wanted can be. Speed is his passion. He races from point to point. In emulation of Leander*and Don Juan,* he swam, I hear, to the opposite shores the other day, or some world-shaking feat of the sort: himself the Hero whom he went to meet: or, as they who pun say, his Hero*was a Bet. A pretty little domestic episode occurred this morning. He finds her abstracted in the fire of his caresses: she turns shy and seeks solitude: green jealousy takes hold of him: he lies in wait, and discovers her with his new rival—a veteran edition of the culinary Doctor! Blind to the Doctor's great national services, deaf to her wild music, he grasps the intruder, dismembers him, and performs upon him the treatment he has recommended for dressed cucumber. Tears and shrieks accompany the descent of the gastronome. Down she rushes to secure the cherished fragments: he follows: they find him, true to his character, alighted and straggling over a bed of blooming flowers. Yet ere a fairer flower can gather him, a heel black as Pluto*stamps him into earth, flowers and all:—happy burial! Pathetic tribute to his merit is watering his grave, when by saunters my Lord Mountfalcon. 'What 's the mattah?' says his lordship, soothing his moustache. They break apart, and 'tis left to me to explain from the window. My lord looks shocked, Richard is angry with her for having to be ashamed of himself, Beauty dries her eyes, and after a pause of general foolishness, the business of life is resumed. I may add that the Doctor has just been dug up, and we are busy, in the enemy's absence, renewing old Æson*with enchanted threads. By the way, a Papist priest has blest them.'

A month had passed when Adrian wrote this letter. He was very comfortable; so of course he thought Time was doing his duty. Not a word did he say of Richard's return, and for some reason or other neither Richard nor Lucy spoke of it now.

Lady Blandish wrote back: 'His father thinks he has refused to come to him. By your utter silence on the subject, I fear that it must be so. Make him come. Bring him by force. *Insist* on his coming. Is he mad? He must come *at once.*'

To this Adrian replied, after a contemplative comfortable lapse of a day or two, which might be laid to his efforts to adopt the lady's advice, 'The point is that the half man declines to come without the whole man. The terrible question of sex is our obstruction.'

Lady Blandish was in despair. She had no positive assurance that the baronet would see his son; the mask put them all in the dark; but she thought she saw in Sir Austin irritation that the offender, at least when the opening to come and make his peace seemed to be before him, should let days and weeks go by. She saw through the mask sufficiently not to have any hope of his consenting to receive the couple at present; she was sure that his equanimity was fictitious; but she pierced no farther, or she might have started and asked herself, Is this the heart of a woman?

The lady at last wrote to Richard. She said: 'Come instantly, and come alone.' Then Richard, against his judgement, gave way. 'My father is not the man I thought him!' he exclaimed sadly, and Lucy felt his eyes saying to her: 'And you, too, are not the woman I thought you.' Nothing could the poor little heart reply but strain to his bosom and sleeplessly pray in his arms all the night.

CHAPTER XXXV

CLARE'S MARRIAGE

THREE weeks after Richard arrived in town, his cousin Clare was married, under the blessings of her energetic mother, and with the approbation of her kinsfolk, to the husband that had been expeditiously chosen for her. The gentleman, though something more than twice the age of his bride, had no idea of approaching senility for many long connubial years to come. Backed by his tailor and his hairdresser, he presented no such bad figure at the altar, and none would have thought that he was an ancient admirer of his bride's mama, as certainly none knew he had lately proposed for Mrs. Doria before there was any question of her daughter. These things were secrets; and the elastic and happy appearance of Mr. John Todhunter did not betray them at the altar. Perhaps he would rather have married the mother. He was a man of property, well born, tolerably well educated, and had, when Mrs. Doria rejected him for the first time, the reputation of being a fool—which a wealthy man may have in his youth; but as he lived on, and did not squander his money —amassed it, on the contrary, and did not seek to go into Parliament, and did other negative wise things, the world's opinion, as usual, veered completely round, and John Todhunter was esteemed a shrewd, sensible man— only not brilliant; that he was brilliant, could not be said of him. In fact, the man could hardly talk, and it was a fortunate provision that no impromptu deliveries were required of him in the marriage-service.

Mrs. Doria had her own reasons for being in a hurry. She had discovered something of the strange impassive

nature of her child; not from any confession of Clare's, but
from signs a mother can read when her eyes are not resolutely shut. She saw with alarm and anguish that Clare
had fallen into the pit she had been digging for her so
laboriously. In vain she entreated the baronet to break
the disgraceful, and, as she said, illegal alliance his son
had contracted. Sir Austin would not even stop the little
pension to poor Berry. 'At least you will do that, Austin,'
she begged pathetically. 'You will show your sense of
that horrid woman's conduct?' He refused to offer up
any victim to console her. Then Mrs. Doria told him her
thoughts,—and when an outraged energetic lady is finally
brought to exhibit these painfully hoarded treasures, she
does not use half words as a medium. His System, and
his conduct generally, were denounced to him, without
analysis. She let him understand that the world laughed
at him; and he heard this from her at a time when his
mask was still soft and liable to be acted on by his nerves.
'You are weak, Austin! weak, I tell you!' she said, and,
like all angry and self-interested people, prophecy came
easy to her. In her heart she accused him of her own
fault, in imputing to him the wreck of her project. The
baronet allowed her to revel in the proclamation of a dire
future, and quietly counselled her to keep apart from him,
which his sister assured him she would do.

But to be passive in calamity is the province of no
woman. Mark the race at any hour. 'What revolution and
hubbub does not that little instrument, the needle, avert
from us!' says THE PILGRIM'S SCRIP. Alas, that in calamity women cannot stitch! Now that she saw Clare wanted
other than iron, it struck her she must have a husband,
and be made secure as a woman and a wife. This seemed
the thing to do: and, as she had forced the iron down
Clare's throat, so she forced the husband, and Clare gulped
at the latter as she had at the former. On the very day

that Mrs. Doria had this new track shaped out before her, John Todhunter called at the Forey's. 'Old John!' sang out Mrs. Doria, 'show him up to me. I want to see him particularly.' He sat with her alone. He was a man multitudes of women would have married—whom will they not?—and who would have married any presentable woman: but women do want asking, and John never had the word. The rape of such men is left to the practical animal. So John sat alone with his old flame. He had become resigned to her perpetual lamentation and living Suttee for his defunct rival. But, ha! what meant those soft glances now—addressed to him? His tailor and his hairdresser gave youth to John, but they had not the art to bestow upon him distinction, and an undistinguished man what woman looks at? John was an indistinguishable man. For that reason he was dry wood to a soft glance. And now she said: 'It is time you should marry; and you are the man to be the guide and helper of a young woman, John. You are well preserved—younger than most of the young men of our day. You are eminently domestic, a good son, and will be a good husband and good father. Some one you must marry.—What do you think of Clare for a wife for you?'

At first John Todhunter thought it would be very much like his marrying a baby. However, he listened to it, and that was enough for Mrs. Doria.

She went down to John's mother, and consulted with her on the propriety of the scheme of wedding her daughter to John in accordance with his proposition. Mrs. Todhunter's jealousy of any disturbing force in the influence she held over her son Mrs. Doria knew to be one of the causes of John's remaining constant to the impression she had aforetime produced on him. She spoke so kindly of John, and laid so much stress on the ingrained obedience and passive disposition of her daughter, that Mrs. Todhunter was led to admit she did think it almost time John should be seeking a mate, and that he—all things considered—would hardly find a fitter one. And this, John Todhunter—old John no more—heard to his amazement when, a day or two subsequently, he instanced the probable disapproval of his mother.

The match was arranged. Mrs. Doria did the wooing. It consisted in telling Clare that she had come to years when marriage was desirable, and that she had fallen into habits of moping which might have the worse effect on her future life, as it had on her present health and appearance, and which a husband would cure. Richard was told by Mrs. Doria that Clare had instantaneously consented to accept Mr. John Todhunter as lord of her days, and with more than obedience—with alacrity. At all events, when Richard spoke to Clare, the strange passive creature did not admit constraint on her inclinations. Mrs. Doria allowed Richard to speak to her. She laughed at his futile endeavours to undo her work, and the boyish sentiments he uttered on the subject. 'Let us see, child,' she said, 'let us see which turns out the best; a marriage of passion, or a marriage of common sense.'

Heroic efforts were not wanting to arrest the union. Richard made repeated journeys to Hounslow, where Ralph was quartered, and if Ralph could have been persuaded to carry off a young lady who did not love him, from the bridegroom her mother averred she did love, Mrs. Doria might have been defeated. But Ralph in his cavalry quarters was cooler than Ralph in the Bursley meadows. 'Women are oddities, Dick,' he remarked, running a finger right and left along his upper lip. 'Best leave them to their own freaks. She's a dear girl, though she doesn't talk: I like her for that. If she cared for me I'd go the race. She never did. It's no use asking a girl twice. *She* knows whether she cares a fig for a fellow.'

The hero quitted him with some contempt. As Ralph Morton was a young man, and he had determined that John Todhunter was an old man, he sought another private interview with Clare, and getting her alone, said: 'Clare, I 've come to you for the last time. Will you marry Ralph Morton?'

To which Clare replied, 'I cannot marry two husbands, Richard.'

'Will you refuse to marry this old man?'

'I must do as mama wishes.'

'Then you 're going to marry an old man—a man you don't love, and can't love! Oh, good God! do you know what you 're doing?' He flung about in a fury. 'Do you know what it is? Clare!' he caught her two hands violently, 'have you any idea of the horror you 're going to commit?'

She shrank a little at his vehemence, but neither blushed nor stammered: answering: 'I see nothing wrong in doing what mama thinks right, Richard.'

'Your mother! I tell you it 's an infamy, Clare! It 's a miserable sin! I tell you, if I had done such a thing I would not live an hour after it. And coldly to prepare for it! to be busy about your dresses! They told me when I came in that you were with the milliner. To be smiling over the horrible outrage! decorating yourself! . . .'

'Dear Richard,' said Clare, 'you will make me very unhappy.'

'That one of my blood should be so debased!' he cried, brushing angrily at his face. 'Unhappy! I beg you to feel for yourself, Clare. But I suppose,' and he said it scornfully, 'girls don't feel this sort of shame.'

She grew a trifle paler.

'Next to mama, I would wish to please you, dear Richard.'

'Have you no will of your own?' he exclaimed.

She looked at him softly; a look he interpreted for the meekness he detested in her.

'No, I believe you have none!' he added. 'And what can I do? I can't step forward and stop this accursed marriage. If you would but say a word I would save you; but you tie my hands. And they expect me to stand by and see it done!'

'Will you not be there, Richard?' said Clare, following the question with her soft eyes. It was the same voice that had so thrilled him on his marriage-morn.

'Oh, my darling Clare!' he cried in the kindest way he had ever used to her, 'if you knew how I feel this!' and now as he wept she wept, and came insensibly into his arms. 'My darling Clare!' he repeated.

She said nothing, but seemed to shudder, weeping.

'You *will* do it, Clare? You will be sacrificed? So lovely as you are, too! . . . Clare! you cannot be quite blind. If I dared speak to you, and tell you all. . . . Look up. Can you still consent?'

'I must not disobey mama,' Clare murmured, without looking up from the nest her cheek had made on his bosom.

'Then kiss me for the last time,' said Richard. 'I'll never kiss you after it, Clare.'

He bent his head to meet her mouth, and she threw her arms wildly round him, and kissed him convulsively, and clung to his lips, shutting her eyes, her face suffused with a burning red.

Then he left her, unaware of the meaning of those passionate kisses.

Argument with Mrs. Doria was like firing paper-pellets against a stone wall. To her indeed the young married hero spoke almost indecorously, and that which his delicacy withheld him from speaking to Clare. He could provoke nothing more responsive from the practical animal than 'Pooh-pooh! Tush, tush! and Fiddlededee!'

'Really,' Mrs. Doria said to her intimates, 'that boy's education acts like a disease on him. He cannot regard anything sensibly. He is for ever in some mad excess of his fancy, and what he will come to at last heaven only knows! I sincerely pray that Austin will be able to bear it.'

Threats of prayer, however, that harp upon their sincerity, are not very well worth having. Mrs. Doria had embarked in a practical controversy, as it were, with her brother. Doubtless she did trust he would be able to bear his sorrows to come, but one who has uttered prophecy can barely help hoping to see it fulfilled: she had prophesied much grief to the baronet.

Poor John Todhunter, who would rather have married the mother, and had none of your heroic notions about the sacred necessity for love in marriage, moved as one guiltless of offence, and deserving his happiness. Mrs. Doria shielded him from the hero. To see him smile at Clare's obedient figure, and try not to look paternal, was touching.

Meantime Clare's marriage served one purpose. It completely occupied Richard's mind, and prevented him from chafing at the vexation of not finding his father ready to meet him when he came to town. A letter had awaited Adrian at the hotel, which said, 'Detain him till you hear further from me. Take him about with you into every form of society.' No more than that. Adrian had to extemporize, that the baronet had gone down to Wales on pressing business, and would be back in a week or so. For ulterior inventions and devices wherewith to keep the young gentleman in town, he applied to Mrs. Doria. 'Leave him to me,' said Mrs. Doria, 'I'll manage him.' And she did.

'Who can say,' asks THE PILGRIM'S SCRIP, 'when he is not walking a puppet to some woman?'

Mrs. Doria would hear no good of Lucy. 'I believe,' she observed, as Adrian ventured a shrugging protest in her behalf,—'it is my firm opinion, that a scullery-maid would turn any of you men round her little finger—only give her time and opportunity.' By dwelling on the arts of women, she reconciled it to her conscience to do her best to divide the young husband from his wife till it pleased his father they should live their unhallowed union again. Without compunction, or a sense of incongruity, she abused her brother and assisted the fulfilment of his behests.

So the puppets were marshalled by Mrs. Doria, happy, or sad, or indifferent. Quite against his set resolve and the tide of his feelings, Richard found himself standing behind Clare in the church—the very edifice that had witnessed his own marriage, and heard, 'I, Clare Doria, take thee John Pemberton,' clearly pronounced. He stood with black brows dissecting the arts of the tailor and hairdresser on unconscious John. The back, and much of the middle, of Mr. Todhunter's head was bald; the back shone like an egg-shell, but across the middle the artist had drawn two long dabs of hair from the sides, and plastered them cunningly, so that all save wilful eyes would have acknowledged the head to be covered. The man's only pretension was to a respectable juvenility. He had a good chest, stout limbs, a face inclined to be jolly. Mrs. Doria had no cause to be put out of countenance at all by the exterior of her son-in-law: nor was she. Her splendid hair and gratified smile made a light in the church. Playing puppets must be an immense pleasure to the practical animal. The Forey bridesmaids, five in number, and one Miss Doria, their cousin, stood as girls do stand at these sacrifices, whether happy, sad, or indifferent; a smile on their lips and tears in attendance. Old Mrs. Todhunter, an exceedingly small ancient woman, was also there. 'I can't have my boy John married without seeing it done,' she said, and throughout the ceremony she was muttering audible encomiums on her John's manly behaviour.

The ring was affixed to Clare's finger; there was no ring lost in this common-sense marriage. The instant the clergyman bade him employ it, John drew the ring out, and dropped it on the finger of the cold passive hand in a business-like way, as one who had studied the matter. Mrs. Doria glanced aside at Richard. Richard observed Clare spread out her fingers that the operation might be the more easily effected.

He did duty in the vestry a few minutes, and then said to his aunt:

'Now I'll go.'

'You'll come to the breakfast, child? The Foreys——'

He cut her short. 'I've stood for the family, and I'll do no more. I won't pretend to eat and make merry over it.'

'Richard!'

'Good-bye.'

She had attained her object and she wisely gave way.

'Well. Go and kiss Clare, and shake his hand. Pray, pray be civil.'

She turned to Adrian, and said: 'He is going. You must go with him, and find some means of keeping him, or he'll be running off to that woman. Now, no words —go!'

Richard bade Clare farewell. She put up her mouth to him humbly, but he kissed her on the forehead.

'Do not cease to love me,' she said in a quavering whisper in his ear.

Mr. Todhunter stood beaming and endangering the art of the hairdresser with his pocket-handkerchief. Now he positively was married, he thought he would rather have the daughter than the mother, which is a reverse of the order of human thankfulness at a gift of the Gods.

'Richard, my boy!' he said heartily, 'congratulate me.'

'I should be happy to, if I could,' sedately replied the

hero, to the consternation of those around. Nodding to
the bridesmaids and bowing to the old lady, he passed out.

Adrian, who had been behind him, deputed to watch
for a possible unpleasantness, just hinted to John: 'You
know, poor fellow, he has got into a mess with his marriage.'

'Oh! ah! yes!' kindly said John, 'poor fellow!'

All the puppets then rolled off to the breakfast.

Adrian hurried after Richard in an extremely dis-
contented state of mind. Not to be at the breakfast and
see the best of the fun, disgusted him. However, he
remembered that he was a philosopher, and the strong
disgust he felt was only expressed in concentrated cynicism on every earthly matter engendered by the conversation. They walked side by side into Kensington
Gardens. The hero was mouthing away to himself, talking by fits.

Presently he faced Adrian, crying: 'And I might
have stopped it! I see it now! I might have stopped
it by going straight to him, and asking him if he dared
marry a girl who did not love him. And I never thought
of it. Good heaven! I feel this miserable affair on my
conscience.'

'Ah!' groaned Adrian. 'An unpleasant cargo for
the conscience, that! I would rather carry anything on
mine than a married couple. Do you propose going to
him now?'

The hero soliloquized: 'He's not a bad sort of man. . . .'

'Well, he's not a Cavalier,'* said Adrian, 'and that's
why you wonder your aunt selected him, no doubt?
He's decidedly of the Roundhead*type, with the Puritan*
extracted, or inoffensive, if latent.'

'There's the double infamy!' cried Richard, 'that a
man you can't call bad, should do this damned thing!'

'Well, it's hard we can't find a villain.'

'He would have listened to me, I'm sure.'

'Go to him now, Richard, my son. Go to him now. It's not yet too late. Who knows? If he really has a noble elevated superior mind—though not a Cavalier in person, he may be one at heart—he might, to please you, and since you put such stress upon it, abstain . . . perhaps with some loss of dignity, but never mind. And the request might be singular, or seem so, but everything has happened before in this world, you know, my dear boy. And what an infinite consolation it is for the eccentric, that reflection!'

The hero was impervious to the wise youth. He stared at him as if he were but a speck in the universe he visioned

It was provoking that Richard should be Adrian's best subject for cynical pastime, in the extraordinary heterodoxies he started, and his worst in the way he took it; and the wise youth, against his will, had to feel as conscious of the young man's imaginative mental armour, as he was of his muscular physical.

'The same sort of day!' mused Richard, looking up. 'I suppose my father's right. We make our own fates, and nature has nothing to do with it.'

Adrian yawned.

'Some difference in the trees, though,' Richard continued abstractedly.

'Growing bald at the top,' said Adrian.

'Will you believe that my aunt Helen compared the conduct of that wretched slave Clare to Lucy's, who, she had the cruel insolence to say, entangled me into marriage?' the hero broke out loudly and rapidly. 'You know—I told you, Adrian—how I had to threaten and insist, and how she pleaded, and implored me to wait.'

'Ah! hum!' mumbled Adrian.

'You remember my telling you?' Richard was earnest to hear her exonerated.

'Pleaded and implored, my dear boy? Oh, no doubt she did. Where's the lass that doesn't.'

'Call my wife by another name, if you please.'

'The generic title can't be cancelled because of your having married one of the body, my son.'

'She did all she could to persuade me to wait!' emphasized Richard.

Adrian shook his head with a deplorable smile.

'Come, come, my good Ricky; not all! not all!'

Richard bellowed: 'What more could she have done?'

'She could have shaved her head, for instance.'

This happy shaft did stick. With a furious exclamation Richard shot in front, Adrian followed him; and asking him (merely to have his assumption verified), whether he did not think she might have shaved her head? and, presuming her to have done so, whether, in candour, he did not think he would have waited—at least till she looked less of a rank lunatic?

After a minute or so, the wise youth was but a fly buzzing about Richard's head. Three weeks of separation from Lucy, and an excitement deceased, caused him to have soft yearnings for the dear lovely home-face. He told Adrian it was his intention to go down that night. Adrian immediately became serious. He was at a loss what to invent to detain him, beyond the stale fiction that his father was coming to-morrow. He rendered homage to the genius of woman in these straits. 'My aunt,' he thought, 'would have the lie ready; and not only that, but she would take care it did its work.'

At this juncture the voice of a cavalier in the Row hailed them, proving to be the Honourable Peter Brayder, Lord Mountfalcon's parasite. He greeted them very cordially; and Richard, remembering some fun they had in the Island, asked him to dine with them; post-

poning his return till the next day. Lucy was his. It
was even sweet to dally with the delight of seeing her.

The Hon. Peter was one who did honour to the body
he belonged to. Though not so tall as a West of London
footman, he was as shapely; and he had a power of making his voice insinuating, or arrogant, as it suited the
exigencies of his profession. He had not a rap of money
in the world; yet he rode a horse, lived high, expended
largely. The world said that the Hon. Peter was sala-
ried by his Lordship, and that, in common with that of
Parasite, he exercised the ancient companion profession.
This the world said, and still smiled at the Hon. Peter;
for he was an engaging fellow, and where he went not
Lord Mountfalcon would not go.

They had a quiet little hotel dinner, ordered by Adrian,
and made a square at the table, Ripton Thompson being
the fourth. Richard sent down to his office to fetch him,
and the two friends shook hands for the first time since
the great deed had been executed. Deep was the Old
Dog's delight to hear the praises of his Beauty sounded
by such aristocratic lips as the Hon. Peter Brayder's.
All through the dinner he was throwing out hints and
small queries to get a fuller account of her; and when the
claret had circulated, he spoke a word or two himself,
and heard the Hon. Peter eulogize his taste, and wish
him a bride as beautiful; at which Ripton blushed, and
said, he had no hope of that, and the Hon. Peter assured
him marriage did not break the mould.

After the wine this gentleman took his cigar on the
balcony, and found occasion to get some conversation
with Adrian alone.

'Our young friend here—made it all right with the
governor?' he asked carelessly.

'Oh yes!' said Adrian. But it struck him that Brayder might be of assistance in showing Richard a little

of the 'society in every form' required by his chief's
prescript. 'That is,' he continued, 'we are not yet permitted an interview with the august author of our being,
and I have rather a difficult post. 'Tis mine both to keep
him here, and also to find him the opportunity to measure
himself with his fellow-man. In other words, his father
wants him to see something of life before he enters upon
housekeeping. Now I am proud to confess that I'm hardly
equal to the task. The demi, or damned monde—if it's that
he wants him to observe—is one that I have not got the
walk to.'

'Ha! ha!' laughed Brayder. 'You do the keeping,
I offer to parade the demi. I must say, though, it's a
queer notion of the old gentleman.'

'It's the continuation of a philosophic plan,' said
Adrian.

Brayder followed the curvings of the whiff of his cigar
with his eyes, and ejaculated, 'Infernally philosophic!'

'Has Lord Mountfalcon left the island?' Adrian inquired.

'Mount? to tell the truth I don't know where he is.
Chasing some light craft, I suppose. That's poor Mount's
weakness. It's his ruin, poor fellow! He's so confound-
edly in earnest at the game.'

'He ought to know it by this time, if fame speaks true,'
remarked Adrian.

'He's a baby about women, and always will be,' said
Brayder. 'He's been once or twice wanting to marry
them. Now there's a woman—you've heard of Mrs.
Mount? All the world knows her.—If that woman hadn't
scandalized.'—The young man joined them, and checked
the communication. Brayder winked to Adrian, and
pitifully indicated the presence of an innocent.

'A married man, you know,' said Adrian.

'Yes, yes!—we won't shock him,' Brayder observed.
He appeared to study the young man while they talked.

Next morning Richard was surprised by a visit from his aunt. Mrs. Doria took a seat by his side, and spoke as follows:

'My dear nephew. Now you know I have always loved you, and thought of your welfare as if you had been my own child. More than that, I fear. Well, now, you are thinking of returning to—to that place—are you not? Yes. It is as I thought. Very well now, let me speak to you. You are in a much more dangerous position than you imagine. I don't deny your father's affection for you. It would be absurd to deny it. But you are of an age now to appreciate his character. Whatever you may do he will always give you money. That you are sure of; that you know. Very well. But you are one to want more than money: you want his love. Richard, I am convinced you will never be happy, whatever base pleasures you may be led into, if he should withhold his love from you. Now, child, you know you have grievously offended him. I wish not to animadvert on your conduct.—You fancied yourself in love, and so on, and you were rash. The less said of it the better now. But you must now—it is your duty now to do something—to do everything that lies in your power to show him you repent. No interruptions! Listen to me. You must consider him. Austin is not like other men. Austin requires the most delicate management. You must—whether you feel it or no—present an appearance of contrition. I counsel it for the good of all. He is just like a woman, and where his feelings are offended he wants utter subservience. He has you in town, and he does not see you:—now you know that he and I are not in communication: we have likewise our differences:—Well, he has you in town, and he holds aloof:—he is trying you, my dear Richard. No: he is not at Raynham: I do not know where he is. He is trying you, child, and you

must be patient. You must convince him that you do
not care utterly for your own gratification. If this person—I wish to speak of her with respect, for your sake—
well, if she loves you *at all*—if, I say, she loves you *one
atom*, she will repeat my solicitations for you to stay and
patiently wait here till he consents to see you. I tell you
candidly, it 's your only chance of ever getting him to
receive *her*. That you should know. And now, Richard,
I may add that there is something else you should know.
You should know that it depends entirely upon your
conduct now, whether you are to see your father's heart
for ever divided from you, and a new family at Raynham.
You do not understand? I will explain. Brothers and
sisters are excellent things for young people, but a new
brood of them can hardly be acceptable to a young man.
In fact, they are, and must be, aliens. I only tell you
what I have heard on good authority. Don't you understand now? Foolish boy! if you do not humour him, he
will marry her. Oh! I am sure of it. I know it. And
this you will drive him to. I do not warn you on the
score of your prospects, but of your feelings. I should
regard such a contingency, Richard, as a final division
between you. Think of the scandal! but alas, that is the
least of the evils.'

It was Mrs. Doria's object to produce an impression,
and avoid an argument. She therefore left him as soon
as she had, as she supposed, made her mark on the young
man. Richard was very silent during the speech, and
save for an exclamation or so, had listened attentively.
He pondered on what his aunt said. He loved Lady
Blandish, and yet he did not wish to see her Lady Feverel.
Mrs. Doria laid painful stress on the scandal, and though
he did not give his mind to this, he thought of it. He
thought of his mother. Where was she? But most his
thoughts recurred to his father, and something akin to

jealousy slowly awakened his heart to him. He had given him up, and had not latterly felt extremely filial; but he could not bear the idea of a division in the love of which he had ever been the idol and sole object. And such a man, too! so good! so generous! If it was jealousy that roused the young man's heart to his father, the better part of love was also revived in it. He thought of old days: of his father's forbearance, his own wilfulness. He looked on himself, and what he had done, with the eyes of such a man. He determined to do all he could to regain his favour.

Mrs. Doria learnt from Adrian in the evening that her nephew intended waiting in town another week.

'That will do,' smiled Mrs. Doria. 'He will be more patient at the end of a week.'

'Oh! does patience beget patience?' said Adrian. 'I was not aware it was a propagating virtue. I surrender him to you. I shan't be able to hold him in after one week more. I assure you, my dear aunt, he's already . . .'

'Thank you, no explanation,' Mrs. Doria begged.

When Richard saw her next, he was informed that she had received a most satisfactory letter from Mrs. John Todhunter: quite a glowing account of John's behaviour: but on Richard's desiring to know the words Clare had written, Mrs. Doria objected to be explicit, and shot into worldly gossip.

'Clare seldom glows,' said Richard.

'No, I mean *for her*,' his aunt remarked. 'Don't look like your father, child.'

'I should like to have seen the letter,' said Richard.

Mrs. Doria did not propose to show it.

CHAPTER XXXVI

A DINNER-PARTY AT RICHMOND

A LADY driving a pair of greys was noticed by Richard
in his rides and walks. She passed him rather obviously
and often. She was very handsome; a bold beauty,
with shining black hair, red lips, and eyes not afraid of
men. The hair was brushed from her temples, leaving
one of those fine reckless outlines which the action of
driving, and the pace, admirably set off. She took his
fancy. He liked the air of petulant gallantry about her,
and mused upon the picture, rare to him, of a glorious
dashing woman. He thought, too, she looked at him.
He was not at the time inclined to be vain, or he might
have been sure she did. Once it struck him she nodded
slightly.

He asked Adrian one day in the park—who she was.

'I don't know her,' said Adrian. 'Probably a superior
priestess of Paphos.'*

'Now that's my idea of Bellona,'*Richard exclaimed.
'Not the fury they paint, but a spirited, dauntless, eager-
looking creature like that.'

'Bellona?' returned the wise youth. 'I don't think
her hair was black. Red, wasn't it! I shouldn't compare her to Bellona; though, no doubt, she's as ready
to spill blood. Look at her! She does seem to scent
carnage. I see your idea. No; I should liken her to
Diana*emerged from the tutorship of Master Endymion*
and at nice play among the gods. Depend upon it—
they tell us nothing of the matter—Olympus shrouds the
story—but you may be certain that when she left the
pretty shepherd she had greater vogue than Venus up aloft.'

Brayder joined them.

'See Mrs. Mount go by?' he said.

'Oh, that's Mrs. Mount!' cried Adrian.

'Who's Mrs. Mount?' Richard inquired.

'A sister to Miss Random, my dear boy.'

'Like to know her?' drawled the Hon. Peter.

Richard replied indifferently, 'No,' and Mrs. Mount passed out of sight and out of the conversation.

The young man wrote submissive letters to his father. 'I have remained here waiting to see you now five weeks,' he wrote. 'I have written to you three letters, and you do not reply to them. Let me tell you again how sincerely I desire and pray that you will come, or permit me to come to you and throw myself at your feet, and beg my forgiveness, and hers. She as earnestly implores it. Indeed, I am very wretched, sir. Believe me, there is nothing I would not do to regain your esteem and the love I fear I have unhappily forfeited. I will remain another week in the hope of hearing from you, or seeing you. I beg of you, sir, not to drive me mad. Whatever you ask of me I will consent to.'

'Nothing he would not do!' the baronet commented as he read. 'There is nothing he would not do! He will remain another week and give me that final chance! And it is I who drive him mad! Already he is beginning to cast his retribution on my shoulders.'

Sir Austin had really gone down to Wales to be out of the way. A Shaddock-Dogmatist does not meet misfortune without hearing of it, and the author of THE PILGRIM'S SCRIP in trouble found London too hot for him. He quitted London to take refuge among the mountains; living there in solitary commune with a virgin Note-book.

Some indefinite scheme was in his head in this treatment of his son. Had he construed it, it would have looked ugly; and it settled to a vague principle that the young man should be tried and tested.

'Let him learn to deny himself something. Let him live with his equals for a term. If he loves me he will read my wishes.' Thus he explained his principle to Lady Blandish.

The lady wrote: 'You speak of a term. Till when? May I name one to him? It is the dreadful *uncertainty* that reduces him to despair. That, and nothing else. Pray be explicit.'

In return, he distantly indicated Richard's majority.

How could Lady Blandish go and ask the young man to wait a year away from his wife? Her instinct began to open a wide eye on the idol she worshipped.

When people do not themselves know what they mean, they succeed in deceiving and imposing upon others. Not only was Lady Blandish mystified; Mrs. Doria, who pierced into the recesses of everybody's mind, and had always been in the habit of reading off her brother from infancy, and had never known herself to be once wrong about him, she confessed she was quite at a loss to comprehend Austin's principle. 'For principle he has,' said Mrs. Doria; 'he never acts without one. But what it is, I cannot at present perceive. If he would write, and command the boy to await his return, all would be clear. He allows us to go and fetch him, and then leaves us all in a quandary. It must be some woman's influence. That is the only way to account for it.'

'Singular!' interjected Adrian, 'what pride women have in their sex! Well, I have to tell you, my dear aunt, that the day after to-morrow I hand my charge over to your keeping. I can't hold him in an hour longer. I've had to leash him with lies till my invention's exhausted. I petition to have them put down to the chief's account, but when the stream runs dry I can do no more. The last

was, that I had heard from him desiring me to have the
Southwest bedroom ready for him on Tuesday proximate.
"So!" says my son, "I'll wait till then," and from the gi-
gantic effort he exhibited in coming to it, I doubt any
human power's getting him to wait longer.'

'We must, we must detain him,' said Mrs. Doria. 'If
we do not, I am convinced Austin will do something rash
that he will for ever repent. He will marry that woman,
Adrian. Mark my words. Now with any other young
man! . . . But Richard's education! that ridiculous
System! . . . Has he no distraction? nothing to amuse
him?'

'Poor boy! I suppose he wants his own particular
playfellow.'

The wise youth had to bow to a reproof.

'I tell you, Adrian, he will marry that woman.'

'My dear aunt! Can a chaste man do aught more
commendable?'

'Has the boy no object we can induce him to follow?
—If he had but a profession!'

'What say you to the regeneration of the streets of
London, and the profession of moral-scavenger, aunt?
I assure you I have served a month's apprenticeship
with him. We sally forth on the tenth hour of the night.
A female passes. I hear him groan. "Is *she* one of them,
Adrian?" I am compelled to admit she is not the saint
he deems it the portion of every creature wearing petti-
coats to be. Another groan; an evident internal, "It cannot be—and yet!" . . . that we hear on the stage. Roll-
ings of eyes: impious questionings of the Creator of the
universe; savage mutterings against brutal males; and
then we meet a second young person, and repeat the performance—of which I am rather tired. It would be all very
well, but he turns upon me, and lectures me because I
don't hire a house, and furnish it for all the women one

meets to live in in purity. Now that 's too much to ask
of a quiet man. Master Thompson has latterly relieved
me, I 'm happy to say.'

Mrs. Doria thought her thoughts.

'Has Austin written to you since you were in town?'

'Not an Aphorism!' returned Adrian.

'I must see Richard to-morrow morning,' Mrs. Doria
ended the colloquy by saying.

The result of her interview with her nephew was, that
Richard made no allusion to a departure on the Tuesday;
and for many days afterward he appeared to have an
absorbing business on his hands: but what it was Adrian
did not then learn, and his admiration of Mrs. Doria's
genius for management rose to a very high pitch.

On a morning in October they had an early visitor in
the person of the Hon. Peter, whom they had not seen
for a week or more.

'Gentlemen,' he said, flourishing his cane in his most
affable manner, 'I 've come to propose to you to join us
in a little dinner-party at Richmond. Nobody 's in town,
you know. London 's as dead as a stock-fish. Nothing
but the scrapings to offer you. But the weather 's fine:
I flatter myself you 'll find the company agreeable. What
says my friend Feverel?'

Richard begged to be excused.

'No, no: positively you must come,' said the Hon.
Peter. 'I 've had some trouble to get them together to
relieve the dulness of your incarceration. Richmond 's
within the rules of your prison. You can be back by
night. Moonlight on the water—lovely woman. We 've
engaged a city-barge to pull us back. Eight oars—I 'm
not sure it isn't sixteen. Come—the word!'

Adrian was for going. Richard said he had an appointment with Ripton.

'You're in for another rick, you two,' said Adrian.
'Arrange that we go. You haven't seen the cockney's
Paradise. Abjure Blazes, and taste of peace, my son.'

After some persuasion, Richard yawned wearily, and
got up, and threw aside the care that was on him, saying,
'Very well. Just as you like. We'll take old Rip with us.'

Adrian consulted Brayder's eye at this. The Hon.
Peter briskly declared he should be delighted to have
Feverel's friend, and offered to take them all down in his
drag.

'If you don't get a match on to swim there with the
tide—eh, Feverel, my boy?'

Richard replied that he had given up that sort of thing,
at which Brayder communicated a queer glance to Adrian,
and applauded the youth.

Richmond was under a still October sun. The pleasant
landscape, bathed in Autumn, stretched from the foot of
the hill to a red horizon haze. The day was like none
that Richard vividly remembered. It touched no link
in the chain of his recollection. It was quiet, and belonged to the spirit of the season.

Adrian had divined the character of the scrapings they
were to meet. Brayder introduced them to one or two
of the men, hastily and in rather an undervoice, as a
thing to get over. They made their bow to the first knot
of ladies they encountered. Propriety was observed
strictly, even to severity. The general talk was of the
weather. Here and there a lady would seize a button-
hole or any little bit of the habiliments of the man she
was addressing; and if it came to her to chide him, she
did it with more than a forefinger. This, however, was
only here and there, and a privilege of intimacy.

Where ladies are gathered together, the Queen of the
assemblage may be known by her Court of males. The
Queen of the present gathering leaned against a corner of

the open window, surrounded by a stalwart Court, in
whom a practised eye would have discerned guardsmen,
and Ripton, with a sinking of the heart, apprehended
lords. They were fine men, offering inanimate homage.
The trim of their whiskerage, the cut of their coats, the
high-bred indolence in their aspect, eclipsed Ripton's
sense of self-esteem. But they kindly looked over him.
Occasionally one committed a momentary outrage on
him with an eye-glass, seeming to cry out in a voice of
scathing scorn, 'Who's this?' and Ripton got closer to
his hero to justify his humble pretensions to existence
and an identity in the shadow of him. Richard gazed
about. Heroes do not always know what to say or do;
and the cold bath before dinner in strange company is
one of the instances. He had recognized his superb Bellona in the lady by the garden window. For Brayder
the men had nods and jokes, the ladies a pretty playful-
ness. He was very busy, passing between the groups,
chatting, laughing, taking the feminine taps he received,
and sometimes returning them in sly whispers. Adrian sat
down and crossed his legs, looking amused and benignant.

'Whose dinner is it?' Ripton heard a mignonne beauty
ask of a cavalier.

'Mount's, I suppose,' was the answer.

'Where is he? Why don't he come?'

'An affaire, I fancy.'

'There he is again! How shamefully he treats Mrs.
Mount!'

'She don't seem to cry over it.'

Mrs. Mount was flashing her teeth and eyes with laughter
at one of her Court, who appeared to be Fool.

Dinner was announced. The ladies proclaimed extrava-
gant appetites. Brayder posted his three friends. Ripton found himself under the lee of a dame with a bosom.
On the other side of him was the mignonne. Adrian

was at the lower end of the table. Ladies were in pro-
fusion, and he had his share. Brayder drew Richard
from seat to seat. A happy man had established himself next to Mrs. Mount. Him Brayder hailed to take
the head of the table. The happy man objected, Brayder
continued urgent, the lady tenderly insisted, the happy
man grimaced, dropped into the post of honour, strove to
look placable. Richard usurped his chair, and was not
badly welcomed by his neighbour.

Then the dinner commenced, and had all the attention
of the company, till the flying of the first champagne-
cork gave the signal, and a hum began to spread. Sparkling wine, that looseneth the tongue, and displayeth the
verity, hath also the quality of colouring it. The ladies
laughed high; Richard only thought them gay and natural. They flung back in their chairs and laughed to
tears; Ripton thought only of the pleasure he had in
their society. The champagne-corks continued a regular
file-firing.

'Where have you been lately? I haven't seen you in
the park,' said Mrs. Mount to Richard.

'No,' he replied, 'I've not been there.' The question
seemed odd: she spoke so simply that it did not impress
him. He emptied his glass, and had it filled again.

The Hon. Peter did most of the open talking, which related to horses, yachting, opera, and sport generally:
who was ruined; by what horse, or by what woman.
He told one or two of Richard's feats. Fair smiles rewarded the hero.

'Do you bet?' said Mrs. Mount.

'Only on myself,' returned Richard.

'Bravo!' cried his Bellona, and her eye sent a lingering
delirious sparkle across her brimming glass at him.

'I'm sure you're a safe one to back,' she added, and
seemed to scan his points approvingly.

Richard's cheeks mounted bloom.

'Don't you adore champagne?' quoth the dame with a bosom to Ripton.

'Oh, yes!' answered Ripton, with more candour than accuracy, 'I always drink it.'

'Do you indeed?' said the enraptured bosom, ogling him. 'You would be a friend, now! I hope you don't object to a lady joining you now and then. Champagne's my folly.'

A laugh was circling among the ladies of whom Adrian was the centre; first low, and as he continued some narration, peals resounded, till those excluded from the fun demanded the cue, and ladies leaned behind gentlemen to take it up, and formed an electric chain of laughter. Each one, as her ear received it, caught up her handkerchief, and laughed, and looked shocked afterwards, or looked shocked and then spouted laughter. The anecdote might have been communicated to the bewildered cavaliers, but coming to a lady of a demurer cast, she looked shocked without laughing, and reproved the female table, in whose breasts it was consigned to burial: but here and there a man's head was seen bent, and a lady's mouth moved, though her face was not turned toward him, and a man's broad laugh was presently heard, while the lady gazed unconsciously before her, and preserved her gravity if she could escape any other lady's eyes; failing in which, handkerchiefs were simultaneously seized, and a second chime arose, till the tickling force subsided to a few chance bursts.

What nonsense it is that my father writes about women! thought Richard. He says they can't laugh, and don't understand humour. It comes, he reflected, of his shutting himself from the world. And the idea that he was seeing the world, and feeling wiser, flattered him. He talked fluently to his dangerous Bellona. He gave her some reminiscences of Adrian's whimsies.

'Oh!' said she, 'that's your tutor, is it!' She eyed the young man as if she thought he must go far and fast.

Ripton felt a push. 'Look at that,' said the bosom, fuming utter disgust. He was directed to see a manly arm round the waist of the mignonne. 'Now that's what I don't like in company,' the bosom inflated to observe with sufficient emphasis. 'She always will allow it with everybody. Give her a nudge.'

Ripton protested that he dared not; upon which she said, 'Then I will'; and inclined her sumptuous bust across his lap, breathing wine in his face, and gave the nudge. The mignonne turned an inquiring eye on Ripton; a mischievous spark shot from it. She laughed, and said; 'Aren't you satisfied with the old girl?'

'Impudence!' muttered the bosom, growing grander and redder.

'Do, do fill her glass, and keep her quiet—she drinks port when there's no more champagne,' said the mignonne.

The bosom revenged herself by whispering to Ripton scandal of the mignonne, and between them he was enabled to form a correcter estimate of the company, and quite recovered from his original awe; so much so as to feel a touch of jealousy at seeing his lively little neighbour still held in absolute possession.

Mrs. Mount did not come out much; but there was a deferential manner in the bearing of the men toward her, which those haughty creatures accord not save to clever women; and she contrived to hold the talk with three or four at the head of the table while she still had passages aside with Richard.

The port and claret went very well after the champagne. The ladies here did not ignominiously surrender the field to the gentlemen; they maintained their position with honour. Silver was seen far out on Thames. The wine ebbed, and the laughter. Sentiment and cigars took up the wondrous tale.

'Oh, what a lovely night!' said the ladies, looking above.

'Charming,' said the gentlemen, looking below.

The faint-smelling cool Autumn air was pleasant after the feast. Fragrant weeds burned bright about the garden.

'We are split into couples,' said Adrian to Richard, who was standing alone, eyeing the landscape. ''Tis the influence of the moon! Apparently we are in Cyprus. How has my son enjoyed himself? How likes he the society of Aspasia?* I feel like a wise Greek to-night.'

Adrian was jolly, and rolled comfortably as he talked. Ripton had been carried off by the sentimental bosom. He came up to them and whispered: 'By Jove, Ricky! do you know what sort of women these are?'

Richard said he thought them a nice sort.

'Puritan!' exclaimed Adrian, slapping Ripton on the back. 'Why didn't you get tipsy, sir? Don't you ever intoxicate yourself except at lawful marriages? Reveal to us what you have done with the portly dame?'

Ripton endured his bantering that he might hang about Richard, and watch over him. He was jealous of his innocent Beauty's husband being in proximity with such women. Murmuring couples passed them to and fro.

'By Jove, Ricky!' Ripton favoured his friend with another hard whisper, 'there's a woman smoking!'

'And why not, O Riptonus?' said Adrian. 'Art unaware that woman cosmopolitan is woman consummate? and dost grumble to pay the small price for the splendid gem?'

'Well, I don't like women to smoke,' said plain Ripton.

'Why mayn't they do what men do?' the hero cried impetuously. 'I hate that contemptible narrow-mindedness. It's that makes the ruin and horrors I see. Why mayn't they do what men do? I like the women who are brave enough not to be hypocrites. By heaven! if these women are bad, I like them better than a set of hypocritical creatures who are all show, and deceive you in the end.'

'Bravo!' shouted Adrian. 'There speaks the regenerator.'

Ripton, as usual, was crushed by his leader. He had no argument. He still thought women ought not to smoke; and he thought of one far away, lonely by the sea, who was perfect without being cosmopolitan.

THE PILGRIM'S SCRIP remarks that: 'Young men take joy in nothing so much as the thinking women Angels: and nothing sours men of experience more than knowing that all are not quite so.'

The Aphorist would have pardoned Ripton Thompson his first Random extravagance, had he perceived the simple warm-hearted worship of feminine goodness Richard's young bride had inspired in the breast of the youth. It might possibly have taught him to put deeper trust in our nature.

Ripton thought of her, and had a feeling of sadness. He wandered about the grounds by himself, went through an open postern, and threw himself down among some bushes on the slope of the hill. Lying there, and meditating, he became aware of voices conversing.

'What does he want?' said a woman's voice. 'It's another of his villanies, I know. Upon my honour, Brayder, when I think of what I have to reproach him for, I think I must go mad, or kill him.'

'Tragic!' said the Hon. Peter. 'Haven't you revenged yourself, Bella, pretty often? Best deal openly. This is a commercial transaction. You ask for money, and you are to have it—on the conditions: double the sum, and debts paid.'

'He applies to me!'

'You know, my dear Bella, it has long been all up between you. I think Mount has behaved very well, considering all he knows. He's not easily hoodwinked, you know. He resigns himself to his fate, and follows other game.'

'Then the condition is, that I am to seduce this young man?'

'My dear Bella! you strike your bird like a hawk. I didn't say seduce. Hold him in—play with him. Amuse him.'

'I don't understand half-measures.'

'Women seldom do.'

'How I hate you, Brayder!'

'I thank your ladyship.'

The two walked farther. Ripton had heard some little of the colloquy. He left the spot in a serious mood, apprehensive of something dark to the people he loved, though he had no idea of what the Hon. Peter's stipulation involved.

On the voyage back to town, Richard was again selected to sit by Mrs. Mount. Brayder and Adrian started the jokes. The pair of parasites got on extremely well together. Soft fell the plash of the oars; softly the moonlight curled around them; softly the banks glided by. The ladies were in a state of high sentiment. They sang without request. All deemed the British balladmonger an appropriate interpreter of their emotions. After good wine, and plenty thereof, fair throats will make men of taste swallow that remarkable composer. Eyes, lips, hearts; darts and smarts and sighs; beauty, duty; bosom, blossom; false one, farewell! To this pathetic strain they melted. Mrs. Mount, though strongly requested, declined to sing. She preserved her state. Under the tall aspens of Brentford-ait,* and on they swept, the white

moon in their wake. Richard's hand lay open by his
side. Mrs. Mount's little white hand by misadventure
fell into it. It was not pressed, or soothed for its fall,
or made intimate with eloquent fingers. It lay there
like a bit of snow on the cold ground. A yellow leaf wa-
vering down from the aspens struck Richard's cheek, and
he drew away the very hand to throw back his hair and
smooth his face, and then folded his arms, unconscious
of offence. He was thinking ambitiously of his life: his
blood was untroubled, his brain calmly working.

'Which is the more perilous?' is a problem put by the
PILGRIM: 'To meet the temptings of Eve, or to pique her?'

Mrs. Mount stared at the young man as at a curiosity,
and turned to flirt with one of her Court. The Guardsmen were mostly sentimental. One or two rattled, and
one was such a good-humoured fellow that Adrian could
not make him ridiculous. The others seemed to give
themselves up to a silent waxing in length of limb. However far they sat removed, everybody was entangled in
their legs. Pursuing his studies, Adrian came to the conclusion, that the same close intellectual and moral affinity
which he had discovered to exist between our nobility
and our yeomanry, is to be observed between the Guardsman class, and that of the corps de ballet: they both
live by the strength of their legs, where also their wits,
if they do not altogether reside there, are principally
developed: both are volage;* wine, tobacco, and the
moon, influence both alike; and admitting the one marked
difference that does exist, it is, after all, pretty nearly the
same thing to be coquetting and sinning on two legs as
on the point of a toe.

A long Guardsman with a deep bass voice sang a doleful song about the twining tendrils of the heart ruthlessly
torn, but required urgent persuasions and heavy trumpeting of his lungs to get to the end: before he had accom-

plished it, Adrian had contrived to raise a laugh in his neighbourhood, so that the company was divided, and the camp split: jollity returned to one-half, while sentiment held the other. Ripton, blotted behind the bosom, was only lucky in securing a higher degree of heat than was possible for the rest. 'Are you cold?' she would ask, smiling charitably.

'*I* am,' said the mignonne, as if to excuse her conduct.

'You always appear to be,' the fat one sniffed and snapped.

'Won't you warm two, Mrs. Mortimer?' said the naughty little woman.

Disdain prevented any further notice of her. Those familiar with the ladies enjoyed their sparring, which was frequent. The mignonne was heard to whisper: 'That poor fellow will certainly be stewed.'

Very prettily the ladies took and gave warmth, for the air on the water was chill and misty. Adrian had beside him the demure one who had stopped the circulation of his anecdote. She in nowise objected to the fair exchange, but said 'Hush!' betweenwhiles.

Past Kew and Hammersmith, on the cool smooth water; across Putney reach; through Battersea bridge; and the City grew around them, and the shadows of great mill-factories slept athwart the moonlight.

All the ladies prattled sweetly of a charming day when they alighted on land. Several cavaliers crushed for the honour of conducting Mrs. Mount to her home.

'My brougham's here; I shall go alone,' said Mrs. Mount. 'Some one arrange my shawl.'

She turned her back to Richard, who had a view of a delicate neck as he manipulated with the bearing of a mailed knight.

'Which way are you going?' she asked carelessly, and, to his reply as to the direction, said: 'Then I can give you a lift,' and she took his arm with a matter-of-course air, and walked up the stairs with him.

Ripton saw what had happened. He was going to follow: the portly dame retained him, and desired him to get her a cab.

'Oh you happy fellow!' said the bright-eyed mignonne, passing by.

Ripton procured the cab, and stuffed it full without having to get into it himself.

'Try and let him come in too?' said the persecuting creature, again passing.

'Take liberties with your men—you sha'n't with me,' retorted the angry bosom, and drove off.

'So she's been and gone and run away and left him after all his trouble!' cried the pert little thing, peering into Ripton's eyes. 'Now you'll never be so foolish as to pin your faith to fat women again. There! he shall be made happy another time.' She gave his nose a comical tap, and tripped away with her possessor.

Ripton rather forgot his friend for some minutes: Random thoughts laid hold of him. Cabs and carriages rattled past. He was sure he had been among members of the nobility that day, though when they went by him now they only recognized him with an effort of the eyelids. He began to think of the day with exultation, as an event. Recollections of the mignonne were captivating. 'Blue eyes—just what I like! And such a little impudent nose, and red lips, pouting—the very thing I like! And her hair? darkish, I think—say, brown. And so saucy, and light on her feet. And kind she is, or she wouldn't have talked to me like that.' Thus, with a groaning soul, he pictured her. His reason voluntarily consigned her to the aristocracy as a natural appanage; but he did amorously wish that Fortune had made a lord of him.

Then his mind reverted to Mrs. Mount, and the strange

bits of the conversation he had heard on the hill. He was
not one to suspect anybody positively. He was timid of
fixing a suspicion. It hovered indefinitely, and clouded
people, without stirring him to any resolve. Still the
attentions of the lady toward Richard were queer. He
endeavoured to imagine they were in the nature of things,
because Richard was so handsome that any woman must
take to him. 'But he's married,' said Ripton, 'and he
mustn't go near these people if he's married.' Not a
high morality, perhaps: better than none at all: better
for the world were it practised more. He thought of
Richard along with that sparkling dame, alone with her.
The adorable beauty of his dear bride, her pure heavenly
face, swam before him. Thinking of her, he lost sight
of the mignonne who had made him giddy.

He walked to Richard's hotel, and up and down the
street there, hoping every minute to hear his step; sometimes fancying he might have returned and gone to bed.
Two o'clock struck. Ripton could not go away. He
was sure he should not sleep if he did. At last the cold
sent him homeward, and leaving the street, on the moonlight side of Piccadilly he met his friend patrolling with
his head up and that swing of the feet proper to men
who are chanting verses.

'Old Rip!' cried Richard cheerily. 'What on earth
are you doing here at this hour of the morning?'

Ripton muttered of his pleasure at meeting him. 'I
wanted to shake your hand before I went home.'

Richard smiled on him in an amused kindly way. 'That
all? You may shake my hand any day, like a true man
as you are, old Rip! I've been speaking about you. Do
you know, that—Mrs. Mount—never saw you all the
time at Richmond, or in the boat!'

'Oh!' Ripton said, well assured that he was a dwarf:
'You saw her safe home?'

'Yes. I've been there for the last couple of hours—talking. She talks capitally: she's wonderfully clever. She's very like a man, only much nicer. I like her.'

'But, Richard, excuse me—I'm sure I don't mean to offend you—but now you're married . . . perhaps you couldn't help seeing her home, but I think you really indeed oughtn't to have gone upstairs.'

Ripton delivered this opinion with a modest impressiveness.

'What do you mean?' said Richard. 'You don't suppose I care for any woman but my little darling down there.' He laughed.

'No; of course not. That's absurd. What I mean is, that people perhaps will—you know, they do—they say all manner of things, and that makes unhappiness, and . . . . I do wish you were going home to-morrow, Ricky. I mean, to your dear wife.' Ripton blushed and looked away as he spoke.

The hero gave one of his scornful glances. 'So you're anxious about my reputation. I hate that way of looking on women. Because they have been once misled—look how much weaker they are!—because the world has given them an ill fame, you would treat them as contagious, and keep away from them for the sake of your character!'

'It would be different with me,' quoth Ripton.

'How?' asked the hero.

'Because I'm worse than you,' was all the logical explanation Ripton was capable of.

'I do hope you will go home soon,' he added.

'Yes,' said Richard, 'and I, so do I hope so. But I've work to do now. I dare not, I cannot, leave it. Lucy would be the last to ask me;—You saw her letter yesterday. Now listen to me, Rip. I want to make you be just to women.'

Then he read Ripton a lecture on erring women, speaking of them as if he had known them and studied them for years. Clever, beautiful, but betrayed by love, it was the first duty of all true men to cherish and redeem them. 'We turn them into curses, Rip; these divine creatures.' And the world suffered for it. That—that was the root of all the evil in the world!

'I don't feel anger or horror at these poor women, Rip! It's strange. I knew what they were when we came home in the boat. But I do—it tears my heart to see a young girl given over to an old man—a man she doesn't love. That's shame!—Don't speak of it.'

Forgetting to contest the premiss, that all betrayed women are betrayed by love, Ripton was quite silenced. He, like most young men, had pondered somewhat on this matter, and was inclined to be sentimental when he was not hungry. They walked in the moonlight by the railings of the park. Richard harangued at leisure, while Ripton's teeth chattered. Chivalry might be dead, but still there was something to do, went the strain. The lady of the day had not been thrown in the hero's path without an object, he said; and he was sadly right there. He did not express the thing clearly; nevertheless Ripton understood him to mean, he intended to rescue that lady from further transgressions, and show a certain scorn of the world. That lady, and then other ladies unknown, were to be rescued. Ripton was to help. He and Ripton were to be the knights of this enterprise. When appealed to, Ripton acquiesced, and shivered. Not only were they to be knights, they would have to be Titans, for the powers of the world, the spurious ruling Social Gods, would have to be defied and overthrown. And Titan number one flung up his handsome bold face as if to challenge base Jove on the spot; and Titan number two strained the upper button of his coat to meet across his pocket-handkerchief on his chest, and warmed his fingers under his coat-tails. The moon had fallen from her high seat and was in the mists of the West, when he was allowed to seek his blankets, and the cold acting on his friend's eloquence made Ripton's flesh very contrite. The poor fellow had thinner blood than the hero; but his heart was good. By the time he had got a little warmth about him, his heart gratefully strove to encourage him in the conception of becoming a knight and a Titan; and so striving Ripton fell asleep and dreamed.

CHAPTER XXXVII

MRS. BERRY ON MATRIMONY

BEHOLD the hero embarked in the redemption of an erring beautiful woman.

'Alas!' writes the PILGRIM at this very time to Lady Blandish, 'I cannot get that legend of the Serpent from me, the more I think. Has he not caught you, and ranked you foremost in his legions? For see: till you were fashioned, the fruits hung immobile on the boughs. They swayed before us, glistening and cold. The hand must be eager that plucked them. They did not come down to us, and smile, and speak our language, and read our thoughts, and know when to fly, when to follow! how surely to have us!

'Do but mark one of you standing openly in the track of the Serpent. What shall be done with her? I fear the world is wiser than its judges! Turn from her, says the world. By day the sons of the world do. It darkens, and they dance together downward. Then comes there one of the world's elect who deems old counsel devilish; indifference to the end of evil worse than its pursuit.

He comes to reclaim her. From deepest bane will he bring her back to highest blessing. Is not that a bait already? Poor fish! 'tis wondrous flattering. The Serpent has slimed her so to secure him! With slow weary steps he draws her into light: she clings to him; she is human; part of his work, and he loves it. As they mount upward, he looks on her more, while she, it may be, looks above. What has touched him? What has passed out of her, and into him? The Serpent laughs below. At the gateways of the Sun they fall together!'

This alliterative production was written without any sense of the peril that makes prophecy.

It suited Sir Austin to write thus. It was a channel to his acrimony moderated through his philosophy. The letter was a reply to a vehement entreaty from Lady Blandish for him to come up to Richard and forgive him thoroughly: Richard's name was not mentioned in it.

'He tries to be more than he is,' thought the lady; and she began insensibly to conceive him less than he was.

The baronet was conscious of a certain false gratification in his son's apparent obedience to his wishes and complete submission; a gratification he chose to accept as his due, without dissecting or accounting for it. The intelligence reiterating that Richard waited, and still waited; Richard's letters, and more his dumb abiding and practical penitence; vindicated humanity sufficiently to stop the course of virulent aphorisms. He could speak, we have seen, in sorrow for this frail nature of ours, that he had once stood forth to champion. 'But how long will this last?' he demanded, with the air of Hippias. He did not reflect how long it had lasted. Indeed, his indigestion of wrath had made of him a moral Dyspepsy.

It was not mere obedience that held Richard from the arms of his young wife: nor was it this new knightly

enterprise he had presumed to undertake. Hero as he
was, a youth, open to the insane promptings of hot blood,
he was not a fool. There had been talk between him
and Mrs. Doria of his mother. Now that he had broken
from his father, his heart spoke for her. She lived, he
knew: he knew no more. Words painfully hovering
along the borders of plain speech had been communicated to him, filling him with moody imaginings. If he
thought of her, the red was on his face, though he could
not have said why. But now, after canvassing the conduct of his father, and throwing him aside as a terrible
riddle, he asked Mrs. Doria to tell him of his other parent.
As softly as she could she told the story. To her the
shame was past: she could weep for the poor lady. Richard dropped no tears. Disgrace of this kind is always
present to a son, and, educated as he had been, these
tidings were a vivid fire in his brain. He resolved to
hunt her out, and take her from the man. Here was
work set to his hand. All her dear husband did was
right to Lucy. She encouraged him to stay for that
purpose, thinking it also served another. There was
Tom Bakewell to watch over Lucy: there was work for
him to do. Whether it would please his father he did
not stop to consider. As to the justice of the act, let us
say nothing.

On Ripton devolved the humbler task of grubbing for
Sandoe's place of residence; and as he was unacquainted
with the name by which the poet now went in private,
his endeavours were not immediately successful. The
friends met in the evening at Lady Blandish's town-
house, or at the Foreys', where Mrs. Doria procured the
reverer of the Royal Martyr, and staunch conservative,
a favourable reception. Pity, deep pity for Richard's
conduct Ripton saw breathing out of Mrs. Doria. Algernon Feverel treated his nephew with a sort of rough

commiseration, as a young fellow who had run off the road.

Pity was in Lady Blandish's eyes, though for a different cause. She doubted if she did well in seconding his father's unwise scheme—supposing him to have a scheme. She saw the young husband encompassed by dangers at a critical time. Not a word of Mrs. Mount had been breathed to her, but the lady had some knowledge of life. She touched on delicate verges to the baronet in her letters, and he understood her well enough. 'If he loves this person to whom he has bound himself, what fear for him? Or are you coming to think it something that bears the name of love because we have to veil the rightful appellation?' So he responded, remote among the mountains. She tried very hard to speak plainly. Finally he came to say that he denied himself the pleasure of seeing his son specially, that he for a time might be put to the test the lady seemed to dread. This was almost too much for Lady Blandish. Love's charity boy so loftily serene now that she saw him half denuded—a thing of shanks and wrists—was a trial for her true heart.

Going home at night Richard would laugh at the faces made about his marriage. 'We'll carry the day, Rip, my Lucy and I! or I'll do it alone—what there is to do.' He slightly adverted to a natural want of courage in women, which Ripton took to indicate that his Beauty was deficient in that quality. Up leapt the Old Dog; 'I'm sure there never was a braver creature upon earth, Richard! She's as brave as she's lovely, I'll swear she is! Look how she behaved that day! How her voice sounded! She was trembling . . . Brave? She'd follow you into battle, Richard!'

And Richard rejoined: 'Talk on, dear old Rip! She's my darling love, whatever she is! And she is gloriously

lovely. No eyes are like hers. I'll go down to-morrow
morning the first thing.'

Ripton only wondered the husband of such a treasure
could remain apart from it. So thought Richard for a
space.

'But if I go, Rip,' he said despondently, 'if I go for a
day even I shall have undone all my work with my father.
She says it herself—you saw it in her last letter.'

'Yes,' Ripton assented, and the words 'Please remember me to dear Mr. Thompson,' fluttered about the
Old Dog's heart.

It came to pass that Mrs. Berry, having certain business
that led her through Kensington Gardens, spied a figure
that she had once dandled in long clothes, and helped make
a man of, if ever woman did. He was walking under
the trees beside a lady, talking to her, not indifferently.
The gentleman was her bridegroom and her babe. 'I
know his back,' said Mrs. Berry, as if she had branded
a mark on it in infancy. But the lady was not her bride.
Mrs. Berry diverged from the path, and got before them
on the left flank; she stared, retreated, and came round
upon the right. There was that in the lady's face which
Mrs. Berry did not like. Her innermost question was,
why he was not walking with his own wife? She stopped
in front of them. They broke, and passed about her.
The lady made a laughing remark to him, whereat he
turned to look, and Mrs. Berry bobbed. She had to bob
a second time, and then he remembered the worthy creature, and hailed her Penelope, shaking her hand so that he
put her in countenance again. Mrs. Berry was extremely
agitated. He dismissed her, promising to call upon her
in the evening. She heard the lady slip out something
from a side of her lip, and they both laughed as she toddled
off to a sheltering tree to wipe a corner of each eye. 'I

don't like the looks of that woman,' she said, and repeated
it resolutely.

'Why doesn't he walk arm-in-arm with her?' was her
next inquiry. 'Where's his wife?' succeeded it. After
many interrogations of the sort, she arrived at naming
the lady a bold-faced thing; adding subsequently, brazen.
The lady had apparently shown Mrs. Berry that she
wished to get red of her, and had checked the outpouring
of her emotions on the breast of her babe. 'I know a
lady when I see one,' said Mrs. Berry. 'I haven't lived
with 'em for nothing; and if she's a lady bred and born,
I wasn't married in the church alive.'

Then, if not a lady, what was she? Mrs. Berry desired
to know. 'She's imitation lady, I'm sure she is!' Berry
vowed. 'I say she don't look proper.'

Establishing the lady to be a spurious article, however,
what was one to think of a married man in company with
such? 'Oh no! it ain't that!' Mrs. Berry returned immediately on the charitable tack. 'Belike it's some
one of his acquaintance 've married her for her looks, and
he've just met her. . . . Why it'd be as bad as my
Berry!' the relinquished spouse of Berry ejaculated, in
horror at the idea of a second man being so monstrous in
wickedness. 'Just coupled, too!' Mrs. Berry groaned
on the suspicious side of the debate. 'And such a sweet
young thing for his wife! But no, I'll never believe it.
Not if he tell me so himself! And men don't do that,'
she whimpered.

Women are swift at coming to conclusions in these
matters; soft women exceedingly swift: and soft women
who have been betrayed are rapid beyond measure. Mrs.
Berry had not cogitated long ere she pronounced distinctly and without a shadow of dubiosity: 'My opinion
is—married or not married, and wheresomever he pick
her up—she's nothin' more nor less than a Bella Donna!'*

as which poisonous plant she forthwith registered the
lady in the botanical note-book of her brain. It would
have astonished Mrs. Mount to have heard her person so
accurately hit off at a glance.

In the evening Richard made good his promise, accompanied by Ripton. Mrs. Berry opened the door to them.
She could not wait to get him into the parlour. 'You 're
my own blessed babe; and I 'm as good as your mother,
—though I didn't suck ye, bein' a maid!' she cried,
falling into his arms, while Richard did his best to support the unexpected burden. Then reproaching him tenderly for his guile—at mention of which Ripton chuckled,
deeming it his own most honourable portion of the plot—
Mrs. Berry led them into the parlour, and revealed to
Richard who she was, and how she had tossed him, and
hugged him, and kissed him all over, when he was only
that big—showing him her stumpy fat arm. 'I kissed
ye from head to tail, I did,' said Mrs. Berry, 'and you
needn't be ashamed of it. It 's be hoped you 'll never
have nothin' worse come t' ye, my dear!'

Richard assured her he was not a bit ashamed, but
warned her that she must not do it now, Mrs. Berry admitting it was out of the question now, and now that
he had a wife, moreover. The young men laughed, and
Ripton laughing over-loudly drew on himself Mrs. Berry's
attention: 'But that Mr. Thompson there—however he
can look me in the face after his inn'cence! helping blindfold an old woman!—though I ain't sorry for what I did
—that I 'm free for to say, and it 's over, and blessed
be all! Amen! So now where is she and how is she,
Mr. Richard, my dear—it 's only cuttin' off the "s"
and you are as you was.—Why didn't ye bring her with
ye to see her old Berry?'

Richard hurriedly explained that Lucy was still in the
Isle of Wight.

'Oh! and you've left her for a day or two?' said Mrs. Berry.

'Good God! I wish it had been a day or two,' cried Richard.

'Ah! and how long have it been?' asked Mrs. Berry, her heart beginning to beat at his manner of speaking.

'Don't talk about it,' said Richard.

'Oh! you never been dudgeonin' already? Oh! you haven't been peckin' at one another yet?' Mrs. Berry exclaimed.

Ripton interposed to tell her such fears were unfounded.

'Then how long ha' you been divided?'

In a guilty voice Ripton stammered 'since September.'

'September!' breathed Mrs. Berry, counting on her fingers, 'September, October, Nov—two months and more! nigh three! A young married husband away from the wife of his bosom nigh three months! Oh my! Oh my! what do that mean?'

'My father sent for me—I'm waiting to see him,' said Richard. A few more words helped Mrs. Berry to comprehend the condition of affairs. Then Mrs. Berry spread her lap, flattened out her hands, fixed her eyes, and spoke.

'My dear young gentleman!—I'd like to call ye my darlin' babe! I'm going to speak as a mother to ye, whether ye likes it or no; and what old Berry says, you won't mind, for she's had ye when there was no conventionals about ye, and she has the feelin's of a mother to you, though humble her state. If there's one that know matrimony it's me, my dear, though Berry did give me no more but nine months of it: and I've known the worst of matrimony, which, if you wants to be woful wise, there it is for ye. For what have been my gain? That man gave me nothin' but his name; and Bessy Andrews was as good as Bessy Berry, though both is "Bs," and says he, you was "A," and now you's "B," so you're my A B, he says, write yourself down that, he says, the bad man, with his jokes!—Berry went to service.' Mrs. Berry's softness came upon her. 'So I tell ye, Berry went to service. He left the wife of his bosom forlorn and he went to service; because he were al'ays an ambitious man, and wasn't, so to speak, happy out of his uniform —which was his livery—not even in my arms: and he let me know it. He got among them kitchen sluts, which was my mournin' ready made, and worse than a widow's cap to me, which is no shame to wear, and some say becoming. There's no man as ever lived know better than my Berry how to show his legs to advantage, and gals look at 'em. I don't wonder now that Berry was prostrated. His temptations was strong, and his flesh was weak. Then what I say is, that for a young married man—be he whomsoever he may be—to be separated from the wife of his bosom—a young sweet thing, and he an innocent young gentleman!—so to sunder, in their state, and be kep' from each other, I say it's as bad as bad can be! For what is matrimony, my dears? We're told it's a holy Ordnance. And why are ye so comfortable in matrimony? For that ye are not a sinnin'! And they that severs ye they tempts ye to stray: and you learn too late the meanin' o' them blessin's of the priest—as it was ordained. Separate—what comes? Fust it's like the circulation of your blood a-stoppin'—all goes wrong. Then there's misunderstandings—ye've both lost the key. Then, behold ye, there's birds o' prey hoverin' over each on ye, and it's which'll be snapped up fust. Then —Oh, dear! Oh, dear! it be like the devil come into the world again.' Mrs. Berry struck her hands and moaned. 'A day I'll give ye: I'll go so far as a week: but there's the outside. Three months dwellin' apart! That's not matrimony, it's divorcin'! what can it be to her but widowhood? widowhood with no cap to show for it!

And what can it be to you, my dear? Think! you been a bachelor three months! and a bachelor man,' Mrs. Berry shook her head most dolefully, 'he ain't a widow woman. I don't go to compare you to Berry, my dear young gentleman. Some men's hearts is vagabonds born—they must go astray—it's their natur' to. But all men are men, and I know the foundation of 'em, by reason of my woe.'

Mrs. Berry paused. Richard was humorously respectful to the sermon. The truth in the good creature's address was not to be disputed or despised, notwithstanding the inclination to laugh provoked by her quaint way of putting it. Ripton nodded encouragingly at every sentence, for he saw her drift, and wished to second it.

Seeking for an illustration of her meaning, Mrs. Berry solemnly continued: 'We all know what checked prespiration is.' But neither of the young gentlemen could resist this. Out they burst in a roar of laughter.

'Laugh away,' said Mrs. Berry. 'I don't mind ye. I say again, we all do know what checked prespiration is. It fly to the lungs, it gives ye mortal inflammation, and it carries ye off. Then I say checked matrimony is as bad. It fly to the heart, and it carries off the virtue that's in ye, and you might as well be dead! Them that is joined it's their salvation not to separate! It don't so much matter before it. That Mr. Thompson there—if he go astray, it ain't from the blessed fold. He hurt himself alone—not double, and belike treble, for who can say now what may be? There's time for it. I'm for holding back young people so that they knows their minds, howsomever they rattles about their hearts. I ain't a speeder of matrimony, and good's my reason! but where it's been done—where they're lawfully joined, and their bodies made one, I do say this, that to put division between 'em then, it's to make wanderin' comets of 'em—creatures without a objeck, and no soul can say what they's good for but to rush about!'

Mrs. Berry here took a heavy breath, as one who has said her utmost for the time being.

'My dear old girl,' Richard went up to her and applauding her on the shoulder, 'you're a very wise old woman. But you mustn't speak to me as if I wanted to stop here. I'm compelled to. I do it for her good chiefly.'

'It's your father that's doin' it, my dear?'

'Well, I'm waiting his pleasure.'

'A pretty pleasure! puttin' a snake in the nest of young turtle-doves! And why don't she come up to you?'

'Well, that you must ask her. The fact is, she's a little timid girl—she wants me to see him first, and when I've made all right, then she'll come.'

'A little timid girl!' cried Mrs. Berry. 'Oh, lor', how she must ha' deceived ye to make ye think that! Look at that ring,' she held out her finger, 'he's a stranger: he's not my lawful! You know what ye did to me, my dear. Could I get my own wedding-ring back from her? "No!" says she, firm as a rock, "he said, *with this ring I thee wed*"—I think I see her now, with her pretty eyes and lovesome locks—a darlin'!—And that ring she'd keep to, come life, come death. And she must ha' been a rock for me to give in to her in that. For what's the consequence? Here am I,' Mrs. Berry smoothed down the back of her hand mournfully, 'here am I in a strange ring, that's like a strange man holdin' of me, and me a-wearin' of it just to seem decent, and feelin' all over no better than a b——a big—that nasty name I can't abide!—I tell you, my dear, she ain't soft, no! —except to the man of her heart; and the best of women's too soft there—more's our sorrow!'

'Well, well!' said Richard, who thought he knew.

'I agree with you, Mrs. Berry,' Ripton struck in, 'Mrs. Richard would do anything in the world her husband asked her, I 'm quite sure.'

'Bless you for your good opinion, Mr. Thompson! Why, see her! she ain't frail on her feet; she looks ye straight in the eyes; she ain't one of your hang-down misses. Look how she behaved at the ceremony!'

'Ah!' sighed Ripton.

'And if you 'd ha' seen her when she spoke to me about my ring! Depend upon it, my dear Mr. Richard, if she blinded you about the nerve she 've got, it was somethin' she thought she ought to do for your sake, and I wish I 'd been by to counsel her, poor blessed babe!—And how much longer, now, can ye stay divided from that darlin'?'

Richard paced up and down.

'A father's will,' urged Mrs. Berry, 'that 's a son's law; but he mustn't go again' the laws of his nature to do it.'

'Just be quiet at present—talk of other things, there 's a good woman,' said Richard.

Mrs. Berry meekly folded her arms.

'How strange, now, our meetin' like this! meetin' at all, too!' she remarked contemplatively. 'It 's them advertisements! They brings people together from the ends of the earth, for good or for bad. I often say, there 's more lucky accidents, or unlucky ones, since advertisements was the rule, than ever there was before. They make a number of romances, depend upon it! Do you walk much in the Gardens, my dear?'

'Now and then,' said Richard.

'Very pleasant it is there with the fine folks and flowers and titled people,' continued Mrs. Berry. 'That was a handsome woman you was a-walkin' beside, this mornin'.'

'Very,' said Richard.

'She was a handsome woman! or I should say, is, for her day ain't past, and she know it. I thought at first—

by her back—it might ha' been your aunt, Mrs. Forey;
for she do step out well and hold up her shoulders: straight
as a dart she be! But when I come to see her face—Oh,
dear me! says I, this ain't one of the family. They none
of 'em got such bold faces—nor no *lady* as I know have.
But she's a fine woman—that nobody can gainsay.'

Mrs. Berry talked further of the fine woman. It was
a liberty she took to speak in this disrespectful tone of
her, and Mrs. Berry was quite aware that she was laying
herself open to rebuke. She had her end in view. No
rebuke was uttered, and during her talk she observed
intercourse passing between the eyes of the young men.

'Look here, Penelope,' Richard stopped her at last.
'Will it make you comfortable if I tell you I'll obey
the laws of my nature and go down at the end of the
week?'

'I'll thank the Lord of heaven if you do!' she exclaimed.

'Very well, then—be happy—I will. Now listen. I
want you to keep your rooms for me—those she had.
I expect, in a day or two, to bring a lady here——'

'A lady?' faltered Mrs. Berry.

'Yes. A lady.'

'May I make so bold as to ask what lady?'

'You may not. Not now. Of course you will know.'

Mrs. Berry's short neck made the best imitation it could
of an offended swan's action. She was very angry. She
said she did not like so many ladies, which natural objection Richard met by saying that there was only one
lady.

'And Mrs. Berry,' he added, dropping his voice. 'You
will treat her as you did my dear girl, for she will require
not only shelter but kindness. I would rather leave her
with you than with any one. She has been very unfortunate.'

His serious air and habitual tone of command fascinated
the softness of Berry, and it was not until he had gone
that she spoke out. 'Unfort'nate! He's going to bring
me an unfort'nate female! Oh! not from my babe can
I bear that! Never will I have her here! I see it. It's
that bold-faced woman he's got mixed up in, and she've
been and made the young man think he'll go for to reform
her. It's one o' their arts—that is; and he's too innocent a young man to mean anythin' else. But I ain't
a house of Magdalens—no! and sooner than have her
here I'd have the roof fall over me, I would.'

She sat down to eat her supper on the sublime resolve.

In love, Mrs. Berry's charity was all on the side of the
law, and this is the case with many of her sisters. The
PILGRIM sneers at them for it, and would have us credit
that it is their admirable instinct which, at the expense
of every virtue save one, preserves the artificial barrier
simply to impose upon us. Men, I presume, are hardly
fair judges, and should stand aside and mark.

Early next day Mrs. Berry bundled off to Richard's
hotel to let him know her determination. She did not find
him there. Returning homeward through the Park, she
beheld him on horseback riding by the side of the identical
lady. The sight of this public exposure shocked her
more than the secret walk under the trees. 'You don't
look near your reform yet,' Mrs. Berry apostrophized
her. 'You don't look to me one that'd come the Fair
Penitent till you've left off bein' fair—if then you do,
which some of ye don't. Laugh away and show yer airs!
Spite o' your hat and feather, and your ridin' habit,
you're a Bella Donna.' Setting her down again absolutely for such, whatever it might signify, Mrs. Berry
had a virtuous glow.

In the evening she heard the noise of wheels stopping
at the door. 'Never!' she rose from her chair to ex-

claim. 'He ain't rided her out in the mornin', and been and made a Magdalen of her afore dark?'

A lady veiled was brought into the house by Richard. Mrs. Berry feebly tried to bar his progress in the passage. He pushed past her, and conducted the lady into the parlour without speaking. Mrs. Berry did not follow. She heard him murmur a few sentences within. Then he came out. All her crest stood up, as she whispered vigorously, 'Mr. Richard! if that woman stay here, I go forth. My house ain't a penitentiary for unfort'nate females, sir——'

He frowned at her curiously; but as she was on the point of renewing her indignant protest, he clapped his hand across her mouth, and spoke words in her ear that had awful import to her. She trembled, breathing low: 'My God, forgive me! Lady Feverel is it? Your mother, Mr. Richard?' And her virtue was humbled.

CHAPTER XXXVIII

AN ENCHANTRESS

ONE may suppose that a prematurely aged, oily little man; a poet in bad circumstances; a decrepit butterfly chained to a disappointed inkstand, will not put out strenuous energies to retain his ancient paramour when a robust young man comes imperatively to demand his mother of him in her person. The colloquy was short between Diaper Sandoe and Richard. The question was referred to the poor spiritless lady, who, seeing that her son made no question of it, cast herself on his hands. Small loss to her was Diaper; but he was the loss of habit, and that is something to a woman who has lived. The

blood of her son had been running so long alien from her
that the sense of her motherhood smote her now with
strangeness, and Richard's stern gentleness seemed like
dreadful justice come upon her. Her heart had almost
forgotten its maternal functions. She called him Sir,
till he bade her remember he was her son. Her voice
sounded to him like that of a broken-throated lamb, so
painful and weak it was, with the plaintive stop in the
utterance. When he kissed her, her skin was cold. Her
thin hand fell out of his when his grasp relaxed. 'Can
sin hunt one like this?' he asked, bitterly reproaching
himself for the shame she had caused him to endure, and
a deep compassion filled his breast.

Poetic justice had been dealt to Diaper the poet. He
thought of all he had sacrificed for this woman—the
comfortable quarters, the friend, the happy flights. He
could not but accuse her of unfaithfulness in leaving him
in his old age. Habit had legalized his union with her.
He wrote as pathetically of the break of habit as men
feel at the death of love; and when we are old and have
no fair hope tossing golden locks before us, a wound to
this our second nature is quite as sad. I know not even
if it be not actually sadder.

Day by day Richard visited his mother. Lady Blandish and Ripton alone were in the secret. Adrian let him
do as he pleased. He thought proper to tell him that
the public recognition he accorded to a particular lady
was, in the present state of the world, scarcely prudent.

''Tis a proof to me of your moral rectitude, my son,
but the world will not think so. No one character is
sufficient to cover two—in a Protestant country especially. The divinity that doth hedge a Bishop would
have no chance in contact with your Madam Danaë.*
Drop the woman, my son. Or permit *me* to speak what
you would have her hear.'

Richard listened to him with disgust.

'Well, you've had my doctorial warning,' said Adrian, and plunged back into his book.

When Lady Feverel had revived to take part in the consultations Mrs. Berry perpetually opened on the subject of Richard's matrimonial duty, another chain was cast about him. 'Do not, oh, do not offend your father!' was her one repeated supplication. Sir Austin had grown to be a vindictive phantom in her mind. She never wept but when she said this.

So Mrs. Berry, to whom Richard had once made mention of Lady Blandish as the only friend he had among women, bundled off in her black-satin dress to obtain an interview with her, and an ally. After coming to an understanding on the matter of the visit, and reiterating many of her views concerning young married people, Mrs. Berry said: 'My lady, if I may speak so bold, I'd say the sin that's bein' done is the sin o' the lookers on. And when everybody appear frighted by that young gentleman's father, I'll say—hopin' your pardon—they no cause be frighted at all. For though it's nigh twenty year since I knew him, and I knew him then just sixteen months —no more—I'll say his heart's as soft as a woman's, which I've cause for to know. And that's it. That's where everybody's deceived by him, and I was. It's because he keeps his face, and makes ye think you're dealin' with a man of iron, and all the while there's a woman underneath. And a man that's like a woman he's the puzzle o' life! We can see through ourselves, my lady, and we can see through men, but one o' that sort —he's like somethin' out of nature. Then I say—hopin' be excused—what's to do is for to treat him *like* a woman, and not for to let him 'ave his own way—which he don't know himself, and is why nobody else do. Let that sweet young couple come together, and be wholesome in spite of him, I say; and then give him time to come round, just like a woman; and round he 'll come, and give 'em his blessin', and we shall know we 've made him comfortable. He 's angry because matrimony have come between him and his son, and he, woman-like, he 's wantin' to treat what is as if it isn't. But matrimony 's a holier than him. It began long long before him, and it 's be hoped will endoor long 's the time after, if the world 's not coming to rack—wishin' him no harm.'

Now Mrs. Berry only put Lady Blandish's thoughts in bad English. The lady took upon herself seriously to advise Richard to send for his wife. He wrote, bidding her come. Lucy, however, had wits, and inexperienced wits are as a little knowledge. In pursuance of her sage plan to make the family feel her worth, and to conquer the members of it one by one, she had got up a correspondence with Adrian, whom it tickled. Adrian constantly assured her all was going well: time would heal the wound if both the offenders had the fortitude to be patient: he fancied he saw signs of the baronet's relenting: they must do nothing to arrest those favourable symptoms. Indeed the wise youth was languidly seeking to produce them. He wrote, and felt, as Lucy's benefactor. So Lucy replied to her husband a cheerful rigmarole he could make nothing of, save that she was happy in hope, and still had fears. Then Mrs. Berry trained her fist to indite a letter to her bride. Her bride answered it by saying she trusted to time. 'You poor marter,' Mrs. Berry wrote back, 'I know what your sufferin's be. They is the only kind a wife should never hide from her husband. He thinks all sorts of things if she can abide being away. And you trusting to time, why it 's like trusting not to catch cold out of your natural clothes.' There was no shaking Lucy's firmness.

Richard gave it up. He began to think that the life

lying behind him was the life of a fool. What had he done in it? He had burnt a rick and got married! He associated the two acts of his existence. Where was the hero he was to have carved out of Tom Bakewell!— a wretch he had taught to lie and chicane: and for what? Great heavens! how ignoble did a flash from the light of his aspirations make his marriage appear? The young man sought amusement. He allowed his aunt to drag him into society, and sick of that he made late evening calls on Mrs. Mount, oblivious of the purpose he had in visiting her at all. Her man-like conversation, which he took for honesty, was a refreshing change on fair lips.

'Call me Bella: I'll call you Dick,' said she. And it came to be Bella and Dick between them. No mention of Bella occurred in Richard's letters to Lucy.

Mrs. Mount spoke quite openly of herself. 'I pretend to be no better than I am,' she said, 'and I know I'm no worse than many a woman who holds her head high.' To back this she told him stories of blooming dames of good repute, and poured a little social sewerage into his ears.

Also she understood him. 'What you want, my dear Dick, is something to do. You went and got married like a—hum!—friends must be respectful. Go into the army. Try the turf. I can put you up to a trick or two —friends should make themselves useful.'

She told him what she liked in him. 'You're the only man I was ever alone with who don't talk to me of love and make me feel sick. I hate men who can't speak to a woman sensibly.—Just wait a minute.' She left him and presently returned with, 'Ah, Dick! old fellow! how are you?'—arrayed like a cavalier, one arm stuck in her side, her hat jauntily cocked, and a pretty oath on her lips to give reality to the costume. 'What do you think of me? Wasn't it a shame to make a woman of me when I was born to be a man?'

'I don't know that,' said Richard, for the contrast in her attire to those shooting eyes and lips, aired her sex bewitchingly.

'What! you think I don't do it well?'

'Charming! but I can't forget . . .'

'Now that is too bad!' she pouted.

Then she proposed that they should go out into the midnight streets arm-in-arm, and out they went and had great fits of laughter at her impertinent manner of using her eye-glass, and outrageous affectation of the supreme dandy.

'They take up men, Dick, for going about in women's clothes, and vice versaw, I suppose. You'll bail me, old fellaa, if I have to make my bow to the beak, won't you? Say it's becas I'm an honest woman and don't care to hide the—a—unmentionables when I wear them —as the t'others do,' sprinkled with the dandy's famous invocations.

He began to conceive romance in that sort of fun.

'You're a wopper, my brave Dick! won't let any peeler take me? by Jove!'

And he with many assurances guaranteed to stand by her, while she bent her thin fingers trying the muscle of his arm, and reposed upon it more. There was delicacy in her dandyism. She was a graceful cavalier.

'Sir Julius,' as they named the dandy's attire, was frequently called for on his evening visits to Mrs. Mount. When he beheld Sir Julius he thought of the lady, and 'vice versaw,' as Sir Julius was fond of exclaiming.

Was ever hero in this fashion wooed?*

The woman now and then would peep through Sir Julius. Or she would sit, and talk, and altogether forget she was impersonating that worthy fop.

She never uttered an idea or a reflection, but Richard thought her the cleverest woman he had ever met.

All kinds of problematic notions beset him. She was cold as ice, she hated talk about love, and she was branded by the world.

A rumour spread that reached Mrs. Doria's ears. She rushed to Adrian first. The wise youth believed there was nothing in it. She sailed down upon Richard. 'Is this true? that you have been seen going publicly about with an infamous woman, Richard? Tell me! pray, relieve me!'

Richard knew of no person answering to his aunt's description in whose company he could have been seen.

'Tell me, I say! Don't quibble. Do you know *any* woman of bad character?'

The acquaintance of a lady very much misjudged and ill-used by the world, Richard admitted to.

Urgent grave advice Mrs. Doria tendered her nephew, both from the moral and the worldly point of view, mentally ejaculating all the while: 'That ridiculous System! That disgraceful marriage!' Sir Austin in his mountain solitude was furnished with serious stuff to brood over.

The rumour came to Lady Blandish. She likewise lectured Richard, and with her he condescended to argue. But he found himself obliged to instance something he had quite neglected: 'Instead of her doing me harm, it's I that will do her good.'

Lady Blandish shook her head and held up her finger.

'This person must be very clever to have given you that delusion, dear.'

'She *is* clever. And the world treats her shamefully.'

'She complains of her position to you?'

'Not a word. But I will stand by her. She has no friend but me.'

'My poor boy! has she made you think that?'

'How unjust you all are!' cried Richard.

'How mad and wicked is the man who can let him be tempted so!' thought Lady Blandish.

He would pronounce no promise not to visit her, not to address her publicly. The world that condemned her and cast her out was no better—worse for its miserable hypocrisy. He knew the world now, the young man said.

'My child! the world may be very bad. I am not going to defend it. But you have some one else to think of. Have you forgotten you have a wife, Richard?'

'Ay! you all speak of her now. There's my aunt: "Remember you have a wife!" Do you think I love any one but Lucy? poor little thing! Because I am married am I to give up the society of women?'

'Of women!'

'Isn't she a woman?'

'Too much so!' sighed the defender of her sex.

Adrian became more emphatic in his warnings. Richard laughed at him. The wise youth sneered at Mrs. Mount. The hero then favoured him with a warning equal to his own in emphasis, and surpassing it in sincerity.

'We won't quarrel, my dear boy,' said Adrian. 'I'm a man of peace. Besides, we are not fairly proportioned for a combat. Ride your steed to virtue's goal! All I say is, that I think he'll upset you, and it's better to go at a slow pace and in companionship with the children of the sun. You have a very nice little woman for a wife—well, good-bye!'

To have his wife and the world thrown at his face, was unendurable to Richard; he associated them somewhat after the manner of the rick and the marriage. Charming Sir Julius, always gay, always honest, dispersed his black moods.

'Why, you're taller,' Richard made the discovery.

'Of course I am. Don't you remember you said I was such a little thing when I came out of my woman's shell?'

'And how have you done it?'

'Grown to please you.'

'Now, if you can do that, you can do anything.'

'And so I would do anything.'

'You would?'

'Honour!'

'Then . . .' his project recurred to him. But the incongruity of speaking seriously to Sir Julius struck him dumb.

'Then what?' asked she.

'Then you're a gallant fellow.'

'That all?'

'Isn't it enough?'

'Not quite. You were going to say something. I saw it in your eyes.'

'You saw that I admired you.'

'Yes, but a man mustn't admire a man.'

'I suppose I had an idea you were a woman.'

'What! when I had the heels of my boots raised half an inch,' Sir Julius turned one heel, and volleyed out silver laughter.

'I don't come much above your shoulder even now,' she said, and proceeded to measure her height beside him with arch up-glances.

'You must grow more.'

' 'Fraid I can't' Dick! Bootmakers can't do it.'

'I'll show you how,' and he lifted Sir Julius lightly, and bore the fair gentleman to the looking-glass, holding him there exactly on a level with his head. 'Will that do?'

'Yes! Oh but I can't stay here.'

'Why can't you?'

'Why can't I?'

Their eyes met. He put her down instantly.

He should have known then—it was thundered at a closed door in him, that he played with fire. But the door being closed, he thought himself internally secure.

Sir Julius, charming as he was, lost his vogue. Seeing that, the wily woman resumed her shell. The memory of Sir Julius breathing about her still, doubled the feminine attraction.

'I ought to have been an actress,' she said.

Richard told her he found all natural women had a similar wish.

'Yes! Ah! then! if I had been!' sighed Mrs. Mount, gazing on the pattern of the carpet.

He took her hand, and pressed it.

'You are not happy as you are?'

'No.'

'May I speak to you?'

'Yes.'

Her nearest eye, setting a dimple of her cheek in motion, slid to the corner toward her ear, as she sat with her head sideways to him, listening. When he had gone, she said to herself: 'Old hypocrites talk in that way; but I never heard of a young man doing it, and not making love at the same time.'

Their next meeting displayed her quieter: subdued as one who had been set thinking. He lauded her fair looks. 'Don't make me thrice ashamed,' she petitioned.

But it was not only that mood with her. Dauntless defiance, that splendidly befitted her gallant outline and gave a wildness to her bright bold eyes, when she would call out: 'Happy? who dares say I'm not happy? D' you think if the world whips me I'll wince? D' you think I care for what they say or do? Let them kill me! they shall never get one cry out of me!' and flashing on the young man as if he were the congregated enemy, add: 'There! now you know me!'—that was a mood

that well became her, and helped the work. She ought
to have been an actress.

'This must not go on,' said Lady Blandish and Mrs.
Doria in unison. A common object brought them together. They confined their talk to it, and did not disagree. Mrs. Doria engaged to go down to the baronet.
Both ladies knew it was a dangerous, likely to turn out
a disastrous, expedition. They agreed to it because it
was something to do, and doing anything is better than
doing nothing. 'Do it,' said the wise youth, when they
made him a third, 'do it, if you want him to be a hermit
for life. You will bring back nothing but his dead body,
ladies—a Hellenic, rather than a Roman, triumph. He
will listen to you—he will accompany you to the station
—he will hand you into the carriage—and when you point
to his seat he will bow profoundly, and retire into his
congenial mists.'

Adrian spoke their thoughts. They fretted; they relapsed.

'Speak to him, you, Adrian,' said Mrs. Doria. 'Speak
to the boy solemnly. It would be almost better he should
go back to that little thing he has married.'

'Almost?' Lady Blandish opened her eyes. 'I have
been advising it for the last month and more.'

'A choice of evils,' said Mrs. Doria's sour-sweet face
and shake of the head.

Each lady saw a point of dissension, and mutually
agreed, with heroic effort, to avoid it by shutting their
mouths. What was more, they preserved the peace in
spite of Adrian's artifices.

'Well, I'll talk to him again,' he said. 'I'll try to get
the Engine on the conventional line.'

'Command him!' exclaimed Mrs. Doria.

'Gentle means are, I think, the only means with Richard,' said Lady Blandish.

Throwing banter aside, as much as he could, Adrian spoke to Richard. 'You want to reform this woman. Her manner is open—fair and free—the traditional characteristic. We won't stop to canvass how that particular honesty of deportment that wins your approbation has been gained. In her college it is not uncommon. Girls, you know, are not like boys. At a certain age they can't be quite natural. It's a bad sign if they don't blush, and fib, and affect this and that. It wears off when they're women. But a woman who speaks like a man, and has all those excellent virtues you admire—where has she learnt the trick? She tells you. You don't surely approve of the school? Well, what is there in it, then? Reform her, of course. The task is worthy of your energies. But, if you are appointed to do it, don't do it publicly, and don't attempt it just now. May I ask you whether your wife participates in this undertaking.'

Richard walked away from the interrogation. The wise youth, who hated long unrelieved speeches and had healed his conscience, said no more.

Dear tender Lucy! Poor darling! Richard's eyes moistened. Her letters seemed sadder latterly. Yet she never called to him to come, or he would have gone. His heart leapt up to her. He announced to Adrian that he should wait no longer for his father. Adrian placidly nodded.

The enchantress observed that her knight had a clouded brow and an absent voice.

'Richard—I can't call you Dick now, I really don't know why'—she said, 'I want to beg a favour of you.'

'Name it. I can still call you Bella, I suppose?'

'If you care to. What I want to say is this: when you meet me out—to cut it short—please not to recognize me.'

'And why?'

'Do you ask to be told *that*?'

'Certainly I do.'

'Then look: I won't compromise you.'

'I see no harm, Bella.'

'No,' she caressed his hand, 'and there is none. I know that. But,' modest eyelids were drooped, 'other people do,' struggling eyes were raised.

'What do we care for other people?'

'Nothing. I don't. Not that!' snapping her finger. 'I care for you, though.' A prolonged look followed the declaration.

'You 're foolish, Bella.'

'Not quite so giddy—that 's all.'

He did not combat it with his usual impetuosity. Adrian's abrupt inquiry had sunk in his mind, as the wise youth intended it should. He had instinctively refrained from speaking to Lucy of this lady. But what a noble creature the woman was!

So they met in the Park; Mrs. Mount whipped past him; and secresy added a new sense to their intimacy.

Adrian was gratified at the result produced by his eloquence.

Though this lady never expressed an idea, Richard was not mistaken in her cleverness. She could make evenings pass gaily, and one was not the fellow to the other. She could make you forget she was a woman, and then bring the fact startlingly home to you. She could read men with one quiver of her half-closed eye-lashes. She could catch the coming mood in a man, and fit herself to it. What does a woman want with ideas, who can do thus much? Keenness of perception, conformity, delicacy of handling, these be all the qualities necessary to parasites.

Love would have scared the youth: she banished it from her tongue. It may also have been true that it sickened her. She played on his higher nature. She understood

spontaneously what would be most strange and taking
to him in a woman. Various as the Serpent of old Nile,
she acted fallen beauty, humorous indifference, reckless
daring, arrogance in ruin. And acting thus, what think
you?—She did it so well because she was growing half
in earnest.

'Richard! I am not what I was since I knew you.
You will not give me up quite?'

'Never, Bella.'

'I am not so bad as I'm painted!'

'You are only unfortunate.'

'Now that I know you I think so, and yet I am happier.'

She told him her history when this soft horizon of
repentance seemed to throw heaven's twilight across it.
A woman's history, you know: certain chapters ex-
punged. It was dark enough to Richard.

'Did you love the man?' he asked. 'You say you
love no one now.'

'Did I love him? He was a nobleman and I a trades-
man's daughter. No. I did not love him. I have lived
to learn it. And now I should hate him, if I did not despise him.'

'Can you be deceived in love?' said Richard, more to
himself than to her.

'Yes. When we're young we can be very easily deceived. If there is such a thing as love, we discover it
after we have tossed about and roughed it. Then we
find the man, or the woman, that suits us:—and then
it's too late! we can't have him.'

'Singular!' murmured Richard, 'she says just what
my father said.'

He spoke aloud: 'I could forgive you if you had loved
him.'

'Don't be harsh, grave judge! How is a girl to distinguish?'

'You had some affection for him? He was the first?'

She chose to admit that. 'Yes. And the first who talks of love to a girl must be a fool if he doesn't blind her.'

'That makes what is called first love nonsense.'

'Isn't it?'

He repelled the insinuation. 'Because I know it is not, Bella.'

Nevertheless she had opened a wider view of the world to him, and a colder. He thought poorly of girls. A woman—a sensible, brave, beautiful woman seemed, on comparison, infinitely nobler than those weak creatures.

She was best in her character of lovely rebel accusing foul injustice. 'What am I to do? You tell me to be different. How can I? What am I to do? Will virtuous people let me earn my bread? I could not get a housemaid's place! They wouldn't have me—I see their noses smelling! Yes: I can go to the hospital and sing behind a screen! Do you expect me to bury myself alive? Why, man, I have blood: I can't become a stone. You say I am honest, and I will be. Then let me tell you that I have been used to luxuries, and I can't do without them. I might have married men—lots would have had me. But who marries one like me but a fool? and I could not marry a fool. The man I marry I must respect. He could not respect me—I should know him to be a fool, and I should be worse off than I am now. As I am now, they may look as pious as they like—I laugh at them!'

And so forth: direr things. Imputations upon wives: horrible exultation at the universal peccancy of husbands. This lovely outcast almost made him think she had the right on her side, so keenly her Parthian arrows*pierced the holy centres of society, and exposed its rottenness.

Mrs. Mount's house was discreetly conducted: nothing ever occurred to shock him there. The young man would ask himself where the difference was between her and the women of society? How base, too, was the army of banded hypocrites! He was ready to declare war against them on her behalf. His casus belli,* accurately worded, would have read curiously. Because the world refused to lure the lady to virtue with the offer of a housemaid's place, our knight threw down his challenge. But the lady had scornfully rebutted this prospect of a return to chastity. Then the form of the challenge must be: Because the world declined to support the lady in luxury for nothing! But what did that mean? In other words: she was to receive the devil's wages without rendering him her services. Such an arrangement appears hardly fair on the world or on the devil. Heroes will have to conquer both before they will get them to subscribe to it.

Heroes, however, are not in the habit of wording their declarations of war at all. Lance in rest they challenge and they charge. Like women they trust to instinct, and graft on it the muscle of men. Wide fly the liesurely-remonstrating hosts: institutions are scattered, they know not wherefore, heads are broken that have not the balm of a reason why. 'Tis instinct strikes! Surely there is something divine in instinct.

Still, war declared, where were these hosts? The hero could not charge down on the ladies and gentlemen in a ballroom, and spoil the quadrille. He had sufficient reticence to avoid sounding his challenge in the Law Courts; nor could he well go into the Houses of Parliament with a trumpet, though to come to a tussle with the nation's direct representatives did seem the likelier method. It was likewise out of the question that he should enter every house and shop, and battle with its master in the cause of Mrs. Mount. Where, then, was his enemy. Everybody was his enemy, and everybody was nowhere! Shall he convoke multitudes on Wimbledon Common? Blue

Policemen, and a distant dread of ridicule, bar all his projects. Alas for the hero in our day!

Nothing teaches a strong arm its impotence so much as knocking at empty air.

'What can I do for this poor woman?' cried Richard, after fighting his phantom enemy till he was worn out.

'O Rip! old Rip!' he addressed his friend, 'I'm distracted. I wish I was dead! What good am I for? Miserable! selfish! What have I done but \make every soul I know wretched about me? I follow my own inclinations—I make people help me by lying as hard as they can—and I'm a liar. And when I've got it I'm ashamed of myself. And now when I do see something unselfish for me to do, I come upon grins—I don't know where to turn—how to act—and I laugh at myself like a devil!'

It was only friend Ripton's ear that was required, so his words went for little: but Ripton did say he thought there was small matter to be ashamed of in winning and wearing the Beauty of Earth. Richard added his customary comment of 'Poor little thing!'

He fought his duello with empty air till he was exhausted. A last letter written to his father procured him no reply. Then, said he, I have tried my utmost. I have tried to be dutiful—my father won't listen to me. One thing I can do—I can go down to my dear girl, and make her happy, and save her at least from some of the consequences of my rashness.

'There's nothing better for me!' he groaned. His great ambition must be covered by a house-top: he and the cat must warm themselves on the domestic hearth! The hero was not aware that his heart moved him to this. His heart was not now in open communion with his mind.

Mrs. Mount heard that her friend was going—would go. She knew he was going to his wife. Far from discouraging him, she said nobly: 'Go—I believe I have kept you. Let us have an evening together, and then go: for good, if you like. If not, then to meet again another time. Forget me. I sha'n't forget you. You're the best fellow I ever knew, Richard. You are, on my honour! I swear I would not step in between you and your wife to cause either of you a moment's unhappiness. When I can be another woman I will, and I shall think of you then.'

Lady Blandish heard from Adrian that Richard was positively going to his wife. The wise youth modestly veiled his own merit in bringing it about by saying: 'I couldn't see that poor little woman left alone down there any longer.'

'Well! Yes!' said Mrs. Doria, to whom the modest speech was repeated, 'I suppose, poor boy, it's the best he can do now.'

Richard bade them adieu, and went to spend his last evening with Mrs. Mount.

The enchantress received him in state.

'Do you know this dress? No? It's the dress I wore when I first met you—not when I first saw you. I think I remarked you, sir, before you deigned to cast an eye upon humble me. When we first met we drank champagne together, and I intend to celebrate our parting in the same liquor. Will you liquor with me, old boy?'

She was gay. She revived Sir Julius occasionally. He, dispirited, left the talking all to her.

Mrs. Mount kept a footman. At a late hour the man of calves dressed the table for supper. It was a point of honour for Richard to sit down to it and try to eat. Drinking, thanks to the kindly mother nature, who loves to see her children made fools of, is always an easier matter. The footman was diligent: the champagne corks feebly recalled the file-firing at Richmond.

'We'll drink to what we might have been, Dick,' said the enchantress.

Oh, the glorious wreck she looked.

His heart choked as he gulped the buzzing wine.

'What! down, my boy?' she cried. 'They shall never see me hoist signals of distress. We must all die, and the secret of the thing is to die game, by Jove! Did you ever hear of Laura Fenn? a superb girl! handsomer than your humble servant—if you'll believe it—a "Miss" in the bargain, and as a consequence, I suppose, a much greater rake. She was in the hunting-field. Her horse threw her, and she fell plump on a stake. It went into her left breast. All the fellows crowded round her, and one young man, who was in love with her—he sits in the House of Peers now—we used to call him "Duck" because he was such a dear—he dropped from his horse to his knees: "Laura! Laura! my darling! speak a word to me!—the last!" She turned over all white and bloody! "I—I sha'n't be in at the death!" and gave up the ghost! Wasn't that dying game? Here's to the example of Laura Fenn! Why, what's the matter? See! it makes a man turn pale to hear how a woman can die. Fill the glasses, John. Why, you're as bad!'

'It's give me a turn, my lady,' pleaded John, and the man's hand was unsteady as he poured out the wine.

'You ought not to listen. Go, and drink some brandy.' John footman went from the room.

'My brave Dick! Richard! What a face you've got!' He showed a deep frown on a colourless face.

'Can't you bear to hear of blood? You know, it was only one naughty woman out of the world. The clergyman of the parish didn't refuse to give her decent burial. We are Christians! Hurrah!'

She cheered, and laughed. A lurid splendour glanced about her like lights from the pit.

'Pledge me, Dick! Drink, and recover yourself. Who minds? We must all die—the good and the bad. Ashes to ashes—dust to dust—and wine for living lips! That's poetry—almost. Sentiment: "May we never say die till we've drunk our fill!" Not bad—eh? A little vulgar, perhaps, by Jove! Do you think me horrid?'

'Where's the wine?' Richard shouted. He drank a couple of glasses in succession, and stared about. Was he in hell, with a lost soul raving to him?

'Nobly spoken! and nobly acted upon, my brave Dick! Now we'll be companions. "She wished that heaven had made her such a man." Ah, Dick! Dick! too. late! too late!'

Softly fell her voice. Her eyes threw slanting beams.

'Do you see this?'

She pointed to a symbolic golden anchor studded with gems and coiled with a rope of hair in her bosom. It was a gift of his.

'Do you know when I stole the lock? Foolish Dick! you gave me an anchor without a rope. Come and see.'

She rose from the table, and threw herself on the sofa.

'Don't you recognize your own hair! I should know a thread of mine among a million.'

Something of the strength of Samson went out of him as he inspected his hair on the bosom of Delilah.*

'And you knew nothing of it! You hardly know it now you see it! What couldn't a woman steal from you? But you're not vain, and that's a protection. You're a miracle, Dick: a man that's not vain! Sit here.' She curled up her feet to give him place on the sofa. 'Now let us talk like friends that part to meet no more. You found a ship with fever on board, and you weren't afraid to come alongside and keep her company. The fever isn't catching, you see. Let us mingle our tears together. Ha! ha! a man said that once to me. The hypocrite wanted

to catch the fever, but he was too old. How old are you,
Dick?'

Richard pushed a few months forward.

'Twenty-one? You just look it, you blooming boy.
Now tell me my age, Adonis!—Twenty—*what?*'

Richard had given the lady twenty-five years.

She laughed violently. 'You don't pay compliments,
Dick. Best to be honest; guess again. You don't like
to? Not twenty-five, or twenty-four, or twenty-three, or
—see how he begins to stare!—twenty-two. Just twenty-
one, my dear. I think my birthday's somewhere in next
month. Why, look at me, close—closer. Have I a wrinkle?'

'And when, in heaven's name! . . .' he stopped short.

'I understand you. When did I commence for to live?
At the ripe age of sixteen I saw a nobleman in despair
because of my beauty. He vowed he'd die. I didn't
want him to do that. So to save the poor man for his
family, I ran away with him, and I dare say they didn't
appreciate the sacrifice, and he soon forgot to, if he ever
did. It's the way of the world!'

Richard seized some dead champagne, emptied the
bottle into a tumbler, and drank it off.

John footman entered to clear the table, and they were
left without further interruption.

'Bella! Bella!' Richard uttered in a deep sad voice, as
he walked the room.

She leaned on her arm, her hair crushed against a reddened cheek, her eyes half-shut and dreamy.

'Bella!' he dropped beside her. 'You are unhappy.'

She blinked and yawned, as one who is awakened suddenly. 'I think you spoke,' said she.

'You are unhappy, Bella. You can't conceal it. Your
laugh sounds like madness. You must be unhappy. So
young, too! Only twenty-one!'

'What does it matter? Who cares for me?'

The mighty pity falling from his eyes took in her whole shape. She did not mistake it for tenderness, as another would have done.

'Who cares for you, Bella? I do. What makes my misery now, but to see you there, and know of no way of helping you? Father of mercy! it seems too much to have to stand by powerless while such ruin is going on!'

Her hand was shaken in his by the passion of torment with which his frame quaked.

Involuntarily a tear started between her eyelids. She glanced up at him quickly, then looked down, drew her hand from his, and smoothed it, eyeing it.

'Bella! you have a father alive!'

'A linendraper, dear. He wears a white neck-cloth.'

This article of apparel instantaneously changed the tone of the conversation, for he, rising abruptly, nearly squashed the lady's lap-dog, whose squeaks and howls were piteous, and demanded the most fervent caresses of its mistress. It was: 'Oh, my poor pet Mumpsy, and he didn't like a nasty great big ugly heavy foot on his poor soft silky—mum —mum—back, he didn't, and he soodn't that he—mum —mum—soodn't; and he cried out and knew the place to come to, and was oh so sorry for what had happened to him —mum—mum—mum—and now he was going to be made happy, his mistress make him happy—mum—mum— mum—moo-o-o-o.'

'Yes!' said Richard savagely, from the other end of the room, 'you care for the happiness of your dog.'

'A course se does,' Mumpsy was simperingly assured in the thick of his silky flanks.

Richard looked for his hat. Mumpsy was deposited on the sofa in a twinkling.

'Now,' said the lady, 'you must come and beg Mumpsy's pardon, whether you meant to do it or no, because little doggies can't tell that—how should they? And there's

poor Mumpsy thinking you're a great terrible rival that
tries to squash him all flat to nothing, on purpose, pretending you didn't see; and he's trembling, poor dear wee
pet! And I may love my dog, sir, if I like; and I do; and
I won't have him ill-treated, for he's never been jealous
of you, and he is a darling, ten times truer than men,
and I love him fifty times better. So come to him with me.'

First a smile changed Richard's face; then laughing a
melancholy laugh, he surrendered to her humour, and went
through the form of begging Mumpsy's pardon.

'The dear dog! I do believe he saw we were getting
dull,' said she.

'And immolated himself intentionally? Noble animal!'

'Well, we'll act as if we thought so. Let us be gay,
Richard, and not part like ancient fogies. Where's your
fun? You can rattle; why don't you? You haven't seen
me in one of my characters—not Sir Julius: wait a couple
of minutes.' She ran out.

A white visage reappeared behind a spring of flame. Her
black hair was scattered over her shoulders and fell half
across her brows. She moved slowly, and came up to him,
fastening weird eyes on him, pointing a finger at the region
of witches. Sepulchral cadences accompanied the repre-
sentation. He did not listen, for he was thinking what a
deadly charming and exquisitely horrid witch she was.
Something in the way her underlids worked seemed to
remind him of a forgotten picture; but a veil hung on
the picture. There could be no analogy, for this was beautiful and devilish, and that, if he remembered rightly,
had the beauty of seraphs.

His reflections and her performance were stayed by a
shriek. The spirits of wine had run over the plate she
held to the floor. She had the coolness to put the plate
down on the table, while he stamped out the flame on
the carpet. Again she shrieked: she thought she was on

fire. He fell on his knees and clasped her skirts all round, drawing his arms down them several times.

Still kneeling, he looked up, and asked, 'Do you feel safe now?'

She bent her face glaring down till the ends of her hair touched his cheek.

Said she, 'Do you?'

Was she a witch verily? There was sorcery in her breath; sorcery in her hair: the ends of it stung him like little snakes.

'How do I do it, Dick?' she flung back laughing.

'Like you do everything, Bella,' he said, and took a breath.

'There! I won't be a witch; I won't be a witch: they may burn me to a cinder, but I won't be a witch!'

She sang, throwing her hair about, and stamping her feet.

'I suppose I look a figure. I must go and tidy myself.'

'No, don't change. I like to see you so.' He gazed at her with a mixture of wonder and admiration. 'I can't think you the same person—not even when you laugh.'

'Richard,' her tone was serious, 'you were going to speak to me of my parents.'

'How wild and awful you looked, Bella!'

'My father, Richard, was a very respectable man.'

'Bella, you 'll haunt me like a ghost.'

'My mother died in my infancy, Richard.'

'Don't put up your hair, Bella.'

'I was an only child!'

Her head shook sorrowfully at the glistening fire-irons. He followed the abstracted intentness of her look, and came upon her words.

'Ah, yes! speak of your father, Bella. Speak of him.'

'Shall I haunt you, and come to your bedside, and cry, "'Tis time!"?'*

'Dear Bella! if you will tell me where he lives, I will go to him. He shall receive you. He shall not refuse—he shall forgive you.'

'If I haunt you, you can't forget me, Richard.'

'Let me go to your father, Bella—let me go to him to-morrow. I'll give you my time. It's all I can give. O Bella! let me save you.'

'So you like me best dishevelled, do you, you naughty boy! Ha! ha!' and away she burst from him, and up flew her hair, as she danced across the room, and fell at full length on the sofa.

He felt giddy: bewitched.

'We'll talk of everyday things, Dick,' she called to him from the sofa. 'It's our last evening. Our last? Heigho! It makes me sentimental. How's that Mr. Ripson, Pipson, Nipson?—it's not complimentary, but I can't remember names of that sort. Why do you have friends of that sort? He's not a gentleman. Better is he? Well, he's rather *too* insignificant for me. Why do you sit off there? Come to me instantly. There—I'll sit up, and be proper, and you'll have plenty of room. Talk, Dick!'

He was reflecting on the fact that her eyes were brown. They had a haughty sparkle when she pleased, and when she pleased a soft languor circled them. Excitement had dyed her cheeks deep red. He was a youth, and she an enchantress. He a hero; she a female will-o'-the-wisp.

The eyes were languid now, set in rosy colour.

'You will not leave me yet, Richard? not yet?'

He had no thought of departing.

'It's our last night—I suppose it's our last hour together in this world—and I don't want to meet you in the next, for poor Dick will have to come to such a very, very disagreeable place to make the visit.'

He grasped her hand at this.

'Yes, he will! too true! can't be helped: they say I'm handsome.'

'You're lovely, Bella.'

She drank in his homage.

'Well, we'll admit it. His Highness below likes lovely women, I hear say. A gentleman of taste! You don't know all my accomplishments yet, Richard.'

'I sha'n't be astonished at anything new, Bella.'

'Then hear, and wonder.' Her voice trolled out some lively roulades.* 'Don't you think he'll make me his prima donna* below? It's nonsense to tell me there's no singing there. And the atmosphere will be favourable to the voice. No *damp*, you know. You saw the piano— why didn't you ask me to sing before? I can sing Italian. I had a master—who made love to me. I forgave him because of the music-stool—men can't help it on a music-stool, poor dears!'

She went to the piano, struck the notes, and sang—

'"My heart, my heart—I think 'twill break."

'Because I'm such a rake. I don't know any other reason. No; I hate sentimental songs. Won't sing that. Ta-tiddy-tiddy-iddy—a . . . e! How ridiculous those women were, coming home from Richmond!

"Once the sweet romance of story
  Clad thy moving form with grace;
Once the world and all its glory
  Was but framework to thy face.
Ah, too fair!—what I remember,
  Might my soul recall—but no!
To the winds this wretched ember
  Of a fire that falls so low!"

'Hum! don't much like that. Tum-te-tum-tum—accanto al fuoco*—heigho! I don't want to show off, Dick —or to break down—so I won't try that.

"Oh! but for thee, oh! but for thee,
    I might have been a happy wife,
And nursed a baby on my knee,
    And never blushed to give it life."

'I used to sing that when I was a girl, sweet Richard,
and didn't know at all, at all, what it meant. Mustn't
sing that sort of song in company. We 're oh! so proper—
even we!

"If I had a husband, what think you I 'd do?
    I 'd make it my business to keep him a lover;
For when a young gentleman ceases to woo,
    Some other amusement he 'll quickly discover."

'For such are young gentlemen made of—made of: such
are young gentlemen made of!'

After this trifling she sang a Spanish ballad sweetly. He
was in the mood when imagination intensely vivifies everything. Mere suggestions of music sufficed. The lady in
the ballad had been wronged. Lo! it was the lady before
him; and soft horns blew; he smelt the languid night-
flowers; he saw the stars crowd large and close above the
arid plain: this lady leaning at her window desolate,
pouring out her abandoned heart.

Heroes know little what they owe to champagne.

The lady wandered to Venice. Thither he followed her
at a leap. In Venice she was not happy. He was prepared for the misery of any woman anywhere. But, oh!
to be with her! To glide with phantom-motion through
throbbing street; past houses muffled in shadow and gloomy
legends; under storied bridges; past palaces charged with
full life in dead quietness; past grand old towers, colossal
squares, gleaming quays, and out, and on with her, on into
the silver infinity shaking over seas!

Was it the champagne? the music? or the poetry?
Something of the two former, perhaps: but most the en-

chantress playing upon him. How many instruments
cannot clever women play upon at the same moment!
And this enchantress was not too clever, or he might
have felt her touch. She was no longer absolutely bent
on winning him, or he might have seen a manœuvre. She
liked him—liked none better. She wished him well. Her
pique was satisfied. Still he was handsome, and he was
going. What she liked him for, she rather—very slightly
—wished to do away with, or see if it could be done away
with: just as one wishes to catch a pretty butterfly, without hurting its patterned wings. No harm intended to the
innocent insect, only one wants to inspect it thoroughly,
and enjoy the marvel of it, in one's tender possession, and
have the felicity of thinking one could crush it, if one
would.

He knew her what she was, this lady. In Seville, or in
Venice, the spot was on her. Sailing the pathways of the
moon it was not celestial light that illumined her beauty.
Her sin was there: but in dreaming to save, he was soft
to her sin—drowned it in deep mournfulness.

Silence, and the rustle of her dress, awoke him from his
musing. She swam wave-like to the sofa. She was at
his feet.

'I have been light and careless to-night, Richard. Of
course I meant it. I *must* be happy with my best friend
going to leave me.'

Those witch underlids were working brightly.

'You will not forget me? and I shall try . . . try . . .'

Her lips twitched. She thought him such a very handsome fellow.

'If I change—if I can change . . . Oh! if you could
know what a net I'm in, Richard!'

Now at those words, as he looked down on her haggard
loveliness, not divine sorrow but a devouring jealousy
sprang like fire in his breast, and set him rocking with

horrid pain. He bent closer to her pale beseeching face.
Her eyes still drew him down.

'Bella! No! no! promise me! swear it!'

'Lost, Richard! lost for ever! give me up!'

He cried: 'I never will!' and strained her in his arms,
and kissed her passionately on the lips.

She was not acting now as she sidled and slunk her half-
averted head with a kind of maiden shame under his arm,
sighing heavily, weeping, clinging to him. It was wicked
truth.

Not a word of love between them!

Was ever hero in this fashion won?

CHAPTER XXXIX

THE LITTLE BIRD AND THE FALCON: A BERRY TO THE RESCUE!

At a season when the pleasant South-western Island has
few attractions to other than invalids and hermits enamoured of wind and rain, the potent nobleman, Lord Mountfalcon, still lingered there to the disgust of his friends
and special parasite. 'Mount's in for it again,' they said
among themselves. 'Hang the women!' was a natural
sequence. For, don't you see, what a shame it was of
the women to be always kindling such a very inflammable
subject! All understood that Cupid had twanged his
bow, and transfixed a peer of Britain for the fiftieth time:
but none would perceive, though he vouched for it with
his most eloquent oaths, that this was a totally different
case from the antecedent ones. So it had been sworn to
them too frequently before. He was as a man with mighty
tidings, and no language: intensely communicative, but

inarticulate. Good round oaths had formerly compassed
and expounded his noble emotions. They were now quite
beyond the comprehension of blasphemy, even when emphasized, and by this the poor lord divinely felt the case
was different. There is something impressive in a great
human bulk writhing under the unutterable torments
of a mastery he cannot contend with, or account for, or
explain by means of intelligible words. At first he took
refuge in the depths of his contempt for women. Cupid
gave him line. When he had come to vent his worst
of them, the fair face now stamped on his brain beamed
the more triumphantly: so the harpooned whale rose
to the surface, and after a few convulsions, surrendered
his huge length. My lord was in love with Richard's
young wife. He gave proofs of it by burying himself
beside her. To her, could she have seen it, he gave further
proofs of a real devotion, in affecting, and in her presence
feeling, nothing beyond a lively interest in her well-being.
This wonder, that when near her he should be cool and
composed, and when away from her wrapped in a tempest
of desires, was matter for what powers of cogitation the
heavy nobleman possessed.

The Hon. Peter, tired of his journeys to and fro, urged
him to press the business. Lord Mountfalcon was wiser,
or more scrupulous, than his parasite. Almost every evening he saw Lucy. The inexperienced little wife apprehended no harm in his visits. Moreover, Richard had
commended her to the care of Lord Mountfalcon, and
Lady Judith. Lady Judith had left the Island for London:
Lord Mountfalcon remained. There could be no harm.
If she had ever thought so, she no longer did. Secretly,
perhaps, she was flattered. Lord Mountfalcon was as
well educated as it is the fortune of the run of titled elder
sons to be: he could talk and instruct: he was a lord:
and he let her understand that he was wicked, very

wicked, and that she improved him. The heroine, in
common with the hero, has her ambition to be of use in
the world—to do some good: and the task of reclaiming
a bad man is extremely seductive to good women. Dear
to their tender bosoms as old china is a bad man they
are mending! Lord Mountfalcon had none of the arts
of a libertine: his gold, his title, and his person, had hitherto preserved him from having long to sigh in vain, or
sigh at all, possibly: the Hon. Peter did his villanies for
him. No alarm was given to Lucy's pure instinct, as
might have been the case had my lord been over-adept.
It was nice in her martyrdom to have a true friend to
support her, and really to be able to do something for
that friend. Too simple-minded to think much of his
lordship's position, she was yet a woman. 'He, a great
nobleman, does not scorn to acknowledge me, and think
something of me,' may have been one of the half-thoughts
passing through her now and then, as she reflected in self-
defence on the proud family she had married into.

January was watering and freezing old earth by turns,
when the Hon. Peter travelled down to the sun of his
purse with great news. He had no sooner broached his
lordship's immediate weakness, than Mountfalcon began
to plunge like a heavy dragoon in difficulties. He swore
by this and that he had come across an angel for his sins,
and would do her no hurt. The next moment he swore
she must be his, though she cursed like a cat. His lordship's illustrations were not choice. 'I haven't advanced
an inch,' he groaned. 'Brayder! upon my soul, that
little woman could do anything with me. By heaven!
I'd marry her to-morrow. Here I am, seeing her every
day in the week out or in, and what do you think she
gets me to talk about?—history! Isn't it enough to
make a fellow mad? and there am I lecturing like a prig,
and by heaven! while I'm at it I feel a pleasure in it;

and when I leave the house I should feel an immense gratification in shooting somebody. What do they say in town?'

'Not much,' said Brayder significantly.

'When's that fellow—her husband—coming down?'

'I rather hope we've settled him for life, Mount.'

Nobleman and parasite exchanged looks.

'How d' ye mean?'

Brayder hummed an air, and broke it to say, 'He's in for Don Juan at a gallop, that's all.'

'The deuce! Has Bella got him?' Mountfalcon asked with eagerness.

Brayder handed my lord a letter. It was dated from the Sussex coast, signed 'Richard,' and was worded thus:

'My beautiful Devil!—

'Since we're both devils together, and have found each other out, come to me at once, or I shall be going somewhere in a hurry. Come, my bright hell-star! I ran away from you, and now I ask you to come to me! You have taught me how devils love, and I can't do without you. Come an hour after you receive this.'

Mountfalcon turned over the letter to see if there was any more. 'Complimentary love-epistle!' he remarked, and rising from his chair and striding about, muttered, 'The dog! how infamously he treats his wife!'

'Very bad,' said Brayder.

'How did you get hold of this?'

'Strolled into Bella's dressing-room, waiting for her—turned over her pincushion hap-hazard. You know her trick.'

'By Jove! I think that girl does it on purpose. Thank heaven, I haven't written her any letters for an age. Is she going to him?'

'Not she! But it's odd, Mount!—did you ever know her refuse money before? She tore up the cheque in style, and presented me the fragments with two or three of the delicacies of language she learnt at your Academy. I rather like to hear a woman swear. It embellishes her!'

Mountfalcon took counsel of his parasite as to the end the letter could be made to serve. Both conscientiously agreed that Richard's behaviour to his wife was infamous, and that he at least deserved no mercy. 'But,' said his lordship, 'it won't do to show the letter. At first she'll be swearing it's false, and then she'll stick to him closer. I know the sluts.'

'The rule of contrary,' said Brayder carelessly. 'She must see the trahison with her eyes. They believe their eyes. There's your chance, Mount. You step in: you give her revenge and consolation—two birds at one shot. That's what they like.'

'You're an ass, Brayder,' the nobleman exclaimed. 'You're an infernal blackguard. You talk of this little woman as if she and other women were all of a piece. I don't see anything I gain by this confounded letter. Her husband's a brute—that's clear.'

'Will you leave it to me, Mount?'

'Be damned before I do!' muttered my lord.

'Thank you. Now see how this will end. You're too soft, Mount. You'll be made a fool of.'

'I tell you, Brayder, there's nothing to be done. If I carry her off—I've been on the point of doing it every day—what'll come of that? She'll look—I can't stand her eyes—I shall be a fool—worse off with her than I am now.'

Mountfalcon yawned despondently. 'And what do you think?' he pursued. 'Isn't it enough to make a fellow gnash his teeth? She's . . .'*he mentioned something in an underbreath, and turned red as he said it.

'Hm!' Brayder put up his mouth and rapped the handle of his cane on his chin. 'That's disagreeable, Mount.

You don't exactly want to act in that character. You haven't got a diploma. Bother!'

'Do you think I love her a bit less?' broke out my lord in a frenzy. 'By heaven! I'd read to her by her bedside, and talk that infernal history to her, if it pleased her, all day and all night.'

'You're evidently graduating for a midwife, Mount.'

The nobleman appeared silently to accept the imputation.

'What do they say in town?' he asked again.

Brayder said the sole question was, whether it was maid, wife, or widow.

'I'll go to her this evening,' Mountfalcon resumed, after—to judge by the cast of his face—reflecting deeply. 'I'll go to her this evening. She shall know what infernal torment she makes me suffer.'

'Do you mean to say she don't know it?'

'Hasn't an idea—thinks me a friend. And so, by heaven! I'll be to her.'

'A—hm!' went the Honourable Peter. 'This way to the sign of the Green Man, ladies!'

'Do you want to be pitched out of the window, Brayder?'

'Once was enough, Mount. The Salvage Man is strong. I may have forgotten the trick of alighting on my feet. There—there! I'll be sworn she's excessively innocent, and thinks you a disinterested friend.'

'I'll go to her this evening,' Mountfalcon repeated. 'She shall know what damned misery it is to see her in such a position. I can't hold out any longer. Deceit's horrible to such a girl as that. I'd rather have her cursing me than speaking and looking as she does. Dear little girl! —she's only a child. You haven't an idea how sensible that little woman is.'

'Have you?' inquired the cunning one.

'My belief is, Brayder, that there are angels among women,' said Mountfalcon, evading his parasite's eye as he spoke.

To the world, Lord Mountfalcon was the thoroughly wicked man; his parasite simply ingeniously dissipated. Full many a man of God had thought it the easier task to reclaim the Hon. Peter.

Lucy received her noble friend by firelight that evening, and sat much in the shade. She offered to have the candles brought in. He begged her to allow the room to remain as it was. 'I have something to say to you,' he observed with a certain solemnity.

'Yes—to me?' said Lucy quickly.

Lord Mountfalcon knew he had a great deal to say, but how to say it, and what it exactly was, he did not know.

'You conceal it admirably,' he began, 'but you must be very lonely here—I fear, unhappy.'

'I should have been lonely, but for your kindness, my lord,' said Lucy. 'I am not unhappy.' Her face was in shade and could not belie her.

'Is there any help that one who would really be your friend might give you, Mrs. Feverel?'

'None indeed that I know of,' Lucy replied. 'Who can help us to pay for our sins?'

'At least you may permit me to endeavour to pay my debts, since you have helped me to wash out some of *my* sins.'

'Ah, my lord!' said Lucy, not displeased. It is sweet for a woman to believe she has drawn the serpent's teeth.

'I tell you the truth,' Lord Mountfalcon went on. 'What object could I have in deceiving you? I know you quite above flattery—so different from other women!'

'Oh, pray, do not say that,' interposed Lucy.

'According to my experience, then.'

'But you say you have met such — such very bad women.'

'I have. And now that I meet a good one, it is my misfortune.'

'Your misfortune, Lord Mountfalcon?'

'Yes, and I might say more.'

His lordship held impressively mute.

'How strange men are!' thought Lucy. 'He has some unhappy secret.'

Tom Bakewell, who had a habit of coming into the room on various pretences during the nobleman's visits, put a stop to the revelation, if his lordship intended to make any.

When they were alone again, Lucy said, smiling: 'Do you know, I am always ashamed to ask you to begin to read.'

Mountfalcon stared. 'To read?—oh! ha! yes!' he remembered his evening duties. 'Very happy, I'm sure. Let me see. Where were we?'

'The life of the Emperor Julian. But indeed I feel quite ashamed to ask you to read, my lord. It's new to me; like a new world—hearing about Emperors, and armies, and things that really have been on the earth we walk upon. It fills my mind. But it must have ceased to interest you, and I was thinking that I would not tease you any more.'

'Your pleasure is mine, Mrs. Feverel. 'Pon my honour, I'd read till I was hoarse, to hear your remarks.'

'Are you laughing at me?'

'Do I look so?'

Lord Mountfalcon had fine full eyes, and by merely dropping the lids he could appear to endow them with mental expression.

'No, you are not,' said Lucy. 'I must thank you for your forbearance.'

The nobleman went on his honour loudly.

Now it was an object of Lucy's to have him reading; for his sake, for her sake, and for somebody else's sake; which somebody else was probably considered first in the matter. When he was reading to her, he seemed to be legitimizing his presence there; and though she had no doubts or suspicions whatever, she was easier in her heart while she had him employed in that office. So she rose to fetch the book, laid it open on the table at his lordship's elbow, and quietly waited to ring for candles when he should be willing to commence.

That evening Lord Mountfalcon could not get himself up to the farce, and he felt a pity for the strangely innocent unprotected child with anguish hanging over her, that withheld the words he wanted to speak, or insinuate. He sat silent and did nothing.

'What I do not like him for,' said Lucy, meditatively, 'is his changeing his religion. He would have been such a hero, but for that. I could have loved him.'

'Who is it you could have loved, Mrs. Feverel?' Lord Mountfalcon asked.

'The Emperor Julian.'

'Oh! the Emperor Julian! Well, he was an apostate: but then, you know, he meant what he was about. He didn't even do it for a woman.'

'For a woman!' cried Lucy. 'What man would for a woman?'

'I would.'

'You, Lord Mountfalcon?'

'Yes. I'd turn Catholic to-morrow.'

'You make me very unhappy if you say that, my lord.'

'Then I'll unsay it.'

Lucy slightly shuddered. She put her hand upon the bell to ring for lights.

'Do you reject a convert, Mrs. Feverel?' said the nobleman.

'Oh yes! yes! I do. One who does not give his conscience I would not have.'

'If he gives his heart and body, can he give more?'

Lucy's hand pressed the bell. She did not like the doubtful light with one who was so unscrupulous. Lord Mountfalcon had never spoken in this way before. He spoke better, too. She missed the aristocratic twang in his voice, and the hesitation for words, and the fluid lordliness with which he rolled over difficulties in speech.

Simultaneously with the sounding of the bell the door opened, and presented Tom Bakewell. There was a double knock at the same instant at the street door. Lucy delayed to give orders.

'Can it be a letter, Tom?—so late?' she said, changeing colour. 'Pray run and see.'

'That an't a powst,' Tom remarked, as he obeyed his mistress.

'Are you very anxious for a letter, Mrs. Feverel?' Lord Mountfalcon inquired.

'Oh, no!—yes, I am, very!' said Lucy. Her quick ear caught the tones of a voice she remembered. 'That dear old thing has come to see me,' she cried, starting up.

Tom ushered a bunch of black satin into the room.

'Mrs. Berry!' said Lucy, running up to her and kissing her.

'Me, my darlin'!' Mrs. Berry, breathless and rosy with her journey, returned the salute. 'Me truly it is, in fault of a better, for I ain't one to stand by and give the devil his licence—roamin'! and the salt sure enough have spilte my bride-gown at the beginnin', which ain't the best sign. Bless ye!—Oh, here he is.' She beheld a male figure in a chair by the half light, and swung round to address him. 'You bad man!' she held aloft one of her fat fingers, 'I 've come on ye like a bolt, I have, and goin' to make ye do your duty, naughty boy! But you're my darlin' babe,' she melted, as was her custom, 'and I'll never meet you and not give to ye the kiss of a mother.'

Before Lord Mountfalcon could find time to expostulate the soft woman had him by the neck, and was down among his luxurious whiskers.

'Ha!' She gave a smothered shriek, and fell back. 'What hair's that?'

Tom Bakewell just then illumined the transaction.

'Oh, my gracious!' Mrs. Berry breathed with horror, 'I been and kiss a strange man!'

Lucy, half-laughing, but in dreadful concern, begged the noble lord to excuse the woeful mistake.

'Extremely flattered, highly favoured, I'm sure,' said his lordship, re-arranging his disconcerted moustache; 'may I beg the pleasure of an introduction?'

'My husband's dear old nurse—Mrs. Berry,' said Lucy, taking her hand to lend her countenance. 'Lord Mountfalcon, Mrs. Berry.'

Mrs. Berry sought grace while she performed a series of apologetic bobs, and wiped the perspiration from her forehead.

Lucy put her into a chair: Lord Mountfalcon asked for an account of her passage over to the Island; receiving distressingly full particulars, by which it was revealed that the softness of her heart was only equalled by the weakness of her stomach. The recital calmed Mrs. Berry down.

'Well, and where's my—where's Mr. Richard? yer husband, my dear?' Mrs. Berry turned from her tale to question.

'Did you expect to see him here?' said Lucy in a broken voice.

'And where else, my love? since he haven't been seen in London a whole fortnight.'

Lucy did not speak.

'We will dismiss the Emperor Julian till to-morrow, I think,' said Lord Mountfalcon, rising and bowing.

Lucy gave him her hand with mute thanks. He touched it distantly, embraced Mrs. Berry in a farewell bow, and was shown out of the house by Tom Bakewell.

The moment he was gone, Mrs. Berry threw up her arms. 'Did ye ever know sich a horrid thing to go and happen to a virtuous woman!' she exclaimed. 'I could cry at it, I could! To be goin' and kissin' a strange hairy man! Oh, dear me! what's comin' next, I wonder? Whiskers! thinks I—for I know the touch o' whiskers— 't ain't like other hair—what! have he growed a crop that sudden, I says to myself; and it flashed on me I been and made a awful mistake! and the lights come in, and I see that great hairy man—beggin' his pardon—nobleman, and if I could 'a dropped through the floor out o' sight o' men, drat 'em! they're al'ays in the way, that they are!——'

'Mrs. Berry,' Lucy checked her, 'did you expect to find him here?'

'Askin' that solemn?' retorted Berry. 'What him? your husband? O' course I did! and you got him— somewheres hid.'

'I have not heard from my husband for fifteen days,' said Lucy, and her tears rolled heavily off her cheeks.

'Not heer from him!—fifteen days!' Berry echoed.

'O Mrs. Berry! dear kind Mrs. Berry! have you no news? nothing to tell me! I've borne it so long. They're cruel to me, Mrs. Berry. Oh, do you know if I have offended him—my husband? While he wrote I did not complain. I could live on his letters for years. But not to hear from him! To think I have ruined him, and that he repents! Do they want to take him from me? Do they want me dead? O Mrs. Berry! I've had no one to speak out my heart to all this time, and I cannot, cannot help crying, Mrs. Berry!'

Mrs. Berry was inclined to be miserable at what she heard from Lucy's lips, and she was herself full of dire apprehension; but it was never this excellent creature's system to be miserable in company. The sight of a sorrow that was not positive, and could not refer to proof, set her resolutely the other way.

'Fiddle-faddle,' she said. 'I'd like to see him repent! He won't find anywheres a beauty like his own dear little wife, and he know it. Now, look you here, my dear—you blessed weepin' pet—the man that could see ye with that hair of yours there in ruins, and he backed by the law, and not rush into your arms and hold ye squeezed for life, he ain't got much man in him, I say; and no one can say that of my babe! I was sayin', look here, to comfort ye—oh, why, to be sure he 've got some surprise for ye. And so 've I, my lamb! Hark, now! His father 've come to town, like a good reasonable man at last, to u-nite ye both, and bring your bodies together, as your hearts is, for ever-lastin'. Now ain't that news?'

'Oh!' cried Lucy, 'that takes my last hope away. I thought he had gone to his father.' She burst into fresh tears.

Mrs. Berry paused, disturbed.

'Belike he 's travellin' after him,' she suggested.

'Fifteen days, Mrs. Berry!'

'Ah, fifteen weeks, my dear, after sich a man as that. He 's a regular meteor, is Sir Austin Feverel, Raynham Abbey. Well, so hark you here. I says to myself, that knows him—for I did think my babe *was* in his natural nest—I says, the bar'net 'll never write for you both to come up and beg forgiveness, so down I 'll go and fetch you up. For there was your mistake, my dear, ever to leave your husband to go away from ye one hour in a young marriage. It 's dangerous, it 's mad, it 's wrong, and it 's only to be righted by your obeyin' of me, as I commands it: for I has my fits, though I *am* a soft 'un. Obey me, and ye 'll be happy to-morrow—or the next to it.'

Lucy was willing to see comfort. She was weary of her self-inflicted martyrdom, and glad to give herself up to somebody else's guidance utterly.

'But why does he not write to me, Mrs. Berry?'

' 'Cause, 'cause—who can tell the why of men, my dear? But that he love ye faithful, I 'll swear. Haven't he groaned in my arms that he couldn't come to ye?— weak wretch! Hasn't he swore how he loved ye to me, poor young man! But this is your fault, my sweet. Yes, it be. You should 'a followed my 'dvice at the fust—'stead o' going into your 'eroics about this and t'other.' Here Mrs. Berry poured forth fresh sentences on matrimony, pointed especially at young couples. 'I should 'a been a fool if I hadn't suffered myself,' she confessed, 'so I 'll thank my Berry if I makes you wise in season.'

Lucy smoothed her ruddy plump cheeks, and gazed up affectionately into the soft woman's kind brown eyes. Endearing phrases passed from mouth to mouth. And as she gazed Lucy blushed, as one who has something very secret to tell, very sweet, very strange, but cannot quite bring herself to speak it.

'Well! there 's three men in my life I kissed,' said Mrs. Berry, too much absorbed in her extraordinary adventure to notice the young wife's struggling bosom, 'three men, and one a nobleman! He 've got more whisker than my Berry. I wonder what the man thought. Ten to one he 'll think, now, I was glad o' my chance—they 're that vain, whether they 's lords or commons. How was I to know? I nat'ral thinks none but her husband 'd sit in that chair. Ha! and in the dark? and alone with ye?' Mrs. Berry hardened her eyes, 'and your husband away? What do this mean? Tell to me, child, what it mean his bein' here alone without ere a candle?'

'Lord Mountfalcon is the only friend I have here,' said Lucy. 'He is very kind. He comes almost every evening.'

'Lord Muntfalcon—that his name!' Mrs. Berry exclaimed. 'I been that flurried by the man, I didn't mind it at first. He come every evenin', and your husband out o' sight! My goodness me! it 's gettin' worse and worse. And what do he come for, now, ma'am? Now tell me candid what ye do together here in the dark of an evenin'.'

Mrs. Berry glanced severely.

'O Mrs. Berry! please not to speak in that way—I don't like it,' said Lucy, pouting.

'What do he come for, I ask?'

'Because he is kind, Mrs. Berry. He sees me very lonely, and wishes to amuse me. And he tells me of things I know nothing about and——'

'And wants to be a teachin' some of his things, mayhap,' Mrs. Berry interrupted with a ruffled breast.

'You are a very ungenerous, suspicious, naughty old woman,' said Lucy, chiding her.

'And you 're a silly, unsuspectin' little bird,' Mrs. Berry retorted, as she returned her taps on the cheek. 'You haven't told me what ye do together, and what 's his excuse for comin'.'

'Well, then, Mrs. Berry, almost every evening that he comes we read History, and he explains the battles, and talks to me about the great men. And *he* says I 'm not silly, Mrs. Berry.'

'That 's one bit o' lime on your wings, my bird. History, indeed! History to a young married lovely woman alone in the dark! a pretty History! Why, I know that man's name, my dear. He 's a notorious living rake, that Lord Muntfalcon. No woman 's safe with him.'

'Ah, but he hasn't deceived me, Mrs. Berry. He has not pretended he was good.'

'More 's his art,' quoth the experienced dame. 'So you read History together in the dark, my dear!'

'I was unwell to-night, Mrs. Berry. I wanted him not to see my face. Look! there 's the book open ready for him when the candles come in. And now, you dear kind darling old thing, let me kiss you for coming to me. I do love you. Talk of other things.'

'So we will,' said Mrs. Berry, softening to Lucy's caresses. 'So let us. A nobleman, indeed! alone with a young wife in the dark, and she sich a beauty! I say this shall be put a stop to now and henceforth, on the spot it shall! He won't meneuvle Bessy Berry with his arts. There! I drop him. I 'm dyin' for a cup o' tea, my dear.'

Lucy got up to ring the bell, and as Mrs. Berry, incapable of quite dropping him, was continuing to say: 'Let him go and boast I kiss him; he ain't nothin' to be 'shamed of in a chaste woman's kiss—unawares—which men don't get too often in their lives, I can assure 'em';—her eye surveyed Lucy's figure.

Lo, when Lucy returned to her, Mrs. Berry surrounded her with her arms, and drew her into feminine depths. 'Oh, you blessed!' she cried in most meaning tone, 'you good, lovin', proper little wife, you!'

'What is it, Mrs. Berry!' lisps Lucy, opening the most innocent blue eyes.

'As if I couldn't see, you pet! It was my flurry blinded me, or I 'd 'a marked ye the fust shock. Thinkin' to deceive me!'

Mrs. Berry's eyes spoke generations. Lucy's wavered; she coloured all over, and hid her face on the bounteous breast that mounted to her.

'You 're a sweet one,' murmured the soft woman, patting her back, and rocking her. 'You 're a rose, you are! and a bud on your stalk. Haven't told a word to your husband, my dear?' she asked quickly.

Lucy shook her head, looking sly and shy.

'That's right. We'll give him a surprise; let it come all at once on him, and thinks he—losin' breath—"I'm a father!" Nor a hint even you haven't give him?'

Lucy kissed her, to indicate it was quite a secret.

'Oh! you *are* a sweet one,' said Bessy Berry, and rocked her more closely and lovingly.

Then these two had a whispered conversation, from which let all of male persuasion retire a space nothing under one mile.

Returning, after a due interval, we see Mrs. Berry counting on her fingers' ends. Concluding the sum, she cries prophetically: 'Now this right everything—a baby in the balance! Now I say this angel-infant come from on high. It's God's messenger, my love! and it's not wrong to say so. He thinks you worthy, or you wouldn't 'a had one—not for all the tryin' in the world, you wouldn't, and some tries hard enough, poor creatures! Now let us rejice and make merry! I'm for cryin' and laughin', one and the same. This is the blessed seal of matrimony, which Berry never stamp on me. It's be hoped it's a boy. Make that man a grandfather, and his grandchild a son, and you got him safe. Oh! this is what I call happiness, and I'll have my tea a little stronger in consequence. I declare I could get tipsy to know this joyful news.'

So Mrs. Berry carolled. She had her tea a little stronger. She ate and she drank; she rejoiced and made merry. The bliss of the chaste was hers.

Says Lucy demurely: 'Now you know why I read History, and that sort of books.'

'Do I?' replies Berry. 'Belike I do. Since what you done's so good, my darlin', I'm agreeable to anything. A fig for all the lords! They can't come anigh a baby. You may read Voyages and Travels, my dear, and Romances, and Tales of Love and War. You cut the riddle in your own dear way, and that's all I cares for.'

'No, but you don't understand,' persists Lucy. 'I only read sensible books, and talk of serious things, because I'm sure . . . because I have heard say . . . dear Mrs. Berry! don't you understand now?'

Mrs. Berry smacked her knees. 'Only to think of her bein' that thoughtful! and she a Catholic, too! Never tell me that people of one religion ain't as good as another, after that. Why, you want to make him a historian, to be sure! And that rake of a lord who 've been comin' here playin' at wolf, you been and made him—unbeknown to himself—sort o' tutor to the unborn blessed! Ha! ha! say that little women ain't got art ekal to the cunningest of 'em. Oh! I understand. Why, to be sure, didn't I know a lady, a widow of a clergyman: he was a postermost*child, and afore his birth that woman read nothin' but Blair's "Grave"*over and over again, from the end to the beginnin';—that's a serious book!—very hard readin'!—and at four year of age that child that come of it reelly was the piousest infant!—he was like a little curate. His eyes was up; he talked se solemn.' Mrs. Berry imitated the little curate's appearance and manner of speaking. 'So she got her wish, for one!'

But at this lady Lucy laughed.

They chattered on happily till bedtime. Lucy arranged for Mrs. Berry to sleep with her. 'If it's not dreadful to ye, my sweet, sleepin' beside a woman,' said Mrs. Berry. 'I know it were to me shortly after my Berry, and I felt it. It don't somehow seem nat'ral after matrimony—a woman in your bed! I was obliged to have somebody, for the cold sheets do give ye the creeps when you 've been used to that that's different.'

Upstairs they went together, Lucy not sharing these objections. Then Lucy opened certain drawers, and exhibited pretty caps, and laced linen, all adapted for a very small body, all the work of her own hands: and

Mrs. Berry praised them and her. 'You been guessing a boy—woman-like,' she said. Then they cooed, and kissed, and undressed by the fire, and knelt at the bedside, with their arms about each other, praying; both praying for the unborn child; and Mrs. Berry pressed Lucy's waist the moment she was about to breathe the petition to heaven to shield and bless that coming life; and thereat Lucy closed to her, and felt a strong love for her. Then Lucy got into bed first, leaving Berry to put out the light, and before she did so, Berry leaned over her, and eyed her roguishly, saying, 'I never see ye like this, but I'm half in love with ye myself, you blushin' beauty! Sweet's your eyes, and your hair do take one so—lyin' back. I'd never forgive my father if he kep me away from ye four-and-twenty hours just. Husband o' that!' Berry pointed at the young wife's loveliness. 'Ye look so ripe with kisses, and there they are a-languishin'!— . . . You never look so but in your bed, ye beauty!—just as it ought to be.' Lucy had to pretend to rise to put out the light before Berry would give up her amorous chaste soliloquy. Then they lay in bed, and Mrs. Berry fondled her, and arranged for their departure to-morrow, and reviewed Richard's emotions when he came to hear he was going to be made a father by her, and hinted at Lucy's delicious shivers when Richard was again in his rightful place, which she, Bessy Berry, now usurped; and all sorts of amorous sweet things; enough to make one fancy the adage subverted, that stolen fruits are sweetest; she drew such glowing pictures of bliss within the law and the limits of the conscience, till at last, worn out, Lucy murmured, 'Peepy, dear Berry,' and the soft woman gradually ceased her chirp.

Bessy Berry did not sleep. She lay thinking of the sweet brave heart beside her, and listening to Lucy's breath as it came and went; squeezing the fair sleeper's hand now

and then, to ease her love as her reflections warmed. A
storm of wind came howling over the Hampshire hills,
and sprang white foam on the water, and shook the bare
trees. It passed, leaving a thin cloth of snow on the win-
try land. The moon shone brilliantly. Berry heard the
house-dog bark. His bark was savage and persistent.
She was roused by the noise. By and by she fancied
she heard a movement in the house; then it seemed to
her that the house-door opened. She cocked her ears,
and could almost make out voices in the midnight stillness.
She slipped from the bed, locked and bolted the door
of the room, assured herself of Lucy's unconsciousness,
and went on tiptoe to the window. The trees all stood
white to the north; the ground glittered; the cold was
keen. Berry wrapped her fat arms across her bosom,
and peeped as close over into the garden as the situation
of the window permitted. Berry was a soft, not a timid,
woman: and it happened this night that her thoughts
were above the fears of the dark. She was sure of the
voices; curiosity without a shade of alarm held her on the
watch; and gathering bundles of her day-apparel round
her neck and shoulders, she silenced the chattering of
her teeth as well as she could, and remained stationary.
The low hum of the voices came to a break; something
was said in a louder tone; the house-door quietly shut; a
man walked out of the garden into the road. He paused
opposite her window, and Berry let the blind go back to
its place, and peeped from behind an edge of it. He was
in the shadow of the house, so that it was impossible to
discern much of his figure. After some minutes he walked
rapidly away, and Berry returned to the bed an icicle, from
which Lucy's limbs sensitively shrank.

Next morning Mrs. Berry asked Tom Bakewell if he
had been disturbed in the night. Tom, the mysterious, said
he had slept like a top. Mrs. Berry went into the garden.

The snow was partially melted; all save one spot, just under the portal, and there she saw the print of a man's foot. By some strange guidance it occurred to her to go and find one of Richard's boots. She did so, and, unperceived, she measured the sole of the boot in that solitary footmark. There could be no doubt that it fitted. She tried it from heel to toe a dozen times.

CHAPTER XL

CLARE'S DIARY

SIR AUSTIN FEVEREL had come to town with the serenity of a philosopher who says, 'Tis now time; and the satisfaction of a man who has not arrived thereat without a struggle. He had almost forgiven his son. His deep love for him had well-nigh shaken loose from wounded pride and more tenacious vanity. Stirrings of a remote sympathy for the creature who had robbed him of his son and hewed at his System, were in his heart of hearts. This he knew; and in his own mind he took credit for his softness. But the world must not suppose him soft; the world must think he was still acting on his System. Otherwise what would his long absence signify?—Something highly unphilosophical. So, though love was strong, and was moving him to a straightforward course, the last tug of vanity drew him still aslant.

The Aphorist read himself so well, that to juggle with himself was a necessity. As he wished the world to see him, he beheld himself: one who entirely put aside mere personal feelings: one in whom parental duty, based on the science of life, was paramount: a Scientific Humanist, in short.

He was, therefore, rather surprised at a coldness in Lady

Blandish's manner when he did appear. 'At last!' said the lady, in a sad way that sounded reproachfully. Now the Scientific Humanist had, of course, nothing to reproach himself with.

But where was Richard?

Adrian positively averred he was not with his wife.

'If he had gone,' said the baronet, 'he would have anticipated me by a few hours.'

This, when repeated to Lady Blandish, should have propitiated her, and shown his great forgiveness. She, however, sighed, and looked at him wistfully.

Their converse was not happy and deeply intimate. Philosophy did not seem to catch her mind; and fine phrases encountered a rueful assent, more flattering to their grandeur than to their influence.

Days went by. Richard did not present himself. Sir Austin's pitch of self-command was to await the youth without signs of impatience.

Seeing this, the lady told him her fears for Richard, and mentioned the rumour of him that was about.

'If,' said the baronet, 'this person, his wife, is what you paint her, I do not share your fears for him. I think too well of him. If she is one to inspire the sacredness of that union, I think too well of him. It is impossible.'

The lady saw one thing to be done.

'Call her to you,' she said. 'Have her with you at Raynham. Recognize her. It is the disunion and doubt that so confuses him and drives him wild. I confess to you I hoped he had gone to her. It seems not. If she is with you his way will be clear. Will you do that?'

Science is notoriously of slow movement. Lady Blandish's proposition was far too hasty for Sir Austin Women, rapid by nature, have no idea of science.

'We shall see her there in time, Emmeline. At present let it be between me and my son.'

He spoke loftily. In truth it offended him to be asked to do anything, when he had just brought himself to do so much.

A month elapsed, and Richard appeared on the scene.

The meeting between him and his father was not what his father had expected and had crooned over in the Welsh mountains. Richard shook his hand respectfully, and inquired after his health with the common social solicitude. He then said: 'During your absence, sir, I have taken the liberty, without consulting you, to do something in which you are more deeply concerned than myself. I have taken upon myself to find out my mother and place her under my care. I trust you will not think I have done wrong. I acted as I thought best.'

Sir Austin replied: 'You are of an age, Richard, to judge for yourself in such a case. I would have you simply beware of deceiving yourself in imagining that you considered any one but yourself in acting as you did.'

'I have not deceived myself, sir,' said Richard, and the interview was over. Both hated an exposure of the feelings, and in that both were satisfied: but the baronet, as one who loves, hoped and looked for tones indicative of trouble and delight in the deep heart; and Richard gave him none of those. The young man did not even face him as he spoke: if their eyes met by chance, Richard's were defiantly cold. His whole bearing was changed.

'This rash marriage has altered him,' said the very just man of science in life: and that meant: 'it has debased him.'

He pursued his reflections. 'I see in him the desperate maturity of a suddenly-ripened nature: and but for my faith that good work is never lost, what should I think of the toil of my years? Lost, perhaps to me! lost to him! It may show itself in his children.'

The Philosopher, we may conceive, has contentment in benefiting embryos: but it was a somewhat bitter prospect to Sir Austin. Bitterly he felt the injury to himself.

One little incident spoke well of Richard. A poor woman called at the hotel while he was missing. The baronet saw her, and she told him a tale that threw Christian light on one part of Richard's nature. But this might gratify the father in Sir Austin; it did not touch the man of science. A Feverel, his son, would not do less, he thought. He sat down deliberately to study his son.

No definite observations enlightened him. Richard ate and drank; joked and laughed. He was generally before Adrian in calling for a fresh bottle. He talked easily of current topics; his gaiety did not sound forced. In all he did, nevertheless, there was not the air of a youth who sees a future before him. Sir Austin put that down. It might be carelessness, and wanton blood, for no one could say he had much on his mind. The man of science was not reckoning that Richard also might have learned to act and wear a mask. Dead subjects—that is to say, people not on their guard—he could penetrate and dissect. It is by a rare chance, as scientific men well know, that one has an opportunity of examining the structure of the living.

However, that rare chance was granted to Sir Austin. They were engaged to dine with Mrs. Doria at the Foreys, and walked down to her in the afternoon, father and son arm-in-arm, Adrian beside them. Previously the offended father had condescended to inform his son that it would shortly be time for him to return to his wife, indicating that arrangements would ultimately be ordered to receive her at Raynham. Richard had replied nothing; which might mean excess of gratitude, or hypocrisy in concealing his pleasure, or any one of the thousand shifts by which gratified human nature expresses itself when all is made to run smooth with it. Now Mrs. Berry had her surprise ready charged for the young husband. She had Lucy in her own house waiting for him. Every day she expected him to call and be overcome by the rapturous surprise, and every day, knowing his habit of frequenting the park, she marched Lucy thither, under the plea that Master Richard, whom she had already christened, should have an airing.

The round of the red winter sun was behind the bare Kensington chestnuts, when these two parties met. Happily for Lucy and the hope she bore in her bosom, she was perversely admiring a fair horsewoman galloping by at the moment. Mrs. Berry plucked at her gown once or twice, to prepare her eyes for the shock, but Lucy's head was still half averted, and thinks Mrs. Berry, ''Twon't hurt her if she go into his arms head foremost.' They were close; Mrs. Berry performed the bob preliminary. Richard held her silent with a terrible face; he grasped her arm, and put her behind him. Other people intervened. Lucy saw nothing to account for Berry's excessive flutter. Berry threw it on the air and some breakfast bacon, which, she said, she knew in the morning while she ate it, was bad for the bile, and which probably was the cause of her bursting into tears, much to Lucy's astonishment.

'What you ate makes you cry, Mrs. Berry?'

'It's all——' Mrs. Berry pressed at her heart and leaned sideways, 'it's all stomach, my dear. Don't ye mind,' and becoming aware of her unfashionable behaviour, she trailed off to the shelter of the elms.

'You have a singular manner with old ladies,' said Sir Austin to his son, after Berry had been swept aside. 'Scarcely courteous. She behaved like a mad woman, certainly.—Are you ill, my son?'

Richard was death-pale, his strong form smitten through with weakness. The baronet sought Adrian's eye. Adrian

had seen Lucy as they passed, and he had a glimpse of
Richard's countenance while disposing of Berry. Had
Lucy recognized them, he would have gone to her unhesitatingly. As she did not, he thought it well, under
the circumstances, to leave matters as they were. He answered the baronet's look with a shrug.

'Are you ill, Richard?' Sir Austin again asked his son.
'Come on, sir! come on!' cried Richard.

His father's further meditations, as they stepped briskly
to the Foreys, gave poor Berry a character which one who
lectures on matrimony, and has kissed but three men in
her life, shrieks to hear the very title of.

'Richard will go to his wife to-morrow,' Sir Austin said
to Adrian some time before they went in to dinner.

Adrian asked him if he had chanced to see a young fair-
haired lady by the side of the old one Richard had treated
so peculiarly; and to the baronet's acknowledgment that
he remembered to have observed such a person, Adrian
said: 'That was his wife, sir.'

Sir Austin could not dissect the living subject. As if a
bullet had torn open the young man's skull, and some
blast of battle laid his palpitating organization bare, he
watched every motion of his brain and his heart; and
with the grief and terror of one whose mental habit
was ever to pierce to extremes. Not altogether conscious
that he had hitherto played with life, he felt that he
was suddenly plunged into the stormful reality of it.
He projected to speak plainly to his son on all points
that night.

'Richard is very gay,' Mrs. Doria whispered her brother.

'All will be right with him to-morrow,' he replied;
for the game had been in his hands so long, so long had
he been the God of the machine, that having once resolved
to speak plainly and to act, he was to a certain extent secure, bad as the thing to mend might be.

'I notice he has a rather wild laugh—I don't exactly like his eyes,' said Mrs. Doria.

'You will see a change in him to-morrow,' the man of science remarked.

It was reserved for Mrs. Doria herself to experience that change. In the middle of the dinner a telegraphic message from her son-in-law, worthy John Todhunter, reached the house, stating that Clare was alarmingly ill, bidding her come instantly. She cast about for some one to accompany her, and fixed on Richard. Before he would give his consent for Richard to go, Sir Austin desired to speak with him apart, and in that interview he said to his son: 'My dear Richard! it was my intention that we should come to an understanding together this night. But the time is short—poor Helen cannot spare many minutes. Let me then say that you deceived me, and that I forgive you. We fix our seal on the past. You will bring your wife to me when you return.' And very cheerfully the baronet looked down on the generous future he thus founded.

'Will you have her at Raynham at once, sir?' said Richard.

'Yes, my son, when you bring her.'

'Are you mocking me, sir?'

'Pray, what do you mean?'

'I ask you to receive her at once.'

'Well! the delay cannot be long. I do not apprehend that you will be kept from your happiness many days.'

'I think it will be some time, sir!' said Richard, sighing deeply.

'And what mental freak is this that can induce you to postpone it and play with your first duty?'

'What is my first duty, sir?'

'Since you are married, to be with your wife.'

'I have heard that from an old woman called Berry!' said Richard to himself, not intending irony.

'Will you receive her at once?' he asked resolutely.

The baronet was clouded by his son's reception of his graciousness. His grateful prospect had formerly been Richard's marriage — the culmination of his System. Richard had destroyed his participation in that. He now looked for a pretty scene in recompense:—Richard leading up his wife to him, and both being welcomed by him paternally, and so held one ostentatious minute in his embrace.

He said: 'Before you return, I demur to receiving her.'

'Very well, sir,' replied his son, and stood as if he had spoken all.

'Really you tempt me to fancy you already regret your rash proceeding!' the baronet exclaimed; and the next moment it pained him he had uttered the words, Richard's eyes were so sorrowfully fierce. It pained him, but he divined in that look a history, and he could not refrain from glancing acutely and asking: 'Do you?'

'Regret it, sir?' The question aroused one of those struggles in the young man's breast which a passionate storm of tears may still, and which sink like leaden death into the soul when tears come not. Richard's eyes had the light of the desert.

'Do you?' his father repeated. 'You tempt me—I almost fear you do.' At the thought—for he expressed his mind—the pity that he had for Richard was not pure gold.

'Ask me what I think of her, sir! Ask me what she is! Ask me what it is to have taken one of God's precious angels and chained her to misery! Ask me what it is to have plunged a sword into her heart, and to stand over her and see such a creature bleeding! Do I regret that? Why, yes, I do! Would you?'

His eyes flew hard at his father under the ridge of his eyebrows.

Sir Austin winced and reddened. Did he understand? There is ever in the mind's eye a certain wilfulness. We see and understand; we see and won't understand.

'Tell me why you passed by her as you did this afternoon,' he said gravely: and in the same voice Richard answered: 'I passed her because I could not do otherwise.'

'Your wife, Richard?'

'Yes! my wife!'

'If she had seen you, Richard?'

'God spared her that!'

Mrs. Doria, bustling in practical haste, and bearing Richard's hat and greatcoat in her energetic hands, came between them at this juncture. Dimples of commiseration were in her cheeks while she kissed her brother's perplexed forehead. She forgot her trouble about Clare, deploring his fatuity.

Sir Austin was forced to let his son depart. As of old, he took counsel with Adrian, and the wise youth was soothing. 'Somebody has kissed him, sir, and the chaste boy can't get over it.' This absurd suggestion did more to appease the baronet than if Adrian had given a veritable reasonable key to Richard's conduct. It set him thinking that it might be a prudish strain in the young man's mind, due to the System in difficulties.

'I may have been wrong in one thing,' he said, with an air of the utmost doubt of it. 'I, perhaps, was wrong in allowing him so much liberty during his probation.'

Adrian pointed out to him that he had distinctly commanded it.

'Yes, yes; that is on me.'

His was an order of mind that would accept the most burdensome charges, and by some species of moral usury make a profit out of them.

Clare was little talked of. Adrian attributed the employment of the telegraph to John Todhunter's uxorious distress at a toothache, or possibly the first symptoms of an heir to his house.

'That child's mind has disease in it. She is not sound,' said the baronet.

On the door-step of the hotel, when they returned, stood Mrs. Berry. Her wish to speak a few words with the baronet reverentially communicated, she was ushered upstairs into his room.

Mrs. Berry compressed her person in the chair she was beckoned to occupy.

'Well, ma'am, you have something to say,' observed the baronet, for she seemed loth to commence.

'Wishin' I hadn't': Mrs. Berry took him up, and mindful of the good rule to begin at the beginning, pursued: 'I dare say, Sir Austin, you don't remember me, and I little thought when last we parted our meeting'd be like this. Twenty year don't go over one without showin' it, no more than twenty ox. It's a might o' time,—twenty year! Leastways not quite twenty, it ain't.'

'Round figures are best,' Adrian remarked.

'In them round figures a be-loved son have growed up, and got himself married!' said Mrs. Berry, diving straight into the case.

Sir Austin then learnt that he had before him the culprit who had assisted his son in that venture. It was a stretch of his patience to hear himself addressed on a family matter, but he was naturally courteous.

'He came to my house, Sir Austin, a stranger! If twenty year alters us as have knowed each other on the earth, how must they alter they that we parted with just come from heaven! And a heavenly babe he were! se sweet! se strong! so fat!'

Adrian laughed aloud.

Mrs. Berry bumped a curtsey to him in her chair, continuing: 'I wished afore I spoke to say how thankful am I bound to be for my pension not cut short, as have offended so, but that I know Sir Austin Feverel, Raynham Abbey, ain't one o' them that likes to hear their good deeds pumlished. And a pension to me now, it's something more than it were. For a pension and pretty rosy cheeks in a maid, which I was—that's a bait many a man'll bite, that won't so a forsaken wife!'

'If you will speak to the point, ma'am, I will listen to you,' the baronet interrupted her.

'It's the beginnin' that's the worst, and that's over, thank the Lord! So I'll speak, Sir Austin, and say my say:—Lord speed me! Believin' our idees o' matrimony to be sim'lar, then, I'll say, once married—married for life! Yes! I don't even like widows. For I can't stop at the grave. Not at the tomb I can't stop. My husband's my husband, and if I'm a body at the Resurrection, I say, speaking humbly, my Berry is the husband o' my body; and to think of two claimin' of me then—it makes me hot all over. Such is my notion of that state 'tween man and woman. No givin' in marriage, o' course I know, and if so I'm single.'

The baronet suppressed a smile. 'Really, my good woman, you wander very much.'

'Beggin' pardon, Sir Austin; but I has my point before me all the same, and I'm comin' to it. Ac-knowledgin' our error, it's done, and bein' done, it's writ aloft. Oh! if you ony knew what a sweet young creature she be! Indeed 'taint all of humble birth that's unworthy, Sir Austin. And she got her idees, too. She reads History! She talk that sensible as would surprise ye. But for all that she's a prey to the artful o' men—unpertected. And it's a young marriage—but there's no fear for her, as far as she go. The fear's t'other way. There's that

in a man—at the commencement—which makes him of
Lord knows what! if you any way interferes: whereas
a woman bides quiet! It 's consolation catch her, which
is what we mean by seducin'. Whereas a man—he 's
a savage!'

Sir Austin turned his face to Adrian, who was listening
with huge delight.

'Well, ma'am, I see you have something in your mind,
if you would only come to it quickly.'

'Then here 's my point, Sir Austin. I say you bred
him so as there ain't another young gentleman like him in
England, and proud he make me. And as for her, I 'll
risk sayin'—it 's done, and no harm—you might search
England through, and nowhere will ye find a maid that 's
his match like his own wife. Then there they be. Are
they together as should be? O Lord no! Months they
been divided. Then she all lonely and exposed, I went,
and fetched her out of seducers' ways—which they may
say what they like, but the inn'cent is most open to when
they 're healthy and confidin'—I fetch her, and—the
liberty—boxed her safe in my own house. So much for
that sweet! That you may do with women. But it 's
him—Mr. Richard—I *am* bold, I know, but there—I 'm
in for it, and the Lord 'll help me! It 's him, Sir Austin,
in this great metropolis, warm from a young marriage.
It 's him, and—I say nothin' of her, and how sweet she
bears it, and it 's eating her at a time when Natur' should
have no other trouble but the one that 's goin' on—it 's
him, and I ask—so bold—shall there—and a Christian
gentleman his father—shall there be a tug 'tween him
as a son and him as a husband—soon to be somethin'
else? I speak bold out—I 'd have sons obey their fathers,
but the priest's words spoke over him, which they 're now
in my ears, I say I ain't a doubt on earth—I 'm sure there
ain't one in heaven—which dooty 's the holier of the two.'

Sir Austin heard her to an end. Their views on the junction of the sexes were undoubtedly akin. To be lectured on his prime subject, however, was slightly disagreeable, and to be obliged mentally to assent to this old lady's doctrine was rather humiliating, when it could not be averred that he had latterly followed it out. He sat cross-legged and silent, a finger to his temple.

'One gets so addle-pated thinkin' many things,' said Mrs. Berry, simply. 'That's why we see wonder clever people goin' wrong—to my mind. I think it's al'ays the plan in a dielemmer to pray God and walk forward.'

The keen-witted soft woman was tracking the baronet's thoughts, and she had absolutely run him down and taken an explanation out of his mouth, by which Mrs. Berry was to have been informed that he had acted from a principle of his own, and devolved a wisdom she could not be expected to comprehend.

Of course he became advised immediately that it would be waste of time to direct such an explanation to her inferior capacity.

He gave her his hand, saying, 'My son has gone out of town to see his cousin, who is ill. He will return in two or three days, and then they will both come to me at Raynham.'

Mrs. Berry took the tips of his fingers, and went halfway to the floor perpendicularly. 'He pass her like a stranger in the park this evenin',' she faltered.

'Ah?' said the baronet. 'Yes, well! they will be at Raynham before the week is over.'

Mrs. Berry was not quite satisfied. 'Not of his own accord he pass that sweet young wife of his like a stranger this day, Sir Austin!'

'I must beg you not to intrude further, ma'am.'

Mrs. Berry bobbed her bunch of a body out of the room. 'All's well as ends well,' she said to herself. 'It's bad

inquirin' too close among men. We must take 'em somethin' like Providence—*as* they come. Thank heaven! I
kep' back the baby.'

In Mrs. Berry's eyes the baby was the victorious reserve.

Adrian asked his chief what he thought of that specimen
of woman.

'I think I have not met a better in my life,' said the
baronet, mingling praise and sarcasm.

Clare lies in her bed as placid as in the days when she
breathed; her white hands stretched their length along
the sheets, at peace from head to feet. She needs iron no
more. Richard is face to face with death for the first
time. He sees the sculpture of clay—the spark gone.

Clare gave her mother the welcome of the dead. This
child would have spoken nothing but kind commonplaces
had she been alive. She was dead, and none knew her
malady. On her fourth finger were two wedding-rings.

When hours of weeping had silenced the mother's
anguish, she, for some comfort she saw in it, pointed out
that strange thing to Richard, speaking low in the chamber
of the dead; and then he learnt that it was his own lost
ring Clare wore in the two worlds. He learnt from her
husband that Clare's last request had been that neither
of the rings should be removed. She had written it; she
would not speak it.

'I beg of my husband, and all kind people who may
have the care of me between this and the grave, to bury
me with my hands untouched.'

The tracing of the words showed the bodily torment
she was suffering, as she wrote them on a scrap of paper
found beside her pillow.

In wonder, as the dim idea grew from the waving of
Clare's dead hand, Richard paced the house, and hung
about the awful room; dreading to enter it, reluctant to

quit it. The secret Clare had buried while she lived, arose with her death. He saw it play like flame across her marble features. The memory of her voice was like a knife at his nerves. His coldness to her started up accusingly: her meekness was bitter blame.

On the evening of the fourth day, her mother came to him in his bedroom, with a face so white that he asked himself if aught worse could happen to a mother than the loss of her child. Choking she said to him, 'Read this,' and thrust a leather-bound pocket-book trembling in his hand. She would not breathe to him what it was. She entreated him not to open it before her.

'Tell me,' she said, 'tell me what you think. John must not hear of it. I have nobody to consult but you—O Richard!'

'MY DIARY' was written in the round hand of Clare's childhood on the first page. The first name his eye encountered was his own.

'Richard's fourteenth birthday. I have worked him a purse and put it under his pillow, because he is going to have plenty of money. He does not notice me now because he has a friend now, and he is ugly, but Richard is not, and never will be.'

The occurrences of that day were subsequently recorded, and a childish prayer to God for him set down. Step by step he saw her growing mind in his history. As she advanced in years she began to look back, and made much of little trivial remembrances, all bearing upon him.

'We went into the fields and gathered cowslips together, and pelted each other, and I told him he used to call them "coals-sleeps" when he was a baby, and he was angry at my telling him, for he does not like to be told he was ever a baby.'

He remembered the incident, and remembered his stupid scorn of her meek affection. Little Clare! how she lived before him in her white dress and pink ribbons, and soft dark eyes! Upstairs she was lying dead. He read on:

'Mama says there is no one in the world like Richard, and I am sure there is not, not in the whole world. He says he is going to be a great General and going to the wars. If he does I shall dress myself as a boy and go after him, and he will not know me till I am wounded. Oh I pray he will never, never be wounded. I wonder what I should feel if Richard was ever to die.'

Upstairs Clare was lying dead.

'Lady Blandish said there was a likeness between Richard and me. Richard said I hope I do not hang down my head as she does. He is angry with me because I do not look people in the face and speak out, but I know I am not looking after earthworms.'

Yes. He had told her that. A shiver seized him at the recollection.

Then it came to a period when the words: 'Richard kissed me,' stood by themselves, and marked a day in her life.

Afterwards it was solemnly discovered that Richard wrote poetry. He read one of his old forgotten compositions penned when he had that ambition.

> 'Thy truth to me is truer
> Than horse, or dog, or blade;
> Thy vows to me are fewer
> Than ever maiden made.
>
> Thou steppest from thy splendour
> To make my life a song:
> My bosom shall be tender
> As thine has risen strong.'

All the verses were transcribed. 'It is he who is the humble knight,' Clare explained at the close, 'and his lady is a Queen. Any Queen would throw her crown away for him.'

It came to that period when Clare left Raynham with her mother.

'Richard was not sorry to lose me. He only loves boys and men. Something tells me I shall never see Raynham again. He was dressed in blue. He said Good bye, Clare, and kissed me on the cheek. Richard never kisses me on the mouth. He did not know I went to his bed and kissed him while he was asleep. He sleeps with one arm under his head, and the other out on the bed. I moved away a bit of his hair that was over his eyes. I wanted to cut it. I have one piece. I do not let anybody see I am unhappy, not even mama. She says I want iron. I am sure I do not. I like to write my name. Clare Doria Forey. Richard's is Richard Doria Feverel.'

His breast rose convulsively. Clare Doria Forey! He knew the music of that name. He had heard it somewhere. It sounded faint and mellow now behind the hills of death.

He could not read for tears. It was midnight. The hour seemed to belong to her. The awful stillness and the darkness were Clare's. Clare's voice clear and cold from the grave possessed it.

Painfully, with blinded eyes, he looked over the breathless pages. She spoke of his marriage, and her finding the ring.

'I knew it was his. I knew he was going to be married that morning. I saw him stand by the altar when they laughed at breakfast. His wife must be so beautiful! Richard's wife! Perhaps he will love me better now he is married. Mama says they must be separated. That is shameful. If I can help him I will. I pray so that he may be happy. I hope God hears poor sinners' prayers. I am very sinful. Nobody knows it as I do. They say I am good, but I know. When I look on the ground I am not looking after earthworms, as he said. Oh, do forgive me, God!'

Then she spoke of her own marriage, and that it was her duty to obey her mother. A blank in the Diary ensued.

'I have seen Richard. Richard despises me,' was the next entry.

But now as he read his eyes were fixed, and the delicate feminine handwriting like a black thread drew on his soul to one terrible conclusion.

'I cannot live. Richard despises me. I cannot bear the touch of my fingers or the sight of my face. Oh! I understand him now. He should not have kissed me so that last time. I wished to die while his mouth was on mine.'

Further: 'I have no escape. Richard said he would die rather than endure it. I know he would. Why should I be afraid to do what he would do? I think if my husband whipped me I could bear it better. He is so kind, and tries to make me cheerful. He will soon be very unhappy. I pray to God half the night. I seem to be losing sight of my God the more I pray.'

Richard laid the book open on the table. Phantom surges seemed to be mounting and travelling for his brain. Had Clare taken his wild words in earnest? Did she lie there dead—he shrouded the thought.

He wrapped the thoughts in shrouds, but he was again reading.

'A quarter to one o'clock. I shall not be alive this time to-morrow. I shall never see Richard now. I dreamed last night we were in the fields together, and he walked with his arm round my waist. We were children, but I thought we were married, and I showed him I wore his ring, and he said—if you always wear it, Clare, you are as good as my wife. Then I made a vow to wear it for ever and ever. . . . It is not mama's fault. She does not think as Richard and I do of these things. He is not a coward, nor am I. He hates cowards.

'I have written to his father to make him happy. Perhaps when I am dead he will hear what I say.

'I heard just now Richard call distinctly—Clari, come out to me. Surely he has not gone. I am going I know not where. I cannot think. I am very cold.'

The words were written larger, and staggered towards the close, as if her hand had lost mastery over the pen.

'I can only remember Richard now a boy. A little boy and a big boy. I am not sure now of his voice. I can only remember certain words. "Clari," and "Don Ricardo," and his laugh. He used to be full of fun. Once we laughed all day together tumbling in the hay. Then he had a friend, and began to write poetry, and be proud. If I had married a young man he would have forgiven me, but I should not have been happier. I must have died. God never looks on me.

'It is past two o'clock. The sheep are bleating outside. It must be very cold in the ground. Good-bye, Richard.'

With his name it began and ended. Even to herself Clare was not over-communicative. The book was slender, yet her nineteen years of existence left half the number of pages white.

Those last words drew him irresistibly to gaze on her. There she lay, the same impassive Clare. For a moment he wondered she had not moved—to him she had become so different. She who had just filled his ears with strange tidings—it was not possible to think her dead. She seemed to have been speaking to him all through his life. His image was on that still heart.

He dismissed the night-watchers from the room, and remained with her alone, till the sense of death oppressed him, and then the shock sent him to the window to look for sky and stars. Behind a low broad pine, hung with frosty mist, he heard a bell-wether of the flock in the silent fold. Death in life it sounded.

The mother found him praying at the foot of Clare's bed. She knelt by his side, and they prayed, and their joint sobs shook their bodies, but neither of them shed many tears. They held a dark unspoken secret in common. They prayed God to forgive her.

Clare was buried in the family vault of the Todhunters. Her mother breathed no wish to have her lying at Lobourne.

After the funeral, what they alone upon earth knew brought them together.

'Richard,' she said, 'the worst is over for me. I have no one to love but you, dear. We have all been fighting against God, and this . . . Richard! you will come with me, and be united to your wife, and spare my brother what I suffer.'

He answered the broken spirit: 'I have killed one. She sees me as I am. I cannot go with you to my wife, because I am not worthy to touch her hand, and were I to go, I should do *this* to silence my self-contempt. Go you to her, and when she asks of me, say I have a death upon my head that—— No! say that I am abroad, seeking for that which shall cleanse me. If I find it I shall come to claim her. If not, God help us all!'

She had no strength to contest his solemn words, or stay him, and he went forth.

CHAPTER XLI

AUSTIN RETURNS

A MAN with a beard saluted the wise youth Adrian in the full blaze of Piccadilly with a clap on the shoulder. Adrian glanced leisurely behind.

'Do you want to try my nerves, my dear fellow? I'm not a man of fashion, happily, or you would have struck the seat of them. How are you?'

That was his welcome to Austin Wentworth after his long absence.

Austin took his arm, and asked for news, with the hunger of one who had been in the wilderness five years.

'The Whigs have given up the ghost, my dear Austin. The free Briton is to receive Liberty's pearl, the Ballot. The Aristocracy has had a cycle's notice to quit. The Monarchy and old Madeira are going out; Demos and Cape wines are coming in. They call it Reform. So, you see, your absence has worked wonders. Depart for another five years, and you will return to ruined stomachs, cracked sconces, general upset, an equality made perfect by universal prostration.'

Austin indulged him in a laugh. 'I want to hear about ourselves. How is old Ricky?'

'You know of his—what do they call it when greenhorns are licensed to jump into the milkpails of dairymaids?—a very charming little woman she makes, by the way—presentable! quite old Anacreon's*rose in milk. Well! everybody thought the System must die of it. Not a bit. It continued to flourish in spite. It's in a consumption now, though—emaciated, lean, raw, spectral! I've this morning escaped from Raynham to avoid the sight of it. I have brought our genial uncle Hippias to town—a delightful companion! I said to him: "We've had a fine Spring." "Ugh!" he answers, "there's a time when you come to think the Spring old." You should have heard how he trained out the "old." I felt something like decay in my sap just to hear him. In the prize-fight of life, my dear Austin, our uncle Hippias has been unfairly hit below the belt. Let's guard ourselves there, and go and order dinner.'

'But where's Ricky, now, and what is he doing?' said Austin.

'Ask what he has done. The miraculous boy has gone and got a baby!'

'A child? Richard has one?' Austin's clear eyes shone with pleasure.

'I suppose it's not common among your tropical savages. He has one: one as big as two. That has been the death-blow to the System. It bore the marriage—the baby was too much for it. Could it swallow the baby, 'twould live. She, the wonderful woman, has produced a large boy. I assure you it's quite amusing to see the System opening its mouth every hour of the day, trying to gulp him down, aware that it would be a consummate cure, or a happy release.'

By degrees Austin learnt the baronet's proceedings, and smiled sadly.

'How has Ricky turned out?' he asked. 'What sort of a character has he?'

'The poor boy is ruined by his excessive anxiety about it. Character? he has the character of a bullet with a treble charge of powder behind it. Enthusiasm is the powder. That boy could get up an enthusiasm for the maiden days of Ops!* He was going to reform the world, after your fashion, Austin,—you have something to answer for. Unfortunately he began with the feminine side of it. Cupid proud of Phœbus*newly slain, or Pluto wishing to people his kingdom, if you like, put it into the soft head of one of the guileless grateful creatures to kiss him for his good work. Oh, horror! he never expected that. Conceive the System in the flesh, and you have our Richard. The consequence is, that this male Peri*refuses to enter his Paradise, though the gates are open for him, the trumpets blow, and the fair unspotted one awaits him fruitful within. We heard of him last that he was trying

the German waters—preparatory to his undertaking the
release of Italy from the subjugation of the Teuton. Let's
hope they'll wash him. He is in the company of Lady
Judith Felle—your old friend, the ardent female Radical
who married the decrepit lord to carry out her principles.
They always marry English lords, or foreign princes.
I admire their tactics.'

'Judith is bad for him in such a state. I like her, but
she was always too sentimental,' said Austin.

'Sentiment made her marry the old lord, I suppose?
I like her *for* her sentiment, Austin. Sentimental people
are sure to live long and die fat. Feeling, that's the
slayer, coz. Sentiment! 'tis the cajolery of existence: the
soft bloom which whoso weareth, he or she is enviable.
Would that I had more!'

'You're not much changed, Adrian.'

'I'm not a Radical, Austin.'

Further inquiries, responded to in Adrian's figurative
speech, instructed Austin that the baronet was waiting
for his son, in a posture of statuesque offended paternity,
before he would receive his daughter-in-law and grandson.
That was what Adrian meant by the efforts of the System
to swallow the baby.

'We're in a tangle,' said the wise youth. 'Time will
extricate us, I presume, or what is the venerable signor
good for?'

Austin mused some minutes, and asked for Lucy's place
of residence.

'We'll go to her by and by,' said Adrian.

'I shall go and see her now,' said Austin.

'Well, we'll go and order the dinner first, coz.'

'Give me her address.'

'Really, Austin, you carry matters with too long a
beard,' Adrian objected. 'Don't you care what you eat?'
he roared hoarsely, looking humorously hurt. 'I dare say

not. A slice out of him that 's handy—sauce du ciel!* Go,
batten on the baby, cannibal. Dinner at seven.'

Adrian gave him his own address, and Lucy's, and
strolled off to do the better thing.

Overnight Mrs. Berry had observed a long stranger in
her tea-cup. Posting him on her fingers and starting him
with a smack, he had vaulted lightly and thereby indicated
that he was positively coming the next day. She forgot
him in the bustle of her duties and the absorption of her
faculties in thoughts of the incomparable stranger Lucy
had presented to the world, till a knock at the street-door
reminded her. 'There he is!' she cried, as she ran to
open to him. 'There 's my stranger come!' Never was a
woman's faith in omens so justified. The stranger desired
to see Mrs. Richard Feverel. He said his name was Mr.
Austin Wentworth. Mrs. Berry clasped her hands, exclaiming, 'Come at last!' and ran bolt out of the house to
look up and down the street. Presently she returned with
many excuses for her rudeness, saying: 'I expected to see
her comin' home, Mr. Wentworth. Every day twice a
day she go out to give her blessed angel an airing. No
leavin' the child with nursemaids for her! She *is* a mother!
and good milk, too, thank the Lord! though her heart 's
se low.'

Indoors Mrs. Berry stated who she was, related the history of the young couple, and her participation in it, and
admired the beard. 'Though I 'd swear you don't wear
it for ornament, now!' she said, having in the first impulse designed a stroke at man's vanity.

Ultimately Mrs. Berry spoke of the family complication,
and with dejected head and joined hands threw out dark
hints about Richard.

While Austin was giving his cheerfuller views of the
case, Lucy came in, preceding the baby.

'I am Austin Wentworth,' he said, taking her hand.

They read each other's faces, these two, and smiled kinship.

'Your name is Lucy?'

She affirmed it softly.

'And mine is Austin, as you know.'

Mrs. Berry allowed time for Lucy's charms to subdue him, and presented Richard's representative, who, seeing a new face, suffered himself to be contemplated before he commenced crying aloud and knocking at the doors of Nature for something that was due to him.

'Ain't he a lusty darlin'?' says Mrs. Berry. 'Ain't he like his own father? There can't be no doubt about zoo, zoo pitty pet. Look at his fists. Ain't he got passion? Ain't he a splendid roarer? Oh!' and she went off rapturously into baby-language.

A fine boy, certainly. Mrs. Berry exhibited his legs for further proof, desiring Austin's confirmation as to their being dumplings.

Lucy murmured a word of excuse, and bore the splendid roarer out of the room.

'She might 'a done it here,' said Mrs. Berry. 'There's no prettier sight, I say. If her dear husband could but see that! He's off in his heroics—he want to be doin' all sorts o' things: I say he'll never do anything grander than that baby. You should 'a seen her uncle over that baby—he came here, for I said, you *shall* see your own fam'ly, my dear, and so she thinks. He come, and he laughed over that baby in the joy of his heart, poor man! he cried, he did. You should see that Mr. Thompson, Mr. Wentworth—a friend o' Mr. Richard's, and a very modest-minded young gentleman—he worships her in his innocence. It's a sight to see him with that baby. My belief is he's unhappy 'cause he can't anyways be nursemaid to him. O Mr. Wentworth! what *do* you think of her, sir?'

Austin's reply was as satisfactory as a man's poor speech could make it. He heard that Lady Feverel was in the house, and Mrs. Berry prepared the way for him to pay his respects to her. Then Mrs. Berry ran to Lucy, and the house buzzed with new life. The simple creatures felt in Austin's presence something good among them. 'He don't speak much,' said Mrs. Berry, 'but I see by his eye he mean a deal. He ain't one o' yer long-word gentry, who's all gay deceivers, every one of 'em.'

Lucy pressed the hearty suckling into her breast. 'I wonder what he thinks of me, Mrs. Berry? I could not speak to him. I loved him before I saw him. I knew what his face was like.'

'He looks proper even with a beard, and that's a trial for a virtuous man,' said Mrs. Berry. 'One sees straight *through* the hair with him. Think! he 'll think what any *man* 'd think—you a-suckin' spite o' all your sorrow, my sweet,—and my Berry talkin' of his Roman matrons!— here's a English wife 'll match 'em all! that's what he thinks. And now that leetle dark under yer eye 'll clear, my darlin', now he 've come.'

Mrs. Berry looked to no more than that; Lucy to no more than the peace she had in being near Richard's best friend. When she sat down to tea it was with a sense that the little room that held her was her home perhaps for many a day.

A chop procured and cooked by Mrs. Berry formed Austin's dinner. During the meal he entertained them with anecdotes of his travels. Poor Lucy had no temptation to try to conquer Austin. That heroic weakness of hers was gone.

Mrs. Berry had said: 'Three cups—I goes no further,' and Lucy had rejected the proffer of more tea, when Austin, who was in the thick of a Brazilian forest, asked her if she was a good traveller.

'I mean, can you start at a minute's notice?'

Lucy hesitated, and then said, 'Yes,' decisively, to which Mrs. Berry added, that she was not a 'luggage-woman.'

'There used to be a train at seven o'clock,' Austin remarked, consulting his watch.

The two women were silent.

'Could you get ready to come with me to Raynham in ten minutes?'

Austin looked as if he had asked a commonplace question.

Lucy's lips parted to speak.. She could not answer.

Loud rattled the teaboard to Mrs. Berry's dropping hands.

'Joy and deliverance!' she exclaimed with a foundering voice.

'Will you come?' Austin kindly asked again.

Lucy tried to stop her beating heart, as she answered, 'Yes.' Mrs. Berry cunningly pretended to interpret the irresolution in her tones with a mighty whisper: 'She's thinking what's to be done with baby.'

'He must learn to travel,' said Austin.

'Oh!' cried Mrs. Berry, 'and I'll be his nuss, and bear him, a sweet! Oh! and think of it! me nurse-maid once more at Raynham Abbey! but it's nurse-woman now, you must say. Let us be goin' on the spot.'

She started up and away in hot haste, fearing delay would cool the heaven-sent resolve. Austin smiled, eyeing his watch and Lucy alternately. She was wishing to ask a multitude of questions. His face reassured her, and saying: 'I will be dressed instantly,' she also left the room. Talking, bustling, preparing, wrapping up my lord, and looking to their neatnesses, they were nevertheless ready within the time prescribed by Austin, and Mrs. Berry stood humming over the baby. 'He'll sleep it through,' she said. 'He's had enough for an alderman,

and goes to sleep sound after his dinner, he do, a duck!'
Before they departed, Lucy ran up to Lady Feverel. She
returned for the small one.

'One moment, Mr. Wentworth?'

'Just two,' said Austin.

Master Richard was taken up, and when Lucy came
back her eyes were full of tears.

'She thinks she is never to see him again, Mr. Wentworth.'

'She shall,' Austin said simply.

Off they went, and with Austin near her, Lucy forgot
to dwell at all upon the great act of courage she was per-
forming.

'I do hope baby will not wake,' was her chief solicitude.

'He!' cries nurse-woman Berry from the rear, 'his little tum-tum 's *as* tight *as* he can hold, a pet! a lamb!
a bird! a beauty! and ye may take yer oath he never
wakes till that 's slack. He 've got character of his own,
a blessed!'

There are some tremendous citadels that only want to be
taken by storm. The baronet sat alone in his library,
sick of resistance, and rejoicing in the pride of no surrender; a terror to his friends and to himself. Hearing
Austin's name sonorously pronounced by the man of
calves, he looked up from his book, and held out his hand.
'Glad to see you, Austin.' His appearance betokened
complete security. The next minute he found himself
escaladed.*

It was a cry from Mrs. Berry that told him others were
in the room besides Austin. Lucy stood a little behind
the lamp: Mrs. Berry close to the door. The door was
half open, and passing through it might be seen the petri-
fied figure of a fine man. The baronet glancing over the
lamp rose at Mrs. Berry's signification of a woman's per-

sonality. Austin stepped back and led Lucy to him by the hand. 'I have brought Richard's wife, sir,' he said with a pleased, perfectly uncalculating, countenance, that was disarming. Very pale and trembling Lucy bowed. She felt her two hands taken, and heard a kind voice. Could it be possible it belonged to the dreadful father of her husband? She lifted her eyes nervously: her hands were still detained. The baronet contemplated Richard's choice. Had he ever had a rivalry with those pure eyes? He saw the pain of her position shooting across her brows, and, uttering gentle inquiries as to her health, placed her in a seat. Mrs. Berry had already fallen into a chair.

'What aspect do you like for your bedroom?—East?' said the baronet.

Lucy was asking herself wonderingly: 'Am I to stay?'

'Perhaps you had better take to Richard's room at once,' he pursued. 'You have the Lobourne valley there and a good morning air, and will feel more at home.'

Lucy's colour mounted. Mrs. Berry gave a short cough, as one who should say, 'The day is ours!' Undoubtedly —strange as it was to think it—the fortress was carried.

'Lucy is rather tired,' said Austin, and to hear her Christian name thus bravely spoken brought grateful dew to her eyes.

The baronet was about to touch the bell. 'But have you come alone?' he asked.

At this Mrs. Berry came forward. Not immediately: it seemed to require effort for her to move, and when she was within the region of the lamp, her agitation could not escape notice. The blissful bundle shook in her arms.

'By the way, what is he to me?' Austin inquired generally as he went and unveiled the younger hope of Raynham. 'My relationship is not so defined as yours, sir.'

An observer might have supposed that the baronet peeped at his grandson with the courteous indifference of one who merely wished to compliment the mother of anybody's child.

'I really think he's like Richard,' Austin laughed. Lucy looked: I am sure he is!

'As like as one to one,' Mrs. Berry murmured feebly; but Grandpapa not speaking she thought it incumbent on her to pluck up. 'And he's as healthy as his father was, Sir Austin—spite o' the might 'a beens. Reg'lar as the clock! We never want a clock since he come. We knows the hour o' the day, and *of* the night.'

'You nurse him yourself, of course?' the baronet spoke to Lucy, and was satisfied on that point.

Mrs. Berry was going to display his prodigious legs. Lucy, fearing the consequent effect on the prodigious lungs, begged her not to wake him. ''T'd take a deal to do that,' said Mrs. Berry, and harped on Master Richard's health and the small wonder it was that he enjoyed it, considering the superior quality of his diet, and the lavish attentions of his mother, and then suddenly fell silent on a deep sigh.

'He looks healthy,' said the baronet, 'but I am not a judge of babies.'

Thus, having capitulated, Raynham chose to acknowledge its new commandant, who was now borne away, under the directions of the housekeeper, to occupy the room Richard had slept in when an infant.

Austin cast no thought on his success. The baronet said: 'She is extremely well-looking.' He replied: 'A person you take to at once.' There it ended.

But a much more animated colloquy was taking place aloft, where Lucy and Mrs. Berry sat alone. Lucy expected her to talk about the reception they had met with, and the house, and the peculiarities of the rooms, and the solid happiness that seemed in store. Mrs. Berry all the while would persist in consulting the looking-glass.

Her first distinct answer was, 'My dear! tell me candid, how do I look?'

'Very nice indeed, Mrs. Berry; but could you have believed he would be so kind, so considerate?'

'I am sure I looked a frump,' returned Mrs. Berry. 'Oh, dear! two birds at a shot. What *do* you think, now?'

'I never saw so wonderful a likeness,' says Lucy.

'Likeness! look at me.' Mrs. Berry was trembling and hot in the palms.

'You 're very feverish, dear Berry. What can it be?'

'Ain't it like the love-flutters of a young gal, my dear.'

'Go to bed, Berry, dear,' says Lucy, pouting in her soft caressing way. 'I will undress you, and see to you, dear heart! You 've had so much excitement.'

'Ha! ha!' Berry laughed hysterically; 'she thinks it 's about this business of hers. Why, it 's child's-play, my darlin'. But I didn't look for tragedy to-night. Sleep in this house I can't, my love!'

Lucy was astonished. 'Not sleep here, Mrs. Berry?— Oh! why, you silly old thing? I know.'

'Do ye!' said Mrs. Berry, with a sceptical nose.

'You 're afraid of ghosts.'

'Belike I am when they 're six foot two in their shoes, and bellows when you stick a pin into their calves. I seen my Berry!'

'Your husband?'

'Large as life!'

Lucy meditated on optical delusions, but Mrs. Berry described him as the Colossus who had marched them into the library, and vowed that he had recognized her and quaked. 'Time ain't aged him,' said Mrs. Berry, 'whereas me! he 've got his excuse now. I *know* I look a frump.'

Lucy kissed her: 'You look the nicest, dearest old thing.'

'You may say an old thing, my dear.'

'And your husband is really here?'

'Berry's below!'

Profoundly uttered as this was, it chased every vestige of incredulity.

'What will you do, Mrs. Berry?'

'Go, my dear. Leave him to be happy in his own way. It's over atween us, I see that. When I entered the house I felt there was something comin' over me, and lo and behold ye! no sooner was we in the hall-passage —if it hadn't been for that blessed infant I should 'a dropped. I must 'a known his step, for my heart began thumpin', and I knew I hadn't got my hair straight— that Mr. Wentworth was in such a hurry—nor my best gown. I knew he'd scorn me. He hates frumps.'

'Scorn you!' cried Lucy angrily. 'He who has behaved so wickedly!'

Mrs. Berry attempted to rise. 'I may as well go at once,' she whimpered. 'If I see him I shall only be disgracin' of myself. I feel it all on my side already. Did ye mark him, my dear? I know I was vexin' to him at times, I was. Those big men are se touchy about their dignity—nat'ral. Hark at me! I'm goin' all soft in a minute. Let me leave the house, my dear. I dare say it was good half my fault. Young women don't understand men sufficient—not altogether—and I was a young woman then; and then what they goes and does they ain't quite answerable for: they feels, I dare say, pushed from behind. Yes. I'll go. I'm a frump. I'll go. 'Tain't in natur' for me to sleep in the same house.'

Lucy laid her hands on Mrs. Berry's shoulders, and forcibly fixed her in her seat. 'Leave baby, naughty woman? I tell you he shall come to you, and fall on his knees to you and beg your forgiveness.'

'Berry on his knees!'

'Yes. And he shall beg and pray you to forgive him.'

'If you get more from Martin Berry than breath-away words, great 'll be my wonder!' said Mrs. Berry.

'We will see,' said Lucy, thoroughly determined to do something for the good creature that had befriended her.

Mrs. Berry examined her gown. 'Won't it seem we 're runnin' after him?' she murmured faintly.

'He is your husband, Mrs. Berry. He may be wanting to come to you now.'

'Oh! Where is all I was goin' to say to that man when we met!' Mrs. Berry ejaculated. Lucy had left the room.

On the landing outside the door Lucy met a lady dressed in black, who stopped her and asked if she was Richard's wife, and kissed her, passing from her immediately. Lucy despatched a message for Austin, and related the Berry history. Austin sent for the great man, and said: 'Do you know your wife is here?' Before Berry had time to draw himself up to enunciate his longest, he was requested to step upstairs, and as his young mistress at once led the way, Berry could not refuse to put his legs in motion and carry the stately edifice aloft.

Of the interview Mrs. Berry gave Lucy a slight sketch that night. 'He began in the old way, my dear, and says I, a true heart and plain words, Martin Berry. So there he cuts himself and his Johnson short, and down he goes —down *on* his knees. I never could 'a believed it. I kep my dignity as a woman till I see that sight, but that done for me. I was a ripe apple in his arms 'fore I knew where I was. There 's something about a fine man on his knees that 's too much for us women. And it reely was the penitent on his two knees, not the lover on his one. If he mean it! But ah! what do you think he begs of me, my dear?—not to make it known in the house just yet! I can't, I can't say that look well.'

Lucy attributed it to his sense of shame at his conduct, and Mrs. Berry did her best to look on it in that light.

'Did the bar'net kiss ye when you wished him good-
night?' she asked. Lucy said he had not. 'Then bide
awake as long as ye can,' was Mrs. Berry's rejoinder.
'And now let us pray blessings on that simple-speaking
gentleman who does so much 'cause he says se little.'

Like many other natural people, Mrs. Berry was only
silly where her own soft heart was concerned. As she
secretly anticipated, the baronet came into her room when
all was quiet. She saw him go and bend over Richard
the Second, and remain earnestly watching him. He then
went to the half-opened door of the room where Lucy
slept, leaned his ear a moment, knocked gently, and entered. Mrs. Berry heard low words interchanging within.
She could not catch a syllable, yet she would have sworn
to the context. 'He 've called her his daughter, promised
her happiness, and given a father's kiss to her.' When
Sir Austin passed out she was in a deep sleep.

CHAPTER XLII

NATURE SPEAKS

BRIAREUS reddening angrily over the sea—where is that
vaporous Titan? And Hesper set in his rosy garland—
why looks he so implacably sweet? It is that one has left
that bright home to go forth and do cloudy work, and he
has got a stain with which he dare not return. Far in
the West fair Lucy beckons him to come. Ah, heaven!
if he might! How strong and fierce the temptation is!
how subtle the sleepless desire! it drugs his reason, his
honour. For he loves her; she is still the first and only
woman to him. Otherwise would this black spot be hell
to him? otherwise would his limbs be chained while
her arms are spread open to him. And if he loves her,

why then what is one fall in the pit, or a thousand? Is not love the password to that beckoning bliss? So may we say; but here is one whose body has been made a temple to him, and it is desecrated.

A temple, and desecrated! For what is it fit for but for a dance of devils? His education has thus wrought him to think.

He can blame nothing but his own baseness. But to feel base and accept the bliss that beckons—he has not fallen so low as that.

Ah, happy English home! sweet wife! what mad miserable Wisp of the Fancy led him away from you, high in his conceit? Poor wretch! that thought to be he of the hundred hands, and war against the absolute Gods. Jove whispered a light commission to the Laughing Dame; she met him; and how did he shake Olympus? with laughter!

Sure it were better to be Orestes, the Furies howling in his ears,* than one called to by a heavenly soul from whom he is for ever outcast. He has not the oblivion of madness. Clothed in the lights of his first passion, robed in the splendour of old skies, she meets him everywhere; morning, evening, night, she shines above him; waylays him suddenly in forest depths; drops palpably on his heart. At moments he forgets; he rushes to embrace her; calls her his beloved, and lo, her innocent kiss brings agony of shame to his face.

Daily the struggle endured. His father wrote to him, begging him by the love he had for him to return. From that hour Richard burnt unread all the letters he received. He knew too well how easily he could persuade himself: words from without might tempt him and quite extinguish the spark of honourable feeling that tortured him, and that he clung to in desperate self-vindication.

To arrest young gentlemen on the downward slope is both a dangerous and thankless office. It is, neverthe-

less, one that fair women greatly prize, and certain of them
professionally follow. Lady Judith, as far as her sex
would permit, was also of the Titans in their battle against
the absolute Gods; for which purpose, mark you, she had
married a lord incapable in all save his acres. Her achieve-
ments she kept to her own mind: she did not look happy
over them. She met Richard accidentally in Paris; she
saw his state; she let him learn that she alone on earth
understood him. The consequence was that he was forthwith enrolled in her train. It soothed him to be near a
woman. Did she venture her guess as to the cause of his
conduct, she blotted it out with a facility women have,
and cast on it a melancholy hue he was taught to participate in. She spoke of sorrows, personal sorrows, much
as he might speak of his—vaguely, and with self-blame.
And she understood him. How the dark unfathomed wealth
within us gleams to a woman's eye! We are at compound
interest immediately: so much richer than we knew!
—almost as rich as we dreamed! But then the instant we
are away from her we find ourselves bankrupt, beggared.
How is that? We do not ask. We hurry to her and
bask hungrily in her orbs. The eye must be feminine to
be thus creative: I cannot say why. Lady Judith understood Richard, and he feeling infinitely vile, somehow held
to her more feverishly, as one who dreaded the worst in
missing her. The spirit must rest; he was weak with
what he suffered.

Austin found them among the hills of Nassau in Rhineland: Titans, male and female, who had not displaced
Jove, and were now adrift, prone on floods of sentiment.
The blue-frocked peasant swinging behind his oxen of a
morning, the gaily-kerchiefed fruit-women, the jackass-
driver, even the doctor of those regions, have done more
for their fellows. Horrible reflection! Lady Judith is
serene above it, but it frets at Richard when he is out of

her shadow. Often wretchedly he watches the young men of his own age trooping to their work. Not cloud-work theirs! Work solid, unambitious, fruitful!

Lady Judith had a nobler in prospect for the hero. He gaped blindfolded for anything, and she gave him the map of Europe in tatters. He swallowed it comfortably. It was an intoxicating cordial. Himself on horseback over-riding wrecks of Empires! Well might common sense cower with the meaner animals at the picture. Tacitly they agreed to recast the civilized globe. The quality of vapour is to melt and shape itself anew; but it is never the quality of vapour to reassume the same shapes. Briareus of the hundred unoccupied hands may turn to a monstrous donkey with his hind legs aloft, or twenty thousand jabbering apes. The phantasmic groupings of the young brain are very like those we see in the skies, and equally the sport of the wind. Lady Judith blew. There was plenty of vapour in him, and it always resolved into some shape or other. You that mark those clouds of eventide, and know youth, will see the similitude: it will not be strange, it will barely seem foolish to you, that a young man of Richard's age, Richard's education and position, should be in this wild state. Had he not been nursed to believe he was born for great things? Did she not say she was sure of it? And to feel base, yet born for better, is enough to make one grasp at anything cloudy. Suppose the hero with a game leg. How intense is his faith in quacks! with what a passion of longing is he not seized to break somebody's head! They spoke of Italy in low voices. 'The time will come,' said she. 'And I shall be ready,' said he. What rank was he to take in the liberating army? Captain, colonel, general in chief, or simple private? Here, as became him, he was much more positive and specific than she was. Simple private, he said. Yet he saw himself caracoling* on horseback.

Private in the cavalry, then, of course. Private in the cavalry over-riding wrecks of Empires. She looked forth under her brows with mournful indistinctness at that object in the distance. They read Petrarch*to get up the necessary fires. Italia mia! Vain indeed was this speaking to those thick and mortal wounds in her fair body, but their sighs went with the Tiber, the Arno, and the Po,* and their hands joined. Who has not wept for Italy? I see the aspirations of a world arise for her, thick and frequent as the puffs of smoke from cigars of Pannonian* sentries!

So when Austin came Richard said he could not leave Lady Judith, Lady Judith said she could not part with him. For his sake, mind! This Richard verified. Perhaps he had reason to be grateful. The high-road of Folly may have led him from one that terminates worse. He is foolish, God knows; but for my part I will not laugh at the hero because he has not got his occasion. Meet him when he is, as it were, anointed by his occasion, and he is no laughing matter.

Richard felt his safety in this which, to please the world, we must term folly. Exhalation of vapours was a wholesome process to him, and somebody who gave them shape and hue a beneficent Iris.* He told Austin plainly he could not leave her, and did not anticipate the day when he could.

'Why can't you go to your wife, Richard?'

'For a reason you would be the first to approve, Austin.'

He welcomed Austin with every show of manly tenderness, and sadness at heart. Austin he had always associated with his Lucy in that Hesperian palace of the West. Austin waited patiently. Lady Judith's old lord played on all the baths in Nassau without evoking the tune of health. Whithersoever he listed she changed her abode. So admirable a wife was to be pardoned for espousing an old man. She was an enthusiast even in her connubial duties. She had the brows of an enthusiast. With occasion she might have been a Charlotte Corday.* So let her also be shielded from the ban of ridicule. Nonsense of enthusiasts is very different from nonsense of ninnies. She was truly a high-minded person, of that order who always do what they see to be right, and always have confidence in their optics. She was not unworthy of a young man's admiration, if she was unfit to be his guide. She resumed her ancient intimacy with Austin easily, while she preserved her new footing with Richard. She and Austin were not unlike, only Austin never dreamed, and had not married an old lord.

The three were walking on the bridge at Limburg on the Lahn,*where the shadow of a stone bishop is thrown by the moonlight on the water brawling over slabs of slate. A woman passed them bearing in her arms a baby, whose mighty size drew their attention.

'What a wopper!' Richard laughed.

'Well, that is a fine fellow,' said Austin, 'but I don't think he's much bigger than your boy.'

'He'll do for a nineteenth-century Arminius,'*Richard was saying. Then he looked at Austin.

'What was that you said?' Lady Judith asked of Austin.

'What have I said that deserves to be repeated?' Austin counterqueried quite innocently.

'Richard has a son?'

'You didn't know it?'

'His modesty goes very far,' said Lady Judith, sweeping the shadow of a curtsey to Richard's paternity.

Richard's heart throbbed with violence. He looked again in Austin's face. Austin took it so much as a matter of course that he said nothing more on the subject.

'Well!' murmured Lady Judith.

When the two men were alone, Richard said in a quick voice: 'Austin! you were in earnest?'

'You didn't know it, Richard?'

'No.'

'Why, they all wrote to you. Lucy wrote to you: your father, your aunt. I believe Adrian wrote too.'

'I tore up their letters,' said Richard.

'He's a noble fellow, I can tell you. You've nothing to be ashamed of. He'll soon be coming to ask about you. I made sure you knew.'

'No, I never knew.' Richard walked away, and then said: 'What is he like?'

'Well, he really is like you, but he has his mother's eyes.'

'And she's——'

'Yes. I think the child has kept her well.'

'They're both at Raynham?'

'Both.'

Hence, fantastic vapours! What are ye to this! Where are the dreams of the hero when he learns he has a child? Nature is taking him to her bosom. She will speak presently. Every domesticated boor in these hills can boast the same, yet marvels the hero at none of his visioned prodigies as he does when he comes to hear of this most common performance. A father? Richard fixed his eyes as if he were trying to make out the lineaments of his child.

Telling Austin he would be back in a few minutes, he sallied into the air, and walked on and on. 'A father!' he kept repeating to himself: 'a child!' And though he knew it not, he was striking the key-notes of Nature. But he did know of a singular harmony that suddenly burst over his whole being.

The moon was surpassingly bright: the summer air heavy and still. He left the high road and pierced into the forest. His walk was rapid: the leaves on the trees brushed his cheeks; the dead leaves heaped in the dells noised to his feet. Something of a religious joy—a strange sacred pleasure—was in him. By degrees it wore; he remembered himself: and now he was possessed by a proportionate anguish. A father! he dared never see his child. And he had no longer his phantasies to fall upon. He was utterly bare to his sin. In his troubled mind it seemed to him that Clare looked down on him—Clare who saw him as he was; and that to her eyes it would be infamy for him to go and print his kiss upon his child. Then came stern efforts to command his misery and make the nerves of his face iron.

By the log of an ancient tree half buried in dead leaves of past summers, beside a brook, he halted as one who had reached his journey's end. There he discovered he had a companion in Lady Judith's little dog. He gave the friendly animal a pat of recognition, and both were silent in the forest-silence.

It was impossible for Richard to return; his heart was surcharged. He must advance, and on he footed, the little dog following.

An oppressive slumber hung about the forest-branches. In the dells and on the heights was the same dead heat. Here where the brook tinkled it was no cool-lipped sound, but metallic, and without the spirit of water. Yonder in a space of moonlight on lush grass, the beams were as white fire to sight and feeling. No haze spread around. The valleys were clear, defined to the shadows of their verges; the distances sharply distinct, and with the colours of day but slightly softened. Richard beheld a roe moving across a slope of sward far out of rifle-mark. The breathless silence was significant, yet the moon shone in a broad blue heaven. Tongue out of mouth trotted the little dog after him; couched panting when he stopped an instant;

rose weariedly when he started afresh. Now and then a large white night-moth flitted through the dusk of the forest.

On a barren corner of the wooded highland looking inland stood grey topless ruins set in nettles and rank grass-blades. Richard mechanically sat down on the crumbling flints to rest, and listened to the panting of the dog. Sprinkled at his feet were emerald, lights: hundreds of glow-worms studded the dark dry ground.

He sat and eyed them, thinking not at all. His energies were expended in action. He sat as a part of the ruins, and the moon turned his shadow Westward from the South. Overhead, as she declined, long ripples of silver cloud were imperceptibly stealing toward her. They were the van of a tempest. He did not observe them or the leaves beginning to chatter. When he again pursued his course with his face to the Rhine, a huge mountain appeared to rise sheer over him, and he had it in his mind to scale it. He got no nearer to the base of it for all his vigorous outstepping. The ground began to dip; he lost sight of the sky. Then heavy thunder-drops struck his cheek, the leaves were singing, the earth breathed, it was black before him and behind. All at once the thunder spoke. The mountain he had marked was bursting over him.

Up started the whole forest in violet fire. He saw the country at the foot of the hills to the bounding Rhine gleam, quiver, extinguished. Then there were pauses; and the lightning seemed as the eye of heaven, and the thunder as the tongue of heaven, each alternately addressing him; filling him with awful rapture. Alone there —sole human creature among the grandeurs and mysteries of storm—he felt the representative of his kind, and his spirit rose, and marched, and exulted, let it be glory, let it be ruin! Lower down the lightened abysses of air rolled the wrathful crash: then white thrusts of light were darted from the sky, and great curving ferns, seen steadfast in pallor a second, were supernaturally agitated, and vanished. Then a shrill song roused in the leaves and the herbage. Prolonged and louder it sounded, as deeper and heavier the deluge pressed. A mighty force of water satisfied the desire of the earth. Even in this, drenched as he was by the first outpouring, Richard had a savage pleasure. Keeping in motion, he was scarcely conscious of the wet, and the grateful breath of the weeds was refreshing. Suddenly he stopped short, lifting a curious nostril. He fancied he smelt meadow-sweet. He had never seen the flower in Rhineland—never thought of it; and it would hardly be met with in a forest. He was sure he smelt it fresh in dews. His little companion wagged a miserable wet tail some way in advance. He went on slowly, thinking indistinctly. After two or three steps he stooped and stretched out his hand to feel for the flower, having, he knew not why, a strong wish to verify its growth there. Groping about, his hand encountered something warm that started at his touch, and he, with the instinct we have, seized it, and lifted it to look at it. The creature was very small, evidently quite young. Richard's eyes, now accustomed to the darkness, were able to discern it for what it was, a tiny leveret, and he supposed that the dog had probably frightened its dam just before he found it. He put the little thing on one hand in his breast, and stepped out rapidly as before.

The rain was now steady; from every tree a fountain poured. So cool and easy had his mind become that he was speculating on what kind of shelter the birds could find, and how the butterflies and moths saved their coloured wings from washing. Folded close they might hang under a leaf, he thought. Lovingly he looked into the dripping darkness of the coverts on each side, as one of their children. He was next musing on a strange sensation he experienced. It ran up one arm with an indescribable thrill, but communicated nothing to his heart. It was purely physical, ceased for a time, and recommenced, till he had it all through his blood, wonderfully thrilling. He grew aware that the little thing he carried in his breast was licking his hand there. The small rough tongue going over and over the palm of his hand produced the strange sensation he felt. Now that he knew the cause, the marvel ended; but now that he knew the cause, his heart was touched and made more of it. The gentle scraping continued without intermission as on he walked. What did it say to him? Human tongue could not have said so much just then.

A pale grey light on the skirts of the flying tempest displayed the dawn. Richard was walking hurriedly. The green drenched weeds lay all about in his path, bent thick, and the forest drooped glimmeringly. Impelled as a man who feels a revelation mounting obscurely to his brain, Richard was passing one of those little forest-chapels, hung with votive wreaths, where the peasant halts to kneel and pray. Cold, still, in the twilight it stood, rain-drops pattering round it. He looked within, and saw the Virgin holding her Child. He moved by. But not many steps had he gone ere his strength went out of him, and he shuddered. What was it? He asked not. He was in other hands. Vivid as lightning the Spirit of Life illumined him. He felt in his heart the cry of his child, his darling's touch. With shut eyes he saw them both. They drew him from the depths; they led him a blind and tottering man. And as they led him he had a sense of purification so sweet he shuddered again and again.

When he looked out from his trance on the breathing world, the small birds hopped and chirped: warm fresh sunlight was over all the hills. He was on the edge of the forest, entering a plain clothed with ripe corn under a spacious morning sky.

CHAPTER XLIII

AGAIN THE MAGIAN CONFLICT

THEY heard at Raynham that Richard was coming. Lucy had the news first in a letter from Ripton Thompson, who met him at Bonn. Ripton did not say that he had employed his vacation holiday on purpose to use his efforts to induce his dear friend to return to his wife; and finding Richard already on his way, of course Ripton said nothing to him, but affected to be travelling for his pleasure like any cockney. Richard also wrote to her. In case she should have gone to the sea he directed her to send word to his hotel that he might not lose an hour. His letter was sedate in tone, very sweet to her. Assisted by the faithful female Berry, she was conquering an Aphorist.

'Woman's reason is in the milk of her breasts,' was one of his rough notes, due to an observation of Lucy's maternal cares. Let us remember, therefore, we men who drunk of it largely there, that she has it.

Mrs. Berry zealously apprised him how early Master Richard's education had commenced, and the great future historian he must consequently be. This trait in Lucy was of itself sufficient to win Sir Austin.

'Here my plan with Richard was false,' he reflected: 'in presuming that anything save blind fortuity would bring him such a mate as he should have.' He came to add: 'And has got!'

He could admit now that instinct had so far beaten science; for as Richard was coming, as all were to be happy, his wisdom embraced them all paternally as the author of their happiness. Between him and Lucy a tender intimacy grew.

'I told you she could talk, sir,' said Adrian.

'She thinks!' said the baronet.

The delicate question how she was to treat her uncle, he settled generously. Farmer Blaize should come up to Raynham when he would: Lucy must visit him at least three times a week. He had Farmer Blaize and Mrs. Berry to study, and really excellent Aphorisms sprang from the plain human bases this natural couple presented.

'It will do us no harm,' he thought, 'some of the honest blood of the soil in our veins.' And he was content in musing on the parentage of the little cradled boy. A common sight for those who had the entry to the library was the baronet cherishing the hand of his daughter-in-law.

So Richard was crossing the sea, and hearts at Raynham were beating quicker measures as the minutes progressed. That night he would be with them. Sir Austin gave Lucy a longer, warmer salute when she came down to breakfast in the morning. Mrs. Berry waxed thrice amorous. 'It's your second bridals, ye sweet livin' widow!' she said. 'Thanks be the Lord! it's the same man too! and a baby over the bed-post,' she appended seriously.

'Strange,' Berry declared it to be, 'strange I feel none o' this to my Berry now. All my feelin's o' love seem t'ave gone into you two sweet chicks.'

In fact, the faithless male Berry complained of being treated badly, and affected a superb jealousy of the baby; but the good dame told him that if he suffered at all he suffered his due. Berry's position was decidedly uncomfortable. It could not be concealed from the lower household that he had a wife in the establishment, and for the complications this gave rise to, his wife would not legitimately console him. Lucy did intercede, but Mrs. Berry was obdurate. She averred she would not give up the child till he was weaned. 'Then, perhaps,' she said prospectively. 'You see I ain't se soft as you thought for.'

'You're a very unkind, vindictive old woman,' said
Lucy.

'Belike I am,' Mrs. Berry was proud to agree. We like
a new character, now and then. Berry had delayed too
long.

Were it not notorious that the straitlaced prudish
dare not listen to the natural chaste, certain things Mrs.
Berry thought it adviseable to impart to the young wife
with regard to Berry's infidelity, and the charity women
should have toward sinful men, might here be reproduced.
Enough that she thought proper to broach the matter,
and cite her own Christian sentiments, now that she was
indifferent in some degree.

Oily calm is on the sea. At Raynham they look up at
the sky and speculate that Richard is approaching fairly
speeded. He comes to throw himself on his darling's
mercy. Lucy irradiated over forest and sea, tempest and
peace—to her the hero comes humbly. Great is that day
when we see our folly! Ripton and he were the friends
of old. Richard encouraged him to talk of the two he
could be eloquent on, and Ripton, whose secret vanity
was in his powers of speech, never tired of enumerating
Lucy's virtues, and the peculiar attributes of the baby.

'She did not say a word against me, Rip?'

'Against you, Richard! The moment she knew she was
to be a mother, she thought of nothing but her duty to
the child. She's one who can't think of herself.'

'You've seen her at Raynham, Rip?'

'Yes, once. They asked me down. And your father's
so fond of her—I'm sure he thinks no woman like her, and
he's right. She is so lovely, and so good.'

Richard was too full of blame of himself to blame his
father: too British to expose his emotions. Ripton divined
how deep and changed they were by his manner. He
had cast aside the hero, and however Ripton had obeyed

him and looked up to him in the heroic time, he loved him tenfold now. He told his friend how much Lucy's mere womanly sweetness and excellence had done for him, and Richard contrasted his own profitless extravagance with the patient beauty of his dear home-angel. He was not one to take her on the easy terms that offered. There was that to do which made his cheek burn as he thought of it, but he was going to do it, even though it lost her to him. Just to see her and kneel to her was joy sufficient to sustain him, and warm his blood in the prospect. They marked the white cliffs growing over the water. Nearer, the sun made them lustrous. Houses and people seemed to welcome the wild youth to common-sense, simplicity, and home.

They were in town by mid-day. Richard had a momentary idea of not driving to his hotel for letters. After a short debate he determined to go there. The porter said he had two letters for Mr. Richard Feverel—one had been waiting some time. He went to the box and fetched them. The first Richard opened was from Lucy, and as he read it, Ripton observed the colour deepen on his face, while a quivering smile played about his mouth. He opened the other indifferently. It began without any form of address. Richard's forehead darkened at the signature. This letter was in a sloping feminine hand, and flourished with light strokes all over, like a field of the bearded barley. Thus it ran:—

'I know you are in a rage with me because I would not consent to ruin you, you foolish fellow. What do you call it? Going to that unpleasant place together. Thank you, my milliner is not ready yet, and I want to make a good appearance when I do go. I suppose I shall have to some day. Your health, Sir Richard. Now let me speak to you seriously. *Go home to your wife at once.* But

I know the sort of fellow you are, and I must be plain with you. Did I ever say I loved you? You may hate me as much as you please, but I will save you from being a fool.

'Now listen to me. You know my relations with Mount. *That beast Brayder* offered to pay all my debts and set me afloat, if I would keep you in town. I declare on my honour I had no idea why, and I did not agree to it. But you were such a handsome fellow—I noticed you in the Park before I heard a word of you. But then you fought shy—you were just as tempting as a girl. You *stung* me. Do you know what that is? I would make you care for me, and we know how it ended, without any intention of mine, I *swear*. I'd have cut off my hand rather than do you any harm, upon my honour. Circumstances! Then I saw it was all up between us. Brayder came and began to chaff about you. I dealt the animal a stroke on the face with my riding-whip—I shut him up pretty quick. Do you think I would let a man speak about you? —I was going to swear. You see I remember Dick's lessons. O my God! I do feel unhappy.—Brayder offered me money. Go and think I took it, if you like. What do I care what anybody thinks! Something that blackguard said made me suspicious. I went down to the Isle of Wight where Mount was, and your wife was just gone with an old lady who came and took her away. I should so have liked to see her. You said, you remember, she would take me as a sister, and treat me—I laughed at it then. My God! how I could cry now, if water did any good to a *devil*, as you politely call poor me. I called at your house and saw your man-servant, who said Mount had just been there. In a minute it struck me. I was sure Mount was after a woman, but it never struck me that woman was your wife. Then I saw why they wanted me to keep you away. I went to Brayder. You know how I hate him. I made love to the man to get it out of him.

Richard! my word of honour, they have planned to carry her off, if Mount finds he cannot seduce her. Talk of devils! He's one; but he is not so bad as Brayder. I cannot forgive a mean dog his villany.

'Now after this, I am quite sure you are too much of a man to stop away from her another moment. I have no more to say. I suppose we shall not see each other again, so good-bye, Dick! I fancy I hear you cursing me. Why can't you feel like other men on the subject? But if you were like the rest of them I should not have cared for you a farthing. I have not worn lilac since I saw you last. I'll be buried in your colour, Dick. That will not offend you—will it?

'You are not going to believe I took the money? If I thought you thought that—it makes me *feel* like a devil only to fancy you think it.

'The first time you meet Brayder, *cane him publicly.*

'Adieu! Say it's because you don't like his face. I suppose devils must not say *Adieu.* Here's plain old good-bye, then, between you and me. Good-bye, dear Dick! You won't think that of me?

'May I eat dry bread to the day of my death if I took or ever will touch a scrap of their money.   BELLA.'

Richard folded up the letter silently.

'Jump into the cab,' he said to Ripton.

'Anything the matter, Richard?'

'No.'

The driver received directions. Richard sat without speaking. His friend knew that face. He asked whether there was bad news in the letter. For answer, he had the lie circumstantial. He ventured to remark that they were going the wrong way.

'It's the right way,' cried Richard, and his jaws were hard and square, and his eyes looked heavy and full.

Ripton said no more, but thought.

The cabman pulled up at a Club. A gentleman, in whom Ripton recognized the Hon. Peter Brayder, was just then swinging a leg over his horse, with one foot in the stirrup. Hearing his name called, the Hon. Peter turned about, and stretched an affable hand.

'Is Mountfalcon in town?' said Richard, taking the horse's reins instead of the gentlemanly hand. His voice and aspect were quite friendly.

'Mount?' Brayder replied, curiously watching the action; 'yes. He's off this evening.'

'He *is* in town?' Richard released his horse. 'I want to see him. Where is he?'

The young man looked pleasant: that which might have aroused Brayder's suspicions was an old affair in parasitical register by this time. 'Want to see him? What about?' he said carelessly, and gave the address.

'By the way,' he sang out, 'we thought of putting your name down, Feverel.' He indicated the lofty structure. 'What do you say?'

Richard nodded back to him, crying, 'Hurry.' Brayder returned the nod, and those who promenaded the district soon beheld his body in elegant motion to the stepping of his well-earned horse.

'What do you want to see Lord Mountfalcon for, Richard?' said Ripton.

'I just want to see him,' Richard replied.

Ripton was left in the cab at the door of my lord's residence. He had to wait there a space of about ten minutes, when Richard returned with a clearer visage, though somewhat heated. He stood outside the cab, and Ripton was conscious of being examined by those strong grey eyes. As clear as speech he understood them to say to him, 'You won't do,' but which of the many things on earth he would not do for he was at a loss to think.

'Go down to Raynham, Ripton. Say I shall be there to-night certainly. Don't bother me with questions. Drive off at once. Or wait. Get another cab. I'll take this.'

Ripton was ejected, and found himself standing alone in the street. As he was on the point of rushing after the galloping cab-horse to get a word of elucidation, he heard some one speak behind him.

'You are Feverel's friend.'

Ripton had an eye for lords. An ambrosial footman, standing at the open door of Lord Mountfalcon's house, and a gentleman standing on the door-step, told him that he was addressed by that nobleman. He was requested to step into the house. When they were alone, Lord Mountfalcon, slightly ruffled, said: 'Feverel has insulted me grossly. I must meet him, of course. It's a piece of infernal folly!—I suppose he is not quite mad?'

Ripton's only definite answer was a gasping iteration of 'My lord.'

My lord resumed: 'I am perfectly guiltless of offending him, as far as I know. In fact, I had a friendship for him. Is he liable to fits of this sort of thing?'

Not yet at conversation-point, Ripton stammered: 'Fits, my lord?'

'Ah!' went the other, eyeing Ripton in lordly cognizant style. 'You know nothing of this business, perhaps?'

Ripton said he did not.

'Have you any influence with him?'

'Not much, my lord. Only now and then—a little.'

'You are not in the Army?'

The question was quite unnecessary. Ripton confessed to the law, and my lord did not look surprised.

'I will not detain you,' he said, distantly bowing.

Ripton gave him a commoner's obeisance; but getting to the door, the sense of the matter enlightened him.

'It's a duel, my lord?'

'No help for it, if his friends don't shut him up in Bedlam between this and to-morrow morning.'

Of all horrible things a duel was the worst in Ripton's imagination. He stood holding the handle of the door, revolving this last chapter of calamity suddenly opened where happiness had promised.

'A duel! but he won't, my lord,—he mustn't fight, my lord.'

'He must come on the ground,' said my lord, positively.

Ripton ejaculated unintelligible stuff. Finally Lord Mountfalcon said: 'I went out of my way, sir, in speaking to you. I saw you from the window. Your friend is mad. Deuced methodical, I admit, but mad. I have particular reasons to wish not to injure the young man, and if an apology is to be got out of him when we're on the ground, I'll take it, and we'll stop the damned scandal, if possible. You understand? I'm the insulted party, and I shall only require of him to use formal words of excuse to come to an amicable settlement. Let him just say he regrets it. Now, sir,' the nobleman spoke with considerable earnestness, 'should anything happen—I have the honour to be known to Mrs. Feverel—and I beg you will tell her. I very particularly desire you to let her know that I was not to blame.'

Mountfalcon rang the bell, and bowed him out. With this on his mind Ripton hurried down to those who were waiting in joyful trust at Raynham.

CHAPTER XLIV

THE LAST SCENE

THE watch consulted by Hippias alternately with his pulse, in occult calculation hideous to mark, said half-past eleven on the midnight. Adrian, wearing a composedly amused expression on his dimpled plump face,

—held slightly sideways, aloof from paper and pen,—sat writing at the library table. Round the baronet's chair, in a semicircle, were Lucy, Lady Blandish, Mrs. Doria, and Ripton, that very ill bird at Raynham. They were silent as those who question the flying minutes. Ripton had said that Richard was sure to come; but the feminine eyes reading him ever and anon, had gathered matter for disquietude, which increased as time sped. Sir Austin persisted in his habitual air of speculative repose.

Remote as he appeared from vulgar anxiety, he was the first to speak and betray his state.

'Pray, put up that watch. Impatience serves nothing,' he said, half-turning hastily to his brother behind him.

Hippias relinquished his pulse and mildly groaned: 'It's no nightmare, this!'

His remark was unheard, and the bearing of it remained obscure. Adrian's pen made a louder flourish on his manuscript; whether in commiseration or infernal glee, none might say.

'What are you writing?' the baronet inquired testily of Adrian, after a pause; twitched, it may be, by a sort of jealousy of the wise youth's coolness.

'Do I disturb you, sir?' rejoined Adrian. 'I am engaged on a portion of a Proposal for uniting the Empires and Kingdoms of Europe under one Paternal Head, on the model of the ever-to-be-admired and lamented Holy Roman.* This treats of the management of Youths and Maids, and of certain magisterial functions connected therewith. "It is decreed that these officers be all and every men of science," etc.' And Adrian cheerily drove his pen afresh.

Mrs. Doria took Lucy's hand, mutely addressing encouragement to her, and Lucy brought as much of a smile as she could command to reply with.

'I fear we must give him up to-night,' observed Lady Blandish.

'If he said he would come, he will come,' Sir Austin interjected. Between him and the lady there was something of a contest secretly going on. He was conscious that nothing save perfect success would now hold this self-emancipating mind. She had seen him through.

'He declared to me he would be certain to come,' said Ripton; but he could look at none of them as he said it, for he was growing aware that Richard might have deceived him, and was feeling like a black conspirator against their happiness. He determined to tell the baronet what he knew, if Richard did not come by twelve.

'What is the time?' he asked Hippias in a modest voice.

'Time for me to be in bed,' growled Hippias, as if everybody present had been treating him badly.

Mrs. Berry came in to apprise Lucy that she was wanted above. She quietly rose. Sir Austin kissed her on the forehead, saying: 'You had better not come down again, my child.' She kept her eyes on him. 'Oblige me by retiring for the night,' he added. Lucy shook their hands, and went out, accompanied by Mrs. Doria.

'This agitation will be bad for the child,' he said, speaking to himself aloud.

Lady Blandish remarked: 'I think she might just as well have returned. She will not sleep.'

'She will control herself for the child's sake.'

'You ask too much of her.'

'Of her, not,' he emphasized.

It was twelve o'clock when Hippias shut his watch, and said with vehemence: 'I'm convinced my circulation gradually and steadily decreases!'

'Going back to the pre-Harvey* period!' murmured Adrian as he wrote.

Sir Austin and Lady Blandish knew well that any com-

ment would introduce them to the interior of his machinery, the external view of which was sufficiently harrowing; so they maintained a discreet reserve. Taking it for
acquiescence in his deplorable condition, Hippias resumed despairingly: 'It's a fact. I've brought you to
see that. No one can be more moderate than I am, and
yet I get worse. My system is organically sound—I believe: I do every possible thing, and yet I get worse.
Nature never forgives! I'll go to bed.'

The Dyspepsy departed unconsoled.

Sir Austin took up his brother's thought: 'I suppose
nothing short of a miracle helps us when we have offended
her.'

'Nothing short of a quack satisfies us,' said Adrian,
applying wax to an envelope of official dimensions.

Ripton sat accusing his soul of cowardice while they
talked; haunted by Lucy's last look at him. He got up
his courage presently and went round to Adrian, who, after
a few whispered words, deliberately rose and accompanied
him out of the room, shrugging. When they had gone,
Lady Blandish said to the baronet: 'He is not coming.'

'To-morrow, then, if not to-night,' he replied. 'But I
say he will come to-night.'

'You do really wish to see him united to his wife?'

The question made the baronet raise his brows with
some displeasure.

'Can you ask me?'

'I mean,' said the ungenerous woman, 'your System
will require no further sacrifices from either of them?'

When he did answer, it was to say: 'I think her altogether a superior person. I confess I should scarcely have
hoped to find one like her.'

'Admit that your science does not accomplish everything.'

'No: it was presumptuous—beyond a certain point,' said
the baronet, meaning deep things.

Lady Blandish eyed him. 'Ah me!' she sighed, 'if we would always be true to our own wisdom!'

'You are very singular to-night, Emmeline.' Sir Austin stopped his walk in front of her.

In truth, was she not unjust? Here was an offending son freely forgiven. Here was a young woman of humble birth freely accepted into his family and permitted to stand upon her qualities. Who would have done more—or as much? This lady, for instance, had the case been hers, would have fought it. All the people of position that he was acquainted with would have fought it, and that without feeling it so peculiarly. But while the baronet thought this, he did not think of the exceptional education his son had received. He took the common ground of fathers, forgetting his System when it was absolutely on trial. False to his son it could not be said that he had been: false to his System he was. Others saw it plainly, but he had to learn his lesson by and by.

Lady Blandish gave him her face; then stretched her hand to the table, saying, 'Well! well!' She fingered a half-opened parcel lying there, and drew forth a little book she recognized. 'Ha! what is this?' she said.

'Benson returned it this morning,' he informed her. 'The stupid fellow took it away with him—by mischance, I am bound to believe.'

It was nothing other than the old Note-book. Lady Blandish turned over the leaves, and came upon the later jottings.

She read: 'A maker of Proverbs—what is he but a narrow mind the mouthpiece of narrower?'

'I do not agree with that,' she observed. He was in no humour for argument.

'Was your humility feigned when you wrote it?'

He merely said: 'Consider the sort of minds influenced by set sayings. A proverb is the half-way house to an

Idea, I conceive; and the majority rest there content:
can the keeper of such a house be flattered by his company?'

She felt her feminine intelligence swaying under him
again. There must be greatness in a man who could thus
speak of his own special and admirable aptitude.

Further she read, 'Which is the coward among us?—
He who sneers at the failings of Humanity!'

'Oh! that is true! How much I admire that!' cried the
dark-eyed dame as she beamed intellectual raptures.

Another Aphorism seemed closely to apply to him:
'There is no more grievous sight, as there is no greater
perversion, than a wise man at the mercy of his feelings.'

'He must have written it,' she thought, 'when he had
himself for an example—strange man that he is!'

Lady Blandish was still inclined to submission, though
decidedly insubordinate. She had once been fairly con-
quered: but if what she reverenced as a great mind could
conquer her, it must be a great man that should hold her
captive. The Autumn Primrose blooms for the loftiest
manhood; is a vindictive flower in lesser hands. Nevertheless Sir Austin had only to be successful, and this lady's
allegiance was his for ever. The trial was at hand.

She said again: 'He is not coming to-night,' and the
baronet, on whose visage a contemplative pleased look
had been rising for a minute past, quietly added: 'He is
come.'

Richard's voice was heard in the hall.

There was commotion all over the house at the return
of the young heir. Berry, seizing every possible occasion
to approach his Bessy now that her involuntary coldness
had enhanced her value—'Such is men!' as the soft
woman reflected—Berry ascended to her and delivered the
news in pompous tones and wheedling gestures. 'The
best word you've spoke for many a day,' says she, and

leaves him unfee'd, in an attitude, to hurry and pour bliss into Lucy's ears.

'Lord be praised!' she entered the adjoining room exclaiming, 'we 're goin' to be happy at last. They men have come to their senses. I could cry to your Virgin and kiss your Cross, you sweet!'

'Hush!' Lucy admonished her, and crooned over the child on her knees. The tiny open hands, full of sleep, clutched; the large blue eyes started awake; and his mother, all trembling and palpitating, knowing, but thirsting to hear it, covered him with her tresses, and tried to still her frame, and rocked, and sang low, interdicting even a whisper from bursting Mrs. Berry.

Richard had come. He was under his father's roof, in the old home that had so soon grown foreign to him. He stood close to his wife and child. He might embrace them both: and now the fulness of his anguish and the madness of the thing he had done smote the young man: now first he tasted hard earthly misery.

Had not God spoken to him in the tempest? Had not the finger of heaven directed him homeward? And he had come: here he stood: congratulations were thick in his ears: the cup of happiness was held to him, and he was invited to drink of it. Which was the dream? his work for the morrow, or this? But for a leaden load that he felt like a bullet in his breast, he might have thought the morrow with death sitting on it was the dream. Yes; he was awake. Now first the cloud of phantasms cleared away: he beheld his real life, and the colours of true human joy: and on the morrow perhaps he was to close his eyes on them. That leaden bullet dispersed all unrealities.

They stood about him in the hall, his father, Lady Blandish, Mrs. Doria, Adrian, Ripton; people who had known him long. They shook his hand: they gave him greetings he had never before understood the worth of or the meaning. Now that he did they mocked him. There was Mrs. Berry in the background bobbing, there was Martin Berry bowing, there was Tom Bakewell grinning. Somehow he loved the sight of these better.

'Ah, my old Penelope!' he said, breaking through the circle of his relatives to go to her. 'Tom! how are you?'

'Bless ye, my Mr. Richard,' whimpered Mrs. Berry, and whispered rosily, 'all's agreeable now. She's waiting up in bed for ye, like a new-born.'

The person who betrayed most agitation was Mrs. Doria. She held close to him, and eagerly studied his face and every movement, as one accustomed to masks. 'You are pale, Richard?' He pleaded exhaustion. 'What detained you, dear?' 'Business,' he said. She drew him imperiously apart from the others. 'Richard! is it over?' He asked what she meant. 'The dreadful duel, Richard.' He looked darkly. 'Is it over? is it done, Richard?' Getting no immediate answer, she continued—and such was her agitation that the words were shaken by pieces from her mouth: 'Don't pretend not to understand me, Richard! Is it over? Are you going to die the death of my child—Clare's death? Is not one in a family enough? Think of your dear young wife—we love her so!—your child!—your father! Will you kill us all?'

Mrs. Doria had chanced to overhear a trifle of Ripton's communication to Adrian, and had built thereon with the dark forces of a stricken soul.

Wondering how this woman could have divined it, Richard calmly said: 'It's arranged—the matter you allude to.'

'Indeed! truly, dear?'

'Yes.'

'Tell me'—but he broke away from her, saying: 'You shall hear the particulars to-morrow,' and she, not alive to double meaning just then, allowed him to leave her.

He had eaten nothing for twelve hours, and called for food, but he would take only dry bread and claret, which was served on a tray in the library. He said, without any show of feeling, that he must eat before he saw the younger hope of Raynham: so there he sat, breaking bread, and eating great mouthfuls, and washing them down with wine, talking of what they would. His father's studious mind felt itself years behind him, he was so completely altered. He had the precision of speech, the bearing of a man of thirty. Indeed he had all that the necessity for cloaking an infinite misery gives. But let things be as they might, he was *there*. For one night in his life Sir Austin's perspective of the future was bounded by the night.

'Will you go to your wife now?' he had asked, and Richard had replied with a strange indifference. The baronet thought it better that their meeting should be private, and sent word for Lucy to wait upstairs. The others perceived that father and son should now be left alone. Adrian went up to him, and said: 'I can no longer witness this painful sight, so Good-night, Sir Famish! You may cheat yourself into the belief that you've made a meal, but depend upon it your progeny—and it threatens to be numerous—will cry aloud and rue the day. Nature never forgives! A lost dinner can never be replaced! Good-night, my dear boy. And here—oblige me by taking this,' he handed Richard the enormous envelope containing what he had written that evening. 'Credentials!' he exclaimed humorously, slapping Richard on the shoulder. Ripton heard also the words 'propagator—species,' but had no idea of their import. The wise youth looked: You see we've made matters all right for you here, and quitted the room on that unusual gleam of earnestness.

Richard shook his hand, and Ripton's. Then Lady Blandish said her good-night, praising Lucy, and promising to pray for their mutual happiness. The two men

who knew what was hanging over him, spoke together
outside. Ripton was for getting a positive assurance that
the duel would not be fought, but Adrian said: 'Time
enough to-morrow. He's safe enough while he's here.
I'll stop it to-morrow': ending with banter of Ripton and
allusions to his adventures with Miss Random, which
must, Adrian said, have led him into many affairs of the
sort. Certainly Richard was there, and while he was there
he must be safe. So thought Ripton, and went to his bed.
Mrs. Doria deliberated likewise, and likewise thought
him safe while he was there. For once in her life she
thought it better not to trust to her instinct, for fear of
useless disturbance where peace should be. So she said not
a syllable of it to her brother. She only looked more
deeply into Richard's eyes, as she kissed him, praising
Lucy. 'I have found a second daughter in her, dear.
Oh! may you both be happy!'

They all praised Lucy, now. His father commenced the
moment they were alone.

'Poor Helen! Your wife has been a great comfort to
her, Richard. I think Helen must have sunk without her.
So lovely a young person, possessing mental faculty, and
a conscience for her duties, I have never before met.'

He wished to gratify his son by these eulogies of Lucy,
and some hours back he would have succeeded. Now it
had the contrary effect.

'You compliment me on my choice, sir?'

Richard spoke sedately, but the irony was perceptible,
and he could speak no other way, his bitterness was so
intense.

'I think you very fortunate,' said his father.

Sensitive to tone and manner as he was, his ebullition of
paternal feeling was frozen. Richard did not approach
him. He leaned against the chimney-piece, glancing at
the floor, and lifting his eyes only when he spoke. Fort-

unate! very fortunate! As he revolved his later history, and remembered how clearly he had seen that his father must love Lucy if he but knew her, and remembered his efforts to persuade her to come with him, a sting of miserable rage blackened his brain. But could he blame that gentle soul? Whom could he blame? Himself? Not utterly. His father? Yes, and no. The blame was here, the blame was there: it was everywhere and nowhere, and the young man cast it on the Fates, and looked angrily at heaven, and grew reckless.

'Richard,' said his father, coming close to him, 'it is late to-night. I do not wish Lucy to remain in expectation longer, or I should have explained myself to you thoroughly, and I think—or at least hope—you would have justified me. I had cause to believe that you had not only violated my confidence, but grossly deceived me. It was not so, I now know. I was mistaken. Much of our misunderstanding has resulted from that mistake. But you were married—a boy: you knew nothing of the world, little of yourself. To save you in after-life—for there is a period when mature men and women who have married young are more impelled to temptation than in youth,—though not so exposed to it,—to save you, I say, I decreed that you should experience self-denial and learn something of your fellows of both sexes, before settling into a state that must have been otherwise precarious, however excellent the woman who is your mate. My System with you would have been otherwise imperfect, and you would have felt the effects of it. It is over now. You are a man. The dangers to which your nature was open are, I trust, at an end. I wish you to be happy, and I give you both my blessing, and pray God to conduct and strengthen you both.'

Sir Austin's mind was unconscious of not having spoken devoutly. True or not, his words were idle to his son: his talk of dangers over, and happiness, mockery.

Richard coldly took his father's extended hand.

'We will go to her,' said the baronet. 'I will leave you at her door.'

Not moving: looking fixedly at his father with a hard face on which the colour rushed, Richard said: 'A husband who has been unfaithful to his wife may go to her there, sir?'

It was horrible, it was cruel: Richard knew that. He wanted no advice on such a matter, having fully resolved what to do. Yesterday he would have listened to his father, and blamed himself alone, and done what was to be done humbly before God and her: now in the reck- lessness of his misery he had as little pity for any other soul as for his own. Sir Austin's brows were deep drawn down.

'What did you say, Richard?'

Clearly his intelligence had taken it, but this—the worst he could hear—this that he had dreaded once and doubted, and smoothed over, and cast aside—could it be?

Richard said: 'I told you all but the very words when we last parted. What else do you think would have kept me from her?'

Angered at his callous aspect, his father cried: 'What brings you to her now?'

'That will be between us two,' was the reply.

Sir Austin fell into his chair. Meditation was impossible. He spoke from a wrathful heart: 'You will not dare to take her without——'

'No, sir,' Richard interrupted him, 'I shall not. Have no fear.'

'Then you did not love your wife?'

'Did I not?' A smile passed faintly over Richard's face.

'Did you care so much for this—this other person?'

'So much? If you ask me whether I had affection for her, I can say I had none.'

O base human nature! Then how? then why? A thousand questions rose in the baronet's mind. Bessy Berry could have answered them every one.

'Poor child! poor child!' he apostrophized Lucy, pacing the room. Thinking of her, knowing her deep love for his son—her true forgiving heart—it seemed she should be spared this misery.

He proposed to Richard to spare her. Vast is the distinction between women and men in this one sin, he said, and supported it with physical and moral citations. His argument carried him so far, that to hear him one would have imagined he thought the sin in men small indeed. His words were idle.

'She must know it,' said Richard sternly. 'I will go to her now, sir, if you please.'

Sir Austin detained him, expostulated, contradicted himself, confounded his principles, made nonsense of all his theories. He could not induce his son to waver in his resolve. Ultimately, their good-night being interchanged, he understood that the happiness of Raynham depended on Lucy's mercy. He had no fears of her sweet heart, but it was a strange thing to have come to. On which should the accusation fall—on science, or on human nature?

He remained in the library pondering over the question, at times breathing contempt for his son, and again seized with unwonted suspicion of his own wisdom: troubled, much to be pitied, even if he deserved that blow from his son which had plunged him into wretchedness.

Richard went straight to Tom Bakewell, roused the heavy sleeper, and told him to have his mare saddled and waiting at the park gates East within an hour. Tom's nearest approach to a hero was to be a faithful slave to his master, and in doing this he acted to his conception of that high and glorious character. He got up and heroically dashed his head into cold water. 'She shall be ready, sir,' he nodded.

'Tom! if you don't see me back here at Raynham, your money will go on being paid to you.'

'Rather see you than the money, Mr. Richard,' said Tom.

'And you will always watch and see no harm comes to her, Tom.'

'Mrs. Richard, sir?' Tom stared. 'God bless me, Mr. Richard——'

'No questions. You'll do what I say.'

'Ay, sir; that I will. Did 'n Isle o' Wight.'

The very name of the Island shocked Richard's blood, and he had to walk up and down before he could knock at Lucy's door. That infamous conspiracy to which he owed his degradation and misery scarce left him the feelings of a man when he thought of it.

The soft beloved voice responded to his knock. He opened the door, and stood before her. Lucy was half-way toward him. In the moment that passed ere she was in his arms, he had time to observe the change in her. He had left her a girl: he beheld a woman—a blooming woman: for pale at first, no sooner did she see him than the colour was rich and deep on her face and neck and bosom half shown through the loose dressing-robe, and the sense of her exceeding beauty made his heart thump and his eyes swim.

'My darling!' each cried, and they clung together, and her mouth was fastened on his.

They spoke no more. His soul was drowned in her kiss. Supporting her, whose strength was gone, he, almost as weak as she, hung over her, and clasped her closer, closer, till they were as one body, and in the oblivion her lips put upon him he was free to the bliss of her embrace. Heaven granted him that. He placed her in a chair and knelt at her feet with both arms around her. Her bosom heaved; her eyes never quitted him: their light as the light on a rolling wave. This young creature, commonly so frank and straightforward, was broken with bashfulness in her husband's arms—womanly bashfulness on the torrent of womanly love; tenfold more seductive than the bashfulness of girlhood. Terrible tenfold the loss of her seemed now, as distantly—far on the horizon of memory—the fatal truth returned to him.

Lose her? lose this? He looked up as if to ask God to confirm it.

The same sweet blue eyes! the eyes that he had often seen in the dying glories of evening; on him they dwelt, shifting, and fluttering, and glittering, but constant: the light of them as the light on a rolling wave.

And true to him! true, good, glorious, as the angels of heaven! And his she was! a woman—his wife! The temptation to take her, and be dumb, was all powerful: the wish to die against her bosom so strong as to be the prayer of his vital forces. Again he strained her to him, but this time it was as a robber grasps priceless treasure—with exultation and defiance. One instant of this. Lucy, whose pure tenderness had now surmounted the first wild passion of their meeting, bent back her head from her surrendered body, and said almost voicelessly, her underlids wistfully quivering: 'Come and see him— baby'; and then in great hope of the happiness she was going to give her husband, and share with him, and in tremour and doubt of what his feelings would be, she blushed, and her brows worked: she tried to throw off the strangeness of a year of separation, misunderstanding, and uncertainty.

'Darling! come and see him. He is here.' She spoke more clearly, though no louder.

Richard had released her, and she took his hand, and he suffered himself to be led to the other side of the bed.

His heart began rapidly throbbing at the sight of a little rosy-curtained cot covered with lace like milky summer cloud.

It seemed to him he would lose his manhood if he looked on that child's face.

'Stop!' he cried suddenly.

Lucy turned first to him, and then to her infant, fearing it should have been disturbed.

'Lucy, come back.'

'What is it, darling?' said she, in alarm at his voice and the grip he had unwittingly given her hand.

O God! what an Ordeal was this! that to-morrow he must face death, perhaps die and be torn from his darling—his wife and his child; and that ere he went forth, ere he could dare to see his child and lean his head reproachfully on his young wife's breast—for the last time, it might be—he must stab her to the heart, shatter the image she held of him.

'Lucy!' She saw him wrenched with agony, and her own face took the whiteness of his—she bending forward to him, all her faculties strung to hearing.

He held her two hands that she might look on him and not spare the horrible wound he was going to lay open to her eyes.

'Lucy. Do you know why I came to you to-night?'

She moved her lips repeating his words.

'Lucy. Have you guessed why I did not come before?'

Her head shook widened eyes.

'Lucy. I did not come because I was not worthy of my wife! Do you understand?'

'Darling,' she faltered plaintively, and hung crouching under him, 'what have I done to make you angry with me?'

'O beloved!' cried he, the tears bursting out of his eyes. 'O beloved!' was all he could say, kissing her hands passionately.

She waited, reassured, but in terror.

'Lucy. I stayed away from you—I could not come to you, because . . . I dared not come to you, my wife, my beloved! I could not come because I was a coward: because—hear me—this was the reason: I have broken my marriage oath.'

Again her lips moved. She caught at a dim fleshless meaning in them. 'But you love me? Richard! My husband! you love me?'

'Yes. I have never loved, I never shall love, woman but you.'

'Darling! Kiss me.'

'Have you understood what I have told you?'

'Kiss me,' she said.

He did not join lips. 'I have come to you to-night to ask your forgiveness.'

Her answer was: 'Kiss me.'

'Can you forgive a man so base?'

'But you love me, Richard?'

'Yes: that I can say before God. I love you, and I have betrayed you, and am unworthy of you—not worthy to touch your hand, to kneel at your feet, to breathe the same air with you.'

Her eyes shone brilliantly. 'You love me! you love me, darling!' And as one who has sailed through dark fears into daylight, she said: 'My husband! my darling! you will never leave me? We never shall be parted again?'

He drew his breath painfully. To smooth her face growing rigid with fresh fears at his silence, he met her mouth. That kiss in which she spoke what her soul had to say, calmed her, and she smiled happily from it, and in her manner reminded him of his first vision of her on the summer morning in the field of the meadow-sweet. He held her to him, and thought then of a holier picture: of Mother

and Child: of the sweet wonders of life she had made
real to him.

Had he not absolved his conscience? At least the pangs
to come made him think so. He now followed her leading
hand. Lucy whispered: 'You mustn't disturb him—
mustn't touch him, dear!' and with dainty fingers drew
off the covering to the little shoulder. One arm of the
child was out along the pillow; the small hand open. His
baby-mouth was pouted full; the dark lashes of his eyes
seemed to lie on his plump cheeks. Richard stooped lower
down to him, hungering for some movement as a sign that
he lived. Lucy whispered. 'He sleeps like you, Richard
—one arm under his head.' Great wonder, and the stir of
a grasping tenderness was in Richard. He breathed quick
and soft, bending lower, till Lucy's curls, as she nestled
and bent with him, rolled on the crimson quilt of the cot.
A smile went up the plump cheeks: forthwith the bud of a
mouth was in rapid motion. The young mother whispered,
blushing: 'He's dreaming of me,' and the simple words
did more than Richard's eyes to make him see what was.
Then Lucy began to hum and buzz sweet baby-language,
and some of the tiny fingers stirred, and he made as if to
change his cosy position, but reconsidered, and deferred
it, with a peaceful little sigh. Lucy whispered: 'He is
such a big fellow. Oh! when you see him awake he is
so like you, Richard.'

He did not hear her immediately: it seemed a bit of
heaven dropped there in his likeness: the more human
the fact of the child grew the more heavenly it seemed.
His son! his child! should he ever see him awake? At
the thought, he took the words that had been spoken, and
started from the dream he had been in. 'Will he wake
soon, Lucy?'

'Oh no! not yet, dear: not for hours. I would have
kept him awake for you, but he was *so* sleepy.'

Richard stood back from the cot. He thought that if
he saw the eyes of his boy, and had him once on his heart,
he never should have force to leave him. Then he looked
down on him, again struggled to tear himself away. Two
natures warred in his bosom, or it may have been the
Magian Conflict still going on. He had come to see his
child once and to make peace with his wife before it should
be too late. Might he not stop with them? Might he
not relinquish that devilish pledge? Was not divine
happiness here offered to him?—If foolish Ripton had not
delayed to tell him of his interview with Mountfalcon all
might have been well. But pride said it was impossible.
And then injury spoke. For why was he thus base and
spotted to the darling of his love? A mad pleasure in the
prospect of wreaking vengeance on the villain who had
laid the trap for him, once more blackened his brain. If
he would stay he could not. So he resolved, throwing the
burden on Fate. The struggle was over, but oh, the pain!
Lucy beheld the tears streaming hot from his face on
the child's cot. She marvelled at such excess of emotion.
But when his chest heaved, and the extremity of mortal
anguish appeared to have seized him, her heart sank, and
she tried to get him in her arms. He turned away from
her and went to the window. A half-moon was over the lake.

'Look!' he said, 'do you remember our rowing there
one night, and we saw the shadow of the cypress? I wish
I could have come early to-night that we might have had
another row, and I have heard you sing there!'

'Darling!' said she, 'will it make you happier if I go
with you now? I will.'

'No, Lucy. Lucy, you are brave!'

'Oh, no! that I'm not. I thought so once. I know I
am not now.'

'Yes! to have lived—the child on your heart—and
never to have uttered a complaint!—you are brave. O

my Lucy! my wife! you that have made me man! I
called you a coward. I remember it. I was the coward—
I the wretched vain fool! Darling! I am going to leave
you now. You are brave, and you will bear it. Listen:
in two days, or three, I may be back—back for good, if
you will accept me. Promise me to go to bed quietly.
Kiss the child for me, and tell him his father has seen
him. He will learn to speak soon. Will he soon speak,
Lucy?'

Dreadful suspicion kept her speechless; she could only
clutch one arm of his with both her hands.

'Going?' she presently gasped.

'For two or three days. No more—I hope.'

'To-night?'

'Yes. Now.'

'Going now? my husband!' her faculties abandoned her.

'You will be brave, my Lucy!'

'Richard! my darling husband! Going? What is it
takes you from me?' But questioning no further, she
fell on her knees, and cried piteously to him to stay—not
to leave them. Then she dragged him to the little sleeper,
and urged him to pray by his side, and he did, but rose
abruptly from his prayer when he had muttered a few
broken words—she praying on with tight-strung nerves,
in the faith that what she said to the interceding Mother
above would be stronger than human hands on him.
Nor could he go while she knelt there.

And he wavered. He had not reckoned on her terrible
suffering. She came to him, quiet. 'I knew you would
remain.' And taking his hand, innocently fondling it:
'Am I so changed from her he loved? You will not leave
me, dear?' But dread returned, and the words quavered
as she spoke them.

He was almost vanquished by the loveliness of her womanhood. She drew his hand to her heart, and strained

it there under one breast. 'Come: lie on my heart,' she murmured with a smile of holy sweetness.

He wavered more, and drooped to her, but summoning the powers of hell, kissed her suddenly, cried the words of parting, and hurried to the door. It was over in an instant. She cried out his name, clinging to him wildly, and was adjured to be brave, for he would be dishonoured if he did not go. Then she was shaken off.

Mrs. Berry was aroused by an unusual prolonged wailing of the child, which showed that no one was comforting it, and failing to get any answer to her applications for admittance, she made bold to enter. There she saw Lucy, the child in her lap, sitting on the floor senseless:—she had taken it from its sleep and tried to follow her husband with it as her strongest appeal to him, and had fainted.

'Oh my! oh my!' Mrs. Berry moaned, 'and I just now thinkin' they was so happy!'

Warming and caressing the poor infant, she managed by degrees to revive Lucy, and heard what had brought her to that situation.

'Go to his father,' said Mrs. Berry. 'Ta-te-tiddle-te-heighty-O! Go, my love, and every horse in Raynham shall be out after 'm. This is what men brings us to! Heighty-oighty-iddlety-Ah! Or you take blessed baby, and I'll go.'

The baronet himself knocked at the door. 'What is this?' he said. 'I heard a noise and a step descend.'

'It's Mr. Richard have gone, Sir Austin! have gone from his wife and babe! Rum-te-um-te-iddledy—Oh, my goodness! what sorrow's come on us!' and Mrs. Berry wept, and sang to baby, and baby cried vehemently, and Lucy, sobbing, took him and danced him and sang to him with drawn lips and tears dropping over him. And if the Scientific Humanist to the day of his death forgets

the sight of those two poor true women jigging on their
wretched hearts to calm the child, he must have very
little of the human in him.

There was no more sleep for Raynham that night.

CHAPTER XLV

LADY BLANDISH TO AUSTIN WENTWORTH

'His ordeal is over. I have just come from his room and
seen him bear the worst that could be. Return at once—
he has asked for you. I can hardly write intelligibly, but
I will tell you what we know.

'Two days after the dreadful night when he left us, his
father heard from Ralph Morton. Richard had fought a
duel in France*with Lord Mountfalcon, and was lying
wounded at a hamlet on the coast. His father started
immediately with his poor wife, and I followed in company
with his aunt and his child. The wound was not dangerous. He was shot in the side somewhere, but the ball
injured no vital part. We thought all would be well.
Oh! how sick I am of theories, and Systems, and the pretensions of men! There was his son lying all but dead,
and the man was still unconvinced of the folly he had been
guilty of. I could hardly bear the sight of his composure.
I shall hate the name of Science till the day I die. Give
me nothing but commonplace unpretending people!

'They were at a wretched French cabaret, smelling
vilely, where we still remain, and the people try as much
as they can do to compensate for our discomforts by their
kindness. The French poor people are very considerate
where they see suffering. I will say that for them. The
doctors had not allowed his poor Lucy to go near him.

She sat outside his door, and none of us dared disturb her. That was a sight for Science. His father and myself, and Mrs. Berry, were the only ones permitted to wait on him, and whenever we came out, there she sat, not speaking a word—for she had been told it would endanger his life—but she looked such awful eagerness. She had the sort of eye I fancy mad persons have. I was sure her reason was going. We did everything we could think of to comfort her. A bed was made up for her and her meals were brought to her there. Of course there was no getting her to eat. What do you suppose *his* alarm was fixed on? He absolutely said to me—but I have not patience to repeat his words. He thought her to blame for not *commanding* herself for the sake of her *maternal duties*. He had absolutely an idea of insisting that she should make an effort to suckle the child. I shall love that Mrs. Berry to the end of my days. I really believe she has *twice* the sense of any of us—Science and all. She asked him plainly if he wished to poison the child, and then he gave way, but with a bad grace.

'Poor man! perhaps I am hard on him. I remember that you said Richard had done wrong. Yes; well, that may be. But his father eclipsed his wrong in a greater wrong—a crime, or quite as bad; for if he deceived himself in the belief that he was acting righteously in separating husband and wife, and exposing his son as he did, I can only say that there are some who are worse than people who deliberately commit *crimes*. No doubt Science will benefit by it. They kill little animals for the sake of Science.

'We have with us Doctor Bairam, and a French physician from Dieppe, a very skilful man. It was he who told us where the real danger lay. We thought all would be well. A week had passed, and no fever supervened. We told Richard that his wife was coming to him, and he could bear to hear it. I went to her and began to circumlocute, thinking she listened—she had the same eager look. When I told her she might go in with me to see her dear husband, her features did not change. M. Després, who held her pulse at the time, told me, in a whisper, it was cerebral fever—brain fever* coming on. We have talked of her since. I noticed that though she did not seem to understand me, her bosom heaved, and she appeared to be trying to repress it, and choke something. I am sure now, from what I know of her character, that she—even in the approaches of delirium—was preventing herself from crying out. Her last hold of reason was a thought for Richard. It was against a creature like this that we plotted! I have the comfort of knowing that I did my share in helping to destroy her. Had she seen her husband a day or two before—but no! there was a new *System* to interdict that! Or had she not so violently controlled her nature as she did, I believe she might have been saved.

'He said once of a man, that his conscience was a coxcomb. Will you believe that when he saw his son's wife—poor victim! lying delirious, he could not even then see his error. You said he wished to take Providence out of God's hands. His mad self-deceit would not leave him. I am positive, that while he was standing over her, he was blaming her for not having considered the child. Indeed he made a remark to me that it was unfortunate—"disastrous," I think he said—that the child should have to be fed by hand. I dare say it is. All I pray is that this young child may be saved from him. I cannot bear to see him look on it. He does not spare himself *bodily* fatigue—but what is that? that is the vulgarest form of love. I know what you will say. You will say I have lost all charity, and I have. But I should not feel so, Austin, if I could be *quite sure* that he is an altered man even now the blow has struck him. He is reserved and simple in his speech, and his grief is evident, but I have doubts. He heard her while she was senseless call him cruel and harsh, and cry that she had suffered, and I saw then his mouth contract as if he had been touched. Perhaps, when he thinks, his mind will be clearer, but what he has done cannot be undone. I do not imagine he will abuse women any more. The doctor called her a "forte et belle jeune femme":* and *he* said she was as noble a soul as ever God moulded clay upon. A noble soul "forte et belle!" She lies upstairs. If he can look on her and not see his *sin*, I almost fear God will never enlighten him.

'She died five days after she had been removed. The shock had utterly deranged her. I was with her. She died very quietly, breathing her last breath without pain— asking for no one—a death I should like to die.

'Her cries at one time were dreadfully loud. She screamed that she was "drowning in fire," and that her husband would not come to her to save her. We deadened the sound as much as we could, but it was impossible to prevent Richard from hearing. He knew her voice, and it produced an effect like fever on him. Whenever she called he answered. You could not hear them without weeping. Mrs. Berry sat with her, and I sat with him, and his father moved from one to the other.

'But the trial for us came when she was gone. How to communicate it to Richard—or whether to do so at all! His father consulted with us. We were quite decided that it would be madness to breathe it while he was in that state. I can admit now—as things have turned out—we were wrong. His father left us—I believe he spent the time in prayer—and then leaning on me, he went to Richard, and said in so many words, that his Lucy was no more. I thought it must kill him. He listened, and smiled. I never saw a smile so sweet and so sad. He said he had seen her die, as if he had passed through his suffering a long time ago. He shut his eyes. I could see by the motion

of his eyeballs up that he was straining his sight to some
inner heaven.—I cannot go on.

'I think Richard is safe. Had we postponed the tidings,
till he came to his clear senses, it must have killed him.
His father was right for once, then. But if he has saved
his son's body, he has given the death-blow to his heart.
Richard will never be what he promised.

'A letter found on his clothes tells us the origin of the
quarrel. I have had an interview with Lord M. this morning. I cannot say I think him exactly to blame: Richard
forced him to fight. At least I do not select him the foremost for blame. He was deeply and sincerely affected by
the calamity he has caused. Alas! he was only an instrument. Your poor aunt is utterly prostrate and talks
strange things of her daughter's death. She is only happy
in *drudging*. Dr. Bairam says we must under any circumstances keep her employed. Whilst she is doing something,
she can chat freely, but the moment her hands are not
occupied she gives me an idea that she is going into a fit.

'We expect the dear child's uncle to-day. Mr. Thompson is here. I have taken him upstairs to look at her.
That poor young man has a true heart.

'Come at once. You will not be in time to see her. She
will lie at Raynham. If you could you would see an angel.
He sits by her side for hours. I can give you no description
of her beauty.

'You will not delay, I know, dear Austin, and I want
you, for your presence will make me more charitable than
I find it possible to be. Have you noticed the expression
in the eyes of blind men? That is just how Richard looks,
as he lies there silent in his bed—striving to image her on
his brain.'

THE END

NOTES

3 *'The Pilgrim's Scrip'*: there was, in 1859, no such book, though Meredith published a volume with that title in 1888. Throughout *The Ordeal of Richard Feverel* Meredith 'quotes' from what was initially a non-existent source, which is imagined to be a collection of thoughts, aphorisms, epigrams, etc., composed and compiled by Sir Austin Feverel.

4 *He had a wife, and he had a friend*: Meredith's first wife, Mary Ellen Peacock Nicolls, eloped, a year before the publication of *Feverel*, with their 'friend', the painter Henry Wallis (see Chronology).

5 *they played Rizzio and Mary together*: that is, Mary Queen of Scots (Mary Stuart, 1542–87), daughter of James V of Scotland, and David Rizzio, her Italian secretary, musician, and lover. Rizzio was eventually murdered, in Mary's presence, by her husband Lord Darnley (Henry Stuart).

love-poem of Diaper's: Sandoe's poetry, Richard's, and most of the other verses attributed to characters in the book, are Meredith's own compositions (like 'The Pilgrim's Scrip'). Mary was of course the name of his first wife, and Sandoe occupies a place in the story roughly equivalent to that of Henry Wallis (see note to p. 4, above) in Meredith's life.

Timon: a misanthropical citizen of Athens who lived about the time of the Peloponnesian War; the subject of one of Lucian's finest Dialogues, as well as of Shakespeare's *Timon of Athens* (1607–8).

8 *caudles*: warm drinks, usually composed of a thin gruel mixed with wine or ale, sweetened and spiced.

10 *epicurean*: devoted to sensual pleasures, with sensitive and discriminating taste in food and wine; after the Greek philosopher Epicurus (third century BC).

Gibbon and Horace: Edward Gibbon (1737–94), English historian, and author of *The History of the Decline and Fall of the Roman Empire* (1776–88); Quintus Horatius Flaccus, Roman poet of the first century BC.

15 *Prince Turnus*: a king of the Rituli, a brave warrior who fought against Aeneas in a dispute over a woman and was killed by him in single combat (Book XII of Virgil's *Aeneid*, first century BC).

Pallas: that is, Athene, the Greek goddess of wisdom, industry, and war.

16 *free-trade farmer*: a farmer who believes that trade and commerce should be left to follow their natural courses, without interference of customs duties, tariffs, or bounties. The issue of free trade was hotly disputed in the 1830s, before Peel repealed the Corn Laws (see Introduction, p. xi).

22 *Bedlamite*: lunatic—as, for example, an inmate of the Bedlam asylum.

tinker: an itinerant mender of household utensils.

24 *mort*: here meaning a great deal.

collier: a ship employed in transporting coal.

Paul: early Christian missionary and author of several New Testament epistles.

pilkins: probably dialect for 'spillikins', long sticks.

30 *Zoroaster*: the Greek form of Zarathustra, the founder of the Magian (dualistic) system of religion; probably an historical personage who has become the subject of legends—a Persian believed to have lived in the sixth century BC.

Fire-worshippers: the Persians of the old religion, who maintained their resistance to the conquering Muslims, were fire-worshippers. Their story is told, for example, in *Lalla Rookh* (1817), a popular series of Oriental tales in verse, linked together by a story in prose, by the Irish poet Thomas Moore (1779–1852).

Guido Fawkes: that is, Guy Fawkes (1570–1606), a conspirator in the unsuccessful Gunpowder Plot fomented by Catholics to blow up the British Houses of Parliament in 1605.

34 *cut his lucky*: that is, taken off, thus 'cutting' the possible cost to himself.

41 *Magians*: wise men; possibly used here in the sense of magicians. Later references in the novel to the 'Magian conflict' refer to the Zoroastrian system of religion (see note to p. 30, above), in which a dualistic conflict between the forces of good and evil, light and darkness, is thought to be constantly waged in the world, centred in man, who is conceived as originally having been created a free agent.

42 *Promethean eagle*: after Prometheus, who in Greek mythology made mankind out of clay. When Zeus oppressed man and deprived him of fire, Prometheus stole it from heaven. In revenge, Zeus caused Prometheus to be chained to a rock, where among other torments a vulture fed on his liver. The name Promethean was later given to a contrivance used, before the introduction of lucifer matches, to obtain fire.

43 *Robin Hood and King Richard*: Robin Hood is the legendary outlaw. If he existed at all, he may have been a contemporary and friend of Richard I ('Cœur de Lion'; reigned 1189–99).

46 *anchorites*: religious recluses, or hermits.

48 *Coleridge's capital simile*: it is difficult to determine exactly which simile Meredith had in mind, but possibly it was one from 'Youth and Age' (1823) by Samuel Taylor Coleridge (1772–1834):

> Dew-drops are the gems of morning,
> But the tears of mournful eve!

Another passage in the same poem characterizes old age as a

> poor night-related guest,
> That may not rudely be dismist;
> Yet hath outstay'd his welcome while . . .

49 *Latude's Escape*: Jean-Henri Latude (1725–1805) was famous for having escaped from the Bastille.

Jonathan Wild: Fielding's novel *Jonathan Wild the Great* (1743).

50 *a Julian, or a Caracalla: a Constantine, or a Nero*: Julian the Apostate, Roman emperor, AD 361–3; Marcus Aurelius Antoninus Caracalla, Roman emperor, AD 186–217;

Constantine the Great, Roman emperor, AD 306–37; Nero Claudius Caesar Drusus Germanicus, Roman emperor, AD 54–68.

51 *Scipio Africanus against the Punic elephants*: a reference to the Roman conqueror of Spain and of Hannibal; the latter employed elephants in his battles against the Romans with great effect during the Punic Wars (third century BC) but was finally defeated at Carthage, in North Africa, by Scipio Africanus (236–184 BC).

53 *celebrated philosopher*: this is Jean-Jacques Rousseau (1712–78), who tells the story in Book II of his posthumous *Confessions*. The girl's name was Marion.

60 *That song about the Viffendeer, etc.*: the vivandière is undoubtedly Marie, heroine of Donizetti's comic opera *La Fille du Regiment* (1840). Set to a libretto by J. H. Vernoy de Saint-Georges, it provided a great vehicle, in London, for Jenny Lind. The girl in the opera is a foundling who follows troops on the march with food for sale and is raised by the French regiment while it is campaigning in the Tyrol. Marie is eventually discovered by her mother, a marquise. The song in question is Marie's jaunty '*Chacun le sait, chacun le dit*', although London may have known it in Italian as '*Ciascun lo dice, ciascun lo sai*'. The scandalous item she is described as wearing is trousers—part of a soldier's uniform. The vivandière also appears in the Waterloo chapters of Stendhal's *La Chartreuse de Parme* (1839), which may have provided some of the inspiration, background, and setting for Donizetti's opera.

68 *Doric*: here meaning a rustic, broad dialect, such as that of the north of England, and Scotland.

hoies: probably a corruption of hoise, meaning tackle or other mechanical appliance.

lucifers: see note to p. 42, above; a friction match usually made of a splint of wood tipped with an inflammable substance ignited on a prepared surface.

74 *goatsucker owl*: a bird supposed to suck the udders of goats.

76 *the old ballad*: a reference to the nursery rhyme

> Robin and Richard were two pretty men.
> They lay in bed till the clock struck ten.

81 *Scythians*: Scythia was an ancient region extending over a large part of what is now European and Asiatic Russia.

82 *Amor*: love.

88 *juice of the juniper*: the juniper yields a volatile oil or juice often used in medicine, in those days, as a stimulant; it is one of the ingredients of gin.

90 *Chatham*: William Pitt, first Earl of Chatham (1708–78), a great Whig statesman and administrator, among other things remembered for the lofty and impassioned eloquence of his parliamentary oratory.

105 *The Titans had an easier task in storming Olympus*: the Titans, in Greek mythology, were the sons and daughters of Ge. They deposed Uranus, and raised Cronos to the throne. Subsequently Zeus revolted against Cronos, and with the help of thunder and lightning hurled the Titans out of heaven. Olympus was regarded as the home of the gods. It was (and is) a lofty mountain standing at the eastern extremity of the range that divided Greece from ancient Macedonia.

109 *Cœlebite search*: after *Cœlebs in Search of a Wife* (1809), a novel by Hannah More (1745–1833); a collection of social precepts and sketches, strung together on the thread of the hero's search for a young woman who possesses the qualities stipulated by his departed parents. Sir Austin, in other words, is looking for the 'perfect' daughter-in-law.

116 *osiers*: willows.

117 *Ferdinand and Miranda*: the romantic young lovers in Shakespeare's *The Tempest* (1611–12) who meet and are betrothed on an island.

Bermoothes: the Bermoothes, in *The Tempest* (I,ii), are the Bermuda islands, discovered by the Spanish in 1509, rediscovered by the English in 1609. It is generally thought that Shakespeare composed most of *The Tempest* in 1611.

Ariel: one of Prospero's ardent spirits in *The Tempest*. Ariel was formerly imprisoned by the witch Sycorax, but released by Prospero through his knowledge of magic. Meredith suggests here that Lucy and Richard are falling under a romantic spell.

118 *Adam, his rib*: that is, Eve. God created her out of one of Adam's ribs, taken from him while he was sleeping; see Genesis, 3:20.

Caliban: son of the witch Sycorax in *The Tempest*, but nonetheless subject to Prospero's powers; a misshapen monster. Caliban is the sole inhabitant of the island setting of the play before the Italians arrive, and remains its sole inhabitant after they leave.

119 *Prospero*: the point is that Prospero, in *The Tempest*, has magical powers (see notes to pp. 117 and 118, above) which can be used to reconcile all differences and make everyone happy; Sir Austin is no Prospero.

121 *Hesper*: that is, Venus, the evening (and morning) star; named for the Greek goddess of beauty and love.

127 *the Borgia's*: the singular suggests Lucrezia Borgia (1480–1519), a great beauty, who had married three times by the age of twenty-two.

128 *the Conqueror*: William I, 'the Conqueror' (1025–87), the Norman who ruled England from the time of his victory at the Battle of Hastings (1066) until his death.

thereanent: concerning business relating thereto.

132 *Blackstone*: Sir William Blackstone (1723–80), the father of modern English law. Ripton would probably have been reading either Blackstone's monumental *Commentaries on the Laws of England* (1765–69) or his *Law Tracts* (1762).

133 *Gavelkind*: the law of land tenure and property division.

136 *Vulcan v. Mars*: Vulcan was the Greek god of fire and the patron of workers in metal, Mars the Roman god of war. Venus was given to Vulcan as his wife, but was unfaithful with Mars (in Greek, Ares).

137 *Brutus*: not the assassin of Julius Caesar but rather Lucius Junius Brutus, the legendary first consul of Rome, who revolted against Tarquin, drove out the old kings of Rome, and later had his two sons put to death for conspiring to restore the Tarquins to power.

142 *Bacchanals*: licentious, ecstatic orgies celebrated in ancient Rome in honour of Bacchus—the Roman name for the Greek god Dionysus.

145 *bantling*: infant.

148 *Arab barb*: a highly bred horse introduced into Spain by the Moors.

screw: a worn-out horse.

151 *Ambrosia*: the food of the Greek and Roman gods.

152 *St. Cecilia*: the patroness of church music; she is supposed to have played the organ, though this idea may be the result of a medieval misinterpretation of a sentence in her Acts.

156 *piquet*: a two-handed card-game played with thirty-two cards (the low cards from the two to the six are excluded).

158 *Silvia*: literally, she of the forest.

Arcadians: from Sir Philip Sidney's *Arcadia* (1590); inhabitants of an ideal region of rural, rustic felicity and pastoral simplicity.

Saurian: reptilian; a term popularly applied in the nineteenth century to crocodiles.

160 *The Huron*: used here in the sense of wild Indian; the Iroquois tribe of the northern United States and southern Canada were once called Hurons.

166 *Apollo*: the Greek god of justice, order, beauty, and art.

Dryope: Apollo, it is said, possessed Dryope by a trick, but Meredith may have confused Dryope with Daphne, who turned into a laurel to escape Apollo. Dryope is the mother of Amphissus by Apollo. In Ovid's *Metamorphoses* (IX, 331, 364, and *passim*) Apollo's affair with Dryope is mentioned. She, too, is eventually turned into a tree. Her name means woodpecker, but traditionally she is associated with the Dryad, or oak nymph.

old Gregorian chants: ancient system of ritual music, characterized by free rhythm and a limited scale; founded on the *Antiphonarium*, of which Pope Gregory I ('The Great', reigned AD 590–604) is presumed to have been the compiler.

170 *ap Gruffudh*: probably a reference to the Gruffydds, kings,

princes, and rulers of Wales between the eleventh and thirteenth centuries, renowned for their fighting spirit and love of battle.

172 *Excalibur*: King Arthur's sword; legend has it that he drew it out of a stone when no one else could, thus becoming king. Literal meaning: cut-steel.

Argus: that is, Argos; in Greek mythology, a monster with a hundred eyes. Hera, jealous of Io, sent Argos to watch her rival, whereupon Zeus slew him. The point here is that the spy Benson has been punished for his labours.

Venus: see note to p. 121, above.

174 *Adonis*: a beautiful youth, whose death and revival symbolize the cycle of life and death, summer and winter, in the vegetable world; a mythological figure. The emphatically middle-aged Berry continues to have an inflated sense of his own attractiveness to women.

177 *Horatian*: see note to p. 10, above. Refers back to Richard's last statement (p. 176 in the text): 'There's no place like home.'

185 *Madam Godiva*: according to legend, her husband (one of Edward the Confessor's great earls) having imposed a tax on the inhabitants of Coventry, she asked him to remit it; he promised to do so if she would ride naked through the streets at noon. Taking him at his word, she directed the people to keep inside their houses and shut their windows—and went for her ride. Peeping Tom, who looked out at her, was struck blind.

Proculus: probably a reference to the Julius Proculus in Livy's history of Rome, a senator and friend of Romulus (the founder and first king of Rome). In Livy's version of the story, Romulus disappeared in a cloud while surrounded by senators. The soldiers thought the senators had killed him, but Proculus assured them that Romulus had ascended to heaven and was now a god—a portent of Rome's future greatness.

187 *I have finished Boiardo and have taken up Berni*: Matteomaria Boiardo (1441?–94), Italian poet of the old chivalry, drew on

the legends of Arthur and Charlemagne. His principal work
was *Orlando Innamorato* (1487), a love story. This was left
unfinished at Boiardo's death, and refashioned by the
Tuscan poet Francesco Berni (1496/7–1535), author chiefly
of facetious and burlesque compositions, whose style was
imitated by Byron in *Don Juan* and *Beppo*. Berni's revised
Orlando Innamorato was for a long time considered superior to
the original. The poem's sequel is Ariosto's *Orlando Furioso*
(1532).

189 *the companion of friend Balaam*: probably a reference to the
materialistic, literal-minded, unimaginative Balak, King of
Moab, whose friend Balaam, inspired and instructed by God,
foretells the happiness of Israel (Numbers 22–4).

190 *fleur-de-luce*: a pun on fleur-de-lis, substituting Lucy's name
into the phrase; literally, lily flower or iris, emblem of the
French royal family.

polypi: jellyfish.

191 *St. Simeon*: Simeon Stylites (AD 390?–459), Syrian ascetic.

220 *pollarded*: used in the sense of a tree whose branches are cut
back to the trunk in order to promote greater growth.

223 *Pegasus*: a winged horse; in Roman mythology it is supposed
by some writers that Bellerophon (son of Glaucus, King of
Corinth) attempted to fly to heaven upon Pegasus, and that
this act of temerity was punished by Jupiter, who caused the
fall of the rider.

Gallia: France.

225 *Fiesco*: this is unclear. It may be a reference to Giovanni Luigi
Fiesco (1523–47), a nobleman of Genoa who disliked the rule
of the Doria family and led a revolt against them (a nice play
on words here, if intended); as the revolt got under way,
Fiesco fell off a galley and drowned. He is the subject of a
play by Johann Christoph Friedrich Von Schiller (1759–
1805; here the name of the character is spelled 'Fiesko').
'Fiesco' could also be a reference to Giuseppe Marco Fieschi
(1790–1836), who attempted to assassinate King Louis
Philippe of France. Either of these readings would mesh with
the other 'libertarian' assassin probably mentioned here,

Lucius Junius Brutus (see below; and note to p. 137, above). Alternatively: in Antonia García Gutiérrez's historical drama about the two doges of Venice, *Simon Boccanegra* (1842), there are two characters named Fiesca (Meredith would naturally use the masculine form here). One marries against her father's wishes and dies in childbirth. The other is the first Fiesca's daughter, raised by her grandfather, who thinks she is an orphan and who lives under an assumed name. The eventual reconciliation between the second Fiesca and her father (by that time doge) provides for a climactic scene in the operatic version of the play by Giuseppe Verdi (1813–1901). In any case, the theme of rebellious young people who resent the rule of autocrats would be what Meredith wants us to remember here.

Lucius Junius: this is somewhat ambiguous. The context (see above) may suggest a reference to the consul of Rome who had his sons put to death (see note to p. 137, above); on the other hand, the form of address may suggest that Richard is prince and heir to the 'throne' of Raynham, Lucius being a mythical king of Britain.

230 *the Morning Star*: that is, Venus (also the evening star). See note to p. 121, above.

238 *Hymen*: in Greek and Roman mythology, the god of marriage, usually represented as a young man carrying a torch and veil.

242 *Milo's trick*: Milo was a celebrated Greek athlete, and immensely strong, a victor in wrestling at the Olympic Games, and a distinguished soldier (sixth century BC). He fell a prey to wolves in the end, his hands caught in the trunk of a tree he was trying to split open.

249 *Dante's Madonna—Guido's Magdalen*: the madonna of Dante Alighieri (1265–1321) is probably the Beatrice of his *Vita nuova* (1290–4), drawn from the girl he loved, Bice Portinari (died 1290). In this poem, Dante sees his beloved as the instrument of his spiritual salvation. Beatrice reappears as the poet's guide in the last book of the *Divina Commedia*, the 'Paradiso'. Guido Reni (1575–1642) was an Italian painter of many biblical scenes whose famous portrait of Mary Magdalene was a Renaissance/Baroque favourite; the repentant saint was a subject often chosen by artists during this period.

253 *Ilium*: Troy; burned by the Greeks at the end of the Trojan War.

Menelaus: King of Sparta, husband of Helen, and a Greek general during the Trojan War.

Helen: the wife of Menelaus; her departure from Greece with Paris sparked the war between the Trojans and the Greeks.

Theseus: legendary king of Athens, destroyer of the Minotaur, and conqueror of the Amazons; husband of Phaedra and father of Hippolytus. He abducted Helen, who was recovered by her brothers, when she was still a child.

Paris: son of Priam, King of Troy, and lover of the Greek Helen; their elopement to Troy provoked the Greeks to make war on the Trojans.

256 *Proserpine*: Greek name, Persephone; wife of Hades and queen of the underworld.

Armida's bowers: in Tasso's *Jerusalem Delivered* (1580–81) Armida is the niece of a powerful magician; she uses her beauty to lure her enemies (Christian knights besieging Jerusalem), through magical powers, into a delicious garden, where they are overcome by indolence.

257 *Nooredeen and the Fair Persian*: from *The Arabian Nights*, tales of Persian origin but Arabian in character, collected in Egypt between the fourteenth and sixteenth centuries, dating as far back as the tenth century. In Sir Richard Burton's edition (1885–8, and thus unavailable to Meredith when writing and revising *Feverel*; but there were other editions) the title of this particular episode is given as 'The Tale of Nur al-Din Ali and Anis alJalis'.

269 *Johnson*: the reference is to Samuel Johnson's great *Dictionary of the English Language* (1755), known too by its shorter appellation, *Johnson's Dictionary*. Note that Meredith, in the preceding sentence, makes Mrs. Berry refer to it as the 'Dixonary'. This was also a common nickname; it is Johnson's 'Dixonary' which Miss Pinkerton invariably gives to scholars departing from her school, and which Becky Sharp throws out of the window of her coach, in the opening chapter of Thackeray's *Vanity Fair* (1847–8).

270 *posseting*: that is, she goes to make a posset, a hot drink of sweetened and spiced milk curdled with ale or wine.

273 *That small archway, etc.*: see Matthew 19: 24: 'And again I say unto you, It is easier for a camel to go through the eye of a needle, than for a rich man to enter into the kingdom of God.'

276 *when Cæsar crossed the Rubicon*: by crossing, with an army, this river in the Apennines separating Italy from Cisalpine Gaul, Julius Caesar (102?–44 BC) overstepped the boundaries of his province and committed himself to war against the Senate and Pompey (49 BC); 'crossing the Rubicon' has come to mean in modern parlance taking an irreversible step.

Acheron: the principal river of Hades in Greek mythology; the Styx is one of its tributaries.

ferryman: Charon, who ferried the shades of the departed over the Styx.

279 *cis-Rubicon*: on this side; that is, on the near side rather than the far side. See note to p. 276, above, on Caesar and the Rubicon.

chalybeate: impregnated or flavoured with iron; e.g., a medicine or spring.

287 *Mrs. Doria Battledoria and the fair Shuttlecockiana*: a reference to the game of battledore and shuttlecock, in which, like modern badminton, the shuttlecock, a small piece of cork or other light material, fitted with feathers, is hit backwards and forwards between two players using a battledore as a racket. The point is that Clara does Mrs. Doria's bidding.

291 *Dian*: the Roman goddess Diana—in Greek mythology, Artemis—goddess of wildlife and of nature; usually represented as a virgin.

Sun-God: in Greek mythology, Hyperion (see note to p. 356, below); or Apollo (see note to p. 166, above).

amazons: a race of female warriors alleged to have existed in Scythia (see note to p. 81, above; also that on Theseus, p. 253, above). More generally, warlike or masculine women.

Saragossa: also Zaragoza; a province of western Aragon in north-eastern Spain.

299 *Penelope*: the faithful, patient wife of Odysseus; instead of returning directly home to his kingdom of Ithaca after the Trojan War, he met with a long series of adventures recounted in Homer's *Odyssey*.

311 *Mammon*: the devil of covetousness (in Aramaic, the word means 'riches').

316 *Beelzebub*: lord of the underworld, prince of the devils; usually described as next to Satan in power.

317 *Mephistophelian humour*: that is, evil humour; Faust, in the German legend, sold his soul to Mephistopheles.

324 *perruquier*: dressmaker, or wigmaker.

326 *Gitana*: gypsy.

329 *Richard Turpin*: a famous highwayman (1706–39); but most romances connected with his name are legendary.

339 *Consequences are the natural offspring of acts*: cf. George Eliot's *Adam Bede*, also published in 1859 (see Introduction): 'Consequences are unpitying' (I,xvi); and: 'The consequences that may lie folded in a single act of selfish indulgence, is a thought so awful that it ought surely to awaken some feeling less presumptuous than a rash desire to punish' (V,xli).

342 *Shaddock*: grapefruit. Meredith believed—and he was not alone—that if any fruit was used to tempt Adam in the Garden of Eden, a study of botanical history suggested that it must have been a grapefruit rather than an apple. The 'Great Shaddock dogma' could be translated as the belief that woman, being more easily corrupted than man, is the root of all evil and invariably the cause of his downfall.

Solent: the channel in southern England dividing the Isle of Wight from the mainland.

343 *Manichee*: a believer in religious or philosophical dualism, of which the principal elements are light and darkness, God and Satan, soul and body; a battle is seen as being constantly fought between the forces of light and darkness, etc., for the possession of mankind. See notes on Zoroaster (p. 30) and Magians (p. 41), above.

Aurora: the Greek goddess of the dawn.

352 *Tritons*: that is, sailors. Triton, a sea deity, was the son of Poseidon (Neptune).

356 *Hyperion*: in Greek mythology, the father of Aurora (see note to p. 343, above), the sun (see note to p. 291, above), and the moon; often taken by the poets for the sun itself. Keats left unfinished a poem called 'The Fall of Hyperion, a Dream' (1819).

Briareus: according to Greek mythology, a hundred-armed giant; generally represented as helping the gods in their war with the Titans (see note to p. 105, above). Meredith refers to Briareus several times subsequently; the idea is that Richard is trying to do too much—as much as if he had a hundred arms—and that he is, to extend the image, over-reaching himself.

caesura: in Greek and Latin prosody, the division of a metrical foot between two words, especially in certain recognized places near the middle of the line; in English prosody, a pause about the middle of a metrical line, generally indicated by a pause in the sense.

362 *Anacreontic*: Anacreon (sixth century BC) was a famous Ionic lyric poet who wrote melodious verses about love and wine; he is said to have died by choking on a grape stone.

365 *Leander*: the youthful lover of Hero, a beautiful priestess, in Greek mythology. They lived on opposite shores of the Hellespont; at night Leander would swim across to meet Hero, who directed his course by holding up a lighted torch. One tempestuous night Leander was drowned, and Hero in despair threw herself into the sea. The story has been treated by poets, most notably in Christopher Marlowe's *Hero and Leander* (1598). Seeing himself as a modern-day Leander, the poet Byron (1788–1824) swam the Hellespont in 1810.

Don Juan: in the epic satire (1819–24) of Lord Byron, the handsome, charming, and unprincipled Don Juan, after a shipwreck at sea, must swim to save himself; he is cast up on a Greek island, where he meets Haidée, the beautiful daughter of a Greek pirate. The pair fall in love but are separated by the girl's father, as a result of which she goes mad and dies (as Lucy will). In other versions of the story (e.g., Molière's and Mozart's), Don Juan is the proverbial heartless and impious seducer.

Hero: see above, under *Leander*.

Pluto: another name of Hades, in Greek mythology the god of the underworld—a gloomy, sunless abode.

Æson: in Greek mythology, King of Iolchus and father of Jason; Æson was restored to youth by the arts of Medea.

376 *Cavalier*: name given to adherents of King Charles I in the English Civil War (1642–52); it suggests swashbucklers, who hailed the prospect of war.

Roundhead: name given to adherents of the parliamentary party in the Civil War (see above); so called from the Puritan custom of wearing the hair cut close, while the Cavaliers (see above) generally wore long locks.

Puritan: in this context, the zealous Protestantism of the Roundheads (see above), whose Puritanism was political as well as religious. More generally, the term suggests extreme strictness in morals.

384 *Paphos*: a city in Cyprus sacred to Aphrodite (Venus; or love). The term Paphian suggests a courtesan, a description which aptly fits Lady Mountfalcon—as well as the action of this chapter.

Bellona: the Roman goddess of war.

Diana: see note to p. 291, above.

Endymion: in Greek mythology, a beautiful shepherd with whom Selene (Diana) fell in love when she saw him sleeping on Mount Latmos. In one version of the myth she causes him to sleep forever, so that she can enjoy his beauty; in another, he obtains from Zeus eternal youth and the gift of sleeping as long as he likes. In Keats' *Endymion* (1818), the allegory represents the poet pursuing ideal perfection and distracted from his quest by human beauty.

394 *Aspasia*: the famous Greek courtesan whose beauty, culture, and wit so captivated Pericles, ruler of Athens, that he made her his lifelong companion (fifth century BC). As in the reference to Paphos (see note to p. 384, above), Meredith emphasizes the moral laxness of this gathering.

396 *Brentford-ait*: Brentford island. Brentford and Chiswick are in the London Borough of Hounslow.

397 *volage*: French, meaning giddy, foolish, fickle, inconstant.

408 *Bella Donna*: Mrs. Berry refers (in an apparently unconscious pun: the epithet also means 'beautiful woman') to the Deadly Nightshade, a plant whose leaves and roots yield a powerful drug; an overdose would be fatal.

418 *Madam Danaë*: in Greek mythology, the daughter of Acrisius, King of Argos. An oracle foretold that the King would be killed by his daughter's son, so Acrisius confined her to a tower to prevent her from becoming a mother. Nonetheless Zeus visited her in her prison, and they sired Perseus. Taking part in some funeral games at Larissa many years later, Perseus, when throwing the quoit, had the misfortune to kill a man in the throng—who turned out, of course, to be his grandfather, Acrisius.

422 *Was ever hero in this fashion wooed?*: see also p. 445, in the text: Meredith paraphrases lines from the famous scene (I,ii) in Shakespeare's *Richard III* (1592–3) in which Richard, Duke of Gloucester, persuades Lady Anne, daughter-in-law of the late Henry VI and widow of his son, Edward, Prince of Wales—both of whom (according to Shakespeare's version of history) died by his hand, or by his order—to marry him. Anne is at first contemptuous, but later gives way. As soon as she is out of earshot, Richard asks:

> Was ever woman in this humour wooed?
> Was ever woman in this humour won?

In *Feverel*, of course, it is the lady who is doing the wooing.

431 *Parthian arrows*: the Parthians were people of Scythian origin (see note to p. 81, above) who came into conflict with the Romans. They were celebrated mounted archers who spread round their enemy, poured in a shower of arrows, and then fled, avoiding close contact, and still shooting their arrows as they retreated.

432 *casus belli*: occasion for war, or act regarded as justifying war.

436 *Samson and Delilah*: the story from Judges, 26, retold by Milton in *Samson Agonistes* (1671), of the powerful man whose

strength was said to reside in his hair; when his wife Dalila perfidiously barbered him, he was taken prisoner by the Philistines. We may note that in the end Samson regains his strength long enough to pull down the Philistine temple, killing his capturers and himself as well; and that he is blind. The tale of the weakened, blind athlete summoning up just enough strength at the last moment to destroy everyone is not irrelevant to the story Meredith is telling in the last third of the novel.

440 *'Tis time!*: reference to Shakespeare's *Hamlet* (1600–1) and the goading of the protagonist to action by his father's ghost, which demands vengeance.

442 *roulades*: florid vocal passages, sung to one syllable.

prima donna: principal female singer in an opera.

accanto al fuoco: fiery or passionate tone, inflection, or accent.

449 *She's* . . . : Lucy is pregnant.

462 *postermost*: swift; in this context, precocious.

Blair's 'Grave': 'The Grave' (1743), by Robert Blair (1699–1746). The poem celebrates death, the solitude of the tomb, and the anguish of bereavement. Some of the later imitators of Blair and his contemporary Edward Young have often been lumped together as the Graveyard School.

485 *Anacreon*: see note to p. 362, above.

486 *Ops*: Roman goddess of fertility and agriculture.

Phoebus: another name given to Apollo in his role of sun-god (see note to p. 291, above), signifying brightness, radiance.

Peri: in Persian mythology, one of a class of superhuman beings—originally malevolent, subsequently good—endowed with grace and beauty.

488 *sauce du ciel*: roughly (from the French), heavenly nectar.

492 *escaladed*: scaled, like a fortification.

499 *Orestes, the Furies*: Orestes was the son of Agamemnon, King of Argos and commander of the Greek army that went to Troy; and of Clytemnestra, daughter of the King of Sparta. Clytemnestra and her lover Aegisthus murdered Agamemnon upon his return from the wars; Orestes avenged his father's

death by slaying his mother and Aegisthus. Afterwards, an outcast, he was beset by the Furies, in Greek mythology the avenging deities. Among other things, the Furies (or Eumenides) executed the curses pronounced upon criminals and tortured the guilty with stings of conscience. Aeschylus (525–456 BC), the founder of Greek tragic drama, wrote his great trilogy around the story of Orestes (*Agamemnon, Choephori, Eumenides*); the Orestes story was also the subject of a play by Euripides (480–406 BC).

501 *caracoling*: that is, half turning, a trick accomplished only by an expert rider.

502 *Petrarch*: Francesco Petrarca (1304–74), poet and father of Italian humanism. Petrarch is perhaps best remembered for his long series of lyrical love poems in praise of Laura.

the Tiber, the Arno, and the Po: Italian rivers.

Pannonian: Pannonia was a Roman province south and west of the Danube, embracing parts of what are now Hungary and Yugoslavia. The province was abandoned by the Romans in the fourth century AD and overrun by barbarians.

Iris: in Greek mythology, the messenger of the gods; the rainbow was supposed to be the path by which she travelled between gods and men.

503 *Charlotte Corday*: Marie Anne Charlotte Corday d'Armont (1768–93); she assassinated Jean Paul Marat, one of the citizen-leaders of the French Revolution, by stabbing him to death in his bathtub in 1793.

Limburg on the Lahn: Limburg is a fairly large town in Hesse, Germany, about thirty miles from Kollenz, and north-west of Frankfurt. It is on the river Lahn, a tributary of the Rhine.

Arminius: German tribal chief (18 BC–AD 19) who incited his countrymen to rise against the Romans, and destroyed the army of Varus in AD 8. He also directed the resistance against Varus's successor, the Roman general and popular hero Germanicus, who was nonetheless able to impose peace on the areas around the Rhine (AD 14).

518 *Holy Roman*: Holy Roman Empire was the name given to the realm of the sovereign who claimed to inherit the authority of

the ancient Roman emperors in the West. It comprised in general the German-speaking states of central Europe from early in the eighth century AD to the nineteenth. The Hapsburgs ruled the Holy Roman Empire for approximately the last 500 years of its existence.

519 *Harvey*: the reference is to William Harvey (1578–1657), who in 1616 first advanced his theory of the circulation of the blood throughout the body. He was Charles I's physician.

538 *a duel in France*: see Introduction, p. xi.

540 *brain fever:* the usual description in those days of inflammation of the brain, as well as fevers that affected the brain in various ways.

541 *forte et belle jeune femme*: French, meaning brave and beautiful young lady.